THE CIRCLE SERIES

WHEN
THERE'S NO
TOMORROW

BY

X. W. KAVANAGH

OTHER NOVELS BY X. W. KAVANAGH

The Circle Series

Freelancing with Freud (The Beginning)
It's Raining In Marrakech (The Union of Souls)

Palmetto Publishing Group, LLC
Charleston, SC

For information regarding special discounts for bulk purchases, please contact Palmetto Publishing Group at Info@PalmettoPublishingGroup.com.

Cover Design and Art by Brandon Wedge

ISBN-13: 978-1-944313-61-6
ISBN-10: 1-944313-61-3

AUTHOR DISCLAIMER

AUTHOR'S NOTES

You will notice as you read **When There's No Tomorrow** that I incorporate foreign language words and phrases, identified by italics font. Such inclusions give special emphasis to actions or other pronouncements, and provide the text with a certain panache—Kavanagh style. As much of **When There's No Tomorrow** occurs in Latin countries, the preponderance of such words and phrases is in Spanish. Included at the end of this book is a Glossary of Foreign Language Words and Phrases that provides the English translation. Instead of inviting a plethora of linguistic objections by those more knowledgeable, I invite you to preface such translations with the words '**as used here**.' So we can all attribute any perceived or known deviations from the spoken word as par for the course for a low IQ coonass Cajun fortunate son.

Of course other words receive italicized treatment besides foreign words and phrases, typically proper names of songs, albums, newspapers and such. I also italicize Will's subconscious thoughts in italics as special insight for the reader.

Finally, you can't read my books without noting the integration of music, both by song titles and some lyrics. After much prodding by readers of **Freelancing with Freud** and **It's Raining In Marrakech**, Hal Rayfield and I have opted to formulate our version of the twentieth century's best songs. This Kavanagh and Rayfield list—you might even read K&R into that—will appear at the end of the next exciting episode of The Circle Series being polished for publication now; **A Rainbow On the Sun**. As expected, Hal and I will shun any and all criticism of our Favorite Songs selections, but at least you'll get a **real feel** for who we are. Until then, enjoy the ride!

X. W. Kavanagh

1

PAYING THE PIPER IN BUENOS

"JESUS THAT HURTS," Will Kavanagh shouted as Dr. Ivan Martinez, purportedly the preeminent orthopedic surgeon in Buenos Aires, reached for a syringe of numbing agent as he began to examine his admittedly badly wounded left shoulder. He had taken a brutal stab there when an Algerian bodyguard had lunged down at him with a *janbiya*, a curved Arab dagger, three days earlier in a deadly rescue mission to retrieve Dominique's mother Ayran in Algiers. Although the mission had ended a qualified success with the rescue of Ayran, then Dominique and, perhaps most importantly, the death of an obsessed Algerian warlord, Will had taken multiple wounds during the mission and it was now time to pay the piper.

Martinez looked at him as he injected the deadening agent and said, "The doctor in Morocco did a good job of closing you up for the trip, but infection is starting and we must get a CT scan of your shoulder. I would recommend not waiting after we have access to the scan results, but proceeding directly to surgery. The sooner we repair the ligaments and clean out any residual infection, the sooner you can begin getting the use of your shoulder back Mr. Kavanagh."

Will didn't even bother checking with Dom and replied, "I agree, let's get this show on the road."

He woke up sometime the next day, his upper body seemingly encased like an Egyptian mummy and opened his eyes to find Dom hovering, "Hello my hero. How are you feeling?"

"A little sluggish; how'd the surgery go?"

"Dr. Martinez said it went very well and that you should regain total use

1

of the shoulder, although your range of motion will be limited for some time as you progress through physical therapy. Want something to drink?"

"Yeah, I'd kill for a beer; how's Hal? Did they operate on him yet?" He asked, knowing that Hal might limp around the rest of his life from the nine millimeter parabellum he took in his lower thigh during the penultimate phase of the mission.

"They prepped him while you were in the operating room, and Dr. Martinez went directly to his surgery after yours. He is resting comfortably. And you can forget about that beer my husband, here's some ice for you to sip on," his ever-protective wife advised.

Satisfied that Hal was taken care of, he remembered an important aspect of the shoulder injury, "How about nerve damage; that wasn't exactly a surgical strike that Algerian made on me?"

"Dr. Martinez brought in Dr. Romero, a skilled neurosurgeon, during the operation and they believe you should regain full use of the shoulder. I do believe there were some very delicate repairs made. That was a violent blow you took Will," she noted as she kissed him sweetly.

He touched her head where she'd taken a nasty blow from the barrel of a pistol wielded by Sandrigan el-Boukhari, the obsessed warlord who was finally very dead. "How about this baby, what can they do to make this better?" He moved his hand across her forehead, touching the scar from a previous bullet ricochet and added, "Are you sure you're not allergic to North Africa?"

"Do not worry yourself about such minor things Will; I will get a plastic surgeon to look at it after the swelling recedes. It is stitched adequately for the time being."

He touched her cheek, glad they could finally relax due to Sandrigan's demise, and told her, "Plastic surgeon indeed Ms. Lefebvre; we've taken one too many beauty marks and tattoos over the past few months."

She smiled furtively and replied, "All minor things love; the important pieces of both of us are still intact for our next important project."

With effort, he leaned to kiss her, "Thank God Sandrigan was aiming high; I can't imagine life with you without access to reproductive organs my dear."

"I actually nudged his arm up just slightly as he was firing to help us with the odds Mr. Kavanagh," she smiled conspiratorially.

"Right, and he rewarded you by pistol-whipping you; it's a good thing I still had a good right arm. I needed it to aim that Walther one last time."

"And you did that perfectly I might add. Now get some rest and we'll see about getting you up and walking. Dr. Martinez says it will help clear your lungs after being immobilized for so long during surgery."

"Hey buddy, how'd it come out?" Will asked Hal as he looked at him in the hospital bed, his right leg suspended from a mechanical sling above the bed to immobilize it.

"How the hell would I know? I can't move shit, and I've got to use a bedpan. Does that answer your question? How about you, how's the shoulder?"

"Thanks to you partner, I still have one. I'll never forget that Colt going off and delivering my ass from between a rock and a hard place," he said with genuine appreciation, remembering how Hal had stepped in from nowhere and put his Colt 1911 .45 pistol under the chin of his attacker and pulled the trigger.

Hal frowned at his buddy and responded, "As long as we're counting saves, don't forget about pulling my ass out of the shit when that bandit got behind me in that casbah bro. I was dead meat if you hadn't plugged him. Thanks ma man."

"Right, you taught me well. I guess we've got some well-deserved R & R coming, n'est pas?"

"God, I'd kill for a scotch," he grunted, his angst well understood.

"All in good time Mr. Rayfield, now take this pill; it's time to begin weaning you off of the morphine," his exotically hot and enchanting fiancée Carmen instructed.

He patted her just beginning to stretch belly and smiled, "No more death-defying missions for you for a while Ms. Fabiano. I believe we both deserve a rest."

Following the operation, Will settled into a pattern of Percodan's every four hours—strictly administered by his vigilant governess Dominique—accompanied by a limit of two glasses of wine in the evening. He was seriously glad they had done their best to make aggressive love to one another every night leading up to the assault, as being badly wounded, having surgery to repair the damage and then working through the pain of recovery had completely slaked his libido. One evening as they finished dinner several weeks later, he looked around for his pal Percodan and the accompanying wine when Dom arrived and said, "Why don't we take a break from the pain killers, see how you can do without it?"

Will grimaced at her and counter-proposed, "Jesus, aren't you a funsucker. Do I at least get my cabernet?" Pouring a generous glass of the local nectar, she curled her finger and led him to the bedroom. He wondered what she had in mind, but followed her and settled into the very comfortable sofa situated in front of the fireplace that would probably be a nice mood-setter in wintertime. Dom sat on the bed so she could have undivided attention.

He shouldn't have been surprised when she launched into her love therapist mode, delivered with her typical medical examiner interrogatory, "I'd like to discuss issues of desire with you Will."

He smiled and nodded, "Alright, shoot Luke."

"Why do you always use that expression Will? It sounds so trite."

"It think it was from a movie called Cool Hand Luke, maybe ten years ago starring Paul Newman," he offered but only received a shrug in return. "Okay, it's American slang for *dîtes-moi*; we all good now?"

"Have you ever considered why you are attracted to certain women as opposed to others?" She asked, devoid of emotion.

Not having a clue where she was taking this, he decided to give her his best bedpan humor, "If they're hot, they're hot."

"So if they're hot, you like them?"

"Pretty much, unless they also happen to be mesmerizing love therapists on the side," he said, knowing it would flatter her.

She deftly parried the compliment, "So if they're hot, you're interested?"

He was becoming slightly uncomfortable with her angle of attack, but took it on, "I guess, but not all women are created equally hot. Would you like some examples of women I consider hot? You know most of them."

"I would be overjoyed, please continue," she replied, her hands posed under her chin like The Thinker statue.

Thinking this was the least threatening exercise in mental masturbation Dom had subjected him to recently he launched, "Okay, Samantha Chessereaux, Christine DeLuca, Penny Martindale and Casey Mooneyhan come to mind instantly. Then I'd have to add Leena Garcia, Au and probably Rose to the mix from the Philippines. Is that enough of a list to start with?"

"It's perfect Will. Do you see any similarities in the seven women you identified?"

He thought over the list, somewhat chagrined that he'd never bedded Casey Mooneyhan, but she was a lesbian so she got a pass, albeit reluctantly. After a few moments he didn't see any pattern, other than nationality, "Other than four are Americans and three are Philippinos, I'm not seeing any differentiation."

"Okay, let's start with the Americans; what is similar about them?"

He quickly saw the pattern and blurted, "They're all blondes."

His paranoia meter was suddenly pegging out—since Dom was a curly redhead—until she replied, "Fine; and the Philippino women, what is special about those three? You must have met hundreds."

He scratched his head as nothing came to mind. On the verge of exasperation he shrugged, "I can't think of a thing Dom, except that they were all tall for Philippinas."

"Okay, let's see if we can break it out culturally. What makes the Philippinas so attractive, considering that you cull the taller ones out for special lust consideration?"

He knew he would have blushed if it had been anyone other than Dom, but they were brutally honest with one another so bombs away, "Their vaginas taste like their skin, salty neutral."

She couldn't hide the smile now, "So you developed a liking for Philippina women because they taste good?"

"Well, I think that's an oversimplification, because when they taste good, they smell that way too," he replied, wondering if perhaps he'd stepped a little over the line.

She couldn't hide the smile this time, "And the American women you listed, what about them?"

Without batting an eyelash, he saw it, "Oh, the blondes typically don't have much pubic hair, just like the Philippinas. Most every blonde I've ever seen naked had very little, what I call a tuft, of pubic hair. And it is generally soft in texture, with typically little if no aroma as well."

Now she was nodding her head as if she had discovered the cure for cancer, "So this taste and smell issue is important to you?"

"Who wouldn't it be important to? Why do you think showers seem to be the universal foreplay exercise?" He declared, thinking he'd stated the blatantly obvious.

She got up from the bed and walked a couple of steps before turning back for the next phase of the inquisition, "But what about Kelly Dupree, she didn't have any smell issues did she? I mean she had what you described as the most beautiful body you'd ever seen; why wasn't she included on your hotness list?"

Not quite seeing the point he blasted away, "Yeah but she had a decently developed bush on her." As soon as he said it, he wondered if the pubic hair was really so important. *Damn, Dom's hitting me up, making me admit the bush is a real turnoff; but man did I want to get in Kelly's pants that night on Johnny's sailboat.*

"So let me see if I get this straight; even if they're drop-dead gorgeous, you gauge ultimate desirability on their pubic hair, or bush as you call it?" He was considering this assessment carefully, wondering what kind of worm hole Dom was herding him towards. *Jesus Christ Kavanagh, your own wife's got a bush, albeit nice and soft; how the hell you gonna dig yourself outa this frigging hole boy?* Dom interrupted his field trip to the frontal lobes with a touch of impatience, "Well?"

"Okay, I guess that's a reasonably fair assessment, but it's not an automatic disqualification factor."

"But based on the list women of you consider hottest, the only real common denominator is their presence or lack of pubic hair?"

He grimaced, more than a little uncomfortable with the exclusionary over-simplification, "It's really hard to say that on a universal basis Dom; but as a general rule I guess that's true, at least for me. You, of course, are my perfect example of the exception to the rule."

She took two steps towards him, stopping right in front of the couch, "It's been a while since we've made love, based on our previous history, don't you think? Those wounds you have really took the bite out of your libido, *n'est pas?*" The furtive smile she was sporting seemed to focus the discussion pointedly.

Her indirect allusion to impotence caused his neck to flush with embarrassment, "Jesus Dom, I'm sorry but I guess they have. I don't think it's a long term fatal issue though." He looked up from the couch, her furtive smile now taking on the sharpened point of defense exhibit one.

As she began taking her clothes off, she admonished, "Long is a relative term Will Kavanagh." When she was down to her black lace panties, she pushed her abdomen right in front of his face and said, "Don't you think it's time we assessed your progress and recovery from those wounds?" With that she slid off her panties as Will gasped; her pubic hair was gone, his mind involuntarily recalling Danielle when she showed up for the Last Dance long ago. Like a bee to a fresh blossom, he grabbed her hips and pulled her to his face, trying but failing in his now finely-honed slow and tantalizing approach to the labia.

Without a clue how it happened, they were on the bed and he was so aggressively prosecuting the D spot that Dom was reduced to uncontrollable moaning and writhing in ecstasy. He moved up to her face smiling, "Now that's one hell of a homecoming present baby!"

She struggled to reply, gulping for breath, "My God, I should have done that long ago; *Mon Dieu!*"

"So you liked the Brazilian wax job? It's sort of your coming out present, so to speak," Dom said as they sat up in bed in utter desolate happiness. His shoulder was aching like hell, and his broken ribs were shooting him the bird, but it seemed almost bearable.

"Hey, absolutely I love it baby. You're bald as a baby's ass down there. What an unexpected treat!" He said, totally ecstatic over the development. "Holy Jesus you made me come like a volcano Dom, but I'm hurting like a mother for it; how about a Percodan?"

She came back from the kitchen with a pill and generous glass of cabernet. She put the Percodan in her own mouth and began crunching it as he looked at her suspiciously. She then began french-kissing him and pushed the crushed pill into his mouth. She then held the wine glass for him to drink which he did with eternal gratification. "Good, it hurt like hell getting it; I would have been disappointed if you hadn't been interested. I must say William, you don't seem to have lost anything as a result of your wounds."

"Hey, I had the ultimate stimulus *n'est pas?* That was one hell of a test of distracted libido, let me tell ya!" He told her, happier than he'd been in a long while. "So where'd you learn to administer medicine like that? You've never done that before."

"You can thank our host Carmen for that little advice on how to get pills working faster; she apparently uses it on Hal who can be somewhat grouchy and demanding." Will merely smiled and nodded as she gave him that sideways glance, "Is mine the first hairless vulva you've encountered?" His eyebrows flexed as she added, "Oh, that's right, Samantha had been shaved; but she didn't endure the Brazilian waxing."

Will was suddenly interested, "So how'd you learn about Brazilian waxing? I've never heard of it before."

"First of all, don't feel like a sheltered puppy; you are no rookie by any means William. I lived in the United States for ten years and never heard the first thing about it. Carmen and I engaged in a small female conspiracy after we changed out of our filthy clothes in the hotel in Marrakech. I couldn't help but stare at her vulva, and that's when she told me about this salon here in Buenos Aires operated by three Brazilian cousins. They claim what we call Brazilian Waxing had been practiced by some inland Indian tribe for centuries for hygienic purposes—which seems to make a lot of sense if you don't regularly bathe, for whatever reason. So basically they sprinkle this talcum powder with a desensitizing agent over the hair after they've shaved it down to a half-inch or so. She then applied molten beeswax with some pine oil mixed in over the hair and covered it with pieces of cloth. When the wax dried she pulled off the cloth—that was the painful part…"

"Wow, so is this a permanent thing?" Will went down for a closer look and nodded, "So getting the hair pulled out didn't leave a rash?"

"Now that would be wonderful if a single treatment solved pubic hair forever. But Leticia said it will grow back in a month, but much finer and softer. This should make subsequent waxings less painful. As for the post-waxing discomfort, Leticia provided a jar of raw shea butter, which is extracted from the nut of some African plant. It must work, as I had the waxing seven days ago and the very aggressive cunnilingus you just inflicted upon my vagina to perfection caused no discomfort."

Will was feeling downright special, "So you did this to test me or was it to wean me from the Percodans?"

"A little of both William, and you passed the libido test with highest marks. The painkillers may take a bit longer, but actually, I had a more selfish motive behind this little exercise."

Now basking in the heavenly emptiness bliss, he innocently asked, "And what would that be?"

"It's time for you and me to have a baby William. We can't do that without your contributions now can we?"

2

COMING TO ARGENTINA
AT THE RIGHT TIME

THEY HAD BEEN IN BUENOS AIRES a few weeks, enough for Hal and Will to im-
merse themselves in aggressive physical therapy to hopefully regain normal
range of motion in their extremities. Carmen's family home in Buenos Aires
was what *Porteños* called a *casa grande*, and was located along *Avenida Junin* in
the 'old money' neighborhood of Recoleta. One morning Will was reading
the English language newspaper, *Buenos Aires Herald*, and grew interested in
the story about international reactions to Argentina's *Dirty War*. He finished
reading the article, which quoted both the London Times and Amnesty International's Annual Report for 1978, and looked up at Carmen. "Carmen, this
article talks about some Dirty War and the plight of *desaparecidos*, or simply
disappeared persons. What's that all about? I certainly haven't seen any signs
of a Dirty War since we've been here."

Dom was now interested as Hal noted, "Jeesh Willy, they actually printed
that in the *Herald*? Videla will certainly want to slap that Editor around."

"Who the hell is Videla?" Will wondered, once again looking at Carmen
for an answer. "And how come Hal knows about this but I don't?"

Carmen shook her head lightly, "I wondered when you would become
interested in Juan Perón's Legacy to Argentina."

"The Dirty War has something to do with Juan Perón?" Will asked, knee-
jerking in reaction. "I thought Perón was wildly popular and died in '74?
What was his Legacy to Argentina?"

Carmen rolled her eyes this time, "Over a thirty-one year involvement
in Argentine politics, which included eighteen years in exile mostly in Spain,

Juan Domingo Perón was able to create powerful leftist and right-wing non-governmental organizations that nearly took the country to the brink of anarchy. He actually precipitated the beginnings of the so-called Dirty War during his final term as President."

"How the hell did he manage to create leftist, which I presume are Marxist, and right-wing NGOs?"

"He was without doubt the most opportunistic of Argentine politicians who ever lived. As an Army colonel in 1943, Perón supported the War Minister against then-President Ramón Castillo, and ended up as head of the insignificant Department of Labour in new President Pedro Ramirez' government. He became the champion of the common laborer, setting up changes to increase hourly wages, have a Social Security system established and supported the birth of national health insurance. Within the year, Perón had the Labour Department elevated to a cabinet-level post. He was assigned as the lead for recovery from the devastating earthquake that leveled San Juan in 1944, including fund raising efforts. This is when he met a minor radio matinee star Eva Duarte…"

"Who became Evita, correct?"

"Correct, and in spite of her glamour she came from humble roots and the common people loved her. So when General Edelmiro Farrell displaced Ramírez as President, he made Perón his Vice President, Secretary of War and Secretary of Labour. Perón so effectively supported and helped organize labor unions that he was the working people's choice for President. General Farrell announced Presidential elections for 1946; in the meantime, Perón incurred the wrath of the industrialists and landowners, who had Farrell depose and imprison him. Evita organized a popular protest known was the October 17ᵗʰ Mobilization that got him released three days later. The day after the Loyalty Day protest Perón announced as Labour Party candidate for the February '46 Presidential elections. He married Eva on October 22, 1945."

"So they finally had a legitimate election?" Will wondered.

"Right, but a bizarre coalition opposed him, and even the US Ambassador Braden came out and branded Farrell, Perón and others Fascists. This made for Perón's famous campaign slogan 'Perón or Braden?'"

"So where did Ambassador Braden get the Fascist thing from?"

"He did not have to fabricate a lot of evidence. As a young military officer,

Pedro Ramirez was sent to Germany in 1911 to train under Kaiser Wilhelm's Prussian Army. When he returned in 1913 he brought home a German wife. Then in 1930, as the military conspired to return to Fascism, Ramirez was sent to Italy to train under Mussolini's army for two years."

"Hold on, I thought you said Farrell and Perón were accused by this Ambassador Braden?" Will pursued, seeing a slight disconnect.

"In 1939, Perón went to Italy as the guest of Benito Mussolini and spent two years touring European countries as a military observer. He concluded afterwards that a social democracy could be a viable alternative to a liberal democracy. Argentina remained neutral during World War II until the very last hour, joining the Allies in March 1945. Argentines were so inclined towards the Germans that when President Ramírez' cut diplomatic ties to the Axis Powers in January 1944, the public outcry got him unseated in favor of Farrell. Farrell and Perón all but issued an open invitation to escaping Nazis after the fall of Hitler's Third *Reich*. His clear tolerance of Fascism and Nazism pretty much confirmed his lean towards the fantasy of social democracy."

"So he got elected in 1946; then what happened?"

"He had the Labour Party renamed as the Perónist Party in 1947 and the unions predictably flourished until Argentina's favorable trade balance— not having to expend huge sums on World War II—resulted in huge imports and inflation set in. Then in 1949 he renewed diplomatic ties with the Soviet Union and began selling them grain, much to the anger of the Americans, who imposed trade embargoes on Argentina and excluded them from the Marshall Plan. Perón moved to repair ties by ratifying Truman's Latin American Policy, thereby freeing up Argentine assets frozen by the US. Perón's reputation was forever ruined in the eyes of the Americans, who viewed his 'Third Way' foreign policy neutrality in the Cold War as a disguise for resurgent communism in the Americas."

"So what happened? You can't piss off Uncle Sam and get away with it indefinitely," Will posed.

"He was reelected to a second term in 1951, largely assisted by the outpouring of sympathy for Evita, who was dying of cancer. He managed to keep the opposing labour and conservative forces placated for over four years until he made the 'Henry VIII Mistake.'"

"What, he wanted a marriage annulled?"

"No, much worse; by 1955 the fifty-nine year old Perón had taken up with thirteen year old Nelida 'Nelly' Rivas, and it was the stuff of gossip in the newspapers. Perón believed the Catholic Church was behind the dissemination of rumors and expelled two priests from the country. The Archdiocese of Buenos Aires responded with the declaration of the Sacred Consistorial Congregation, which Perón perceived as excommunication from the Holy Roman Church. He called for a rally of support the next day at the Plaza de Mayo, a common political ploy for Presidents in trouble. While he was addressing the throng, the Navy attacked the crowd with fighter/bombers, killing more than three hundred civilians. Though the Perónists ransacked every Catholic Church and Cathedral in response, three days later the leaders of the three military services led the *Revolución Libertadora*. The Junta took power on September 16, 1955, and Perón narrowly escaped with his life, but not Nelly, to Venezuela in exile."

"So these early supporters of Perón were leftists, given the union angle, *n'est pas?*"

"Actually, the *Montoneros* were a far left Catholic Perónist group, took up armed insurrection against the Junta and were a viable force until Isabella Perón finished them off in 1975."

"Where's Isabella come into the picture?"

"Perón's stay in Caracas was only two years, as his host President Jiménez fell from favor and was ousted in 1958. Perón fled to Panama, where he met an Argentine nightclub singer named Maria Estella Martinez, who became Isabella Perón. Spain agreed to take him in but only if he married his mistress, and that's where he remained until beckoned back by his champion Héctor José Campora in 1973. On the day of his return, millions of supporters crowded Ezeiza Airport to welcome him home. Left wing snipers opened up on the crowd, killing thirteen and wounding over three hundred in what became known as the Ezeiza Massacre. The reaction to the attack was overwhelming, and Perón replaced Campora on the ticket as he and Isabella won with over sixty percent of the vote."

"So for eighteen years—with Perón in exile—Argentina somehow got by without any major upheavals?" Will asked, wondering if Perón was an incendiary ingredient.

"It would seem that way, but he had cultivated right wing associates as well as Marxists during his time in exile. Rumor had it that the *Montoneros* were so enraged by Perón's budding friendship with Fidel Castro and Che Guevara that they labeled him an enemy of the Holy Roman Church. This association is believed to have led directly to the Ezeiza Massacre that welcomed Perón home in 1973. So within a year of his return to power, Perón had the economy working well and inflation under control. Then José Rucci, the Secretary General of the Confederation of Labor was assassinated in front of his home by commandos who never took credit for his death. That's when Perón unleashed José López Rega, ostensibly the Minister of Social Welfare, to form a paramilitary death squad; hence the *Alianza Anticomunista Argentina*, or Triple A, was born. Within a year, Triple A had grown in numbers and was making such progress against the *Montoneros* that they went underground."

"This was technically the beginning of the Dirty War, although Jorge Videla gets disproportionate credit. Early in 1973 after Peron's return, the Guevarist ERP, or *Ejército Revolucionario del Puebla* of Argentina, began large scale anti-government attacks in and around Buenos Aires."

"In a strategy shift, the ERP abandoned urban combat to secure a large land area as a base of operations. This new base was the sparsely populated northwestern Province of Tucumán. The entry of the ERP into the struggle became the primary target of the *Batallón de Inteligencia 601*. Perón died on the First of July, 1974, and Isabell became President, although not a good one. López Rega was her closest supporter and confidant, and she in turn issued annihilation decrees which specified the annihilation of all left wing subversion. This was officially the start of the Dirty War, where essentially the constitution was set aside to deal with the insurgents."

"So what role did you play in the Dirty War Carmen?" Will wondered. "You were in the 601 Intelligence Battalion, and they were totally devoted to the eradication of the ERP, correct?"

"First of all, I was recruited from college into the *Secretaria de Inteligencia de Estado*, or SIDE, as my father was close friends with SIDE Secretary Carlos Alberto Martínez. As 'Uncle Carlos' had known of my academic record and hardened personality traits, I was hired or recruited during my second year of college. I was able to master National Intelligence School in five months, as opposed to two years. Within months I attended the US Army's School of the Americas at Ft Gulick, near Colon in the Panama Canal Zone, with two Directors from the Under Secretariat for Foreign Intelligence. There were also representatives from the intelligence services of Bolivia, Chile, Paraguay and Uruguay there for the presentation by the Commander, US Southern

Command, General Bengood. He spoke for over an hour about the need to stop the spread of communism and openly encouraged military *coup d'états* to regain control from leftist leaders supported by the Cuban DGI's export of revolutionary fronts."

"That was the day we learned of Operation Condor, where cooperation between Southern Cone intelligence agencies would gain better visibility of the overall Cuban/Soviet plan that was being executed in each of our countries. That was the day I met Chilean Colonel Manuel Contreras, Augusto Pinochet's military intelligence leader and soon to be Head of DINA, the *Dirección de Inteligencia Nacional* set up under Pinochet."

"So you sort of zoomed up inside the SIDE as it were," Hal half asked, shocking Will. "Which personality traits were hardened by the way?"

Carmen smiled sickly, "My total distrust of males led every Director and Division Head within SIDE to believe I was incorruptible. This was especially so since my family was wealthy and I could not be bought out."

"Wow, so you were the first female operative SIDE ever recruited other than the honey trap candidates, eh?" Will asked with a smile.

"If you're asking if there were any unattractive female agents within SIDE, you are correct Mr. Kavanagh."

"Fair enough, my black widow friend. But I gotta tell ya, the last forty minutes has been like drinking through a Spanish fire hose. Jesus Christ, it sounds as if the Commander-in-Chief of the Army here sprung a *coup d'état* every time a civilian President lost control of the economy..."

"That is a point very well taken William; since World War II, there have been nineteen Presidents of Argentina, and eleven of them came to power via *coup d'état*..."

"So the guy on the throne now, Videla, has quelled the enemy, made it safe in Argentine society again and has managed to stay alive for three years. He sounds like the rock of Gibraltar compared to some of his predecessors."

"Perhaps, but the rock has a very large crack in it; the *desaparecidos*. Forget international rebuke for the moment; how long do you think this Junta can withstand the growing cries from thousands of Argentines of foul play perpetrated by the Triple A and the 601 combined?" She looked at Hal suddenly and shook her head, "Please forget you heard that last sentence Harold."

"Right, so they're living on borrowed time, until they get desperate enough to invade the—what'd you call them—the *Malvinas*?" She started to scold him so Will took a different tack, "So how'd you make the transition to the 601? I thought Hal called it a Commando Brigade when we first met."

"Dammit Willy, I was trying to use words you'd understand bro. You haven't been around Colonel Jepson yet, but when you do you're gonna occasionally hear the term 'sheep-dipped.' In the case of the CIA and the Delta Force, the CIA sort of subcontracts its muscle jobs, also known as wet work, to Delta Force. So when the shit hit the fan in Argentina, the SIDE needed help with wet work, or at least I think that's what Belen is gonna tell us."

"That is actually a close approximation to what happened in late 1974. Up until that time I had been operating as an assassin for SIDE's 34 Directorate. Even though Allende was President of Chile, Pinochet ran the military, and the intelligence service was DINA, the Army Intelligence Directorate. The Marxist, or Maoist, insurgency in Chile is called MIR, for *Movimiento de Izquierda Revolucionaria*, or Revolutionary Left Movement. What SIDE discovered was that the leaders of MIR and ERP couldn't seem to stay hidden in the trenches for long periods of time, the most likely reason being boredom. They of course insisted they needed to meet face-to-face with their counterparts or other unit commanders. We found it both interesting and convenient that almost all of the meetings took place in Cordoba, Santiago or Conception…"

"Now hold on a goddamn minute, Ms. Belen Fabiano," Will said as he pointed at her. "How the fuck could a Marxist guerilla force continue to be viable when the fucking President is a card-carrying communist? I mean, they shoulda been dancing instead of fighting, right? Hell, you'd think he'd appoint the MIR leader as his Secretary of State," he blurted out as Hal had to turn his head in laughter.

"Willy, sometimes I just have to suck it up and surrender to your Cajun world view brother," Hal told him as Carmen frowned.

"From all reasonable appearances, your logic should be correct. But the MIR was not united on how they wanted to change their world. During Salvador Allende's Presidency the MIR focused on prior government villains instead of Allende. They rallied to his side on September 11, 1973, but Pinochet's attack was too well coordinated for any reinforcements to reach *La Moneda* in time. Pinochet promptly purged the Army of anyone sympathetic to Allende after the *coup d'état*."

"Okay, I get it; the MIR coordinating committee couldn't agree that the sun was rising," Will said as Dom began chuckling. "I think I interrupted your Southern Cone socio-political tutorial Belen. So you were doing assassinations in three cities over two years? You must have indeed become a black widow shadow assassin my dear."

"During this period I mastered the art of disguise, obviously. When Perón returned for his third term as President, the ERP shifted focus from an urban guerilla force to a rural one, hoping to take control of most of remote Tucumán Province along the Andes. Although the Army sent in their Airborne and Mountain troops, López Rega was pressuring the Army Commander Videla to form a special commando unit to clean up the ERP free of constitutional rules of engagement. Such restrictions might include the Army's *raison d'être*, the defeat of foreign invaders. The fact that the ERP members were communist terrorists made the creation of the *Batallón de Inteligencia 601* seem reasonable. The guerillas had wreaked havoc over the Argentine economy and society for years, so killing them was no different than killing rats. My part of the 601 was targeted assassination, so the shift from SIDE to the 601 was not difficult, until they ran out of worthy targets. I advised the 34 Directorate that my skills were no longer needed in the 601 so I was commended and sent to 32 Directorate for International Political, Economic and Social Processes."

"Do what?" Will asked. "What the hell did you do in 32 Directorate?"

"I was one of SIDE's two representatives to the Conference of the American Armies in Managua in 1977. We were accompanying Junta members General Orlando Agosti and Admiral Emilio Massera to advise the Somoza Regime on how to improve the effectiveness of their National Guard. Obviously, the Sandinistas are prevailing in spite of Somoza's efforts."

"That's fucking amazing," Will said as Dom even shook her head in disbelief. "So did you end up in Nicaragua or did they come down to Argentina?"

"Neither; on the trip back south Admiral Massera asked me to look into a rather curious American with intelligence ties who had taken a trip to the *Islas Malvinas* while we were in Managua. They made an unscheduled stop in Caracas to drop me off; ostensibly with official business at the Argentinian Embassy. I promptly flew to Aruba to investigate this mystery man. When I spotted him at the bar at the Hyatt Regency in Aruba, he actually tried to approach me romantically. I only thought he was overly confident at that point."

"So you were smitten when you left Aruba, even if you hadn't given up on homicide as an option," Will joked. "So how did you exit the Argentine intelligence apparatus?"

"I made an appointment with General Otto Carlos Paladino, Secretary of SIDE in 1977, told him we had destroyed all of the Republic's enemies during the Process of National Reorganization and that I wanted to step down as I had served my country to the fullest of my abilities. He agreed and signed my discharge paper from SIDE before I left the office."

"And you never had to report back to the Admiral Massera about that commando?"

"Of course I did, and I told him that our CIA mole Marty Lindstrum had sent him down to sniff around but had heard nothing about our secret Operation Sol while he was in Stanley, East Falklands. Operation Sol was a probing foray by the Army in 1976 where fifty soldiers landed and established an outpost on the frozen island of Southern Thule. In case you've never heard of Southern Thule, it is the southernmost of the South Sandwich Islands. The British did take notice and advised the Junta to leave quietly, but I believe it is lost in negotiations. So I left and went and found my lover," Carmen told them as Will shook his head in wonder.

"I'll be goddamned; I never in a million years woulda thought that. So I guess it's all safe now here in Argentina?"

"For patriots that hate communism it sure is," Carmen told him and kissed the top of his head.

"That's good to know, but this Herald article seems focused on these *desaparecidos*, what they refer to as persons who simply disappeared. From what you've told me so far, Argentina reacted to essentially a multi-front insurgency and defeated it. Why is Amnesty International raising such a stink?" Will wondered as Dom nodded her head. Will smiled, "What, you think my brain's asking the right questions?"

"Yes, but you may not like the answers William," Dom replied as she nodded towards Carmen.

Carmen exhaled with resignation, "If the Process of National Reorganization the Junta pursued had stopped when they defeated the ERP—much as I did when there were no more targets—the Dirty War may have become a forgotten unpleasantness. Emotions were running very high when José Rucci, the Labour Union chief, was assassinated. Juan Perón ordered the Defense Ministry to find the remaining Montoneros and wipe them out. Then Isabella became so frustrated with the urban chaos the ERP was propagating that she issued the annihilation decrees, and didn't bother putting a leash on José López Rega to determine how efficiently he was executing her orders. To Rega and Videla, the Army Commander, this was not only a military operation but a chance to reform Argentinian society. In their view, the eradication of subversion meant not only the guerillas' activities, but also what we would refer to as political dissent. So to them, the new National Reorganization Process required eradicating the Perónists, the unions, paramilitary radicals and basically any leftist organization."

"Jesus, so all they wanted left in Argentina were patriotic conservative-minded Catholics? Now that's a utopia that ain't ever gonna happen so long as free will prevails," Will offered as Hal shook his head.

"Right," Carmen replied, "but I left out an important attribute; the remaining Argentines could have no proclivity towards socialism or even social justice. So in addition to killing all or the vast majority of the Perónist Montoneros, the Chilean MIR Revolutionary Left Movement, the Uruguayan Tupamaros and finally the Guevarist ERP, they also arrested tens of thousands of civilians, denied them due process and imprisoned them. These civilian targets included union activists, left wing university faculty, opposition news purveyors, any university student who had joined a Socialist Workers Party and all of their personal enemies. Another Company of the 601 Intelligence Battalion ran the prisons that housed these leftist-minded civilians, torturing and killing many of them—sometimes brutally. Admiral Massera ran one of the most notorious of the prisons at the Navy Mechanics School a few kilometers from our house. So that is the part of the Process that is the Dirty War; taking care of bothersome political opponents in conjunction with the counterterrorism sweep."

"So this Junta now has no enemies to fight except for international human rights opinion, eh?"

"You have boiled it down to its essence William. While buildings were being blown up, ships sunk and innocent civilians slaughtered in indiscriminate bombings, the Junta's detention of 'sympathizers' was considered acceptable. Now that hostilities have ceased, families of the imprisoned and murdered *desaparecidos* have begun making thousands of inquiries as to the status and location of the persons arrested. Obviously, some have complained to Amnesty International and they have taken on the *desaparecidos* as their latest *cause célèbre*."

"So the Junta has succeeded except they can't provide a status or location of however many thousands they murdered along the way. How does this story end Belen?"

"Admiral Massera was one of the original Junta members and reportedly ran the Defense Ministry during the first two years when things got very dirty. Do you recall that Massera was so interested in the *Islas Malvinas* that he had me check out a CIA surrogate that had recently visited Stanley?"

"Sure, which resulted in the renunciation of your lifelong commitment to celibacy," Will said as Hal high-fived him.

"The drumbeat of accusations will only grow as more of the families come forward and demand an accounting for the *desaparecidos*. Admiral Massera has already left the Junta and the Navy and is essentially hiding from the aftermath; but recovery of the *Islas Malvinas* was his sacred life's goal. At some point the Junta will try to deflect this growing and untenable criticism by invading the Malvinas to restore national pride that has been a festering wound since 1820. Of course they will fail, and that will be the end of the Junta," she said with such assurance that Will and Dom were shaking their heads.

"Wow, how many Argentines are clairvoyant like you Ms. Fabiano?"

"Too many I am afraid, but the good news is that it is once again safe to live here in Argentina, *n'est pas?*"

"*Si Señorita!*"

3

OPPORTUNITY KNOCKS FROM AFAR

THEY WERE TOASTING THEIR FIRST TASTE of Scotch whisky since Tangiers when the Lightweight Satellite Terminal, or LST-5B, their mobile satellite communications unit—or SAT phone—gave its familiar trill. Hal picked up the handset happy to hear from afar, "Hey Alex, what's shaking at ROUST on this fine day?"

Since it was the first call they'd had on the LST-5B in a week, Will plugged in the remote jack as Alex reported, "Hey, your buddy Pierson wants to get in touch. You got the number out in LA?"

"Yeah, I got it partner, thanks for the heads up. Any clue what Dan the Man's got cooking?"

"I don't think it's anything operational; he said he needed to hook up this 'stone fox' out at Great West with Kavanagh. That's all I got on it Boss."

"Okay buddy, thanks; you get the transfer notification yet on the Caymans account?"

"Sure did, our ship came in and Rico and I are happy campers. *Muchas gracias, compadre.*"

"Roger that, you two certainly earned it; over and out."

Earlier in the week, Carmen and Dom had taken what appeared to be a girl's vacation to the beach and flown up to the Cayman Islands on a special charter flight Carmen had arranged through friends within the intelligence community. Utilizing her contacts to great avail at the airport, she was able to covertly smuggle the three million in dollars from the Ksar takedown aboard in wine cases for the trip to the offshore banking island of anonymity. Once there, she had deposited the cash into Hal's Destination Partners account and

20

distributed shares to Rico, Alex, herself and Will. Hal had taken action earlier to have Carmen and Will named as directors in the corporation. By doing this, she had saved tens of thousands in 'transaction fees' otherwise charged by the unsavory middlemen who transformed cash into account credits. The cost of the charter flight was a pittance compared to the loss they would have incurred laundering Sandrigan's ill-gotten gains otherwise.

Hal had them linked into Dan Pierson post-haste and got his attention, "Hey buddy, did you get a little black plastic card from American Express in the mail?"

"Hey man, is it good to hear your voice! Hell yeah I got the card; what's behind it?" Pierson's contributions to the takedown in Algiers were huge, especially having brought Vinnie and the Huey in for air support.

"We discussed it, and there's a hundred thousand USD thank you on the other end of that black magic. Don't spend it in the States though."

"You have got to be shitting me! Thanks man, as much as I move around that is huge!" Pierson all but shouted.

"You earned every penny of it brother; my home boy Willy is now a huge believer in Mossberg's, let me tell you. He's actually the one I'm making this call for, but I wanted to make sure you got your little reward. Standby one Daniel."

"Hey Rambo, what's shaking in Tinsel Town?"

"Hey Will, hope you guys are on the mend; never can tell when the call of duty beckons. Listen, you remember that smoking ass hot woman Kelly? She says she's a friend of yours, and the way she says it makes me wonder. Anyway, the head of the studio apparently wants her to get with you about putting together a book or a screenplay or something about both your court-martial and the kidnap/rescue op we did in Algeria. She's pretty hyped about it, and she seems to think there's a chance she can sell it as a movie concept, but she's got to get—and these are her words—the straight skinny from the horse's mouth. Anyway, she's chomping at the bit to talk to you."

"Okay Dan, thanks for the intel. Can you patch me through to her or do I need to call her number?"

"Standby one Will, happy trails."

"Hey Dan, did you ever find out how to get ahold of Will?" Kelly Dupree, the Cossack minx asked when she came on the line.

"Hey baby, how's my Cossack Queen?"

"Will Kavanagh, is this you?"

"You bet, how you doing at Great West? Three months and Zig's probably designated you MVP; I can only imagine you're driving the boys crazy on the lot."

"Ha, how are you doing? I heard through a secure grapevine that you were involved up to your eyeballs in a certain kidnap and rescue mission recently."

"There may be some truth to that rumor; who's interested?"

"I don't know what flipped his button, but Zig Kowalski is hot to trot for developing it into a screenplay for an action movie. Either Dan Pierson or your buddy John Chessereaux got to him and he's all abuzz. Where are you by the way? Dan thought maybe you were in North Carolina."

"We are in beautiful downtown Buenos Aires my dear, enjoying the Argentinian summertime. How exactly does Zig propose to make this little project come to fruition?"

"The easiest way—yeah right—is to write a book and then adapt a screenplay from it, at least that's the normal route a story takes to becoming a movie."

"Hmm, sounds like a lot of work; how do you plan to execute Mr. Kowalski's pipedream?"

"Zig wants me to 'get in bed,' those are his words not mine, with Will Kavanagh and Hal Rayfield and get this story on paper. I am to magically appear where you are and camp out there whenever I can get a commitment from you; that is, if you're interested?"

"What's in it for me?" He posed as Dom magically appeared; no doubt the business deal attracting her like a remora to a shark.

"That's negotiable Will, but I'd suggest you consult an attorney about it. I guess there are plenty of hotels there; I've never been to Brazil."

"This is your geography lesson for today Kell; Buenos Aires is in Argentina, another 2000 miles south of Brazil. It's a long-ass plane ride, but it sounds like you'll be here for a while when you start the Vulcan mind meld. As for hotels, forget it; you're hot little ass is staying in this large estate that Carmen's family owns. There's plenty of room, and if we have to collaborate on writing a book, we need to be close proximity-wise. Hal's here too, and we're both recovering from war wounds, so we should be a captive audience until the cabin fever takes us out. I'll call my attorney now and get back to you soon. Sounds like we're going to be working together; I never thought I'd be personally involved in delivering the goods on that court-martial, but I can probably do a credible job on it. Did Trip ever get that Trial Record to you?"

"He was true to his word; I got it last week and have been reading through it. Nobody will believe the paperwork complexity involved with one of those things. Listen, I'll pass on the potential good news to Zig; he wanted to know when we finally found you. If Dan Pierson hadn't been working here, I don't know how long it would have taken. How's Dom?"

"She's doing well; she got a mild concussion during the op and has a pretty nasty scalp wound, but we're actually going to be working on parenthood issues here shortly. I'll be in touch after I consult with that attorney you suggested. Don't drive the guys too crazy, Bye."

———

"Hey buddy, how in the world are you? Dan Pierson gave the entire Board of Directors a debrief on that little black op you pulled off in Africa. Man, you are one famous motherfucker! Where are you by the way? Dan lost sight of you when he choppered out of that compound you guys blew the shit out of," Johnny Chessereaux said in rapid fire, no doubt glad to hear from his son's godfather. "By the way, did that raven-haired minx Kelly get ahold of you?"

"Dom, Hal Rayfield, his fiancée Carmen and I are at Carmen's family's mansion in Buenos Aires. Carmen's pregnant and Dom and I are working on it. I just spoke to Kelly and she laid out the rough sketch on the court-martial and black op development projects. I needed to speak to an attorney, so who better than my armpit buddy? Besides, I figured nobody knows the industry better than you. What's the best way to approach this from my interest, straight cash advance for the story?"

"Okay buddy, by the way, can you get Dom on this call, we need to cut her in, especially since it was her mother who's kidnapping precipitated all the action."

Will motioned Dom to pick up the remote headset and then replied, "She's on the line Johnny. So what's in my best interests?"

"Hi Dom, how are you? Is your mother okay?" Johnny inquired.

"We are all fine John, but healing from our battle wounds, as Will calls them. How is Samantha and that precious little Willy?"

'They're all doing fine; Willy's growing like a weed. Thanks for asking. So here's the lowdown on me representing you; it's a dicey situation since I'm on the Great West Board."

Will was moving into engineer mode now, "Why is it dicey Johnny? I guess you're supposed to represent their interests, not mine?"

"Right, the two are competing interests unless I make them a little rain along the way. If you agree to sell the movie rights of the stories to Great West—as opposed to another studio—then I can represent you in the follow-on battle over compensation. What do you think?"

"Okay Johnny, here's how I see things; if Great West hadn't provided significant material support for that operation, it would never have come off, or possibly been successful. So Dom and I owe Great West—and you in particular—for essentially saving our bacon. So as far as I'm concerned, we're staking our claim with Great West out of loyalty if for no other reason."

"It's a good thing you called me Will; you never want to say those kind of words to someone you can't trust. This town is not about loyalty, but about the almighty bottom line. In the immediate instance however, I believe that is a prudent business decision on your part. Now that we've concluded the assignment matter, I need to ask you; how are you guys sitting with cash? Are you broke, do you need the liquid assets up front?"

"No Johnny, I married a wealthy, sensual woman. So what's the best deal if we don't need the cash up front; a percentage of the net?"

"At least you're thinking along the correct lines. Never, ever think net; that's after the studio gets their cut and unless you've got 'The Godfather' for sale, there's no guarantee there will be a net profit. What you want is a percentage of the gross, that way you get yours sort of like an expense item on the books."

"Okay, sounds smart. What kind of percentage is normal; that is if the owner of the work is properly represented?"

"It depends, but the hardest deal I've ever seen was Brando demanding five percent, but he took no salary either, so it was a toss-up for the studios. Obviously, you're not a marquee movie star, but we may just have one playing the part of Will Kavanagh before this is over. I'd say ask for two percent of the gross and they'll come back at you with one and a half, which is where you want to end up. These sharks can't fathom going in at the projected price up front, you've got to barter with them. So what do you think?"

He looked at Dom who merely nodded her head, "I just consulted with Dom at length, and we are in agreement with your advice. Tell Zig you have reprised your role as rainmaker and that the film is his at 2% of gross for the rights. You might mention that the book isn't even written yet, so it's not merely a shell game, but that significant work will be required for us to get 'his' story delivered. That should keep him from thinking he's getting hood-winked."

"Jesus Kavanagh, are you a frustrated lawyer? Man, you adapt to this dealing dance pretty quickly."

"This will be our daughter's trust fund John, and I believe we have de-cided in her best interest," Dom intoned.

"Daughter I didn't know you already had a child? Where was she when you guys were out here?"

"That was some serious projection Johnny; we're just working on the con-ception end now. What's next?" Will asked, fending off Dom's swat.

"I'll present your proposal to the Board this week and we'll have the rep-resentation and artistic copyright agreement documents couriered out to you. By the way, I need your contact information in Argentina. Give me the num-ber you're calling from."

"This one won't work, but I'll get that and relay it back to Pierson. Hey, you and Sam ever been to Argentina? And Kelly's got to get down here too. Why don't you guys come on down and stay for a week. We've got plenty of room, and everyone involved in that black op knows you are the critical contact that made that little suicide mission work out. I'll not soon forget that 'case of francs' you left for us; man, did you know the lay of the land there or what! That's how we paid for the boat ride across the Med to Algiers."

"That's not a half-bad sounding plan Will. I suppose Kelly's got to take most of an office with her to get that screenplay moving. I'll let you know how we're going to solve the logistics when I call you back after the Board meeting. Man, I'm actually excited about this. I will be in touch Will; hang in there Dom and good luck with that daughter-in-the-making. Bye."

———

They were lounging around the pool the next morning when Henrietta the housekeeper approached, "There's a telephone call for you *Señor* Kavanagh."

He frowned at her hatefully, "How many times do I have to tell you Hen-rietta, my name is Will!"

Peering at him none too righteously she replied, "Very well, *Señor* Will, you have a call."

He grimaced, the ribs sending a reminder as she got up, "I guess that's better. Jesus, you *Porteños* are so formal."

Will picked up the phone and it was Johnny, excited as hell. "Hey buddy; it's a go on the screenplay. I've got Zig with me, so how about get Dom and Hal for a conference call. Can you do that?"

"Hey Zig, how are you? Didn't think I'd hear from you, maybe other than for a rematch on the links," he said, figuring the new boy better not kowtow to the major domo from Hollywood.

"Yeah, you damn sandbagger," came the bellowing voice. "We hear life's been interesting for you. Do you have Mr. Rayfield and your wife with you?"

"Standby one, I'll get everybody on the squawk box," he said, thanking his lucky stars that Hal had thought about getting one of those fancy phones he'd only seen in big wig's offices. Hal and Dom were already moving, having picked up that something big was astir. As they headed towards the study— which had been converted to their office—Will saw Carmen, "Hey this is Johnny Chessereaux and his boss Zig Kowalski on the phone. I want you in on it too, since you were the marksman that sprung the Ksar sweep and are our host."

"Okay Zig, I've got my wife Dominique, Hal Rayfield and his fiancée Carmen Fabiano with me. Go ahead."

They heard some suppressed chattering in the background before Zig came on the line, "We need to limit this call to the principals Will; I don't know about Ms. Fabiano."

Will glanced at Hal and Carmen, but couldn't tell they were doing anything other than watching the grass grow. Will shrugged and responded, "Well Zig, Carmen only took out Sandrigan's second-in-command in a daring escapade in Algiers, and she was the sniper that sprung the entire takedown in Ksar, so I believe she belongs in this conversation. And if you were to cast her equitably, you'd have to sign Michelle Pfeiffer to play her role."

They could hear laughter in the background as Zig said, "Okay, okay Will; you don't mince a lot of words do you? Ms. Fabiano is welcome to this conversation, but I want to speak with you and Mrs. Kavanagh privately before I get off. So John made the pitch to the Board just now, and it's a lead-pipe cinch. We want your story and I plan to make a blockbuster out of it as soon as it's ready for a screenplay adaptation. And even though I'm reluctant to pay an unknown like a veteran, your shyster attorney here has convinced me I can count on you; so I'll give you your damn point and a half. What we want to do is send our assistant producer to wherever you are and the two of you can wrangle over whether you want to write a book or go directly to a screenplay. It's better if the book has been published in advance; stimulates interest and all that, but it's not mandatory. However you do it, I want a fast track to begin production on this—whatever you call it—in six months. Think you can support that?"

Without looking at anyone, Will replied, "I think that might be doable, at the outer stretches of reason, but I want these three partners of mine on the clock at ten large a month and we support your assistant producer while he's in Argentina extracting this story so far as lodging, meals and transportation go. We'll assign movie rights to Great West, but we retain publishing rights to the book. Should you desire on-set consultative advice, we'll negotiate that separately. Did I miss anything?"

They heard a *phew* in the background and Zig responded, "Yeah, apparently the college trust fund for your first born! Damn Kavanagh, you're almost as bad as your Svengali Chessereaux here. Okay, I'll bite the bullet since I'm compressing production here. Are you sure you need three assistants for this; ten large a pop?"

"I don't know Zig, Hal here only stuck a .45 caliber Colt under the chin of Sandrigan's body guard—who had just stabbed me through the shoulder—and blew his brains into a Jackson Pollock mural on the ceiling. And Dominique is the only surviving soul who can describe the actual kidnapping, so yeah, I believe their participation is paramount to pulling this compressed project, as you put it, off successfully. This is going to take a lot of work."

"Yeah, yeah, I get it. You must have programmed your attorney extraordinaire here; he used almost those same words to sell us the dream. Alright, you got your assistants, so what do we call your little band of marauders?"

Will looked around the room, got the Italian army salute, so he shot from the hip, "Why don't you call us Circle Entertainment? When does all of this begin?"

"Now I believe we're done with general business; I want to speak with you and Mrs. Kavanagh privately."

Hal didn't say a word as he high-fived Will leaving the room, and Carmen stopped to give him a sensuous hug, which he tried but failed to slough off. He hit the mute button and said: "Looks like we've got a little project; let me see what the fuck Zig wants now." As the door closed, he hit the button and said, "Okay Zig, it's just Dominique and I here. What do you want to talk about?"

Without mincing words he launched directly into a surprising query, "The production assistant isn't a he, it's Kelly Dupree, and I know you have some history with her Will."

Will looked at Dom who smiled but said nothing, "Right, she and I are friends."

"Well, that's what I want to talk to you about, but I'd rather direct this to Mrs. Kavanagh. I won't mince words here ma'am, so I don't know if you are aware of the fact that Will and Kelly are close friends. I met her when he brought her in for John's son's baptism. Now she's one smart cookie, and she's got skin thick as leather; Jesus she's had to fight off damn near every would-be Romeo at Great West. And I believe she's squared away and wants to make a go of it in the movie business. But I won't subject your marriage to the constant pressure if you think her presence will be a problem between you and your husband."

Without a moment's hesitation Dom replied, "Thank you for your concern Mr. Kowalski; I suspect few in your business would be so thoughtful as to even care. But Will and I got to know Kelly in the Philippines where she was working as a stewardess, and I consider her a close personal friend. I am aware of the past association between she and Will, and I can assure you that will not be a factor in working with her on this project, however closely that may be during the research and writing portion. We would be happy to host Kelly here at the estate, and we will provide space as necessary for her to work and organize her efforts."

"Good, but I've got to tell you, she is such an attractive woman that most wives would feel differently. I'm going to give this project the green light, so you can expect to hear from Kelly soon. Please let me know when you're going to be in LA again; I want to meet you and show you some Hollywood hospitality."

They heard another scuffling and Johnny came back on, "Damn Kavanagh, who did you think you were talking to? I've never heard anyone deal with Zig like that! Man, you've got a set of brass balls buddy; your ass wouldn't last two days doing that around here. Three assistants at $10,000 a month? Nobody's ever pulled off anything like that, but I gotta tell you, the look on Zig's face when you mentioned that Jackson Pollock mural was priceless. He actually looked aghast! You are a negotiating demon Mr. Kavanagh."

Will rolled his eyes slightly, "Right Johnny, if you'd just gone through the shit we did in Africa, you'd think talking to Zig was a walk in the park. Watching a Berber dagger coming down at your face has a tendency to recalibrate one's perspective. And besides, he called us; we didn't go seeking his largesse."

"Yeah, I guess you're right; I sure wouldn't want to play poker with your ass!"

"I'd probably be a walk in the park compared to Dom. So when is all of this going to start?"

"Hey, that's the good part. Zig's so amped about this that he's letting me borrow the studio bird to bring Kelly and her stuff down, along with the representation papers and the artistic rights agreement. And Sam is so excited to get to Argentina and see you guys; I think the farthest south she's ever been is Cozumel. Is there enough room to bring Willy? If not, I'm sure Dad will be happy to keep him."

Dom immediately piped up, saying, "John Chessereaux, don't you dare come down here without your son. Will and I can't wait to see the three of you."

"Good, Zig obviously wasn't sure you'd be so accommodating of Kelly, and I've got to admit that I'm a little surprised myself. Anyway, I need to scoot; you got anything else?"

Will glanced at Dom and rolled his eyes, "As a matter of fact Johnny, since Circle Entertainment was just conceived during this phone call, we need to formalize its structure as a corporation. I want you to take us on as your clients, and you can bring those papers with you as well. It would seem the Caymans would be a good place to incorporate, and you can set Dom up as President and the other three of us as directors. If you get shaky on that, set it up in Delaware, and you can get most of the particulars on the directors from Destination Partners."

"Destination Partners, what the hell is that?"

Will paused to consider the indirect links to the intelligence world, but figured they survived in the open so he told him, "That's Hal's corporate shield; the training school is under it, as well as some other operations. Carmen and

I are now directors of Destination Partners as well. If you need any other information for the paperwork, fax it to me and we'll turn it around quickly."

"Damn, my other boss is going to be pleasantly surprised that we made some rain for him on this endeavor as well. I'll get my Girl Friday on it and we'll have something to you soonest; man, what a day!"

Will looked at Dom afterward and smiled, "So Kelly Dupree's going to be our working companion. Who'd have thought that would happen?"

She was smirking when she replied, "Do you think you can keep it in your pants William? The two of you seem to get along well, and I wouldn't want to find you holed up in some bedroom while you're supposed to be feverishly getting this story down on paper."

He burst out laughing and said, "Keep it in your pants? Holed up in some bedroom? Feverishly getting this story down? You are hilarious Mrs. Kavanagh, and I would venture that 'holed up in some bedroom' restriction would apply only if you weren't there with us. I seem to recall that she reminded you of a certain Reiki practitioner."

"Now, now William; we are a married couple now, and we don't participate in ribald sexual escapades like that any longer.

He gave her the wrinkled forehead scowl of consternation, "Well let's see Mrs. Lefebvre, I seem to recall a night not too long ago when you castigated me for not wanting to be the King of Paris by engaging in a *ménage a quatre*."

She gave him the Mona Lisa smile and concluded, "We shall see William; business before pleasure."

"My thoughts exactly."

That night, Will got everybody together after dinner and said, "Alright, we've got to figure out a plan of attack on this, so I'll take the lead for now and be the facilitator. The way I think we can make it work is that we should probably brainstorm the steps of the operation and I'll reduce them to outline form. Once we've got that, we can start fleshing out the bullets under each segment of the op. So I guess we start at ROUST when Bob Kellor came in with the bad news; any objections?"

They were all looking at him with exasperated expressions when Dom said, "As much as I don't like revisiting it, I believe the screenplay should start with the unwise tryst with Sandrigan in Rabat."

Hal and Carmen looked at her in confusion, so Will filled them in, "Actually, Sandrigan's kidnapping of Dom precedes her mother's, so that's got to be a precursor as well. Okay you two, the reason Sandrigan was interested in kidnapping Dom in the first place was because she had a one night tryst with him in Rabat, maybe five or six years ago, and he became insanely possessive of her when she rejected his overtures for a permanent assignation. This obsession laid dormant until he saw her in Mustafa's camp in Er Rachidia maybe seven or eight months ago. He snatched her—to the eternal ire of Mustafa—from the camp and flew her to Algiers, where he proceeded to torture her unmercifully. Kellor got the alert via the CIA that Dom was in the safe house in Tangier, so he went there and accompanied her to Manila. There we reunited and soon stumbled across Hal and Dan Pierson in a casino. That should take us up to the start of the infiltration and the combat operation."

Dom was looking at him disconsolately, "I believe you forgot to mention that two years after the ill-fated and poorly advised tryst, I met an Air Force officer in Colorado and things got complicated."

Without thinking Will blurted out, "Jesus, what the hell does that have to do with the black op?"

"Everything Will, you were the reason it happened," she replied, and the look on his face must have been telling, because Hal and Carmen were suddenly looking at him like they were in some movie theater watching a show.

"No honey, you were the reason it happened. It was your mother that got kidnapped, remember?"

Unfazed, she replied, "And she and I would both be dead right now if you hadn't made it turn out otherwise."

"What about Hal, and Carmen, and Johnny, and Kellor and Rico and Alex and Rambo, and......"

She took over and continued, "And Keith, and Trip, and Leena, and Mustafa and Mando Chu, and even Marty Lindstrum. What did all of them have in common Will?"

"They were all in the right place at the right time."

"But why were they all in the right place at the right time? That would seem so unlikely that the odds would have to be astronomical," Dom insisted. For the very first time since this whole impossible confluence of events had unfolded, it dawned on him. Will was humbled by the fact that he had been by far the luckiest man in the universe.

He closed his eyes and approximated the meditation pose, "Okay, I might have been the swizzle stick, but I definitely wasn't the machine. I will agree that I had some fortuitous friendships that facilitated the outcome, but so did you Dom. Could we have pulled it off without Mando Chu or Mustafa?"

Hal finally—mercifully—got them off of this daisy chain and said, "Dammit Willy, don't you see that it probably couldn't have been pulled off with all of us living through it if each person hadn't played their role. Chalk it up to chance or fate or whatever, but don't we need to put an outline together?"

———

Two days later, they had put together a fairly comprehensive outline, and each of them took segments to begin fleshing out the details. Will was surprised when Johnny called, as it was nine o'clock at night, "Working late tonight counselor?"

"Naw, I'm calling from home. Sam's so excited about the trip that she threatened my life if I didn't let her in on the call. Okay, I've got the agreements ready for your signatures and Kelly's got her office materials together; Pierson got them palletized for her to help with the transport. Jesus, Zig's got her set up with word processing equipment, a copier, fax machine, the latest phone available and something called a Picturephone that AT&T developed; don't ask me how it works, 'cause I don't know. I've never seen him this interested in a project; hell, he only makes it to the lot if Sean Connery is on set. It wouldn't surprise me if he actually wants to go down to Argentina to meet the development team. He even pulled Pierson back in after that Jackson Pollock remark. Pierson said he didn't see it, but that he helped patch up your shoulder so you could fly that Cessna out of there. How the hell did you stand the pain Will? Man, I'd have been ready for a morphine pump or something."

"Ever heard of dexies Johnny?"

"Dexies? No what are they?"

"Dexedrine is a brand name for dextroamphetamine. Anyway, Rayfield jammed two down my throat and I was flying so high I didn't even notice the shoulder until I got shot. Then I was hurting all over."

"Got shot? Jesus Will, what the fuck? That was some fucking dangerous mission. Where'd you get shot?"

"In that fucking warehouse in Ksar el Boukhari, you know, the carpet factory where Sandrigan staged his drug and gun smuggling operation? Luckiest two pistol shots ever fired; that fucking Sandrigan nailed me and Hal from a good forty yards with two fucking shots!"

"You have got to be shitting me! What I meant was where did he hit you on your body?"

"Oh, I took one in the ribs, but thank God I had a thick bound ledger book in my coat. It took the velocity off of the round. So when are you guys getting in? I guess you're taking the Great West chariot?"

"Actually, I bartered with Zig; Jesus, do you know what first class airfare is between LA and Buenos Aires? Anyway, Great West is shooting some adventure film in Peru, so they've got a chartered Federal Express DC-10—sounding familiar—headed out with the set gear. Hell, you'd think we'd need one to get all of Kelly's stuff down there. So the deal I cut is that Sam, me and Willy—along with Kelly—are riding in the forward flight deck of the FedEx cargo jet. It's definitely not spacious and we'll have to fend for ourselves, but we get to fly back first class on Pan Am."

Will rolled his eyes, nodding his head, "So when are you getting in Johnny?"

"Damn, the day after tomorrow, but I better let Sam take the phone or she's gonna hit me. See you soon bro!"

"Johnny, wait! What about the incorporation of Circle Entertainment?"

"Damn Kavanagh, I'm losing my head. We got you incorporated in the Cayman's no sweat. I'll bring along those papers to sign as well; here's Sam."

As Dom was catching Sam up with a condensed version of the North African invasion--as it had humorously come to be called—Will figured it might not be a bad idea to check in with Kelly and see what was happening behind the scenes, below the Board of Director's level. Grating his teeth at the seemingly endless gossipy chatter going on between the two admittedly compatible hotties, Will grabbed the sat phone and promptly had Kelly's number ringing. When she answered on the fourth ring, he deadpanned in his most demure voice, "Hey baby, ready for the Southern Hemisphere?"

"Hey yourself cowboy! Talk about timing, I just walked in the door. What's going on?"

He was almost ashamed of his inability to shake the image of Kelly, riding her and spanking her ass to beat the band, from his mind but finally snapped out of it. "Nothing much, working my ass off putting an outline together laying out a precise sequence of the entire North African invasion, that's all. Would that be something my Cossack Queen might be interested in seeing—you know—maybe to show the boss and prove Kavanagh ain't blowing smoke up his ass?"

"Man would it; what's it gonna cost me?" Will was suddenly lost in a frontal lobes field trip, re-enacting how she had come completely apart during the G spot exploration. He didn't notice how zoned out he was until she asked, "Well?"

"Sorry Kelly, my mind was completely in the gutter thinking about what it was gonna cost you. Actually, I was hoping you might be able to provide me with the straight skinny, you know from the horse's mouth?"

She was laughing her ass off when she replied, "And what exactly would you like to know Mr. Kavanagh?"

"Well, I've only talked to the CEO and his right hand man about the project, but I don't see what's going on behind the scenes. Listen, we've already finished the negotiations, so don't worry about spilling the corporate beans. Tell me what you know from putting that lovely little ear to the ground."

She was laughing again, "My God, are you horny Will? I haven't heard you this animated in forever!"

That snapped him out of his reverie enough to respond, "Actually no, but it may be negotiable."

This spun her back into that sexy laugh, but to her credit, she pushed on, "So what did you want to know? Maybe how Zig was telling his CFO to do it and shut up after you got those assistant fees negotiated?"

"Nah, I know I bumped his blood pressure on that 'cause he was pissed on the phone about it. He backed off when I told him the assistants brought realism to the project."

"Do you mean the part about the Jackson Pollock mural on the ceiling? I was in his office when he was telling Warren Banding about it on the phone; I didn't know you two were acquainted?"

"Yeah, we played golf together that morning you shanghaied my ass with those Cossack restraints. Man was that some way to wake up!"

"William, when is the last time you had sex? You sound certifiably Kavanesque!"

This made him hoot with laughter, "Kavanesque? Wow, a new low, I am so ashamed. So did Warren talk to you about the court-martial? He was locked onto that like a heat-seeking missile when we talked about it after the round at Torrey Pines. Actually I believe he was more interested in the way Philippino women threw themselves at dashing bachelor American officers."

"If you keep this up, I'm going to call Dom up and see if they've got you on some experimental pain-killers or something..."

"Yeah, it's called a Brazilian wax job; ever heard of it?"

"A what?"

"Apparently it's the next big thing to hit America; think getting rid of those pubic hairs of yours and having bald vulva. Whatcha think?"

"Have you been drinking?"

"Do you still have that nice little bush of pubic hair?"

Now she got noticeably defensive, "What if I do?"

"Get your ass down here and get rid of 'em; all on me baby doll." Will's brain snapped and he redirected, "Banding got real interested in the court martial project when I told him the lead-in to the unpleasantness was going through a hundred women in a year. I think you and I sorta sniffed around that on the plane ride into Frisco when I met you."

"Well, that would explain why Warren has agreed to co-produce the court-martial project. You have become a man in high demand Mr. Kavanagh."

"So I'll have another shot at working with the hottest producer in Hollywood again? Man, I'm getting your sweet ass out of LA for that one too!"

Will was enjoying the banter so much he didn't notice Dom walk in behind him, "You had better be talking to Kelly Dupree William!"

Startled by her stealth approach, he recovered enough to reply, "Actually this is Crystal the Call Girl; I don't know how she tracked me down, but I think she knew Johnny too..."

"Hello Kelly, how are you? Looking forward to getting away from the madness?" She listened for a moment and said, "I know, he's misbehaving tonight. He's crowing about the outline that he brow beat out of us the last two days, but I'm glad we made the effort. We had to grapple around serendipitous confluence a while before we locked down on the sequence of events in what he calls the North African invasion. Yes, I believe we do, hold on," she said and then signaled for him to grab the remote headset.

"Okay Will, here's the straight skinny; Zig Kowalski's coming down to Buenos Aires himself later this week. You have him so buzzed up that he wants to meet and discuss the North African invasion, as you call it, in person with each of you. I'll be there with a tape recorder, you can bet your sweet ass. I think I know what he wants to do; I believe he wants to be the Executive Producer for this movie. He has not done that in twenty years according to my boss, who is the Producer and has been around the business forever. What do you think?"

Without a moment's hesitation he replied, "I think I'd better call Johnny and make sure he brings our golf clubs out with you on the plane. Who's coming with him; CEO's don't travel alone, somebody's got to carry the bags?"

"He's bringing his son-in-law Carlos; he's the Production Assistant to God now. Hey, if you talk to John, don't mention anything about Zig coming down to Argentina. I was sworn to secrecy, probably because he's making John fly down on the FedEx bird with the swine."

"Fuck 'em," Will said, but was immediately scolded by Dom, then continued, "I don't think Zig would be petty about it because Sam is coming, but I ain't gonna lose any sleep over it; you guys will be traveling in the first class deck behind the cockpit, so the only thing you'll miss is catering, movies and obnoxious fellow passengers. Better plan for that, I think it's 12 hours flying time, but it sounds like you're breaking it up by stopping off in Lima. We'll be at the airport to greet you guys, so is there anything else, Dom?"

Dom gave him that look of disgust—which meant of course she had something else—and said, "Tell me Kelly, did Zig Kowalski talk to you at all about being circumspect in your behavior while you're down here?"

They both detected a nervous little laugh as she said, "How'd you know about that?"

Will was suddenly interested, so he sat back and listened to Dom pursue the interrogatory. "Because he insisted on talking to Will and I in private, and proceeded to ask me—specifically excluding Will—whether I was aware of the history between you and Will, and did I feel comfortable with you coming down here. He all but said that I should be concerned about you working so closely with Will. I just found it suspicious that a Hollywood CEO would give one bit of a damn about whether his people's behavior is a concern."

"Well, you two have got to keep this on the QT; it would seem that every heterosexual male at Great West has made at least one pass at me, including his son-in-law Carlos. Carlos didn't want to take no for an answer, so he ended up getting what Will would call Cossack restraints."

Kelly paused long enough for Will to jump out of his seat, "You gotta be shitting me? What'd he do, grab your ass?"

"He wishes he would have, because then he could have scooted away from me before I kicked his sexist pig ass. No, he reached around me when he was supposedly pulling a chair out for me in the commissary—that's what they call the cafeteria on the lot—and started pawing my left breast."

She paused to catch her breath so Will offered, "Yes I remember it fondly. I take it he didn't get as warm a reaction as I did?"

Dom was slapping his wounded shoulder when Kelly replied, suppressing another giggle, "Nowhere near as warm. I stomped on his foot and grabbed his arm and twisted it behind his back, resulting in him yelping loud enough to draw attention, and he did a very poor job of covering up by limping out and complaining about his broken foot."

Will was hooting with admiration, "So this somehow tied back into them not traveling down here on the same conveyance as you and the Chessereauxs?"

"Right, but in his attempt at a clumsy cover-up—he knew the grapevine would get back to Zig—he told Zig that we had a lover's spat, and begged forgiveness for his indiscretion."

"You have got to be shitting me! He told Zig that? So what happened?" Will all but shouted.

"Well, your buddy John Chessereaux told him that he couldn't believe that I would fuck an ugly man—you've seen Carlos right?—when I could have anybody on the lot, including the actors and him. Doesn't he know he's married to a goddess? Anyway, Zig is having misgivings about who's telling the truth, but he remembered when you and I flew down to San Diego together. So he felt compelled to make sure he wasn't sending his 'home wrecker' assistant producer down to facilitate a divorce between his two most important partners, as he put it."

"Well, at least Zig hasn't come after you, has he? That could make for a difficult business decision on your part; I mean Zig's not exactly Tom Cruise."

"No, he's kept his hands off of me. He's taken up with this insanely beautiful model from Brazil, so he's occupied thank God. What'd you tell him when he asked Dom?"

"I told him we had met you while you were working in the Philippines and that we were good friends. I further insisted to him that you stay in our place to facilitate the development of the script. I believe he understands that I must naively be unaware of this cravenly torrid love affair you're conducting with my husband when you see him every twelve months or so."

After she stopped laughing Kelly wrapped up, "Alright, I think I've given you guys the straight skinny, at least as much of it as I know. Can you fax me that outline Will? That'll give me a leg up on what you guys already have etched into your DNA after that mission."

Will smiled wickedly at Dom when he asked, "You got anything left tonight…"

"What kind of question is that?" Kelly interrupted, huffing on the edge of an attitude.

He was laughing when he finished the sentence, "…or do you want me just to fax it to your office?"

"Will Kavanagh, I am going to twist your tit when I see you; you are a very naughty boy! These guys in Hollywood can't hold a candle to your level of bullshit. Yeah, go ahead and fax it to this same number, I'll set up the machine; give me two minutes. If I don't talk to you again, see you two on Thursday."

As he was faxing the outline, Dom looked at him with a scowl, "And just how do you think you're going to swing a golf club with that shoulder Mr. Kavanagh?"

He grimaced and groaned when he thought about what a full swing with a golf club would feel like. "Hey, if I can't play, I'll have to drive the cart. Johnny always says I'm his good luck charm on the golf course. He won't need my score to help anyway; he'll probably kick both their asses with his ball."

"Well, I believe you made a wise decision by calling Kelly, in spite of your seeming inability to behave around her. It is important to know what we're facing from the other side," Dom observed.

"Hey, we're partners in crime, what can I say?"

4

HOLLYWOOD VISITS ARGENTINA

THE POSSE—AS THEY NOW REFERRED to themselves plus their most connected allies—drove the Fabiano's Mercedes out to Ezeiza International Airport to meet the incoming guests. They leased a limousine for the guests' ride back to *Casa Fabiano*, rather than drive two vehicles. They also arranged for a covered step van to haul Kelly's 'office pallet' back to the casa. Ezeiza International Airport was a good twenty-plus miles from central Buenos Aires, and had been built during Juan Peron's first presidency to handle the long distance jets and their longer takeoff and landing requirements. Jorge Newbery Airport, which was a smaller, older airport along the banks of the Rio de la Plata, and within a mile or so of *Casa Fabiano*, had a shorter runway and handled mostly domestic flights within Argentina. The trip out to Ezeiza was more a demographic case study as they left the luxury of Recoleta and passed through descending levels of wealth as the neighborhoods turned into barrios the further they traveled. It was also a very slow trek out through the rather claustrophobic congestion in the barrios. Will shook his head and grumbled, "Damn *Señorita* Fabiano, it would seem helicopter service between Recoleta and Ezeiza would be a booming business here among the wealthy *Porteños*."

"You are correct Will, as the trip to Ezeiza is never pleasant unless made at night. There is an *autopista* planned around Buenos Aires City that will somewhat replicate the Capital Beltway around Washington."

"Yeah, but that doesn't sound like it helps Recoleta. They're gonna need an *autopista* to connect into or near the central business district if there's ever gonna be relief getting to Ezeiza," Will offered as Hal seconded the opinion.

"Yes, the government has opened bids for National Route One to connect central Buenos Aires to the Beltway," she was telling them as they entered a modern restricted access highway.

"Jesus Christ, now this is what I'm talking about; where the hell did this Dulles Access Road come from?" Will asked in wonder as they left heavy traffic behind and accelerated along the four lane divided highway after crossing a major intersection.

"Dulles Access Road?" Carmen asked, shaking her head.

"Yeah, when the US government opened Dulles Airport in the early 60's it was located like twenty-five miles from the White House in Northern Virginia. US Route 50 through Falls Church was the only road linking it at the time, so they opened the Dulles Access Road connecting into the Beltway at the same time they opened the airport," Will told her, glancing at Dom and closing his eyes. "What a fucking memory that was, my first trip out to Dulles."

"I see," Carmen nodded, "so we have some similarities here. We are now on *Autopista Ricchieri*, which is very analogous to your Dulles Access Road. It is a restricted access highway that connects Ezeiza Airport to the boundary between Buenos Aires City and Province, which was that intersection we just passed." She started to turn back around but suddenly jerked and stared at him accusingly, "You almost got away with that comment, *Señor* Kavanagh. What happened on your first trip to Dulles Airport, and when did you make it?"

Will just smiled at her before glancing at Dom, "That's right, that was way before we ran into Hal and Dan in Baguio, and was probably when you were 'cleaning up the trash' for the 601 Belen. Damn, that seems like ten years ago, doesn't it baby?"

"Yes, it actually makes me shiver to recall it Will," Dom added.

"Well what the fuck happened Willy; are you gonna keep us in suspense up here?" Hal grouched, honking at a taxi that cut them off.

"Sorry, it just recalls one of the darkest moments in my life. Dom and I had been carrying on this affair for, say, four months when she came to DC for a Realtor Convention. Instead of it being the grand lovers' reunion, it turned into the most trying time of my life; the court martial was years in the future…"

"Hold on, you mentioned a grand lovers' reunion; where the fuck was Danielle while all this was going on?" Hal wondered.

"Oh, let's see, the trip to Dulles actually lit the fuse for the final detonation of that toxic relationship, as Dom tagged my marriage to Ms. Chessereaux. Danielle was already seeing this guy that she worked for at the

Census Bureau, and I had stopped caring about her long before I met Dom in Denver. So anyway, the FBI had begun an investigation of Dom based on IRS disclosures of money she'd sent to her brother in Morocco. Of course, Alain turned out to be involved with a nationalist Bedouin guerilla group the FBI considered Marxist-inspired, so they brought the hammer down on Dom. Perhaps this was the origin of 'no good deed goes unpunished.' Anyway, then-Colonel Melson came to her DC hotel room on the afternoon of June the Fifth, and advised her of the results of the investigation, from which she was exonerated—thank God. The bad news was she'd hired a 'facilitator' to expedite her passport processing in Rabat years earlier and the fucking INS declared her a persona non grata for living and thriving here with an invalid passport. So Melson delivers this painful pronouncement that she had six hours before being deported from the US on an Air France flight back to Morocco. It was bad, but could have been worse…"

"What the fuck coulda been worse than being booted from the country with six hours' notice?" Hal suddenly screeched.

"Treason is considerably harsher than deportation, wouldn't you agree Hal?" Dom posed as Carmen had now turned in her seat to listen to the most riveting story she'd heard in years.

"Holy fuck, so they actually considered you a supporter of Soviet-sponsored insurrection in Morocco?" Hal screeched, shaking his head in disbelief.

"Yes they considered it, but found no indication that I knew of my brother's ties to the Atlas Triad. Alain did not have an internationally recognized bank, so I wired the money to the Moroccan Recovery Fund's account at the Bank of Zurich in Rabat. I even underwent a polygraph to prove that to them," Dom related as Will closed his eyes from the memory.

"Jesus Christ, I had no idea; so what happened next, after Melson's pronouncement?" Hal asked, his eyes glued on the rearview mirror.

"We spent our six hours wisely, as there was much to discuss. Will did not mention that he'd been warned to avoid any contact with me following my deportation or be charged with conduct unbecoming an officer by the Air Force," Dom told them as she squeezed Will's hand and noticed a tear dancing on his eyelid. "But we survived it and reunited to become the happiest couple in the universe."

"You are correct love, but Danielle was lying in wait for my ass when I got back to the apartment in Suitland boudreau, and she was loaded for bear,"

Will noted as he kissed Dom sweetly. "Oh, Dom didn't mention that June Fifth was her thirty-fourth birthday and that she stunned me by revealing she was Sigmund Freud's great-granddaughter during that little sojourn. She also gave me a book that ended up explaining it all when I finally got around to reading it."

"What the fuck did Danielle say when you walked in?" Hal asked, now in the middle of the most intense soap opera in his life.

"Now that's kinda interesting; Dom's convention was at the DC Grand Hyatt I think, and as we were leaving the hotel to drive out to Dulles we ran into Danielle's boyfriend in the elevator…"

"You knew this man was conducting an affair with your wife?" Carmen asked in disbelief.

Will looked at her sideways, "Carmen, that marriage was long over by that time, and Dom had convinced me Tommy Halderon was my ally, not my enemy. So yeah, we were actually friends, and I knew he was fucking Danielle and actually felt sorry for the poor bastard. So we run into Tommy in the elevator on his way to make a presentation to the Realtor's Convention that night on Urban Demographics, as I recall. To say that he was interested in Dom would be an understatement of note. By the time I got back to the apartment Danielle wanted to know where the hell I'd been and who the hell was Dominique?"

"Holy Jesus, you didn't have a gun in the apartment, did you?" Hal asked in quasi-terror.

"No, but I told Danielle I had just bid adieu to the only woman who had ever loved me unconditionally and I really didn't feel like fighting about it…"

Hal shivered, "Man, I'm glad I wasn't on the same continent."

"So she tried to pull her little dick dance but I wasn't having any part of it. I told her I wished her and Tommy all the best, that I had finally found a woman who loved me more than life itself, grabbed two beers from the fridge and locked myself in the spare bedroom."

Dom was snickering now as Will and Carmen stared at her. "Sorry, when Will mentioned 'a woman who loved me more than life' it reminded me that the day they got married was the last time she ever performed oral sex with him. I asked him if she did not even like him."

"Weeeellllll," Will said with a smile, "that trend turned around in a big way when I got back to Gastineau from Denver—remember we made love like two banshees the night before AND Danielle had put on a good dozen pounds. So when I walk in from eleven hours on the road, Danielle was hornier'n I'd ever seen a woman. I pulled a couple of Freelancing tricks out of the hat to save my severely damaged Johnson, and she came so hard she was screaming her head off to the considerable interest of her parents. That seemed to unlock her interest in fellatio, as she began inhaling me whenever possible after that."

"Holy fuck," Hal yelled as he pulled into a parking space. He turned in his seat and shook his head, "So you didn't know how to turn a woman on until your dalliance with Dom?"

Will shot him the bird, "In the grand scheme of things, what you just said is very much true. But once you learn the D spot and the elevated fulcrum buddy, there's no turning back. I'll never forget Greg Chessereaux slapping me on the back and asking what I wanted to drink when we got back downstairs. I told him 'make it vodka straight up' as that's what Dom used to bridle my passion when I was a Freelancing apprentice. Now Greg's a diehard bourbon man and all but demanded I tell him where I'd learned to drink vodka straight up. Danielle was watching me like a hawk, so I smiled, apologized and told him to give me one of whatever he was drinking. Catherine the Shark even murmured to me that she was impressed when Danielle dragged my ass back upstairs."

"So how'd it end in Washington?" Hal asked, completely unconcerned about why they were at the airport.

"Danielle moved out a week later to Tommy's place, 'until she could get settled' I believe were the words. She stopped by to pick up her mail a couple of weeks later on a Saturday morning, and I'd completely forgotten she was stopping by. I'd been up all night long engaged in total debauchery with this smoking hot blond I met through the guy in the apartment next door. So Danielle's standing there with an attitude when Crystal the Call Girl answers the door buck naked. Now Crystal was blond, maybe my age and smoking ass hot with an incredible body. Danielle was pissed but was also kinda jealous and interested in Crystal. She told me later that she almost turned around and came back in to pursue a possible *ménage*."

Hal was laughing, "When the hell did she tell you that *ménage* crap? I thought it was sign the papers time after that."

"Well, she did come by my fucking married housing unit—I finally made it through their priority list a week after Danielle moved out. The fucking neighbors were sniping at me about a bachelor living in married housing. So anyway, she comes by to sign papers and get the keys to my beloved Datsun 280Z and is dressed to kill. Turns out Crystal the Call Girl had turned her on but good, so she was gonna find out all the tricks during the Last Dance." Will started hooting with laughter, slapping his thighs as Dom merely smirked.

"What's so funny?" Hal demanded, leaning over the front seat by now.

"Crystal the Call Girl's primary erotic interest area and contribution to the maturation of Kavanagh was anal sex, and I absolutely had trouble holding on to her when she exploded from the G spot stimulation. The fucking neighbors were banging on walls, threatening to call the cops and all. So fast-forward to the property settlement night when sweet Danielle rolled over after orgasming her brains out six times for the final rodeo doggy ride; let me tell you brother, I gave her the surprise of her life!"

"Jesus Christ Willy, what the fuck happened?" Hal yelled as Carmen looked at him strangely. "Okay, I can figure out what happened at the—oh fuck it, what happened?"

"Danielle Chessereaux found out what it's like to be fucked that night brother. She screamed so hard when we enjoyed our last orgasm together that my neighbor Major Dudley Do-Right and his homely wife were banging on my front door wanting to know if a murder had been perpetrated. Shit, I was bleeding from the front shoulder where Danielle had bitten me trying to cope with the shuddering from the fulcrum explosion so they were suspicious. Then Danielle walked up behind me wearing my tee shirt and a pair of hot black lace panties, hid behind me and told them we had missed seeing each other. And that was it for Danielle Chessereaux buddy."

"I never knew that's how you two parted company," Hal nodded. "So no harm, no foul?"

"Are you kidding? I'm married to the most desirable woman in the world who is my love mentor. Other than killing obsessed drug lords I'm in heaven brother," Will said as Hal high-fived him.

Reacting to a noise, Carmen pointed out the windshield, "I think that's your friends coming in. Didn't you say they were flying in on a Federal Express plane?"

"Yeah, and they won't be coming into the passenger terminal," Will offered as Carmen read the road signs, all in Spanish.

"We must pull out of the commercial terminal lot and drive over to the general aviation side, to the north of the main terminal," she said as she pointed to a sign directing traffic to the Ezeiza fixed base operator.

It was a reasonable drive over to the FBO as Will looked around, "Damn, this airport is huge. The FBO looks bigger than many airport terminals I've been to." He was a bit like a child in wonderland, "Hey, there's the FedEx bird taxiing over, so let's follow it."

At the gate to the General Aviation parking ramp, Carmen let loose a fusillade of Spanish as the gate guard raised the bar and allowed the Mercedes into ramp area. As they pulled around to the huge McDonnell Douglas DC-10 Will noted, "Man is it nice coming into the General Aviation side of an airport or what? That is the way to travel."

Hal looked around at him scornfully, "It's a hell of a lot better than some modes of travel we utilize, at least when the shit's hitting the fan."

Will shook his head no, "Hey buddy, I seem to remember a bird just like this got some very valuable cargo to Tangier for us not too long ago."

"That's why I keep you around Willy boy," he nodded, "you tend to moderate my ill memories of fun rides on C-47s, you little asshole."

"Yeah, but you were carrying a 9mm parabellum in your leg at the time, and I'm not sure any ride would have been fun Harold."

As the forward cargo door of the FedEx DC-10 opened, an FBO scissors lift slowly crawled towards the opening as the operator guided it underneath the side of the huge bird. Thankfully, the FBO had a set of truck-mounted mobile stairs pulling up to the forward port-side personnel door as the pilot was shutting down the engines. The Posse was standing by the Mercedes as Kelly came running down the stairs, quickly scanned the area and took off straight for the welcoming committee. Thinking that it had been three or four months since they'd seen her, Will smiled and opened his arms to welcome her as Dom leaned against the car. To his surprise, Kelly raced right past him, offering a "Hey Will" and flew into Dom's arms, the two of them doing a reasonable job of not embarrassing themselves in front of the crew.

Will stared at the two, feeling miffed when a pair of arms snaked around him and that luscious voice purred, "Hey baby, been missing me?"

He turned to find Samantha Chessereaux tightening her hold as she began a most inappropriate kiss, causing instant karma in his loins. "You will never know Sam, you will never know. Damn it's good to taste you again woman." She smiled mischievously as he tried to banish riotous thoughts, summoning unknown resolve to redirect the conversation, "Where's my little Willy?"

Her deceptive smirk was telling as she turned her head, her hands holding his hips in the erotic embrace. He silently cursed the growing erection as she replied, "He's with his Daddy; come on, he's been grunting for you."

"Grunting huh?" Will said as he took the little guy in his arms, "Hey *mi Chico favorito*, how you been? Welcome to Argentina!"

The little tyke was probably five months old by now and excitedly grunted, "Unny, unny!" He hugged Will's neck tightly until Will leaned back to take a close look at the blonde haired little tiger.

"Unny huh? I think you look more like your Momma Willy, and that ain't all bad *Chico*!"

He looked at Sam mystified as she unlocked the code, "That's as close as he can get to Uncle Will; you are now Unny. What do you think Mr. Kavanagh?"

"I am very impressed; according to those near my mother, I didn't utter my first word until I was three years old! Willy must be a prodigy!" He twirled him around in the air as Willy laughed, "I think we've got to get him a cousin sometime soon. Dom and I are working on it." As he twirled Willy around the second time, his shoulder buckled and he let out a guttural roar to keep from collapsing to the tarmac in agony.

"What's wrong Will?" Johnny asked as he swooped in to grab Willy.

The tears were pulsing down his face, "Just overdid it a little buddy. I sort of forgot I just had surgery on that shoulder two months ago. Damn it, how much can Willy weigh at five months?"

"He's gonna be the size of Johnny according to the pediatrician," Sam told him, now doting over Will but clueless as to what to do. "What can I do to help you Will?" Will managed to glance up at her through the pain and half-smiled.

"Right now Sam, I need drugs baby."

Now Dom and Kelly were hovering as Dom kneeled down on the tarmac, "Are you alright Will? You shouldn't be lifting like that."

"I know babe, I just forgot. Jesus, Willy can't be more than fifteen or twenty pounds. Damn that hurts; got any Percs in your purse?" As she looked down to find one, Will glanced over her shoulder to see a most unexpected face, "Well I'll be damned, if it ain't my shield Rambo; how in the hell are you doing bro?"

Dan Pierson reached down to position his hand under Will's good arm and lifted him up, saying, "I see you're not quite ready for prime time just yet Will. How you doing other than the battle scars?"

Ignoring all manner of decorum, Will gave him a half bear hug with his right arm, "Shit, I'm alive thanks to you Rambo. What the hell are you doing down here?"

"I brought down the pyro package for the shoot in Peru, and since you and mean streak were down here in sunny Argentina…"

Will caught a flash of a left hook swinging towards Dan's head, which he easily dodged and Hal caught him in a modified bear hug, limping on his repaired femur. "Damn it's good to see you Dan the Man; how they hanging?"

"Must I call the authorities to report child endangerment?" Dom registered with aplomb. They looked at her mystified until she continued, "Your language is inappropriate in front of this child. Now if you gentlemen would like to continue this revelry, I suggest you do so outside earshot of Will's godson."

Will rolled his eyes but paid penance, "We'll do better baby." Looking back at Pierson, he resumed the query, "So how long you gonna be on the ground bro? Carmen's put us up in palatial splendor down here. Tell us you can come stay and play for the night?"

"Zig would like us to do a BA-turnaround, but the flight crew's burned, so we've gotta RON," he said as Will high-fived Hal in celebration of their Posse's opportunity to socialize for the first time since the wedding.

Dom stepped in with her arms across her chest, her expression one of righteous indignation, "BA-turnaround, flight crew's burned, R-O-N; please explain?"

Will turned his head so she wouldn't see him rolling his eyes, as Dan patiently explained, "Sorry Dom, it's flight operations jargon. Mr. Kowalski would love nothing more than if we just refueled here, turned around and headed straight back out. That ain't gonna happened because the FedEx flight crew has exceeded the allowable crew flying hours and we must rest-over-night here in Buenos Aires."

"So what the fuck are we waiting for?" Will shouted, suddenly ecstatic that he would be able to party hearty with Pierson, his most cherished commando buddy.

The look of shock registered on Dan's face just before Will felt the hard slap to the back of my head, so he turned with considerable angst to find Dom shaking her hand, pointing the other one saying, "What must I do to reign in this language of yours William, put you on Freelancing restriction?"

He managed to suppress the anger just enough to reply, "No, I've got it under control babe. Where was that Percodan?"

"What's Freelancing?" Pierson asked.

"I'm sure Ayako's got some similar sexual framework with you bud. You ready to head out? What do you need to do to secure the plane?"

"Nah, we've got to unload Kelly's pallet off the bird," he said as they turned to see the FBO scissors lift extend upward until it was even with the cargo deck, maybe ten feet off the tarmac. Once the copilot signaled the lift operator that he was at the correct height, he began cheating the lift in until the edge was almost touching the fuselage.

"How the hell you gonna do that?" Will wondered, not seeing any fork trucks around.

Dan was smiling as he ran back up the stairs and appeared in the cargo bay guiding a palletized cargo box onto the scissors lift with an electronic pallet jack. Pierson made hand signals to the lift operator who eased the lift up until it had the weight of the pallet secure. Dan pulled the pallet jack back inside and watched the operator lower the cargo box. As soon as it was safely down, the outward opening cargo door swung back down and clicked shut. When Rambo got back on the ground he looked around, "How far is the palace of splendor from here?"

"It's a decent ways bro, think LAX to Burbank Airport, with traffic," Will said as the Pilot and First Officer descended the portable steps. He pointed to a panel truck approaching the scissors lift, "That truck will deliver the cargo box for us, so no sweat." Something about the First Officer looked familiar as Will asked, "Hey, who's the copilot of this beast; he looks familiar?"

"Last name's Brunson, and he was telling us some wild ass stories about the Philippines," Rambo said as Will started walking towards the two men. "Hey, you don't know the guy, do ya?"

Will walked up to the two men and said, "Excuse me, but one of you resembles a relentless cunthound I knew at Clark Air Base. What the fuck are you doing flying FedEx birds Jiffy?"

"Well I'll be goddamned, if it ain't Willsome of Leena the Screama fame. What the fuck are you doing in Buenos Kavanagh?"

"Recovering from some war wounds Jiffy Jeff; just when the fuck did you get out of the war and start flying buses for FedEx?" Will asked as the rest of the crowd walked towards them.

He rolled his eyes and shook his head, "Thanks for reminding me of an infinitely forgettable portion of my life Willsome. I repeat; what the fuck are you doing standing here on the tarmac at Ezeiza International?"

Will shook his head no, "You first; when did you get out and into FedEx? Sure seems kinda seamless employment-wise."

"They ended up letting me out ten months shy of my commitment because DoD was slimming down. My fucking wife Brandy split on me the day of my last TDY to Ramstein, drained the accounts and left me high and dry. Thank God I'd stayed in touch with Kibby Blanton; you remember him?"

"Yes Jeffrey, I was the last wish his daughter Connie had before leaving Clark. What'd Kibby do, hook you up?"

Brunson was now grinding his teeth, "I'll try to forget you told me that little piece of intel you raging asshole!"

"Touché, please proceed with FedEx DC-10 transition from F-111s?"

"So Colonel Blanton knew the CEO of Federal Express and made some magic happen with some excellent referrals. So I separated from the Air Force on December 15th and flew my first flight as a quote/unquote 'copilot' in early-January when Great West Studios chartered the bird for that movie set in Tunis."

Now the crowd was circling, with Rambo and Dom being the most curious. "Is he actually a friend of yours?" Will turned to see Kelly Dupree staring with an attitude. Will's mind did a dozen back flips trying to decipher the comment.

"Holy fuck, do you two know each other?" Will was so dumbstruck he was only able to duck at the last moment to avoid Dom's slap. He shrugged and pantomimed that he'd do better.

"Yes, unfortunately," she replied, staring a hole through Brunson.

Will didn't care as he jumped at Jeff, giving him a right-armed bear hug,

"Damn it's good to see you again Jiffy. What's the deal with Kelly; what the heck am I missing here? Was this something that preceded my arrival at the Palace?"

"Yeah, by about a week," he said before looking at Kelly. "Kelly, I was honest with you and I don't think I humiliated you; why can't we be friends? That was a tough twelve hours aboard the plane trying to avoid your death stares on that flight deck. Why are you here in Buenos Aires?"

"Oh, you didn't know your friend Will here was tied into the most interesting people?" Kelly offered as Will was almost terrified to see the lover's quarrel spark openly.

"Jesus Christ, will somebody make sense of this? Jeff Brunson left me in charge of the Palace in September 1976, and I met you Kelly on a TIA flight in November '78." He looked at Kelly and raised his eyebrows, "Time to help you're old buddy out here Kell; what don't I know?"

"What she's too polite to mention is that she and I were an occasional item when she came into Clark before you arrived there Will," Jeff provided with some embarrassment.

"Well, then why are you two facing off like two hockey players at center ice at the start of a game? What didn't work out right?" Will asked just as Dom pulled his sleeve, both of them shaking their heads in dread. "Okay, my wife just told me something didn't work out between you two. Why is that still an issue three years later?" When nobody said anything Will got impatient and turned to Kelly, "Didn't we establish love and trust between us?"

"Yes, and you're right Will; this is a childish little tantrum that I've let fester far too long," Kelly admitted. She held out her hand to Jeff and said, "Hi Jeff, I'm sorry we had to part with such angst, but we're old enough and mature enough to let it be bygones, right?"

Brunson's face was splotchy red from the encounter as he held out his hand, "You will never know how much I appreciate what you just said Kelly. You're the first woman who's ever forgiven me for anything. Thank you, from the bottom of my heart. I never meant to hurt you; I didn't know we were exclusive lovers. If it's any consolation, not paying close attention to our relationship was next to the worse decision I ever made."

Kelly turned her head to smirk at Will and replied, "Good; since we're all staying together tonight, we don't need any outstanding quibbles. Now what exactly did you mean when you said it was next to the worst decision you'd ever made?"

"I think that'll wait until we get to Carmen's place Kelly," Dom said as she leaned in to whisper something in her ear.

Kelly exploded with laughter and shook her head no, "Not even in the same ball park Dominique." She turned to Rambo and said, "Are we going to wait for my gear or will they deliver?"

Two men in khaki uniforms walked up as Rambo turned to Carmen, "This is a pallet of work-related gear; think you can satisfy their curiosity?"

Carmen pulled Will over when she replied, "I'll take care of the customs inspector, but Ms. Dupree's presence here will not remain a secret considering the volume of 'work-related gear' she's bringing in. I'll get rid of him, but I'm going to provide cover by being her sponsor."

"Good by me Carmen; it's actually the truth; let's just hope 'no good deed goes unpunished' doesn't apply to the *Porteños*," Will offered.

"I happen to know him so we're fortunate," she said just as she turned and engaged in a blithering exchange in Spanish with the two men. As one began stamping passports, Carmen took the other by the elbow and said, "Aleandro, I'd like you to meet my friends Mr. and Mrs. Chessereaux and Ms. Kelly Dupree who just arrived from the United States. John, Sam and Kelly, I'd like you to meet Inspector Aleandro Rojas. Aleandro is a friend of the family and welcomes you all. He is especially happy that you chose Buenos Aires as the site for your work on the history of the country Kelly."

Kelly had on her most inviting smile as she shook his hand, "Thanks so much Inspector; I hate setting up shop without the tools of the trade, so to speak." Her overture seemed to confuse the Inspector as Rambo handed him a clipboard with a bill of lading for the 'virtual office' pallet. He pulled a small metal device from his leather pouch and precisely stamped the bill of lading.

"How long do you plan to be here writing your book *Señorita?*"

"I'm not sure Aleandro," Kelly replied, batting her eyes at him, "it could take a while if I do any traveling around your country."

Aleandro smiled, took his pen and wrote *'Indefinido'* in the middle of the stamp and handed the clipboard back to Rambo. "Do enjoy your stay in Argentina Ms. Dupree," he said, nodded to the Chessereaux' before saying a few indecipherable words to Carmen and left.

"Are we all clear?" Will asked her.

Carmen cut her eyes at him, "Please *Señor* William, do not attempt to portray naivety; it is not becoming for someone possessing a lizard brain such as yourself. The Interior Minister will no doubt hear about this international novelist being hosted at *Casa Fabiano* before the sun sets."

Will looked at Brunson, "Come on Jiffy, you two can help us set up Kelly's office at *Casa Fabiano*."

———

Hal and Carmen rode back in the limousine they'd 'borrowed' to get the visitors in from the airport as Will and Dom had Rambo, Jeff and the pilot Barry Oswalt in the Mercedes. "So Jiffy, what was the deal with Kelly? I've known her for a few months, and Dom and I even took her and Mary Claiborne by the Palace for a no-notice-hospitality-check one night when I got back from the court-martial."

"Kelly was back at Clark?" Brunson asked in surprise.

"Hell yeah, she and Mary were at Mongolian BBQ Night when Dom and I walked in, so when Trip joined us we made it a merry little band of expatriates. Kelly didn't seem like she knew about the Palace and its reputation when Dom and I drove her over. What gives here? Man, you hide things pretty well."

"Okay, I got to Clark in September 1975, and the Palace was a totally different place than what Billy Rafferty and I turned it into…"

"Billy Rafferty, why does that name sound vaguely familiar?" Will interrupted.

"Because he was Leena Garcia's 'Clark Connection' before you got there; he musta been decent to her since it took three months for her to look for a replacement—that would be you Willsome…"

"Now hold on a minute Jiffy; how did the Palace change after you and Billy Rafferty teamed up?" Will wondered, curious as to how much worse it could have been.

"Before it was a way station for geographic bachelors; they kept the tradition going by appealing to married guys on short tours. You know, twelve months at Clark and they didn't have to uproot the families. But then Billy recruited my ass in and we decided the WESTPAC sexual revolution would be centered out of the Palace. When you showed up we turned it into the zenith of debauchery brother. Never, ever have so many good-looking women hovered around that place!"

"Okay, you and Billy were the junta of the revolution, got it," Will nodded, now that it made sense.

"Right, anyway, when I first got there the TIA stews always came to the Palace Parties; some of 'em would even take a day off to be there for the parties. Even the pilots would come in with them. So Billy and I had Marie and Leena on a home-and-home rotation, and the second Palace Party we had during my tenure Kelly, Mary and Janice Caine showed up. Kelly and I hit it off and she stayed the night. So she'd make it to Clark in bursts—like once every three weeks when she could trade off with another stew in the WEST-PAC Loop. So the last Palace Party before you got there is when the cat fight happened. I don't know if you remember Frizzy…"

Will almost stopped the car as he turned his head to look in Brunson's eyes. "You motherfucker, don't tell me, nah, it couldn't be. I seem to remember this tall, very shapely thin cargo driver's wife who played naughty games when hubby wasn't around. She actually frizzed her hair up into a quasi-Afro, which was pretty odd for *haoles*. I'm sure you're not talking about the most lusted after dependent wife in the history of the US Air Force?"

"Try to maintain normal breathing Willsome. So of course we made sure the O'Club women's bathrooms and the dependent school teachers' lounges were plastered with fliers to maintain our equal opportunity status. So Frizzy comes in with her rat pack of cargo driver wives in tow, spots my ass and drags me straight into the little parlor to the left. She tells me she heard I was good in the sack so why didn't we give it a go? She even knew about the work bench for Christ's sakes, so she met me there five minutes later transformed into some nymphomaniac. She was going crazy and she had this thing for anal sex."

"I only have fond memories of the work bench as well as the mirrored ceiling tiles Jiffy; Dom even got to experience that waterbed with me on my farewell tour. So what happened at this party, did Kelly show up to surprise you or something?" Will asked, as it seemed to be playing out in his brain.

"Exactly; she normally called me from Hickam or Kadena when she was coming in, but this time decided to surprise me. Anyway, when Frizzy came in with her gal pals she had a head of steam, launched into my ass as soon as she got to the bedroom, ripped off my clothes and pushed me right onto the water bed. And that's the one and only time I didn't lock the bedroom door…"

"Oh, *Mon Dieu*, poor Kelly," Dom said, closing her eyes and shivering slightly.

"It was really pretty ugly, as Frizzy was on her knees on the waterbed at the zenith of a climax when Kelly opens the door and just stood there staring. Of course Frizzy came out of her screaming peak in semi-shock and jumped off of me yelling 'God Jeff, do people always enter without knocking?'"

"Oh Jesus Christ," was all Will could offer as Barry Oswalt even made an *ughh* sound.

"So Kelly told her, 'Actually I thought I shared an interest with him but I see I was mistaken—about the bedroom and Jeffrey Asshole Brunson. Fuck you Jeff and the horse you rode in on.' I threw on some gym shorts and caught up to her outside on the carport, feeling totally helpless. I told her I was sorry but if she'd called I woulda been a better host. So she smiles and took a step towards me, like she was gonna kiss me. Instead she hit me with a right cross and then kicked me in the nuts as hard as she could. I was lying on the carport concrete when she stormed off yelling 'Fuck you Jeff Brunson, I don't ever want to see your face again.' And that Sir William, was the last time TIA stews ever set foot in the Palace; we became two-timing, unscrupulous bastards that'd fuck a hole in the wall after that."

"And you never saw Kelly again until today's flight?" Dom asked, clearly shaken.

"Nope, but I'll tell you this much; I don't know how you got her refocused, but I'm eternally grateful. Jesus, she seemed almost like her old self just now. What'd you two do to her, relationship counseling for single lovelorn women?"

Dom was about to reply when Will held up his hand, "Jiffy, please tell me the two of you hadn't fallen in love." Before Brunson could blow him off he added, "Did the words 'I love you' ever come up in pillow talk between you and Kelly?"

"No, never Willsome, and that's the God's truth. I heard her tell Mary one time over the phone that she was excited about seeing her boyfriend, but she never ever said those three words—which as you recall were specifically verboten around the Palace."

"Well, apparently she put more weight on the definition of boyfriend than you did, or else you considered it solely a geographic demarcation. Regardless, branding the Palace a 'no fly zone' for all the TIA stews seems just a bit vindictive. By the way, you mentioned Janice Caine; did you ever hit on her?" Will asked as he glanced at Dom, flexing his eyebrows.

"Oh yeah, along with every other fighter pilot at Clark; Jesus, now that was one smoking hot woman!"

"Let me guess, you weren't cool enough for her, right? By cool I mean you wouldn't smoke a reefer with her or drop a Quaalude to make things crazier. Did I totally miss the mark Jiffy?"

"How the fuck did you know that? Did Kelly pass along that intel?"

"Nope, I learned that one painfully along with four other officers after she brought an ounce of cocaine into Clark, packed and sold it and then turned state's evidence against us at general courts martial. That's what you were giving the affidavit about me for to the Area Defense Counsel at Lakenheath."

Brunson was suddenly nodding his head, "So that's what was going on eh? We heard there was a big drug bust at Clark but nobody knew anyone involved…"

"Except you Jiffy, and only as acquaintances. Of the five of us, I was the only one who was acquitted; as a matter of fact I met Kelly on the flight back to California for the trial. After the trial she helped me get my head back together, since my career was kaput what with the publicity and all…"

"Get your head back together, what the fuck does that mean? Did you and Kelly…"

"Yes Jeff, we spent the weekend in Diego where my godson was christened—that was him you hauled down here—and that's when I introduced her to Zig Kowalski, the CEO of Great West Studios over dinner after the baptism. She's worked her ass off for them, and in three short months is already an Assistant Producer. She's here to help us write a book and a screenplay about the North African Invasion. In case that doesn't ring any bells, you hauled Hal, Carmen, Rico and Rambo—the guy you call Dan Pierson—to Tangiers with our weapons load, then beat feet to Tunis to offload the props, pyro and other equipment for that war flick."

"Holy shit; that was your black operation Dan promised me to secrecy about?" Will merely nodded before Brunson added, "I hope I'm not being a prick, but why isn't Kelly pissed at you too if you're married now and the two of you were, you know, close friends in Diego a few months ago?"

They were pulling into the mansion grounds when Will glanced back at Brunson, "That story could take three days Jiffy, but the short version is I had been told Dom was killed in Morocco over a year before, so I was just trying to keep life between the lines. When I got back to Manila the next night, three of the greatest guys a man could ever want as friends had Dominique waiting to surprise me in the bar at the Manila Hotel. Trust me, there weren't any cat fights when Dom met Kelly; Kelly couldn't believe she was alive because I'd bared my soul to her and she knew Dom was my salvation, my soul mate and my love mentor. She and Dom hit it off really well, so we're all good friends now. Welcome to my world buddy."

When they got to the house Hal twisted Johnny's arm to join him for a cocktail on the patio as Sam retreated with Henrietta to get Willy situated. Remarkably, the step van had stayed up with the Mercedes and the cargo box arrived at the same time the hosts and guests did. Carmen offered up the library for Kelly's office as Jeff and Barry helped Rambo set up the equipment, Kelly providing specific placement instructions. When they were finished with the heaviest of the moves, Will smiled and told them, "Wanna take a look at my world?"

When they walked into the study that had been transformed into the 'Incubator' as Will called it, the visitors were mesmerized. Jeff and Kelly were so focused on the good guy and bad guy pyramids on the white board they bumped into one another. Will was watching closely as Kelly acted like she'd backed into wet paint, "So Kelly, why did you lead Dom and me on like you'd never been to the Palace that night you met Chancy and Rose? You know, right after you met Dom risen from the dead at the O'Club Patio at Mongolian Barbeque Night?"

She put the death stare on, but Will just gave her the finger prompt, "Bad memories."

Will glanced at Dom and nodded at Kelly. "Kelly dear," Dom began, "Will and I both love and respect you, and I think the prior weekend with him in Diego changed your perspective on Clark Air Base, my husband for sure and probably life in general. Did you fear that telling us the truth would somehow make Will doubt your friendship?"

"The short answer is yes; Mary had already told me that Will and Jeff were close friends, so I didn't want to destroy the buzz we were all on by bringing up unpleasantness," she said, as Will nodded his head, her explanation making a lot of sense.

Will suddenly snapped around, "How'd Mary know Jeff and I were buds? I met her on my very first flight to Clark out of Hickam in early '76..."

"And she wanted to jump your bones from that moment on big boy,"

Kelly said with an impish grin.

"It only took her two and a half years and me being depressed border-ing on schizophrenia, but we finally scratched that itch. So how'd she know and pass to you that Jeff and I were close buds? You guys had already put the Palace off-limits, so I never saw her except on TIA flights." Will glanced at Jeff, "By the way Jiffy, Mary Claiborne was the star witness in my court mar-tial—she completely gutted the government's OSI agent that testified against me." He looked back at Kelly, "So?" His lizard brain kicked in as he shook his head, "In my wildest dreams I could imagine that since you and Mary shared all intel—especially concerning bedroom metrics—that she told you Trip and I had enlisted her as our secret atomic bomb witness against Janice and the OSI agent." She smiled as Will connected the dots, "Dammit woman, you already knew who I was when I met you on the plane that night! Now that's not playing fair Ms. Dupree."

Kelly glanced at Jeff before she answered, "Quite surprisingly, you dis-played more honest loyalty than any man alive after she put that sales pitch on you coming in to Hickam that night…"

"Holy shit, you were on that flight?" Will asked in amazement.

"Yep, and she thought you were maddeningly straight; you were in love with that younger woman and wouldn't even accept Mary's offer of a very private lingerie show in Honolulu."

"Why call it a commitment if you don't mean it? I know Mary wanted to fuck me blind but there wasn't any right time to do it until I was banished from Christine DeLuca's life. I still felt some slight pangs of conscience, as the two of you happened so soon after my relationship with Christine imploded. Only weeks later did Dominique point out to me that I couldn't turn love off and on with a light switch."

"So are we good now, you and me?" Jeff asked, hoping Kelly had been softened up by his former Palacetinian.

She smiled at him and said, "Will?"

Brunson looked at Will in frustration as he held up his index finger, "Jef-frey, I believe that Kelly has reassessed her hatred of you now that she knows you've experienced complete evisceration by a woman who professed uncon-ditional love turning on you as badly as Brandy did. Now if you were to look at Kelly and convince her you would never abuse love again, I think she'd accept that you and I are spiritually enlightened humans."

"So getting your soul ripped in half is somehow equal to spiritual enlightenment?" Brunson asked in obvious disbelief.

"Well, either you turn into Colonel Kurtz' heart of darkness or become spiritually enlightened. Those are the two possible outcomes Jiffy."

He actually opened his arms as Kelly allowed him to hug her. With his head over her shoulder he pled the ultimate mea culpa, "Kelly Dupree, I'm so very sorry that I treated our friendship with casual disregard; and I will never ever forsake a love relationship again."

She pulled back to look in his eyes, touched his face with both hands and kissed him sweetly on the lips. "Good; go and sin no more Jeffrey Brunson."

5

BIRTHING BUSINESS IN BUENOS

"So what's this place?" Johnny asked as they took their seats in a semi-private room inside La Cabrera, one of the best restaurants in Buenos Aires.

Hal nudged Carmen to provide the *tourista* spiel so she smiled and complied, "This is one of our favorite restaurants John. The food is excellent, but the beef is especially good here. Let me know if you need help with the menu."

Will looked around the table, assessing how much unvarnished truth could be wielded and considered the FedEx crew. The only 'outsiders' were Sam and Johnny, but they and Kelly were so far into the facts of the North African invasion that it didn't seem right to be overly exclusionary in their dinner conversation. Carmen had convinced Sam that she could entrust Willy's safekeeping to Henrietta back at the house so that she and Johnny could have a night out on the town for dinner. He looked at Jeff and Barry, "Okay Jeffrey and Barry, I don't know if you've sniffed around the edges on this little initiative we're taking with Hollywood, but at least Brunson's been associated with Circle Entertainment before. That's the name of the new company we formed to deal contractually for the development and distribution of extreme action adventure stories—all completely mythological. When you hear the word 'Posse' it is comprised of Carmen, Dominique, Hal, Daniel and myself. Of course if you hear me use the word Rambo, think Dan Pierson. Kelly and Johnny boy are down here specifically to get a movie storyline started that will hopefully become a profitable venture at the box office. What you may hear over the next hour or so could contain references to this mythological black operation that allegedly took place fifty-eight days ago. I'd like you both to swear that you will not divulge any aspects of this mythological black op until granted permission by either me or Carmen."

"You're speaking in riddles Willsome; are you talking about the North African Invasion? If so, Barry was Pilot on the trip into Tunis that refueled at Tangiers."

Will stared a hole through him, "And?"

"And I so swear to keep my lips zipped regards whatever's discussed at dinner tonight," Brunson said with authority. "Now can we order some appetizers, I'm fucking famished bro." Will merely looked at Barry, waiting.

"I so swear that I will not disclose details of this mythological black op overheard at this table tonight. Can we now get a cocktail?"

Kelly was sitting between Dom and Dan, so Will tempted fate by suggesting, "Hey, why don't you and Dom trade seats Dan? That way I can dig the goods out of you without threatening the language police." Dom gave him such a scathing look that he immediately relented, "On second thought, maybe everyone has an interest in the conversation. So what happened back at Great West? Are you now the go-to guy for things that go boom Daniel?"

As he began to reply Will caught a very discreet wink from Kelly and glanced just enough to see her make an almost imperceptible nudge towards Johnny. He rolled his eyes in disgust thinking they couldn't speak frankly just because Johnny was on the Board, but Pierson didn't pick up on the high level intrigue, "We actually made budget on the pyro addendum in Tunisia, which means they didn't have to delay shooting for supplemental HE shipments. Bottom line is I think Mr. Kowalski's okay with me so far."

"Fuck HE shipments," Johnny interjected, "when he found out you were there for the takedown in Algiers he lost any care about that Tunis war flick; he wanted to know what happened at that casbah in Algiers. Man, when you gave that report to the Board I thought we were going to have to call a doctor in to check his vitals." Johnny then leaned into Kelly and asked, "Did he tell you he's going to be the Executive Producer for this film? He hasn't done that since I was in high school, at least!"

Without a moment's hesitation, Kelly pretended it was news and said, "No, he didn't mention anything about that. How's he going to have the time?"

As Johnny shrugged, Dom looked at Dan and asked, "How's Ayako doing, and where is she? You two are still together, aren't you?"

"She's back visiting her parent's in Osaka," he said smiling, "and yes, we're still together from a spiritual perspective at least. Now that I'm based in LA, we're talking about her moving there and setting up house together. I hope it will be marginally better than it is now, given my travel schedule." He looked sadly at Hal and said, "Some things never change, eh buddy?"

Hal looked at him in puzzlement and inquired, "So where from here, Lima?"

"Yeah, the film there is about some revolutionary hero, so there's a decent pyro package. Shooting doesn't start for another few days, so I could take a blow down south where Barry says there's not a papal war zone in the brewing."

Dom and Will were immediately on alert, "What papal war in the brewing?"

Dan shrugged, then nodded to Barry Oswalt who told them, "All I know is that there's some politically active priest or something, his name is Villaponteau, in Colombia and he sees his role as uniting the lands south of the US as some exclusive Catholic archdiocese. All other religions in the region, especially those trying to exert influence, are apparently on his radar scope."

"The Catholics want to dominate South America and are wielding power to discourage other religions? I can hardly believe my ears Barry. Where the hell does a Catholic priest become so hell bent on conquest?" Will wondered as he glanced at Carmen.

Dom had a studied look on her face when she added, "The Spanish sent in their Conquistadors in the 1500s to conquer the Americas. Cortés and Pizarro were the famous ones, and I believe the imposition of Catholicism was begun at that time. Why in the world is this coming back after almost 600 years?"

Sam was listening closely and offered her perspective, "My father's family came from Ireland, and there has been trouble there between the Catholics and Protestants for decades and now is all but a civil war. But I thought that was contained on the island of Ireland, or at least within the United Kingdom."

"So what Protestant religion is predominant in Ireland?" Will asked, mildly curious as his brother Colton had been a Lutheran missionary in Nicaragua for the last couple of years.

"The Church of England, the Anglicans or what we know as the Episcopalians have a presence in Ulster, officially called Northern Ireland…"

"How so?" Pierson interrupted.

"Certainly you've heard of the Scots-Irish?" Dan nodded so she continued, "The English forcibly migrated thousands of poor Scotsmen and their families to Ulster, promising them land. These Anglicans became the initial targets for the Irish Catholics."

Pierson slapped his forehead, "Got it, before they began exporting terror to London and anywhere they could annoy the Brits. Please continue Sam, as Tonto seems most interested."

"When the Vatican wouldn't grant Henry VIII an annulment in the 1500s, England broke off from the Catholic Church and formed its own religion. The Irish chose to stay with the Holy See, and it seems as though they've been at each other's throats ever since," Sam explained, and Will was surprised by her grasp of history. *Jesus you idiot, just because she's hotter'n a sunspot and evaporates your definition of adultery doesn't mean she isn't intelligent.*

"So this Catholic priest Villaponteau is now acting like a Conquistador, is that what you're saying?" Will asked Barry.

"Dude, I have no idea. All I can tell you is that this priest is stirring up the pot in Colombia, and I wouldn't be surprised to find some coziness with the drug cartels before it's over," he said, prompting all of them to look at him strangely.

"What in the hell do the Catholic Church and the drug cartels have in common?" Hal all but stammered.

Dom was nodding her head in the affirmative when she opined, "Power, influence and control. If a man of the cloth could bring himself to ignore the moral implications of the drug trade, he could ally himself with some powerful networks of influence."

Hal was nodding with introspection when he peered at Barry with a dead serious look on his face, "What's this guy's first name Barry; I think we need to become more aware of this man?"

"Juan, his name is Juan Villaponteau."

Will glanced at Dom and then Carmen and finally Hal, satisfied that the Posse had stored the intel. "Anyone want appetizers while we ponder which size *bife de lomo* we want?"

Carmen was giving Will the evil eye as she spoke to the waitress in Spanish. "Maria our waitress says the chef will be tested with your Oysters Rockefeller recipe William. How do you want to play this?"

"Come on Belen; you know me almost as well as you know Harold." Will replied as he turned to Maria. "Maria, please ask the *chef de maison* to come see me when he has a free moment, *sí?*"

The chef showed up wiping sweat from his face but smiling, "¿En qué puedo ayudarle, *señor*." After Carmen confirmed the chef understood English well enough, Will laid it out precisely how he wanted the oysters prepared and presented.

"How many do you desire *Señor*?"

Will sized him up, "I think you got the message loud and clear Julio. See that blond goddess over there?" Will pointed at Sam as Julio nodded, "Okay, she's an oyster bogart from the get go, so she'll take two dozen by herself. So let's figure on five dozen for starters; sound reasonable?"

"And if they are as good as you expect *Señor*?"

"Then they'll become your number one selling appetizer in the world Julio. You'll be looking for me to partner with. Go and do the right thing ma man."

6

DEBRIEFING THE NORTH AFRICAN INVASION

AFTER HAL AND WILL GOT BACK from taking Jeff, Barry and Dan to the airport, Will looked at Carmen, "I'm telling ya Belen, commuter helicopter services is a growth business opportunity here in Buenos." He then led Sam, Johnny and Kelly to the study where they had set up the research area and intoned, "Welcome to our operations center, what we have dubbed the Incubator, for hatching out this story on the North African invasion."

As Johnny, Sam and Kelly were perusing the outline documents and the drafts of the sections Hal, Carmen, Dom and Will had been working on, Johnny stopped in front of a large whiteboard that displayed a sort of operational pyramid, with dual towers for the good guys and the bad guys. Sourcing from whatever pictures were available, the images of each with their real names and nicknames conjured up, some with a bit of humor. Johnny pointed to one picture and asked, "Who the hell is Obi-Wan?"

Dom smiled, "Mando Chu is my trusted mentor and lifelong friend who may have been as instrumental as you in assisting us in the mission."

"I see, and this one is the Devil himself," he said, pointing to the picture of Sandrigan.

"Actually, we considered Lucifer to be more appropriate; Satan's angel," Dom provided with a touch of angst.

"Casanova?" Sam asked, pointing to the picture of Alex. Will picked up the query with a smile, "Alex is Hal's Operations Manager at the school in North Carolina and a Greek stud who made the mistake of hitting on Dom a bit too stridently."

Kelly pointed to the picture of Dan Pierson, "Yeah, we all know Rambo here, and I think I agree with the moniker." She lighted on the picture of Rico, "Hey, who's this Che? He's kind of cute, is he married?"

Dom glanced at Will smiling, "No, he's an assassin."

"So are they mutually exclusive, being married and an assassin?"

"I guess not, Carmen here is the most deadly assassin in the Western Hemisphere," Will replied.

Kelly looked at Carmen inquisitively, "No way; she's way too hot to be an assassin."

Will glanced at Hal, who was smirking proudly, "Carmen can get next to any heterosexual man in the universe. And if he's hot to trot like Ouzo there," he said, pointing to the picture of Khalil Sidi, "then he won't even notice the 10cc of succinylcholine entering his bloodstream. And to think he took that shot just for a chance to kiss sweet Carmen; sux instead of sex for Sidi."

Kelly looked at Hal disbelievingly, but shook it off, "So is Che married?"

Dom fielded the question this time, "No he's not Kelly. Do I detect an untoward interest?"

"How can you tell from a picture? Maybe I'll get a chance to meet him at some point," she said, and Will was smiling as Dom nodded.

Kelly stopped at the good guys pyramid and pointed to the pictures at the top of Will and Dom, "This almost looks like some kind of twisted family tree. And that reminds me, due to the fact that we've got identities to protect, this book should probably be a work of fiction." She looked at Will and said, "Who do you want to be?"

He rolled his eyes and picked a name out of the cloud, "Oh, call me Tony Marantz; that seems a far enough cry from Xavier Kavanagh."

Everyone was nodding their approval when she continued, "That was easy. So what do you think we should call the book? I've heard you refer to the operation as the North African invasion before, but do you have any ideas for the name of the book? My guess is it would have a fair chance of being the movie title as well."

Hal put his two cents in with, "What's wrong with the North African invasion?

Kelly scrunched up her face, pondered it and replied, "I guess it generally describes what you did, but it's non-specific as to the operation. I mean, you didn't invade the whole of North Africa, just Algeria, right?"

Will suddenly broke into the giggles, earning a frown from Kelly, so she inquired, "Something strikes you as funny William?"

"I'm sorry Kell, it's just that the way you said it reminded me of what officer's get instead of venereal disease," Will told her, still chuckling.

She shook her head, "Oh, non-specific urethritis, I get it. So we need to think about this title thing; so Algeria invasion, Algiers invasion, Ksar invasion. None of them seem to reach out and grab me."

Dom frowned just as Will was about to respond, so he altered course and said, "Maybe we need something more esoteric, you know, not the name of the black op, but something tangentially related."

This earned him confused stares from Johnny and Sam, but Kelly seemed to pick up on it and proceeded, "Well the boat ride was through the Mediterranean, maybe there's something there."

Risking her ire by stomping on her brain-storming suggestion, he countered, "Jesus Kelly, that's just as non-specific as North Africa almost."

Dom was about to reign him in when Kelly raised her palm and said, "No, Will's right. Let's think about specific parts of the picture. Where did things start out?"

Dom, Carmen, Hal and Will all threw up their arms with that, and finally Dom explained, "We had a two hour discussion, what Will called a daisy chain and Hal called a circle jerk, before we finally came to the conclusion that it started with Adam and Eve." When the laughter subsided, she added, "For purely operational purposes, it began in Tangier. Does that help?"

Will was shaking his head and thought out loud, "I don't know about Tangier; not much action happened there except Hal pulling that Colt 1911 and pointing it at Marty Lindstrum. I'm still not sure if he would have pulled that trigger; I for one was so pissed at the bastard that I was pulling for the hammer to drop."

That comment brought a smile and a high-five from Hal before Kelly redirected, "Okay, maybe the beginning of the op wasn't eventful enough. How did it end, other than three of you being wounded?"

Without looking at the others for input, Will blurted out, "We were sitting in a Hilton suite beat to shit, but it was cold and raining in Marrakech, so we jumped at the chance to come to sunny Argentina."

Kelly suddenly got an excited look on her face and said, "Hey, I think you hit on something. How about 'Raining in Marrakech'? Now that's got panache!"

Will looked at Dom knowingly and opened his palm toward Kelly, "Actually Kelly, Will and I have used a phrase very similar to that before. We signaled alarm to one another by saying 'It's Raining in Marrakech.' I believe you've found your title."

"Alarm, huh?" she said as she nodded her head, "sounds about right for this crowd. So 'It's Raining in Marrakech' it is. Whew, I feel like I've already done a day's work!"

"Right, we'll pick this back up tomorrow when Zig and Carlos arrive in their chariot," Will said as Kelly narrowed her stare at him. He nodded his head no as she shot him the bird.

———

"How you doing Zig, welcome to Buenos Aires," Johnny said as Zig and Carlos came rambling out of the jetway from their Pan Am flight at Ezeiza International the next afternoon.

"Jesus, that was a hell of a flight," he replied, causing Hal and Will to roll their eyes since he had made the ten hour flight in the throes of first class luxury.

"So how you feeling Mr. K, ready to rumble?" Will asked as he tried but failed to elude Zig's bone-crusher handshake.

"Actually, they just fed us lunch before we landed, so I'm feeling pretty good. Let's go launch into a dump on this African invasion story; I've only heard it from your buddy Pierson, and I know you two saw a lot more of it than he did. Where are we staying by the way? My secretary said something about private accommodations, but I ain't staying in no hovel."

As Will shook Carlos' hand he looked back towards Zig, "Fear not oh sacred one; Sir Rayfield is providing you with the best room in Argentina this evening. You'll be staying in the same place where our research team is located."

He grunted, "This better not be some honky tonk Kavanagh; I don't sleep well in rat holes you know."

Will smiled as he opened the door to the Mercedes, thankful for the heads up Kelly had given them about his 'surprise' visit to Buenos Aires that had been formally announced by his secretary's call the day before. "Let us sweat the small shit Zig; you are now in the land of the *Porteños*. Are you ready to dive into 'It's Raining in Marrakech?'"

"Hell yeah, that's why I flew all the way to Antarctica Kavanagh."

"Well, it's a bit of a jaunt into the city so why don't you scan through this outline we've been working on Zigster?" Will said as he handed Kowalski a stapled booklet with nearly a hundred pages of details the Posse had captured.

"Jesus, you guys have been busy down here; let me know when we're at this castle, won'tcha?"

When they got to *Casa Fabiano*, Carlos and Johnny huffed the luggage in as the women greeted Zig, making him feel like a prince on a world tour. Ushered directly to the Incubator room, Zig was immediately drawn to the whiteboard with the players mapped out in pyramids. "So this is the madman, eh?" he asked, tapping the picture of Sandrigan. He looked at Carlos, "Wouldn't Omar Sharif be the perfect cast for this guy?"

"I don't know Zig, what kind of budget were you thinking about?" Carlos replied, no doubt wondering what Sharif's bottom line would be to play the dastardly antagonist.

Ignoring him, Zig went across the board to Carmen's picture, who they'd dubbed Angel for her soothing takedown of Sandrigan's second-in-command. He tapped it and looked back at Carmen, "So you're the mystery woman, eh? Did you know that Kavanagh here told me we'd have to cast Michelle Pfeiffer to do you justice? Now that I've met you I believe he was telling the truth."

Carmen merely smiled, furtively glanced at Will and replied, "I'm quite flattered Mr. Kowalski, but I really don't care who plays that role as long as I have nothing to do with the project other than assist you in developing the screenplay."

Zig looked at her askance, "And why is that Ms. Fabiano?"

Hal and Will saw her flinch and started to answer his question when Carmen calmly raised her hand to settle them. "I'm a very private person Mr. Kowalski. I can be effective in the things I do primarily because no one knows who I am." She glanced down at her stomach, just beginning to bulge slightly and continued, "And besides, we've got a baby on the way and we've got other protective interests to consider."

Zig nodded, seemingly accepting her reply, "So tell me why they dubbed you the Angel?"

Hal told them of the insertion of Carmen and Rico into the International Metals Conference, during which Khalid Sidi met his maker. "And she was back at the Tangier safehouse in time to hear our CIA asshole," Hal said, pointing to the picture of Marty Lindstrum, "tell us that he reluctantly believed we had nothing to do with Sidi's death simply because Dan Pierson wasn't with us."

"Pierson? Why the hell would he say that?" Zig bellowed.

"Because he thinks Pierson is the most effective counterintelligence agent in the world Zig; you've got one hell of a technical guy there," Hal explained, giving his buddy the plug.

He shook his head as he glanced at Carlos, "That guy is working things out for us in Peru now; maybe we should keep an eye out for him in the future."

"So what would you like to hear about now Zig?" Will asked.

He looked at Dom and said, "Why don't we start with why this guy kidnapped your mother and take it from there?"

After Dom had run down the basics of the scenario—impressing Will by starting with the tryst in Rabat with Sandrigan—Zig looked at her and said, "Obsessive son of a bitch wasn't he?"

"You have no idea how obsessive Mr. Kowalski; when he had an opportunity during a chance encounter three years later, he kidnapped me and took me to his casbah in Algiers and brutally tortured me for weeks," Dom related as Will began squirming. Even now, with the bastard damned to hell, it bothered him to think about what he had done to his blessed angel.

"So this casbah, is it the same...." he asked, but Will interrupted.

"Right Zig, the same casbah he took Dom to after swapping her for Ayran at the mosque in Algiers. And Dan Pierson had his buddy Vinny the Huey pilot level the place right in front of our eyes with two hundred high explosive 40 millimeter rockets. If you could have seen what that looked like lying on the fucking ground, looking up to see the smoke trails tailing through the sky above our heads like fifty fighters pulling contrails at thirty thousand feet, it was one motherfucking sight I'll never forget for the rest of my life. Jesus the starburst explosions against the walls of the casbah were like the most bizarre lightning storm you ever saw. Then the fucking house gas tank went and all hell did break loose....." Will said, drifting back to sitting on the ground watching the final destruction of Sandrigan's lair.

The room was silent when he glanced up from his daydream, everyone waiting for him to come back and finish the story. "The starbursts exploding on the house with every rocket impact was the most incredible fireworks show I have ever seen, maybe except the 4th of July Bicentennial Show at the Washington Mall in 1976." Will glanced at Hal and smiled, "But when the last forty hit the mansion some shrapnel musta penetrated this huge fucking propane tank on the side of the house. Now when that fucker blew it was like a fucking sunspot, the fucking yard suddenly feeling like some furnace and then the motherfucking casbah started leaning to the left and then totally collapsed into a pile of white hot rubble."

He snapped out of his reverie and finished, "But that bastard had already flown out with Dom in a Cessna by then, so it was no time to sit back and admire the majesty of that fucking hell house implode on itself. Jesus, I'd a collapsed right there if Kemosabe hadn't throw a couple of dexies down my throat."

"Yeah, but no woman was ever gonna be tortured and raped in that house again, let me tell ya," Hal added as Will gave him a high-five.

Zig looked at the sling holding his shoulder immobilized and asked, "So some time before that is when you saw that Jackson Pollock mural?"

Will looked at him confused until Hal jumped in, "We chased Sandrigan—who had Dom and was making his way to a secret tunnel entrance—through the house, and it was no walk in the park. Willy here saved my ass when one of the Algerians got behind me; I thanked my lucky stars that I had taught that boy how to fire a Walther, I can tell you that."

"Right, so how did his shoulder end up in a sling?" Zig wondered.

"Oh that; okay Zig, imagine being in that house which had been under combat attack for a good twenty minutes before we got there. After Willy nailed that bandit who had me dialed in for hell, we started clearing rooms one at a time. It was fucking pitch black and hotter'n a furnace, the smell of cordite and death was damn near overwhelming. I didn't want to lose sight of Willy again, so I grabbed his belt and we all but crab-walked through the house, clearing one room at a time. When we got to what was Sandrigan's bedroom, Willy stumbled over a corpse on the floor just as this Algerian bodyguard hiding in the shadows lunged at him with a curved Arab dagger, slicing right down through his shoulder."

Now Will smiled and held his hand for Hal to let him finish the scene, "So I'm laying over this dead body, the hot pain searing down my chest like liquid fire from where the knife got me and I look up to see the fucking Algerian raise up to finish me off with another lunge from that dagger. I don't know how many times you've faced death totally helpless but there was nothing for me to do except watch my life end, that fucking *janbiya* already arcing down towards my face. And then it was like Jesus rising from the grave, my own fucking miracle played out right before this dagger skewered me right down the throat."

Will glanced at Carmen and nodded, "Now I don't know if anyone's ever told you this Zig, but for some reason your mind goes into a slow motion warp right before you're about to enter the zone, you know, that zone where it's kill or be killed; what Dom and I call mortal combat. So as this dagger's coming down at me time slowed down to like one frame a second—probably my brain telling me to pay attention to my last moments of life. But then the most confusing thing I've ever seen happened; Hal stepped in from nowhere, it was behind me I guess, like it was a fucking nightmare transforming into a wet dream. Suddenly the barrel of his Colt .45 1911 cannon was pushed under the Algerian's chin and he pulled the trigger. Although the blast was deafening, I was paralyzed by the dream happening in front of me and looked up when the Algerian's head exploded to see this God-awful splatter appear on the ceiling above us. It reminded me of a Jackson Pollock mural I had seen in the Metropolitan Museum of Art when I was a teenager in New York City." Will looked at Hal, gave him a high-five and concluded, "Man did this old basketball buddy ever come through and save my bacon that day!"

"But not your shoulder Willy," Hal grimaced.

"So you guys were basketball buddies? When was that?" Zig asked, as all of the visitors leaned in to hear the answer.

"Hal was the basketball star at my high school Zig; we've known each other damn near our whole lives. I was just the bench warmer who cheered him on," Will explained as Kelly looked on with a smirk.

Hal sneered at his old buddy, "Yeah right you little asshole; you were banging that Danielle Chessereaux like a screen door in a hurricane dammit…" The room exploded in uproarious laughter as Will winked and pantomimed TOUCHÉ. "Anyway, Willy was hitting it so hard he didn't give a shit about anything. Now that I think about it, you are the luckiest bastard I have ever known!"

Will smiled meekly, "I was that day in Algiers buddy, and I'll never forget it either."

As they were eating some delicious club sandwiches for brunch, Zig cut to Dom, "So we've heard from the guys here what it was like on the ground at that casbah, but I'm interested in what the situation was like from your eyes. I'm sure it's quite different from theirs."

Will looked on with interest, as did everyone else, as they hadn't completely debriefed Dom on the episode from her perspective. She smiled furtively at Will, "The ride into Algiers was rough, as we had to go through a storm that was coming in off of the Mediterranean. Will and I had our last intimate moments together not long before we landed, and were very nervous as we made our way to the mosque. When we got there Sandrigan appeared from the other side with Maman; as we exchanged places I noticed Maman was looking very frail. When I finally looked up, Sandrigan smiled at me and then smirked at Will before berating him as a weakling. Will just stared at us until Sandrigan shifted his gaze to the balcony," she related, pausing to smile. "Hal was standing at the balcony railing wiping off the blade of a K-Bar military knife. Sandrigan's mood changed immediately as he thrust me in front of him as Will drew his Walther. He then backed out of the mosque with me as his shield and threw me into the back seat of a car and jumped in behind me. There was another car of Sandrigan's men and they took off flying away from the mosque with our car following."

It was Carlos that held up his hand for a pause and asked, "So what were you doing up on that balcony, Hal?"

Will nodded in admiration as Hal explained, "Sandrigan must have had a terrible jealous streak, because he had one of his henchmen stationed up on the balcony holding a Dragunov sniper rifle aimed at the back of Willy's head. He didn't even hear a thing until that K-Bar was slicing across his neck, but at least the bastard didn't have to suffer long. I apparently interrupted Sandrigan's plan for Will to go out with a bang, and that's why he was staring up at me as I cleaned off the knife."

Sam was shivering with disgust, but Dom didn't seem to notice as she continued, "When we got to the Liberation Highway, Sandrigan's cars sped up dramatically, and as I tried to look out the rear window to see if anyone was following us, Sandrigan grabbed me and began frisking me roughly. I asked him what he was looking for and he slapped me hard across the face and said, 'You think I trust you Dominique, my pretty lusty whore? You will not escape me this time. I will enjoy teaching you the lesson of your life.' I wanted to spit in his face, but I knew I had the stiletto in my boot and vowed to keep myself calm and hopefully alert enough to use it when the opportunity presented itself."

"What stiletto? You had a weapon on you?" Kelly asked, suddenly energized.

Dom stood up, walked over to a table in the corner of the room, opened the center drawer, picked up something, returned to her seat and held it out for Kelly to see. "This is the object that liberated Sandrigan from his means of raping another woman ever again." As Kelly held out her hand to take it, Dom looked into her eyes and opened the stiletto, the pointed blade's sudden appearance startling Kelly as she jumped back slightly. Dom's stare never left Kelly's eyes as she intoned, "Be careful dear, this is a dangerous weapon."

As Kelly took it gingerly and carefully examined it, Zig, Johnny and Sam crowded around her to look at the knife. "So this, uh, stuff on the knife, is that what I think it is?"

"It's Sandrigan's blood, and it is our eternal reminder that bastard will never rape another woman or torture another human," Will said, looking Dom in the eyes as he said it.

Zig took the knife from Kelly, tested its balance and said, "It really doesn't seem that nasty a weapon to me. I mean, I've seen a lot more scary knives than that."

Carmen looked at him dispassionately and asked, "May I?"

Zig handed it to her, "Be my guest."

"So you think this is a minor weapon Mr. Kowalski?" She asked as she closed it up, the blade disappearing into the handle as she did.

"Well, I mean it is kinda skinny and all, but……"

Before he could finish the sentence Carmen seemed to shift her hand forward as the knife sailed right over Zig's shoulder and flew across the room, impaling the spot between the one and two of the twelve on the wooden clock face. Carmen, Dom, Hal nor Will moved as they watched the others duck and dodge, making excited gestures in wide-eyed amazement. Zig's face turned red, but he restrained himself enough to get up, walk over to the clock, pull the knife out with some effort and cleverly ask, "Is there something significant about twelve o'clock I should be aware of?"

Will actually rolled his hand out to Carmen with exaggerated drama, "That's the moment I parachuted out of an antiquated cargo plane in cloud cover over Ksar el-Boukhari to begin the takedown of Sandrigan's operational drug and weapons base."

"And this knife had something to do with this takedown?" He asked, struggling to connect the dots.

"At the end it certainly did Zig. Dom planted that knife in Sandrigan's scrotum all the way to the hilt, but the lucky bastard didn't have to hang around and figure out what a life without balls was gonna be like," Will replied, a smirk leaking out around his lips.

Zig actually reached to grasp his crotch, recovered and asked, "Why not?"

"Because Will blew the bastard's brains out before he could think about slitting my throat," Dom said, leaning over and planting a rousing kiss on his lips.

"So you bagged this bastard warlord Lucifer, but you got a bum shoulder out of it?" Zig pursued.

"Try a nine millimeter parabellum to the ribs sometime Zig, it's downright invigorating," Will said, rubbing his mending ribs, "but we've gotten away from Dom's experience with Satan's henchman."

Carmen reached out to Zig with her left hand, "May I?"

Zig handed the stiletto back to her carefully, but she didn't take her eyes off of him as she closed the knife and flicked her wrist towards him once again. As the visitors ducked, Will barely noticed her right hand slipping it into Dom's pants pocket. Zig looked around in wonder and asked, "Where is it?"

"Put away Mr. Kowalski; one can't be too careful around children."

"The high-speed chase along the Liberation Highway ended as we turned off to begin wildly careening through residential neighborhoods towards his casbah. Sandrigan had a hand-held radio to speak with the other driver, trying to determine how to lose the car that was apparently following us. At the next intersection, the lead car took a left and our car took a right, but I managed to catch a glimpse at the car following us—which I hoped Will was in—turn to follow our car. Sandrigan cursed and shouted into the radio to find us on some boulevard. A few blocks later I heard gunshots as Sandrigan pushed my head down and told me to stay down. After that I didn't see anything until we arrived at his casbah, but his tortured shouts over the radio indicated that something had happened to the other car."

"Your husband had just shot the fuck out of their trail car, that's what was causing the asshole to shout on the radio. Damn Willy, you stepped up to the plate son!" Hal added.

"Right," Will pointed to his ears, "that's why you're still shouting eh?"

"I noticed that," Sam interjected, "did you experience some hearing loss Hal?"

Hal flinched as Carmen whispered something in Spanish to him, so Will glanced around the table and nodded. "Hal was pushing our Renault Fuego as hard as she'd go, but the trail car got off a lucky shot and blew out the back windshield, pissing Hal off royally. He said something like 'shoot that damn AK Willy,' so I aimed the AK-47 out the back window and held the barrel down as best I could while I emptied the clip on full automatic. Now I know that sounds like rock and roll to some, but inside that Renault Fuego with its sixty-three horsepower, it was damn near as deafening as a howitzer. I remember laughing at Hal as the trail car pulled over, steam billowing from the hood of that monster Mercedes and yellin', 'What'd you say?'"

Hal scribbled something on a sheet of paper, shot Will the bird and held it up; it read 'Lesson Learned: wear earplugs for takedowns.'

Dom looked at them with newfound understanding and continued, "Our car slowed down for what I presumed was the casbah, but Sandrigan told the driver to stop because there was a car stalled just outside on the street. I heard some panicked discussion as the car jerked again and we slammed on brakes under the portico. Sandrigan was shouting instructions to his bodyguards to stay in place and shoot anyone that followed us into the compound. He then grabbed me and threw me in front of him to go into the house."

"So Sandrigan didn't notice that there was a shootout going on at his casbah?" Hal wondered.

"Oh yes, as soon as we entered the house there were shell casings covering the entranceway and the smell of gunfire was prominent along with blue smoke hanging everywhere. What happened in there?" Dom asked.

"All hell broke loose. So you didn't see Dan Pierson lurking off to the side when you got out of the car?" Hal asked.

"No, Sandrigan was forcibly shoving me forward to enter the house as quickly as possible. So he pushed me in front of him until he saw the shell casings and then he pulled me to his body, wrapping an arm around my neck as he told me to move. As we passed the kitchen I saw a body on the floor, and there was another one just inside the bedroom. I heard someone call out to him as he shoved me towards his secret escape passage, and one of his men rushed in the bedroom and asked if he was alright. Sandrigan told him to conceal himself next to the door and kill anyone that came in. He then opened the door to his secret tunnel that leads to the airstrip in back of the property. I heard a commotion and looked back, but it was too dark to tell what was going on. I thought I heard Will shout, but that was replaced by a loud gunshot. As Sandrigan was setting the keypad inside the door to the tunnel, I caught a glimpse of Will but Sandrigan quickly closed the door and said, 'You'll never see that boy again; perhaps in hell.'"

"He set a booby trap for us that Hal spotted just before I opened that door, so what happened next?" Will asked, Hal nodding with anticipation at the new perspective.

"We quickly traversed the tunnel, but the guard at the opposite end was dead on the ground. Sandrigan pulled out a pair of plastic handcuffs and put them on me, then threw me up into one of the airplanes and buckled me in place. We were just taking off above the house when I caught another glimpse of Will, but it was too late to do anything but hope I lived long enough to have a chance to kill my tormentor."

"So what'd the house look like from the air?" Hal asked.

"There was a huge hole blown into the back of the house where the dining room was, and there were some bodies in the yard. Oh, and the garage looked like it was drunk, leaning to the side like it wanted to fall over. I remember wondering why it was painted gray until I took another look and noticed the back of it was missing," she explained.

"Pierson got close enough to give it a C-4 welcome. So how was the ride to Ksar; did Sandrigan talk to you?" Hal wondered.

Dom nodded and said, "It was actually a very stressful ride, as the weather was horrendous and the plane was bucking constantly. That added to the frustration of the handcuffs and made for a dreadful journey. Sandrigan was unable to establish radio contact with his factory at Ksar, so he was in a truly foul mood. He slapped me hard twice during the flight when I told him that he had finally met his match in my American hero. I knew I was infuriating him, but I didn't care because I loathed him so completely. When we flew over the factory, there was smoke coming from a couple of buildings but the property looked reasonably normal. There weren't any bodies lying on the ground. When we landed, Sandrigan became truly homicidal when there was no one to greet us, so he dragged me off into that hangar building where the drugs were stored. Once we were out of the airplane, the sound of gunfire was very noticeable, but it didn't sound like there was a lot of automatic fire— just single shots sounding sporadically."

Hal was rocking slightly in his chair, his recollection beginning to meld with hers as he inquired, "Mustafa was implementing his 'law of the desert' by then. So how did the shootout with Will and I go down?"

"There were gaps in the bales of marijuana on the shelves, and Sandrigan peered through them to get a fix on your whereabouts. When I saw Will I yelped, but Sandrigan slapped me again and put one hand around my mouth as he began edging us out towards the end of the aisle. When we moved out from the packed storage racks, I saw Will and Hal coming up the center of the building between the aisles with their guns drawn. Sandrigan saw them at the same time and told Will that he would deliver his whore to him begging, and then he fired two shots at them. My heart completely imploded when I saw both Will and Hal fall to the floor, and I couldn't for the life of me understand how he had hit them both from that distance. As Sandrigan dragged me towards the door at the back of the building I beat him with my cuffed fists cursing him for shooting my husband, but he scowled at me before everything went black. I must have been knocked unconscious, because I wasn't aware of anything until I opened my eyes behind the building, slumped on the ground. Something told me to retrieve my knife because we had to be getting close to the end of the nightmare. I pulled it out of my boot and managed to cut through one side of the handcuffs, the motion signaling Sandrigan that I was conscious again."

"But you weren't alone, were you?" Will told her, no longer asking.

She grasped his hand, squeezed it and finished the epic, "No my darling, you and Mustafa were standing right in front of me, weapons trained on Sandrigan. I thought it ironic that Sandrigan now was holding a curved dagger to my throat, as I planned on showing him a dagger as well in short order. I peered into Will's eyes, blinked downward so that he saw the stiletto in my hand and he nodded just perceptibly. Sandrigan gave his final pronouncement that he was going to deliver me to Will in no condition to ever make love to him again, but Will just looked at him and said, 'Hey!' At that moment I extended the stiletto and swung it backwards with my right hand as hard as

I could. As soon as I felt Sandrigan flinch a gun went off very loudly and the knife flew away from my throat. I jumped to the side and looked back at Will, who took two steps forward and said, very calmly, 'Goodbye Sandrigan el-Boukhari.' I watched the bullet blow the back of that bastard's head away and have never felt a greater sense of relief in my life. Will had delivered me from evil, as he had been delivered at a previous time himself. I clutched him and found him badly wounded and barely able to move, and my heart exploded as I thought I was losing him once again. He told me he was hurt, but that he was alive, and I can't remember what else happened because I was holding on to him and never wanted to let go the rest of my life."

The tears were rolling down Will's face as he took her into his arms, clutched her tightly and buried his face in her neck. "I love you more than anything Dominique. If that was it, if that was the end for me I knew one goddamn thing; we weren't going to live in fear of that bastard anymore."

Will looked up finally to see everyone wiping their eyes, even Zig Kowalski. He shook his head just slightly and said, "Damn, I think we all could use a drink after that!"

As they got up to fix the drinks, Henrietta and her daughter came walking into the kitchen with bags of food, placed them on the counter and began arranging everything in a buffet-style serving line. Hal's curiosity was getting the best of him when he asked, "And what *Porteño* delight have we here *Señora* Henrietta?"

She frowned and replied, "It's time for you to experience the *Porteños el bufet, Señor* Harold."

There must have been twenty different containers of all manner of meat entrees, vegetable sides, warm bread and a couple of deserts. Henrietta was slapping at Will's wrists as he ventured in for a taste test of the delicious looking pork ribs. As they were finishing off the last of the scraps, Zig looked at Carmen and said, "Now this is the way to do a smorgasbord if I ever saw one. I'm beginning to like it here in Argentina!"

"So no shabby treatment so far Mr. Kowalski?" Will ventured with a chuckle.

"We ain't made it to the golf yet, so I'm withholding final judgment. Is there any other part of the Algerian operation that we need to know about before we break for the night?"

Will looked at Carmen and said, "We only got into the Ksar side of the operation at the very end. Now Hal may have heard it, but I've never gotten a debrief on how that key part of Sandrigan's demise unfolded. Would you like to take us through it Belen?"

She nodded and began, "Our part really began when Reda, Mando Chu's explosives expert, and I left with Mustafa in his car from Tangier. The passage through the mountains was treacherous, and we were exhausted by the time we got to Er Rachidia. I'm not sure our piece of the operation would have been possible without the satellite phone set, as we had no way of knowing when the CIA cargo plane was to arrive otherwise. After a fitful night's sleep, the C-47 arrived the next morning, and I was greatly relieved to find two operable parachutes in the plane."

Dom raised her hand slightly and asked, "Fitful night in Mustafa's camp? Did everyone behave?"

Carmen lips betrayed a hint of a smile as she told them, "In spite of Hal's assurances to Mustafa that I could take care of myself, word apparently did not filter down to all of his men, as one pursued me to Mustafa's aunt's home where I was to stay for the evening. I was questioning Bedouin manners when he approached me and grabbed my shoulder to get my attention. When I turned around, he touched my face and said something, but it was in Arabic and I didn't understand him. He leaned in closer to kiss me so I slapped him, figuring that was a universal signal to retreat. When he didn't, I had to provide him with a suitable incentive to behave and everything worked out fine."

"Suitable incentive?" Will asked, breaking up into laughter.

Now she did smile, "A moderate kick to his groin seemed to rescue his manners for the rest of the evening. There were 40 fighters with Mustafa for the trip, and the plane was crowded by the time everyone and their weapons were aboard. Charley, the pilot, quickly noted that I had the best command of English, so he invited me to sit in the co-pilot's seat in the cockpit. The flight over to Ksar took about two hours, and it gave me a chance to discuss the positioning of the plane for the parachute drop with the pilot; jumping into a cloud layer is a risky evolution, but with the strong winds we had to estimate the best spot for me to eject from the plane—landing in the factory grounds would have been disastrous. I did not exit the cloud layer until right before my feet touched the ground, and I was alarmed at the close proximity of a radio transmission tower to my landing spot."

"Tell me about it," Will interrupted, "we almost hit that same tower when we exited the clouds in the Cessna. So you made the jump by yourself? Wasn't that kinda risky?" He asked and instantly recognized the idiocy of the statement. "I mean, what if you'd gotten hurt or killed in the jump? There was no backup?"

Carmen merely nodded, "One of Mustafa's men, Brahim, had made a parachute jump before, so he went out the door first. I was deeply impressed by his courage."

"Damn, so you did have some backup. Did Brahim make the landing okay, I mean without any injuries?" Will wondered.

"Yes, at least no disabling ones; he suffered only a twisted ankle, but he was key to taking out a nested group of Algerians later," Carmen replied and paused before continuing. "So as I was setting up the rifle, I heard the call to noon prayers from within the town and knew the timing was perfect if I could locate the spotter guards who were manning the tower vantage points. After eliminating those two, I closed up the M24 and began climbing down towards the factory as the C-47 rolled up to the hangar door at the airstrip. I reconnoitered the barracks building and found a large number of the guards saying noon-time prayers and set off in search of Reda to evaluate the possibility of employing plastic explosives to take out the barracks. Once Reda set the charges up, we backed off a distance and he detonated the plastique. At that point several fire fights broke out, mostly with guards not in the barracks, and four of them successfully holed up in the factory building and effectively stymied Mustafa's men with their field of fire. I was able to gain access to the factory building and neutralized the residual nest of guards. Two of Mustafa's men were killed by a booby trap protecting access to the subterranean storage rooms; this seemed to enrage him, so he instructed his men to kill all of the Algerians."

Sam looked on horrified and asked, "So they just killed them all in cold blood?"

"Mustafa correctly determined that survivors could both identify the attackers as well as seek revenge, so his decision made good tactical and strategic sense," she answered without any show of emotion.

"Oh Jesus, I hope I didn't fuck up," Will said.

Carmen looked at him with concern, "Fuck up how Will?"

"When I went out to find Mustafa to begin packing up the plane with the goods, I stopped him from shooting a wounded teenage girl so that she could tell everyone in Ksar that Sandrigan and his men no longer controlled them," he said, rolling his eyes at the potential for revenge that he had precipitated.

"What's wrong with that? What harm could one girl do?" Sam asked in disbelief.

"That girl could foster much animosity and pledge revenge as a blood oath," Dom replied, shaking her head sideways. "I realize that sounds tragically cold-blooded, but this was a combat operation targeting a deranged killer. I fervently hope that tactical intrusion does not come back to haunt us in the future."

7

WHAT A DAY FOR A DAYDREAM

AT BREAKFAST THE NEXT MORNING, Zig was wolfing down his third waffle when he suddenly thought of something, "Hey, where we playing today? I guess they got decent courses down here?"

"Here's the plan of attack for today Zig," Will explained, "the military actually has a premiere course on Campo de Mayo, which is like their Fort Meyer and Andrews Air Base altogether where the Army and Air Force headquarters are located. Carmen's brother is best friends with the Deputy Minister of Defense, and he's invited you to play as his guest."

He looked at the sling holding Will's tender shoulder immobilized and said, "So how we gonna play if you're all gimped up? I just know Chessereaux must have some sandbagging scheme to put the shaft to us."

Will looked at Hal and said, "Think you can bail me out here buddy; can you swing with that leg?"

"Yeah, I can probably hit the ball, but I can't walk 18 holes; I gotta have a cart if I'm gonna play," he said, sounding like a good sport considering the shot he'd taken to his leg.

Zig rolled his eyes, "Right, I can see your ass shooting par and taking it to us like Johnny Boy did at Olympic last month. What's your handicap Rayfield, and don't be bullshitting me."

It was almost hysterical how Zig assumed being the CEO of one of dozens of studios back in Hollywood meant he was the king of the world, even around the most lethal black op commandos in the Western Hemisphere. "Well, when I last played six months ago I shot an 82, and that was at Andrews Air Force Base; it's a pretty decent course, but it ain't Augusta National."

"I feel something crawling up my ass here. So what's the game John? And don't hand me any of that Captain's Choice shit."

Johnny smirked, well attuned to Zig's incessant posturing before golf outings. "Okay, we'll make it best ball for say, another half point on Will's take for the movie rights."

The bulging veins on his forehead bespoke the spike in his blood pressure, "Goddamn it Chessereaux, if you're gonna be like that, we'll make it hundred dollar Nassau; good by you?"

Johnny had already told Will that their point and a half could easily play out to a million and a half US given the movie's complexity, so he was unusually magnanimous when he said, "That works for us; you about ready to go check out Campo de Mayo?"

He was nodding his bald head in the affirmative, "Hell yeah, I need to hit some balls if you're gonna be a shark today. Carlos hasn't swung a club since Olympic; let's hit the trail."

As they were heading out, Johnny looked at Will, "What are your plans for today? Want to come keep score?"

He smiled at Johnny as he shared the plan, "Nope, I'm using my day off to take a Perc and mix some Pina Coladas by the pool. Zig about squeezed every last morsel out of my brain yesterday."

Hal looked at him with intense envy before turning to Carmen, "What's the plan for dinner this evening babe?"

"I thought we'd do something special for our guests tonight since they're leaving tomorrow. Do you think *bife de lomo*, *pomme frittes*, sautéed spinach and garlic bread might appeal to everyone?"

"Hell yeah, we got some already?"

Zig picked up on the conversation and asked, not without rancor, "Hey what's this lomo shit, you trying to put off some mystery meat on me?"

Carmen and Dom were laughing out loud as Hal replied, "No Zig, *bife de lomo* is Argentina's finest grass-fed beef filet mignon. We've got a huge grill, called a *parilla*, out back that we can socialize around while we're grilling 'em. Sound good to you?"

"Grass fed eh? Sounds good, what's our tee time? I need to hit some balls before Chessereaux scalps my ass."

As he leaned in to kiss his hot fiancée goodbye, Hal intoned her, "Better get some Grand Marnier while you're at the market babe, this crowd can get rowdy."

She glanced at Will with a sly grin when she replied, "I'll take care of everything honey; you gentlemen have a good time."

"Hey, careful with that gentleman stuff, Chessereaux is with us," said Zig as he laughed so hard he started coughing.

———

As the guys were leaving, Will looked over at Carmen putting the dishes away and once again thought what a magnificent piece of ass she probably was in bed. Even three months pregnant, with her stomach just starting to bulge slightly, she was smoking ass hot. Maybe it was being pregnant that made her seem vulnerable; Lord knows he actually feared the woman when she spoke. Hal wasn't wrong when he labeled her the most dangerous woman in the world.

"Whatcha thinking about cowboy?" Kelly said as she draped herself around him with a sensuous hug.

Thinking he'd throw her off her game, he told her, "Sex."

Carmen gave them a furtive glance when he said it, but Will was distracted when Kelly sat in his lap, "Well what a coincidence, so was I."

Ever since Dom had admonished that there was to be no fooling around while Zig, Johnny and Sam were in Buenos, the lust was simmering just below the surface. Will looked at her, kissed her none too meekly on the lips and replied, "And which fantasy were you playing out in that pretty little head of yours?"

Without missing a beat, she replied, "Oh, I was thinking about that pretty little head of yours."

Her clever rejoinder caught him by surprise, as the erection party came to life, much to his chagrin. Carmen was now looking at the two of them suspiciously, "My, you two are being somewhat suggestive today."

With that, Kelly swung around and straddled his lap, making small thrusts at his crotch with a wicked smile. "Oh I don't think there's any suggestion at all." With that she launched into a devastating french-kiss, as Sam walked into the room, took one look at them and broke into a huge grin. "Well, my, my. I see the good friends are warming up."

"It's not what it looks like Sam..." was all he got out.

"Yeah, I bet it looks better without any clothes on," she said as she rolled her huge breasts across his shoulders.

Will was wondering how much estrogen he could stand when Dom walked in and said, "You look outnumbered William; how's your shoulder?"

He rolled it to test, "It's still a little tight babe, maybe a Perc will loosen it up."

Carmen turned around and said, "Didn't you say you were going to fix pina coladas out by the pool today?"

"Yeah, so what? You worried about me passing out?"

She reached up into one of the kitchen cabinets, selected a bottle, took out a pill and walked over to him, "Here, take this. It's milder than the Percodan, and you won't get overwhelmed drinking the pina coladas."

He started to grab it from her, but instead she casually pushed it into his mouth and held up a glass of water, saying, "Let us help you with your recovery today Will; you need a vacation from recuperation."

"Okay, enough playing around," Dom intoned, "everybody go change into swim suits. We might as well take advantage of this nice day and get some sun."

"I've got to go to the market and get the *lomos* for dinner. See you all in a little while, and try and behave while I'm gone," Carmen said as she grabbed her wallet and was vanished.

Will was blending up the second batch of pina coladas when Dom cautioned him, "I've got to go inside for a minute. I don't want you three getting into any mischief while I'm gone either. I expect to see you fully clothed when I come back, is that clear Mr. Kavanagh?"

He was already feeling happy, but not drunk, "Go ahead babe, I promise I'll still have my clothes on when you get back."

He was kicked back on a chaise lounge, minding his own business soaking up some rays enjoying the day. Sam walked up behind him, stroked his ear, causing his sunglasses to almost fall off. He playfully slapped at her, "Hey, you heard the Zen master, no fooling around. I am being a good boy today. That little pill Carmen gave me has mellowed my ass out but good."

Shrugging as if she could care less, she pointed to a walled enclosure, "Hey, what's that over there?"

Will looked where she was pointing and saw the privacy wall comprised of five foot cedar fence boards. "I don't know, let's have a look."

As they entered the enclosure, he was surprised to find a huge hot tub. Kelly swooped in behind them, smiled furtively and bent down to flip a switch on the control panel located along the outer coping of the fiberglass tub. The tub's jets immediately began boiling up, the forced air warm currents appealing to his repaired shoulder invitingly. He looked at the two 'temptresses,' as Penny Martindale had labeled them and offered, "Shall we?"

Heedful of Dom's warning, he stepped into the hot tub with his polo shirt on, figuring he'd be in compliance with her specific rules of engagement. He smiled inwardly that she hadn't mentioned hot tubs being off limits.

His temptress associates however, not being so constrained quickly pulled off their tiny bikini swimsuits and plunged in, splashing and laughing.

Will was sitting at a corner, the warm water jets blasting his shoulder and ribs from two directions, and was feeling whole again for the first time since the North African invasion.

His Zen-like field trip to the frontal lobes was badly disrupted when Kelly insisted, "Here, let me help you with that shirt." She looked down at his surgically-repaired shoulder, noting the still pink scar tissue and said, "My God Will, that's a hell of a scar."

"Yeah, it wasn't much fun getting it either." As she pulled the shirt up over his head to alleviate stress on the shoulder, he nodded his head no, "Hey the rules of engagement are….."

"Here, let me help you with those trunks, they seem to be getting in the way," Sam said as she pulled off his swimming trunks.

His interest in Dom's rules of engagement were badly compromised as Sam straddled his waist and they totally vaporized when she began french-kissing him with incredible passion. It suddenly became apparent that he'd lost control of his life as a nominal erection instantly morphed into a blue-steel hard on. Totally overwhelmed by his penultimate fantasy, he searched those galactic blue eyes and confessed, "Jesus Christ I've missed doing this with you woman."

She was wearing that Mona Lisa smile when she shifted to allow the water's buoyancy to position her directly above him, easing down over the blue steel erection, causing both of them to shudder dramatically. He had no other thought in the world until Kelly appeared next to them, rubbing and caressing Sam's breasts. Will closed his eyes and luxuriated in the incredibly erotic dream, the sensual aura completely engulfing him. He suddenly sensed a shadow blocking the sun, so he looked up and saw Dom smiling at them. Dread quickly overtook him but she merely wagged her finger, "You're such a naughty boy."

With that she took off her swim suit and joined them in the hot tub, all but inhaling Kelly as the two of them unleashed the restraints of mixed company. *Mixed company, did I just redefine that term? For now it means two husbands who might otherwise object.* With Dom otherwise focused, he smiled at Sam, "Hey, this is my dream day; I must be in heaven. Never in a million years did I foresee the three of you naked at the same time. Am I one lucky motherfucker or what?"

She responded by turning up the urgency dial, now well into her high speed finish routine, the water splashing up around them from the frenetic copulation. Will was distracted from Sam's urgings by another shadow blocking the sun. He grabbed Sam's hips to momentarily slow her and looked up to find Carmen fully dressed, a frown on her face, no doubt disgusted by the sexual hijinks playing out in her hot tub. "I'll be right back."

He looked back at Sam shaking his head, "Man, I hope we didn't fuck up."

Sam smiled furtively once again, leaning back and playfully faking a backstroke in the tub. Will saw the opportunity and put a full frontal attack on her exposed labia, resulting in instant karma. Sam was within a hair of climaxing when she reined it in and sat still on his lap, the two of them panting and flushed. He merely winked at her, "What's up; not ready to go over the edge of complete abandon Samantha Diane Herrington?"

She stared at him apparently surprised at his control, "Not yet."

They heard a splash and saw Dom and Kelly desperately flailing at one another, neither Sam nor Will sure how the D spot played out underwater.

Just as Will's engineering mind thought he had it figured out, he turned around to find Carmen standing at the edge of the hot tub, a terrycloth robe wrapped around her. She leaned down and had two yellow pills in her hand, "You think I need more?"

She smiled furtively, "Oh, these aren't painkillers; these are from Hal's stash. They give you more lead in your pencil."

Will shrugged and said "Wow, you must really put it to him if he needs pills, or does it take that long to excite you Ms. Fabiano?"

He opened his mouth for her to put them on his tongue, "No, there's a faster way."

"Oh yeah, Dom showed me your expedited delivery method the other night with a Percodan." He smiled flexing his eyebrows, "So I finally get to french-kiss the invulnerable, unapproachable Carmen Fabiano, eh?"

With that, she dropped her robe and was buck naked. Will just gasped at her body; she was rock solid, with medium size breasts, but she had the most incredible nipples he had ever seen. She got into the hot tub beside him and put the two pills in her mouth. He saw her chew down and then she initiated the french-kiss he'd so badly wondered about. Her mouth was now wide open as she transferred the crushed pills to his. He smiled at her and offered, "Thanks, I guess; you never answered my question Carmen Belen Fabiano."

By now, Sam had moved out of the way as Will glanced around to see the other three women watching the interplay between he and Carmen as if it were some soap opera drama.

"So you think you can excite me with little difficulty Mr. Kavanagh?" She said it with a certain flippancy, which had the opposite effect on Will. *Okay, I see where this is going, and I'm gonna show her a little Freelancing with Freud if I can keep my shit together.*

He angled his head towards her and narrowed his stare, "So, you've been around Dominique Lefebvre for two months now and she's not imparted the nuances of Freelancing with Freud to you?"

She rolled her eyes, "I take it these are sex tricks that result in elevated screaming?"

"Most of the time, why?"

"Because you drive my Harold to the edge of insanity imagining what you two are doing. This is when he reaches for his little yellow pills."

Will glanced back at Dom, who was smiling wickedly, as Carmen jerked his head back to look at her. He gave her one of her own upjerks of the head and smiled, "We shall see *Señorita.*"

She straddled his lap and conjured up almost hypnotically erotic accented English, "What's your hidden sexual fantasy Will Kavanagh?"

He felt the other women's eyes boring through him, trying to gauge Dom's self-image as she closely observed him seducing this woman, his unrequited object of pure lust. Carmen pulled his chin to gain his full attention as he surrendered the truth; fuck the consequences, "You are."

She smiled furtively, glancing down at their union, "Good."

She began moving her pelvis around his lap, as he quickly found the most sensitive nerve-packed square inch of skin on her body and massaged it gently. *Thank you sweet Jesus for allowing me to live this long; I will forever believe in the power of positive thinking and second chances.* She never stopped staring into his eyes as her breathing became labored. He gently began exploring until he found her D spot. Her eyes took on a smoky resolve as her pelvis began thrusting very slightly. Now she fondled his stainless steel erection, as they both reacted to the growing excitement breath for breath. She stopped rotating her hips and asked, "How do you want to take me?" He was smiling now, her curiosity obvious.

Without further discussion he asked, "Oh, you mean the first time?"

"There will only be this one opportunity for you to impress me with your manhood *Señor* Kavanagh."

"Fair enough, guess I'd better get it right then; turn around and put your arms over the edge of the tub, I want to take you from behind."

This seemed to please her, so she did as he requested and looked back, "And what now?"

He reached up around her and got a hand on each nipple and gave her a moderate squeeze, pulling on them lightly. Her moan of pleasure told him he'd guessed right. As he entered her, she let out a whimper and seemed to push back against him. He slowly built her into a frustrating frenzy of anticipation; her moans shifting to huffs, like the first phase of hyperventilation. He imagined her greatest fear and smiled inwardly as he reached up and tickled her throat, producing a distinct gasp. He started riding her in circular motions as she once again began to push back, the huffs now turning to soft pleadings.

Knowing fright might set her off, he put his hand back to her throat and gently closed his fingers around her neck, focusing on the soft skin of the nape. When he did so she gasped for breath and began bucking against him so hard he wondered how long she could keep it on the edge before collapsing into orgasm. He grabbed her hips and threw her hard sideways, resulting in loud insistent pleading. Carmen was about to lose that control she guarded so selfishly, as Will focused his thoughts on anything but the startling effect she was having on his ego. He let go of her hips as one hand found her left nipple while the other her magic launch button. She was somehow balanced on the verge of insanity when he gave her a hard thrust upwards; pinching her nipple hard while simultaneously massaging the upper reaches of the labia. He heard Carmen swearing—the tide inevitably overtaking her now—as she continued to lunge, reaching back to pull him in tighter. She finally exhaled and half-collapsed, still emitting little yelps. She was radiating sexual fire down below, like a nuclear furnace around him. She looked over her shoulder finally, swore in Spanish then asked through clenched teeth, "You did not climax?"

"Of course not," he said as he glanced back at Dom and flexed his eyebrows. "I am Dominique Lefebvre-trained Ms. Fabiano. That was Part One of our audition, *n'est pas*? If you liked the introduction, Part Two just might be the ultimate sexual fantasy, *sí*?"

She moved so fast she startled him. She was suddenly straddling his lap and kissing him as if the world was going to end. He finally pulled back from her, "Well, was it worth the wait?"

Now she was challenged, her pride showing, "Very much so *Señor* Kavanagh; I was not prepared to allow you to overwhelm me, but you did so. How do you propose we execute this Part Two?"

"I'm gonna lay down on that bathrobe on my back and you're going to join me. Is this something you might be interested in?"

"Oh my God, he's going to show her the fulcrum," Sam blurted out, unable to suppress her excitement.

Carmen was instantly alert, "What is this fulcrum she speaks of?"

"She's been there before Belen, and she swore she saw God that night. Is this perhaps too much excitement for my *Porteño* lover?"

Carmen gave Sam a whimsical look, "If Samantha can handle you, so will I."

Will liked this position so much more because he could watch her facial expressions and ravish her body with his eyes, now already coated with sweat, the tub water wiped off when they got out. In spite of herself, the earlier orgasm had superheated her furnace, and she was doing her best to slam an orgasm out of him when he grabbed her hips and stopped her pelvic motion. Between panting breaths, she asked, "What are you doing? I was almost there."

As he slammed her hips backward the first time, her eyes showed alarm as he smiled, "We shall see." By the third violent impact at the fulcrum Carmen was beginning to open and close her eyes, bleating in Spanish. On the next push back he slammed up into her as violently as he could and that was it; Carmen began shaking involuntarily as she forcefully squirted onto Will's stomach, the viscous splattering up onto his chest. She was now in a ballet split trying to maximize penetration as he thrust up into her with considerable vio-lence. *Come on baby, you can't hold it inside any longer. You're gonna have to forget about the audience and focus on your own soul for the next minute or so.* She let out a scream and began swearing in Spanish as she absolutely tried to crush Will with her overheated erogenous fire pit. He thrust up into her one last time and com-pletely lost it, the intensity of the orgasm totally blinding his soul. When he opened his eyes she was down on his chest, her arms around his neck pleading in Spanish. He felt her sides and smiled; the cool wet clamminess of a cold sweat shiver. He turned his head and kissed her neck, "So how'd you like the elevated fulcrum?"

She acted like she didn't want anyone to hear as she kissed his ear, "*Mío Dios,* I have never felt anything like that in my life Will. *Mío Dios,* you made me climax harder than all the times in my life together. How did you do that?"

He found her ear and whispered, "Have you ever ejaculated before Belen?"

"What? What are you talking about?"

"Look at my stomach," he told her and watched the reaction.

Now she was embarrassed, "I am completely shamed; I have never ever done that before."

"It's nothing to be ashamed of Carmen; you just completely lost control of yourself when your soul rejoiced, and I might add, you inspired the bejesus out of me!"

"*Mon Dieu,* she more than inspired me too," said Dom, swooping in to kiss Carmen passionately. This had the unintended effect of revving Carmen's engine up again as Dom saw it and backed off.

"My God, that was unbearably erotic. I had an orgasm just watching the two of you. I must say, you kept that lust very well concealed William; are you happy now?" Will turned to look at Carmen who was still planted firmly on him, waiting for a final kiss. By the time she rolled off, he looked down at his Johnson in disbelief. *My God, what the hell was in those little yellow pills?*

"Sure, what's next?"

"Me, you up for your love mentor?" She asked, smiling.

For some strange reason he felt immediately aroused and the erotic scene she had just witnessed had obviously stirred all three of the female observer's libidos to a frenzy. And so things continued on Will Kavanagh's magical fantasy tour, as Dom finally screeched, "Damn you Will Kavanagh; that was not playing fair, you just wait!"

He smiled at her, "So Ms. Fabiano's loss of composure affected your libido?"

It quickly became obvious that Sam was sitting on a hair line trigger, what with having been all but tortured as a sideline spectator. She completely lost her senses when he gave her the Everest launch, climaxing like a small volcano. Like a fuse suddenly lit, Sam slammed her body down with brutal effect, concluding the elevated fulcrum, coming so hard she shouted as she gave off a guttural, agonizing scream. He was sucking on those incredible areolas when they both exploded with the combined fury of a tactical nuclear weapon.

Thankfully, Dom had gone to the bar and mixed another batch of pina coladas which they hungrily inhaled as Carmen fed him another pill. "Jesus woman, what are you trying to do to me?"

She smiled seductively and replied, "We just don't want you to give out at any critical juncture. I would hate for Kelly to miss out on what I experienced, *usted semental.*"

He looked at her with a scowl until Dom told him, "*Usted semental* is *vous taureau stud* in Spanish."

He nodded his head and looked at Carmen, "That's so nice of you to say Ms. Fabiano, but I would like to impart classic Kavanesque wisdom." She prompted him with the finger roll, "I could never even contemplate such a performance—pills or no pills—if I wasn't with the four most alluringly sensuous women in the Southern Hemisphere."

Seeming to catch his second, or third wind, he looked at Kelly and said, "What's your pleasure my dear?"

"In spite of Mrs. Chessereaux' seeming intransigence, I think it's about time for the Midnight Cowboy to ride again."

"Well," he smiled somewhat drunkenly, "never up never in for the G spot my dear." Once he got into rhythm behind her, she started writhing and grunting so violently that Dom and Sam were helping control her motion, the restriction of which seemed to only enhance her violent conclusion. As Will climaxed one final time, he just managed to tell her with a dose of glee, "The

Midnight Cowboy rides the Cossack Queen once again!"

Will woke up with a start, shaking his head, wondering if he had dreamed it all. He looked down and saw that he was dressed, his clothes dry just as they had been before the hot tub episode began. He reached up and felt his sunglasses, but suddenly noticed his face was sunburned. He looked around, and Kelly and Sam were sitting in their chaise lounges just as they had been, reading books and listening to a radio playing some kind of funky jazz. He got up and walked over to the hot tub, which was turned off, no evidence of water splashed on the coping, nothing. Beginning to wonder if he was losing his mind, Dom walked up behind him, "Hey, how's sleepy head doing; you feeling better now?"

"Better than what?" He asked, wondering what kind of crazy charade they were playing on him.

"Better than you were when you went to sleep; we thought you had too much to drink with that painkiller. Are you feeling hungover?"

He shook his head and said, "I'm a little groggy, but I'm fine."

"Good, you needed some rest after the week we've had," she replied sweetly, softening him with her compassion.

Will just rubbed his head in disbelief, "Jesus Dom, I had the most realistic dream. Man did we ever break your rules of engagement. And it seemed so real, but I guess the mind can play some strange tricks, *n'est pas?*"

"Yes, I believe the mind can create some extraordinary fantasies," she offered.

"But it seemed so real Dom," he looked at her, totally helpless.

"Oh come on Will, you know we all have fantasies."

"I think I just had the greatest one of all time," he said, finally accepting the truth.

"But you can't believe everything you dream, can you?" Dom had that foxy smile as she winked and brushed her hand across his crotch.

"Hey, watch it," he yelped as his sore member tingled in response.

She looked down at his pants and said, "Now that must have been some fantasy!"

8

UNEXPECTED GUESTS AT CASA FABIANO

"So how'd it go on the links today?" Will asked his disheveled looking companions as they sauntered into the house from their excursion to Campo de Mayo.

"That goddamn sandbagging buddy of yours limps around like he can hardly stand upright and then he shoots lights out," Zig reported as Will looked at Hal with raised eyebrows.

"Jesus Zig, what can I say, I liked the course," Hal offered with an embarrassed smile.

He was growling, no doubt ready to take another bite out of Hal when he remembered something, "Hey, is your brother-in-law coming over for dinner? I kinda liked his buddy; sneaky little bastard around the greens though."

"I take it you're referring to Danny Rojas, who snaked us for fifty bucks? And I believe they're both coming. Oh shit!" Hal said and looked wide-eyed around for Carmen, "Hey honey, did you get enough *lomos* for a couple more folks? If not, I'll go get some more."

She rolled her eyes, "Of course I did; I suspected you might bring home some wayward golfing friends, knowing you were playing with my brother. I had the butcher cut up two whole loins, so we have plenty."

He snaked his arm around her waist, his hand resting on her hip; as Will's mind flashed back to his lusty daydream. "What would I do without you baby? Thanks for thinking ahead. Did you get some wine and the Marnier?"

She pecked on the lips, "Of course I did." She then scrunched her nose slightly, "And I believe you need to shower up and get Campo de Mayo off of you Mr. Rayfield."

He pinched her ass, earning a slap on his arm, "Maybe we should both take a shower; can't get too clean, right?"

"Perhaps later, my wounded, smelly warrior; now go!"

They were kicked back, relaxing with cocktails on the backyard patio when Hal noticed Will's face, "Jesus Christ Willy, what'd you do, fall asleep in the sun today? You look like a fucking raccoon."

"Yeah, Dom was giving me the devil for drinking the Pina Coladas with the Percs, so I've heard enough grief for one afternoon. Your fiancée just snickered but Henrietta saved my life. She cut some stalks from her Aloe vera plant, and the juice takes the sting away; Henrietta's good people bro, she looks out for us wounded warriors."

Hal nodded, "You're getting the hang of it around here if you've figured out Henrietta's more than just a housekeeper Tonto." They turned to find Roberto, Carmen's brother, walking over with two men in sport coats. "We so missed you on the course this afternoon Will," Roberto offered with faux sympathy.

Will stood to greet them, "Hey, I'd a been there if I could've. This shoulder's not quite ready for a prime time golf swing just yet." He glanced at the two men with Roberto and offered his hand, "Hi, I'm Will Kavanagh. I don't think I've had the pleasure of your acquaintance."

As they shook hands, Roberto had a sheepish look on his face, "Will, please meet Special Agents Lucas Torres and Rodrigo Carbon. They are with the Presidential Security Unit."

Will tried to stifle the alarm he felt, "Taking the night off guys?"

Hal limped up just as Lucas replied with a polite smile, "Actually, we are what you might call the 'advance team.' We inspect the premises of any location *El Presidente* is to visit. I apologize for the short notice, but we only found out *El Presidente* was coming to *Casa Fabiano* one hour ago."

Hal and Will both shook their heads slightly, as Will confirmed what he thought he'd just heard, "The President is coming here tonight? Why would he be coming to *Casa Fabiano*?"

Lucas looked slightly embarrassed and shrugged, "I am not sure why *El Presidente* Videla is coming here sir, but you may wish to ask Minister Rojas, as he will be with him." He faced Hal directly, "May I seek your indulgence

Señor Rayfield; as Agent Carbon and I must inspect the premises?"

Hal nodded with a glance at Roberto, whose family owned the estate, "By all means Lucas, is there anything we can do to assist?"

He smiled tightly, "That will not be necessary *Señor*; please excuse us sir, we will be as discreet as possible."

As the agents walked off, Carmen appeared behind them, "Who are they?"

Will looked at Roberto accusingly, "Yeah Roberto, why is the President coming here tonight?"

Carmen's eyes were burning through her brother when he replied, "Daniel Rojas called me thirty minutes ago and said President Videla would like to meet *Señor* Kowalski. I know that The President is making great efforts to promote culture and the arts now that the *Revolucionarias* have been dealt with. I can only presume he wants to meet the CEO of a major Hollywood studio. I apologize if I have made this situation awkward for you *mi querida hermana*. Who knows, this could be a good association for us all."

Carmen looked at Will and gave that little upjerk of her head, "In the study, now *por favor*."

With Hal, Dom and Will settled, she shut the door and launched into Hal with both feet, "Do you have any idea how we're going to explain Mr. Kowalski's presence here to the President?"

Dom looked like she had been slapped, "Oh my God, how did this happen?" As she did there was a knock on the door. Roberto opened the door cautiously and entered with a slightly embarrassed expression.

"Sorry, but I need to bring you all up to speed on several items before *El Presidente* Videla arrives," Roberto said as Carmen nodded her head towards a seat.

Dom was not to be deterred, "So how did this happen?"

Hal was unrepentant, "All I can tell you is that Zig and Danny Rojas, who turns out to be Deputy Defense Minister Daniel Rojas, hit it off on the golf course today and Roberto invited him along for dinner. How the hell the President made the invite list I ain't got a clue."

"He probably wants to promote Argentina to Hollywood would be my guess," Will offered, "but that doesn't matter. What is Zig doing here, at least for public consumption? And for that matter, what are we doing here?"

"I am *Porteño* by birth, so that explains our being here," Carmen stated, "but Kowalski's presence could be problematic."

"Hey, we didn't invite him, and he showed up on his own. My suggestion is let me be the reason Zig's here, since I'm writing the book he intends to make a blockbuster out of and Executive Produce. I hope we can sell it," Will offered with obvious misgiving. He remembered something vague before it crystallized in his mind, "Damn, remember the other day when that Customs Inspector approved the 'virtual office' pallet of Kelly's equipment?" He looked at Carmen and asked, "Wasn't it you who said the Interior Minister would know about the American novelist staying at *Casa Fabiano* by that evening?"

She nodded, "That may have set off a slight curiosity, but the golf match with Daniel Rojas today lit the fuse, as my fiancé is prone to say." She then looked at Roberto and tried but failed to smile, "What can you tell us that will shield us from danger, *mi hermano?*"

Roberto had a look of concern on his face as he exhaled and crossed his legs nervously, "I take it you have educated our guests regards the Process of National Reorganization?"

"Yes, Belen explained Peron's 'Legacy to Argentina' a few days ago. I saw an article in the Herald about missing persons," Will offered up. "Hal here even thought the Editor of the Herald might get in hot water about the article."

Roberto nodded and shrugged, "You are most insightful Harold; I would be very surprised if *Señor* Robert Cox remains as Editor of the Herald through the end of this year. The government will not harm him in any way, but the fact that he ran that story will make him a target of all of the military Junta's enemies. He will be pressured to publish more of their accusations and such, and this will no doubt be accompanied by death threats. No party to this so called Dirty War has fought fairly my friend."

"So what do we need to know about the Dirty War to keep from snagging tripwires while the President is present tonight? By the way, what do his friends call him, you know, his peers? Do they call him Jorge, or what?" Will asked as everyone nodded.

Roberto chuckled slightly, "Most people call him *El Presidente*, but his closest allies refer to him by his first name Jorge."

"That's kinda key Roberto; you pronounce George 'hōr hā' here in *Porteño*-land?" Will asked as Hal rolled his eyes. "Hey boudreau, I didn't know if maybe his wife and best buds call him Rafy or what."

Roberto started laughing, "You are correct in your pronunciation of Jorge Will, but I have never heard anyone refer to him as Rafy. Mr. President is probably safe."

"Okay, we've got the name all figured out; what has been hidden from us that we do not know and could make Jorge feel uncomfortable if we were to discuss it?" Will pursued.

Roberto almost rolled his eyes this time, "First of all, Videla is a fairly religious Catholic, as is his wife and family. He is from Mercedes, a city some one hundred kilometers west of Recoleta. He and his wife Alicia had seven children, one of whom was born with congenital mental retardation and died in a hospital some eight years ago at age nineteen. Videla is very much orthodox in some of his beliefs, one of which is the sanctity of the unborn child. This has now grown into a huge public...oh, I do not know the word..."

"Shitstorm?" Will offered as Dom grimaced.

"Exactly, his interest in unborn children has grown into a public relations fiasco..."

"How in the hell could the unborn child in the womb be a PR nightmare?" Will asked in disbelief. Dom was now angling her head in disapproval, "Sorry, I didn't think about the issue of abortion."

"Now you have discovered the tripwire *Guillermo*," Carmen interjected. "Abortion to Videla is the worst form of sin. He refuses to allow a pregnant woman to be killed, and this has caused the upheaval."

Now Will was totally confused as Roberto picked up, "Okay, *mi amigo Guillermo*, what if the woman is a captured leftist revolutionary bent on destruction of the Republic?"

"Ah," Will nodded, "so how many times has this happened to cause it to become a political shitstorm publicized by Amnesty International?"

"A few hundred from what I understand," Roberto said as everyone but Carmen shook their head in disbelief.

"Damn, what the hell, is it mandatory for leftist or Marxist females to be pregnant?" Will blurted out as Hal winced.

"Ah, now we come down to the crux of the matter; efficiency in execution—literally—*Guillermo*. When Videla and the Junta took over they did so as

a last resort; the country was at the edge of anarchy due to the urban bombings, assassinations and kidnapping of wealthy industrialists. As their reason
for dethroning Isabella Peron, the military Junta stated that a concerted campaign would be undertaken to kidnap, torture and kill anyone regarded as
being part of or supporting the left wing guerilla groups…"

"My God, just what the North Vietnamese said we did not have the will to
do to prevail in Vietnam. Well I'll be damned," Will said in near admiration.
He looked at Dom and tried to peer into her soul, "Do you remember that
movie 'Apocalypse Now' where Colonel Kurtz told Captain Willard about the
Viet Cong going into the villages where the Americans had inoculated all of
the children for polio?"

"Not really, what does that have to do with…"

"With the National Reorganization Process?" Will finished for her. "In
the movie, the Viet Cong had come back after the Americans left and cut
off the inoculated arm of every Vietnamese child and left them in a pile. It
hit Kurtz as the most incredible will to win imaginable. Now I don't equate
the Junta's 'efficiency' with the Viet Cong's barbarism, but I see the absolute
incredible will the Junta was willing to push forward to defeat their version of
the Viet Cong." Will was nodding when he turned to Roberto, "So the Junta
found the country riddled with leftist-leaning people, or did it get ugly with an
expanded definition of enemy?"

Roberto was seeing Will in a totally different light, "I must watch this
movie, this 'Apocalypse Now,' if it is that intense. But you are correct in your
assumptions; left-wing guerilla groups became more widely defined as anyone dissenting from the Junta's policies. So thousands of people were arrested—and Belen knows about this—and tortured and many were killed. The
'baby stealing' became a real public relations nightmare, even though Videla
thought he was preserving the sanctity of the unborn by having them adopted
by eager and willing families."

"I guess it's just a technicality that most adoptions involve voluntary
abandonment of the child by the mother," Will offered sarcastically. "But of
course, if she was a *Montonero* or a Guevarist ERP member, she had forfeited
her right to choose. Sorry, but I can sorta see this thing from either side man."

"Videla will love you because of that; the international community is not
quite as inclined as you towards accommodation," Roberto offered.

"Well, a hundred years from now, when all the fucking limp-wristed left-wing liberals are dead and gone, I think history will judge Rafy Videla in a much more positive light. I mean he and the Junta did step in and save Argentina from anarchy, right? They saved the country but probably got a bit heavy-handed with political opposition. But dammit, the bottom line is they saved Argentina from the Cuban surrogates' Marxist revolution, so I tend to lean toward the Junta saving the Republic," Will pronounced prophetically.

Carmen sat on the arm of his chair and put her hand on his shoulder, "I believe you have stated irrefutable logic if it were not for the *desaparecidos mi querido Guillermo*. The mothers of the adopted babies were mostly enemies, but the twenty thousand disappeared persons is the legacy of Emilio Massera from which Jorge Videla cannot hide."

Will put his palms together and bowed slightly so quickly Roberto did not notice, but his tone was contrite now, "Of course *Señorita*, the voice of reason that insures the entire karmic circumstance is visible; *muchas gracias mi querida Belen*."

She leaned over and kissed him on top of the head before whispering something to him.

"What the hell was that?" Hal grouched. "I leave for one afternoon and suddenly my fiancée is your moral compass?"

Will stared down his best friend, "I believe Belen became my conscience the night you first admitted you loved her Kemosabe." Hal rolled his eyes but finally nodded his understanding, "Good, so does Rafy drink at all? Is he high-strung or uncomfortable in social settings?"

"He has escaped four assassination attempts thus far, so he is a bit on the focused side; I've never seen him completely relax socially," Roberto explained. "But I believe his intention in coming here is to do what he can to lift Argentina above the ugliness of the Dirty War, which is now over and done with. He is focused on improving the near-ruined economy and wants to inspire culture and the arts where he can. He even appointed a non-military officer as the Minister of Tourism and Culture last year after she was the *titiritero* for planning and executing the World Cup soccer tournament."

"Whoa, whoa, whoa," Will held his hands up in the time out signal. "What the hell is a *titiritero*; damn if it doesn't sound sexual?"

Carmen smiled at the implication, "Rosita Cabrera was much like the Tonto for the World Cup matches."

Will shook his head, "So she was the swizzle stick that stirred the drink?"

Roberto laughed, "Now I don't know what you mean Will; but Rosita was the puppet master, perhaps the behind-the-scenes enabler who did all the work for some military officer who took credit?"

"Ah," Will nodded in understanding, "the shitty little projects officer eh? I was a SLPO when I was a lieutenant, but it sounds as if this Rosita earned recognition and reward." Roberto nodded with a smile as Will narrowed his stare on Belen, "So is there a sexual component?"

"The Tourism Minister is what you coonass Cajuns would call a 'hot momma' I believe," she provided as Dom's eyebrows flexed.

"Which brings up another very relevant point Roberto," Hal said as everyone turned to look at him. "What you just said about the Tourism Minister kinda implies that all key positions within the government are trusted military officers of the Junta members. How in the world is Danny Rojas the Deputy Defense Minister if he didn't come up through the military ranks? Does he have pictures of Jorge with Evita in his younger days?"

"If he did he would have disappeared by now, *no crees*?" After the laughter dissipated he continued, "Daniel Rojas is from Cordoba, and earned a degree in metallurgical engineering before joining the Defense Ministry's, oh, *cómo se llama eso Belen?*"

"CITEFA," she replied as Will gave Hal the Italian army salute.

"Does it have anything to do with scientific and technological research centers?" Will offered.

"Exactly, that is what CITEFA is for the Defense Ministry. Daniel excelled at CITEFA and gained the Director's ear, convincing him that the future of Argentina's Air Force and Naval aviation was dependent on the transition to jet aircraft. He made this assertion right before Argentina bought its largest aircraft carrier, so he was treated somewhat as a prodigy and promoted to the Assistant Minister for Planning at headquarters. He soon found himself in front of Defense Minister Lanusse to sell his proposal which was bought into all the way to the President. Within months Daniel Rojas was attending the Inter-American Defense College in Washington, where over ten months he made key friendships with other foreign students and the American Security Assistance Agency. When he returned to Buenos Aires, Daniel Rojas had the preliminary agreement worked out for Argentina's purchase of the Douglas Skyhawk jet. Within months he was in California watching the first of the Skyhawks taking off from their production plant for the long flight south to

Argentina. When he returned he was made the Assistant Minister for Systems Acquisition by General Lanusse…"

"So this General Lanusse was Danny boy's rabbi, *no es?*" Will asked as Hal tried to slap him.

"I am unsure about the rabbi reference, but Rojas became the darling of the generals at Edificio Libertador. In early 1973, he arranged the purchase of the French Dassault Mirage as Argentina's primary fighter interceptor. Then President Lanusse rewarded him by naming him Deputy Defense Minister…"

"Man, it's nice to become indispensable," Will nodded. "I take it the, uh, Libertador Building is like the Pentagon?"

"*Precisamente*, and when the current Junta rose up in 1976, Daniel Rojas was the only senior staff director who survived the upheaval at Edificio Libertador and Campo de Mayo. He is now Videla's wonder boy as well since the American embargo was imposed by your President Carter," Roberto educated them.

"Wow, so Danny boy's been able to work around the embargo, eh? What's he done, gotten in bed with the French, Brits and the Israelis?" Will wondered as Hal narrowed his stare.

"*Una vez más, precisamente*; he is now showing the Junta how to survive after the divorce with the *Norteamericanos*," Roberto said as there was a knock at the door.

Carmen opened it to find Henrietta, "Sorry to bother you *Señorita*, but Special Agent Torres wishes a word with *Señor* Roberto."

As Roberto stood up he looked around, "Are we all properly briefed now on tripwires and land mines?"

"Yeah, that was one hell of a dump Roberto; *muchas gracias mi amigo*," Will said as he left to coordinate with the Presidential Security agent.

———

Twenty minutes later Carmen had the five visitors join the Posse in the Incubator Room. "Alright everyone," she began, "we just learned that tonight we are entertaining not only Deputy Defense Minister Daniel Rojas, but also President Jorge Videla. As best we can tell, the President's interest in coming here is your presence Mr. Kowalski. Argentina's been through a most divisive civil war that ended a couple of years ago and now he's focused on rebuilding society and improving the economy. Your position as CEO of Great West

Studios may well be seen by the President as an opportunity to improve both the economy and culture, as well as begin workarounds to the US President who many hope will be replaced next year…"

"So this President is trying to shape his future as much as possible; sounds smart to me," Zig offered as everyone nodded.

"Right, but the problem we have is explaining the presence of the Great West senior representatives at *Casa Fabiano*. As everyone is aware, Will, Hal and I were deeply involved in an unsanctioned paramilitary operation to rescue Dominique's mother in Algeria this past January. I believe we covered our tracks as well as possible—the Algerians apparently don't even know who to complain to about the incursion. It is imperative to our collective health and safety to limit this knowledge to as few people as possible." She looked at Zig and continued, "I realize that you and Carlos came here to obtain in-depth information about the raid from each of us, as this will prepare you for your upcoming project of overseeing the creation of the associated motion picture. I would propose that you came here to interview Will in detail, as he is the author of record for 'It's Raining in Marrakech.' Carlos accompanied you to consider casting possibilities for the characters, and Kelly is here to work with Will in developing the screenplay for scripting. Your golfing affliction resulted in your introduction to Minister Rojas today, and we hope the President's interest is primarily due to your position as CEO of Great West Studios. Have I left anything out? Are there any other issues we need to discuss? If not, I must assist Henrietta with dinner preparations."

9

PLAYING HOST TO EL PRESIDENTE

THE SMALL CONVOY OF VEHICLES pulled into the circular drive of *Casa Fabiano* to disembark their passengers as Roberto patiently waited, assuming hosting duties for the evening. He bowed just slightly as he reached for President Jorge Videla's hand. "Welcome to our home *Su Excelencia El Presidente*."

Videla shook his hand warmly, "I hope I haven't made your life too much of a bother this evening Roberto. Daniel told me of your visitors, and I wanted to meet them in person before they left Argentina."

"Please come inside and meet everyone," he said, gesturing his VIP guest towards the front door.

"It is my pleasure to introduce my sister Carmen and her fiancé Harold." As Will caught his first glimpse of Jorge Rafael Videla, he was a bit surprised. Jorge was possibly five feet eight inches tall, was trim and carried himself very erectly. His prominent moustache looked a bit like an overgrown Hitler-style bottle-brush, but Jorge smiled easily and seemed to be pleased to 'have the night off.' Although Roberto had warned that Videla liked to wear his uniform whenever in public, tonight he was wearing an open-collared light blue shirt, dark grey trousers and a navy blue blazer. *Hmm, he's been in the job long enough now that he doesn't feel insecure without his uniform shield. Hell, he's dressed like a guy in Georgetown for Christ's sakes!*

Carmen curtsied just slightly as she reached for his hand, "It is indeed a pleasure to meet you President Videla. It is an honor to have you in our home." She then turned to her visitors, "These are our guests from the United States Your Excellency. This is Mr. Zbignew Kowalski, and his son-in-law Carlos Santine, visiting from Los Angeles. Also from California are our dear friends John and Samantha Chessereaux and Kelly Dupree." After Videla had warmly greeted them Carmen finished the introductions by saying, "And these are our newlywed friends William and Dominique Kavanagh. Please come out to the patio and let us offer you some refreshments."

Will was impressed when Videla detoured on his way to the patio to walk into the kitchen and warmly greet Henrietta, who was deeply embarrassed by the attention. "So what would you prefer to drink Mr. President?" Carmen asked, playing hostess quite remarkably. Will had rarely seen her so outgoing, with the exception of that lusty dream that repeatedly flashed before his consciousness.

"You are so kind Mrs. Rayfield," he replied, then turned towards Zig and said, "I'll have whatever Mr. Kowalski is drinking if that would be convenient."

Hal had assumed the role of shadow escort for Defense Minister Daniel Rojas, saying "What'll it be for you Danny?"

The informality caused everyone to flinch, but Videla looked at him and smiled, "I see that a round of golf has worked wonders in overcoming excessive formality Daniel; perhaps I should take up the game. Do you think it might help me?"

"Only if you need another source of unbridled frustration Mr. President," Will offered as Dom winced.

Videla hooted with laughter and replied, "Perhaps you are correct Mr. Kavanagh; I believe I have quite enough of those sources already."

"Please call me Will Mr. President, everyone else knows me by that name," he said and was immediately rewarded with a nudge of disapproval from Dom.

Then the President requested an almost unbelievable breech in protocol, "If you all would oblige me one indulgence for this very intimate evening, I would consider it an unaccustomed gift if you could address me by my given name Jorge. I so tire of the strictures of formality that come with this office I hold."

Will smiled broadly as he touched his shoulder and told him, "As you wish Mr. President."

The rear of the Fabiano estate opened into a large manicured lawn shielded by a tall masonry perimeter fence. Between the rear of the house and the Olympic-size pool was an open-sided covered patio that formed a large casual entertainment area. To one side of the patio was a massive grill, perhaps fifteen feet in length with a masonry base and attractive chimney penetrating through the roof of what looked like the classiest porch Will had ever encountered. *No high-fallutin' outdoor grill rooms like this in Cajun country.* He was impressed that Roberto was assuming the role of *grillmeister* for the evening, not pawning off the work on the hired help. As he excused himself to tend to the fire that was already set, Hal escorted everyone to a beautiful handcrafted wooden bar and fixed the drinks. "So what'll it be Zig? Sounds like President Videla's following your lead."

Before Zig could answer Videla held a hand up and with a deliberate voice insisted, "Perhaps I did not make myself perfectly clear earlier. I would not want to have to resort to threats to have you accommodate a simple request by a humble native of Mercedes: my name is Jorge while I am sharing your hospitality. Are there any questions?"

Will looked at Zig with a shit-eating grin, "So what are you and Jorge having to drink Zigster?"

Kowalski's face blushed immediately as he raised his hand to slap him, but Kelly intervened like the moderator she had become by putting her arm through his and pointedly telling Hal, "That'll be two bourbons on the rocks Hal."

After they had settled into the impressive leather chairs surrounding the bar, Videla broke the ice by asking, "So Zig, I understand that you are the Chief Executive of Great West Studios in Los Angeles. If I might be so bold as to ask, what brings you to Buenos Aires?"

Without missing a beat, Zig replied, "I have been in preliminary discussions with Will here," he nodded, "about adapting a screenplay from a novel he is writing. I believe it has great potential as an action adventure film, so I took the opportunity to 'get away from it all' for a few days to come down and discuss it with him in person."

Videla smiled knowingly as he said, "What I would give to be able to 'get away from it all for a few days,' as you put it. What is the novel about?"

Will was impressed as Zig launched in feet first, "Mr. Kavanagh seems to have a penchant, a gift as it were, for very creative—albeit imaginary—action adventure stories. This one is along the lines of the Israeli commando operation that freed hostages from the airport at Entebbe, Uganda."

The President was suddenly alive with enthusiasm, "The Raid on Entebbe, but of course. That was one of my favorite action movies!" His expression was similar to that of a kid on Christmas morning as he leaned forward and asked conspiratorially, "Would you be giving too much of the plot of this movie away to tell me where it is based, fictionally of course?"

Will felt his anxiety level peg out as he risked the shortest of glances at Dom, who was also on full alert. Anticipating that Zig was rapidly exhausting his layers of plausible deniability Will leaned towards the President, "Actually Jorge, it's also set in Africa. My wife Dominique is from Morocco, and we began developing the story while we were visiting her family there a couple of months ago." Figuring he'd better wrap the lie up tightly, he added, "As a matter of fact, Hal and I didn't survive a skiing adventure in the Atlas Mountains there and elected to come here, in sunny Argentina, to recuperate."

Videla rolled his drink around the crystal highball glass before venturing his next query, "So is this novel you're writing also about rescuing hostages?"

Will smiled as he shook his head, "Nothing so dramatic as the raid on Entebbe. This one was more of a family conflict. Entebbe was a planeload of passengers. That movie convinced a lot of people that the Israelis are deadly serious and are not to be fucked with."

Although Hal appeared shocked by Will's profane assurance, Videla simply turned to him and smiled, "I take it people are learning the same thing about you Mr. Rayfield."

Will thought Hal was displaying credible survival instincts when he posed, "I'm afraid I don't know what you mean Mr. President."

Videla's poker face showed no gives as he stared intently into Hal's eyes. "I'd like to shake the hand of the person who killed Sandrigan el-Boukhari; may that bastard rot in hell. I believe I am sitting in the presence of such a person. Would you care to enlighten me further?"

Will was clearly impressed with his buddy's aplomb as he leaned forward slightly, "You already have Mr. President, and he's writing this book."

Now Videla had the prize he had sought by coming to *Casa Fabiano*. "Could you possibly freshen this drink for me Hal?"

When Hal rose to fix the drinks, Jorge gave Will a hint of how imposing his thousand yard stare got when he was deadly serious. "You don't know this, but Sandrigan supplied the poison that killed my beloved niece Maria Lacoste while she was vacationing in Nice, France. When I sent one of my counterintelligence people to confirm this story," he was saying but paused to glance at

Carmen, "Sandrigan had him nearly decapitated when his throat was slit. I considered this a direct affront to the reputation and the civility of the citizens of the Republic of Argentina."

Will was nodding his head, appreciating an uncle's angst but now more than a little concerned how Videla had heard about Sandrigan's demise. "Our embassy in Algiers provided all of the information that was available from news sources following the operation that sent Sandrigan to hell where he belonged. I wondered who had the resources to mount such an attack, and was completely stymied until Colonele Blanco advised me that at least part of the attack had the distinct signature of one of his, no, he indicated she was his finest, operative from the *Batallón Inteligencia 601.*"

"And this operative happens to be my fiancée," Hal said, connecting the dots as he handed Videla his drink.

Everyone was still sitting on pins and needles as Videla sought out further answers to the mystery. "I understand you are under no obligation to advise me, but I am very curious as to what infraction Sandrigan perpetrated to bring about this incredibly successful operation you no doubt completed."

"He kidnapped my mother in Morocco and demanded that I be exchanged to secure her freedom," Dom said.

Jorge was absorbing this when something clicked in his brain. "Why did he kidnap your mother; and insist that you be exchanged for her?"

"Sandrigan had a demonic obsession to possess me and then brutally murder me. I am not proud of this, but several years ago we had been one-night lovers in what was the biggest mistake of my life."

"And these people at this *parilla,*" he said, opening his hands outward, "were able to overcome the most powerful warlord in Northern Africa?"

Without blinking she told him, "Do not ever underestimate the power of good to conquer evil President Videla." She leaned down and draped her arms around Will's shoulders, kissed him on the forehead and continued, "This man loved me more than any human rightly deserves to be loved, and together—all of us—we were able to overcome this satanic bastion of evil. It very nearly killed us, but we prevailed and I will not stand before you and say that I regret one thing we did to rid this world of evil incarnate."

"Where are you going Will?" Jorge Videla asked as Will stood and headed for the bar.

"Dom?" he asked, reaching for the Grand Marnier bottle.

Carmen assisted her in setting the small crystal snifters down in front of everyone. After Will had poured a shot in everyone's glass, he lifted his and said, "I'd like to propose a toast to the inevitability of love. It is the only imperative that invariably prevails."

Jorge stood to touch his glass, quickly followed by everyone present as he nodded his head at Will in appreciation, *"De hecho mi valiente amigo, Salud, Salud!"*

Will didn't feel the least bit ashamed as he put down his snifter and wrapped his arm around Dom, kissing her passionately. When they broke for air he looked at Videla and gave him the little upjerk of his jaw, "I understand that you also had to prevail over evil Jorge, and from what I read not everyone appreciates what it's like to have your entire life and civilization under attack by Soviet-inspired subversives bent on rending the Republic of Argentina into chaos. Well guess what Jorge Rafael Videla; fuck them. I will stand with the man who defends his birthright and his family. Am I perfect, are you? To hell with Amnesty International if they can't quite absorb why the Argentine people were unwilling to lie down in front of the motherfucking Guevarist ERP. I am your friend Jorge, and I don't really care one damn bit if I'm the only swinging dick this side of the equator who knows it's true, but you, *mi amigo*, are a hero. You saved Argentina from collapse. War is never pretty, and the Viet Cong taught us this lesson in Vietnam; if you're not willing to kill every person that opposes you then you do not possess the will to win. You Jorge, possessed the will to win and you succeeded." He grabbed his snifter and raised it high, "Here's looking at a man of conviction. Cheers to you Jorge Videla who never lost the sight of Christ in the rearview mirror!"

They clicked glasses, slung back the cognac and threw the glasses into the fireplace. Jorge locked one of his arms around Will, the smile now seemingly permanently affixed. "My, how you improve a person's spirits Will Kavanagh!" Will nodded then glanced over to see Carmen, Dom, Kelly and Samantha whistling and cheering, "Here, here!"

As they were finishing the absolutely delicious, melt-in-your-mouth *lomos*, Jorge looked at Will and said, "I would like to offer every accommodation in supporting your efforts while you are here in Argentina Will. This nation could not be more solidly behind helping in any way we can." He turned to Zig and made his sales pitch, "Mr. Kowalski, it would be a personal favor and a salute to our Republic if your studio would consider movie production efforts here in Argentina for this or any other films you produce."

"I would be most humbled if you would agree to come to *La Casa Rosada* tomorrow evening for dinner and meet Rosita Cabrera, our Minister of Tourism, so that she can extend her personal invitation and express her willingness to collaborate in making this business relationship mutually rewarding."

"We'll be there Jorge, and I might add that I am overwhelmed by your hospitability. I had no idea this trip south would be so rewarding," Zig said as he glanced at Will, nodding his appreciation.

As he turned to leave at the front door, Videla smiled at Kowalski and said, "It would seem you keep good company Zig; these people you associate with are truly special." He turned to Carmen, took her hand and bent slightly to kiss it. "And thank you so much for being the perfect host here in *Casa Fabiano* Carmen; I haven't had such an uplifting evening in many years, *buenas noches*."

———

After the presidential party left, the Fabiano clutch were sitting around the parilla, drinking another round of Marnier in celebration when Carmen told them, "This evening did not happen the way I thought it would, but I cannot imagine a finer outcome. Well played my fellow conspirators."

"I guess we're out in the open now, eh?" Will said with more than a little trepidation.

Hal surprised him—he the harbinger of guarded anonymity—by overruling Will's paranoia. "Oh, I don't think our shit's out on the street here Willy. So the President, the Defense Minister and the 601 Battalion Commander know about us. I'd say we've got a direct line into Videla via Danny, our golfing buddy. This might actually be a good place to set up a satellite ROUST office."

"So you see a potential for business bonus down south, eh?"

"Right on, but Videla shocked the shit out of me by knowing about Sandrigan's demise, and linking us into it especially. But it is indeed unfortunate that we could not hide the fact that Carmen is the Argentine angel of death," Hal posited.

10

DANCING WITH THE DICTATOR

AT LA CASA ROSADA

"So what do you think of this shit?" Zig Kowalski muttered to Will as they walked under an arch of drawn swords into the grand entrance hall of *La Casa Rosada*.

"Probably not on the itinerary your secretary typed for you, eh?" He replied, super-impressed with the pomp and pageantry President Videla rolled out for them.

As they crossed under the last of the swords, Jorge Videla was waiting for them beaming, his wife at his side in anxious anticipation. Gone was the Georgetown casual feel at *Casa Fabiano*; Videla was decked out in full military regalia—his lieutenant general's mess dress—and looked very sharp. *Damn, I guess they only have three stars for the highest ranking military guy here in Porteño-land.* Neither Zig nor Will could believe they were treating them like visiting heads of state, but had to admit they shared a common interest; the enemy of my enemy is my friend. Back at *Casa Fabiano*, it had been decided that Circle Entertainment would present as small a footprint as possible; hence Zig, Carlos, Kelly and Will were the only ones from last night's impromptu dinner in attendance.

"Welcome to our Government House ladies and gentlemen," a beaming President Videla announced. "May I present my lovely wife Alicia Raquel Hartridge, and Rosita Cabrera, the Minister of Tourism," he said as they paused to greet them warmly.

When they got to the banquet table, Will was humored to see that the seating had Zig and Carlos to the left of Videla and he and Kelly to the right of Alicia. Rosita sat beside Carlos, which was probably a good matchup. Being wedged between two interesting females seemed like the perfect arrangement to Will, but he could tell by Zig's glances that he really wanted Kavanagh all but hovering between him and the President. *Well you can't always get what you want....*

He peered at the first lady as discreetly as possible and considered Alicia the perfect counterpoint to Jorge; she was probably mid-forties, well preserved with a fit body, and to his surprise was fairly attractive. Her long brown hair was coiffed in an attractive bun drawn up behind her head, and her skin was remarkably smooth. "So what were you in your previous life before being the First Lady of Argentina?" He asked, earning a discreet poke in the ribs from Kelly. *What's that? So little Miss Dupree is feeling frisky tonight, eh? We'll see how she likes two playing that game!*

Using the tablecloth as a fence he slipped his left hand up Kelly's skirt until he felt the soft flesh of her thigh and smirked at her. He looked back as Alicia replied, "Actually Jorge and I have been blessed with seven children, so in that previous life you mentioned I was a college student." Will tried to hide his shock, reconsidering Roberto's value as a pre-briefer. "We had our last child in 1966, so I've been a fairly devoted mother and then shifted into being a professional soldier's wife." She pawed at Will's sleeve, "I dabble in art, mostly charcoal sketches when some scene impresses me greatly. How about yourself *Señor* Kavanagh, what is your favorite endeavor?"

As he leaned slightly towards Alicia, knowing he'd convey sincerity by doing so, he swept his hand back under Kelly's dress and flitted his fingers across her crotch. He then replied with conviction to the First Lady, "From the sounds of it, we both enjoy sex." Alicia looked startled so he added, "Actually, I prefer not getting shot at, but in my spare time I seem to get myself into tricky situations."

Kelly suddenly lurched forward, let out an 'Oh,' as Alicia looked around at her assuming she had further insight into Will's odd response. "Do you know about any of these 'tricky situations' *Señorita* Dupree?"

There was no discreet way she could move his hand out from under her dress as she blushed slightly and replied, "They seem to happen with an unsettling randomness."

They both frowned at Kelly, but Will decided to bail her out, "Kelly and I have been collaborating on a manuscript for the past few days. She is Mr.

Kowalski's golden girl for screenplay adaptations."

Alicia glanced back at Zig, affording Kelly an opportunity to sweep his arm out from under her dress before the First Lady looked back at them. "So you both work for Mr. Kowalski's studio in Hollywood?"

Finally freed from her constraints, Kelly offered, "I work in the Production Department at Great West, but Will is working as a consultant for this particular project."

The First Lady looked at him strangely, some of the dots beginning to connect no doubt, and she said, "Jorge mentioned something about a rescue…"

Just as she was about to make him very uncomfortable with her interrogatory, a band they hadn't noticed to the side of the banquet room began playing a classical but seductive rhythm and the beat of the song seemed suddenly compelling. Will watched with amusement as Jorge stood and opened his arm towards his wife who looked back and asked, "Do you tango *Señor* Kavanagh?"

He was shaking his head no, "I saw a movie a few years ago called 'Last Tango in Paris,' but I've never even seen anyone dance the tango."

"Watch closely and I'll tango with you after I dance with my husband," she said as she took Jorge's hand and waltzed out to the dance floor.

"Just what the hell is wrong with you Kavanagh? Trying to drive me crazy? Goddamn you to hell doing that sitting next to the First Lady of Argentina!" Kelly groused at him once the first couple left.

"Oh, a little cranky, huh? Well, we'll have to talk with Mrs. Kavanagh about that when we get back to the castle," he replied, discreetly tweaking her breast.

"Oh no, you know what the rules of engagement are; no playing while the guests are in town," she implored, but the look on her face betrayed her.

"Perhaps we can find a muzzle for a certain overly enthusiastic Hollywood producer that appears to have a head of steam built up." Then looking into her eyes he smirked, "I haven't had a shot at the Cossack Queen since the Philippines; this is beginning to take on the aura of a special celebration my dear!"

"Oh that's so much bullshit Kavanagh, you just had…." she said but suddenly truncated her tirade.

"I just had what? I don't recall breathing heavily with you since before the wedding. Now I might have a dream or two about you from time to time," he offered, unable to shake the incredibly graphic daydream he had about Kelly and the coven of hot temptresses.

She smiled seductively and replied, "Yeah I bet; we'll see William." Quickly shifting her focus over his shoulder she asked her boss, "Have we arrived at any collaborative arrangements with our Argentine cohorts?"

Zig slipped into Alicia's chair and said, "Jesus Christ, Videla wants us down here so bad he's exempting our operations from taxes and they'll provide the extras for free. Talk about an incentive; what do you think we can shoot down here Will? I mean it's not exactly Africa."

He pondered this for a moment before responding, "We could probably shoot most of the front end of the movie down here in Buenos, but when things shift to Ksar the terrain looks a lot more like desert. Well, sort of like the desert meeting the mountains. The foliage here is too lush to replicate Algeria, but if we shoot it in the winter down here it shouldn't be too noticeable. Why don't we ask them if there's a more desert-like area here in Argentina? I for one sure like the Argentines more than the Arabs; at least they like to drink." He shook his head suddenly and added, "Oh, and the Argentines don't have any issues with pork; man, think about breakfast without bacon for three months!"

Zig was nodding his head when he remembered something and said, "Come on, let's talk to Rosita; she knows the place."

When they got down to where Rosita and Carlos were sitting, Will was pleasantly surprised that upon closer inspection Rosita was a fairly hot Argentine. She had a dark complexion and very dark eyes, and her hair was almost jet black, just like Kelly's. He was subliminally pondering her hot body and fantasizing about her sexual nuances when she addressed him, "Hello Will, it's nice to finally chat with you…"

"What's that mean? That *Señorita* Cabrera was something more than a tourism specialist during the Reorganization?"

She tried to hide it but he caught it for just a second; that glance secretly sizing up her opposition. *Damn, was she in SIDE with Carmen?* "Of course I had qualifications for the job *Señor*…"

"Yeah, like SIDE? I'll bet you'd make one hell of an assassin, or at least you could since you could get next to any heterosexual male in the world,

Señorita Minister."

She cut her eyes at him again, "Please Mr. Kavanagh, I was most fortunate to have been the deputy organizer of the World Cup last year. I got to meet a lot of foreign visitors and," she said as she pulled in beside him conspiratorially, "we won the World Cup. So how is it you *Norteamericanos* summarize it, to the victor go the spoils?"

"Actually Rosita, I think Julius Caesar coined that phrase, but I might be wrong. So you spent some time in 34 Directorate before the World Cup?"

The reference to 34 Directorate did it. She tugged at his coat sleeve until they had a bit of separation, "Will, I know you are close friends with Belen, so please do not cause unnecessary reflection on the past." She pulled up to his ear and whispered, "It works both ways Will." As she eased back down Kelly was on them like glue as Will rolled his eyes. "Carlos tells me you are an incredible writer. Have you published any books?"

Jesus Christ, she's a damn man-eater. He couldn't seem to wipe the grin off his face, "So here's the deal Rosita; we need a location that simulates dry desert, not unlike the high plateaus of the American western plains. Is there such terrain in Argentina?"

His apparent disregard for her inquiry resulted in throwing her hands open and up and at him. Will just looked at her in disbelief, "Did you just blow me off?" *I cannot believe this woman has such moxy; damn, I bet she's dead red for bed Fred.* "Actually Rosita, that was a yes or no question; I'm not sure how 'fuck off' fits into the reply. Care to help out a dumb ass *Norteamericano?*"

His half-hearted apology was canceled out by the profanity, but she recovered enough to say, "Yes, Mendoza and Rio Negro provinces have similar topography in the western portions leading up to the Andes. Why do you ask?"

"How accessible are they? Are there any cities with airports in the western portions of these provinces?" Will was three questions ahead of her, focused on the bottom line. *I have got her ass tied into a knot. Come on Rosita, get your shit together if you're gonna play in the big leagues.*

She was obviously put off by his disregard for her inquiries but doggedly hung in there, "Yes, Mendoza is the capital and is located in the western portion of Mendoza province. And San Carlos de Bariloche is located at the foot of the Andes in Rio Negro. Why do you ask, do you want to go there?"

"Probably," he replied, his lizard brain now fully engaged, "can we easily travel to either of these places? Do you have airplanes available?"

This seemed to fluster her, but he gave her credit for not buckling, "I'm sure we could arrange that; when do you think you might want to travel?"

"Hey, could Danny Rojas help us out with the air transport? I know he'd help us any way he could, so long as we keep losing to him at golf," Will assured her, not losing one molecule of inertia with the solution unfolding before them.

"You know Minister Rojas?" She exclaimed, her eyes narrowing as the conversation seemed to strike some resonant chord. *Jesus, is she fucking Danny Rojas?*

"Sure, he might even want to go with us too; get him out of *Edificio Libertador* for a day. I guess we need to coordinate this with Jorge, huh?" Will asked, looking back at Zig and giving him the high sign nod with two thumbs up.

"Are you referring to President Videla?"

"Yeah," he looked out at the dance floor and noticed Jorge and Alicia dancing with dramatic flair. "Wanna go dance?"

He looked at her with interest as she tried to decide if lust or duty would win out; she seemed to get sort of a hot flash, waving her hand in front of her face. Undeterred, he offered her his hand as invitation, but the song the first couple were dancing to suddenly ended. Will had to give Rosita credit for effort as she rebounded enough to ask, "Do you tango?"

He smiled at her, "No, not at all. This is kind of new music for me."

"So what kind of music do you like to dance to?" She asked with a devilish grin.

He shook his head in defeat, "Listen, I'm not really much of a dancer like these tango professionals. I actually prefer slower music; you know stuff that's got a bit of soul."

The conversation seemed to elicit some hidden self-confidence in her as she leaned in, "What kind of slower music. Do you have a song you like in particular? Perhaps we could have it played for you; that is if you would like to dance with me."

Kelly suddenly leaned over his shoulder, Will involuntarily rolling his eyes, as she happily provided the answer, "He's got a real soft touch for Hall and Oates 'Sara Smile.' But that's not going to happen with this band."

Rosita gave Will an impish grin, tapped her chin twice and told them, "I'll be right back; the band isn't our only resource."

"So what do you have lined up for us Kavanagh? I couldn't tell what you were kibitzing with that Tourism Minister about; Jesus, she's actually pretty hot," Zig asked with an excited look on his face.

"She said they've got terrain like the high plains here in Argentina, and we're going to check them out. Might have to lean on Danny Rojas for air transport, but I think we might just be able to do all of the location shooting here in Argentina. Probably have to shoot it during their winter to match the foliage with any reasonable similarity though," Will reported as if he'd been there scouting scenes for two weeks.

"Damn Kavanagh, one setup for all of the location shooting? That'd simplify things dramatically, to say nothing about the savings to gross; damn good work!"

"Hey, it ain't a lock yet; we've got to see if we can make Argentina look like the Atlas Saharan mountains. But if it were me, I'd sure like shooting here better than northern Africa."

"So when are we going to check out these high plains?" Zig asked, surprising the hell out of Will.

"Did I just hear Zbignew Kowalski say WE? You want to go check out possible shooting locations? Aren't you getting down in the weeds a bit for a CEO Zigster?"

Kelly and Carlos seemed to wilt away when he said it, but Zig looked at him with a bemused grin, "Hell, I'm five thousand fucking miles from home now; what's a few hundred more to lock down the most unpredictable part of the entire project?"

Rosita tapped Will on the shoulder and said, "I found this *Sara Smile* song you are apparently a 'soft touch' for. Shall we dance to it?"

Will was smiling like it was his first birthday, reaching for her hand as the first chords of the song played over the sound system. His growing interest in the foxy Tourism Minister was rudely interrupted when an arm appeared over his shoulder as Kelly took his hand and warned Rosita. "Actually, he gets sort of out of control dancing to this song, and it might embarrass you. I'll dance with Will instead."

He looked at Rosita with an embarrassed shrug, "Mommy dearest says I can't dance with you. Please forgive me Rosita."

As they were walking away to the dance floor, Rosita was standing there with her arms across her chest, scowling at them. Kelly leaned into Will with a snicker, "Mommy dearest?"

"I might embarrass her? Do you think she's a virgin or a lesbian?"

"No, I'm counting on her being neither; and your ass is not getting across the breakers with Mrs. Kavanagh tonight Willy boy."

Instead of slowly acclimating to one another, Kelly immediately clutched him like a grape vine as soon as they began dancing. He kissed her ear and warned her, "Rules of engagement Dupree; do not kiss me or the entire diplomatic relationship between America and Argentina will disintegrate—got it?"

She licked her tongue up the side of his neck all the way to the ear out of spite, "Yeah, I got it cowboy. Now show me how you danced with Samantha."

It quickly became apparent that Kelly and he could synchronize almost magically, as he began testing her out by swirling her around and back to the enchanting music. She began singing the lyrics in his ear and held him so close they could have easily swapped skin. Will decided to give her the ultimate synchronicity test and began twirling around and around, but Kelly was staying with him step for step, as light on her feet as a pixie. He was in sky high state of glee when he told her, "Damn Dupree, we're dancing like we're one person."

All he heard back was a childish giggle as she squeezed him in delight. They had gone around the entire dance floor twirling and settled back into a slow grind when he felt a tap on his shoulder. Will looked to see Rosita standing beside them, "Do you mind if we dance Mr. Kavanagh?"

He looked at Kelly and said, "Thank you so much for the dance Ms. Dupree."

Will held out his hand to take Rosita's, like a normal dance partner would, but she smiled wickedly and put her arms around his neck as he drew her in tight to see if she had the moxy to hang with Kavanagh. Much to his surprise, Rosita showed no apprehension snuggling up like they were lovers. He kissed her neck and took her for a test spin with a few twirls but she was glued to him like a shadow. "You surprise me Rosita," he whispered in her ear, "we have never danced together before and yet it seems so familiar. You are an extraordinary dancer, and I really enjoy cutting the dance floor with you, Minister of Hotness."

She stunned him when she kissed his ear, her tongue tickling as she did, "No Will, I'm the one who is thrilled. God you smell so good I could just lick you." Will almost laughed as she seemed to redirect herself, "I saw the way you danced with your friend. Tell me, are you two lovers?"

He pulled back to look her in the eyes, their trunks tight together now as she dropped one hand to his waist for leverage. She seemed to be casually aggressive, which appealed to him greatly. *It's always easier dealing business with a woman if she wants to screw your brains out.* "No Rosita, we are just good friends." He thought about it for a second and added, "I don't think she and I have ever danced together before."

This time she actually nibbled on his earlobe, "I'm not sure I believe that."

As the last chords of the song played out, he kissed her neck right below her earlobe eliciting an involuntary shiver. "If I weren't a married man I would make an indecent proposal to you Rosita. Thank you so much for the dance; you redefine sex on the dance floor *Señorita*."

She leaned her head around to look him in the eyes, pecked him on the lips and smiled, "I can assure you Will Kavanagh, it would not be indecent at all. I very much enjoyed sex on the dance floor with you as well."

By the time they got back around to the banquet table, Zig and President Videla were slapping each other on the back as a waiter held out a box of cigars for them. Videla looked at Will and with a hearty laugh said, "I understand you and Rosita have already discussed potential movie production locations Will. I have decided to accompany you on the trip to Mendoza and Bariloche tomorrow. I don't get out of Buenos Aries often enough. This is a great night for Argentina!"

He looked back at Rosita, put his arm around her shoulder and told her, "See what one little dance can do?"

She looked and nodded at President Videla, and then smiled provocatively, "Yes, I believe I do. Shall we go call Minister Rojas about transportation? I have an office just down the hall."

Kelly suddenly appeared at his side and said, "I think I'll go with you. I need to let the office back in Los Angeles know Mr. Kowalski won't be returning tomorrow."

As they were heading back to Rosita's office Kelly tugged his coat sleeve as he looked at her with a tinge of annoyance, "What's up?"

"You know what's up, you fucking snake Xavier; if I'd have let you go to that office with her you two would have been fucking in thirty seconds. That woman wants to eat you alive Will Kavanagh, don't you get that? Oh and that was the most provocative I have seen you dance since the night you imploded with Samantha in Diego. Really William, you are a married man!"

"I believe you are exaggerating my dear. I had no such intentions with regard to Ms. Cabrera, and I believe that if you could watch a videotape of the two of us dancing it couldn't have been any less erotic than the clutch with Mrs. Chessereaux." He remembered something and said, "And for your information, I think I've only danced twice since the Diego implosion as you call it. One of them was my wedding reception, thank you very much!"

She was sneering at him, looking for some sign of insincerity but didn't detect it, "Well, even if you hadn't made the move I'm sure she would have had your pants off by now! Are these Argentine women all oversexed?"

"Oh let me see Kelly; are all American, Philippino, Moroccan, Japanese and now Argentinian women all oversexed? No way, I believe it's a matter of situational ethics."

"Oh, and how so?" She inquired with an attitude.

He laughed, pinching her ass as he provided the secret revelation, "If you don't mind, it don't matter."

———

"So that's it Dom, the evening went swimmingly for all concerned," Will told her after Zig and Carlos headed off to bed.

"Is that so; why is there lipstick on your earlobe? Was that part of the swim?" She asked, trying to keep a straight face but sending him into a paranoiac grimace.

"That's because the Tourism Minister for the great Republic of Argentina couldn't seem to keep her hands off of the *Norteamericano* adventure writer," Kelly intoned as he gave her a hateful scowl.

"Now come on Dupree, we hashed out a plan that may just keep all of the shooting locations for Marrakech here in Argentina. I know you missed out on the incredible fun of Algeria, but trust me, Argentina has it all over Muslimville." She didn't respond so he completed his report to Dom and Hal, "I thought we accomplished a lot tonight, although I didn't expect the President to want to escort us out to the hinterlands."

Kelly hooted with laughter as they began to question her sanity, "When you referred to the President as Jorge I knew Rosita was going to soil her panties."

"So this Rosita's the Tourism Minister, eh? What did she look like?" Dom asked, now interested in Kelly's insights.

"Oh, she's hot. And when Will danced with her she clung to him like a vine. It was a pretty salacious scene actually."

Carmen suddenly became energized, "You are talking about Rosita Cabrera, correct; who is now the Minister of Tourism?"

Will looked at her, knowing Carmen's thumb on the pulse of the *Porteños* was second to none, "Yeah, as a matter of fact, I figured if she didn't come through the Defense Ministry she musta been a spook. Spooks hide in spider holes, so I knew I had to unnerve her before I started in with the movie scene blitzkrieg. But when I was giving her the old left-right-left warmup she pulled me aside and cautioned me to ease up on references to SIDE and mentioned the word Belen. I take it she is an old comrade?"

Carmen's expression turned cold, "How in the world did you make that association?"

"She's got the same furtive glance that most operatives less skilled than you give when sizing up the prey. I spotted it when I angered her by answering a question with a question."

Kelly began hooting, "Oh, I can just see this. 'Hey Will, I heard you're a famous writer.' So you tell her, 'Do you blush before or after we start talking about sex?' How'd I do?"

Carmen acted like Kelly wasn't in the room, waiting on him, "I kinda hit her on bona fides and she said she was the deputy organizer for the World Cup. Now I gave her props for that, since that means she did all the work and got little of the thanks except being named Tourism Minister. But these Junta types don't reward work with titles UNLESS the hard worker is a trusted veteran. She didn't strike me as a soldier in the mountains, so I figured she was SIDE. She confirmed it by denying it and we were then able to pursue our discussion of shooting locations up close to the Andes."

Carmen was now smiling furtively, "I don't believe anyone has seen her with a man in public for the past two years; there were rumors that she is gay."

Before Will could say a thing, Kelly jumped on the band wagon, "Well, she may be, but I can assure you that she wasn't while she was dancing to *Sara Smile* tonight! There is no doubt in my mind that she would have stripped Will's clothes off as soon as she closed the door to her office if I hadn't been playing bodyguard."

Carmen was nearly incredulous, "I'm having a hard time believing my ears."

Will just rolled his eyes, "Carmen, maybe Rosita responds to animal magnetism from either sex. Give the gal some credit; she sure as hell wasn't honking on Carlos!" Even Kelly had to give the devil his due on that one. "Besides, when I mentioned Danny Rojas hooking us up with air transportation to the Andes tomorrow I saw another give on her face. If she hasn't been seen with a man, maybe she's carrying on with Danny on the sly. You know, like having an affair of the heart, which would take her ass off the street."

Carmen nodded, "Your powers of observation can be quite scary at times William."

"So who wants to go on the magical mystery tour tomorrow?" Will looked at Carmen, remembering her penchant for discretion and asked, "Laying low for this one Belen?"

She looked at him thoughtfully and replied, "Actually, President Videla and Minister Rojas know of my association with this group and Argentine intelligence, so I see no reason to hide from them. My family has an *estancia* in Bariloche, so this will be an opportunity to visit there without having to endure commercial transportation."

"So it's the merry band of adventurers off to the hinterlands tomorrow; hopefully we can lock down on the best place to shoot the Ksar scene, short of going back to Africa," Will said, wrapping up the discussion.

After Hal and Carmen had gone up for the evening, Dom looked at Will but asked Kelly, "So did William misbehave this evening? It sounds as though there was some untoward attraction between him and this Tourism Minister."

Kelly smirked at him before she replied, "Well, he probably wasn't totally out of line with Rosita, but there was no doubt what her intentions were. He was way over the line, however, when he snaked his hand up my skirt while sitting next to and talking with the First Lady!"

Will grimaced as Dom looked at him in disbelief, "What did you think you were doing William? Could you not contain the devil in you, even in front of the President?"

He shrugged and tried to defend myself, "Hey, she elbowed me without provocation when I asked Alicia what she did for a living, so I figured payback's hell. Besides, she's a big girl, she can handle it."

Dom turned to Kelly and inquired, "So there was more mischief than meets the eye, *n'est pas?* It sounds as though impressive progress was made at the dinner; well played you two."

Kelly glanced at Will, then turned to Dom and made her indecent proposal, "Actually Dom, William here kinda tripped a little switch in me while he was misbehaving under the table. Think maybe we can buddy up, you know, chase the horns away?"

Dom patted her hand lightly, "Let's allow our visiting guests a chance to vacate the premises before we do any of that Kelly. It'll only be a day or so."

This caused Kelly to put out her pout lip, so she growled at him and said, "Fair enough, but keep William here at bay."

He smiled at her and replied, "Heaven forbid I act like a normal, heterosexual male. I will be on my best behavior; wouldn't want to make you any crankier when you don't get your way Kelly D."

11

MAKING PLANS FOR THE FUTURES

"So what do you think Zig?" Will asked as they flew over the mountainous terrain on final approach into San Carlos de Bariloche. They had flown around western Mendoza province and lunched in Mendoza, but the preponderance of vineyards and other agriculture—while giving Mendoza its DNA of sorts—didn't equate to the parched character of Ksar el-Boukhari well at all.

Zig was more laid back than Will had ever seen him. "I like this area we're flying over; does it seem at all similar to the mountain village where that final incredible scene played out? You know the Ksar place where you finally take down Lucifer? What do you think, I mean you were there?"

"I think either place could do in a pinch, but for some reason I like this whole area around Bariloche. It just seems to have character or something, you know, like you just stepped into South Tahoe or Breckenridge," Will told him, looking around at Dom for her reaction. "What do you think Dom; does this Bariloche place have a Colorado feel to it?"

"Yes it does, even from the air." She pointed to the west and the snow covered peaks of the Andes, "The mountain configurations are markedly different, but there is the definite feel that we are in the hilly country adjacent to an overwhelming mountain range." Will could tell she was somewhat taken with it and gave her the little upjerk as a prompt. "It's just that the commercial development of Colorado around the ski resorts is overwhelming. Here the Andes seem to be a long backbone down the west coast of the continent as opposed to the huge cluster of upscale ski resorts in the Northwest Region of Colorado."

Will nodded his head, "This place we're flying over feels comfortably familiar for some reason baby."

"Will is right, at least for most of us *Porteños*. Bariloche reminds many people of a Bavarian village. There are in fact a number of Germans who moved here before and after Germany was defeated in World War Two," President Videla added. Jorge had agreed with Will's suggestion through Rosita that *El Presidente* not show the colors today, as civilian clothes would make him much less visible. Will had collaborated with Rosita and Carmen about the prior assassination attempts earlier when Dom had Jorge mesmerized with her tutorial of good versus evil. They were able to travel with a minimum of notice by flying in the military plane without any uniformed personnel around. Of course SIDE and the Presidential Security Unit were covering everything closely, albeit discreetly. Will found it interesting when Carmen let on that the Presidential Security agents were all former members of the 601 Intelligence Battalion. Deploying her usual cunning, she had ascertained this the day the 'advance team' showed at *Casa Fabiano*, having chatted with both agents whom she knew from her 'undercover' days. Will had fun with her, simulating Torres and Carbon's antics when they saw Carmen now had a *fiancé*.

"Nazis? The Nazis fled to Argentina and hid out in Bariloche?" Will asked, as his lizard brain suddenly shifted his focus. *That's right; my brother Colton told me the Pope's own staff in Vatican City acted as enablers for the Nazis to escape the dragnet we set for them.* Will looked at Videla and offered a theory, "I have heard rumors that the Holy See was so frightened by the Godless communists that he danced with the devil named Hitler, knowing his purported tolerance of formal religions separated him from the heathens in Moscow."

"I am beginning to admire your associates that pass rumors," Videla said as he chuckled. "Many of the most villainous ones were caught by the Israelis, but the lesser ones managed to escape, bring liquid assets here and live meaningful lives," Videla continued.

"Money talks, eh?" Will offered but felt he was possibly criticizing what was likely a complex issue for the Argentines, many of who were of European lineage.

"Unfortunately you are correct Will. Let's go over to the lake so you can see the area from the higher ground. I believe you all will like it," the President said.

They had walked out onto the smoothly paved marina breakwater that looked out over a pristine lake, reminding the visitors of Lake Tahoe. The air was so clear and clean that Will felt his soul rejoice at the glorious change from the dusty smog of Buenos Aires. Remembering the muddy Rio Plata, he looked at Carmen and asked, "This is a beautiful lake Carmen, what's the name of it, Lake Bariloche? I can understand why your parents like to stay here compared to Buenos."

She smiled and corrected him, "No, this is Haupi Lake, and my family's *estancia* shares its shoreline a few kilometers west of here."

Will was intrigued that Carmen and Rosita seemed to bond, and he wondered if Carmen could ever shake the spy network embraced during her time with SIDE and the 601 Battalion. "Rosita, we don't necessarily need a lake front property for the scene we have in mind, but there's a chance Haupi Lake could stand in for the Mediterranean." Remembering the final takedown of Sandrigan's casbah he thought out loud, "What might be ideal is an old masonry estate that is in disrepair and otherwise ready for demolition prior to some wealthy *Porteño* building their dream mansion." He glanced at Hal and continued, "We could give the baby one hell of a sendoff."

Rosita was looking at him with studied consternation, "There might just be such a property here in Bariloche that is targeted for demolition. What size would the property need to be? I am sorry, oh, how much land around the house would be ideal for the scene you have in mind?"

He looked at Hal, who gave him the Italian Army salute, "I'd say that Sandrigan's estate was around five acres, but that's just the fenced in area, not including the airstrip. What do you think Kemosabe?"

Rosita peered at him strangely, but Carmen quickly did some math conversion and rescued her confessor, "About two hectares, that is what the casbah grounds in Algiers included."

Now Rosita nodded knowingly, made a note in her calendar and replied, "Okay, I will canvas the properties in Bariloche and see if we can locate something suitable."

President Videla walked up us as they were turning to head back, "So what do you think of Bariloche?"

"I like it a lot, and I can assure you that I will return to this place; it just feels like home for some reason. Rosita will screen the local real estate market to see if she can find a suitable property that can be demolished in conjunction with the scene of the cataclysmic destruction of Sandrigan's casbah."

Videla looked at her as they engaged in a frenetic conversation in Spanish, "I believe we can find something suitable Will; are you sure that it must be destroyed in conjunction with the filming?"

His question flashed him back to the destruction of Colonel Kurtz' stronghold at the end of 'Apocalypse Now,' but Zig nudged Carlos and asked him, "We won't need to destroy a mansion to shoot the final scene at Algiers, do you think?"

Carlos glanced at Will, shrugged and replied, "I wasn't there, so it's hard to say, but we can do a lot with pyro that can simulate destruction."

"Yeah, but nothing can give the true impact of a house going up in an explosive attack like we witnessed. Now I ain't saying it can't be done, but it almost seems like it would be the ultimate sexual release for the whole fucking enchilada to vanish, don't ya think?" He told them, feeling he had communicated his eyewitness opinion as clearly as humanly possible.

Zig's deep furrowed forehead reflected his shock at the vulgar manner Will had conveyed his opinion, but to his credit Videla nodded in agreement, "Yes, I believe you are correct Will. We will see what we can find."

As they drove further west on *Circuito Chico*, or Route 77, they passed a large golf course on Lake Haupi's shoreline. "That is the Llao Llao Social Club at Punta Verde," Carmen told them. "It's not much further to *Estancia Fabiano*."

Dom looked at Will, "Buenos Aires is enough like old Algiers that we could probably find the right place to film the car chase scene, what do you think?"

"Yeah, I think you're right, but......" his complete train of thought was disrupted as he looked out the window and stared, unable to believe his eyes."

"What is it Will? What's wrong?" She asked with concern.

Hal looked to where he was staring and exclaimed, "Jesus Christ Willy, I would have never believed it."

Now Carmen was curious so she looked at the little valley about a mile to the south of the road and gasped, "My God, I cannot believe it. That is part of the *Estancia!*"

There was no road off of the highway leading to the cluster of buildings in the relatively sparsely vegetated valley, so they transferred to four-wheel drive jeeps at *Estancia Fabiano* and rode over the trail to the valley. "So what is this place Carmen?"

"This is a cattle processing facility that is most active during the summer months, with December being the peak slaughter season. As we are entering fall now, activity here is mostly limited to putting up hay and grain for feed during the coming winter months."

"So what do you think Carmen, can you see the Atlas Carpet Factory here?" Will asked the question everyone who had been at Ksar el Boukhari seemed in agreement on.

"I absolutely can; we could even clear a landing strip over there if we need to," she said, pointing to the south of the cluster of buildings.

Will motioned for Hal and Dom to join him to wrap up locations, "Okay, so we've got at least a rough understanding of how we're gonna shoot the boat ride in, the casbah implosion and the carpet factory takedown. Any ideas on where we might shoot a romantic interlude that ended with sux instead of sex?"

Carmen's eyes seemed to light up as she offered, "Of course; there is a garden behind La Cabrera, the steak house we ate at in Buenos Aires. It actually reminds me of the park beside Farouk's, the restaurant where *Señor* Sidi had his last taste of ouzo."

Will turned to find Zig, and the five of them along with Kelly went to form a conference circle around President Videla as Will summarized the group's suggestions, "Okay Jorge, I believe we have identified locations within Argentina for all of the exterior scene locations that need to be shot in conjunction with 'It's Raining in Marrakech.' I also believe that shooting here will make the movie a brighter spectacle than if it were shot in North Africa, and I know everyone connected with the filming will enjoy being here. I really, really like it here in Argentina."

Videla smirked at him, then looked at Zig and asked, "It would seem that Mr. Kavanagh has summed up the day's investigation succinctly. Shall we celebrate?"

Back at the *Estancia*, everyone got to meet and socialize with Carmen's parents, George and Carlita Fabiano. Carlita had been initially unhappy about the no-notice visit by the President, but had used the hour or so the group visited the cattle processing facilities to prepare a veritable smorgasbord of delicious heavy *hors d'oeuvres*. As the crowd was inhaling the wonderful *tapas*, each had a large glass of *Estancia Fabiano* cabernet sauvignon to savor. Will glanced at Carmen and winked, impatiently waiting for Videla to comment. After finishing off half of his wine glass he looked at Carlita and smiled, "The tapas is delicious *Señora* Fabiano, but I must admit this cabernet is unusually rich and pleasant to the palate."

"That is most kind of you to say *mi Presidente*; we take great care and pride in our wine-making here at the Estancia," George Fabiano replied, unable to hide the pride in his own creation.

"I would say this cabernet is equal to or superior to any in the world; but then again, I am biased," he said with a chuckle. He looked at Zig and asked, "What do you think Zig; how does the *Estancia Fabiano* wine measure up against other vintages?"

"Actually, I was just noting that it is as good as any wine from the Napa Valley in Northern California." He turned and flexed his eyebrows, "What do you think Kelly?"

She winked at Will and smiled, "Why don't you tell President Videla what you think Will?"

Will touched glasses with Videla and smiled, "*Salud*." After they took another sip Will was ready to launch, "Here's the deal Mr. President, me and some of my compatriots have come to the same conclusion about Argentinian wine. We think there is an opportunity for introducing the American public to the wonderful vintners here in the Andean country. My group of associates thinks there is a wonderful opportunity to export Argentinian wine to the US; but we just recently broached the subject, and have no experience with the import/export business. In particular, we are not so sure how duties and tariffs would affect the viability of such an enterprise."

Videla looked at Rosita and entered into a fast-paced exchange of Spanish that sounded to Will as if it was slurred they spoke so quickly. He looked back to Will, "How is it that you continue to propose activities that are high on our list of economic priorities?"

Will glanced at Carmen before responding, "Okay Jorge, here's the deal; we have noted opportune airlift possibilities in the short time we have been in Argentina. For instance, a jumbo jet flew into Ezeiza a few days ago to drop off cargo and I was able to confirm they were flying back to the US empty. Now anybody can tell flying empty jumbo cargo jets thousands of miles just ain't good business. So while savoring some delicious Argentinian cabernet it hit me; why not fill the empty planes up with wine and export it to the US?

Sound like a reasonable initiative given Argentina's efforts to revitalize her economy?"

"And how do you envision this export effort to work Will? There must be other 'issues' to deal with besides the Argentinian vintners?"

"Well, we ain't got all that worked out just yet Jorge, primarily because it's gonna require setting up an import company on the receiving end. Now Hal here is the Chairman of a diversified corporation in Delaware, so creating a subsidiary isn't too difficult. There are obvious hurdles to success but these are not insurmountable if we can entice a single celebrity to champion our product; whatdya think?"

Videla smiled as he held his glass for Hal to refill it. "I think you are one opportunistic businessman is what I think. We would love to see Argentinian wine become commonplace on the dining tables of our *Norteamericano* friends. Do you foresee governmental resistance to your export/import efforts?"

Will rolled his eyes before replying, "Okay, you might as well know the true feelings of most *Norteamericanos* Jorge. There ain't a US citizen sitting at this table that can tolerate the sight of Jimmy Carter, and the next President will be the opposite of Carter; we're all tired of having a leader without a set of *cojones*. Now I know that's gonna take another year and a half, but the clusterfuck he's gotten America into in Iran is gonna sink his presidency. So the long and short of it is that relief is in sight regards peanut man Carter, but will we be viewed as somehow taking advantage of native entrepreneurs?"

"I see, so you believe the regulatory issues will not be overwhelming on the US end. How can an operation like you propose possibly exist without offering some compensating benefit to the Americans? Do you understand my concern?" Videla asked, and Will only smiled and shook his head in admiration.

"Jorge, you are indeed a wise man; and I for one am most impressed with your grasp of these back-scratching nuances. So your question to me is 'of what benefit is it to America to import any country's wines, especially since we produce so much of it ourselves?'"

He shook his head vigorously as the Fabianos looked on with amazement, "Exactly; how does your proposal make sense to say, the US Secretary of Commerce?"

"Well, we've got these distressed distilleries in Kentucky and Tennessee that produce distilled spirits, mostly from corn mash. Now if we were to set up an agreement with a few struggling bourbon whiskey distillers it would only benefit these economically distressed coal mining states, and at least offset the importation of Argentinian wine that WE suspect will compete well."

"So, to sum up this grand business proposition; you want to export Argentinian wine and import American bourbon?"

"Well," Will stretched in his chair as he glanced at Hal, "bourbon's got its fans but we were thinking a better-rounded offering of distilled spirits would better serve all tastes. So, with due consideration of existing licensing agreements, the exchange would be your wonderful and abundant fermented wines for distilled spirits which are not produced in Argentina. So whatdya think?"

"So Argentina vintners benefit and American distilleries benefit; what could possibly spoil the logic of that proposal?"

"Tariffs and duties," Will announced, not expecting Videla to acquiesce without consulting his trade minister.

Videla nodded his head in agreement. "Import tariffs are meant to protect national industries from untoward competition. Distilled spirits is not a key industry in Argentina, so I see no conflict. What of the competition with California wines?"

"The US already imports more French wine than California produces, so demand will always tip the scale. Of course, the French wine is more expensive because of the import duties, but it sells very well among the wealthy. We will look into the obstacles on the receiving end. Do you see it as possible that *Estancia Fabiano* Vintners and others could have their wines exported without significant trade barriers on this end?" Will asked as Carmen cleared her throat. Will glanced at her and added, "Sorry, I'm not asking you to absolve the laws of Argentina Jorge, just trying to let you know how we're thinking, sir."

"I like the way you think Will; I have already instructed Rosita to confer with the Trade and Commerce Ministry about this export initiative, and to relay to them that I think it bodes well for our wine producers. It also has the unseen benefit of promoting Argentina in a positive light. I would pursue the 'due diligence' portion of this proposal via your partners in the US." He looked at Rosita and smiled, "It would seem imposing on the hospitality of the Fabianos has uncovered interesting opportunities with our *Norteamericano* guests, *si*?"

"Indeed Mr. President," she replied with a sly smile at Will.

12

COMING OUT OF HYPERDRIVE

As THEY WAITED FOR ZIG'S RETURN flight at Ezeiza, Will had never seen the man in such a positive, upbeat frame of mind. Gone was his cynical, sardonic hard edge that seemed permanently infused in LA. He looked at his hosts smiling, "Well, this turned out to be one hell of a trip Kavanagh. I've never been invited to the White House for dinner; shit, I'm beginning to like these Argentinos better than most Americans."

"*Porteños*," Carmen added with a smirk.

"They call Argentinians *Porteños?*"

She rolled her eyes as she gave the CEO some local insight, "Argentines who reside in Buenos Aires are referred to as *Porteños*."

He smiled at her, "You guys will never be strangers in Los Angeles, I can assure you of that." He then eyeballed Kelly, "I want to hear from you directly on progress; no middle man. WE are going to make this one hell of a blockbuster."

"Right, to say nothing of boosting the international beverage industry," Will added with a wink. He turned to Johnny, "Hey Johnny, think you can get your swami to reveal the pitfalls of this import/export endeavor?"

"Sure, I can get that rolling; it's making rain for the firm. Who the heck you gonna get to run the operation in the States?"

Will looked at Sam and gave her the upjerk, "What you doing besides raising my godson and keeping the spa busy sculpting that body of yours?"

She glanced nervously at Johnny before responding, "Not a whole lot, why? Are you thinking about getting me involved in this wine import business?"

"Can't fool you Samantha Herrington; you already know about wine, so with your good tastes, Johnny's legal snake eyes and our draft business plan you can digest it and give us your thoughts. Whatcha think?"

"So I'd be sort of your startup consultant? I can't see us moving to the East Coast because of this import/export business," she said, a hint of dread showing.

Will grabbed her face with his hands, "Samantha, nobody's talking about dragging you OR Johnny boy away from Diego and Great West my dear. It's just that you're the one with time on your hands, and you need to put that business brain of yours to work before rust sets in. We'll work the hard parts about finding the operators once we've proven the concept. You're gonna help me, aren't you?" Now he had his hands on her hips, pulling her in for a peck on the lips.

"Of course I'll do anything to help you guys Will. It's been one hell of a vacation to the Southern Hemisphere. Don't be a stranger, okay?"

Zig seemed impatient once again, listening to Will enlist Sam in his web. Glancing at Johnny, he reverted to his junkyard dog roots, "Come on you sandbagger; let's head back to the rat race."

Will took Willy from Henrietta and gave him one last smack on his fat cheek, "See you soon Willy; you like Argentina?"

To everyone's amazement the little guy replied, "*Si* unny." He held his arms out to Henrietta and laughed, closing his eyes in excitement. "*Addee Whailuh Dee.*" Carmen stared at Henrietta in astonishment.

"You already have a five-month old *Norteamericano* boy speaking *Español Abuela Diaz?*"

"Why, what'd he say?" Sam was wondering, about to pee her pants.

Carmen smirked at her, "Your son William tried very hard to say *Adios Abuela Diaz*, which means 'Goodbye Grandmother Diaz.' He was probably thinking 'Bye bye, Granny Diaz.' It would seem he has taken to *Señora* Henrietta, *si?*"

Sam was beside herself, "He only speaks three words in English, and one of those is Unny." She gave Henrietta a warm hug and smiled, "We must return sometime so he can properly thank his Granny Diaz. Thank you so much for looking after our little Willy Henrietta."

"It was indeed my pleasure *Señora* Samantha; he is a good boy. Bring him back anytime," Henrietta said as she kissed the top of the child's head one last time.

That night in bed, finally relaxed with the visitor's departure, Dom looked at Will, "That was some visit, *n'est pas*? Now it is time for you and I to do what we must to have a baby William. Are you prepared for this?"

She was rapidly elevating his happiness level when there was a knock on the door. He smiled as he shook his head at Dom, "Do I detect an interested guest?"

She merely gave the head jerk, "Let her in; I believe she's also glad the visitors are gone."

After an incredibly intense and passionate interlude, Dom banished Kelly off to her bedroom and admonished her that they had work to do and this was not a care-free libidinous holiday.

Things proceeded smoothly the following week as they mapped out detailed action sequences for each of the major scenes; planning in Tangier, Carmen's deadly seduction in Algiers, the swap at the mosque, the takedown of the casbah and the penultimate ending in Ksar. When they broke for lunch on Friday, Carmen's mental exhaustion was obvious, "Does that about do it for Marrakech?"

Will nodded with empathy, "Yeah, I think Kell's got about everything she needs for the screenplay, why? You ready to look at something else besides our pretty faces?"

She stood up, walked to him and stroked his whiskered face with two fingers, "Yes Will, it's time for your friend Harold and I to get married." She patted her slightly swelling stomach and added, "We must do this before it becomes a matter of familial embarrassment."

Will looked like she had insulted him, "Only family members?"

"Well, I'm gonna need my best man Willy boy," Hal said with a smile. He then looked to Carmen for her input.

"Dominique, would it be too much of an imposition for you to serve as my Maid of Honor?"

Dom launched into her arms, "It would not be any imposition whatsoever Carmen; I would be most honored to be your Maid of Honor. When do you plan to marry?"

"Hal and I are going to Bariloche for a week or so to plan the ceremony. My parents are there so I will hopefully be able to make peace without coming to blows with dear *Madre* who knows nothing of the pregnancy. I'd really like to keep this as small as possible."

Will shook his head in disgust at the thought of Hal smuggling his parents in for the wedding, "Okay, so we'll see you guys back in a week with all the plans set for the wedding. It's amazing that it took twenty-nine years for a woman to put the hook in you buddy-ro."

"Fuck you Willy; at least I didn't jump out of the crib married." Before Will could conjure up a proper rejoinder Hal added, "Hey, I take that back; you had more than a little help with that conspiratorial bitch Danielle." He looked at the three of them wistfully and asked, "What are you going to do Kelly; head back to LaLa land?"

"Actually, I should head back now to keep Zig from calling a press conference over Marrakech, but I think I'll take advantage of being down here to work up the draft screenplay for Will's court-martial while I have a window of opportunity. Warren Banding's going to be waiting as soon as Zig let's up on Marrakech to get that started, and Lord knows where I'll find the four of you if I wait."

Hal was nodding his head at Will as he acknowledged her wisdom, "You are a wise woman; take advantage of having my homeboy in one place while you can."

Dom hugged her again, making Will twitch slightly, and told her, "Don't you worry about a thing. Enjoy your time in Bariloche; and good luck keeping the wedding down to a small service. Will and I were fortunate to hold ours down to one hundred invitations."

"I would consider it the greatest triumph in my family's history to contain the wedding to one hundred people. Would you like to come and join us? Perhaps when you finish the other script with Kelly? You know we would love to host you in the Argentine Rockies if you possibly could."

Dom shook her head and replied, "We'll see how things go with the court-martial script. I'm sure we'll be in touch to assess progress."

———

As Roberto came and picked up Carmen and Hal for the ride out to the airport, Kelly wrapped her arms around Dom and Will, "How about a little relaxation in the hot tub? It's time for a break, don't you think?"

'Relaxation in the hot tub' translated into the most lascivious conduct perpetrated at *Casa Fabiano* in recent memory, as the three of them were reduced to limp noodles within an hour. "How about some pina coladas?" Will suggested.

The next week went smoothly, as Kelly had digested the court-marital Record of Trial impressively, and they were able to quickly transition between the major procedural steps of the process, inserting personal and emotional anecdotes where appropriate. Early on she had led the three of them in a perverse version of brainstorming to come up with a working title for the project. "So what is strange about having cocaine in the Philippines?"

Will looked at her like she was a zombie, rolled his eyes and replied, "Duh, what's strange is you can't get any there; it's a South American crop—coca— you know. So the source of the spark is half a world away."

"Hey, jungle's jungle right? What makes the Philippines different from the coca growing areas in South America?"

Will walked over to the Atlas of the world in the study and looked at the two countries. Picking up a tape measure and checking the scale of the map, he got a rough approximation, "Okay, Manila is about 11,000 miles from Bogotá, which makes it damn near on the other side of the Earth from one another. Let's check the latitudes."

After eyeballing the city placements he announced, "Bogotá is roughly at 5 degrees and Manila is at 14 degrees, but the Philippine archipelago extends all the way down to 5 degrees so they're approximately on the same band of the globe."

"How about elevations for the two cities Will, can you get that from the map?" Dom asked.

Grabbing a notepad, he did some quick calculations for metric conversion and reported, "Okay, Bogotá is a little more than 8,600 feet above sea level, and Manila is obviously at sea level. Now when we were in Baguio, we were at the highest inhabited part of the Philippines at about a mile high, or 5,200 feet. So Colombia is obviously higher in elevation, and from what I remember the coca cultivation takes place in the jungles at elevation in Colombia, Peru and Bolivia."

"So it snows in Colombia and not in the Philippines; how does that help us?" Kelly asked in exasperation.

He laughed and told her, "The only snow you get in the Philippines is the dry powder kind, if you're lucky. Clint Roberts confused me the first time he called it blow. Hell, we joked about being blinded by a snowstorm of cocaine. It was one of the ultimate fantasies there, and the most difficult to experience, that's for sure."

"So the ultimate fantasy, since you were already living the other one, was to experience being snowblind in the Philippines?" Dom asked.

"That's it baby, but just talking about it almost got me convicted of a felony. No telling what it'd have been like to be snowblind in the Philippines."

Dom looked at Kelly and smiled, "Congratulations Kelly, I believe that, in spite of long odds, we have our working title for the court-marital project."

13

A FLY IN THE OINTMENT

As THEY WERE DRIVING KELLY OUT to Ezeiza Airport for her flight back to LA, Will thought about what a strange week it had been since the three of them had the house to themselves. Carmen had given Henrietta the week off to be with her family, so they had adopted a fairly organized approach to work every day; Dom and Will alternating cooking duties, with forays out to restaurants when they couldn't stomach leftovers or just didn't have time. Kelly had all but moved into their bedroom, although she still kept her clothes in her bedroom.

The second day after Hal and Carmen left for Bariloche, she and Dom went shopping and came back with food, intoxicants and some interesting looking red velvet rope restraints they had found in some sex toy shop. These had been deployed during evening hijinks, although Dom declined to be tied up what with the torture at Sandrigan's casbah still on the edge of her consciousness. On her last day in Buenos, Dom took Kelly to Salón Rio, Leticia Alvarez' waxing studio in Palermo Soho, for a full Brazilian Waxing. Though she was a bit tender and slightly reddened around the pubic region, Will told Kelly she now looked like a true Playmate.

Kelly was so paranoid that the restraints might be discovered in her luggage that she had them mailed back to her condo in LA. All in all it was probably the closest Will would ever get to experience being a king with a harem. He doubted many kings had women as sultry and sensuous as Dom and Kelly, and for sure not as stridently independent.

On the drive out to Ezeiza, he was smiling thinking about the fantasy of it all when Kelly interrupted his field trip to the frontal lobes, "Whatcha thinking about William?"

He snapped out of it to smile, "Sex."

"Well what a coincidence, so was I."

"Haven't you two had enough sex for a week?" Dom wondered.

"So what kind of ribald thoughts are you conjuring up in that pretty little head of yours?" Will asked her, tweaking her thigh.

"Oh, I was thinking about that pretty little head of yours," she told him, smiling lasciviously as she stroked his crotch.

He shook his head slightly, glanced at her and said, "Damn, I just got the weirdest sense of déjà vu. Didn't we have this same conversation that morning after the guys left for golf?"

She sidled over to him, wrapped her hand around his aroused member and smirked, "Hey, not bad for someone who conked out on pina coladas and Percodans later that day. I'm going to miss you guys, can you tell?"

He deliberately stroked his hand right up her crotch, "Actually, I was wondering what they call the women in a harem. I figure this is as close as I'll ever get to experiencing one."

She squeezed down on his swanse deliberately, got right next to his ear and dared, "I think they call them concubines, but don't try that shit on Dom or I if you want to keep this hanging in your lap."

"Hey, hey, hey, I'm good. I don't even want to know how to spell that thing you mentioned. That's how far away I'll keep that thought from daylight. Jesus, it was just a passing fancy; I mean, you asked me right?"

"Right cowboy, just as long as you keep making us happy, everything will be just fine," she said with a hint of an attitude.

"Come to think of it, I don't think this is the way the participants in a harem interface. No harm no foul, right?" He said, giving them his best shit-eating grin.

As she gave him one final squeeze she kissed him salaciously and purred, "Good boy."

Will took his trusty Pentax into the terminal as the skycap dragged Kelly's bags. They had decided to keep the Great West office equipment, as it seemed likely they would be working back and forth for the foreseeable future. When Zig heard the proposal he immediately endorsed it, no doubt seeing it as a means to further cement their affiliation. As they were waiting at the gate for the Pan Am flight announcement, Will looked at a hungry skycap and winked, "Can you take a picture of us *por favor*?"

After he took three insurance shots Will thanked and tipped him, and as he turned to look at the Departures Status Board on the wall someone said, "Hello Will."

He turned to find Deputy Defense Minister Daniel Rojas extending his hand as he broke into a huge grin, "Hey Danny! How the heck are you? Are you flying out?"

He motioned Will over to a secluded spot, "Actually, I'm flying to Los Angeles on the Pan Am flight."

"Whoa, Los Angeles and not Washington, eh? Is this business or pleasure Minister Rojas?" He asked with a conspiratorial smile.

Rojas looked up to find Dom and Kelly excitedly hug him and blushed slightly before continuing, "Actually, it's business and that's a pleasure. I'm going up to personally coordinate certain aspects of the motion picture memorandum of understanding with the Studio. President Videla thought it untoward for him to travel personally, so I am his representative."

Will looked at him, wondering what in the world could be so complicated that it couldn't be done over the phone. He let it slide by telling him, "Are you taking your golf clubs? Zig wants revenge on your ass bro."

He laughed and nodded, "Of course I'm taking my clubs Will. What self-respecting deputy defense minister could conduct business without them?"

"Hey, do you mind if we get a picture of the four of us? Scrapbook material for when we're old and gray," Will asked.

"Not at all," he said as the skycap reappeared to shoot four more frames.

"Have a nice trip Danny, see you when you get back," Will said, waving to him goodbye as he held Kelly back from following him onto the plane.

"What's the matter Kavanagh, already missing your harem?"

"Yeah, you wish you hot little minx. Listen, something's not kosher with Danny's trip to LA; how about work him for some details on the flight out. You used to be a stewardess, I'm sure you can figure how to get next to him."

"Oh, you want me to take one for the team?"

"Hey, whatever the heat will bear baby; I'll leave surveillance and counter-intel details to you. What I'm most interested in is why he would be going to LA and not Washington; he's the Deputy Defense Minister remember? That seems more than a little strange to me, especially since there's an arms embargo in effect. Maybe I'm being paranoid, but how about keep an ear to the ground babe."

"I will do just that Mr. Kavanagh; take care of my soul sister here," she said, and then kissed him aggressively, all but biting his lower lip. She then kissed Dom tenderly and headed off to her first class seat back home.

As they watched her head up the jetway, Dom clutched him and nodded, "You're right Will; it does seem strange that Danny's going to LA. I wonder what that's all about?"

"Jesus I hope there's not trouble in paradise," he shivered.

"Time will tell my husband. Are you ready to go live like a normal couple again?"

He rolled his eyes, gave her an incredulous look and responded, "When have we ever lived like a normal couple the first time?"

14

GETTING SERIOUS ABOUT PARENTHOOD

THE NEXT MORNING THEY WENT for their initial consult with Dr. Robert Calvatori, who according to Carmen was singularly the preeminent obstetrics physician in Argentina. Calvatori was one handsome guy, early thirties and about six feet tall, an athletic physique and long flowing black hair that he combed back around his head. Will wondered how many of his patients secretly harbored lustful thoughts about him, but erased the thought figuring it was at least 100 percent. "How are you Mrs. Kavanagh and I trust you are Mr. Kavanagh? I am so pleased to see you both for the consult; many Argentine husbands find it distasteful to be seen at an obstetrician's office."

Will shook his hand, liking him instantly, "Well, this isn't going to be a typical situation I can assure you Doc. I would all but bet you that Dominique and I will both require enhanced procedures to pull off this pregnancy, but we are totally committed to bringing a baby into this world. So where do we begin?"

"Your enthusiasm is compelling. Could you tell me why you believe you both have fertility issues?"

Will nodded to Dom, so she took the lead, "I suffered a serious injury as a child and have endured polycystic ovary syndrome my entire adult life. My gynecologist in Morocco determined that I have only one functioning ovary, and my menstrual cycles have been sporadic since puberty."

The doctor looked at her in amazement and finally said, "That is the most thorough diagnostic statement any patient has ever presented to me. I can only say that I am beholding to the excellent medical consultation you

142

have sought previously Mrs. Kavanagh."

She smiled perfunctorily, "It's my body and my life doctor, so it is my responsibility to have a clear understanding of my health condition."

He nodded and told her, "Indeed." He then looked at Will, "And what is your medical condition Mr. Kavanagh, at least as it pertains to reproduction?"

Will laughed until he thought he'd puke, Calvatori's query caught him so off guard. Noting Dom's scowl he recovered enough to say, "Some would say oversexed, but I was diagnosed with impeded sperm motility factor in my early twenties and was advised by an urologist that I could not conceive without incubative intervention."

He again nodded his head appreciatively and replied, "Once again, I am almost at a loss to describe my relief to find a couple who present their pathology so succinctly."

"So where do we go from here? What's next for us doc?" He wanted to know.

"First of all, I'm going to examine both of you and take some blood and tissue samples. Upon examination of the results, I will have a follow-up consultation with you and we will determine the proper course of action that will give you the greatest probability to conceive. Agreed?"

Will raised his hand up to high-five the stud doc, but Calvatori just looked at him strangely, so he lowered his hand and replied, "Dude, you must've gone to the same school of 'what's happening now' as I did. I admire a man who knows how to set up a plan. Where do we sign up? Carmen really knew what she was talking about sending us to her savant."

In spite of the lingering scent of a confused look, he nodded his head, "I presume you are referring to Ms. Fabiano?"

"That's the one bro, three-plus month's pregnant and still hotter'n a sunspot, but about to become Mrs. Rayfield. How many stone foxes are that hot when they're knocked up?"

He was suddenly chastised by Dom as she snapped, "Will Kavanagh!"

Calvatori finally got his act back together. "Excuse me, I'm not quite used to the level of American slang you present Mr. Kavanagh."

Dom sneered at him and turned to the doctor and explained, "I apologize for my husband's inability to contain his colloquialisms Dr. Calvatori; please excuse his inappropriate pronouncements."

To Will's amazement, Calvatori held up his hand and insisted, "No, no,

I have never had a patient discuss such things with me so openly. Your husband's candor is most welcome."

"See, he's a squared away doctor," Will told her. "You know Carmen wouldn't sick us on a bones that didn't have his shit together!" He nodded at Calvatori and proposed, "Listen Doc, why don't you come over to our place for a *lomo* on the *parilla*?"

Now Dom was furious, standing up and all but shouting, "Will Kavanagh, leave this office right this minute. We are trying to have a serious discussion about fertility here, or did you forget that?"

Calvatori surprised them both when he said, "I've never been referred to as a bones before, but I would like to reserve your invitation for after we have determined a treatment plan for the two of you. Now Mr. Kavanagh, would you excuse us while I examine your wife?" He saw the scowl on his face and smiled, "And would you ask Lita to step into the exam room when you leave?"

———

"Will Kavanagh, you sometimes amaze me with your incredible prosaic euphemisms. How could you possibly have known that Dr. Calvatori would want to come to the house for *lomos*?"

"Hey, he's a stud from the get-go babe. It's a shame Kelly blew town; she might fall in love like all of his patients no doubt do."

"As much as I want to strangle you, I also wish Kelly could meet Dr. Calvatori. If I were unattached, I believe I would…."

"You would what? Change his life inalterably? I don't think so my dear, but I get it; he's a hot stud. Here's the deal, he is our pathway to bringing another Kavanagh into this world. I am once again impressed with Carmen's sense of value. Calvatori is a class act."

"What am I going to do with you Will Kavanagh?"

"Oh I don't know," he replied, looking at her furtively, "love me, live with me, and make love to me desperately?"

She crept over for a kiss and purred, "Maybe not in that order."

15

MAKING WEDDING PLANS
ON THE SLY

"THAT'S RIGHT BRO, there's a fox in the henhouse," Will told his buddy Hal after calling the *Estancia* in Bariloche.

"Danny Rojas? I can't believe this conspiracy theory Willy; Jesus, that's one squared away motherfucker if I've ever met one. Why do you think he's up to no good?"

"If you happened to be say, Deputy Defense Minister of some obscure South American country with shaky residual relationships to the Third Reich, and you went off to do business in the US which has an arms embargo imposed against you, and it wasn't in DC, what would you think?"

"You think they're our enemy or something? What have you been drinking partner, obviously something stronger than the wine," answered his closest of buds.

"Hey, I may be all wet around the ears, but I don't think so. First of all, fucking Jimmy Carter put the arms embargo on 'em two years ago, right? Why would Argentina be playing nookie with the *Norteamericanos*? What's to gain here?" Will posed with a healthy dose of conjecture.

"I don't know Willy, but you've got my attention. I can't think of anything the Argentines are into that would require counterintelligence snooping all the way back to the States. Man, especially with regards to Danny Rojas; I thought he was one of us! Unless there's something we don't know about…"

"Well, since they bought a brood of Douglas A-4 Skyhawks in the past five years I'd think they'd be thinking logistics support bro. Now the embargo can't be helping them with spares and all; maybe Danny Boy is looking for the old end around. Whatdya think?"

"What I think is the FMS weenies at the Security Assistance Agency would look down upon such devious spares stocking. Jesus Willy, if you were, say Israel or Brazil, would you wanna piss off the FMS guys in the Pentagon by selling spares to Argentina?"

"You make an excellent point Kemosabe, but he's heading to the epicenter of US aircraft manufacturing by some odd coincidence."

"And I can't ignore your point bro. What do you think honey?"

Hal's deference to Carmen was surprising, but her response was even more so, "The Junta that Videla led in '76 has already lost one of its founding members; Admiral Emilio Massera has retired and all but vanished. Rumors would lead one to believe Massera was in charge of military operations the first two years of the Reorganization Process, and he and Videla were at odds constantly. It is no small secret that the military is the keeper of the never extinguished embers concerning our sovereignty over the Falkland Islands. Should anything come of this, Argentina would suddenly become the pariah of the South Atlantic and Britain would be thrust into the confrontation. If they are serious about this childish ploy, it could put Argentina in a position of trying to influence the Americans before the British come calling for support. After all, the Americans are the ones with the huge aircraft carriers that can project deadly force globally."

"My God, how could this be happening?" Will gasped out loud, obviously shocked that Rojas—who seemed like a tight friend—could turn on them so quickly.

"I believe we are all experiencing overexposure to celebrity here," Dom intoned. "The only reason we're having this conversation about Daniel Rojas is because we have befriended him and have access to him in social settings. Therefore if he does something that appears odd, we overreact—what William refers to as knee-jerking. What if he has some secret relationship with a woman elsewhere? We would be guilty of severe overreaction merely because we know him and feel comfortable asking him very personal questions about his travel and intentions."

"That's a good point, I hadn't thought of it that way," Will offered.

"Yeah Willy, just like you didn't think it was odd to assemble a throng around the President of Argentina—the leader of the military Junta no less— and address him as Jorge. We're lucky he tolerates you well," Hal said, not hiding his criticism of what otherwise would appear unprofessional conduct. "Jesus man, the guy did preside over the Dirty War, right?"

"Actually, I'm sure he tolerates us because we are a means to an end Patton; bringing Hollywood and the attendant international exposure to Argentina is where he wants this to lead. And now he's hearing preliminary discussions about us doing legitimate business with his ailing economy. But hey, it's a wonderful place, so why not?"

"On another subject Carmen, Will and I met with Dr. Calvatori yesterday, and we both were impressed with his professionalism. Thank you so much for the referral; we are going to see him tomorrow for the exam results and develop a treatment plan if William can throttle his damning Louisiana bent for wanting to make every male he encounters a coonass Cajun good old boy," Dom said with more than a tinge of vitriol.

"Hey, it's in our blood Dominique, and I seem to recall that you married him," Hal offered in Will's defense.

"And it was the best decision I ever made. Now if I can just endure William's penchant for reducing human interactions to fraternity campfire chitchats we might just discover his preeminence as a physician. By the way, what have the two of you decided about wedding plans?"

"Now that has become a very delicate matter Mrs. Kavanagh. Perhaps I should allow my fiancée to address that subject," Hal replied as Will and Dom looked at each other strangely.

The discomfort in Carmen's voice was apparent as she unveiled the unpleasant truth. "When my parents found out I was pregnant, they reacted as if I were some promiscuous teenager. They seem to feel as though the fact that I am pregnant with Hal's child to be scandalously gossip-worthy considering their station in life and their friends. The good news is that I have succeeded in my desire for a small wedding ceremony. Hal has already arranged for his parent's to arrive one week from tomorrow. We will be married in the San Isidro Cathedral in Buenos Aires by Bishop Luis Jorge Martin. My parents have refused to invite any of our extended family due to the pregnancy. I had at least wanted to have my aunts and uncles, along with a few friends at the ceremony. I admit to being a bit discouraged concerning my parents'—especially my mother's—reaction."

"Who'd you want to attend?" Will asked, clearly put out. "Fuck invitations; the Cathedral is an open house of worship, right?"

They could hear Carmen exhale before saying, "I cannot create severe animosity within my family by openly subverting their plans. I'm leaving this phone call now my friends, but Harold would like to speak with you further about something."

"Tonto, you got the lizard side of your brain engaged?" Hal asked.

"I am here Kemosabe. So eight days from now, the wedding will be held at San Isidro at what time?" Will asked.

"Sixteen hundred hours."

"Okay, the ROUST staff, Pierson and Ayako, Kelly and Bob Kellor. Anybody I'm missing?" Will asked, scribbling the names down.

"Those are the prime guys. Listen, if the Fabiano's catch wind that I'm setting up some alternate wedding party they will not be happy. So I need you to..." he was saying before Will interrupted.

"Got it Kemosabe; we'll set everybody up in the Alvear Palace Hotel and book the penthouse for an 'after reception' party. We'll set you two up with the Honeymoon Suite. Where were you planning on heading out for the honeymoon?"

"Good point; how about booking us a suite at the Conrad Punta del Este Resort for three days," he said in almost a whisper.

"Damn bro, black op, eh? Alright, tell me, are the Fabiano's planning on a reception after the wedding?" Will asked, knowing he couldn't let his best friends be penalized because of Carlita Fabiano's traditional Catholic mores.

"Yeah, but it's gonna be a low key thing back at the mansion," Hal quickly advised.

"Fuck 'em; I'll schedule the limo to pick you two up at the Cathedral and stick with you for the drop-off at the Alvear. I'll go ahead and book you round-trip first class to Punta; three days on the ground, right? I'll set up a rental car at the airport in Punta; you want a sport model to wheel around in?"

"Jesus Willy!"

"Hey, your ass is only getting married once; if you change your mind later she'll kill you. Might as well do it right, eh?" Will told him as Dom slapped him in the back of the head.

"I don't know how to thank you brother," he offered sheepishly.

"Oh, this ain't outa my ass bro; this is Circle Entertainment overhead all the way. But between you and Carmen, there are a lot of people who are alive today because of your skill and friendship. Truth be known, we could probably fill up the Cathedral with people indebted to you two. This is the least we can do to make your wedding memorable."

"Besides being my best man?" He offered sheepishly.

"I wouldn't miss being there for the world brother." Dom was about to have a fit, "Hold on buddy, Dom wants to say something."

"Hal Rayfield, I feel terrible that you and Carmen have run into this tradition-bound moral code. I would say the Fabianos were being totally unreasonable if I were not a Bedouin of a Muslim society that is far more restrictive. That is why I eloped for my first marriage and quite likely why we never considered Marrakech when I married your Cajun home boy. Please let Will and I worry about getting the right friends in for this blessed event. And please tell Carmen I will be there providing all the strength she needs as her Maid of Honor."

Now Hal was on the verge of tears, "Dom, if it weren't for you demonstrating your love for Willy, this marriage would have never taken place. I was so completely wedged into my self-satisfied ego that it took you to make me acknowledge how much she means to me and how much I love her. You will always be our angel."

"It had to happen Hal; you two were so obviously in love that all it took was a gentle nudge. Now you will have a baby as evidence of that love. Take care; we both love you very much."

"Thanks for everything. And best of luck with the fertility specialist," he said in parting.

"We'll see how the treatment plan works out; we'll call and let you know. Good luck in Bariloche!"

16

A CRASH COURSE IN FERTILITY ENHANCEMENT

"WELCOME BACK MR. AND MRS. KAVANAGH, it's good to see you again. I have the exam results and I believe we need to discuss the possibilities you are facing. Please have a seat," Dr. Calvatori said as he pointed towards a sofa in his office.

"Okay doc, whatcha got?" Will asked, ready for the straight skinny.

Calvatori tried to hide a smile when he told them, "Ordinarily I prefer to discuss the individual results with each patient privately, and I would ordinarily refer you to an urologist specializing in fertility treatments Mr. Kavanagh. However, considering the extant pathology diagnoses you each presented in our initial consult, I feel comfortable addressing aspects of fertility from both sides of the conception picture. May I begin with you Mrs. Kavanagh?"

Dom nodded so he continued, "Blood samples confirm the impaired endocrine function associated with polycystic ovary syndrome. The computed tomography scan we took shows complete obstruction of one fallopian tube and a non-functioning ovary on that side as well. The existence of menstrual cycles, however intermittent, indicates at least a partial functioning of the remaining ovary and its associated fallopian tube. This is very good news, as it indicates the probability that ovum are being expelled by your functioning ovary."

He turned to Will and advised, "Your sample analysis indicates normal sperm volume but a slightly impaired motility factor. I do not believe this should present a significant impediment to fertilization Mr. Kavanagh. I am curious; why did you indicate that motility was an issue during our initial con-

150

sult? Were you told this by another physician in the past?"

Will assessed Jonathon Calvatori, trying to decide if he gave a rip, but figured he'd give him the option, "Do you really want to hear a no-bullshit human interest story Doc?"

Dom threw her head back, rolling her eyes as she muttered Arabic curses under her breath. She was about to let Will have it with both barrels when Calvatori held his hand up and smiled. "Yes, I am very much interested. Please continue with this human interest story Mr. Kavanagh."

Will gave Dom a fake 'I-told-you-so' smile as she had the temerity to shoot him the bird in front of Calvatori. Unfazed Will laid it out, "Here's the deal Doc; I had to get married at the end of a shotgun when I was seventeen because my back-and-forth girlfriend got pregnant. She miscarried—thank the good Lord—but we never used birth control so she got curious after a year or so and we got tested; this was while I was a sophomore at college. So the urologist tells me I've got impaired motility factor and that I probably had it since birth. He also mentioned the adverse effects of marijuana smoking on motility—which I was doing a bit of at the time—but I sloughed it off as inconsequential when he surmised it was congenital. The important implication for me—and the cheating bitch didn't deny it—was that she'd gotten pregnant by a guy who jilted her for a hot blonde, and then roped my gullible ass into marrying her. Now ain't that some shit?"

The doctor's eyes were wide with surprise but Will gave him props for his next question, "I take it Mrs. Kavanagh was not the cheating bitch?"

He nodded excitedly, blew Dom a kiss and told him, "Not this one, that's for damn sure!"

He nodded his head and gave the next part of his script, "Very well Mr. Kavanagh, we have determined that your fertility problems do not represent a formidable impediment to impregnation." He turned to Dom and continued, "However Mrs. Kavanagh, yours are problematic bordering on improbable."

Her shoulders drooped in resignation as Will reached out to comfort her, but the Argentinian Julio Iglesias intervened by saying, "I do not believe, however, that it is impossible. Would you be willing to consider a technique that is undergoing clinical testing at the moment? It has not been approved for widespread application, but I am one of the physicians involved in the clinical testing that is taking place here in Argentina."

The look on Dom's face was like a hungry child pleading for bread, so

Will answered for her, "So what does this technique involve Doc?"

He got a deadly serious look on his face as he told them, "The technique is referred to as zygote intrafallopian transfer. It involves the extraction of an ovum—or egg—from Mrs. Kavanagh's ovary, fertilizing it in our laboratory with your sperm and then placing it surgically into the fallopian tube to gestate. It is referred to as experimental and investigational by the American Medical Association, but it is undergoing similar clinical testing in the United States concurrently with our tests."

Dom was locked in on the doctor's face as she asked, "So this is the only realistic chance we have of conceiving a child with my egg and Will's sperm?"

He had a look of resignation on his face, "In my professional opinion that is the only way you can reasonably expect to conceive a child."

"So where do we sign up Doc?" Will answered for the both of them.

Calvatori shook his head slightly and replied, "You two are a remarkable couple. You have just in the last minute completely ignored the denial that is so inherent in typical couples. I am truly impressed with the both of you."

"Impressed how Doc? That we know the truth and had fast-forwarded past the bullshit years ago? Listen ma man, after I dodged that bullet of having to raise another shitbird's child, I promised myself I would never, ever even consider the possibility of bringing a child into this world. But guess what? I met a woman who taught me I had a soul, and who showed me she loved me unconditionally. So guess what old Kavanagh's attitude is now? I've seen the light, and we know we've got serious impediments. But Carmen said you're the wunderkind so we're putting our stock in you. What's the process sequence?"

The doctor looked at him like he was a mad man, but recovered enough to shake his hand with a bewildered gaze, then shifted to shake Dom's. She snickered, got up quickly and gave him a hug, "We'll do everything we possibly can to make this successful Dr. Calvatori. I feel truly blessed to have found you."

He went back to a cabinet and found two stapled sets of papers, then turned and handed one to each of them. "These are the patient preparation steps that I absolutely insist upon to maximize the chances for success of this very complex procedure. I have found that if the patients, I'm sorry, the parents, aren't willing to present themselves in the best possible physical condition then the odds for a successful conclusion are lessened. Are you both willing to try this?"

Will scanned the instructions, which looked like something Hal's secret agent school should mail to matriculating students for the combat training course. "Let's see here Doc, no alcohol except wine for the next two weeks; Jesus, I guess that leaves out vodka and Grand Marnier. No smoking! You have got to be shitting me!" He looked at Calvatori in disbelief, wondering how smoking could influence sperm motility. The doctor merely looked at Will with a snick of a smile, so he continued down the list, "Limited red meat, okay, fruits and vegetable, no big deal. No recreational drugs, I guess that leaves off the alcohol. What's this about vitamins? Is this something you provide?"

"It's all included within the fee Mr. Kavanagh," he replied.

"Hey, that reminds me; what's this gonna cost us? Investigational and experimental sounds like it could be kinda expensive," Will asked, wondering how bad this was going to deplete the coffers.

"Don't pay any attention to my husband Dr. Calvatori. He was raised to be a frugal person and I love him for it, but the fee is not even a remote consideration for either of us. What about sexual intercourse? How do we prepare for the ovum and sperm extraction appointment?"

"Sex as you usually partake for the next ten days and then no sexual intercourse for three days prior to the extraction. Will this be a problem for you?" Calvatori asked with a barely disguised grin.

Dom seemed to ignore his question as she glanced down the list, "What is this medication Clomid? I am not familiar with it. Everything else looks like dietary supplements targeting specific body systems."

"I was about to cover that with you. Clomid is the brand name that clomiphene is marketed by its patent holder, Sanofi, of England. It is designed to stimulate the development of ovum cells already in the ovaries, and greatly improves the odds of successful ovum extraction."

Dom was nodding her head in assent, but Will wasn't giving in without a plan of action and milestones, "So here's the deal Doc; we do this boot camp regimen for two weeks, do the deed and wait for the results. Now this could be three fucking months based on Dom's menstrual cycle. I take it there's some rabbit test you can do in the interim, right?"

This time he snickered, but caught himself as he told them, "Yes, seven days after the procedure I will perform a urinalysis on Mrs. Kavanagh to determine whether she is pregnant. We actually don't use the 'rabbit test' as you call it anymore."

"So since my magnanimous bride has so readily agreed to whatever your terms for remuneration might be, here is mine; if she's pregnant when you check the golden flow, your ass is coming out to *Casa Fabiano* for some *bife de lomo*, whatdya say to that?"

He extended his hand to shake and responded, "I accept your invitation Mr. Kavanagh, whether the first impregnation is successful or not. I somehow get the impression that I will be seeing the two of you many times again, and I look forward to visiting with you socially. You are possibly the most engaging patient I have ever met during my entire tenure as a physician."

Will looked at him closely, wondering if it was possible, but discounting the chances told him, "If I didn't know better I'd call you a Coonass. You would love it in Louisiana Doc; those Cajun gals would be all over your ass!"

Now he did laugh as he became animated for the first time, "These Cajun gals would possibly be seeking impregnation samples?"

"I knew you were a Coonass dammit; hell yeah they'd be extracting samples, but not for impregnation, I can guarantee you that!"

17

THE LONG AND WINDING ROAD

DOM AND WILL WERE STANDING ACROSS the altar from one another, smiling as the bridal processional played and a resplendent Carmen Fabiano was escorted up the aisle of the San Isidro Cathedral on the arm of her father George. When they got to the altar, Bishop Luis Jorge Martin asked something in Spanish to which George replied and turned to sit next to his wife Carlita. As she reached out for Hal's hand to take her place beside him, Will scanned the nearly empty cathedral, smiling just perceptibly at Harold Senior and Janie Rayfield, Alex Manatos, Rico Suarez, Rose Cordes, Dan Pierson, Ayako Tanaka, Kelly Dupree, Bob and Rose Kellor, Johnny and Sam Chessereaux and most importantly of all Ayran Lefebvre and Mando Chu. Besides her parents, Carmen's *Porteño* friends in attendance were limited to her brother Roberto and Danny Rojas. Surprisingly, Ayran nor Mando had any difficulty understanding the 'moral barrier' that the Fabianos had thrown up in front of the 'blessed union,' in spite of the fact that both bride and groom were twenty-eight years of age. In spite of such however, they both recognized that the child Carmen was carrying was far more important than any societal expectations.

As Will stood and listened to the priest conduct the entire ceremony in Latin interspersed with Spanish, he wondered what Hal must be thinking, uncertain when to insert his input when called for in the vows. There were a fair number of opportunities for the audience to provide refrains to the priest's incantations, but only the *Porteños* along with Rico and Rose did so. When it came time to recite the vows, Carmen recited them as the priest had intoned and smiled with true love into Hal's eyes as she did so. After the priest cited the vows for Hal to repeat, also in Spanish, he merely turned to face her,

155

stared into her eyes and said, "Carmen Belen Fabiano, I take you as my bride in the sanctimony of marriage and vow that I will always love you, protect you and be with you, in sickness or in health. I love you more than anything in the universe baby."

The Bishop looked at Hal with a mystified smirk, nodded his head and continued with the presentation of the rings. After what seemed an extended ceremony, the Bishop finally proclaimed *"Gracias a Dios,"* and Carmen and Hal turned to walk triumphantly down the aisle as all of the visitors broke with solemnity strictures and began applauding the happy couple.

The Bishop followed them to the steps of the Cathedral as they darted into an anteroom near the back of the church. As the Bishop was greeting each of the attendees, Roberto Fabiano pulled Will aside, "I can only apologize for the strict nature of my family's interpretations of morally acceptable behavior. I do not share this interpretation, obviously. You and your friends have rescued what would have been a very subdued celebration of a truly great event. Please invite your friends over to the Casa for a celebration of the marriage. Can you do this for me?"

He looked Roberto directly in the eyes, as serious as he'd ever been and replied, "No Roberto, I cannot do this for you. But I will do it for your wonderful sister, who by the way has saved my life twice now. And I will do it for my best brother friend in the world, who saved my life and deserves to celebrate on his wedding day."

"I am sorry Will, I do not know what to say," Roberto said, clearly humiliated.

"Hey, it wasn't your fault Roberto; you're an upfront guy and I like you. Will the Bishop join us?" Will asked as Dom hovered, monitoring his conversation closely.

"Of course; it is one of his opportunities to be free of the bonds of the Cathedral," he smiled.

"Okay, we'll see you over there." Will turned back and glanced over Roberto's shoulder to assure privacy. "Roberto, I have never known what you do for a living, but I assumed you were part of the Fabiano SA business enterprise. The reason I'm telling you this is we are giving serious consideration to setting up an import/export business between here and the US. Would you have any interest whatsoever in being our Argentine managing partner?"

Dom suddenly appeared like a shadow as Roberto smiled, "I wondered who you trusted enough to approach as your Argentine partner..."

"Don't you think *su querida hermana* would insure the trustworthiness of our partner?" Will asked with an impish grin but suddenly heard what Roberto had said. "So, Belen has already discussed this with you perhaps?"

He shook his head no, "Actually President Videla called me to inquire about *Estancia Fabiano Lagar*'s readiness to participate in such a venture. To say I was surprised would be an understatement..."

"So what'd you tell Jorge? He was sitting right there when we first seriously discussed the mechanism of the arrangement while eating *tapas* at *Estancia Fabiano*."

"I told him we would be proud to ship our wines to the US for export. I am unsure of the volumes you plan to ship, but the *lagar* is a large one."

"It's hard to say, but I sweet-talked Samantha into doing exploratory market research for us. Later tonight I want to speak with you and Bob Kellor at the Alvear penthouse. He doesn't know it yet, but I'm gonna give him the same pitch I gave you; he's retiring from the military and would be perfect as our *Norteamericano* managing partner."

Now Roberto was nodding, "I am very much interested in pursuing this venture with you Will. Tell me, are you looking for investors in your business plan?"

"Quite possibly, but the exact portfolio of the import side has not yet been finalized..."

"That is a brilliant move, importing distilled spirits into the country to offset the cash flow implications. Jorge was quite taken with your business development ideas."

"Right, and the ultimate profitability achieved by each business unit will largely depend on the marketing abilities of the managing partners. Are you up for the challenge *mi amigo* Roberto?"

"*Si*, we will discuss this further after the reception at *Casa Fabiano*."

"Well how does it feel to be a married man?" Will asked the groom as they leaned back against padded stools at the bar set up in the Alvear Palace Hotel penthouse.

"You actually pulled this thing off you motherfucker! I could not believe the way Carlita was hugging and kissing you when we left their house. You, my friend, have rescued a catastrophe in the making and turned it into the happiest day of my life!"

"The difficult is challenging; the impossible calls for Kavanagh's Posse!" He said as a pair of arms wrapped around him.

Expecting Samantha Chessereaux was perpetrating one of her typically embarrassing and inappropriate welcomes, he was pleasantly surprised to find Carmen Fabiano Rayfield in his face, smiling radiantly. She kissed him long and hard on the lips and said, "Thank you for making this such a wonderful day for us Will. I cannot believe everything worked out between you and my mother!"

"You are referring to Carlita the pliable matriarch, right? She's a piece of cake compared to Zig Kowalski. What'd you think of those extemporaneous vows your hubby came up with? I kinda went off script when Dom and I got married, but I thought the Bishop was gonna faint when my homeboy lit off straight from the heart!"

"I actually thought they were very much heartfelt and appropriate," a voice came from behind them. Ayran Lefebvre was standing next to them with a huge smile, "If it weren't for you two, I am sure I would not be alive to celebrate this day. I am so happy to be here to witness your exchange of love for one another. I feel so much happiness that you will now bring the symbol of that love into the world." Carmen hugged her warmly and kissed her cheek before Ayran continued, "And thank you so much for leading my Dominique towards the possible miracle of such a symbol of her love with my Will. May God bless you both."

As she walked away, Mando came up to shake hands with Hal and Carmen, who gave him a warm hug instead. "What you two did to help my dear friend Ayran and her angel will never be forgotten. My God bless your lives as you go forward now to lead another into the ways of love."

After everyone had a chance to visit with the newlyweds, Will discreetly pulled Bob Kellor off to the patio outside the penthouse as Dom engaged Rose Kellor in rapturous conversation. "Bob, you remember meeting Carmen's brother Roberto, don't you?"

"Sure," he said with a smile as the two men shook hands. As they settled into chairs in the pleasant evening air Bob flexed his eyebrows. "Why do I think this little discussion is not innocent?"

"How long before TOPCAP snatches you into retirement?" Will launched without delay.

"Two months, and most of that will be terminal leave if I can train my replacement…"

"Bullshit, nobody can replace Bob Kellor at TJAG; they'll probably have to establish a new section just to handle your connections Chief," Will said as a waiter brought them Johnnie Walker Black on the rocks.

"Do what; did Melson already get ahold of you?"

"No Bob, I just know your capacity for absorption based on the Buzzards Point project. You remember that don't you, snatching victory from the jaws of defeat?"

"Boy do I," he said, looking up at the sky and smiling. "And then I sent you off to the wonderful world of pussy as I recall; any regrets?"

"Do what, did I hear you correctly *Señor* Kellor?" Roberto suddenly blurted, sloshing his drink.

"Dammit Bob, now you've got Roberto off track," Will fumed. He looked at Roberto and summarized, "I was forlorn lonely after my first marriage ended in divorce when Bob here suggested I get assigned to the Philippines. It had a reputation as the wonderful world of pussy, and let me tell ya big fella, Bob Kellor knew what he was talking about. To answer your next question, Dominique—who'd been killed in Africa I'd been told—turned up magically in Manila right before I left the Air Force thanks to this guy on my right. So, *mi amigo* Roberto, *Señor* Kellor and I go way back in the trust department, *comprende?*"

"*Si*, so have you had a chance to discuss the proposal with him?"

"No," Will replied and turned to Kellor. "Bob, we are very seriously considering establishing an export/import operation between Argentina and the US. Argentina makes wines as good as or better than California, and the time is right to introduce it to America. This is partly because the President, Jorge Videla, is a friend and is especially interested in improving the economy here and supporting the arts and culture. Great West Studios has been down here, met and traveled with Videla, and have committed to shooting the location scenes of 'It's Raining In Marrakech' here in Buenos Aires and down in Bariloche—the Argentine equivalent of Vail, Colorado…"

"Do what?"

"Right, you're Harry Strock in the movie, and it's gonna be a blockbuster. Shooting begins in a couple of months. In the meantime, I spotted the planes bringing in movie studio gear flying back to the US empty and *voila*, why not fill 'em up?'"

"Jesus Christ Kavanagh, are you serious?" Kellor asked, shaking his head. "How much whiskey have you had?"

"This is my first one, why?"

Roberto whistled for the waiter and had a large glass of cabernet sauvignon in front of Kellor within two minutes. "Please, try our cabernet; this is from my family's winery outside Bariloche."

Bob took a sip and looked up, evaluating the bouquet before swallowing. "It's certainly friendly smooth," he said before taking a larger swallow. "Damn, that's some extremely good cabernet Will. I'd rather drink that than the Bordeaux vintages."

"Good, so we've established bona fides," Will said, moving the conversation along. "Supply on this end is no problem; Roberto has signed on unofficially as our managing partner in Buenos, and it's his headache to work through tariffs and duties. Now we come to your part…"

"Somebody's got to market this in the US; is that my part?"

"We can't expect you to accomplish that alone. We—meaning you, me and Roberto—have got to draft up a business plan. Then we'll know if we need angel investors like *Señor* Fabiano here. Part of the plan is gonna be our marketing scheme in the US. We figure Napa Valley's got the Left Coast all but sown up, so our initial target market's gonna be the Northeast. Whether we want to introduce it through restauranteurs or retail sales establishments is open to discussion. The only catch is the retail side will require advertising, and that eats up capital fast. When we do decide to launch, we're gonna get a big fucking LA name—like Michelle Pfeiffer—to be our spokesperson." Will saw the grimace and added, "Bob, Zig Kowalski's got LA wired up tight and he was also there for the discussion with Videla. Don't worry about Miss Hot Legs for the moment. We've got to come up with a penetration scheme. While you and Sam Chessereaux are hatching that out, Roberto and I've gotta figure which distilled spirits haven't been exclusively licensed by their distillery or distributor for Argentina. That becomes our target for export to Argentina; we can't take stuff out without bringing stuff in, otherwise we get a trade imbalance and the motherfucking profiteering *Norteamericanos* get the bad press. Are we all good now?"

"Holy Mother of God," Bob exclaimed as he finished the glass of red wine. "So you hatched this after watching an empty plane take off…"

"To fly 5000 miles and eleven hours back to the US for its next assignment. Now you talk about wasted capacity!" Will's mind was a blur, "Didn't you tell me in Tangier that you'd grown up in Tennessee?"

"Sure, why, you need somebody who knows sour mash?"

"Hell yeah," Will said as he gave him a high-five. By now Hal had snuck out onto the patio as Will handed him a Cohiba Lancero and a lighter. "Harold was with us when we did our first sniffing around the whiskey available in Buenos Aires. Now we may not be one hundred percent on mark, but we know what a very popular restaurant does and doesn't stock in their bar. It turns out that Jack Daniels Black Label is the only bourbon they carry, and it's damn popular among the businessmen that stop over after work and casually discuss business while eyeing the lovely lasses. Same with Johnnie Walker Black and Chivas Regal; in fact, the distilled spirits seem to be available here on a specialized basis." Will looked at Roberto, "Why do the businessmen drink Black Jack and Johnnie Black almost exclusively Roberto?"

"There is a perception, perhaps from international travel, that those are the best of the bourbon and scotch brands."

"Is it also a matter of cost? The waitress at La Cabrera said the young dudes only drink cheap vodka when they drink spirits. How bad are the excise taxes and import duties on distilled spirits?"

"They are what you might term severe, and they definitely affect the access to distilled spirits," he said with a grimace on his face.

"Dammit Roberto, you're our eyes and ears; what is it?"

"Well, the moral strictures of the Catholic church frown on hard spirits as alcoholic beverages. I believe we may be facing a morally-imposed barrier here."

"Can't be as bad as the Protestants; hell, they don't allow their daughters to dance for Christ's sakes!" Hal interjected.

"Come on, it's just a matter of silk degrees. The damn holy rollers back in the states are closet drinkers, but here in *Porteño*-land the consumption of wine is all but embraced. At least we don't have that hurdle to clear." Will looked once again to Roberto, "I got the feeling that Videla wants to jump start this economy. Are distilled spirits really that big of a deal with the Holy Roman Church?"

He shook his head, "No, not really, especially since the dangerous drugs have become available. Distilled spirits are legal, but cocaine, heroin and such are considered the public safety monsters now. I believe we can bring about a softening of the barriers on distilled spirits in Argentina. We will still have to be concerned about the cost differential between spirits and beer or wine."

"Not if those excise duties can be negotiated, say with an assurance of a million cases of Argentine wine escaping north to the benefit of the local *lagars*, wouldn't you think?"

Roberto was narrowing his stare as he lit a Lancero, "You have one devious business mind Guillermo."

"Right, then the brands of spirits lower than the premium stuff can be sold at a reasonable price and we've got our chance." Roberto was shaking his head yes now, so Will looked at Bob, "Does this sound like something you'd be willing to tackle once you step aside from being Keith Melson's flying buttress?"

When he stopped laughing he held out his hand, as Will, Roberto, Bob and Hal shook hands encircled like warrior grips. "That's what I'm talking about gentlemen!"

After most of the guests had gone to their rooms for the evening, Hal, Will, Dom and Carmen were about to toast with the drink of happiness when they noticed movement at the elevator. To their surprise, Roberto came out leading Danny Rojas and President Jorge Videla, who was surprisingly wearing a business suit. Will reached to pour up three more snifters of Marnier, turning to offer each of the guests one as they were warmly welcomed. Jorge took a sip, nodded appreciatively and said, "I didn't want either of you to think I didn't appreciate what you did to rid this world of Satan's evil. I salute you now and all of Argentina salutes Mr. and Mrs. Harold Rayfield."

"That's very kind of you to say Mr. President," Hal replied, shaking his hand a second time.

Jorge put his hand on Carmen's shoulder and told her, "After what you did for this country, please let me know if there is anything I can do to help you. Congratulations on your wedding day, and may you experience many years, no a lifetime, of marital happiness."

After sharing a small snifter of cognac with them, Videla pardoned himself to leave, not wanting to detract from the Rayfield's wedding day. As he turned to leave he glanced at Will, "Come, walk with me Will."

When they got across the room next to the elevator Videla stared Will in the eye, "I understand you have enlisted Roberto here in your business scheme. I heartily concur with this most incisive decision on your part to include a very well-connected *Porteño*. He has informally suggested a new look at our duty and excise policies in light of the potential benefit to Argentine businesses. You are indeed an industrious young man Will."

Will grasped Videla's hand and quickly shifted to the warrior grip, pulling Videla slightly towards him. Videla immediately looked to his side and nodded his head no to a rapidly approaching bodyguard. "Jorge, I like you and I respect you; you are a true patriot. You will make the right decisions as you pursue efforts to improve the average Argentine's quality of life. Whether this little venture succeeds or not will not affect my opinion of you. Have you ever shaken hands like this before?"

"No, I have not; does it have some special meaning?"

Will leaned in, smiling, "You bet; this is the warrior's grip, and I only share it with fellow warriors. May God be with you Jorge Videla, *mi buen amigo*."

"And with you *Guillermo* Kavanagh; as always, I find myself smiling after I've been in your company."

Will shook his head, "Is that a good thing?"

"*Si*; until we meet again *mi buen amigo*."

"*Auf wiedersehen* Jorge."

18

EMBRACING ZYGOTE
INTRAFALLOPIAN TRANSFER

WILL WAS ALMOST ABLE TO DEAL with humans normally by the time they arrived back for the penultimate day of anticipation at Dr. Calvatori's fertility clinic. The clinic, aptly named *Circulo de la Vida Realce*, or CIRVIDAR, was on *Avenida* Humboldt in Palermo's trendy Hollywood subdivision. Will had been especially interested when Carmen told them it meant 'Circle of Life Enhancement.'

Most aspects of the 'training regimen' the doctor had given them were relatively easy to accommodate, but not smoking had damn near killed Will. This was the first time he had gone for as long as twelve hours without smoking since his sophomore year in college. Interestingly, he had been prone to intermittent bouts of bronchitis until his Air Force Reserve Officer Training Corps' Summer Camp roommate's smoking had intrigued him. Every doctor he'd ever known had bristled at this fact, but grudgingly admitted his immune system had risen up to thwart the invader. He had shown the utmost resolve at Hal and Carmen's wedding reception, handing out Habana cigars and not smoking any himself.

He actually had a slight case of the shakes the first couple of days *sans* tobacco, but this had eased off to mere snarkiness and eventually a void of terrible longing. He grudgingly came to understand but not discount the psychological aspect cigarettes served in his life. They were the ultimate 'after' anointment and reward; not smoking after meals and after sex was damn near debilitating. He looked at Calvatori with a dispassionate frown as he welcomed them, "Why hello Will and Dominique, are you ready to proceed to the next big milestone?" Vanished was the formality portrayed during prior visits. One night around the *parilla* was what the shrink ordered for Jonathan Calvatori; he became a trusted friend, and after viewing a shot of Kelly from their wedding pictures he was more than a little interested in meeting her.

"Hello Jonathan, it's so nice to see you," Dom said as she hugged him and planted a kiss on his cheek.

He looked at Will with an inquisitive smile, "And how are you doing Will? You haven't backtracked on the tobacco have you?"

He muscled up his best shit-eating grin and replied, "I'll be fine JC just as soon as I do my duty here. I'm gonna smoke a damn cigarette a foot long in one toke for Christ's sake!"

Dom was already frowning at him, as she had hoped the temporary injunction would lead to a permanent cessation. Calvatori bailed her out by saying, "Please do not do that until we have confirmed that Dominique is indeed pregnant Will. We may well have to attempt the insemination more than once."

He rolled his eyes to the heavens, wondering how he was going to get some sweet relief when Dom put her arms around his waist. "You need a reward Will; I have just the thing in mind for you tonight. Please do this for us?"

"Oh, alright; where's that petri dish Doc?" He offered in abject, clearly disinclined resignation.

Jonathan couldn't restrain the smile that was sneaking out. "Actually, in light of the motility issue, we will collect your sperm in this," he said, holding out a glass petri dish with a cover.

Will frowned at the surgical gloves he was wearing, "Any chance I can get some assistance with this? Otherwise it's gonna be pure fantasy you know Jon." He smiled furtively at Dom, "I don't see any magazines."

Jonathon was nodding his head no with conviction, "We must maintain strict sterility to maximize the chances of success Will. I'm sorry, but no oral sex by an enabling assistant would be possible because of the significant potential for contamination by the saliva. I am sorry."

To his amazement Dom suggested, "Perhaps I can be with my husband for this sperm extraction Doctor?"

Will looked at her with a huge smile on his face, "Damn right; a hand job would beat the hell out of conjuring up some temptress from my past!"

Dom narrowed her gaze and replied, "I don't believe we need to go there

William." She then turned to Jonathan and offered, "Perhaps I can assist Will in this without violating sterility standards?"

"Oh baby, Jesus," Will exclaimed as Dom extracted the sample with a practiced touch. He was smiling through the aftershocks, stroking her hair, "Now that's the way to give a sample baby."

She smiled knowingly as she screwed the top onto the glass dish, a surprising volume of milky semen captured ready for the next step. As she popped off the surgical gloves Calvatori had insisted she wear to insure sterility, she said, "Clean up and get yourself dressed my darling. I'll deliver this sample so that we can begin our journey."

Will was bored to tears in the waiting room, having given up on engaging Lita in sociable conversation with her darting in and out so. Browsing through an old copy of Playboy magazine, he wondered what the chances were of finding the one Samantha Herrington had graced when Jonathan came walking out. "So how'd it go?" Will asked with uncertainty.

"The ovum extraction went very well Will; Dominique's ovary responded to the Clomid and my laboratory assistant is impregnating the egg now. Would you like to go get a bite to eat? We should be ready for the insemination of the zygote in about an hour," he advised.

"So how's Dom doing? Were there any complications?" He asked, fully alert bordering on concern now.

"We put her under mild sedation for the extraction, which can be somewhat uncomfortable. Oocytes, or ovum, are microscopic, and the procedure required hypodermic intrusion into the ovary. She is resting comfortably and the insemination procedure will be much less problematic," he advised, not unlike a professor in a college lab.

"So where is she? I need to see her," Will asked, his paranoia growing now that he knew more about the extraction procedure.

"Of course you can Will; follow me back to the operating room."

"Operating room? Jesus, I had no idea this was so complicated!"

Jon stopped, put his hand on Will's shoulder and said, "Will, this is cutting edge technology we're dealing with here. We must take every precaution to hopefully insure success." He reached for a set of scrubs and said, "Put these on and let's get you back there."

"Hey baby, how you feeling?" Will cooed as he stroked Dom's hair.

She smiled at him, puckered her lips so he'd kiss her and replied, "I'm fine

Will. Did Jonathan tell you about the procedure?"

"Yeah baby, and it looks good so far. How was the pain? He said they gave you some sedation."

"I'm fine Will, but it was nothing I wouldn't endure a thousand times for us to have this baby."

He looked at the IV dripping into her arm, the stirrups resting at the bedside, "I don't know babe, it looks pretty involved. Jonathan said it'd be another hour before the insemination. You gonna be alright?"

She nodded excitedly and told him, "I'm fine Will; why don't you go get something to eat?"

He nodded at her and said, "Yeah, I might just do that; these old copies of Playboy and Hustler aren't exactly keeping me entranced. You want me to get you something?"

She reached out and grasped his hand with that pixie grin, "You already have Will, you gave me the one thing I couldn't get myself; a part of you."

"So how are you feeling my wonderful bride?" Will asked, peering sideways at her slumped against the door as they drove back to *Casa Fabiano*. His question sent his mind into deliberation, doing a quick calculation, and couldn't believe they had been married a mere four months. It seemed like a lifetime of drama had unfolded since that day they pledged 'Forever' in front of the world in Gastineau.

"I'm sleepy," she muttered, the sedative no doubt still working its magic.

"Don't you worry about a thing, Mrs. Kavanagh; I will oversee your welfare until you come back," he said, stroking her face tenderly.

She bolted upright in the seat and all but shouted, "Come back from where?"

He patted her thigh and intoned reassuringly, "They gave you a sedative for the procedure babe; I'll look after you until you come back from being sleepy. Aren't you glad you have me?"

She slumped back against the door, closed her eyes and smiled, "Every day of my life Will Kavanagh, every day....."

When they got home—strange that *Casa Fabiano* was now home—he helped Dom to the bed, took off her clothes and tucked her under the covers. He looked at her and offered, "Want something to drink hon?"

She half-opened one eye and said, "Come stay with me Will, just for a little while."

He shucked his clothes and climbed in, snuggling up like spoons as she purred, "Mmmm."

In spite of his plans to fix Dom some soup, he opened his eyes suddenly, glanced at the bedside alarm clock and grimaced that they had been asleep for two hours. When she felt him stir, she rolled onto her back and said, "Thank you for staying with me Will; I needed to be held."

"Think nothing of it my dear; want some soup?"

She had a confused look on her face, "How did you know that is what I wanted? I would love some."

"Right back."

When he got back with the soup, Dom was looking down at her stomach, inspecting the bandages so he put the bowl down and joined her examining the incisions closely. She had a small vertical cut below her navel and two smaller ones farther down by her bikini line. "Do these hurt? Jonathan sent along some painkillers for you to take when the anesthesia wore off."

She grimaced slightly as he reached for the bottle of pills and gave her one. Nodding in thanks she asked, "Did you bring some soup?"

As he fed her the soup, he went down the post-op plan of action, "Okay, no tub bath for three days, showers only. Take pain meds as needed. Resume normal eating as soon as post-op nausea subsides. No sex for four days. Did I leave anything out?"

She smiled furtively at him, "I don't remember anything in the instructions prohibiting me from participating in oral sex Mr. Kavanagh. You haven't smoked yet, have you?"

Her question suddenly reminded him that he wanted a cigarette so badly he could almost smoke one without lighting it. Will controlled his angst enough to reply, "No sweets, no smoking for me. Why don't we wait and see how you're feeling in a few hours before deciding whether you need the aggravation of one-sided sexual activity."

She casually rubbed his crotch as she smiled, "Just as long as you don't start missing that harem, or make any lusty calls to San Diego."

Her allusion to Samantha gave him pause, but he ignored it enough to reply, "I'm fine Dom; eat this and rest. We'll see how things look a little later this evening, okay?"

The next morning Will contemplated their immediate future and saw nothing pressing in Buenos Aires, "How would you like to take off to Bariloche for a few days? The Rayfields are back there again following their repose in Punta del Este." He allowed the lizard to sneak up on him, "Dammit, they must know Bariloche is the place to be—even with the parents."

"Do you think that's wise so soon after the procedure?" Dom wondered.

After getting clearance from Dr. Calvatori and making the airline reservations, they called *Estancia Fabiano*, catching Carmen by surprise. "You are kidding me? You've already had the implantation procedure?"

"Yes Carmen, and everything is going according to expectations; so Will and I are flying down to Bariloche tomorrow if you two are going to be there."

"We'll be at the airport to meet you! Hal will be very happy to have his Cajun companion around," she actually gushed.

19

SOMEBODY'S GAMING THE SYSTEM

"Welcome back to Bariloche partner," Hal said as he slapped Will's back, sloshing wine out of the glass he was holding to celebrate their arrival.

"Dammit you prick, that shoulder's not up to Cajun punishment yet, but I guess we had to test it out, eh?" Will said as he slammed Hal in the stomach with a hard right hook, making his mending ribs vibrate with pain.

The remainder of the wine was now covering them both as the women hooted with laughter, Dom announcing their verdict, "I hope you two can survive a few days around each other."

"No problemo Dominique, just glad to see my homeboy," Hal said as he locked an arm around Will's neck in a stranglehold.

Will shrugged off his arm and asked, "So what's been happening around Bariloche?"

"I think Carmen has found our surrogate casbah my friend; wanna stop by and check it out?"

"Oh hell yeah; let's go see what you found," Will said excitedly as he hugged Carmen's neck, careful to avoid her growing belly. He looked at her, remembering the vivid, erotic dream they'd had together, "When are you going to stop being a smoking hot woman Carmen; the day before you give birth?"

She smirked at him, "Please Will, I'm four months pregnant; even your friend Harold has begun to take notice."

He looked at Hal and gave him a narrowed stare, in obvious disbelief that Harold thought she was losing her sensuality. Rayfield tried but failed to defend himself, "Hey, I've got to start thinking of the welfare of my child, don't you think?"

170

The drive in from the far eastern outskirts of Bariloche had Will's project planning DNA revving, "So is the casbah located close into civilization? I wonder about permits; you know, disrupting the neighbors and all?"

Hal looked at him like he was demented, "Willy, I am married to the most connected *Porteño* this side of Buenos Aires, and she's now best buds with Rosita Cabrera. Now do you really think permitting is gonna be a big deal?"

Will remembered Rosita fondly—especially the manner in which she'd completely discounted the indecent proposal—and asked, "So how's Rosita doing? Has there been further evidence of heterosexual leanings?"

Now Carmen brandished that diabolical smirk, "It seems as though the Tourism Minister and the Defense Minister have indeed taken a liking to-wards one another."

Dom was the first to strike, "Isn't Danny Rojas married?"

Will didn't even hear her question, "Damn, I completely forgot to call Kelly and ask her about her intelligence-gathering mission on the flight back to LA."

"Jesus Willy, don't you think she'd a called if she had anything?" Hal surmised.

"I think Will is right; we should call Kelly and see how she's doing. I would love for her to come back down here so that she could meet Jonathan Calva-tori," Dom said as Will nodded his head in assent.

"Jonathan Calvatori? So the doctor has become more than a professional acquaintance at CIRVIDAR?" Carmen asked with a heavy dose of curiosity.

Dom looked at Will, smirked and replied, "Are you kidding? Ten minutes around Will and he had the choice of either becoming a 'homeboy' as he puts it, or banishing us from his life. My husband has a hard time behaving around what he calls stud males; it's some Cajun predisposition to enlist them into his 'good old boy' alliance."

Will exhaled and offered his side, "Listen, when I meet a sculpted stud who's got the key to the kingdom and he don't act like God's gift to the world, he's got coonass potential. JC certainly responded to therapy." His lizard brain suddenly kicked in as he added, "Hey, we might just have a reason to get Kelly back down here if we've locked down the last of the filming locations."

———

"Damn bro, I do think this is it," Will said in amazement as they turned into the driveway of the former Catalano estate. "That separate garage is ideal for the guard boarding house." He looked back at Carmen and asked, "What's the story on this property? Is it abandoned?"

"I wouldn't call it abandoned, but it has been on the market for over a year with no serious offers tendered. The elderly matriarch of the Catalano family died last year, and none of the children are interested in living here in Bariloche. Rosita arranged for the sale of the estate to a *Porteño* who wants to build a new mansion with a view of the Andes. There is still an estate manager on the premises, Pablo Herrara, so you can ask any questions you like."

"So Pablo, are there any tunnels leading out of the house?" Will asked the caretaker as they toured the impressive but very old mansion.

Pablo smiled as he looked to Carmen, who joined him in an energetic exchange in Spanish before she looked at Will and said, "There is a tunnel entrance leading off of the back of the house that was used as a discreet entry point for romantic interludes many years ago."

Will nodded his head, "Couldn't stay out of the company ink, huh? No problem, sounds like we've got our secret tunnel to the airstrip." He turned to Hal and asked, "So whatdya think buddy? Could this be the movie version of the casbah?"

"Man, there aren't but us six shooters, Dom and her mother that even remember what Sandrigan's casbah looked like that day before it was transformed via fire and brimstone. Everyone else is in the afterlife; so I guess if we think it's right, and the permit's not a problem, we're about set."

"Okay, let's go call Kelly on the sat phone," he said, wrapping up the Catalano property tour.

"Hey baby, how's my favorite Hollywood producer doing?" Will asked once Kelly answered her phone. Hal had shown some technical ingenuity by rigging up a twelve foot piece of telephone wire with RJ11 jacks on both ends. The 'cutout' was now plugged up connecting the auxiliary port on the sat phone unit to a regular speaker phone, thereby thwarting Will's ability to privately check out his former concubine.

"Why hey yourself Comrade Kavanagh. To what do I owe the pleasure of your attention this fine afternoon?" Kelly brandished.

He was pondering what he could get away with when Dom shook her head and twitched her index finger at him, "Hello Kelly, it's so good to hear your voice dear. I take it you have been quite busy since you returned to Los

Angeles?"

"You wouldn't believe it; between writing the edits to the screenplay and attending casting calls for the actors it's been a blur. Could you hang on for a sec; Zig wanted me to let him know the minute I had you on the phone. He's taken on this movie as his major opus, being CEO is now a side job. Can I just call you back?"

"No babe, we're on the sat phone. Before you bring Kowalski in, we need to talk to you about a couple of things," Will told her, the conspiracy obvious.

"Okay, go ahead. What's the matter, wondering what I learned on the flight back up to LA?"

"As a matter of fact, we're quite curious about that Kelly," Dom replied.

"Well, I knew one of the stewardesses from my TIA Pacific days, and she got me seated next to Danny for the flight. I was thinking about my idle comment to Will about taking one for the team as it became clear that he badly wanted me to be his 'full-service escort' in LA once we got there. I would say Danny Rojas is the epitome of a 'geographic bachelor' in every sense of the term. The fact that he's married was an automatic deal breaker for me; I'm not saying it can't happen, but Danny is far from irresistible. I agreed to be his date to this aerospace conference dinner, as he needed some 'arm candy' to impress his marks. I was amazed at how he cozied up to the Grumman and McDonnell-Douglas CEOs. Did you know he was in LA on a military aircraft mission?"

Carmen was nodding knowingly when Will replied, "No, but I'm not surprised; Jimmy Carter imposed an arms embargo on Argentina two years ago. Our best guess is he's hunting for spares and replacement parts for the Douglas Skyhawks they bought before Carter branded the Dirty War as a Southern Hemisphere human rights holocaust. Did he mention any plans on heading to Washington afterwards? If he was on a shopping trip, you'd think he'd have sucked up to his contacts in the Pentagon, especially the foreign military sales guys."

"Now that is interesting, because he asked me—no he made me promise him—not to discuss his dealings with the aircraft industry to anyone from Washington. I got the definite impression that he wanted to accomplish whatever mission he was on completely under the radar."

"So he didn't even meet with Zig about the movie memorandum?" Dom asked. "As I recall, that was the solely stated purpose of his visit."

"Oh yeah, he met with Zig almost as an afterthought the morning he was flying back. The memorandum signing was just a ceremonial thing at best. By the way, how's that coming?"

"That's really what we called about. I guess it's time to bring Zig in," Will said, figuring they had covered the delicate matters.

Dom grimaced at him and said, "Kelly, before you bring the CEO onto the call, I wanted to tell you that Will and I have completed the first important step in our plan to become parents. And you wouldn't believe....."

"You are kidding me? Are you pregnant Dom?" She all but shouted. *Why in the hell are women always excited about pregnancy? I know we're on a mission, but Hal sure didn't act like he'd won the lottery. Must be some genetic thing—probably some chromosomal architecture of estrogen—that makes women want to populate the world. Lord knows I made the one-time exception for Dom when I learned her chances were so bleak. Okay, maybe it makes a difference because of our karmic history.*

"We'll know in a week dear. But that's not what I wanted to discuss with you. Our fertility specialist, a Dr. Calvatori is the most insanely interesting man I've met," she was saying but glanced at Will before continuing, "since I ran into Mr. Kavanagh. He is single and was most intrigued when we showed him a picture of you. We would love you to meet him. What do you think?"

"Now that does sound interesting; a fertility specialist? Let me get Mr. Kowalski on the phone and see if he wants to cut me loose for another scamper down south of the border."

"Okay, Kelly tells me we've got the principals of Circle Entertainment on the line, so how's it going in lovely Argentina?" Zig said by way of introduction.

"It's going well Zig," Will told him, "we just visited the mansion in Bariloche that Carmen and Rosita Cabrera found and our overall reaction is quite favorable. This is where the takedown of Sandrigan's casbah would be shot, and Hal, Dom and I think it's a great location. We can probably shoot the landing in Algiers harbor at the Bariloche Marina on the Haupi Lakefront, and Carmen has offered up the cattle and livestock processing area for the Ksar carpet factory assault scene. If we shoot Farouk's restaurant scene at La Cabrera in Buenos Aires, we've got all location shooting rounded up inside Argentina."

"So what's this mansion gonna cost me? I gotta live with a budget even though I'm the boss ya know," Zig wondered.

"Rosita and I have arranged to have the property sold to a *Porteño* who wants to tear it down and start his Andes mansion from the ground up. The Tourism Minister has arranged for the necessary explosives permits, so it would appear that whatever modifications to the exterior of the mansion would be the only out of pocket costs on that scene to Great West Studios," Carmen reported.

"Man, you guys do good work, you know that? Okay, here's what I want to do. I'd come back down myself, but I've got three other movies in production this very moment, so I can't just fly away. I want Kelly back down there to lock down production details, including any memoranda that might not be covered by the agreement Danny Rojas and I signed. I think Pierson's still in Peru wrapping up that La Paz shoot, so I'll reroute him down there for the advance pyrotechnics package planning while he's close by. Jesus, that flight between LA and Argentina is brutal, even in first class. Hey, I gotta run, are we all straight?" Zig asked as an afterthought.

"Yeah Zig, we're good. We'll talk to Kelly and Pierson about their travel schedules," Will said in closing.

After Zig had left, Kelly came back on the line, "It sounds like everyone's on the same page, but I can't leave here before next week. Is that pushing the envelope?"

"Nah, that works for us. Call us when you've got the flight scheduled and we'll make the follow-on to Bariloche for you. Take care babe; nice detective work with *Señor* Rojas."

20

SCORING A MOVIE IN THE ANDES

LATER THAT EVENING, as they were rabidly inhaling king crab legs, Will looked at Carmen, "So where do you get king crab legs down here? In Denver they flew them in from Alaska."

"Our source is obviously closer than Denver's was. Puerto Montt is only one hundred sixty kilometers from Bariloche across the Andes Mountains. Seafood exports are becoming a major economic resource for Chile. We also get very good salmon from there," she advised.

"A hundred miles, and that crosses the Andes huh? Sounds like a lot of up and down; what's the elevation here in Bariloche?"

She did some quick mental calculations and reported, "Bariloche is about 2800 feet above sea level, and the highest mountain you see there," she pointed out the window to a barely visible snow-covered peak, "is a little over 11,000 feet. Puerto Montt is obviously at sea level, so it is a bit of an up and down airplane ride from here. We are fortunate to be so close to the Pacific coast, in spite of the Andes barrier between us."

"Yeah, gives you a nice variation from the beef, but it's hard to complain about steaks as good as they are here in Argentina," Will offered as Dom readily agreed.

"To say nothing of the wine, right partner?" Hal added.

Will raised his glass to toast his buddy but was interrupted by Carmen. "When were you going to mention to me that you've enlisted Roberto as your Argentinian connection with the export/import business?"

Will glanced at Hal with alarm before responding, "Uh, I kinda figured Roberto was the only trustworthy *Porteño* we knew, so we had a heart to heart the day you guys were married. Did I make the wrong move Belen?"

176

"No, but only by good fortune; you must learn to trust me on such matters in my own country William."

Will now found himself in the uncomfortable position of almost pleading his case, "Well Jesus Christ Mrs. Rayfield, Roberto tutored us in the straight skinny before Videla showed up at *Casa Fabiano* so I figured he was a straight shooter. Sorry, I certainly didn't mean to remove or avoid you in the process; you know I consider you my conscience, *n'est pas?*"

"As well as a Director of CEI; and you should not allow distractions make you forget that. Let's just say we are most fortunate that my brother is not cut from the same fabric as Daniel Rojas."

Will smirked furtively, "Oh, in all the excitement the night you got married, I totally forgot to cut you in Belen. Jorge pulled me aside at the penthouse elevator alcove and agreed to take a hard look at excise and tariff issues in light of the fact that native *Lagars* would benefit from our business initiative. He even said the restrictions had been put in place to protect local businesses from imported goods." She rolled her eyes so he added, "Of course, distilled spirits like bourbon and scotch don't seem to be native specialties, so the import side is also non-threatening from Videla's perspective."

"And what else did *El Presidente* 'casually mention' that the Directors of CEI might be interested in?" Dom asked, making Will feel she and Carmen were a tag team.

"Well, I think I got a bodyguard to go for his pistol when I pulled him in for the warrior grip, but he and I respect one another. He told me that I was indeed a wise businessman for involving Roberto Fabiano in our venture."

She finally smiled, "I am personally amazed that you have been able to cultivate such a close working relationship with a man otherwise known to be cold, distant and even flippant."

"Johnny Boy's working the incorporation papers even as we speak *mi querida hermana*. As for Rafy Videla, don't you think he is susceptible to charm, especially when so many others are attacking his motivations? It helps that I happen to agree with him philosophically; no prostituting this soul to get the big guy on board Belen."

"I suppose success is the mistress of fortuitous timing, *si?*"

As they were sitting on the patio, admiring the Andes the next afternoon, Hal was strumming on his guitar, "Willy, it's time we figured out some music to accompany the scenes in the movie; you know give it some poignant emphasis."

"Hey, that's not a half-bad idea. Did you have anything particular in mind?"

"I just can't get the Rolling Stones *Gimme Shelter* out of my mind Tonto. I hear it playing every time I think of when we were sliding sideways into that driveway, the bullets flying everywhere and me pushing your head down. What do you think?"

Will thought about the opening bars of *Gimme Shelter* and remembered the abject terror he was feeling at the time. He shook his head in wonder, "Man did you ever get that score right on the money." He laughed and added, "So from this day forward hot landing zones and Gimme Shelter go hand in hand, eh?" Hal high-fived him, obviously in agreement. "Let's take this from where the movie scenes start—you know, the safehouse in Tangier—and see if anything comes to mind, okay?"

Hal dialed back the scenes in his head, "Alright, we're sitting around the table at the safehouse in Tangier and Marty Lindstrum's pissed me off so bad I pull the Colt 1911 and chamber a round." He rubbed his chin to consider the homicidal mood Lindstrum put him in, "How about Bob Dylan's *Knockin' on Heaven's Door*, what do you think?"

Will shook his head in agreement, "Perfect. Let's write these down as we go so we can give them to Kelly when she gets down here. So we're motoring across the Mediterranean that night. How about Phil Collins' *In the Air Tonight*, whatdya think?"

"Damn, that's fucking perfect Willy; I'll never forget your sorry inconsiderate ass getting it on like a banshee while the rest of us sat around jerking off." he said, throwing a guitar pick at him. "So the next big scene would be when we're entering Algiers harbor in the middle of that storm. How about the opening bars of AC/DC's *Hells Bells*, whatdya think?"

"Damn right, and we can continue that song, without the vocals, right through the prisoner exchange at the mosque. Good going. What's next Kemosabe?"

"The car chase across Algiers, what's right for you?"

"Either Leon Russell's *Stranger in a Strange Land* or Joe Walsh's *Rocky Mountain Way*, I can't pick a favorite for that scene," Will thought out loud.

"Hell, put 'em both down, either one's perfect. Let the music guy and Zig figure it out. So we're chasing Sandrigan's Mercedes through the streets and you finally come through and blast the shit out of the chase car behind us."

He rocked his head for a minute and said, "Why in the hell can't I get the opening chords of Led Zeppelin's *When the Levee Breaks* out of my head when I think of that AK-47 blasting off on full automatic next to my ear?"

"Who knows, it might've been playing on the radio, but it is spot on buddy." Will shuddered slightly remembering his indoctrination into a hot LZ as Hal put the car into a sliding lunge through the front gates of the casbah. "Dude, you made the ultimate musical score with the Stones' *Gimme Shelter* for the hot LZ scene. I can envision Mick Jagger wailing away just as the windshield explodes in a million pieces, 'Ooh, see the fire is sweepin',' our very street today.' Damn, how'd we ever live through that one?"

"Fate, destiny, karma, who knows? We're standing in Sandrigan's casbah foyer and I'm desperate to keep you alive; what the hell fits there Tonto?"

"How about the Rolling Stones' *Paint It, Black*, you know, 'I see a red door and I want it painted black.' We can have the doors to the casbah painted red for the scene."

"Damn Willy, I can even see it when Jagger yells those last words later in the chorus as that Algerian guard stabs you. Good going bro."

He rubbed his very sore shoulder when Hal mentioned it. Dom had insisted that they begin each day in Argentina with a yoga session, and though traumatic at first, the yoga had slowly improved his range of motion in the shoulder. Now, if he could just smoke a damn cigarette. He nodded at Hal, "Okay, so Sandrigan and Dom escape through the tunnel and we're back outside when the Cessna flies over us with that bastard smiling at us sardonically. We gotta have something for that scene; it's too poignant."

Hal was rocking gently when he offered, "How about Bill Withers' *Ain't No Sunshine (When She's Gone)*? Think that about fit your mood at that moment?"

"Perfect. So we're flying through the damn cloud cover over to Ksar, I'm juiced on the dexies and we start coiling down in a corkscrew hoping we don't hit a mountain before the cloud cover breaks. What fits?"

"Jesus Willy, that's a lead-pipe cinch; it's gotta be Lynyrd Skynyrd's *Free Bird*. What else could it be?"

He grimaced at his buddy who was calling every scene like the song was written for it. "Oh I don't know Hal; the Allman Brothers *Whipping Post* comes to mind. I wasn't feeling particularly confident as we went down in that death spiral."

"Yeah, you're right, put 'em both down. So we're entering the warehouse by the airstrip at Ksar. Wouldn't want to miss putting a score to this scene; we're both still trying to recover from it. Damn that Sandrigan was either lucky or good with those two shots," he said as he rubbed his knee where the scar tissue was hardening. "So whatdya think, Jimi Hendrix' *All Along the Watchtower*? Is that perfect or what?"

Will high-fived Hal for the perfect selection and said, "So that leaves us with the penultimate scene behind the warehouse with Sandrigan holding that dagger at Dom's throat and me and Mustafa trying to figure out an angle to shoot the bastard without hitting Dom. We gotta do this one right bro. What's it gonna be?"

"What else could it be? The Doors *(This is) The End*," he exclaimed in victory.

As they rallied the women to report the results, Will looked at Hal and said, "Man, we have got to put together a list of the greatest songs of all time. It can be OUR favorite songs, to hell with the critics. I'd say between the two of us we've got a fair ear for perfection."

He pulled his wife around him for a sweet embrace, "We've also got a fair eye for perfect women as well young Kavanagh."

21

A DEPUTY MINISTER USED TO GETTING HIS WAY

THEY WERE SITTING IN DR. CALVATORI'S OFFICE, no longer relegated to the waiting area when he walked in with a huge smile on his face, "I am most pleased to announce that you are pregnant Mrs. Kavanagh! Congratulations!"

Will swept Dom up in his arms and began a slow, joyous spin as he told her, "I can't believe it Dom, we actually did it!" She had completed the urinalysis test twenty minutes earlier, and they had been on pins and needles awaiting the outcome. He was almost doing cartwheels in his mind thinking about the Marlboro Light he was going to fire up as soon as they got home.

She was crying tears of joy when she kissed him unashamedly and replied, "Yes Will Kavanagh, we did it; and Jonathan was the magician that brought it about."

He half let her go and grabbed Calvatori around the shoulder with his other arm, "You were right down the line bro; you knew what you were doing. And guess what? We've got the perfect celebration for you boudreau. Our smoking ass hot friend Kelly is coming into town tomorrow and we get to see if there's magic between the two of you!"

He was smiling from ear to ear as he finally succumbed to a high-five, "I look forward to meeting her; you have clearly impressed me that she's a very interesting woman. What time should I arrive?"

Will glanced at Dom's ecstatic face and told him, "Oh what the hell, make it about six thirty; we can have a cocktail while we catch up on the news from Hollywood."

"So may I bring along some wine for dinner?"

"You bet, and you know we'll be grilling *lomos,* so do your best to impress," he told him as they headed out the door, their feet not quite touching the floor.

When they arrived at *Casa Fabiano,* Hal and Carmen were waiting in the driveway. They took one look and started dancing, "Congratulations Mr. and Mrs. Kavanagh! We couldn't be happier for you."

Will grabbed Hal's hand, "Damn bro, Argentina must be the incubator! Now we get to face up to life's biggest challenge together—fatherhood!"

Hal grimaced at his bud raining on the parade as he shook his head and pointed towards the patio, "Get your ass inside and let's have a drink; I found some 21 year-old Macallan just for the occasion."

The women joined them with a glass of chardonnay as Will torched up a glorious Marlboro and inhaled deeply. He glanced at Dom to see if she would scold him, but she merely smirked as he exhaled the wondrous blue stream. He narrowed his gaze on Carmen, "So what have we discerned from our *Porteño* brethren?"

She cut her eyes at him, launching his brain to the hot tub dream encounter, gave him the upjerk and narrowed her stare. "It seems as though the *Norteamericanos* have discovered Minister Rojas' plans—what you refer to as 'the old end around'—and have subtly indicated their disinterest in directing him toward allies that may have the same combat aircraft as Argentina. Minister Rojas has countered this move with an overture to the French, who were more than happy to entertain export of their Dassault Mirage Dagger fighter/bomber aircraft."

"Damn, that's a lot of intel from pillow talk Carmen," Will noted with a hint of intrigue.

"You apparently impressed Rosita greatly William. She was especially interested to know that your wife's pursuit of parenthood issues has cast a pall over the erotic nature of your relationship. This would become more compelling the farther along the pregnancy developed. I would say she's quite smitten with you Mr. Kavanagh."

He smiled sheepishly at Dom, "Hey, anything I can do to help the team. I wonder if that's gonna affect Danny boy's relationship with us?"

As if providence was playing out before them, the doorbell rang. They were all but stunned when Hal brought Danny Rojas into the den and announced, "Guess who was in the neighborhood?"

As they all warmly greeted him, Hal asked, "Hey, what'll it be to drink Danny. Will and I were just having some single malt scotch whisky."

"That will do nicely Hal, thank you for your hospitality."

"So what brings you to the neighborhood Danny?" Will asked after they all were settled with drinks.

"Actually, I came by to discuss a matter of potential benefit to your business initiatives here in Argentina," he replied, having the net effect of having broken wind loudly.

"And what business initiatives might those be Danny?" Hal obliged as he dared a glance at Will, wondering if Rojas was alluding to their export/import initiative.

He smiled at them as if all was well with the world, "Why your import/export license application for Andean Precious Stones of course."

They all looked at each other mystified and it was Carmen, the Argentine sponsor of the corporation who ventured, "I am sorry Minister Rojas," the imposition of formality quite noticeable, "how is the issue of business licenses a matter of interest to the Deputy Ministry of Defense?"

He smiled dutifully and nodded, "Oh, I believe matters of strategic importance are common to national as well as commercial interests. Wouldn't you agree?"

Will wasn't seeing the tiger behind the pussycat face, but Carmen looked at him with cold calculation and inquired, "What matter of strategic importance can we help you with Minister Rojas?"

"I desperately need someone to make a reconnaissance visit to the Falkland Islands and ascertain their defensive posture," he said so matter-of-factly they were stunned.

"And how could we, mere common *Porteños*, assist in such an endeavor?"

Will thought Danny's smile was borderline condescending when he replied, "A mere common, but highly-trained, *Porteño* and her American spouse could make a business trip to Port Stanley and be otherwise invisible from a strategic perspective."

She was narrowing her gaze on him now, "And under what pretense would such an obscure couple travel to the Falkland Islands during the least hospitable months for tourist visits?"

He smiled, flexing his eyebrows as he gave his glass to Hal for a refill. "It would seem that Andean Precious Stones has experienced a windfall and is considering investing in oil futures in the seas surrounding the Falkland Islands."

The gambit was now becoming clearer, but Carmen was having nothing of it, "And why would Andean be remotely interested in oil futures associated with the Falkland Islands?"

His smile had become sickeningly superficial, "It would seem that certain precious stones to be marketed by Andean have—shall we say—an uncertain provenance. Such custom tariff concerns would vanish, and all import and export restrictions permanently removed in consideration of assistance provided to the Republic."

Will glanced at Dom, the threat clear and present concerning the diamonds expropriated from Sandrigan's subterranean vault, for which they had every intention of marketing under Andean. The profit and subsequent reinvestment they had planned with Andean was clearly endangered by Rojas' knowledge of their existence. The creases in Hal's forehead reflected their collective shock that Danny Rojas knew anything about the gemstones secretly smuggled into Argentina. Their growing concern grew to the cash also brought in, but Carmen's clandestine trip to the Cayman's soon after they arrived removed that as a concern in the immediate discussion. Carmen shrugged resignedly as she pursued, "I can only presume my husband and I will somehow become experts in offshore oil exploration prior to our arrival in Port Stanley? I would think such late-developing interest in oil exploration around the Falklands would be a matter that would attract immediate attention, especially from *Porteños* who have no existing link to the petrochemical industry. Would it not be less noticeable if we were investigating Falkland's wool for use in the Fabiano S.A. garments and fashion enterprises?"

Rojas hesitated, rubbed his chin thoughtfully and agreed, "Of course, and since you two endured the journey to get there, you will tour West Falkland Island to get a feel for its ability to sustain these wool imports in the volume Fabiano S.A. has in mind. Do you have any further questions that I might help you with?" Rojas asked, his sincerity as pliable as sheetrock mud.

Hal couldn't help himself when he asked, "So how did you know that diamond trading was a strategic interest of Andean Precious Stones Danny?" Will noted the look Carmen gave him could have killed weaker creatures.

"The same way I knew that you entered the country with three million US dollars Hal. Do not underestimate the surveillance capabilities of the

Secretariat of State Intelligence. I believe Mrs. Rayfield was under their employ when the two of you met."

The near homicidal stares of Hal and Carmen spoke volumes, so Will interjected myself, grabbed Danny's hand and offered, "So we're partners now, eh?"

"So it would seem Will, so it would seem."

———

"How in the hell?" Was all Hal could get out of his mouth once Danny Rojas, their new partner in counterintelligence, had left with a satisfied smirk on his face.

"Ernesto, our trusted attorney of course," Carmen implored.

"Ernesto Gortez, your former compatriot, now retired from SIDE?" Hal all but shouted.

"Yes Hal," she said with sobering realization, "they must have really pressured him for information. I hope that he is alright."

"Hell, he's probably drinking champagne right about now. Why would Danny hurt him?"

She nodded her head, "You're right Hal; I should have seen this coming. But I cannot believe the trip to Port Stanley could be that difficult. I don't see us having a real choice in the matter."

They all agreed reluctantly that Danny had delivered the *coup de grâs*, but Dom wasn't shrinking, "What comes around goes around. Mr. Rojas has played his card, and I doubt he is holding that many more in his pocket. This Falklands Island concern must be paramount to the Argentine government right now."

"You make an excellent point Dominique; President Videla is known to show no interest in the Malvinas. This initiative must be coming from the generals and admirals at *Edificio Libertador*..." Carmen was saying when Will interrupted her impatiently.

"Dom has hit the nail on the head folks; Danny Boy is operating outside the ropes on this little Falklands snooping. I would even risk a bet that Jorge would not be pleased to learn of this. So Rojas' boss, the Defense Minister, and his service chiefs must be giving Rojas work direction. From where I sit, it seems to indicate trouble in paradise."

22

GETTING THE GOOD NEWS OUT

"THAT'S RIGHT, YOU TWO ARE GOING to be grandparents," Will told his ecstatic parents after he got them on the phone for the big announcement.

"I cannot believe my ears Will! You have made your mother a very happy person. Is Dominique nearby?"

"I'm right here Mrs. Kavanagh, how have you been?" Dom asked as she pecked her husband on the lips.

"We're doing wonderfully now! Our first grandchild; I am so thrilled for you Dominique. When are you coming back home?" She trilled, the sniffling obvious.

The allusion to 'home' gave Dom pause, so Will answered, "Actually Mom, the conception was a complicated process due to an injury Dom suffered in childhood, and we had to go through an assisted insemination routine to conceive. Now everything is fine and proceeding as expected, but we need to stay close to our acclaimed fertility doctor for at least the first trimester."

"Assisted insemination routine? I'm not familiar with this process, but I've heard of artificial insemination. Is that what you did?"

Dom had recovered enough to resume her explanation, "Actually Mrs. Kavanagh, Will and I participated in an experimental process known as zygote intrafallopian transfer—what the doctors refer to as ZIFT. It involved harvesting an egg from me, fertilizing it with Will's sperm and surgically implanting the fertilized egg for gestation. We completed the transfer ten days ago and just this afternoon received notification that the fertilized egg is now developing into a fetus. It is indeed a wonderful thing, and neither Will nor I ever anticipated having a child, so we are very, very happy."

"Oh I can't wait to tell the family this wonderful news," she gushed.

"Hey Mom, why don't you let us call Alex and let her know; she's kinda expecting special consideration since she took me under her wing for the wedding and all. Do you know how to get into contact with Colton?" When he asked, Will was suddenly embarrassed that he had not considered it important enough to have his brother's contact information in case he needed to locate him on short notice.

"All we have is a number at the church where he works in Nicaragua. I don't even know if he's got a phone where he lives," she offered with a trace of forlornness.

"How about give me that number for the church, just in case we need to find him in a hurry. I guess it's in Managua?" he asked, reaching for a pen.

"Yes Will, that's the place he told us, I think it might be the capital down there. I can't wait to tell the family; they thought you'd gone off and become some kind of adventure seeker or something. Where are you going to live? You aren't going to stay down there in South America, are you? How am I going to spoil my only grandchild?"

"Mom, Mom, Mom, we've got nine months to work through the details on that. But we do have to call the other new first time grandmother and let her know the news. You two take care; we'll be in touch to let you know how things are going. I love you both very much. Bye."

"Well, that seemed to go fairly well," Will told his beaming bride who had taken up residence straddling his lap for the entire phone call.

The burgeoning erection made her smile as she came clean, "Those first few days after the procedure were agony for me Will; I wanted to reward you so badly for being so disciplined during the lead-up to the process."

He smiled at her, pecked here lips and replied, "Fear not my fair maiden, for you have once again acquitted yourself admirably in the reward department. I have been in a sperm replenishment program ever since we passed the three day sexual moratorium."

"So no regrets?"

"Why would I? Once Dominique Lefebvre sets her eyes on you, your life is gonna change in a big way!"

She looked at him furtively, "And that is perhaps the most exclusive club in the world Mr. Kavanagh. Feeling special?"

"Every day of my life baby, every day!"

"Good, let's call Maman and make her a happy person as well."

"Hello Maman...." was all Will understood once Dom got Ayran on the phone in Marrakech. The excited ferocity of the Arabic fusillade being bandied about made him think the Navajo code-talkers of World War II fame had nothing on these two women. After about ten minutes—and no less than a million Arabic words later—Dom looked at him like a kid in a candy store, "She's thrilled Will, and she wants to speak with you!"

"Hello Aryan, how are you? This is some news, eh?"

"Oh Will, I cannot even begin to tell you how thrilled I am to hear my dear Dominique so happy. This is beyond anything we ever thought possible. Incredible things have happened since my daughter met you," she said, making him momentarily recall some of the 'incredible things' that had transpired. He involuntarily reached for his shoulder to rub it.

"As long as we live through them Ayran; how have things been in Morocco? No mention of the kidnapping adventure in the news I trust."

"Nothing whatsoever; Mando even arranged for Alain to visit me here in Marrakech, and he had his friend Mustafa with him. I wasn't aware that you were friends with Mustafa Will."

He was about to tell her how he knew Mustafa when Dom entered the conversation again and blistered his ears with yet another volatile Arabic remonstration. After the apparent explanation Ayran said, "I understand you gifted an airplane to Mustafa Will; he flew it here to Marrakech with Alain as a passenger. How is it that you touch so many people's lives?"

"I'm merely the benefactor Ayran; Mando Chu and Mustafa had everything to do with permanently erasing the scourge of Sandrigan el-Boukhari from our lives. And those two are admirers of your daughter, as am I. I believe that many people who had love in their hearts—and refused to let evil prevail—worked together to make our lives safe and happy once more."

"I once again see why my daughter, my precious Dominique, loves you so Will; when you speak you tell the truth. I am so happy that she met you," she said, the tears becoming evident.

"And now we have the opportunity of welcoming another generation of Bedouins into the world Ayran. I love you so much for giving me Dom to share my life with. I hope to see you soon. Take care."

After they hung up, Will looked at his pregnant wife and said, "One more call, this time to Pensacola and we'll be finished with the first and most important phase of notifications."

She was nodding her head NO as she put her finger under his chin and said, "I believe we have an appointment in the horizontal position Mr. Kavanagh. And that supersedes the phone for the moment."

"Hey, who am I to argue with progress?"

"That's right Alex, you're gonna be an aunt," Will told her, feeling comfortably numb and once again an empty shell casing.

"I cannot believe my ears Willy! How did this happen?" She blurted out, and the silence must've been deafening because she quickly rebounded. "That didn't come out the way I meant it. What I meant to say was how did you pull that off? I remember talking to you about that miscarriage you had with Danielle and the sperm deficiency thing? Did all of that go away?"

He laughed and told her, "No Alex, all of that didn't go away, and Dom had even bigger issues with fertility. I want you to read up on an experimental fertility treatment called zygote intrafallopian transfer—ZIFT is the acronym. Basically, we had one of Dom's eggs fertilized with my sperm in a laboratory and the fertilized egg—that's what they call a zygote—was surgically implanted back into her and now we've got a growing fetus. So you'll have a nephew or a niece in, say, eight months or so"

"Wow, I've never heard of that. So what does Mom think? Have you already told her?"

"She's on top of the world Alex, and is already trying to force me into nesting considerations," he said, quietly wondering where the nest was ultimately going to be located himself.

"So this ZIFT thing, this experimental thing you did, it really works, eh?"

"It did for Dom and I; why, you thinking about parenthood? How's Casey doing by the way?" He wondered, remembering what a hot tamale his sister's lover was.

"Actually, we've been talking about the possibility of surrogate parenthood for a little while ourselves. You know she's always liked you."

"I know Alex, and I like Casey too. We go back a ways; you could've done far worse in finding a mate, that's for sure," he admitted, not having to bend the truth one iota.

She snickered and dropped the bomb, "That's good, because we've been talking about a male donor a lot, and we don't want to use a sperm bank. You are the only man we could agree on as somebody we'd be happy with as a donor. So whatdya think?"

"Jesus," he knee-jerked, "I barely get one on the way and you want me to do it again? You know we're in Argentina babe. When were you two hoping to make this happen?"

"Oh no time real soon," she laughed, "you can imagine what kind of scuttlebutt a pregnant single Air Force Captain would invite. She's been able to keep her personal life under wraps for quite a while now."

Will was painfully aware of the official military disinclination towards homosexual behavior—including prosecution under the military code—so it was almost remarkable that Casey had been able to live her two lives so separately for four or five years. "Yeah, she's pulled off a Houdini, that's for sure. You'll recall how vigorously they pursued your brother for merely chatting about cocaine?"

"Boy do I ever, I've still got that newspaper from Sacramento. Do you ever hear from that other woman in the photo; I think her name was Mary?"

"Yeah, Mary Claiborne is her name. Dom and I ran into her a week after the trial over in the Philippines, but we've sort of lost touch since. Now her stewardess friend Kelly—you met her at the wedding—she's working with a Hollywood studio now and we are in almost daily touch with her and her boss about a movie deal."

"Movie deal; what's that all about? And isn't Kelly that black-haired doll that was complaining that you were off the market? How's Dom feel about all of that? Are you being a good married man Willy? I saw the way that blonde Samantha woman from California was dancing with you at the reception; you and women!"

"Hey, I do the best I can for someone who was fortunate to meet and fall in love with the perfect woman. That would be my wife in case you're having doubts Alexandra."

"Okay, I'll lay off, but don't be a stranger; let us know how things are going down there. Love ya bro."

23

THE FALKLANDS BECKON AS KELLY MEETS THE DOCTOR

"So how are we going to play this?" Will asked later that evening.

"What choice do we have Will? We must play the Defense Ministry's game for the time being," Carmen said in resignation.

"And how the hell are we gonna keep from being his little pawns in this damn idiotic game of chicken they're gonna propagate with the British? Just answer me that? How the hell does this shit happen? There ain't a snowball's chance in hell that Argentina will prevail once they invade or take over the Falklands. History is pretty clear on how that Empire reacts when confronted. And we can only speculate on how the Americans are going to react. Jesus Christ!"

To his enduring shock, Carmen got up, came to where he was sitting, put her arms around his shoulders and said very calmly, "This isn't your war Will."

He jerked, throwing her hands off and protested, "Hey, we're with you and you're getting sucked into this damn mess. Didn't you parachute into Ksar already pregnant to bail us out a few months ago?"

She returned her hands to his shoulders and replied, "Calm down Will. You are correct that Argentina seems to be moving towards this impossible situation, but it remains to be seen if we are also taken with them."

"Jesus honey," Hal said, also frustrated, "those assholes see you as a counterintelligence operative extraordinaire and they could give a shit if you're five months pregnant with our son. What do we have to do, leave Argentina to shake them off of you?"

Will couldn't tell if he imagined it, but a tear seemed to leak out of Carmen's eye as she replied, "If we have to do that to protect our child Hal, that is exactly what we will do. Now I have made some inquiries, and Fabiano S.A. is interested in obtaining some quality Falkland's wool for their manufacturing business. The southern part of Argentina is a solid market for heavy winter clothing. So I believe we can execute the immediate part of Mr. Rojas' plan without stirring suspicion. Let's make this trip and see where we are with the Minister."

"What is the temperature like in the Falklands this time of year Carmen? Is it safe for you to travel this far into the pregnancy?" Dom inquired.

Carmen looked at her and smiled, "I'm fine for travel Dom." She then nodded and continued, "Have you given consideration to having a priest bless your child while it's in the womb?"

Dom looked at her with a confused expression, "No, I've never heard of that. Is that something that is common in the Catholic Church?"

Carmen rolled her eyes in clear exasperation, "No it is not; in fact it is a somewhat controversial blessing in the eyes of the Vatican. The Archbishop of Buenos Aires is known to be somewhat of a renegade when it comes to matters of substance to families."

"Well that is interesting; can't have too much good will conferred upon a child in this world. Sounds like something reserved for the anointed though," Will offered, figuring their Lutheran/Bedouin backgrounds might not endear them to the Catholics.

Carmen sneered at him, "I believe the spirit of the child is the sanctity that is being blessed Will. I don't think your religious affiliation is an impediment to receiving the blessing."

Will glanced at Dom and they nodded, agreeing to look into this blessing soonest. He looked back at Carmen as his lizard brain engaged, "Hey, is there some unholy union between the Junta and the church here in Argentina? I remember Roberto telling us about the 'baby stealing' as part of the Reorganization Process. Now you tell us the Catholics in Argentina are particularly concerned about a child in the womb. From what I can piece together, Videla was too religious to allow Massera to kill pregnant women before they gave birth, and apparently made sure the babies were adopted by well-off families. Am I seeing clearly or through a prism?"

Carmen actually got up and put her arms around his neck, "No Will, once again you are seeing right through the fog that obscures everyone else's vision. Peron angered the Vatican so badly when he evicted two priests over the 'Henry VIII Fiasco' that they embraced Videla—already a strict Catholic—with open arms, to the chagrin of the rest of the world. It is indeed a paradox of sorts that the man many view as a murderous dictator is accepted as a keeper of the faith of the One God."

Will held her face in his hands as he kissed her sweetly on the lips, "Well, I'd say we've found our little alliance that's gonna keep my Conscience from being abused."

She smiled in wonder, "Is that what I am to you, your conscience?"

"Yes Carmen; when I take a step in the wrong direction you are there to redirect my focus." He leaned in close and whispered in her ear, "And sometimes my soulmate is the beneficiary of such mentoring, love."

She shook her head mischievously, "I knew the day I met you that I would not be able to treat you like the rest. You do not allow people you want to become close to the option of psychological distance."

"That's because you're the ultimate hybrid that Hal saw and was willing to risk his life to pursue. You are at once irresistibly exotically erotic and at the same time coldly calculating. Such a person must always be my friend if I can possibly charm them. I am indeed a fortunate son."

"Well damn Willy," Hal echoed, "in that we totally agree!"

Carmen was now curling around Will as he looked at her curiously. "To what do I owe this unusual intimacy?"

She just smiled nodding, "Once again your entrepreneurial inspiration has borne fruit Guillermo. The Air Force took delivery of a new larger and faster helicopter for Presidential Airlift Support, and Roberto was able to convince President Videla—over Daniel Rojas' objections—to sell it to Fabiano SA."

Will's eyes were narrowed now, "And exactly how did *Señor* Fabiano outduel Deputy Minister Rojas for the chopper?"

She gave off a sexy carefree laugh, her arms around his neck, "You are the golden child it would seem Xavier. Roberto mentioned to President Videla that YOU thought a commercial helicopter commuter service between downtown Buenos Aires and Ezeiza would have widespread appeal to visiting foreigners and wealthy Porteños. Videla immediately saw the brilliance of the plan, as he himself takes his Presidential helicopter to Ezeiza—perhaps more for security than convenience. Regardless, your friend...is it true that you all but swore to him almost nose to nose that he was *mi buen amigo?*"

"*Si, esto es verdad*. After telling him that, he confided in me that he always has a smile on his face after being in my presence. Of course, I asked him if that was a good thing," Will said as everyone broke up laughing. "So, I take it there is now a Fabiano SA subsidiary for charter copter flights, home-based out of Jorge Newbery?"

"Capital Air Services opened for business yesterday, benefiting hugely by the recent retirements of Colonele Arturo Fox, Presidential pilot since Videla became President, along with his maintenance supervisor. We are their first charter tomorrow to Ezeiza and will return us to Jorge Newbery after our trip south. Are you feeling pleased with yourself?"

"So Danny Boy lost out in this tug of war, eh? What'd he want it for; doesn't the Air Force have choppers? What model helicopter is it, by the way?"

"*Gaucha* is a Bell Twin Huey, I believe it is a Model 212, specially configured for VIP transport, reducing passenger capacity from fourteen to eight, with luggage. It became available when the Air Force took delivery of the new *Aérospatiale* AS332 Super Puma last month," Carmen advised them as Will opened his palm, waiting. "Oh, President Peron noticed during his last term as President that nearly every general officer in the Defense Ministry had his own helicopter assigned. This was noted as the same officers insisted they needed additional funds for helicopters to fight the ERP. He then decreed that only the President would be assigned a dedicated transport helicopter, further irritating the military. Apparently, Minister Rojas hoped to use the Bell 212 to transport visiting dignitaries but Videla overruled him and had Libertador sell the helicopter to Fabiano SA at its straight-line depreciated value based on the purchase price. It has been maintained to perfection, so we got a great deal."

"I am impressed Belen; a very good strategic move on Fabiano SA's part. By the way, with a pilot, mechanic, maintenance facility and office, that's a lot of overhead. What's the cost of a flying hour?" Will asked as Hal nodded.

She gave him her trademark, riotously erotic upjerk, "Roberto is no fool; he exercised his friendship with the owner of Plata Aviation, the fixed base operator at Jorge Newbery, to use their facilities, offices and reservations system for a fixed monthly fee. As you know, this controlled start-up costs greatly. Still, operating costs per flying hour are around seventy-five US dollars, or about eighty-two thousand Argentine pesos."

"Jesus, now I see why the economy is Videla's number one priority; has inflation ever been this bad?" Will asked in amazement.

"No, we are now in the worst of it."

"Well, I guess that means international transactions take place in gold bullion?" Will asked out of the clear blue.

"Jesus Christ Willy, where'd that come from?" Hal asked with a snarl. Will merely held his hand open to Carmen for the response.

"Once again, you see through the fog William; all international transactions are negotiated in ounces of gold; the Central Bank maintains a huge stock of bullion, as you might imagine."

"No sweat; so a trip from Jorge Newbery to Ezeiza is seventy-five US, or is it dependent on whether there's a charter waiting at Ezeiza?"

"For us it will not matter; we pay actual costs for our personnel ferrying. Plata Aviation maintains counters at Ezeiza's commercial and FBO terminals, so the hope is that once we are known there will be more two way traffic thereby lowering the cost to passengers."

Will held his hand up for her to high-five, but Carmen merely stared at him with a smirk. "Oh, I get it, saluting my Conscience must be more personal than high-fiving?" She merely nodded her head as Will took her in his arms, leaned her over like an ice skater might and gently pecked her on the lips. "Damn nice business venture Mrs. Rayfield."

She kissed him back before launching from his arms, "I must pack for this God-forsaken trip to *Isla Malvinas*." Will began snickering as she turned on him like a cobra, "I hope it rains every day while I'm gone *Señor* Coonass."

———

"Hey baby, welcome back. Did Zig spring for first class this time?" Will asked Kelly as she walked off of Pan Am's flight from LA.

"Are you kidding?" She hissed as she air-kissed him. "I had to use every frequent flier mile in my account to upgrade. How you doing cowboy?"

He looked around, wondering how long the greeting between she and Dom would take, but she finally came up for air, "So what's on first base?"

"Damn, ten hour flight and loaded for bear? I'm impressed. Carmen and Hal just took off out of here for parts south, so checking out the restaurant for a shooting scene is out unless you're hungry," he offered up.

"So when are they getting back? Sounds like a couple of days in BA with my buds; damn, it's my lucky break! Parts south? What the hell's south of here? I thought BA was next to the South Pole?"

Will grimaced at her lack of geographic acumen, "For you general fund of knowledge Ms. Dupree—Jesus, and you used to be an international stewardess—the Falkland Islands are approximately 1200 miles southeast of BA out in the Atlantic Ocean. And before you ask, they grow some of the finest wool in the world, and Carmen's family's clothing line is interested in obtaining a reliable source."

"Business trip *humph*? So we're all alone in BA for the night? Hot damn, you guys do entertainment right!" She all but danced with glee.

"Actually Kelly, we're having Jonathan Calvatori over tonight for steaks on the *parilla*. He's looking forward to meeting you," Dom provided.

This seemed to get her mind off of the harem track enough to reply, "Yeah, that might be interesting; he's hot you say?"

"You be the judge of that Kelly, but if I weren't married to Will…." Dom said, letting the ending trail off to parts surmised.

"Right, and his ass woulda been in North Africa dodging knives and bullets for New Year's instead of yours truly!" Will told them, figuring he'd level the playing field.

"Now, now William, there's no reason to be overly jealous here; I made my decision and am quite happy with you," Dom offered in recompense.

"Good, let's go get the *parilla* ready for the evening's performance; I bet the Cossack Queen will meet her match tonight!"

As they walked out of the Ezeiza terminal Will flagged down a cab. "Jesus, we're taking a cab back to *Casa Fabiano*?"

"Perish the thought, my Cossack Queen; for visitors as important as you we're taking a helicopter back. The taxi's to get us over to the FBO where the Bell 212, dubbed *Gaucha*, is awaiting our arrival."

"Welcome back to *Casa Fabiano* Jonathan," Will said as he opened the door to the fertility wunderkind.

"It's good to see you in such a good mood Will, how are you?" He asked, sporting a white dress shirt open at the collar, a blue blazer and surprisingly, black designer jeans. Taken in total, Will didn't see how Kelly was going to keep her clothes on much past dinner.

"Come on back and have a drink buddy," he offered as they made their way to the patio.

"Hello Dominique," he said as she wrapped herself around him, "it's so good to see happy patients. But I suppose you are no longer a mere patient are you?"

"Jonathan, I'd like you to meet our friend Kelly," she said turning to 'the candidate.' "Kelly, this is Jonathan Calvatori, our friend who also happens to be the most renowned fertility specialist in the Southern Hemisphere."

Jonathan looked like he had been shot with a tranquilizer dart, but to her credit, Kelly remained composed enough to offer her hand and say, "Hello Jonathan, it's so nice to meet you."

For some insane reason, Will flashed back to the night he met Malina Garcia at the Palace, with her playing coy in spite of the fact she was sharpening her mental knives planning how she was going to carve him up. He must have been replaying the squeezebox portion of that evening when Dom said, "Will, are you going to fix Jonathan something to drink?"

He snapped out of it to say, "What'll it be buddy? Scotch, bourbon, you pick the poison." After Jon told him he'd prefer scotch, Will brushed up past Kelly and whispered in her ear, "Don't tease him too bad Kell, I've been where he is before."

Jonathan looked at Will like he wanted to follow him off to the bar in the worst way, but Dom grabbed his arm as he started to lean and escorted him back to the chairs by the *parilla*. When Will got over to them, Jonathon grabbed the single malt and sucked down a healthy snort, surprising Will enough to glance at Dom. She took the lead and asked him, "So do you have any other ZIFT couples in treatment right now Jonathan?"

This seemed to shock him back to reality, so he smiled, "No other ZIFT cases in the induction phase such as you and Will, but there are many other clients with issues not quite as complex as yours."

"So where are you from Jonathan?" Kelly asked with a demure smile. Will wondered if she might in fact be somehow immune to Calvatori's charm, but decided she was just jaded from overexposure to every man in Hollywood trying to get in her pants.

"Actually, I was born in Mendoza, which is in the western part of Argentina, have you ever heard of it?" He asked politely, no doubt used to people not having heard of his hometown. Gastineau came to mind as an example.

She smiled knowingly, "Actually, we flew there and ate lunch at this nice little restaurant called Cantina La Rambla when we were scouting shooting locations in western Argentina a few weeks ago. Did you go to medical school there?"

"No, I went….what were you doing in Mendoza, if you don't mind my asking?" He finally heard what she said and shook his head, "I know of this place, Cantina La Rambla, and it is one of the best bistros in Catalan Centre. I'm almost amazed that you were in my home province."

"We were looking at possible movie shooting locations. So did you go to medical school there?" Her interrogation manner reminded Will of Samantha Herrington's total intimidation of poor Johnny Chessereaux' that fateful day at LAX.

"No, actually I went to medical school in the United States, at Johns Hopkins University. Have you heard of it?" He replied, seeming to regain some semblance of wits about himself.

"Duh," Kelly deadpanned, "have I heard of the most famous medical training institution in the United States? I think so."

Jonathan looked to Will desperately for translation help so he told the hero of CIRVIDAR, "She's impressed Jonathan."

"So where are you from Kelly?" He asked in return. Will glanced at Dom because neither of them had heard a lot about her family.

"I was born in Wichita, Kansas, where my father worked in an aircraft plant," she smiled, just barely turning her head to pantomime 'GOTCHA' at Will.

"So where the hell did the Cossack Queen come from? This sounds like a disconnect to me bigtime Dupree," Will blurted out, but was immediately chastised by the scowl Dom gave him.

Now Kelly frowned at him, no doubt from the Cossack Queen remark and enlightened them, "My father was part of the French occupation force in Berlin after the war, and he met my mother who was a translator for a Russian general. Their romance was very hush hush because the Russians mistrusted the Allies so. My father parlayed some contact he made with an American pilot he knew to get a job and a visa to the United States. So there Mr. Cajun boy, put that in your pipe and smoke it."

"Well that would explain a lot of things," Will quickly added. Seeing the need for an out, he offered, "How about giving me a hand with the *parilla* Jonathan. How would you like your steak Kelly?"

She smirked at him, "Oh, I'll have it like Jonathan likes his; can't be a wimp around the men now can I?"

"So whatdya think big boy, did we set you up or what?" Will asked Jonathan once they got over to the grill and outside earshot of the women.

"Oh Kelly is something; she is far different from these *Porteño* women, I can assure you of that. I am not sure that I have ever seen a woman with jet black hair and blue eyes. I do not think that you and Dominique have misled me about her incredible beauty."

"Right, right, right; so what do you think? Can you visualize a spot of heavy breathing with that minx?" He asked, baiting the trap. Upon further reflection, Will didn't need to bait the trap, as he recalled pursuing her wantonly their first night alone in San Diego. *Jesus Kavanagh, that seems like a decade ago, and it was what, six months in the past? Man has my life been a blur.*

He laughed and said, "I can visualize a bit more than that Will. But the fact that she lives and works in Los Angeles causes me concern. I wouldn't want to fall head over heels in love with someone I could never be with."

Will looked at him with a jaundiced eyeball, put his arm around the Mendozan's shoulder and told him, "As your attorney I advise you to strike while the iron is hot ma man. Those long term considerations should not impede short term objectives, especially during the audition stage. If I wasn't married to Dom, Kelly'd be on my short list, I can assure you of that. And I wouldn't give a shit where she lived!"

He smiled at Will and replied, "We shall see Will. I take it she will be in Buenos Aires for more than one night, yes?"

Will saw where he was going with this, so he relented, "Nah, she'll be here a couple more days before we head west out to Bariloche. I wouldn't waste too much time if I were you bro."

At this Jonathon's eyebrows were dancing as he told him, "I'll keep that under advisement Will. I like my steak medium rare. Do you think we can prepare it properly?"

"Fear not Lancelot, for you are with the grill *meister!*"

As they were inhaling the first bites of the delicious *lomos*, Kelly sneered at Will, "Jesus Kavanagh, I've seen cattle get hurt worse than this and pull through. Whatdya do, pass it over the grill and sprinkle holy water on it?"

He looked at her hatefully as Jonathan tried mightily not to spit steak across the table onto Dom's lap, "Oh, I'm sorry Miss Wuss, let me take it back and return with a fucking hockey puck. I thought someone from the Midwest would appreciate tasty beef but I was obviously mistaken. You apparently subscribe to the Larry Bird 'Country Hick from French Lick' school of beef preparation—ruint!"

Dupree was pissed now, standing with her hands on her hips and cast the challenge, "Wuss huh? Well the next time your sorry ass is in LA I'm taking you to my favorite sushi bar. We'll see how sophisticated your tastes are Mr. Coonass Cajun Bayou Boy!"

Her reference to sushi gave him pause, shaking his head no, "Hey, I don't eat bait. At least singe the outer edges for Christ's sake!"

"Yeah right; I'll eat this poor wounded steer, but your ass is not getting out of the sushi challenge!"

He looked at Jonathan sheepishly and told him, "I told you she was a spirited woman Jonathan; I just didn't know she was so cranky about her beef."

"Will Kavanagh! Am I going to have to put you on Freelancing restrictions? Now you apologize to Kelly this very minute. I will not tolerate such behavior in front of guests!" Dom grouched, and Will knew he was in the dog house.

"Uh, so sorry *Señorita* Kelly, I was apparently showing off in front of our distinguished guest, and I apologize for my rude behavior. Now can I please go convert that perfect beefsteak to trail jerky for you?"

"Mr. Kavanagh!" Dom all but shouted this time.

Now rolling his eyes, he glanced at Calvatori, forced to apologize once again. Jonathon held his hand up instead, "So what is a Freelancing restriction? You responded so abruptly that I must find out what magic inducement that entails."

"Your heart's in the right place Jonathan, I admire your instincts."

———

"So what do you think happened?" Will asked a disconsolate but very naked Kelly Dupree as they were lounging in bed not thirty minutes after Jonathan departed, professing to having had the time of his life.

"Oh, why do you even go there Will Kavanagh? You obviously scared him off so that you could have your harem back together again," ranted the severely bent-out-of-shape temptress.

"Now Kelly, I can't condone William's childish behavior tonight, but I didn't get the impression that Jonathan had anything but a wonderful time meeting you," Dom offered in his defense.

"Oh, but you don't know what advice he was giving that Adonis god when they were over by the grill together. What is it about you men? Can you never get over the fact that you're not the be-all-to-end-all?"

"Actually Kelly, I told him to strike while the fire was hot, but he's apparently too well-mannered to go after the prize on the first date."

"Bullshit, and I'm going to screw you so hard you'll never think about playing frat boy games on me again Xavier. I for the life of me cannot understand men and this ridiculous petty jealousy!"

"Do you think it's outside the realm of possibility that Jonathan came to meet you because Will and I had promoted your desirability to him so pointedly? Perhaps he wanted to get to know you a bit before he suggested anything more intimate. I realize that is alien for someone like Will, but Jonathan is from a different culture. Remember, they are very religious down here," Dom cautioned.

Kelly looked at Will hatefully, her primal instincts refusing to give him the benefit of the doubt. She softened her response however, "Well maybe, but how long does it take for the sexual revolution to get down to Argentina? Man was I ever ready to take him there."

"All in good time my dear; is not paradise worth waiting for? Now if you have no other indictments to falsely convey, I've had a long day and I need my beauty rest. Goodnight my Queen."

"And you can forget that shit," she said as she rolled him over onto his back. The Cossack Queen from Wichita then proceeded to make her case for why he could delay slumber, at least for a while anyway.

24

CLOSING THE DEAL IN BUENOS AIRES

"So this is the place Carmen thought would be perfect for one of the scenes in the movie. Do you know the proprietor per chance?" Will asked Rosita Cabrera as he launched into a perfect Caesar salad.

Kelly and Dom were watching her suspiciously, very much aware of Rosita's untoward interest in him. To her credit Rosita smiled, "Of course I do; this is one of the most popular restaurants in Buenos Aires. Why do you want to shoot the scene here?"

"Actually, Carmen was the one who said this place reminded her of the, uh, location in Algiers that an important event took place. She also said the garden outside may be appropriate for the takedown."

"Oh, are you alluding to where she eliminates Sandrigan's second-in-command?" She asked, all but flooring them with her knowledge of potentially dangerous information. "The restaurant was Farouk's I believe, not far from the Casbah where you were exchanged for your mother in the mosque?"

"Yeah, that's the scene. I didn't realize that Carmen had discussed the, uh, particulars with you about it," he replied, a slight blush running up his neck.

"I know the information is delicate; I suppose I should be more circumspect." She leaned into him and whispered, "That's not all Belen told me about. You are a very interesting man Will Kavanagh."

Feeling the stares of Dom and Kelly burning through him, he smiled, "I am when I can keep from getting shot, that's for sure. Did Carmen tell you that Dominique and I are expecting our first child?"

Rosita turned to Dom, offering her hand, "I am so happy for you both

Dominique, congratulations. Is there anything I can do to help you here in Buenos Aires?"

To his surprise, Dom smiled at her and nodded, "Carmen was telling us about this Catholic ritual of blessing of the child in the womb, and I was interested. Do you know of any priests here in Buenos Aires who perform such a blessing? Will and I feel as though we can use every advantage."

She smiled beguilingly and nodded her approval, "As a matter of fact, my godfather is the Archbishop of Buenos Aires. Would you like me to ask him to perform this blessing for you? Are you both Catholic?"

Dom's downcast look spoke volumes as she exhaled, "No, we are not Catholic, but we are very interested in obtaining the blessing. I am Moroccan, of Bedouin and French ancestry, and Will is an American raised in the Lutheran church. Is it possible to obtain such a blessing without being a follower? Carmen convinced us that it was important to give the child every possible advantage coming into this dangerous world."

Rosita looked at Will, then back at Dom and told them, "I will speak to my godfather about you, and I will let you know if he is amenable to offering this blessing. I agree that an unborn child should have every advantage possible coming into this world."

Will was impressed that she seemed genuinely interested, and then wrapped it up by saying, "Good, Carmen and Hal will be back tomorrow and we can schedule our trip out to Bariloche. You will be accompanying us, won't you?"

She smiled at him with just a hint of mischief, "Oh, I wouldn't miss that trip for anything. I am under orders from President Videla to insure that every aspect of the movie is coordinated. He doesn't want to hear of any local issues interfering with the movie's progress."

"*Muy buena*, so we're in good hands," he smiled and shook hers, only to be rewarded with a kiss on the cheek.

"I don't know, I don't think I trust that woman around you Will," Kelly said after they were in the car on the way back to *Casa Fabiano*.

"Jesus Kelly, you're not my wife for Christ's sake! She is just magnetically drawn to me like many other women in this world. Why do you parse her out for special condemnation?"

"Well, there's nothing wrong with your self-image Mr. Kavanagh. What sets her apart is her barely veiled interest in fucking your brains out. Is that plain enough for you to understand?"

He rolled his eyes and exhaled loudly, "Yes, that's plain enough, I get it; but I'm not gonna fuck Rosita Cabrera. Did you forget that I'm married to the perfect woman?"

"And if I hadn't magically appeared to accompany you back to her office that night at the Presidential Palace? Do you think being married to the perfect woman would have shielded you from the onslaught Rosita had in mind for you?"

"I would hope so; I mean it was the Presidential Palace you know. I thought she was very helpful agreeing to speak with her godfather about blessing our child, don't you?"

"Oh, remarkably so; no doubt currying favor for when your perfect wife is ripe with child. Sometimes you amaze me with your naivety William," she all but grunted.

"Well, I certainly won't have to worry about all of that with my protector of the chalice around. Now when is Rambo getting in?"

"Oh shit, he's due in this afternoon. Can you get us that helicopter ride over to the airport?" She asked as Will rolled his eyes; he'd chartered the chopper for the jaunt out to pick up Rambo when they got in with Kelly the day before.

"I am your slave Dupree, do with me as you will," he deadpanned.

"Yeah right, but I'll have to admit you responded to the call like a champ last evening," she said, reminding him of his thwarted desire for sleep, finally passing out from the ribald sex at oh-dark-thirty.

"It would not have worked out for you to have been here when we were preparing for seed transfer, I can assure you of that!"

"Life is all about timing William."

———

Later that evening it was Hal, Carmen, Dom, Pierson and Will at the house, kicked back and enjoying the rare comradery. Kelly was out with Jonathan for dinner, and they all hoped the two would hit it off and make a shambles of Jon's Argentine morality. "So what did you find in the Falkland Islands?" Will asked, truly curious.

"That's the most boring fucking place on the planet Willy. Jesus I couldn't wait for the plane to take off. There's nothing there but a bunch of stinking ass sheep farms. Man, talk about a nothing existence. Why in the hell would anybody even want the fucking place?" Hal summed up.

Carmen frowned at him, "Apparently it's the oil reserves that interest them. Oil imports represent a strategic weakness for both the military and the economy."

"Okay, so Rojas isn't going to back down from extorting us when he needs a snoop again. What can we do to reduce our footprint of visibility?" Will pondered.

"Well, getting out of his face might help some. We could move our nest to Bariloche for the time being," Hal offered, looking at Carmen.

"That might actually help, but Will and I need to stay close to Dr. Calvatori for at least a couple of months. We need something to discourage him from seeing our pregnant friend as a counterintelligence asset," Dom offered.

Dan Pierson looked up from his bottle of Barba Roja Red Ale and offered, "Better hope they don't turn to the Russians for outside help. I know that Carmen is the best, so they might just play the outside trump card if she's not around."

"Jesus, the fucking Russians, just what we need here in beautiful sunny Argentina." Will glanced at Carmen, "I thought Operation Condor was all about removing communist-inspired revolutionaries from the Southern Cone. Why would Videla shift totally towards them when there are other options?"

Carmen was on her feet and in Will's face instantly, snatching the collar of his shirt. "How do you know about Operation Condor?"

Will grimaced trying to remember as Carmen's glare bore into his soul. "Uh, I seem to recall the day I met you Harold was trying to establish your bona fides with me and the hottest Latina I'd ever laid my eyes on surmised that Allende's suicide was assisted."

"Rumors *Guillermo*," she hissed hot breath at him, "please get specific with Condor, *por favor?*"

"Is pregnancy exacerbating your paranoia meter Belen?" Will asked as he twisted his head and leaned towards her. "Within weeks of our arrival, your tutorial on the Dirty War ended with you in Panama listening to the SOUTHCOM three star pound Condor into you as the best means of stonewalling Cuban Marxist hegemony. You even told us you met the DINA colonel who became SIDE's foremost ally in Operation Condor."

She released his shirt and leaned in until their noses were touching, "I see that I must be careful what I tell you William; you have this remarkable ability to synthesize facts but I never mentioned Condor. Where did that come from?"

Will glanced at Hal and gave him the Italian army salute, "What the fuck, you want me to record every damn conversation as an evidence trail Belen? Hell, Dom and Hal were sitting right there when you told us SOUTHCOM was pitching Condor bigtime for the Agency. What's the matter, you afraid of shadows suddenly?"

Her expression indicated she was contemplating wounds that didn't leave marks, so Will took a chance and put his hands on her face. "Jesus Carmen, it was in the same article that complained about the Dirty War and the baby stealing." She nodded as he exhaled and glanced at Hal, "Did the Editor of the Herald ever feel the heat over that article?"

"Now that is an incredibly timely question Willy," Hal nodded his head. "According to Roberto, Robert Cox, the Editor of The Herald survived an assassination attempt on his life last week, and his wife was nearly kidnapped two days ago. He'll be heading out of Argentina soon bro; he has stirred up the embers a bit too brightly."

"Where would he flee to?"

"From what Roberto told me, the Herald is owned by this publishing firm in Charleston, South Carolina. That sounds like Cox' landing zone; hell, he's been in Buenos for twenty years I hear."

The foreign reference triggered Will's lizard brain, "Speaking of outside influences, how's that bishop doing, you know the Conquistador guy? You heard any rumblings out of him lately? My brother's in Nicaragua working as a missionary for the Lutheran Church."

Pierson took a long pull on his beer, "I haven't heard of any overt moves, but that big church guy down here is apparently powerful enough to keep Villaponteau from edging his nose southward."

"The big guy down here; you mean the Archbishop?" He asked, thinking that Rosita's godfather was who they were talking about.

"Yeah, Acosta; he's the Archbishop of Buenos Aires. He's something like the head bubba for the Catholic Church in South America," Pierson advised them.

Will looked at Dom as he pondered, "So the Archbishop has considerable influence with the Junta, eh?"

"Will, I thought you'd already established the connection between the circumspect Videla and the church when we were discussing the baby adoption part of the Dirty War," Carmen noted as Will nodded.

"Now look who's got the eidetic memory."

"Oh yeah, they wouldn't dare do anything without consulting with the Archbishop," Rambo hypothesized. "Now maybe Brazil is different because of the Portuguese, but they're all Catholic, and you can bet your ass they wouldn't sneeze without the Archbishop's tacit approval."

"Now that is interesting Rambo; I believe you have enhanced our general fund of knowledge by coming down and educating us on these church-state interrelationships."

———

"So how'd it go sweet cheeks; did Romeo finally come around?" Will asked Kelly as they were eating breakfast the next morning. She had surreptitiously snuck back into the house sometime during the night after they had gone to bed.

She smiled furtively and came clean, "Yeah, finally without his Cajun buddy twisting him to the side. He was, however, what I would call somewhat reserved regarding bedroom activities."

"Jesus Christ Dupree, you couldn't seduce him into hedging his sacred link to the abolitionists?"

She laughed this time and offered, "Only because I am somewhat strident about getting my own way. His Catholic upbringing makes it much more difficult to let loose, so to speak."

"Give him time Kelly," Dom urged. "I'm sure someone visiting from the Valley of the Dolls—as Will puts it---would find things somewhat constrained around the *Porteños*, Rosita Cabrera notwithstanding."

"I'm afraid time is the one commodity I don't have a lot of here in Buenos. He is such a nice guy, and my God what a body!"

"That's my girl; I knew you could make him see the light," Will pumped as he gave her a hug.

She shrugged and dropped the unexpected modesty bomb, "I have never known another man to resist fellatio. He actually made me feel like I was somehow inadequate."

Will now frowned at her with genuine pity, "I don't know Kell, you may be right. He may have some structural defect if he doesn't like a blow job!"

The five of them rendezvoused with Rosita at La Cabrera for lunch, and the maître d' was becoming a friend, "Ah *Señor* and *Señora* Kavanagh, how nice to see you again. Your friend the Minister is waiting for you; please follow me."

Instead of showing them a table, he led them back past the kitchen and opened a door for them to enter. As they walked in a man in his late forties with a growing midriff got up and greeted them, "Hello, and welcome back to La Cabrera. I am Roberto Torrez, and this is my restaurant. Minister Cabrera has told me about your plans, and we are most excited."

The link between the restaurant name and Rosita's surname connected suddenly as Will turned to her, "Hello Rosita, is there some connection, perhaps a family affiliation with this restaurant?"

To his surprise, she got up and hugged him, kissing him chastely on the cheek, "Aren't you the suspicious one Mr. Kavanagh? And no, I am not related to the Torrez family. The restaurant takes its name from the section of Buenos Aires it is located in." She then dutifully shook everyone else's hands in greeting as Roberto asked them to sit in his comfortably appointed office.

"Now hold on here *Senorita* Tourism Minister, I thought we were in the Soho subdivision of Palermo. So Cabrera is like a neighborhood within Palermo Soho?" Will pushed the navigational issues. He could instantly tell that he'd lit off a stink bomb by their reactions.

"I realize that you are trying to establish your landmarks here in Buenos Aires Will, but Roberto would not like to think of his fine establishment being part of the debauchery of Palermo Soho," Rosita advised him.

"Sorry, no insult was intended," Will said as he inwardly noted the distinction. "So have you explained to *Señor* Torrez why we are here?"

"Please, I insist that you call me Roberto, as everyone else does. Rosita has just been explaining to me that you would like to use our place of business in conjunction with a movie you are planning. Let me say to you before we get into details that I am honored and flattered to host your filming here in Argentina."

"We really want to insure that we disrupt your normal business as little as possible Roberto. What are your hours of operation?" Kelly asked, quickly assuming her role as movie producer.

He shrugged and replied, "When we first started La Cabrera it was open every day except Sunday, as we hoped to allow our employees a day of rest,

including the owner! As fortune would dictate however, the restaurant became popular among tourists, and the cost in lost revenues by shutting down
on Sundays represented a business imperative that we could not ignore. There
was also the issue of losing customers to our competitors. So we are open every day except Easter Sunday and Christmas Day."

"And what are your slowest days, from a revenue generation perspective?"
Kelly pursued.

"Mondays and Tuesdays are slowest for business, with the tourists providing adequate traffic to justify opening on those days."

She was nodding her head, making notes in her day planner, "Okay, so
early in the week is best so far as disruption to normal business is concerned."
She looked around at the rest of them and asked, "Are there any other details
we need to ask Roberto about, at least that you can think of now?"

Will was shaking his head no when Carmen asked, "What time of day
does your evening dinner traffic become heaviest? Are the tourists like *Porteños*,
in that they eat late?"

Roberto was nodding his head as he responded, "Yes, I would say our
heaviest dinner traffic occurs between 8:30 and 10:00 most nights. Is this going to be a problem?"

Will looked at Carmen as the light bulb came on and blurted, "Hey, that's
right, wasn't it about at dusk when you met Ouzo at Farouk's?"

She smiled whimsically at him, "Very good Mr. Kavanagh." Then she
turned to Kelly and Roberto, "I believe we can get the filming crew in and
out of here before the evening guests arrive. If we have the set ready to shoot
around dusk, I believe we can complete the interior shooting before the prime
business hours."

Kelly was all but ecstatic as she gushed, "Great! So we've got the restaurant scene locked. I can't wait to try a La Cabrera hamburger." She pointedly
stared at Will and said, "I bet they'll cook it long enough so it's not still wailing
in terror!"

He was trying to figure out how to slap her on the ass under the radar
when Carmen asked, "Can we take a look at the garden behind the restaurant
now Roberto? There is a continuation of the restaurant scene that takes place
outside."

Will made sure he was the last person out of Roberto's office so he could
thank him for his cooperation. This positioned him nicely to sneak up behind

Kelly and pinch her on the ass, causing her to shriek as everyone turned around to see what the commotion was about. Will swept right past them to the garden and asked Carmen, "So whatdya think?"

As she looked around she was shaking her head in the affirmative, and finally looked at Roberto, "This garden is lovely, just as I remembered it. It will do nicely for the movie scene. Tell me, do you have dinner guests here in the garden?"

Now it was Roberto's turn to ponder, as he finally replied, "Depending on the weather, there may be a group of younger people who come here soon after work for libations. During the cooler months, almost no patrons use the garden tables."

Will looked around with newfound respect and smiled, "So this is where the Happy Hour crowd comes, eh? This place would be perfect for an office party."

"Happy hour?" Roberto repeated, apparently never having heard the term before.

Will smiled at him and winked, "Right, Happy Hour Roberto; you may want to consider focusing on the social aspects to prospective clients. You know who I'm talkin' about; the young ones who work in the offices around here and can't wait until four-thirty to get the hell out of dodge? As a jaded fighter pilot once explained to me, sitting in a bar after a hard day's work; 'Hell Kavanagh, if you don't believe in life after death, just be here at four-thirty tomorrow for the proof!'"

Will watched him closely as the translation made its way through his brain and he finally burst out laughing, his eyeballs bulging hugely. He actually slapped Will on the back, narrowly missing his mending shoulder, "I will have to give that strong consideration to promote early evening business Will. Thank you for telling me about this Happy Hour."

As they were eating lunch for the second consecutive day at La Cabrera, Will noticed three young women sitting at the bar having a cocktail and smoking cigarettes. Kelly caught him eyeballing the hotties, leaned into him and grouched like a schoolmarm, "Down boy; have you completely forgotten your manners?"

By now Dom was also looking at him suspiciously so he gave them a glimpse inside the lizard brain, "I wonder what it's like to be drinking around some hotties, sort of like those three, and they don't speak English and you don't speak Spanish. Man, I wonder how frustrating that could be?"

Dom rolled her eyes before she responded, "I believe it wouldn't make much difference, the way you look at women who 'qualify' according to the Kavanagh Rules of Engagement. The look of lust is its own universal language William, and there is no doubt you would succeed in transmitting your intentions."

He nodded at her, figuring he'd test her theory, "Okay, when we finish eating, you guys leave and I'll go test out the theory. Are we all good with that?"

"No we are not!" Dom and Kelly replied in unison as Rosita and Carmen looked to see what transgression had been perpetrated.

Will was haggling with the maître d' as they left, refusing to accept Roberto's largesse of providing lunch on his nickel, when Rosita walked up to him. "It's alright Will, the Ministry of Tourism picked up the bill for lunch; you are not imposing on Roberto's charitable interests."

He raised his eyebrows and leaned down to her ear, "Good, I'm not a big believer in free lunches." He discreetly pushed a twenty dollar bill in the maître d's pocket as they turned to leave the restaurant. Rosita once again cozied up to him, "I spoke with my godfather, Archbishop Acosta, and he has agreed to provide the blessing for your child."

Will leaned into her further, inhaling the delight of her enticing perfume and smiled at her, "Thanks babe, what time does the man want to see us?"

She smirked as Dom ventured back to see what the holdup was about. Rosita played it well, "The Archbishop will see you at 11:00 tomorrow morning in his private office in the Metropolitan Cathedral. Do you need directions on how to get there?"

Dom's entire personality changed as she drew Rosita into a warm hug, "We'll find it Rosita, and thank you so much for doing this for us. I cannot believe we will have the opportunity to meet the Archbishop!"

She smiled at them and offered, "Well, it seems as though you have already befriended the President of Argentina, so why not the Archbishop? By the way, those two men are close personal friends, so be careful how casually you speak around him."

Dom none-too-delicately pulled on Will's shirt collar, "Oh don't worry, I'll make sure that Mr. Kavanagh here is on his best behavior."

She nodded towards Pierson and asked, "So who is your friend, the one named Daniel?"

Will was favorably impressed with Rosita's newfound, trailblazing spirit, but Dom quickly interjected, "He's a very dangerous man Rosita, and he's in love with one of my best friends."

Undeterred by the warning, Rosita looked again towards Pierson, who by all appearances looked completely at ease but was no doubt reconnoitering the street, "He's an interesting man, and a rather handsome one as well. If I didn't know better I would think he is surveilling the street for possible danger."

Will cozied up to her once again and told her, "I like your instincts Rosita."

25

THE MAGICAL BLESSING OF THE CHILD IN THE WOMB

"So you two are having an audience with the Archbishop of Buenos Aires?" Carmen asked dumbfounded once they were on their way back to the house.

"He's going to bestow the blessing of the child in the womb for us, can you believe it?" Dom chortled.

Carmen glanced at Will and advised, "I would be careful with extemporaneous remarks around His Excellency Will, especially any profanity-laced truisms from your past."

"Yeah, no problem; I wonder if he knows about his charlatan priest Villaponteau in Colombia?" Will wondered out loud.

"Do not bring that up Will, or he might suspect you have some connection to the drug cartels. We must be circumspect in our conversations about such matters," she cautioned.

"Yeah, I can see your point. So you guys gonna head on out to Bariloche? Dom and I can catch a flight out after the meet with Acosta," he proposed.

"No, actually I want to return to La Cabrera with Hal and Dan and scope out the particulars for the Algiers restaurant scenes. With Kelly along, we can map out most of the production details while you two are with the Archbishop."

———

"So how are we gonna play this Dom?" Will asked as they drove over to the incredibly impressive Metropolitan Cathedral, the headquarters of the Buenos Aires Archdiocese.

She looked just the slightest bit shaky when she turned and said, "I think it would be disingenuous for us to refer to him as 'Your Excellency' or 'Your Grace.' Perhaps we can strike a neutral ground by calling him Archbishop Acosta. What do you think?"

"Sounds good; how are we gonna receive the bestowing, you know, just sit there or kneel down in front of him so he can touch us? I'm out of my league considering my Lutheran roots," he offered helplessly.

"Let's just play that by ear. We've got to see what kind of person he is; if he's too intractable in his interactions it may be awkward to kneel. I am a good judge of these things; take my lead," she suggested.

He patted her thigh and replied, "Okay, and speaking of leads, man am I ever glad Carmen told us about the alms deal. Who would've known we're supposed to bring some gift in return for the blessing? That could have been embarrassing if the Archbishop was expecting something and we gave him the Italian army salute; Jesus!"

Dom shook her head, "Have you ever thought about what that 'Italian army salute' that you keep bandying about jokingly represents?"

"Sure, the Italians had a knack for surrendering during World War Two, so hands raised up empty became the sign. You think Acosta doesn't know about that?"

"And exactly where is the Vatican located Will?"

"Rome of course...oh, okay I get it. So these Catholics might not think it's as funny as some others do. I will make every attempt to restrain myself dear. What would I do without you?"

"Precipitate international incidents resolved only by the United Nations? I can only imagine where that totally random sense of humor you have would land you without some reasonable constraints. But I'm glad to be the one to help you through the gauntlet Mr. Kavanagh."

"Me too," he said as he leaned over for a careful kiss, not wanting to muss the makeup.

"Wow, this place is something! There must be a lot of rich Catholics around Argentina," he said as they sat in the anteroom awaiting their audience with the Archbishop. "They've restored the place nicely since the ransacking by the Peronists in 1955, that's for sure." The oil paintings of aged political and religious heroes festooned the hallways and walls of the incredible 'back offices' of the Metropolitan Cathedral. "I wonder if he wears all those robes and all, you know so we can kiss the ring?"

Dom swatted at his arm as she scolded, "Will Kavanagh, behave!"

A man walked up to them, whom Will assumed was the Catholic equivalent of a secretary and smiled, "Mr. and Mrs. Kavanagh, how nice to meet you. I am Guillermo Acosta; won't you come and join me in my office?"

They were both stunned at his informal manner, but followed him into a large office, richly appointed and settled into two chairs that looked like they should have been at a dining room table. The thought crossed Will's mind that they weren't being ushered into the plush stuffed leather ones in the corner lest they overstay their visit with His Excellency. Acosta took a more comfortable looking—like it'd been sat in a lot—chair directly across from them, smiled and began, "My goddaughter told me that you are expecting a child, and I am thrilled for the both of you. She also told me that you are both visitors to Argentina; could you tell me where you are from?"

Dom took the first shot and replied, "I am from Morocco Your Excellency, and I am the daughter of a Bedouin mother and a French military officer. Although I was baptized in the Holy Roman Church in Casablanca, I have been raised as a Bedouin and have not practiced the faith of Catholicism."

He nodded and looked at Will, who launched, "So here's the deal Archbishop Acosta," he said but glanced at Dom to make sure he was within social parameters. "I'm a Cajun boy born in Gastineau, Louisiana, and my grandfather is a Lutheran minister. I've lived an interesting life and was transformed by my chance meeting with this woman four years ago in Colorado. I am a sinner but haven't worried too much about it, as I figure everyone is at least stained by the curse. So I'm here in front of you today because I feel as though you are a holy man who can grant certain reformative powers to this child we are about to bring into this world. But make no mistake about my intentions as a father sir; I am as committed to bringing her up in a Christian way as any man you have ever seen before you."

He nodded at Will thoughtfully and turned to Dom, "So you have chosen this man Dominique? What do you think of his fitness to be a father to your child?"

She glanced at Will with a tinge of guilt in her face before responding, "He is as he says father, a sinner and imperfect, but are we not all imperfect in the eyes of the Lord? I love this man more than life itself, and he has proven to me beyond doubt that he is committed to me and to the welfare of this child

I bear. I have already gone to the ends of the earth with him and he has not left me wanting or questioning his resolve in our love. I would implore you to consecrate this child that I bear so that he or she may live in this world as a child of God, free of the influences of the Satan."

His eyebrows flexed and he paused, and then continued with a surprising query, "So you have seen the face of Satan?

Dom looked at Will questioningly as he gave her the nod, so she turned to look directly into Acosta's eyes, "This man has saved the world from the angel of Satan Your Excellency."

Acosta looked at Will closely and asked, "So I have heard of your encounter with this Satan's angel Mr. Kavanagh. Are you willing to proclaim Jesus as your savior before myself, Dominique and the world?"

Will shivered as he told him, "Your Grace, I am not proud of the fact that I have broken the Ten Commandments once again, this time in what I consider the most egregious of infractions, but I would do it again to save my soul mate from the evil this Satan perpetrated upon her. I am but a sinner Archbishop, and I seek absolution."

He was crying when the Archbishop laid his hand upon his shoulder, leaned down and kissed his cheek and said, "You are forgiven William, as I say before God, the Holy See and the World. There are certain moments in the course of humankind when we are confronted with a choice, and you have made the correct one in this circumstance. I am moved to tears that you have survived this quest and have lived to help create this living monument to the resurrection of Christ, the love of mankind."

Will didn't know what to do but grab him in his arms and hug him, but was surprised when Dom joined as they were all shedding tears of grief and joy seemingly at the same time. Will looked up at him through a haze of tears and asked, "How did you know?"

He nodded with a measured smile, "Jorge Videla is my step-brother Will…" He noticed Will's look of curiosity and smiled, "Jorge's parents Eugenio and Maria adopted me when I was a toddler after my own parents died tragically. I knew of your situation before you arrived. I must say that I am humbled by your love for this woman," he said as he nodded to Dominique, "and your devotion to what is right in the world. If only we had a thousand like you to lead the fight against evil. Now before I invest this blessing upon your blessed child, is there anything I can possibly do to make your life better?

That is, other than granting you some material windfall?"

His reference to money made Will laugh, but he recovered enough to reach into his vest pocket and hand him the envelope with the $1000 in cash. "If it would be possible Your Grace, could you possibly see that this modest gift is given to the children who most need it? We would be eternally grateful." And then Will Kavanagh—on autopilot now—did the almost unconscionable thing and reached out, took Acosta's hand and kissed his ring signifying his position as a Cardinal in the Holy Roman Church.

Acosta reached down, grabbed Will under the armpits and lifted him back into the chair, "It will so be Will. Now tell me, is there anything that I can do for you?"

He was thunderstruck, but his mind was working and he remembered Carmen's plight with Rojas. He decided this might be his only opportunity to affect the outcome and took the chance. "Actually Your Grace, there is a matter of some great importance to Dom and I that you might could help us with."

The Cardinal was nodding, giving him the prompt when Will abandoned all pretenses and launched into saving one his truest friends. "Our friend Carmen Fabiano Rayfield is an Argentine who was formerly a member of the Argentine intelligence service SIDE, as well as the 601 Intelligence Battalion."

He nodded indicating that he should proceed, so Will told him straight up, "So Carmen was the most extraordinary agent SIDE or the 601st ever had, or so I've been led to believe. But anyway, she's a friend of ours and was critical in the takedown of Sandrigan el-Boukhari—oh shit, I don't know if you…"

He smiled at him and interrupted, "Do not worry Will; Jorge Videla has told me about your involvement in the elimination of Mr. el-Boukhari, please continue."

"So anyway Archbishop, Carmen's the wife of my best friend from high school, and she's now five months pregnant with their first child and Danny Rojas is trying to make her his counterintelligence agent seeking surveillance and Lord knows what else concerning the Falkland Islands. Jesus Christ Archbishop, she's five months pregnant, don't you think they could forget about her and give her a break? Shouldn't her child have the same chance as ours? Just because she's the most feared assassin in the free world shouldn't make her exempt from a little consideration. What do you think?"

He looked at Will with considerable consternation before responding, "I think that you are a very loyal friend Will. And I agree that Mrs. Rayfield's child should have the same consideration as yours to come into this world without terror. I will make some communication to see what I can find out about this matter. Is there anything else I can help you with before we have our blessing?"

Will knew he was risking certain death by going there—but things seemed to be going smoothly so far. He took a deep breath and asked, "I have heard unsettling rumors about a Catholic Bishop in Colombia. Is it the goal of the Holy Roman Church to exert influence over the political matters of sovereign states?"

Instead of seeming insulted, he merely asked, "And what has attracted your attention towards Archbishop Villaponteau Will?"

"I have heard that he is aggressively pursuing the banishment of all other Christian influences within his realm of authority," he said as Dom reached out to his arm in protest.

Acosta narrowed his gaze at Will and asked, "And why would this pursuit, if it were possible, concern you Will? Do you have an interest in matters ecclesiastical?"

He shook his head and answered, "No sir, it's just that my brother Colton is a Lutheran missionary in Central America, and I was wondering if this pursuit could potentially affect him."

"I see. I can only say that Archbishop Villaponteau is a most energetic representative who is sincerely committed to the spread of the Christian faith. Now, are you prepared to receive this most important blessing?

Dom was anxiously shaking her head in assent when Will paused and made yet another inquiry, "I gotta ask Archbishop; I heard from other sources that this blessing of the child in the womb is not necessarily commonplace within the Catholic Church. Why do you do it? I mean, it's gotta make you seem a renegade or nonconformist. Am I way out of bounds—as my wife thinks—by inquiring Cardinal Acosta?"

He actually looked mildly shocked, but recovered enough to explain, "I consider this blessing paramount to the embodiment of positive influences within the soul of the fetus Dominique is carrying. This is a supreme consecration, and the fact that you have sought this for your child speaks highly for your love and desire for this child to grow and prosper. Now, may we continue?"

Will blushed and all but pleaded, "Of course, Your Grace."

Dom and Will knelt down in front of Archbishop Acosta, bowed as he laid a hand on each of their heads and spoke directly from the Spirit of the Lord:

> "God, Author of Life, bless we pray, this unborn child,
> give constant protection and grant a healthy birth that is
> the sign of our rebirth one day into the eternal rejoicing
> of heaven.
>
> Lord, who have brought to this woman the wondrous
> joy of motherhood, grant her comfort in all anxiety and
> make her determined to lead her child along the ways
> of salvation."

He then paused, and after a moment continued:

> "Lord of ages, who have singled out this man to know
> grace and pride of fatherhood, grant him courage in his
> new responsibility, and make him an example of
> justice and truth for this child."

When Will looked up, Guillermo Acosta was beaming and holding his arms open as Dom and he rose to embrace him. After a moment he told them, "It is God's grace that we have met, Dominique and Will. I can only wish you the best in the coming months." He then looked at Will suspiciously and said, "I will look into this matter concerning Mrs. Rayfield. I believe that she deserves the same consideration as you in bringing her child into this world without undue conflict. Thank you for coming to see me today."

Dom and Will were all but too shocked to respond, but she managed to eke out, "No, thank you for seeing us Archbishop Acosta, all three of us."

———

"Was it just me, or were we in the presence of God back there," Will asked as they were driving away from the Cathedral, still tingling from the experience of the audience with Acosta.

Dom reached out to hold his hand and told him, "No Will, it wasn't just you. That was one of the most magical moments of my entire life. I cannot believe what just happened to us."

Will shook his head slightly to clear the cobwebs and told her, "I don't believe, other than at our wedding, that I have ever experienced anything like that." Then coming to his senses added, "Other than, perhaps, the night you told me 'This is the first and last time you are ever fucking me Will.' That was nearly transcendental."

"How can you remember such things Will Kavanagh?"

"Because Dominique Lefebvre, that was the last innocent question you ever asked me. After that I was completely drawn into your being. I didn't know it at that moment, but I was totally immersed in your vortex after you uttered those words. God am I one lucky motherfucker or what?"

"That wasn't a question Will," she admonished.

"'After tonight, we'll be making love, do you understand the difference?' I believe that was the question you posed Ms. Lefebvre, and yes I knew the difference then and I certainly understand it now. I cannot believe that I was so fortunate that you chose me to be the one."

"Actually, you chose me Will. How else could I have been willing to turn my back on my marriage and my life if I hadn't made a conscious decision to trade my life to be with you?"

"I chose to be with you? I thought all I said was 'Orange juice?' How can you translate that mere statement into the proposition that I chose you? Was I that wanting? Was I that desperate to change my life?" As the words left his mouth, he knew that she was right, that he was so ready to change his life that when he saw her in front of him, he was nothing but a fish about to bite a worm. "Okay, you're right, I was so wanting that I was perhaps vulnerable, but you were the unattainable sophisticated exotic woman. There was no way I could ever have interested you."

"And what were you wanting of Will?" She asked, the therapist once again assuming her role.

"A trusting relationship with another human, a bond I could have no fear of remorse over, ever again. But I was such an egotistical bastard that I needed that person to be someone that I—no, that everybody else—looked at and lusted after as well. I needed a woman, a person who I could be proud of, who I could wear on my arm like a million dollar bracelet. I needed someone who could make me whole again. No, I needed someone to make me whole for the very first time. And it couldn't be anybody but you Dom. How the hell did we ever meet?"

"Destiny Will, that's the only explanation that makes sense. I believe with all my heart that we knew each other before—in a past life—and that the moment our eyes met we were frozen into the inevitable love that has unfolded between us."

He smiled at her and offered, "Like a hell-bound train?"

She leaned over to kiss him and said, "We've avoided that conductor once my love; let's not tempt fate, shall we?"

He looked at her with newfound admiration and surmised, "I think I flew straight into your soul when we climaxed together that first time, but it was so alien to me that I was terrified. I believe that you have taught me to embrace rather than fear such a union."

"You have learned well Will. Every day is a thrill ride for us now."

"I'm the luckiest man in the world Dominique. And every day is indeed a thrill ride."

26

THE ARGENTINES SALUTE
THEIR HEROES

"So how did things go with the Archbishop?" Carmen pounced as they got out of the Mercedes at *Casa Fabiano*. Hal was pretty excited as well as they parked the family vehicle, noticing the chauffeured limousine for the airport jaunt.

"Come on, you can tell us on the way over to the airport. This one's close by, so no chopper rides today bro. We've already got your bags in the trunk, so let's scoot," Hal said, ushering Will and Dom into the limo.

Will was all smiles as Dom launched, "It was magical Carmen. He is a very interesting and sincere person. Will and I both felt moved by the presence of the Lord as he bestowed the blessing. He is very concerned about the welfare of children. I suppose I should not have been surprised by that, but I had some doubt considering that Catholic clergymen do not marry."

Will gave Carmen's knee a squeeze as he told her, "And thank you for the heads up on the alms deal. When he asked if there was anything he could do for us, it reminded me that I had that envelope in my pocket."

She looked at Will suspiciously and inquired, "So what did you say when he asked if he could intone some favor? I only hope that you did not get too relaxed around His Excellency."

He looked at her, figured they'd let destiny play out regards his request concerning Carmen's situation and replied, "Are you kidding me? You guys had put the fear of the Lord in me regarding playful banter with the head bubba. I totally watched my language Carmen Belen." Will looked out the limo and pointed to the mud-colored water along the shoreline and asked,

"So what's this body of water to our right? Some bay off the Atlantic Ocean?"

Carmen looked over at the ugly lake, "No, that is the *Rio de la Plata*. It is formed by the confluence of the Parana and Uruguay Rivers just above Buenos Aires, and it always looks muddy like that."

Beating back his innermost fantasy of catapulting her into infinite orgasm he replied, "Parana River? I remember that there are some very deadly fish called piranha. Where does the river flow in from?"

She looked at him whimsically, no doubt surprised at his interest in the geography and explained, "Its source is in the Brazilian interior, and you are correct that the deadly carnivorous species piranha is native to its upper reaches."

He had to hide the smirk as he considered how much she had in common with the species, "So they stay upriver? No danger being eaten alive down here I hope?"

She merely smirked, "Not from fish I wouldn't think; besides, if we want to go into the water we can fly over to *Punta del Este* in Uruguay on the Atlantic Ocean. It's one of the most beautiful beaches in South America."

"Uruguay," he asked, "how far is that from here?"

"The capital Montevideo is about one hundred sixty kilometers from Buenos Aires. Now tell me more about this encounter with the Archbishop William..."

"Hey, we're here, come on, we can continue this conversation inside," Hal said as the limo driver had a skycap instantly on their baggage.

When they met up with the rest of their traveling troupe at the *Aerolíneas Argentinas* departure gate at Jorge Newbery Airport, Carmen was not to be put off any longer. "So William, I am curious, how did you manage to control yourself around Cardinal Acosta?"

"Carmen, you warned me and I watched my language as closely as possible, but the Archbishop is a pretty impressive guy. I really respect him and he was super friendly. I was a modicum of good Cajun behavior."

Now Hal guffawed, "A modicum of Cajun behavior?"

Dom couldn't restrain herself and reported, "'Jesus Christ Archbishop, oh shit, I don't know if you' might to some seem a bit relaxed in conversing with a Cardinal William. But I was almost stunned that he didn't even seem to notice." She then looked at Carmen and asked, "You don't think they—I mean the religious hierarchy—converse in such ways in private, do you?"

"Jesus Willy, you actually said 'oh shit' in front of the Cardinal? My God boy, what in the hell did you think you were doing? And what could you possibly have been talking about to slip up like that?"

Will stared at Hal dead seriously, "It might interest you to know Harold that His Grace knew about the takedown of Sandrigan el-Boukhari; and when my brain tripped over this revelation those two words slipped right out. Now I know it might have been inappropriate, but shit happens bro."

Now Carmen became alarmed and urgently inquired, "How in the world did Archbishop Acosta know about Sandrigan el-Boukhari?"

"He told us his step-brother, Jorge Videla, told him about it. What's more interesting is that he all but blessed me for shooting the bastard and even said the world would be better off with a thousand more like me. I was superimpressed with his grasp of love versus hate. He's a squared away dude," Will observed.

Carmen was looking at him strangely, no doubt assimilating this information when she continued, "So what was the blessing like?"

Dom took over and told her, "It was almost as moving as our marriage vows."

"So what does a Cardinal wear when he's in his office Willy? Did he have one of those strange looking hats, you know like the Ku Klux Klan wear back home at their rallies?"

"Nah, he had on a charcoal business suit with a reddish-purple shirt and one of those white dog collar type things priests wear. But he had an impressive looking cross hanging on his chest with an expensive looking chain. All told, I was kinda surprised that he looked as normal as he did. But there's nothing normal about that guy's view of spirituality, I can assure you of that."

"So you tried to treat the Cardinal like he was a homeboy? Jesus Willy, talk about making a claim for Louisiana being the home of the redneck!"

Will was about to shoot him the bird when Dom interceded, "Actually Hal, Will kissed the Archbishop's ring after he granted him absolution for killing Sandrigan. I was very moved by his piety and reverence around His Grace. I do not believe he embarrassed anyone today, even for being an expatriate Coonass Cajun. I was proud of my husband."

Now Will did shoot Harold the bird, but instantly regretted it when Rosita snuck up behind him, "I certainly hope you didn't demonstrate that hand signal to my godfather today."

Will blushed slightly as he told her, "No Rosita, I reserve such signals for my closest associates. But there is one thing I am curious about, and since you're a fish-eater you might know. I have always been hung up on wiring diagrams; you know organization charts. So how is this Catholic worldwide organization structured? It seems like there's a lot of people called Archbishops. Is there a pecking order, I mean, are all Archbishops created equal? And what the hell is a Cardinal? I thought Archbishops were the head honcho for like a country or a region. Can you help me out here?"

She looked at him strangely, "Fish-eater?"

He instantly regretted distracting her with the colloquialism, "Yeah, in America Catholics eat fish on Fridays, and so fish-eaters is American slang—but apparently only for non-Catholics. So how about this organization thing, I didn't even think to ask Archbishop Acosta about it."

She smirked at him and explained, "Actually, I try and avoid red meat on Friday's as well." She then paused to collect her thoughts and continued, "I studied for a year in the United States, so I will try and relate the Holy Roman Church in political terms for you. Archbishops oversee a geographic area and are directly responsible for ministering to their followers, sort of like the governors of the individual states."

"So there's more than one Archbishop in Argentina? I thought Acosta was the big dog?"

"Actually there are three Will, but the population supported within an Archdiocese does carry some weight regarding political influence within the College of Cardinals. So the Archbishops minister to their followers, somewhat like a governor administers a state. Now unlike your American political system, each of the Archbishops also has a secondary responsibility as a member of the College of Cardinals. This would for you mean that each governor was also a senator. Within the Holy Roman Church, the College of Cardinals elects the next Pope when one dies or steps down. The Pope must be selected from within the serving Cardinals below the age of eighty. Does that help?"

"Actually, it makes electing the next Pope a lot simpler. No having to wait for the tally from five hundred million Catholics' votes certainly facilitates the election. By the way, I really liked your godfather; he's a neat guy."

Now she looked at him suspiciously, "I've never heard anyone refer to him as a neat guy before. Did everything go as planned during your meeting?"

"You bet Rosita, just ask him if he remembers us the next time you talk to him. It got pretty intense there for a while," he was telling her with a smirk as their flight to Bariloche was called. "I'll let Dom tell you about it on the flight down to Rio Negro Province *mi querida Ministria*."

"So why is the Deputy Minister of Defense requesting me, no he issued it in the form of an instruction, to deliver Mr. and Mrs. Rayfield and Mr. and Mrs. Kavanagh to his office the moment we get into Buenos Aires?" Rosita demanded of Will as they awaited the *Aerolíneas Argentinas* return flight to the capital.

It had been quite a productive two days on the ground in Bariloche, as Pierson and Carmen worked feverishly with Kelly to identify production needs, including construction requirements and blast zones at the two primary filming sites. If they could get some cooperation from a passing weather system to roil up Haupi Lake, Dom was confident that Great West could even shoot the boat scene of the landing in the port of Algiers in Bariloche as well.

"Rosita, I have no idea. What could be so pressing that we 'must' be there for this meeting?"

"I don't know, but *Aerolíneas Argentinas* has indicated that the flight into Jorge Newbery will be boarded with no delay. Whatever it is must be awfully important," she related.

Carmen pulled at Will's shirt cuff to whisk him aside, "I don't have a good feeling about this Will. Did you upset the Archbishop somehow?"

"Uh, could I have a word with you and Harold in private William?" Kelly asked from behind them as Will looked at Hal and grimaced.

They each grabbed her by an elbow and escorted her to a nearby alcove. "Why is my paranoia meter pegged out Kelly?"

"Oh, I didn't want to get into all this but in light of the sudden invitation you two need to know everything…" She paused to wait for their irritation to surface but they merely looked at her as Hal opened his hand and twirled his index finger. "Uh, oh dammit, why am I so damn…shit…anyway, Danny Rojas wanted me to be his full-service escort when we got to LA…"

"Right, you told us about that; what part's missing from your original version?" Will asked, his arms folded across his chest as he snuck a glance at Carmen who did not look pleased.

She shook her head in embarrassment or revulsion before answering, "Okay dammit, Danny wanted to sleep with me pretty badly and made an impassioned overture, including the fact that Great West was benefiting so much from Argentine hospitality AND the fact that I was not married or attached. I told him I didn't sleep with married men because I didn't have to, and that seemed to set his Latin temper off. He accused me of being in love with you and could not understand how Dom was blind to it. He even had the nerve to tell me his relationship with Rosita had suffered considerably since your arrival in Buenos. Now she seems to have shifted her focus to Dan, which can't help the jealousy monster that's stirring in Rojas' mind. I'm so sorry I didn't have the balls to tell you before."

"Fuck it," Will said as he looked at Hal. "You told us now, so we've still got a chance to react. Whatdya think Kemosabe, could we be looking at an ambush between the airport and The Libertador?"

"We gotta move fast; can't take that chance," he said as he pulled Kelly along until they were with the group again. Everyone was looking at them fearfully when Hal exhaled loudly and began, "Okay Rosita, it's time that we all stop hiding secrets. Kelly just told us Danny Rojas has fingered Willy here as his romantic obstacle between his desires to have Kelly AND whatever the two of you have going on." Her temper was about to get the best of her when Hal glanced at Carmen and nodded. Carmen stepped behind Rosita and whispered something as Rosita nodded in response.

"It is true; why are you now making a spectacle of it?"

"Because we've got to take a motorcade over to Libertador from Newberry, *sí*? Could Rojas possibly pull off an ambush without his military bosses knowing? Think very hard before answering that question Rosita, because if the answer is no, the ambush could be part of a coup to remove Videla. Call me a wild paranoid idiot, but we're all still alive because of it."

She glanced at Will, then at Kelly and finally at Carmen. She launched into the most incoherent dialogue in the history of the Spanish language as the two women were no doubt sharing every instinct they'd ever developed in the spy trade. She looked up as she began to walk, "I must make one emergency call and then we will know the truth."

Will moved into Carmen's face, "I take it she's calling *la Secretaria de Inteligencia de Estado*?"

Hal saw where this was going, his face reddening, "Honey, why don't you make a call to Arturo Fox at Capital Air Services and see if the *Gaucha* is available for a short hop to Edificio Libertador? I take it there's a helo pad at

Libertador?"

She nodded and took off towards a pair of pay phones. Will's lizard brain was flashing red warning signals, "Okay, we'll have to—the Posse and Rosita—exit the jetway at the ground crew access stairs and catch a lift over to the FBO. Rojas probably has some schmuck greeting us at the arrival gate, but fuck him; once we're vanished his plans go up in smoke. Danny Rojas just made the shit list in my book brother; can't let missing out on a hot woman change your allegiances."

Hal was shaking his head as Kelly and Dom were looking on with dread. "Kelly giving him the stiff arm didn't change his allegiance Tonto, it just stiffened his resolve. There's more in play here than meets the eye bro."

Will opened his mouth to allow the word to exit, "Lindstrum?"

"Who else?" Hal replied as Carmen came walking back up to them.

"Okay, Arturo will be waiting for us at the jetway stairs with a Plata Aviation minibus. He will call in the helicopter's flight plan while he does the preflight. We are indeed fortunate that he is so connected into the Presidential Protective Service," she said as Hal seemed to shrink with relief.

"Hey, didn't you say Danny lost out in Fabiano's pitch to get that Bell 212? Maybe he's making a list of things to hate me for, *n'est pas?*" Will offered as Hal rolled his eyes and shook his head yes. "Damn, could he order us over to Libertador to kill us?"

Carmen was about to answer him when Rosita came running up to them, more stunned than out of breath. "Rojas has formed a *culto* of former 601 Battalion 'augmentees' who helped run the interrogation facility at *Escuela de Mecánica de la Armada*..."

"The what?" Hal asked, saving Will the effort.

"She's talking about military soldiers and sailors that were temporarily assigned to the 601 Battalion's interrogation and torture facility at the Navy Mechanics School. After the worst of the 'arrests' were made and resolved, the augmentees were sent back to their units, apparently unhappy at the loss of stature and importance," Carmen quickly explained. "That's also where most of the donors to the baby adoption program were incarcerated."

"So Rojas has his own little army, is that what you found Rosita?" Will asked, hoping he'd guessed right.

"Yes, very much so; in fact our motorcade from Jorge Newbery was to pass right in front of the Navy Mechanics School..."

Will was eyeing her now with a hint of a smirk, "Why do I think that the phone call you just made will result in the disbanding of this *culto* that Danny Boy has formed up?"

"Because you are both a beguiling and shrewdly paranoid man *Guillermo*; but what an incredibly unique combination." Will glanced at Dom before Rosita regained her focus, "Deputy Minister Rojas was acting on orders of the Minister of Defense when he beckoned us, so I believe we are safe once we reach Libertador."

Will was shaking his head in approval as he leaned into Rosita, "Damn woman, you've got moxy too; I like you more the longer I know you *Señorita*."

"Alright, I think we've got the survival plan, so let's get on the bird and see what awaits us at Libertador," Hal said as he herded the throng toward the departure gate at the Bariloche Airport.

When the AA flight landed at Jorge Newbery, they were met by Arturo Fox in the jetway and escorted down a stairway to the Plata Aviation minibus. Will looked at Kelly and Pierson as he started down the steps, "We'll see you back at the house after we discover what surprise Danny Rojas has in store for us."

On the short drive down the parking apron to Plata Aviation Arturo glanced at Carmen sitting beside him in the front passenger seat. "What have you done to gain Daniel Rojas' ire Belen?"

She smiled as she touched his arm, "At least part of it was losing the *Gaucha* to Fabiano SA Arturo. What else have you learned since we spoke on the phone?"

He snickered as he shook his head, "It would seem that Daniel Rojas has indeed maneuvered himself into the indispensable delivery boy, yes?" Carmen rolled her eyes towards the back seat and Arturo nodded. "It would seem that *Señor* Rojas' wings have been clipped considerably, but his association with the arms dealers will assure his survival, albeit on a very short leash."

"*Muy beuno* Arturo," Carmen said with a sultry chuckle.

"This is the Libertador Building; it is the headquarters of the Ministry of Defense and the military staffs. It is quite an impressive edifice, yes?" Rosita asked as Arturo skillfully hovered the Bell 212 over the landing pad and slowly descended.

Will almost subconsciously corrected her, "*N'est pas*."

She seemed insulted by his tone of voice, "What do you mean?"

He leaned towards her, "The French add the parenthetical expression '*n'est pas*' to the end of almost any sentence that poses a simple question. Try it on for size."

A clever smile grew on her face as she nodded at him, "*Le Edificio Libertador* is quite impressive, *n'est pas?*"

He held his open palm in front of her as she looked at it, then the light came on in her eyes as she slapped his hand none too gently. "I believe I like this expression."

"Got a bit of panache, *n'est pas?*"

They were met at the helicopter landing pad by an Argentine Army officer, but their rank insignias were so foreign Will had no idea what his grade was. Rosita solved the puzzle when she introduced them, "Good afternoon, General Pastador. It is my pleasure to introduce you to Carmen and Harold Rayfield." After the General greeted them warmly, Rosita turned and said, "Dominique and Will Kavanagh, I'd like you to meet General Pastador, the Chief of the General Staff of the Armed Forces of Argentina."

He surprised all of them when he held his arm out to lead them across the short path to the imposing entrance. "I understand you two gentlemen are former members of the United States Armed Forces. It is very gratifying to have fellow warriors associated with such celebrations."

Hal and Will looked at each other and asked, "Celebrations?"

Pastador merely smiled, pushed the button for the elevator and said, "It is a surprise that I believe you will enjoy." *Damn, if they're sending the General Staff Chief out to play butler this must be some to do.*

The General ushered them into an opulently appointed office suite on the top floor. Entering the Defense Minister's office, they all stopped in stunned silence to see President Jorge Videla walking towards them, his hand extended. "Welcome to Edificio Libertador. I am so happy that you could join us here for this special occasion."

The confusion on their faces was very apparent, so he explained, "The time is well past due for two richly deserved awards of recognition. Would you please follow me for the conferring of our nation's humble appreciation?"

Videla ushered them over to a spot in front of three flags, the one in the center recognizable as the national banner of the republic. As they made their way over, Will noticed Danny Rojas standing to one side in front of a small podium, smiled and winked, "Hey Danny, uh *excusez-moi*, how are you today Deputy Minister Rojas?"

He smiled but didn't reply as President Videla cleared his voice to begin the ceremony. He picked up what looked like a heavy cloth necklace from an elegant dark wood table and began, "Carmen Belen Fabiano Rayfield, it is my pleasure on behalf of a grateful nation to bestow upon you the Argentine Nation to the Heroic Valour in Combat Medal." He then held up the necklace, which was a light blue heavy cloth collar with a white border and there was a medal with what looked like a German WWI star hanging as a pendant. As he put it around Carmen's neck and secured it he said, "Deputy Minister Rojas, will you please read the commendation that accompanies this highest military award in the Republic of Argentina?"

They were all standing there with gaping mouths as Danny read the citation in Spanish, which Hal and Will assumed was done intentionally to obscure the specific nature of Carmen's clandestine accomplishments. They watched with interest as a tear crept down the side of her face, but Hal had to give her props as she wasn't embarrassed in the slightest at the show of emotion. As Danny finished the citation, she smiled at Videla as he shook her hand and concluded, "Thank you for all you have done for our nation Carmen. Your contributions will always be remembered heroically by those still in the service of their country."

At this, Carmen curtsied slightly and said, "Thank you Mr. President."

He smiled at her like a proud father, then leaned down to pick up the other necklace and stood directly in front of Will, "Xavier William Kavanagh, it is my pleasure on behalf of a grateful nation to bestow upon you the Argentine Order of May. This Order recognizes your support of our most sacred interests." He then held up the necklace, which was a bright red cloth collar with a white border, with a superimposed starburst pendant with a circular shield in the middle commemorating a presumed national hero.

Will lowered his head slightly as Videla secured the collar around his neck. Deputy Defense Minister Rojas read the accompanying citation, "Xavier William Kavanagh, for valor in connection with heroic ground operations in direct support of the compelling interests of the Republic of Argentina, it is my distinct honor as the President of the Republic of Argentina to confer upon you the Order of May. A grateful nation hereby commemorates your unselfish actions taken at great risk to safety and your very life."

Now it was Will's turn to cry, as the tears leaked down both sides of his face. Jorge Videla smiled and shook his hand vigorously. "Thank you William, may every Argentine see, but perhaps not know, that you are our ally in the war against evil."

Forsaking all protocol conventions, Will reached out and enveloped President Videla in a bear hug. Jorge Videla was clearly joyful as he said in a hushed tone, "It would seem you have made friends in high places Will. Guillermo Acosta sends his regards."

Will let go of him, wiped the tears from his face and looked him in the eye, "So it was Archbishop Acosta that...."

Videla put his finger to his lips to silence the Order of May awardee, "Guillermo was quite impressed with both you and Dominique Will. I understand he gave you absolution for your sins. The Order of May is our way of further absolving you of any misgivings you may have regards ridding the universe of that madman."

Will had to ask, "And the Medal of Valor for Carmen?"

The President glanced at her, leaned in closer and whispered, "She should never have to worry about whether her debt to her country has been paid in full. Guillermo sends along his best wishes for both children."

Will shook his head in complete overwhelming amazement, "If I had a bottle of Grand Marnier with me Jorge, we'd have a shot and celebrate this appropriately."

He only smiled as he held out his arm and intoned, "And now, if you would be so kind as to accompany me to the *Círculo Militar*, we shall do just that!"

Will turned back to tell everyone else the plan, but found himself in Carmen's face as she wrapped her arms around his neck. "I suppose things worked out for everyone, *n'est pas?*" He said but was quickly silenced as she kissed his lips.

Will kissed her back smiling for a living now, "Better than we could have hoped, that's for sure. Jorge wants us to go celebrate with him at the *Círculo Militar*, which I suppose is a fancy Officers' Club."

She pointed to her swelling belly and said, "Perhaps just a taste."

As Dom and Will walked out arm in arm, the tears were once again flowing as she told him, "What a day Will, can you even believe it?"

He kissed her none too chastely before replying, "Not in my wildest dreams could I have imagined this. But I can tell you that Guillermo Acosta will always be on our Christmas card list!"

When he came up for air someone had their hand on his arm. He looked around to find Rosita Cabrera's face a rush of excitement. "I cannot believe this Will; how did you manage to pull off this miracle?"

He assumed a professorial stance, his hands clasped behind his back, "And what would make you describe this as a miracle *Señorita?*"

She just bunched her fist at him before launching into an embrace, her nose on his earlobe, "I should inflict injury upon you for withholding the truth from me." She then had the temerity to lick his neck, of which Dom was no doubt taking note.

"Do what," he posed in faux anger, "weren't you the one who was haranguing me about not behaving properly in front of your godfather?"

"You fool many with that diabolical mind *Señor* Kavanagh," she said before glancing at Dom and adding, "*n'est pas?*"

Dom was playing it demurely, replying simply, "*Mais oui.*"

Carmen obviously overheard the exchange, turning slightly to glance at Will before telling Rosita, "No Rosita, *no diabólica; que es su cerebro de lagarto.*"

Rosita flashed back at Will as Rojas was calling them onto the elevator, "So, it is this lizard brain that has deceived me, *n'est pas?*"

"*Sí,*" Will replied as he popped her discreetly on the butt.

———

The surprises didn't stop as they made their way to the *Circulo Militar*, riding with President Videla in his Presidential Limousine the few short blocks back towards the airport. Will noted with interest that Danny Rojas didn't rate the Presidential limo, but was in the lead car in the convoy. As they passed a large citadel, Videla pointed it out, "That is the Navy Mechanics School; perhaps you have heard of it recently?"

Will glanced ever so discreetly at Carmen before replying, "Yes sir, as a matter of fact we flew to the Libertador to avoid passing it on the way in."

Videla looked at Will with what seemed like admiration, "How did you detect the betrayal?"

Will now looked around and smiled, "Jorge, look at the people in this limousine; together we were able to detect Rojas' plan and avoid it. We did not make it to Buenos Aires by mistake or chance, *mi buen amigo.*"

"Indeed; I am seeing the evidence more clearly every day. I want to apologize for seemingly luring you into this trap, but I can assure you that Deputy Minister Rojas' duties will be limited to his field of expertise in the future." He looked directly at Carmen and added, "Neither Rojas nor anyone from my government will come seeking your participation in any clandestine or other military activities *mi heroina* Belen."

"Thank you so very much Mr. President," the words immediately followed but it was Hal speaking them.

"Indeed, your child should have every opportunity to grow up happy and loved, as I did."

———

The *Circulo Militar* was at least the most opulent Officers' Club Will had ever seen, as it seemed to be three huge stone buildings linked together, with an awesome iron gate they passed through before entering the vast hall. When they entered the small but beautiful meeting room all four of them were stunned to see Kelly, Dan Pierson, Roberto Fabiano, Jonathan Calvatori, Archbishop Acosta and most surprisingly Henrietta Diaz, the *Casa Fabiano* maid. "What's this?" Kelly asked as she fingered the collar hanging around Will's neck.

"Something called the Order of May; Jorge just presented it to me at the Libertador Building. I will not apparently be prosecuted in Argentina for the events depicted in *It's Raining In Marrakech*."

She tried mightily not to overdo the smoldering kiss that was destined to follow, failing miserably until he discreetly leaned back to tell her, "And I believe the collar you see dangling from Carmen's neck means she is officially retired from her military responsibilities to the Republic of Argentina."

Remembering his deal with Jorge regards Marnier, Will nabbed a waiter in a stunning white uniform and asked, "Can we get some Grand Marnier, *por favor?*"

Instead of replying he nodded over Will's shoulder at President Jorge Videla holding two snifters, smiling, "I believe this is what you were looking for Will."

Will held up one finger for him to wait, looked around until he found Carmen and told her, "We've got one more part of the ceremony to complete Mrs. Rayfield; come, walk with me."

Jorge looked momentarily confused when Will brought Carmen to where he was standing. Will smiled at him, took the snifter Videla proffered and handed it to Carmen. "And now Mrs. Rayfield, I believe it is our earthbound duty to offer you a 'sip' of Grand Marnier. It is my uncommon pleasure to salute the newly retired former clandestine operative and most feared assassin of SIDE and the *601 Batallón de Inteligencia*. I'd sure hate to be on the other side of the war from you Belen!"

Jorge saluted her and intoned "Here, here!" Carmen took her one sip of Marnier, and then closed her eyes to savor the bouquet. When she looked up again she was smiling, but instead of handing it to Will she placed the rim of the snifter on his lips, "And now Mr. Kavanagh, I believe it is our earthbound duty to salute the reluctant crusader whom I will always know as the truest of friends. Here, here!"

He instantly remembered the craven dream where the two of them had made perfect harmony. She must have detected his lust-driven thoughts as she aggressively tried to force him to drink the entire snifter, as he tried but failed to keep from dribbling Marnier down his chin. He wiped his face with his sleeve as he looked at Jorge and told him, "What a day Mr. President; I am truly overwhelmed."

"Good, I'm sure you remember Archbishop Acosta?" He said as they turned to see Acosta walk to them.

Will shook the Archbishop's hand warmly and smiled, "Would it be out of line for you to join us in a taste of cognac Your Excellency?"

"Not at all Will, but just one," he said as Will eyeballed the waiter giving him the high sign for another snifter of Marnier. "Are you pleased with the outcome of today's ceremony?"

Will looked at him deadly serious, touching the Cardinal's shoulder for emphasis, "To tell you the truth Cardinal Acosta, the Order of May was never sought nor even expected in my wildest dreams. But I can assure you that I will be forever in your debt for your involvement in getting Carmen Belen Fabiano released from her seemingly interminable link to the counterintelligence world. She is almost as another sister to me, and I fear that she would have separated herself from her home, her nation of birth if that's what it took to allow her child to have a chance to enjoy a normal life. So thank you from the bottom of my heart sir."

"You have both earned it. By the way, I have discreetly inquired about Archbishop Villaponteau and can tell you that he is aggressively pursuing a program to reach out to the needy in the northern part of this continent and his activities are promoting much good. If I may ask, how did you come upon word that his mission in Colombia was a potential threat to other Christian efforts in the region?"

Will glanced momentarily at Pierson, who was at that moment being dominated by a very engaging Rosita Cabrera, and his eyes locked on Will's as he turned back to Acosta to reply. "If you would forgive my overly protective manner Your Grace, I overheard—no I eavesdropped onto—a conversation concerning the influence of the drug cartels in Colombia, and the apparent competition for influence between the cartels, the government and the church in that area. With my brother working as a missionary in Nicaragua, I made the association without considering the likelihood of its veracity. I apologize if I have disparaged the image of the Church sir."

He finished off his Marnier in a slug and nodded, "No apologies are necessary Will. If you ever have any misgivings about any matters relating to the Church, I would appreciate it if you would contact me directly so that I can give you my studied insight. I may have access to information that you find surprising. Here is my card with my personal number. Please do not hesitate to contact me if you feel the need."

Will took the business card and was impressed with the raised letter printing. He looked up to ask, "You are a very busy man Cardinal Acosta; why are you being so kind to me? I am the one beholden to you for bestowing a blessing upon my unborn child."

He touched Will's shoulder as he moved to depart the celebration, "Do not forget that I absolved you for ridding this world of Sandrigan el-Boukhari. Maria Lacoste Videla was my niece as well as Jorge's. You will always have a friend in me William Kavanagh; please do not forget this."

Will knew he was exceeding every hint of social graces when he reached out and caught the Cardinal's coat sleeve. Acosta looked back at him quizzically, "Was there something else you wanted to discuss Will?"

Will leaned into him and smiled, "Your Grace, my associates and I are contemplating an import/export business dealing with alcoholic beverages. I guess what I'm asking is, does this cause undue alarm within the Archdiocese?"

"Are you asking if I want another shot of cognac, or did you not know the Order of May comes with a lifetime exemption from both personal and corporate taxes, tariffs and duties for its recipients?"

Will just stared at Acosta, his brain suddenly not working. "How many of us are there Your Grace?"

"I believe you are by far the youngest of the seven living recipients, so please be safe my friend *Guillermo* Kavanagh."

Will grabbed his hand to shake, kissed his ring once again and smiled, "You have been uncommonly kind to my friends and I Guillermo Cardinal Acosta; we shall not forget the communion of spirit with the Holy Roman Church."

"Good," he said and leaned in one last time, "and please be safe Will; I hope to hear from you again soon."

27

A CELEBRATION TO REMEMBER

IT WAS A HERO'S DREAM when they got back to *Casa Fabiano*, as everyone repaired to the downstairs game room where Pierson and Jonathan were squared away in a to-the-death game of Ping-Pong while Kelly and Rosita had taken up roles as leering Ping-Pong groupies. Will was sitting on the couch between Dom and Carmen, each with arms draped around his shoulders as Hal monitored his brandy snifter, replenishing it with Grand Marnier if the cognac level dropped noticeably. Carmen pushed her Heroic Valour medal at him and insistently inquired, "I'd give a month's stipend from Great West to know what you said to Guillermo Costa to make this happen Will Kavanagh?"

He leaned into her and kissed her for the umpteenth time, "I merely asked why your baby shouldn't have the same freedom from danger as ours Carmen. He is a sensitive guy and took it from there."

"I somehow think you are understating the facts, so I will defer to Mrs. Kavanagh to find out the truth about this mysterious turn of events," she said, slapping his thigh.

"It's as he said Carmen; Archbishop Acosta somehow overlooked William's casual nature to see that you and Hal deserve to bring this child into the world without undue pressure from your intelligence colleagues to go out on life-threatening missions."

"Well, I will always be indebted to you for bringing the two most influential men in Argentina around to this point of view. I never thought I would see this happen," she said as she once again leaned in to Will for a kiss. He realized it was all in celebration, but couldn't quite bring himself to stop replaying that dream where the two of them communicated in the purest form.

"Hey, it's a done deed. So now what is our next crusade, as you put it?"

"For now, it's waiting for this child to announce his arrival to the world. How about the Kavanagh's; what are your intermediate-term goals?'"

"You know, I hadn't really given that much thought. I suppose we can resume our plans for doing business here in Argentina now that the danger of Danny Rojas appearing in the middle of the night is no longer a constant threat."

"Here's to the future William, without that particular worry," Carmen said as she kissed he and Dom rather demonstrably.

"Oh, in all the celebration I almost forgot to tell you what Cardinal Acosta whispered in my ear as he was leaving the *Circulo Militar* today," Will said and pretended to get very interested in the ping-pong match that was eliciting strong competitive instincts from Jonathan. He expected Rambo to never give up, but the obstetrician showed a lot of heart in his desperate flails for gets and winners. His ploy had its predictable results.

Dom suddenly moved away from him as Hal snatched his brandy snifter. Carmen threw him on his back on the couch and promptly straddled him, her hands loosely around his neck. "Why don't you share the Cardinal's whispered words with your fellow directors *Señor* Kavanagh?"

Will thrust his abdomen up into hers with a wicked smile, "How about we get naked and have this discussion; Hal and Dom might give us a pass since we're the heroes and all."

Now she tightened her grip around his neck, causing his face to flush from the blood flow restriction, "How about you tell us this secret that the Archbishop passed to you instead?"

He managed to gasp, "Come on, be reasonable; is the deal negotiable?"

She tightened her grip as Hal and Dom grimaced, "Not at this time *Guillermo*; now if you want to remain conscious, I suggest you tell your closest friends about the message from His Grace."

"Alright, let me up," he said in a barely audible voice. She let up but kept her hands on his throat, "You know, I could get used to having you straddle my crotch like this…" As she tightened the grip he waved her off, "Okay, okay, *no mas*. Guillermo Acosta was leaving when I caught his sleeve and asked him if the Church had any concerns about our little import/export business involving alcoholic beverages. It was a daring overture, but bore fruit for CEI."

"Dammit Willy, I'm gonna let her flatline your ass if you don't spill the damn beans," Hal grouched, his head right above Will's.

"So Acosta leans in to me and says, 'Do you ask because you wish me to drink more cognac or did you not know that members of the Order of May—I found out there's seven of us alive—have lifetime exemptions from all Argentine personal and corporate taxes, tariffs and duties?"

"You have got to be fucking shitting me!" Instead of Hal, it was Kelly and Dan Pierson echoing from across the room.

"That's what Cardinal Acosta said, so I guess that's a good thing so far as doing business in Buenos Aires, *si*?" Will said as Carmen dropped onto him and engaged in the most shameless of romantic attacks. He noticed the erection party had started and smiled, "Do we move this to the bedroom now that I've made CEI some serious rain?"

"Sex, is that all you think about Will Kavanagh?" Carmen chided him even as she pressed her abdomen onto his growing erection.

"It is when you're lying on top of me inspiring a revolutionary erection party."

She let him up and rolled her eyes, "William, we must be circumspect in our marital vows, *n'est pas*?"

He rolled his eyes as she pulled him into a sitting position, "Well, if we can't have sex at least give me my Marnier back Rayfield."

Rosita was now sitting in his lap, smiling wickedly, "Belen told me you and President Videla were having a private chat on the ride over to the *Circulo Militar*. As I was relegated to the lead limousine enduring hateful glances from Daniel Rojas I believe we would all be interested in this chat between *muy buenos amigos, n'est pas*?"

"Wow, blending *anglais, español and francais* now, are we?"

"*Si*, now spill the beans, as Senor Rayfield insisted."

"When we were passing the Navy Mechanics School he pointed to it and was very impressed that we discovered and averted Danny Rojas' little ambush plan. Now he didn't provide all of the detail your SIDE informant did, but he did say that Deputy Minister Rojas would be focused solely on his duties from now on." Will looked at Hal, "I wonder why Videla didn't just squash Rojas' *culto* and make the threat go away?"

"Because he had SIDE surveilling the conspirators and would have had them killed had we not subverted Rojas' plans. The lizard brains in this Posse as you call it are very keenly focused on survival, and I am very much impressed."

"Good, so Danny Rojas has been removed as a serious threat to our livelihood," Will said with a smile. "Time to celebrate for sure!"

⸻

The onslaught of Marnier wrecked Will out early that night, so to say he was surprised when he went down to breakfast the next morning was clearly an understatement. He walked in to find Kelly totally engrossed with feeding waffles to Jonathan and then questioned his own sanity; he could swear that Rosita was sitting in Dan Pierson's lap kissing and flailing herself on him. It was clear that at least two of the four couples had hooked up with vigor since he'd last seen them before he lost consciousness last evening. *God, I've been hungover before, but stepping into another planet is new even for me!* "And how is everyone doing this fine morning? Better than my Grand Marnier-saturated brain is no doubt."

"Did you know that Daniel enjoys rock climbing?" Rosita asked as she swooped in yet again for a shameless French-kiss with Pierson. Will looked at Dom, but she merely shrugged so he looked over at Kelly, who now had taken up position not only in Jonathan's lap, but was straddling him face to face.

"Did I miss something during my affair with a Grand Marnier bottle last evening? I don't seem to recall Rosey and Rambo being quite such chummy friends."

"Actually it was closer to three bottles Will, but did you know that Rosita is an archery champion?" Pierson asked as he neglected to avert another erotic advance from the Tourism Minister.

"I'm gonna walk back out and when I come back the world is gonna make sense to me; see y'all soon," Will stammered as he got up and walked back to the den.

Dom caught up to him and explained, "I know this is sudden Will, but it seems that Dan and Ayako have been having some problems. He told me that she refused his proposal of marriage because he engages in such life-threatening missions and she couldn't live worrying about him anymore. It is indeed tragic, but Dan seems to have walked into a very convenient Argentinian opportunity."

"I'll say, but Kelly and Jonathan seem to have overcome whatever misgivings she had about his cultural stigmata. Damn, I get drunk one night and the world changes by breakfast?"

"Yes, and you may be hungover but you are still the recipient of the Order of May, and have the eternal backing of both the President of Argentina and the Archbishop of Buenos Aires. I am so proud of you that words cannot do me justice."

"Right, but more importantly Carmen is free of the curse. Okay, I'm better. Man do I ever need a waffle and some bacon in the worst way!"

As Will was crunching through the twelfth slice of bacon, he finally looked up and said, "So Rambo, when do you have to head out?"

"Actually, I'm thinking of heading back over to Bariloche with Rosita. We need to look at the waterfront pier side locations to get camera angles for the port landing in Algiers," he said the words but they somehow seemed alien, like someone had taken over his body. Will could not come to grips with Rambo's casual nature. He had never seen Dan Pierson so relaxed and unfocused on his heretofore eternal intrepid, sinister insistence on insuring the security of his surroundings.

Shaking free from that surreal mind fuck, he looked at Kelly and inquired, "So let me guess; the Circle of Life Enhancement Clinic has decided to shut down for two days while you and Jonathan accompany the two lovebirds out to Bariloche?"

"Hey, it's movie business, so as the Producer I must insure that all is recorded for travel preps once we get back to LA. Would you now like to assume the role of Producer Mr. Kavanagh?"

"Nope, just trying to make sure I'm available to get everyone to the airport on time for their flights. Would you mind passing me the syrup?"

"Oh don't worry about us Will; your benefactors have assured that ground and air transportation is provided for anything having to do with *It's Raining In Marrakech*. A limousine instead of taxis is what President Videla insisted at the celebration yesterday. We are prospering from your fame *Señor* Kavanagh!" Rosita said as she pulled Rambo's face into her cleavage.

"Glad I could be of service; now could you please pass the syrup?"

28

KICKED BACK AT PUNTA DEL ESTE

"You seemed a little grumpy with our guests William, are you sure you're not missing your harem? I mean you have this pregnant wife and all," Dom tested him.

"Are you kidding me? I'm happy for them; I mean we had two grumpy women all but ready to face off twenty-four hours ago and now all is well," he responded, figuring Dom was checking his recovery from the Marnier hangover.

"It does seem almost miraculous that those two couples could come together in such short order."

"Come together?" Carmen chuckled as she appeared from nowhere. "That's an interesting choice of words. I assume you are referring to the budding lovebirds." She looked at Will and said, "I believe you had more to do with it than you think distinguished member of the Order of May."

"Oh, how so?"

"Well, I overheard Jonathan telling Kelly that he enjoyed the fellatio more than anything in his life earlier this morning. And I was shocked when Rosita asked Dan if he'd learned any tricks from you while I was making coffee. If I didn't know better, I would bet that you and she had been intimate."

"Please, don't put those kinds of thoughts in Mrs. Kavanagh's head, Belen. I mean it's not like she's the only woman who's ever wanted to fuck me but my marital commitments trumped wanton lust."

"They're already there William. Do you know she told me in wondrous terms last night about dancing with you at *La Casa Rosada*? She even admitted having sex with you on the dance floor was almost as thrilling as the real thing. I cannot believe you were able to have *Sara Smile* played there. I actually became convinced that Kelly might well have prevented you from being seduced by her that evening in her Palace office," Dom snickered.

His efficient deflection was Carmen, "Well, it would seem that our concerns about our cohort being jerked back into the dark side have subsided. Perhaps we should reconsider providing training services to the Argentines once again. Did you speak with Danny Rojas after the ceremony?"

"No, he seemed a bit reserved to me," she answered.

"So it would surprise you that he handed me his business card at the reception and asked me to call him next week about readiness issues?" Hal said, surprising them as he walked in from the kitchen.

"Great, do you really want to deal with Rojas on any basis now that his little assassination plot has been exposed to the daylight?" Will wondered.

Carmen smiled at him and proposed, "Perhaps it's time for you two to experience the wonders of Punta del Este."

Will tried mightily to translate before asking, "So what's it the east point of?"

"Uruguay of course, and they have the best beaches south of Copa Cabana."

———

"So what do you think?" Carmen asked as they dropped into chaise lounges laid out on the pristine white-sand beach in front of the Playa Marriott the next afternoon.

"Wonderful, I see why this is popular. It seems so different from Buenos Aires," Dom noted as she basked in the sunshine. They were fortunate to arrive on a warm day, as the temperature was a nice 75 degrees. The complete swap of the seasons with the calendar in the Southern Hemisphere was still hard for the Cajuns to assimilate at times, but the spring and fall months were similar.

"Hey, what are those people doing?" Will asked as two bathers seemed to float above ski boats plowing across the water maybe a hundred yards offshore.

Carmen looked to where he was pointing, "They're parasailing; I have never done it, but it looks like fun."

Hal was already out of his chair as he signaled Will to follow, "We'll be right back."

"So how was it?" The women asked breathlessly as the homeboys walked back to their chaise lounges an hour later. They had reluctantly paid the exorbitant fee of twenty bucks, and the boat operator wanted it in US dollars, but the view had been spectacular.

"Great until we had to come back down; do you know how cold the Atlantic is this time of year?" Hal replied as he shivered inside of two large beach towels the hotel had provided.

"At least we can get some sun on the beach," Carmen offered.

"Yeah, I haven't been in the sun this much since I got burned by the pool a month ago in the back yard," Will said, and then remembered the incredible sensuous dream that included a simmering encore with his buddy's assassin wife Carmen.

"Put some sunscreen on Will; I remember that day, your face was peeling for a week afterward," Dom said as she reached for her beach bag.

"Yeah, and that was some unannounced visit we got from Jorge Videla that night too," he remembered. He worked his shoulder around trying to get comfortable until it dawned on him, "Damn, I keep forgetting I had surgery on that shoulder not too long ago."

"Yeah, tell me about it; when we were getting up on those skis my knee was reminding me of the same thing," Hal said with empathy. He then considered the friendships they had cemented amongst the elite and added, "Well, the Videla sunshine surprise seems to have worked out alright. Now we've got two anointed heroes in Circle Entertainment. I'd say we've got Argentina about covered."

———

They were relaxing in the living room of their suite that night when the sat phone trilled, prompting Hal to grumble, "I wonder what this is all about?" He grabbed the headset, flipped the switch and said, "What's cooking Alex? All well with ROUST?" He listened for a minute and groused, "What the hell does Marty Lindstrum want with me? I thought I'd said goodbye to that bastard." After another pause he said in resigned disgust, "Alright, I'll call him, thanks for letting me know, and you can take it to the bank that I don't mean that; over and out partner."

Carmen was shaking her head with apprehension as Will grimaced, "Not Lindstrum again? I thought we had paid that bastard off enough to keep him fat, dumb and happy for a while."

"Hey, it's Rayfield. Whatcha got?" Hal said almost grinding his molars.

"No Marty, I don't plan on being anywhere around Panama in the near future, why?"

He listened for a minute and snared, "And why would the Falklands bullshit possibly interest me Marty? I've insulated myself from that political hot potato."

"Hmm, alright, since you're being an unrepentant asshole about it, I'll see you in Panama in two days. This is coming off the top though, no free rides."

He looked at Will and got a homicidal scowl on his face, "What the fuck does Kavanagh have to do with ROUST?"

"Okay, okay, calm down. We'll be there."

After he dropped the headset, instead of speaking he got up and went directly to a bottle of Johnnie Walker Black scotch, poured himself a healthy snort and shot it straight down. When he sat back down the flush on his face spoke volumes about spiking blood pressure, but he got it under control enough to tell them about the latest net being cast. "Lindstrum wants to talk to the two of us in person, in Panama of all places. He must want to get out of DC in the worst way; otherwise it'd be all the way up to Camp Peary for us."

"What the hell does he want to talk about? And why me, I don't owe him shit. We paid his ass twenty million for the plane ride to Ksar. What's he got over us?" Will wondered.

Hal looked at him like he was a zombie and replied, "ROUST, that's what he's got over us Will. Remember, the profit center of Destination Partners? We can't count on a black op pumping a few million into the good and welfare every year, now can we? I can only presume it has something to do with the Falkland Islands, based on his letting that destination leak out in the conversation. I wonder what's got his shorts in a dither?"

"Perhaps someone at Grumman is complaining to some Senator that Argentina has opted to go with Avions Dassault Harold. I could envision many millions in lost revenue. These things could easily cause questions to be raised within political circles. I would even hazard a guess that you're the easiest person outside the Agency for him to reach out and touch within Buenos Aires at the moment. Please be careful, you know we are too tightly connected to the leadership of this country," Carmen cautioned.

"Oh shit, that's exactly what's in play. His station chief down here probably caught wind of the medals, or at least of the friendship with Videla, and relayed that back to Langley. Hell, they know nobody can sell shit to the

Argentines, and Jimmy Carter ain't exactly making friends for the Agency. Fuck, what are we gonna do to insulate ourselves from that?" Hal said, all but in a panic now.

"Too late for that bro; from where I sit our travel options are either sunny Panama or Antarctica. I suppose we're always gonna be somebody's target," Will offered reluctantly. "Better Marty Lindstrum than Sandrigan el-Boukhari, right?"

"You are too naïve Willy boy; at least we could kill Sandrigan, albeit with considerable effort. We can't take out the entire CIA. We'll just have to deal with the bastard the best we can. I guess this vacation is about to come to an unfortunate end."

"Oh come on Hal, the water was too cold to swim in anyway." He shook his head, a thought failing to materialize. Dom saw this and got behind him, rubbing his temples and giving him a shoulder massage.

"What is it Will; what were you trying to remember?"

"Thanks baby; you've done it again. I was thinking that Rojas might have been encouraged by Lindstrum—or even bankrolled—for the motorcade hit on us. Rojas probably can't figure out how he got doubled-crossed, so he had to give Lindstrum the bad news and bend over…"

"Damn Willy, that's exactly what triggered this off. Now Danny Boy's lost his lifeline into the power brokers since Videla slapped his hand and demanded he be their arms merchant gofer and nothing more. So now Marty wants an alternate pipeline into *La Casa Rosada* since his boy down here was probably plugged up to Rojas like a shadow," Hal said, giving Will a high-five.

"Well," Carmen summed up the situation, "at this point the *Isla Malvinas* is just a dream in a general's head; there are no active plans to invade, and I doubt Jorge Videla would accede to such a plan. Martin Lindstrum is trying to anticipate problems that are at best years away from being transformed into action."

"We'll put that right up on the front line of defense baby," Hal replied sarcastically and was rewarded with an orange in the stomach.

He was wiping up the juice and smiling deceitfully, "Damn, if we ever get destitute we can get you a tryout with the Atlanta Braves baby."

———

The new lovers were no doubt having the time of their lives, so they decided to extend their stay in Bariloche for another day. Hal and Will would be gone when they got back, so damage control was in order, except for Pierson, who definitely needed to know the lay of the land. Will was thinking over the possible topics Lindstrum could hit them with when Dom asked him, "Don't you think it's almost humorous that the most renowned fertility doctor in the country is suddenly unavailable to his patients because he is practicing conception techniques?"

"Hey, I'm glad he met someone to walk him out of that cave of sexual repression he resided in. And I can't think of a more attractive tour guide than Kelly Dupree. He's a lucky guy," Will mused. "Hell, if you don't believe that just ask the hundreds of swinging dicks at Great West that have hit on her for months now."

"But what of the future of that relationship Will?"

"Damn, we miraculously pull the Adonis god out of his trough of innocence and you're suddenly worried about the long-term prospects? Jesus Dom, what were ours when we were at that stage? You gotta live and let live. What will be, will be, *n'est pas?*"

"I suppose you're right, but I so want Kelly to find someone she can love and have a life with."

"Yeah, I get that, and I hope for the same thing. But I ain't gonna lose sleep over it; Kelly seems to be doing pretty well for herself. When I met her six months ago she was a stewardess making loops around the Pacific. Things are going well for her Dom."

"Until you stepped into her life and introduced her to Zig Kowalski. You certainly are a catalyst William," she said with admiration.

"So now we gotta concoct a cover story. Here's the deal; Lindstrum contacted Alex about a big project, and we agreed to meet in the middle where Marty, the ROUST guys and Hal and I could be equally inconvenienced. Are we all good?" Will asked, turning to Hal for his input.

"So it's a ROUST board meeting? That's not too bad, and the emergent nature is a big client project. Good going Tonto. I can guarantee you that Lindstrum's proposal won't be that easy to react to," Hal observed.

"Why do you think that Hal? Sometimes you seem to edge to the overly cynical," Dom observed.

He got up, kissed the top of her head and provided the truth according to Rayfield. "If it was that easy he'd never have even called me. We're the extreme problem solvers, remember?"

29

YOU CAN RUN, BUT YOU CANNOT HIDE

"So what's the fucking emergency about Marty?" Hal asked with undisguised hostility sitting across from his CIA fair weather associate in the parlor of his suite in the Panama City Hilton. The flight up had been almost tolerable after Hal spitefully booked first class seats that he would charge to the client. Traveling 'up' along longitudinal axes seemed far easier than traversing eight time zones going east to west. Even so, being jerked northward 3300 miles still entailed six and a half hours flying time.

"Funny question coming from you Rayfield," he replied over a *Cuba Libre*. "I seem to recall a frenzied call for information about a certain Sandrigan el-Boukhari some four months ago. And you didn't relent until you had sucked me for every last drop of intel I had on Algeria."

If there's such a thing as holding in place from an aging perspective, Lindstrum seemed to have reached the age where his appearance didn't change. He still wore that silver-white hair pulled back long, almost touching his shoulders as if he were a latter day Jimmy Buffet, the only difference being about thirty years and the tailored suit. He seemed to have lost some of his midriff; making Will think he probably had gastric ulcers from all the stress he subjected to both himself as well as any others unfortunate enough to deal with him. *At least the bastard's not asymptomatic like that asshole Colonel Nakajima in Hawaii; that fucker had to be the world's most infectious stress carrier. So if the ulcers are killing him he ain't gonna be on top of his game. Maybe what we need is a little blind man's bluff using Jorge today.*

"Right, and I paid you twenty million in fuzzy dreams for the privilege, so what's got your knickers in a knot now that we had to fly to Panama to learn?"

Lindstrum leaned back, took a long pull on his rum and coke and continued, "Yeah, and that code book you brought out was worth its weight in gold." He slurped out the last of his cocktail, sucking on an ice cube with that dastardly smile, "It would seem that you have planted yourself in the epicenter of a coming hurricane down in Argentina." He then pointedly looked at Will, "And I have it from a reliable source that you my friend are the latest recipient of the Argentine Order of May. You seem to be in a very interesting position Mr. Kavanagh; best buds with the Dictator as it were."

Will rolled his eyes and then looked at him like the piece of shit he was, "So you would be surprised to learn that the two events are related? Were you aware that the President's niece died of an overdose from Sandrigan's smuggled poison? Or that one of their top operatives was garroted when he went to Algeria to investigate the basis for this young woman's demise?"

His eyebrows rose as he replied, "Actually no I didn't; but knowing that isn't going to help me satisfy the inquisitive nature of the players in this mess."

"And who might they be?" Hal snorted.

"Oh I think you can figure that out Rayfield; one of them might be Jorge Videla's counterpart, as well as the heads of both legislative bodies. You my friends are smack in the center of the tempest." Will chanced a glance at Hal and blinked his left eye, already suspicious of Lindstrum's purported clients that had no names. Hal actually nodded back, thinking the closest Marty Lindstrum ever came to an elected Senator was his gofer executive assistant.

"I'm tired of playing your fucking games Marty. What the fuck do you want?" Hal shrieked, his impatience now glowing. The reference to senior U.S. government officials however, was somewhat problematic.

"I want to know when they're going to invade, and what their mobile force capabilities are. This information could be quite valuable in a certain country's positioning with, say, the United Kingdom and its Prime Minister."

"What the fuck is the CIA and DIA doing in the Land of the Pampas if you don't already know the answers to those questions Marty, tell me that?" Hal was rip snorting mad, but Will had to agree that it was the DIA's mission to know about such military capabilities.

As he fixed another cocktail, not bothering to ask his guests if they desired one, he started firing up his patented version of bad cop/bend over. "The *Porteños* have clammed up on our guys assigned down there; being away from

Washington at least buffers you from Jimmy Fucking Carter…"

Will burst out laughing, "Let's see Marty, from what little we've heard over the international news, Carter's managed to give away the canal we're sitting next to, thrown Taiwan under the bus, picked the wrong side in Iran and shut off military aid to Argentina, our most hospitable partner for Operation Condor. He sounds like a perfectly wonderful purveyor of accommodation; what's not to love?"

He sneered and rolled his eyes, "You left out Executive Order 12036, coming up on its seventeen month's anniversary. In case you hadn't heard, Carter took Ford's prohibition on political assassination one step further to no assassination by a US employee—zip, nada, nowhere, no how."

Will caught Hal trying to contain a laugh, "So what, you want us to knock off Khomeini since Jimmy says you can't?"

"And you can forget about that shit Marty; we ain't carrying out your dirty work by proxy. Find somebody who's not a citizen for that shit," Hal added.

"We're not asking you to kill anyone Rayfield," Lindstrum replied calmly, "but it would seem your Cajun associate Kavanagh has managed to make friends with the most powerful people in the Republic of Argentina."

"Listen Marty, I've already told you that taking down Sandrigan earned us respect with the Argentines. But you wasted a trip down to sunny Panama City bud, 'cause Will and I ain't playing turncoat spy on the country that has taken us in with open arms," Hal parried.

He smiled at them and delivered the *coup d'état*, "So you would be surprised that Deputy Defense Minister Rojas—that's right, your golfing buddy Danny from Libertador and Campo de Mayo—was offering you two up as bait while trying to leverage my boss in the deal to get his airplane logistics tail working again?"

Will looked at Hal, a flex of his eyebrows the only indication that Lindstrum had precipitated barely disguised shock, "And what would Deputy Minister Rojas offer up that could make us bait?"

"That you knew he was surreptitiously seeking American help in obtaining Douglas Skyhawk replacement components and spares and neglected to advise your native country because you had found life in sunny Argentina much to your liking. There's a process in place for defense security cooperation, and he was obviously attempting to subvert the rules as well as President Carter's arms embargo."

"What the fuck Marty?" Will blurted out. "Even if that were true, which it ain't, how is that against the law? Me not picking up a telephone and telling you there's a renegade Argentine military systems acquisition guru in search of jet engines is somehow against the law? I don't get it."

"What are you saying?" Hal asked, now totally tuned in.

"Oh, I think the FBI would consider treason an indictable offense, don't you?"

Their heads were reeling from the allusion to treason, which carried cataclysmic repercussions. Will reined it in enough to say, "So what do you really want us to do Marty?"

"All I want is for you to get on the inside of your good pal Danny Rojas—the hot Tourism gal Cabrera would seem the easiest angle—and signal back when the Argentines plan to invade the Falkland Islands. Do you somehow think that's traitorous on your parts? You took an oath when you were commissioned Kavanagh, and just 'cause you're out don't mean you're free to swap allegiances. I mean, he enlisted your smoking hot friend Kelly Dupree to provide cover so he could surreptitiously meet with mainline defense contractors didn't he?" Now he looked at Hal and offered the final straw, "And wasn't he insistent that your pregnant wife be thrown into the fray, totally unconcerned about the welfare of your child?"

"This is bullshit Marty," Will said without emotion, "Rojas is on your little payroll, isn't he? At least that's the scuttlebutt circulating around Buenos amongst the spooks."

He turned on Kavanagh like a cobra about to strike, "And you somehow managed to fuck that little relationship up. Cappeletti still can't figure out how you got Rayfield's wife exempted from Rojas' stable, but the bottom line is that he's become golfing buddies with Alexandr Novikov. Care to guess what Novikov's in charge of?"

"I'm gonna take a wild ass guess here Marty and say he ain't the military attaché of the Federal Republic of Germany's embassy," Will offered as Hal looked at him strangely.

Lindstrum actually bared his teeth, "Nice try, but you've managed to fuck that up too. One of our most reliable contacts in Andean Argentina went to ground after Videla and a bunch of Federales showed up snooping around Bariloche for some movie you're involved in."

"You're speaking in riddles Marty," Will shrugged, "I don't know any of these people you're referring to." He thought of something Lindstrum had said and nodded his head, "You said Cappeletti still can't figure out how the 601 Intelligence Battalion lost their assassin. Is he your station chief in Buenos?" Before Lindstrum could answer Will snapped his fingers, "Hey, when we were in Bariloche with Videla, he talked around the influx of Nazis at the end of World War II. So your contact is one of these Germans living off of stolen Jewish wealth?" Now he held up his hand and smiled, "So Colonel Novikov is the KGB Rezident in Buenos Aires and Rojas is playing tiddlywinks with him? I wonder why; we heard they bought a bunch of fighters/bombers from Dassault when we wouldn't play ball with them. It wouldn't seem they need MiGs or Bears anymore."

"So now you see why I'm leaning on you two expatriate but well connected Americans in Argentina. Cappeletti's lost his 'in' with Rojas since we stiff-armed them with the embargo, and the Deputy Defense Minister has a new friend with Alexandr. Our sometimes source Schmid has gone to ground and we're in need of information from the Southern Cone…"

"So fire Cappeletti and get somebody down there that knows how to play hardball Marty," Hal offered with a smile.

"Goddamn it Marty, Videla's focused on the damn economy and Massero—who was the supposed *Isla Malvinas* champion—was fired from the Junta. Nobody's beating that drum now Lindstrum, so why don't you just tell us the truth? Sorry, I know you're immune to it, but what you really want is a surrogate station chief since this Cappeletti can't make friends in *Porteño*-land, right?" Will laid it out so deliberately that Hal tried to hide the grimace. "Here's the fucking deal Lindstrum, you bet the limit on Rojas taking us out in that motorcade hit and all he got from it was cut off from every goddamned swinging dick in Edificio Libertador and a short leash to suck dicks getting French, Israeli or Russian arms." Will saw the near shock on Lindstrum's face and knew he had him. "Now just because you lost your Deep Throat at Libertador and your piece of shit station chief can't tango with the *Porteños* ain't my problem boudreau. That's right, we know you're swinging at outside curve balls bozo, but here's a magic piece of intel for your starving soul. The fucking Argentine Air Force hasn't ever fought a war; how the hell do you think they stand a motherfucking chance against the Brits? You're so fucking stupid or Cappeletti is that you're dreaming this Falklands shit up. Ain't nobody even whispering *Isla Malvinas* to Jorge Videla, and he'd fire 'em if they did."

"I've had enough of your shit, both of you, and I'm finished playing around with you unpatriotic asses. Now the Attorney General's Assistant Director for National Security has provided our Deputy Director for Operations with a finding of probable misconduct and criminal intent to commit treason against both of you. The reason the FBI's not here arresting you now is that I convinced them I could discuss this with you and come to an accommodation that disproved their finding. I believe the description of your options can best be termed checkmate gentlemen."

Hal's face flushed dramatically as he looked to the heavens and said, "Oh fuck! Okay Lindstrum, what if...."

"What if we tell you to go to hell and embrace sodomy as your new definition of sex?" Will interrupted.

Lindstrum actually smiled at him, "I would think that's exactly where you and your wives and your unborn child would reside once this implodes on you."

Will rubbed his chin, looked up at the ceiling and nodded his head, "Let's see Marty, it would seem the source of the AGA's findings is you, and you alone. Doesn't that seem to lack corroboration for the Justice Department to come out with guns blazing Harold?" Hal just looked at him crazily as he got up and fixed his own drink. Will looked at Lindstrum and shrugged, "So since it's your credibility that's on the line Marty, you'll probably be interested in the pictures we've got of the C-47 loaded with heroin, and your pilot standing by the loading door smiling. We've got pictures of you at the safehouse in Tangier negotiating with the four of us. And, oh yeah, we've got a tape of you agreeing to send us the C-47 in exchange for twenty million in heroin. I also took pictures of the pages of that code book I gave you, so that's in play as well. Now Marty Fucking Lindstrum, do you really want to roll the dice motherfucker?"

His face turned beet red as he scowled at Will, the hypertension peeking as he hesitated, looked up, and finally replied, "You know Kavanagh, I don't know why you keep Rayfield around. You are the most cunning bastard I think I've ever run into."

Will smiled at Hal and said, "Why do you think he makes me come to important business meetings? Here's what we will agree to do. If we learn of anything regarding Argentine intentions of invading the Falklands AND that appears to have direct implications for involvement of American forces, we will contact you immediately to let you know. Otherwise, this is a misunderstanding between two allies of the United States. We are for all practical purposes neutral in this childish disagreement. And in spite of whoever in Washington wants to try and steer this thing from the sidelines, it ain't gonna happen with our help. I've already secured the pictures and tapes in a safe deposit box in the Cayman Islands. And you can stuff that treason shit away where the sun don't shine. Hal and I are honorably discharged veterans of the United States Armed Forces. So what's it gonna be buckwheat?"

He just smiled, nodding his head in surrender, "I think I'll have another drink. Vegas wouldn't stand a chance against you guys."

———

They were able to catch a flight back to Buenos Aires an hour later, the first class tickets saving their asses as those were the only open seats on the plane. The flight crew was securing the doors as a lovely blonde stewardess asked the two solicitously, "What'll it be gentlemen; coffee, tea or a cocktail?"

Will gazed at her wantonly but recovered enough to say, "Oh make it a couple of Johnnie Walker Blacks on the rocks."

"So I gotta ask Willy, what gave him away?"

"Danny Rojas is forever indebted to the Fabianos for his life and his position. Even if he were willing to risk that, something as insignificant as knowing he wanted airplane parts ain't Security Council agenda item worthy. That was a complete bluff—since it's obvious that any country with four dozen Skyhawks needs spares—and any lawyer worth his weight in sand could beat the rap that not disclosing that knowledge constituted treason. It was a lead-pipe cinch that he was bluffing."

Hal high-fived him as the truth became crystal clear, "So you out-bluffed Marty Lindstrum? I cannot believe it!"

"When everything's on the line, what have you got to lose? Welcome to you first hot landing zone in poker table diplomacy Harold."

"Man, did I ever underestimate your ass Willy Kavanagh! We actually won!"

"And Marty Lindstrum paid for first class tickets to take it up the ass. This war ain't over by a long shot; drink up partner!"

Three stiff scotches did the trick in first class, and both of them were able to get a few hours' sleep on the way back to Ezeiza. It was dusk when they made it over to Plata Aviation at Ezeiza, but Arturo Fox was there waiting for them next to the *Gaucha*.

"Welcome back gentlemen; I was a bit startled when the Eastern Airlines courtesy desk in Panama called to advise of your early arrival. Do I take it things went well, or very bad?"

Once they cleared Ezeiza control Arturo led in with the lead punch, "Roberto has sold the *Gaucha* and Capital Air Services to his sister Carmen; I take it this was a decision made suddenly during your trip to Panama, yes?"

"What the fuck, over?" Hal knee-jerked as he turned to Will and gave him the Italian Army salute.

"So why are you telling us this instead of Belen Arturo?" Will asked, obviously in better touch with his senses than brother Rayfield.

"Because the paperwork associated with the transfer must be made promptly to insure proper documentation. Roberto had filed temporary operating permit applications for the helicopter and the corporation in order for me to fly you two to Ezeiza for the Malvinas trip."

"Okay, so why the emergency; isn't there an allowable period to operate with the temporary permits?" Hal wondered, still showing signs of high paranoia.

"There is, but the Air Regions Command of *Fuerza Aérea Argentina*, the Argentine Air Force, has operational control of all *aeroparques* and Buenos Aires—and Jorge Newbery in particular—fall under the Central Air Region. Some anonymous caller to *Casa Militar* complained that Capital Air Services was being granted special dispensation due to insider connections."

Will reached over and put a hand on Hal's arm, silently suggesting that he calm down. "Okay, so who do we have to see and what do we have to do when we get to *Aeroparque* Jorge Newbery?"

Arturo exhaled noticeably, "*Gracias a Dios* you are taking this so well Will. I must take you directly to the Deputy Commander of the Central Air Region's office for you to provide identification and sign documents."

"Let's see if I'm following Arturo; the Air Force is like both the airport owner and the federal aviation administration combined, and they operate this Air Regions Command from an office directly under the Air Force Chief of Staff at Libertador. How am I doing so far?"

"I cannot believe you understand this; most *Porteños* cannot and give up."

"Arturo, I'm not *Porteño*, and Hal and I have been through some shit before. Where's this office of the Deputy Commander?"

"That is the good news; Colonele Beneifico Cargaza is the Deputy Commander for the Central Air Region and he has an office at the east end of Jorge Newbery, right across the airfield from Plata Aviation. He has agreed to wait until we arrive."

"So you say an anonymous whistleblower called *Casa Militar* and said Capital Air Services was being unfairly favored. Why do I suspect that person may be Danny Rojas?" Will asked as Hal grimaced and shook his head.

"I would guess that you are a mystic perhaps," he said, chuckling. "Worry not my friend, for Colonele Cargaza is also the Deputy Commander of *Agrupación Aérea Presidencial*; he also commands the *Destacamento Aeronautica Militar Aeroparque*, so this does not present a large problem."

Will considered what Arturo had said and tried to make sense out of the Spanish, some of the words seemingly familiar. "Okay, let's try this in English Arturo; your buddy Beneficio is the local honcho of the President's Airlift Group, designated as a military aviation detachment at Newbery?"

"Exactly, I am amazed at your quick adaptation to *Español Guillermo*."

Hal was looking at Will shaking his head as he made the next assumptions, "Okay, in my wildest dreams, you used to have Beneficio's job and he was maybe your copilot when flying Air Force One?"

"How did you figure this out? In Argentina, we call the President's dedicated aircraft Tango 01 instead of your more famous Air Force One. The detachment is located here at Newbery because this is where Tango 01 is assigned; maintenance and other special unit aircraft are assigned to El Palomar Air Base eighteen kilometers west of Newbery."

Hal was now on board, "So what precipitated this sudden change of ownership within the Fabiano family? Did Will being awarded the Order of May have anything to do with this?"

"No, it is the only reason for making the change. In addition to charging a monthly *aeroparque* access fee, the Central Air Region also extracts an assessment per takeoff and landing of all aircraft using the airport. With an official exemption, Capital Air Services is required only to file a monthly summary of departures and arrivals, as well as passengers transported. This data is collected by the Air Region to influence possible future governmental subsidies for runway lengthening and possible terminal expansion."

"So what did Capital Air Services buy the *Gaucha* for Arturo? Have you seen the documents we must sign? They're not in Spanish, are they?" Will blasted as they neared Jorge Newbery.

"Insurance actuarial tables show the Bell 212 with an expected service life of seventeen years. The Air Force bought *Gaucha* in 1973 for three point three million US dollars. Based on the straight-line method of depreciation, Capital acquired the helicopter for eleven-seventeenths of the purchase price, or two point one four million US dollars. This is quite a windfall, because if the sale were based on flying hours, the price would have likely been much higher. The *Gaucha* is pampered and *El Presidente* flies mostly fixed wing aircraft to distant destinations."

"So I have to sign it to gain Capital the tax shelter, but you're too savvy a guy to allow that to happen Arturo. I bet either you or Jorge Videla insisted that all directors of Circle Entertainment International sign the sales and incorporation papers to mask the obvious; am I correct?" Will asked as Hall muttered something unintelligible out the window.

"*Si Señor*; I intend on flying the *Gaucha* for several more years *mi buen amigo*."

As Arturo landed the *Gaucha* outside the Capital Air Services hanger, the mechanic rolled up on a tractor they referred to as *la mula*. Arturo had dropped the retracted wheels below the skids as they approached, so they looked back to see the *Gaucha* being tugged by the mule into its comfortable quarters inside the hangar, safe from the weather or dangerous animals—like whistleblowers.

30

WHEN WORD SPREADS FAST

THE VISIT TO THE PRESIDENTIAL AIR GROUP (AAP) had been a bit like old home week for Arturo Fox, as it was immediately obvious that he and Colonele Beneficio Cargaza were indeed long time comrades in arms. "So, Arturo told me that he knew—no, that he was *un buen amigo*—of a member of the *Orden de la Sociedad de Mayo*, and even though we are longtime friends I thought he was joking me. And then this arrived from *La Casa Rosada* today, and I am completely overwhelmed with admiration. It is indeed a pleasure to meet you, a hero, William Kavanagh."

Will was quite surprised as he shook hands, "Nice to meet you too Colonel Cargaza; may I see this document that arrived from The Pink House?"

Cargaza thumbed through a small stack of papers, selected one and handed it to Will. "Please take no offense *Señor* Kavanagh, but I must see some proof of identity to process these documents the *Fabiano Sociedad Anónima* sent me to certify." As Will scanned the certificate, the only words he recognized were his name and the date. "Also *Señor* Rayfield, if I could possibly trouble you to show me some identification, as you are also a Director of this company, Circle Entertainment International, that is to become owner of record for Capital Air Services?"

As Cargaza had his secretary photocopy the passports Will looked at Hal, "I suppose this is the Certificate of Award; kinda strange when you can't read it, eh?"

Arturo chimed in with the answer, as Hal and Will wondered just how close Colonel Fox was to the Fabianos. "No Will, that is THE Testament of Bestowment of the Order of May. Since you are not a native, you cannot appreciate how rare and awe-inspiring it is to meet someone who was conferred this honor."

"Actually I asked Cardinal Acosta about it and he said I was one of only seven living members of the fraternity, er, society. Maybe I'll learn Spanish just to be able to read it," Will joked as he caught another designation that had puzzled him. "Exactly what is *Fabiano Sociedad Anónima*? I've seen Fabiano S.A. before, but never knew what the SA stood for."

"Ah, you and most *Porteños* are equally stymied by this legal designation *Señor* Kavanagh. *Sociedad Anónima* literally means anonymous society in Spanish. As used in the Argentinian business world it means a publicly owned and traded joint stock company. It is analogous to the English plc, or public limited company," Beneficio explained.

"Please, if we are to be friends Colonel Cargaza, you must call me Will, as that is my name, and *mi mejor amigo* is Hal. Are we agreed?"

Now Cargaza laughed, "Anyone who calls El Presidente 'Jorge' is due such a request Will. Please, I am Beneficio."

Will couldn't help himself, "So does your wife call you Benny? You gotta know about Elton John's song 'Benny and the Jets' *si*?"

He looked a bit shocked, "No, no one has ever called me Benny before, and I have not heard this song but am aware of Elton John."

"So Benny, it sounds like I must send you a gift then. What papers must we sign *mi buen amigo Colonele*?" Will said as Hal tried but failed to suppress a laugh.

"I told you he was somewhat unorthodox but infinitely likeable Beneficio," Arturo said as he slapped the Colonel on the back.

"Indeed; I have the Certificate of Title to Capital Air Services S.R.L., a wholly-owned subsidiary of Circle Entertainment International, LLP. As you can see, Roberto Fabiano has signed the transfer of title line, with the bill of sale a separate document. Please sign above your printed names gentlemen and this will complete the transaction." Will pointed to the S.R.L. as Beneficio nodded, "Yes, Capital Air Services is a business enterprise classified as a *Sociedad de Responsibilidad Limitada*, or a limited liability corporation where the stakes are divided evenly among the partners."

Next Beneficio pulled out an ink pad and stamped the bottom of the signature page, then signed and dated it. "Oh, so you are a Notary Public as well as the Deputy Commander of the AAP?" Will asked, curious as to how many titles Cargaza held.

"Actually we call such public officers *Escribano Publico* in Argentina, but they are roughly the same responsibilities as your Notaries in the U.S. And yes, you are correct that I hold several titles jointly, but the *Escribano Publico* responsibility is more useful in my job as Deputy Commander of the Central Air Region…"

"Ah," Will surmised as he nodded, "the part where you are the mayor of *Aeroparque* Jorge Newbery, *si*? I take it we must complete some forms associated with our use of facilities and doing business under the Plata Aviation banner?"

"Your Certificates of Airworthiness and Authorization as a Public Conveyance were greatly facilitated by your employment of *Señor* Fox and *Señor* Juan Principe. I do not know of finer or more competent leaders within the *Aeroparque* Will."

Will looked at Arturo, "The mechanic is Juan Principe? We have not had a chance to meet him yet." Will smiled furtively, "Was he perchance your senior maintenance superintendent for Tango 01?"

Arturo was shaking his head at Benny, "Yes, Juan was my indispensable Chief of Maintenance for Tango 01."

"So, was he your go-to top dog, you know, a Chief Master Sergeant? I have known several E-9s and they saved my ass as a young lieutenant," Will confessed as Benny and Arturo bent over laughing.

"Yes Will, Juan retired a few weeks after I did as a *Suboficial Mayor*, or what you call the Chief Master Sergeant, the highest enlisted rank in the FAA."

"And finally, this is the Operations and Utilization Agreement between the Central Air Region, *Aeroparque* Jorge Newbery Center, and Capital Air Services S.R.L. The Testament *La Casa Rosada* forwarded will of course exempt your company from any use or access fees, other than public conveyance liability deposits. We request that you have your *Contador Público Certificado*," he saw the lost look in Will's eyes and continued, "sorry, we request that your accountant that prepares your company's annual statements provide a report on passenger activity and business sortie activity by Arturo in *Gaucha*."

"So are we all done here?" Will asked as he glanced at Arturo. "Do we get copies of all of these documents?"

Beneficio half-smiled, "The Ministry of Justice handles incorporation matters, and that was completed prior to the purchase of Capital Air Services. All other functions are ultimately regulated by the Ministry of the Economy, and they shall mail you the formal copies of these documents upon processing them through registry. Would you care to take unofficial copies with you; I have an office copier?"

"Yeah, if you don't mind Benny, that would be most helpful. If your federal government's anything like ours in the US, you never send them jack shit without keeping a copy of proof of compliance!"

"What was that about public conveyance liability insurance Beneficio?" Hal asked as Will cursed himself for not asking. "In the U.S. we would make that payment to a private insurer; does the government assume liability for all public conveyances?"

As Cargaza handed them the copies he smiled, "You are a wise man to keep copies Will." He looked at Hal and offered, "Since you are a visitor you may not know of Argentina's infrastructure struggles Hal. Most of the country outside of Buenos Aires City is rural without significant bases for taxation. You will not find the network of interstate highways and urban rail transit here, as the provinces cannot raise revenue to construct them. All infrastructure improvements are made slowly by need from the federal government. Capital Air Services is the only commercial aviation corporation in the country besides the fixed base operators at the airports. Since the FAA Air Region Command oversees all aviation issues it also serves as the central insurer for liability purposes."

"Damn, I learn something new here every day Beneficio," Hal replied as he and Will shook their heads.

"Do not let this overly worry your parent company gentlemen," Beneficio continued, "with a single conveyance in its material state, coupled with the excellent maintenance and flying skills of Arturo, the public liability conveyance fee assigned to Capital Air Services will be the minimum rate." He saw that the conversation seemed to cast a pall over the two and smiled, "Come, I will show you Tango 01 on the way out. By the way, Roberto left the Mercedes for you in the VIP parking section of the commercial terminal."

———

As they walked across the Jorge Newbery Passenger Terminal to the parking lot, Will heard a familiar voice, "Well speak of the devil, if it's not Will Kavanagh here to greet us!"

He turned around just in time to find Kelly Dupree launching into his arms, happy as clam, "How did you two know we were coming in on this flight? You must be psychic."

"Actually Kelly," Will replied as he kissed her lightly on the lips, "we had to come over and sign some papers for Capital Air Services with the airport authorities." He then turned to shake hands with Jonathan and asked, "So what's next on the calendar for my favorite OB/GYN practitioner?"

"Kelly and I are heading over to have dinner with my sister; she wants to meet this mystery woman I have all but abandoned my medical practice over. So did you really come to sign papers with the Air Region Director?"

"Well, it did include negotiating user fees and access taxes," Will offered, interested that the 'cover' story they had concocted for their clandestine meeting with the CIA had been nicely overtaken by events. Even so, it was nine o'clock in the evening as Will glanced at his watch before saying, "Wow, you *Porteños* do eat dinner late; that's very European I believe. Someone told me the Spaniards don't eat dinner until ten most nights!"

Now Kelly was on max alert, narrowing her stare on him as she inquired, "And where did this so-called negotiation take place Mr. Kavanagh? You and Harold seem to be out past office hours."

"Um, down at the east end of the airport," he replied, then quickly looked at Rambo and asked, "we all set with the pyro package for the casbah implosion?"

"Hold on here," Kelly refused to let it go, "what office is at the east end of the airport?"

"Jesus Christ Kelly, weren't you listening when Jon mentioned the Air Regions Director? Jorge Newbery happens to be in the Central Air Region, and it's important enough to have its own mayor. Oh, and the guy is dual-hatted as the Presidential Airlift Group Deputy, and he gave us a tour of Tango 01, Argentina's equivalent to Air Force One." He watched until she gave up the interrogation and looked at Rambo, "Well, all done with planning things that go boom?"

"Oh yeah, we're done on this end with the planning phase," he replied, curiously eyeing Hal as he spoke. "You guys got transportation?"

Will grabbed Rosita for a hug and a peck on the cheek, "Sure, you guys need a lift?"

Rosita hugged him tightly for a moment, before she released her embrace to answer, "I've got to go by my office and leave the President a short report on how things are going with the Production plans. I'll see you all later this evening."

After they saw Kelly, Jonathan and Rosita off at the taxi stand, the guys headed out to the parking lot to get the Fabiano's 'spare vehicle,' normally parked in the four car garage at *Casa Fabiano*. Carmen's parents spent months at a time at *Estancia Fabiano* in Bariloche, returning to Buenos Aires during the winter months that were less severe than at altitude next to the Andes. This was the first time he'd had a shot at Pierson *sans* Rosita since the 'awards' day, so Will jumped him, "So I assume you're looking forward to shooting this movie Rambo. Man, when you hook up, you do it large; the Tourism Minister? Man, she is smart and hot!"

He smiled at Will, slapping him on the back, "Yeah, and I'm giving you the John Havlicek Award buddy. Man did you ever set me up!"

"John Havlicek Award?"

"Yeah, the sixth man who's not on the court, but whose presence is always felt by the opponent. Jesus Will, that woman had the hots for your ass so bad she was primed for me, I can tell you that!"

"'Had' is the operative word there Rambo. I see you turned her attention around remarkably."

He snickered self-consciously and reported, "I couldn't help but pick up on the fact that Kelly was leading Jonathan into the land of emancipation. Let me tell you bro, Rosita needed no such indoctrination."

Will nodded his head, glad to see Pierson relaxed and happy, "She's a good dancer too. Listen, that story I told back there about a negotiation meeting was partially bullshit."

Pierson glanced at Hal as they got in the car before replying, "Yeah, I kind of figured you guys coming into the airport at night without your wives was a sure sign of trouble. What's up?"

Hal turned in his seat and said, "Marty Lindstrum decided it was time to lean on us. It seems his station chief down here isn't competent enough to tell them when the Argentines plan to invade the Falklands."

"Let me guess; your sudden access to the highest levels of the administration seemed like a better information conduit than his organization on the ground here?"

Will looked at Dan in the rear view mirror and added, "And the son of a bitch had the gall to try and extort us with a treason gambit."

"Treason, you have got to be shitting me! What the hell did he think he had on you; illicit carnal knowledge with foreign national wives?"

"Who are both pregnant," Hal added for emphasis. "No buddy, he tried to convince us that Danny Rojas' little aircraft hunting expedition to LA was something we should have reported in the national interests."

"Am I missing something here? Argentina's not playing snatch-an-island from the US! That sounds pretty far-fetched to me."

Hal slapped Will lightly in back of the head, "Willy here agrees with you, and he damn near gave Lindstrum a heart attack when he told him to roll the fucking dice motherfucker!"

Pierson was sounding confused again when he asked, "Roll the dice? You called his bluff by convincing him Rojas' hardware acquisition program was above board?"

Now Hal was hooting with laughter as he spilled the beans, "I learned something new about Willy's imagination today Rambo. He actually convinced Lindstrom that we had him on tape selling us air support for twenty million in heroin! Can you imagine the hemorrhoid attack that fucker had? After that, Lindstrom didn't mention aircraft again. I wish I had a recording of that meeting!"

"So Lindstrum already knew about the Order of May award?"

"Yep, I think he'd have fired the station chief if he couldn't come up with that much," Hal replied. "He also told us Carmen's retirement had soured his boy Cappeletti's relationship with Rojas, who's since taken up with the KGB Rezidentura Novikov."

"I think you left out the part where we exposed his participation with Rojas in the motorcade hit Kemosabe. That fucker was completely flat-footed after we laid that one on him."

"Holy shit, so you basically told him he was neutered so far as Argentina is concerned?"

"Well, Danny Boy has been cut out of the loop and the Station Chief is totally ignored, so we were his last chance for romance. Harold here got his first intro to a hot LZ in high stakes poker, let me tell ya."

"I don't know Hal, it seems as though your presence down here is becoming apparent to the *Norteamericanos*. Now I know Will got the heat deflected off of Carmen with the *Porteños*, but damn, you solve one problem and another one appears."

Will nodded his head in agreement, "Just like that whack-a-mole booth at the county fair bro; it's hard staying on a level playing field."

After they got through debriefing the trip to Dom and Carmen, Will looked at her and winked, "How did transferring the title to Capital Air Services become a five alarm emergency? All was quiet when we left."

She rolled her eyes before responding, "Didn't Arturo tell you an anonymous caller had complained about preferential treatment?"

"Well, by transferring it to CEI, all we did was move it from one Fabiano to another. Certainly the tax thing didn't light the fire, *n'est pas?*"

She shook her head in exasperation, "William, the tax thing as you call it shifted the focus from Capital Air Services to a decorated national hero. It was quite simply one of Dominique's wisest surreptitious moves."

"Benny sorta explained what an S.R.L. was in Argentina; I think the legal expectation is 'equal shares' and 'equal stakes.' How's that all work out since you're the one who paid two point one million US for the *Gaucha?*"

"Actually William, I borrowed some capital from the family nest egg and WE will pay it back on an 'equal stakes' basis. I understand you got an education in third world infrastructure tonight? Now you know why flying to distant places is the only viable option—there are no interstates."

"Whoa, feedback from the Fox eh? I didn't know until the ride in from Ezeiza how tight Arturo Fox was linked into the Fabianos. I think it's time for a celebration drink after the pow wow in Panama." As they were pouring cognac the sat phone trilled.

Hal exhaled noticeably as he said, "Hey buddy, how's life in Carolina?"

He quickly plugged up the connection to the speaker phone as Alex replied, "Apparently quieter than it is in South America. How'd things with Marty Lindstrum work out? I know when he calls it's bad news."

"Willy here took care of Marty's untoward interest in our affairs, quite impressively I might add. So you just concerned about our state of mind, or were there more pressing matters?"

"Actually, Bob Kellor called in to find out how to get to Kavanagh. He said General Melson that Will's friends with wants to chat. Here's the number for the guy; Bob said he's in Hawaii if you still want to call tonight."

"All right, thanks partner, talk to you later," Hal said ending the call.

"How about let me take this one alone buddy, I have no idea what Keith wants," Will asked as everyone but Dom got up and left the study.

"Yes sir, Kavanagh here; how are you Keith?" Will asked as Brigadier

General Keith Melson picked up the phone.

"Jesus Will, that was fast! I just spoke with Bob Kellor not ten minutes ago. Where are you?" Will signaled Dom to pick up the handset so that she could participate in the conversation.

"We're in Buenos Aires sir, and I've got Dom on the phone with me."

"Hello Keith, it's so good to hear from you. How have you been?"

"My gosh, I didn't expect to hear your voice Dom! How have you been since the war by the shore in Africa? Bob Kellor's been on the mend, but he said Will and you were hurt as well."

"We are fine Keith; Will and Hal Rayfield had surgery once we got to Argentina, but they are well enough now to have gone parasailing at the beach this past week. Are you still in Hawaii?"

"Yes, but not for much longer, I'm sorry to say. I have been tapped to head up the USAF Judiciary, so I'll have to head back to DC after only twelve months here in the land of perfect weather. I am so relieved to hear that you both are doing well; Bob told me how dicey things were in Algiers."

"Yeah, but he missed out on the excitement in Ksar el-Boukhari; I took a bullet through the ribs at the end of that drama." Will remembered the proposition after Hal and Carmen's wedding, "Hey, did Bob mention that I tried to hogtie him into being our rep for a little import/export startup?"

"Are you kidding me? I have never seen Bob Kellor so pumped about anything like that before; it's like he just became a father for the first time again. How in the world did you get into the spirits business?"

"He didn't tell ya? We saw a chartered FedEx bird leaving Buenos empty heading back to the States and that was my inspiration. By the way, we just started an air taxi service company to shuttle pax between the Buenos tourist district and the international airport three ZIP codes away. Now that one may take years to recoup the cost of the chopper, but driving between Ezeiza and the tourist district could render many wealthy Americans pre-suicidal." Will looked at Dom, who was giving him the high sign, "Dom's got some news for you Keith."

"Will and I are going to have a baby Keith! Can you believe that wonderful news?"

They could hear him choke up as he replied, "I am thunderstruck; congratulations to the both of you. When are you expecting the new Kavanagh to join us?"

"Hold on a minute Keith," Will said and looked at Dom, flexed his eyebrows and whispered "Godfather?"

She was smiling when she asked him, "Keith, would it be too much of an imposition if Will and I asked you to be the godfather to our daughter?"

"I would be honored Dom. So you already know it's going to be a daughter? How far along are you?" He asked, as Will frowned and shook his head at her presumptive nature.

"Actually, that was some serious gender projection Keith. Dom's in the first month, so we've got eight months to get ready for 'her' indoctrination into breathing air."

"Well that's just wonderful. Do you think I could impose upon you there in Argentina?" They were suddenly energized at the prospect of hosting Keith in Buenos Aires.

"Sure, when are you coming into town? You will stay with us while you're here of course," Dom said, putting her foot down.

He started laughing and told them, "I'm sorry if I gave you the impression that's how I wanted to impose upon you. I must admit, I'd rather be at your place than what I'll be doing for the next week. What I was alluding to is would it be too much of an imposition for you to meet with a friend of mine in Buenos Aires?"

"Sure, who is it? Are they playing tourist or something? We could have them over for some Argentine beef steaks," Will offered.

"No," he laughed, "it's not like that Will. I'd like you to meet with Charlie Richardson. He's an old buddy of mine that I got to know during the 'Law of the Seas' negotiations in Brussels."

Will's blood pressure spiked as he suddenly recognized the name, "Oh shit, not the US Ambassador to Argentina? Is that the Charlie Richardson you want me to meet with?"

"One and the same Will. He actually called me after one of his people told him that the President of Argentina had bestowed the Order of May upon you. Are you aware of the fact that very few living people are members of that Order?"

Will felt the second twinge of paranoia hit him involuntarily. "So why would the US Ambassador call his old Brussels buddy Keith Melson when he found out some obscure *Norteamericano* was awarded the Order? What am I missing out on here?"

"My God Will, going through that court-martial sure sharpened your paranoia meter, I'll say that. But you are well-served by it, as he had you checked out within the government system to find out who you were. When he saw that you'd been in the Air Force, he called me to do some reconnoitering for him. Obviously, he called the right person since we have history together. I hope I didn't betray your trust by letting him know about our background together."

"Nah, you could never betray me Keith; you are the reason Dom and I are together now to have this child. What's Richardson's interest in me; casual, or is there more to it? I've already been approached by a certain alphabet agency in the past two days, and it had to do with my affiliation with certain ranking members of the Argentine hierarchy.'"

"I didn't know that obviously, but Charlie wants to meet you because you apparently are better connected than any American in the country. Care to tell me how this came about; or am I prying?"

"Not at all Keith; you can ask me anything. I told you on the airplane over the Pacific that night that I trusted you with my life, so I have no secrets from you. Well, no important ones at least. So here's a synopsis for you: after the North African Invasion, as it's been dubbed, the CEO of Great West Studios caught wind of it because one of our teammates works for them. So they hunted me down and made an offer Dom and I couldn't refuse to write and help produce a movie project called *It's Raining in Marrakech*. The studio CEO, Zig Kowalski, got so energized about the project that he personally came down to Argentina to debrief the key players, who were all here in one place recuperating from wounds. So Jorge Videla, the President, shows up at our house one night after Zig played golf with the Deputy Defense Minister and proceeds to interrogate us about the operation, which we had colluded to lie to him about. You can imagine my shock when he said, almost out of the clear blue, 'I'd like to shake the hand of the man who killed Sandrigan el-Boukhari. And I believe I'm in his presence.' It turns out he lost a niece to a drug overdose in the south of France, and he traced the drugs back to Sandrigan. So to sum it all up, he left the house that night thinking we all were heroes of the Republic of Argentina. He and the Archbishop have helped solve some ticklish problems for us."

"The Archbishop; you're not referring to Archbishop Acosta are you? How in the world did you meet him?" Keith asked, clearly on the edge of disbelief.

Will figured it was time for a break, so he nodded to Dom, his tag team partner, "Will and I became interested in receiving a blessing for our child, and a friend told us about an almost renegade blessing of the child in the womb. The Tourism Minister, who had an untoward interest in William, throttled her lust enough to ask her godfather, Guillermo Acosta, if he would be willing to bestow such a blessing, and he agreed. I would have to say Keith, that aside from our marital vows it was the most incredible moment Will or I have ever experienced. During the course of the meeting with the Archbishop, Will asked him if he could help out our friend, whom the Argentine intelligence community would not leave alone even though she's five months pregnant. We left the meeting ecstatic, and didn't even think about it again until we were whisked off a commercial flight to meet with the Defense Minister at their Pentagon. President Videla was waiting in the Defense Minister's office to bestow the Order of May to Will, and a Heroic Valour medal to our friend Carmen. Apparently the military treats winners of the medal as retired persons, and we hope that Carmen is not further pressured into exposing her child to the dangers of this dark fairy tale Falklands fiasco."

"My God, I feel like I should take notes! So life hasn't leveled off to boring for the two of you just yet, eh? Now that I know what you just told me, I can see why you are of interest to Charlie Richardson. I doubt there is another American alive who is close personal friends with both the President and the Archbishop. I'll call Charlie back and let him know he's not dealing with some radical activist loosened on his area of responsibility. If he still wants to meet you, do you have a preference for how and when that should take place?"

"Yeah Keith, he gets to meet me just like you did. No meetings at his palatial office in the Embassy, no cameras or other publicity of any type. If we have to meet with him, we'd rather do it in our house like we did with Jorge Videla. I'll cook him a steak on the *parilla*; think he'd go for that?" Will asked, hoping to keep this to a low key meet.

"You call the President of Argentina Jorge? My God Will, how did that happen?"

"Oh, let me see Keith. I seem to remember a certain lieutenant colonel telling a shaved-tail second lieutenant one time to 'call him Keith and that's an order.' It was much the same with Videla, but it became much more personal with the death of his niece in play. And I probably made it into his top ten when he confirmed I'd pulled the trigger on Sandrigan. By the way, Archbishop Acosta hasn't asked me to call him Guillermo yet, so I just refer to him as 'Your Grace.'"

"All right, I'll call Charlie and pass on a sanitized version of why you're there in his domain. What number can I reach you two at? It seemed like a circuitous path going through Bob and his contact from the dark side."

"Hey, we both need to stay in touch. I guess Bob Kellor is gonna be our common denominator for a while as we both move around, but here's the number at Carmen's family mansion we call *Casa Fabiano*. It's great to talk to you Keith, and best of luck on becoming TJAG; it couldn't happen to a more deserving officer."

31

A STRATEGIC FRIENDSHIP WITH THE AMBASSADOR

"THAT'S RIGHT; THE AMBASSADOR wants to come meet us. When are you guys getting the hell out of Dodge? I'll stiff-arm his ass until you're gone so we don't have to get into fifty questions about how I know everyone," Will told the assembled throng when everyone had reconvened for breakfast the next morning. *Casa Fabiano* was taking on a definite Circle Entertainment flair, but Will knew he'd better embrace it because no one knew when the eight of them would be together again under one roof.

"Rambo and I are heading out tomorrow, so we shouldn't be too much of a headache by having the swine around while you smooze with His Excellency the Ambassador Extraordinary and Plenipotentiary. Maybe we should call Samantha Chessereaux down to make the place more inviting for His Highness," Kelly said as Will surveyed the damage he'd cause if he slung her over his knee and spanked her right in front of everyone. To their credit, Jonathan and Rosita were wearing long faces knowing their new lovers were blasting off to LA in mere hours.

"Okay, as much as I—to say nothing of our *Porteño* friends here—don't want to see the two of you go, I know you both will be back for the production shooting in a few months. So Ms. Dupree, I will resist the temptation to lay you right over my knee and spank your unrepentant, intemperate ass and embarrass my wife and Jonathan."

Kelly sneered at him contemptuously, "I dare you."

The challenge caught him wrong, so in a blur he grabbed her and had her over his lap, spanking her and enjoying it immensely until Dom stopped him

272

in mid-flail, "Will Kavanagh, stop that right this minute! You have company!"

He reigned it in enough to smile at Jonathan sheepishly and say, "Sorry bro, but she's one spirited woman. Sometimes she trips my wire and I gotta respond."

Will discreetly pinched her ass none too lightly as he helped Kelly back up. Jonathan seemed spellbound, "Oh, I am well aware of her spirited ways Will, but who is this Samantha woman that she mentioned? I do believe I'd like to meet her, as the mere mention of her name seemed to inspire significant reactivity in you."

Dom took over and told him, "You really don't want to know Jonathan. It's probably a miracle you haven't already met your Samantha."

They had just gotten back from dropping Kelly and Dan at their gate for the return flight to LA, the chopper ferry to Ezeiza and return to Jorge Newbery having made it bearable. Henrietta approached them and reported, "There is a gentleman who would like to speak to you on the phone *Señor* Will."

"A gentleman with no name?" Will wondered.

"He only said that he is from the United States Embassy here in Buenos Aires."

"Will Kavanagh," he said by way of a neutered greeting.

"Hello Mr. Kavanagh, I am Ron Cappeletti with the Embassy here in Buenos Aires. Ambassador Richardson asked me to contact you about a meeting with him."

"Right, are you his appointments secretary?" He asked, wondering how he could make Cappeletti's life miserable.

"Actually, I'm with the embassy staff handling security matters for the ambassador. I believe you are aware that the ambassador wishes an appointment with you?"

"Let me guess; are you nominally the Cultural Affairs Attaché?" He asked, knowing the CIA Station Chief was often times masqueraded as the cultural staffer.

"That is one of my jobs here in Argentina. When would you be available to come meet with Ambassador Richardson?"

"Okay Mr. Cappeletti, here's the deal; I ain't coming there, and you can tell the Ambassador that ain't the agreement I had with Keith Melson. So if you can't do better than that, you obviously don't understand or care that I didn't ask to meet His Excellency."

"I see," he replied an octave lower, "and what do you propose instead Mr. Kavanagh? I believe you are a United States citizen, are you not?"

"You know Cappeletti, you're gonna piss me off throwing out those idle threats. Now either act like a human or I'll tell you to stuff it just like I did your rabbi Marty Lindstrum. Now if the big dog wants to come share a meal with me, I suggest you have him call me so that we can arrange it man to man; got all that?"

"Yes I believe I read you loud and clear Mr. Kavanagh. We will be in touch."

"You seemed very abrupt with that man Will, what did he say to you?" Dom asked after he all but slammed the handset down onto the receiver.

"The fucking Ambassador sicks his CIA Station Chief on me to remind me I'm an American citizen and that I should kowtow straight in there at his beck and call. Well fuck him and the horse he rode in on!" Will ranted, feeling better instantly.

"Perhaps the CIA Chief has responsibilities for the Ambassador's personal safety Will, did you consider that? Argentina cannot be a safe place for the American Ambassador considering the antagonism your President has focused on the Junta."

"To the casual observer that might seem logical, but I know the security guy's a low paid functionary compared to the CIA Chief of Station. I wonder if Marty Lindstrum got to his ass?"

"Well, even if he did you haven't met this man, so you can't be sure he's cut from the same cloth. Don't you think you should meet him before passing judgment?"

Will reached out to hug her as he reconsidered, "Of course you're right baby, it's just that I've never met a real human being who works for the CIA. Besides, he was probably Lindstrum's front man in the motorcade hit we flew over on the way to Libertador." He was working up a head of steam when he noticed Dom's look of disapproval. "Okay, I promise I'll wait until I meet him to consider whether he deserves humane treatment."

"Thank you my husband, I will reward you later," she said, and the thought made him immediately reach out and pull her into his lap. They were both getting in the mood when the phone rang again, but he let Henrietta answer it, not wanting to seem too anxious.

She poked her head around the corner and said, "There's a *Señor* Charlie Richardson on the phone for you *Señor* Will."

Will picked up the phone and said, "Yes sir, how are you today Ambassador Richardson?"

"I'm fine Will, and I'm sorry if you and Ron Cappeletti got off on the wrong foot. I've been in touch with Keith Melson about you, and he's told me some quite frankly amazing stories. I would love to meet you and your wife Dominique when it would be convenient for the two of you."

"Now that's more like it; whatcha doing tonight?" Will posed, figuring he'd check out his sincerity.

"I've got nothing scheduled but a boring reception for the Portuguese Ambassador's wife's Glee Club. Do you think you could rescue me from that?" He all but pleaded, and Will instantly knew he would like him.

"Damn right we can! How about come over to our place for cocktails and the best grilled *lomos* in BA? Whatcha think?"

"What time?" He asked, as Will danced a jig around the telephone table.

"Six thirty if that's not too early for whisky; you bringing heat?"

Will could hear him hesitate before answering, "I apologize Will, but considering the current political situation in Argentina, I must travel with protection. Is that too much of a problem?"

Will considered his worries, "Now that I think about it, Americans with high visibility are targets here; hell, they had a motorcade hit out on me on the way to Libertador a week ago. We figured it out and choppered in; flew right over the bastard's heads at the Navy Mechanics School. You're right, you do need protection sir."

"Ron Cappeletti is my best trained agent within the house Will…"

"So your Military Attaché didn't serve a tour in Vietnam?"

"*Phew*, General Melson told me you go straight for the jugular. The attachés are not expected to provide counter-terrorism cover Will."

"Man, it's hard to believe the CIA's the best you got, but you do need heat with you sir. Whoever it is will need to be equally armed in our house, so why don't you bring Cappeletti with you? My wife thinks I was too hard on him and should give him a chance. Is he as big an asshole as the other pricks I've met in his organization?"

"You don't mince words do you? Keith Melson warned me that if I couldn't take the heat, don't bother contacting you. I may be wrong, but I think you and Ron can find common ground. Keith told me you're a real patriot, so I know you're a red-blooded American boy."

"Coonass Cajun refugee is what I am sir, and we look forward to meeting you face to face at six thirty!"

"That seemed to go well. Am I to understand the ambassador is vulnerable to becoming a good old boy?" Dom asked as she passed a warm hand across his susceptible nether region.

"We'll see, but I think the odds are in our favor. Do we have any *lomos* Henrietta?"

"*Si Señor* Will; how many should I plan for dinner?"

"Make it six; do I need to go to the market?"

"I will go instead *Señor* Will; is there anything else you need?"

"How about a couple of bottles of Grand Marnier, and see if they've got the Macallan 21 year-old scotch. You got money, right?"

"Do not concern yourself with such matters *Señor* Will. The Fabiano family has trade accounts with every major supplier in the city of Buenos Aires. I will return soon."

After she left he turned to Dom and said, "Care to accompany me for a spot of heavy breathing my dear?"

"I thought you'd never ask."

———

"Hello Will, and you must be Dominique? I am so happy to meet you both," a casually dressed man in his late forties and a full mane of graying hair announced as Will opened the front door.

"It's good to meet you Ambassador, please come into our home away from home." He looked to the man accompanying him and said, "And you must be Mr. Cappeletti, welcome to our humble abode."

After the customary hand shaking Will and Dom led them to the patio and continued the introductions, "Ambassador Richardson, I would like you to meet our hosts here, Carmen and Hal Rayfield."

He shook their hands warmly and offered, "And this is Ron Cappeletti, who works as a security specialist on my staff."

Hal gave him a roundhouse handshake, half pulling him across the room and said, "How ya doing Ronbo? Glad you could make it."

Cappeletti considered him closely and replied, "It's my pleasure Mr.

Rayfield, and so nice to meet you also Mrs. Rayfield."

The ambassador held up his hands and said, "Okay, I can see we need to set some ground rules, if you'll forgive my taking over Will. I insist that you call me Charlie and my associate is Ron. Now did you mention earlier some scotch whisky might be available Will?"

"Only if Macallan 21 suits your taste," Hal chimed in, heading for the bar to make the drinks.

"Aren't you ladies joining us?" Ron asked, trying to fool them into believing he was at least part-human.

"Actually our obstetrician cautioned against excessive alcohol ingestion during our pregnancies, but please feel free to enjoy yourselves gentlemen," Carmen said with noticeable grace and candor.

After they had settled into chairs with the drinks, Will blasted a shot across the bow, "So why did you want to meet me Charlie?"

The Ambassador shook off the shock to reply, "Boy was Keith Melson ever right about you. Actually, I wanted to personally meet the man who seems to have curried the favor of President Videla within a month of setting foot on the shores of his country."

Will nodded his head and told him, "Actually, I believe the currying started before we got here."

"You mean with the demise of Mr. el-Boukhari?"

"Exactly, but we had no idea anyone in Argentina either knew about that or really gave a shit until Jorge Videla walked into this house the same way you did one week ago tonight."

"And shortly thereafter you became the first American citizen to ever be awarded the Order of May. I would say he was very impressed indeed."

Will shook his head no, "It ain't me Charlie, I just happened to cap the bastard that sold the crap that his niece overdosed on in Nice, France. The enemy of my enemy is my friend."

"That's quite prophetic, but how are you going to maintain neutrality in light of the debacle the Argentines are getting themselves into over the Falkland Islands?" Cappeletti suddenly enjoined.

The departure from civility hit Will like one of Hal's right hooks. He took three breaths to calm himself before answering, "Unless my hearing failed me Cappeletti, you just questioned my ability to sustain allegiance to my country. If you really want to know the answer to that question—but let me warn ya, it'll be with the gloves off—I suggest we get Marty Lindstrum on the phone and see how he came to understand how the cow eats cabbage."

"How does that possibly pertain to the Falklands, can you answer me that?" Cappeletti replied as Will felt his blood pressure rising.

He smiled sarcastically, "Excuse me Charlie; I've got to deal with an ill-informed disciple of the Agency's most erratic renegade." He stared Cappeletti down now, "For your general fucking fund of knowledge supervisory agent Cappeletti, when Admiral Emilio Massera was dismissed from the Junta last year the primary focus on the *Isla Malvinas* vanished, as he was both the Rasputin of the Dirty War AND the keeper of the flame for *Malvinas* reclamation. Jorge Videla is firmly committed to gaining some semblance of normalcy over this runaway economy and has no interests in conquest, other than bringing arts and culture back into Argentina."

"That's not what we're hearing from our sources on the ground, or from Washington. Are you somehow omniscient Mr. Kavanagh?"

Will was spitting nails when he looked at Hal and told him, "Right, you keep on listening to Danny Rojas and see where that gets you!" Will was now fighting mad, "Matter of fact, why don't you ring Lindstrum's ass up right now and put him on the speaker Kemosabe? After they missed us with the motorcade hit last week you'd think they'd be a bit more humble. We might as well get all of these spooks out into the open so we can have them all on the same page with the same answer, whatdya think?"

"I'll have him on the horn momentarily Tonto," Hal said as he got up to head over to the sat phone.

Charlie stood up and said loudly, "Please guys, let's not ruin the evening shall we? Ron made a mistake challenging your patriotism, but I desperately don't want to go back to that Glee Club recital. Is there something that can make this work?"

Will looked at Cappeletti trying mightily to keep the sneer off his face, "Well, are you gonna be Marty's sycophant are or you gonna be a human; it's your choice buckwheat."

"Jesus was he right when he said you two don't take any prisoners. Listen, I'm cool with it if Ambassador Richardson is. I just get nervous when Americans come down here and get too cozy with the natives."

Now Hal was ready to take Cappeletti for three rounds in the ring. Will thought he saw steam escaping his ears as Hal stood over him and growled,

"You mean like my wife who's five months pregnant? Are those the kinds of natives we're getting too cozy with? Just who in the fuck do you think you are Cappeletti, some master race or what? I thought we answered those questions when Hitler ate a Luger for breakfast. If your stinking ass ever even got close to a woman as extraordinary as my wife you'd fucking faint. Now if you can't see the light that we're all humans here, you can get the fuck out of my house!"

To their enduring surprise Ron Cappeletti got a frightened look on his face, "I totally apologize Hal, and to you Carmen. I did not mean that the way it came out and I am humiliated to enrage you like this in your own home. Now can I start over, possibly with a refill on this scotch?"

"I think he's coming around partner, let me fix the drinks," Will said as he took his glass and went to the bar. As he walked by he winked at Hal; hell, they'd both have thrown the bastard out if Charlie Richardson wasn't a potentially key contact. *You never know when you're gonna need somebody in the State Department who's not an automaton.*

Richardson wiped a bead of sweat off his forehead as he asked, "So how did you become friends with Archbishop Acosta? He won't even be seen in the same place as me, so I thought he was biased against non-Catholics."

"No, he's biased against insincerity. If you go to him seeking his help, he's the most accommodating person in the world Charlie. I have a suspicion that we Americans don't go seeking people's help very often. We tend to try and tell them what's best for them, and that don't cut it," Will philosophized based on his own very recent experience.

"I can't imagine what kind of help you needed from the Archbishop; are you Catholic perchance?" Charlie pondered.

"Nope, but Dom and I saw the importance of having our unborn baby blessed in the light of God. You may not know this, but Guillermo Acosta is one of the only—if not the only—Cardinal with the balls to even espouse such a thing. So he didn't care that we were Arab Bedouin or Lutheran or what; he saw the object of the blessing as the child in the womb. Pretty unbiased guy, wouldn't you say?"

"I'm beginning to get a totally different impression of the Archbishop, I must say," Charlie espoused.

"Good, you two ready for some *lomos*?"

They were hungrily making their way through the filets when Will looked at Charlie and asked, "So have you heard anything about the craziness in Colombia? We picked up a rumor that the Catholics were trying to reinforce their position of influence in the northern most part of the continent."

"Now that is an interesting subject that no Catholic wants to talk about."

He had their undivided attention when Hal followed up, "How so?"

"Well, this is just rumor—I heard it during a meeting of the regional ambassadors—but the Ambassador to Colombia told me that the Catholic Archbishop up there had made some overture to the FARC; ever heard of them?"

"Yeah, the FARC and the ELN are the two major revolutionary movements in Colombia, right?" Hal said, suddenly razor focused.

"Exactly, and this priest is apparently aligning himself with the FARC. I guess he thinks they'll win or something," Charlie replied, and they were all listening very closely.

"Choosing sides huh? Now that could make for some strange bedfellows," Will conjectured.

Charlie smiled when he imparted his final tidbit of wisdom, "It's always about women, money or influence. I'd say that priest has cast his lot with the one most likely to succeed."

"Now that makes perfect sense," Dom observed as Will looked at her knowingly.

Will saw the opening, "So this Ambassador to Colombia, is he a squared away guy like you that I would call on in a desperate moment?"

Charlie Richardson actually crossed himself before he replied, "You're treading some very sensitive ground Will; I hope you know that. Members of the Foreign Service form a sort of fraternity based on the demands of being the titular U.S. representative on foreign soil without any real local authority. Hence we must develop influence by nurturing accommodation with the host government leaders. As you can imagine, that's not really hard in a places such as Tokyo, London, Ottawa or Oslo, but when the host nation doesn't trust us to begin with, political chasms can seem all but insoluble. When they're our avowed enemies, success is measured far differently. But when the very lives of the Embassy staff are constantly threatened for whatever reason, serving in the Foreign Service is very stressful—as you can imagine. Now I wouldn't say that Tom Drake is any less patriotic than myself..." he seemed to pause to formulate his next thoughts.

"But?" Will prompted.

Charlie rolled his eyes and shook his head, "But Tom Drake is counting the days until he can leave Bogotá; only his Military Attaché staff are away from the Embassy on a regular basis."

Hal was suddenly rocking back and forth, shaking his head knowingly. Will glanced at him waiting but Hal kept whatever he was thinking to himself. "So, Tom Drake's like a drafted rifleman in Vietnam, eh? Who's the trusted soul one relies on in Colombia?" Will asked, totally uncertain what the Ambassador might say.

Charlie looked at Cappeletti and asked, "Could you give us a second Ron; I'm not going to embarrass myself if I can avoid it." Once Cappeletti walked out to inspect the far reaches of the back yard Charlie leaned in close and said, "There are only three forms of authority not owned by the cartels in Colombia; the Catholic Archbishop Villaponteau is by all reports a righteous man. The CIA as you might suspect finds the cartels too alluring to pass up on the seduction; they're in similar businesses. You didn't hear this from me, but there is only one man who is respected as incorruptible and feared by the cartels; his name is Bernard Jepson, and he's the Colonel in charge of the U.S. Army's 7th Special Forces Group. That's why the Military Attaché staff is always in the field; they're running interference or communications for whatever operation Jepson has going on."

Will suddenly glanced at Hal, remembering the damn near synergy between ROUST, Camp Peary and Camp Mackall at Fort Bragg. Hal shook his head just perceptibly not to comment. Will glanced back at Charlie and said, "That's very interesting information to know Charlie." He glanced back to make sure Cappelletti wasn't close by and told him, "Good luck with Ron and his xenophobia; that doesn't seem like a marriage made in heaven for an Embassy staffer, especially in a country with women as incredibly alluring as Carmen here."

"He's my cross to bear Will; you are everything Keith said you would be and I'd consider it an honor to be your friend," the Ambassador said as he handed Will a business card. "That's my personal number that rings on my desk at the Embassy or at my residence. You call me if you ever need anything, okay?"

Will looked at the classy business card, remembered Acosta's and smiled, "I might just take you up on that Charlie; this is a strange world that we're living in."

After Richardson and Cappeletti left, the four of them were in the study, Will all but staring a hole through Carmen. "So it would seem—at least from the Foreign Service perspective—that the Holy Roman Church is the only steadfast bulwark one can count on in this dangerous world."

"Maybe for public appearances sake, but the only steadfast bulwark in this dangerous world is Bernie Jepson, and don't you ever forget that Tonto," Hal offered.

"Damn, I guess it's good I haven't had to meet him yet, eh?"

"Oh, he knows all about you Willy, and he still can't believe you one, killed Sandrigan, and two, lived to tell about it. You graduated into the world of the noteworthy when we took that bastard out, let me tell ya. But as Dominique is just about to explode to tell you, we took out Sandrigan primarily because of Mustafa's Bedouin army. When Mustafa's not around, you'd better hope the Bear's objectives are the same as yours."

"I'll keep that in mind Kemosabe, but when he doesn't have a dog in the race we've gotta find the enemy of our enemy, *n'est pas?*"

"Willy, you have just coined the mantra of Circle Entertainment my friend," Hal said as he held up his rocks glass for the final toast of the evening. "May we always be able to find the enemy of our enemy."

"Here, here."

32

CIRCLE ENTERTAINMENT SHOWS THEIR APPRECIATION

THEIR LIVES SEEMED TO SETTLE into a new but different pattern after the crew left, so Dom and Will embraced the opportunity to do the simple things, specifically improving their health and continuing to recover from the near-death experiences in Africa. Each day began with yoga and this almost naturally pointed them back in the direction of meditation. Based on Dom's incantations Will made a concerted effort to reduce the number of cigarettes he smoked every day, negotiating it down to after meals and after sex. He couldn't be sure she had agreed to these limits to further incentivize bedroom sports, but it was a win-win situation all the way. The Fabiano's neighbors had a tennis court in their back yard and never used it once their teenage children left for college, so the Kavanagh's accepted their invitation to use it several times a week. All four of the Posse became much more interested in taking long walks and they were actually improving their golf games. Will and Dom were relaxing one day at the 19th Hole of the Buenos Aires Golf Club when he spotted a familiar face and told Dom, "I'll be right back." He furtively snuck up behind Rosita Cabrera, nattily attired in very form-fitting golf togs, put his hands over her eyes and said, "Guess who?"

The look of disdain she had when she threw his hands off and turned around ready to kill made him suspect that perhaps such goosing wasn't normal for *Porteños*. When she saw it was Will, her expression quickly changed as she gave him a huge hug, "Hello Will Kavanagh, I haven't seen you in weeks. How are you?"

He looked at her suspiciously, "What's the matter Rosita; forget who your friends are?"

She spotted Dom across the room, put her hand on his shoulder and whispered, "What you just did would provoke a fight among *Porteños*, but I assume this is normal behavior among you *Norteamericanos?*"

"Who knows, it was you so I figured you wouldn't mind. Come on over and say hello to Dom."

After they greeted each other warmly, they sat down as Will made the first interrogatory, "And just how are you and Rambo doing? Heard from the boy lately?"

She gave him a funny look, "Why do you call Daniel by that name, Rambo? Is that a middle name that I do not know?"

Will shook his head in disbelief, "So you never saw the Sylvester Stallone movies about John Rambo's adventures?"

"Of course, he is the macho commando who annihilates his enemies when he gets mad. What does that have to do with Daniel?"

He glanced at Dom and winked, then turned to Rosita and just sat there looking at her, waiting for the thought to assimilate. She scrunched up her face, "Daniel is nothing like that. Do not tell me that my dear sweet Daniel is a violent man."

"And he is a timid lover who is afraid of emotional interactions?"

She blushed slightly and tried again, "Of course not, but I cannot believe he is as you say. He is quite skilled in the planning of motion picture productions. Are you sure we are talking about the same person."

He gave her the Italian army salute and offered, "Well perhaps it's not an absolute comparison; I've never seen Rambo get mad. He's really quite good at doing his job, whatever that might entail."

"He never gets mad? I believe you are exaggerating Will Kavanagh."

Will leaned into her until his head was buried in her hair, "Having a hard time believing he's capable of the same violence you were? Come on Rosita, you're a big girl now, and you have big man appetites, *sí?*"

She considered him as if he were a viper before smiling, "*Sí*."

He patted her lovely thigh, "That's my girl; when are the two of you getting back together? He seemed quite taken with you."

Now her expression turned to a huge smile, "Was he now? As a matter of fact, I have a trip planned to Las Vegas for a Tourism conference and we plan to rendezvous there."

"I'm glad to hear that Tourism Minister, it would seem the gaming industry is of interest?"

"Very much so, and we have much to learn from you *Norteamericanos*."

"I actually found you to be an incredibly resourceful person when you had *Sara Smile* played at *La Casa Rosada*. And I can say beyond any doubt that you are one of the best dancers I have ever been paired with."

Now she did break into a wide grin, "I was later asked by President Videla if we were close friends when he and his wife saw us dancing. I told him you were more than a little impressed with their skill at the tango." She turned her attention to Dom and asked, "How is the pregnancy progressing Dominique?"

"Quite well, and thank you for inquiring. I would like to get back in touch with your godfather and see if there is something else we can do to help his mission here in Argentina. He was most accommodating in helping our friend Carmen gain some semblance of peace in her life. How would you suggest we approach the Archbishop about such a matter?"

"Would you like to speak with him now? The manager of the golf club is a close business acquaintance, and I am sure we could use his office."

"That is most gracious of you Rosita, are you sure it wouldn't be too much of an imposition? When were you going to play golf?"

She smirked at her, "I am a member here, and the starter will allow me latitude in such matters. Please follow me."

"*Tio Guillermo, esta soy yo Rosita*," was as much of the conversation as Will picked up when Rosita called her godfather the Archbishop. The fusillade of Spanish that ensued reminded him somewhat of listening to Dom and her mother blast away in Arabic, but at least he could pick up a few words in Spanish.

After their greetings were concluded, she handed the phone to Dom and said, "He's delighted to hear from you Dominique."

"Hello Archbishop Acosta, how are you?" She listened for a moment and continued, "You have been a Godsend with regards to the plight of my friend Carmen Rayfield. Will and I are so beholding to you for the help that......"

Will looked at Rosita, figuring he'd get the debrief later on the half of that call he couldn't hear, and asked her, "So you really had no clue about Rambo, huh?"

She slid over next to him and half-whispered, "Are you telling me he is an agent with the CIA? I cannot believe such a thing Will; he is the most fun person I have ever been around."

He smiled furtively at her and replied, "Yeah, he was pretty impressed with you too. Now I don't want to fill that pretty little head of yours with all kinds of hateful thoughts, but suffice it to say that no one—and I mean no one—will ever fuck with you when you're around Dan Pierson. I'd go to war with that guy anytime; at least anytime I had to." He remembered her question and added, "Rosita, it'll be a cold day in hell before Rambo ever sucks up to the CIA. He is a self-made man, and I am most fortunate that he respects me. He pretty much saved our ass in Algiers, I can assure you."

She playfully slapped his wrist, "I am not used to men saying such things to me Will, but I must say that it is reassuring to know he can protect himself."

"From men at least Rosita, I'm not so sure about smoking ass hot *Porteños* who also happen to be killers in the business world. I don't know for sure, but Pierson might have met his match with you!"

She peeked at Dom, who was totally immersed in the phone call, moved in tighter and whispered, "So what was this woman like that Daniel was in love with?"

"She was a smoking-ass hot Japanese woman; beginning to see any similarities here?"

She narrowed her gaze trying to figure it out, "He doesn't like American women?"

Will laughed before thinking back. *Damn, maybe Rambo does have Ameriphobia, but Rosita seems to have broken the yellow fever streak in him.* She finally nudged him so he responded, "No, he won't waste his time with women unless they're super intelligent and smoking-ass hot. Feeling special?"

"I believe so Mr. Kavanagh. Thank you for telling me this," she purred as she leaned in to kiss his cheek.

"Hey, you earned it. If I hadn't been married, I'd have been on your ass like white on rice!"

She batted her eyes at him, "I'm not completely sure what you just said, but I believe I should be flattered."

"That you should Rosita, that you should."

"So what'd the Cardinal have to say?" Will asked Dom on the drive back to *Casa Fabiano*. The Country Club was all the way across Buenos from Recoleta, on the other side of Camp de Mayo.

"Before we get into that, I'd like to know what you and the Tourism Minister were all huddled up talking about. You know I don't trust that woman William."

"Jesus Dom, she's all but in love with Rambo, give me a break! She actually wanted to know what kind of woman he was in love with before."

"And you told her about Ayako? I cannot believe you would betray such a confidence Will. And besides, I am not sure that relationship is completely over just yet."

"Of course I didn't tell her about Ayako, except that they shared the common traits of super intelligent and smoking-ass hot. She cannot get her head around the fact that Pierson is Rambo though."

"I don't think there's an urgent need for her to know too much of the truth on that front."

"Don't forget that she was one of Carmen's peers within SIDE and the 601; that Rosita is no naïve gal, let me tell ya. So how'd things go with *Tio Guillermo*?"

———

"Hello Kelly, how are you today?" Dom said in greeting as Rosita and Will sat around the speaker phone in the Fabiano study.

"I'm doing better now; it sure is good to hear your voice. Were your ears burning or something? I was just telling Dan Pierson that we should be ready to load up the sets and head down your way in about a month. Are you guys ready to head out to Bariloche?"

"You know we will be waiting anxiously for your arrival. I am glad that Dan is there with you, is there any chance we could get the two of you and Mr. Kowalski on this call? I've got Will and Rosita here with me and we would like to discuss an interesting business proposal."

"Are you kidding? He'd stop a board meeting to talk to you guys; he's planning on coming down for the first few days of filming. Hold on, I'm going to transfer this call over to his office. We'll be back on the line in a couple of minutes."

"How are my *Porteño* friends doing, isn't that what you call yourselves now?" Zig's raspy brogue came blasting over the speaker phone.

"Hey Zig, how's the golf game? I might be well enough to take you on by the time you get back down here, that is if Kelly's prediction about your interest in the shooting schedule was on the mark," Will said, baiting him with small talk for the coming push.

"Your ass is giving me strokes this time Kavanagh; I don't take a whipping lying down! And you can bet your ass that Zig Kowalski is gonna be on set for the first day of shooting. What's up?"

"I have found a most interesting investment opportunity down here, and was wondering if we could get some of our fee shifted to the front," he told him, trying to set the hook.

"Well, that's not exactly what we talked about initially, but you guys have busted your ass to get the screenplay ready. Whatcha looking for?"

"I don't know, at least a hundred large, maybe two if you could swing it," he ventured.

"Weellllll, I might, and I repeat might, be able to swing a hundred large, but $200K might be pushing it. We've got three wraps waiting to lay the proverbial golden egg. Which reminds me, whatcha got that looks so interesting? You find a gold ore vein or something?"

"Better than that Zig. We, and I mean Circle Entertainment and Great West Studios, have an opportunity to make a real difference down here in Argentina. Did you know that half of the Argentines live below the poverty level?"

They could hear him exhale before he replied, "That's really unfortunate Will, and I have sympathy for their plight, but we all came up through the tough parts. Why is that a business proposition for me? Sounds like you've decided to help 'em, huh?"

"Right Zig, Dom and I and Carmen and Hal have decided to do something to pay back the welcome these folks have put out for us. Now here's the deal: Circle Entertainment has already been the recipient of a major dispensation by the government and the Archbishop of Buenos Aires, so we're all in. But if you'd like to step in and stand beside us—maybe going fifty-fifty—Argentina is willing to make it worth your while. There are a lot of poor folks that need help down here."

They could hear the '*whew*' in the background before he said, "So we're talking a hundred large outa Great West to match your hundred. What the hell is it gonna go to? And how the hell does that make it worth my while? I'm all ears Kavanagh," he said, throwing down the gauntlet.

"Actually Zig, I've got Rosita Cabrera here with us to address that question, Rosita?"

"Hello Mr. Kowalski, first of all I would like to say that we look forward to the filming of *It's Raining in Marrakech*." Will suddenly realized that Kelly and Pierson were licking their lips for the shooting to start as well, with nightly ventures into the heavy breathing realm with their Latin lovers. "President Videla is quite excited about the initiative the Kavanagh's and Rayfield's have brought forward. If Great West Studios would also like to participate—as an equal partner with them—the Republic of Argentina will extend the tax-free provision of our existing agreement to cover all future film production efforts your studio might consider. And we will provide a fifty-fifty share line on the cost of all extras required in conjunction with the filming."

"Damn, you guys are playing hardball, I'll say that," he offered in what Will hoped was excitement. "What exactly is the money going to be used for? I'm kinda antsy on the prospect of it slipping off into some politician's hands, no offense intended Rosita."

Dom jumped into the conversation by telling him, "The money would go to procure baby food, diapers and infant formula, all of which are in critical short supply among the poor in the slums around Buenos Aires."

"So the government's trading tax credits for baby food? How are you gonna insure it don't get siphoned off to some black market or something?"

"Because the Catholic Relief Services branch here, *Cáritas Argentina*, will administer the distribution without any administrative costs whatsoever. All we have to do is get the critical products to *Cáritas Argentina* and they will distribute them," Rosita advised him.

"Rosita, please forgive me for sounding like I don't trust my own mother, but what assurances would we have that the church wouldn't pay inflated prices or be subject to bribery buying the goods?"

Will jumped in with both feet, "That's part two of the request; we want the goods bought in the U.S. and flown down here, say on a chartered FedEx DC-10 cargo bird that otherwise might be loaded with set props and such. Who knows, FedEx might even be willing to chip in the flight to get their name on the list of charitable businesses helping out with the humanitarian relief."

"Damn Kavanagh, you get settled someplace and you turn into a missionary. I can just see the taxes and export tariffs eating up my legal staff—your buddy Chessereaux—for weeks trying to iron that mess out. And who's gonna arrange all of this stuff up here? You coming back to the States to oversee it?"

"Ambassador Richardson has assured me that the State Department will coordinate the rescission of all sales taxes and export tariffs associated with this humanitarian effort."

"Damn Kavanagh, you know the Ambassador? And just how did you pull off all of this magic smoke and mirrors shit? I ain't ever seen the State Department move faster than a glacier in my whole life."

"So it would surprise you that we discussed this with Charlie Richardson over after-dinner drinks on the same patio you met Jorge Videla on, eh? Or that Rosita's Godfather Guillermo, also known as Cardinal Acosta, is ready to change his mind about the unholy entertainment industry because of your prospective involvement?"

"Damn Kavanagh, I shoulda known you'd never make a pitch unless it was a lead-pipe cinch. Okay, count me in for the hundred large. That makes two hundred thousand as the funding source for this humanitarian thing. Jesus, I wonder how much stuff can fit on a DC-10?"

"Why don't you let Kelly and Dan figure that out for us? And I'm sure you've got folks in your Purchase Department that buy these kinda things from vendors all the time. Hell, they might even be willing to cut us a break on the price for shared billing on the project."

"So you're suddenly dumping this in my lap, eh? I knew you were gonna stick it to me somewhere along the line Kavanagh. I gotta a movie studio to run for Christ's sake!"

"Now Zig, would I do that to you anywhere other than the 18th green? For your information, the President wants Dom and I, along with his Tourism Minister here to come to LA to get the details hashed out, and we're bringing a leading Argentine obstetrician with us to certify the need in case USDA or HHS gets their shorts in a dither over it."

Before he could object again, Rosita added, "And the President has instructed me to have the Ministry of Tourism cover all associated expenses with this trip to Los Angeles Mr. Kowalski."

They could hear him slam the table with his palm as he all but shouted, "All right dammit, you've boxed me into a corner Kavanagh. I will have my CFO wring the books out to see if we can do a little more than a hundred. And make sure you bring your clubs with you to LA, 'cause I'm getting three a side from your sandbagging ass this time!"

"Bullshit, we're playing even up Kowalski. Now here's the real deal;

we ain't flying those DC-10s back empty Mr. CEO," Will told him as Rosita started rubbing his forearm.

"Hold on, something's coming to me now. Oh yeah, Johnny Boy wasn't available one day when I called him because he and his goddess wife Samantha were doing some wine tasting in Napa Valley. I asked him what the fuck and he said they were performing 'due diligence' on some cockamamie import/export venture you'd dreamed up. What's that all about?"

"We're just doing our part to help Jorge Videla get the Argentine economy kick started again Zigster. Those poor vintners along the Andean range could really benefit from a *Norteamericano* interest in their delightful vintages."

They waited twenty seconds as Kowalski apparently rewound the film in his brain. "Damn, that was some outstanding red wine you served with those lomo things. Is that what you're talking about importing?"

"Yep, and Johnny Boy and Sam were doing a taste comparison with a few bottles we sent back with them. Their conclusion is the Andean wines are at least on par with Napa Valley. It's time to turn the wheel big daddy."

"Damn, you're turning into a regular business incubator down in *Porteño*-land Kavanagh."

"Didn't Kelly or Rambo already spill the beans?" Will put his hand over the phone as he laughed with Rosita and Dom.

"Spill what beans; what the fuck are you on about now?"

"Zig, don't you remember threatening my life because of the traffic between downtown Buenos and the airport?"

"Geez, I had almost forgotten about that Chinese water torture," he said as Rosita couldn't stifle the hoot as she laughed her ass off. "So what'd you do, magically extend the runway of that runt airport next to the Casa by reclaiming wetlands or something?" Now Kowalski was laughing so hard that he began coughing.

"Yeah, or something; turns out the Air Force upgraded the *El Presidente's* equivalent of Marine One, so we bought the cast aside superbly maintained chopper with few flying hours on it. Next time you fly in, we'll ferry you to the *tourista* district via Capital Air Services, the first commuter helicopter business ever opened in the Republic of Argentina. How you like them apples?"

"Wow, now that is something the wealthy tourists will want to take advantage of; how you gonna advertise it? Now that'll eat your profit center up in a heartbeat," he said and began laughing, then coughing again.

"Zig Kowalski, haven't you ever heard of Travel Magazine? I mean it's only published in LA, right?"

"Yeah, so what?"

"So we mail in four dozen complaints about the horrid commute between Ezeiza International and the Buenos tourist district. Then we front an ad on the facing page about Capital Air Services; 'avoid the hassle in the air-conditioned splendor of a VIP helicopter.' We think it'll catch on over time."

"Shit, I'd pay a C note right now for avoiding that nightmare."

"Right, so seventy-five USD sounds like a bargain, *n'est pas?*"

"Okay, I'll wait to hear from Kelly about your arrival plans. This is really a supreme public relations angle Kavanagh."

"Right, to say nothing of the newborns who'll be fed? Later on Zigster!"

Dom apparently forgave Rosita her latent lust for her husband as they all hugged and kissed in celebration after the call. Will didn't even have to ask, as Dom came running back with the snifters and a bottle of Grand Marnier. As they were mellowing out after the first glass, Rosita shook her head in wonder and asked, "Is that the way all business calls happen in America? I had trouble believing you were carrying on a serious conversation at times."

Will filled her glass back up as he told her, "Are you kidding me? That was probably the most successful and friendly business conversation I have ever been involved with! Man, we had every answer for him before he asked it. FedEx is still the wild card though."

Dom snuggled up to him and said, "And just when did you talk to Dr. Calvatori about this business trip William? And what certifications are you talking about?"

He merely looked at her and smiled, "Don't you think we've got some new fans with Kelly and Jonathan about now?"

He was still looking at her with his best shit-eating grin when Henrietta poked her head in and said, "*Señorita* Dupree is on the phone, and she asked to speak with all of you."

Will punched in the speaker phone button, "*Casa Fabiano.*"

"And just when did you talk to Dr. Calvatori about this business trip William? And what certifications are you talking about?"

"Actually, I was gonna leave that up to you Kelly; and as for the certifications…" he said as he opened his hand towards Rosita.

"The Office of the President has asked the Ministry of Health to request Dr. Jonathan Calvatori to provide international certification of need relative to the impoverished residents of greater Buenos Aires."

"I see, and the relief planning group coming from Argentina will include Rosita Cabrera and Jonathan Calvatori? This sounds like some espionage operation. Did you know anything about this Dom?"

She clinked glasses with Rosita as she responded, "As my husband is fond of saying Kelly, 'ask me no questions, I'll tell you no lies.'"

"Hey, I'm not complaining, as government intervention is probably the only way Jonathan will leave his practice again for two days. I have never seen Zig Kowalski get whipsawed like that before, especially for a charity project! That was incredible!"

"Actually, you can prepare for our arrival by having someone reach out and touch Gerber, Pampers and Enfamil, and see what they're willing to do to cut us some slack. By the way, is Rambo there?"

"Right here bro, that was some performance. And that was some supporting job there Ms. Cabrera! I look forward to hosting you here in Los Angeles," said an obviously happy Pierson.

"Okay Rambo, FedEx is the wild card in all of this. How about reach out and touch your main man and see if they're amenable to helping out. If push comes to shove, we'll get a bird at Great West's rates. That'd be the worst case scenario for air freight. Think you can take that one on?"

"I can talk to their freight scheduler, but I'm not linked into the head shed like your buddy John Chessereaux. Did you know he was college buds with their CEO? Now that'd be how to approach them."

"Alright, I guess I'd better make that call. We'll plan on coming up next week after we hogtie Jonathan into a travel commitment. Does Johnny have an office at Great West?"

"He does, but I don't know if he's in LA. By the way, thanks for being the travel agent with the most down there; I can hardly wait!"

"John Chessereaux," came the familiar voice over the speaker.

"Johnny boy, how they shaking? Hey, don't answer that question, I've got a couple of reputable women here with me," Will told his attorney as Dom tried to kick him.

"Well if it's not the elusive Mr. Kavanagh! Who you got with you?"

"Dom and the Argentine Minister of Tourism, *Senorita* Rosita Cabrera and she's hot; just ask Rambo..." Both women were slapping at him as he said, "Dammit this is a business call; stop stripping my clothes off 'til we're finished with Johnny boy."

"Don't you believe a word he said John Chessereaux," Dom insisted with an attitude. As she said it Will glanced at Rosita, wondering what barriers she might have to a little trio fun.

"Why not?" Johnny said as both women's faces began blushing and he blew Rosita a kiss.

"Just kidding, listen here bro, we need an airlift favor from FedEx and Pierson just told me your thicker'n thieves with the CEO. He owe you any favors?"

"FedEx eh? That would be my old Stanford buddy Brant Stringer, who I did bail out with an alibi not too long ago. What's cooking? Not airlifting guns into another hot spot I hope?"

He grimaced at Rosita and rolled his eyes, "Nothing nearly so dramatic as all that. What we've got is a humanitarian project to bring in a planeload of baby food, diapers and infant formula into Buenos Aires to be distributed to the poor children in the slums around here. And it might be of interest to know that the Zigster has rogered up at least a hundred large in a share matching deal with Circle Entertainment. So whatcha think?"

"Zig's in? Hell yeah, I'll make that call. So I guess you want round trip from LA to Buenos Aires?"

"One way from LA to BA; but I'm working on a plane load of superior wine for them to haul back from South America. If he bites the round trip, my first shipment gets a trade deal extraordinaire. Either way, I get my first shipment of bona fides in via air express rather than wait a month for a slow boat to make it up the Atlantic. Think he'll bite?"

"There's only one way to find out. Let me call you back; I don't know if he's in the office. By the way, how'd you get Zig to sign up for a charity deal? He wouldn't even give his mother a chance if she wanted one."

"We made him an offer he couldn't refuse JC. Only one way to appeal to Zig Kowalski; prove it's good for his bottom line. By the way, Dom, Rosita here and I will be in LA coordinating this thing next week. Let's try and find some time to get together with the Chessereaux' clan while we're up there."

"You're coming into SOCAL? Sam will be beside herself to see the two of you, and so will our little Willy. I'll be back after I find Brant."

—

When Johnny rung off Will smiled slyly at Rosita, "Rosita, have you ever given consideration to sex with another woman?"

"Of course not; that is disgusting," she stammered as Will and Dom just looked at her and smiled. "Why would you ask me such a crazy question?" She sounded repulsed but her body language betrayed her. "What woman would you even suggest that I might do such a thing with?"

Will leaned towards her for a slow kiss on the lips, "Dominique." She looked at Dom and considered her for a long moment before Will interrupted her thoughts, "I'll make this easy on you Rosita; what if Dominique and I were to entertain you? Would that seem more interesting?"

"I, I'm, I've never even considered such a thing," she said as Will remembered Carmen thinking Rosita was a lesbian.

"Here's the deal Rosita, you kinda lit a fuse in me the night I met you, and Kelly thought the same thing happened to you. With this in mind, what do you think of Dominique as a woman? To me she's pure sexual joy."

"So what you're suggesting is…"

"Exactly."

33

DOING SOME GOOD WITH
'HELP THE HELPLESS'

ON THE FLIGHT TO LA, the four of them huddled up around the bar in the back of the first class section of the Pan Am 747 to chat. Jonathan's diaper rash still wasn't completely healed from being jerked out of his practice for the trip, but the assurance that he would leave LA a spent shell casing somewhat attenuated his guilt for abandoning his patients for a few days. "So you see any problems associated with distribution of the goods to the people in the slums Jonathan?"

"Actually, you probably couldn't have selected three items more critical to postnatal survival, especially among the poor. The prepared food and diapers will be immediately put to use, but the infant formula could be problematic."

This caught Dom by surprise as she asked, "How is the dispensation of infant formula problematic Jonathan. I thought you were the one who championed the infant formula to counteract the nutritional condition of poor mothers breast-feeding their babies."

He nodded his head in assent then continued, "It absolutely is, however the infant formula must be reconstituted with water, and clean water is nearly non-existent in the barrios."

"So we've got to figure out how to get it to them premixed with water, is that what you're saying?" Will pondered, the problem already firing up his industrial engineering core.

"That would be ideal, as the mother could merely shake the suspension to redistribute the formula. But how could that occur on a large-scale basis?"

"Well, it seems as though the soda and beer bottlers have mastered that problem. Why don't we enlist them in this effort? You know, have the infant formula combined, blended and bottled under sanitary plant conditions?"

"That is a brilliant idea! Perhaps we could identify a benign additive that would keep the formula suspended in the solution. Do you happen to know any important bottlers?" Jonathan posed.

"Not off the top of my head, but I betcha our friends in the Catholic Relief Services could reach out and touch someone. Let's look 'em up in LA; think you could track that down through your contacts Rosita?"

She smiled as the light bulb came on in her head, "Of course, Coca-Cola is already a significant sponsor of *Caritas Argentina*, so we can surely approach them through my *Tio Guillermo*. If we could somehow enlist the support of their *Norteamericano* headquarters, it would incentivize their further participation in our humanitarian effort."

"Very good Rosita, that is an excellent idea," Jonathan beamed as he reached out to shake her hand. This made Will wonder how the two of them would get along socially, like without any clothes on. Rosita's semi-aggressive behavior towards males would no doubt intimidate Jonathan.

He was musing over this when Jonathon rousted Will from his lizard fog and asked, "Do you think we can find a source into the Coca-Cola headquarters Will?"

"We'll punt that one to the Great West Studios' publicity maven; let her earn her keep in launching her major domo Zig's entry into the philanthropic world. So did you contact the Catholic Relief Folks before we left Rosita? If they've got an office in LA, that would seem a focal point for publicity over this. I'm sure Zig will hit us up over getting his portly countenance in front of some cameras in exchange for his largesse," he noted, anticipating as many angles as possible before face-off time.

She surprised him with her vigilance, "The Catholic Relief Services is headquartered in Baltimore, Maryland, and I am not sure about any offices they may have in Los Angeles. I do know that the Cathedral of Saint Vibiana is the administrative headquarters for the Archdiocese of Los Angeles."

Will held his hand up for a high-five, as she showed spunk by slapping it with vigor, "I love it when a plan comes together."

———

The BA travelers were surprised by the greeting committee that awaited them at LAX; in addition to Kelly and Dan Pierson—no doubt anxious to escape with their Latino paramours—was Sam, Johnny and Willy Chessereaux. The scene must have looked like long lost lovers finally reuniting as the coupling quickly ensued. Will was thinking the presence of the *Porteños* would rein in Sam's usual wildly inappropriate greetings, but Dom blew past them all, grabbed little Willy from Johnny and began twirling him around in the air. Will turned back to grab Dom's carryon bag but was suddenly put under a full assault by Sam, who flew into his arms, looked him in her eyes and said, "Welcome back to California!" He knew resistance was futile as she delivered a withering kiss that immediately inspired an insurrection in his groin. He managed to pry away from her just far enough to tell her, "Jesus Sam, later. I want you to meet some friends from down south."

She got right into his eyes and purred, "Later huh? I'm holding you to that."

By the time they separated, Will was flushed and slightly out of breath, and turned to find Kelly and Jonathan looking at them expectantly. "Hey baby, have we got a list for you. Jonathan, I'd like you to meet a dear friend and the mother of my godson Samantha Chessereaux."

Sam narrowed her eyes, then flexed her eyebrows and offered, "Hello Jonathan, please call me Sam. And you are?" She trailed the question off, looking down at Kelly holding his hand.

"Jonathan Calvatori, and I am not totally sure why I am here other than I am Dominique's obstetrician," he said, slightly star struck, but Will gave him props for at least being able to speak.

"Obstetrician?" She all but yelled. She turned with a scowl and said, "And just when were you going to tell me and John about this turn of events Mr. Kavanagh?"

"Figured we'd wait 'til we got here I guess," he driveled off, not having thought about informing the Chessereaux' about the pregnancy.

She was raring up to take a bite out of him when Dom came up holding Willy, "I see you've met Jonathan, our fertility specialist and Kelly's boyfriend. Have you met Rosita?"

They turned to find Pierson and Rosita, already moved off to a spot behind a column making out like two teenagers. Johnny ignored them, "Hey buddy, welcome back to the land of the living. Man am I glad to see you in one piece!"

Will held up an index finger, looked back at the two lovebirds and issued a subtle but insistent command, "Rambo!"

They walked up, smiling and flushed as Will introduced them, "Rosita, I'd like you to meet our dear friends Johnny and Samantha Chessereaux. And that little fellow Dom is holding is my godson Willy. Johnny, Sam, Rosita is the Minister of Tourism for the Republic of Argentina and is here to help close the loop on a humanitarian project we've tripped off down in Buenos Aires."

Johnny looked at Will and asked, "Does the project have a name yet?"

He rolled his eyes, half-pissed they hadn't talked about naming it and blurted, "Oh what the hell, how about 'Help the Helpless?' That's what it's all about."

Once they got their bags, Johnny asked "So what are your plans for to-night? We're staying at the condo in Century City. Why don't you guys come stay with us? You've been there; you know the lay of the land."

Will slapped himself in the forehead, "Jesus Christ, I didn't even think about lodging." He looked back at the two lovebird couples and said, "But apparently Dom and I were the only ones I should have been concerned about. Are you sure you don't mind putting us up?"

Now Sam entered the fray, "Will Kavanagh, I will never speak to you again if you don't come stay at our place while you and Dom are in Los Angeles. What are your plans right now?" Will looked at his watch, which told his body it was eight o'clock at night *Porteño* time, but it was still a bright sunlit afternoon outside.

"Damn, it feels like supper time but we gained four time zones on the way in. I don't know what our plans are Sam, I'm at a bit of a loss; jet lag maybe?" He then heard a female clearing her throat rather loudly.

They turned to find Kelly staring, tapping her shoe "Uh, Mr. Kavanagh, your co-conspirator in 'Help the Helpless' is waiting breathlessly for your arrival at his office in Burbank. I would suggest we move out smartly."

He turned to Johnny and said, "Looks like Zig's lying in wait, so we gotta head over to the studio. We'll come to the condo after he's finished with us, maybe go over to that steak house across the street. By the way, what'd you get from FedEx? Their vig is gonna affect how much product we can move."

"Hey, hey, hey, my buddy Brant knows how to return favors. Air freight is gratis if we give FedEx a plug with 'Help the Helpless.' They'll even collect the goods from the three manufacturing plants for us. Whatdya think about them apples?"

Will high-fived him as he closed his eyes, raised his fists and yelled, "YES." His lizard brain wasn't asleep however, so he ventured, "What if we fill up that empty DC-10 on the flight back and divert it to Northern Virginia for offload—maybe Dulles. Whatdya think?"

"For your first import delivery of wine? I think Brant would accept an offer of variable operating costs for such a trip. You already got a receiving unit in Fairfax or something? I incorporated International Delights in the Caymans as we agreed, but the U.S. business address is the Destination Partners office in Wilmington, Delaware."

"I gotta check in with Bob Kellor about that; he was marching off with much zeal when I last heard a report about him." Will then turned to Pierson, "It looks like we gotta daisy chain the pickup on the charity goods; you good to go on playing loadmaster escort?"

He looked at Rosita with a grin and said, "No sweat Kemosabe, as long as the big boss says it's a go."

Will turned back, gave Willy a blurble kiss on his fat cheek and told him, "We'll see you in a little while big guy; will that be okay?"

He started laughing at his Uncle Will, "Unny Wim."

"See you guys later; I'll call as we're leaving Zig's office."

"Hey, it's rush hour LA Kavanagh; it'll take you 'til midnight to get to Great West. Chris Campion is waiting for you guys at the General Aviation Terminal," Johnny told him as everyone looked at him aghast.

"Jesus Christ, who would have thought we needed a plane from LAX to Burbank?" Will grunted, shaking his head in disbelief.

Johnny just shrugged his shoulders, "It's twenty-eight miles, mostly up 101 with two million cars at rush hour Will. Welcome to our world."

Dom was instantly alert, "John, perhaps William failed to advise you in all the excitement, but Circle Entertainment sort of inherited a helicopter commuter air service. Capital Air Services' primary focus is shuttling passengers from the International Airport you traveled through and the central downtown airport in Buenos Aires. If you recall, the commute becomes somewhat stressful when you enter Buenos proper."

"You gotta be shitting me," Johnny swore at Will. "You set up a corporation without me? What about the vig down there? I can imagine their licking their chops with a Yankee raking in pesos from touristas."

Rosita stepped forward, smiling furtively, "I take it you are not aware that *Señor* Kavanagh is a hero of the Republic, no?" When Johnny gave her the Italian Army salute she added, "He was bestowed the Order of May by President Videla a few weeks ago, and so earned a lifetime exemption from all personal and business taxes, tariffs, duties and fees. It would seem his rescue of Dominique's mother—and the ensuing shootout with the North African drug lord—has made him a national treasure."

"Jesus Christ, so Argentina is a free ride for CEI operating out of Buenos Aires? Man I can hardly believe my ears." He turned to Will and demanded, "What the hell did you do to become Argentina's national hero?"

Dom stepped in, looking up to stare into Johnny's eyes, "He killed that bastard Sandrigan el-Boukhari, who had provided the poison the President's niece overdosed on in Nice. So John, the enemy of my enemy is my friend, *n'est pas?*"

Pierson had Rosita with him in his Jeep, so Dom and Will caught a ride over to the Atlantic Aviation parking lot with Kelly and Jonathan. As they pulled out of LAX parking lot number four, Jonathan was in a daze, no doubt his first visit to LAX. "It's alright honey, we just have to go to the other side of the airport," she said as she saw him looking at huge jets taking off right in front of them. "It's okay Jonathon, there's a tunnel under the runways so we don't have to dodge 747s," she joked as Dr. Calvatori's concerned expression demonstrated faith was in play.

Finally he turned and asked, "So that is the Samantha woman Kelly was kidding you about right before you spanked her?"

"One and the same brother, one and the same; what'd you think of her?" Before he could answer Will added, "You did a hell of a lot better than me bro; I was speechless for five minutes after she walked into my life from Gate 29, I think. My tongue was too thick to form words." He exploded into riotous laughter before countering his claim, "Of course that was twenty-four months, a baby boy and a marriage ago. She's really let herself go to the dogs in the interim; whatdya think?" Dom was now laughing so hard she was beating Will with both hands.

"She is incredibly striking, and I couldn't help but notice that she looked like a model that was the centerfold in an old issue of Playboy magazine." He seemed to flush before adding, "Please excuse my unsolicited opinion, but the two of you seem quite friendly towards one another." This time it was Kelly who erupted into hysterics, nearly crashing through the entry gate to Atlantic Aviation. She was watching Will closely in the rear view mirror, knowing he'd confessed at his wedding reception that he and Dom had reoriented Sam's sexual inclinations.

"How could I forget about your magazine collection in the sperm collection room? If you saw her without any clothes you'd think she looked exactly like that Playboy model."

He narrowed his gaze and said, "You must have a vivid imagination Will."

He glanced at Dom, saw Kelly using the rear view mirror like a submarine periscope and burst out laughing. Finally he replied, "That I do, Jonathan, that I do."

———

"So let me get this straight, between the four of you, you've figured out how we can get all of the baby stuff donated by the manufacturers, collected and flown to Buenos Aires free of charge and are scheduling a press release about a news conference kicking this all off in front of the Los Angeles Cathedral?" Zig said as he recapitulated the rapid fire briefing Kelly, Pierson, Rosita and Will had presented.

"That's about right Zig, but we've still gotta get Coke on line and that's the wild card right now." Will cautioned, not wanting Kowalski to think they'd laid a done deal on his desk. CEO's must manage their world.

"So if you magicians have got a line for all of this stuff free, why do you need my hundred grand? I got other things I can do with that kinda dough."

Will shook his head like Zig didn't understand English, "We ain't got the reconstitution part figured out yet Zig. Hell, we might have to spend the money on high-impact plastic for the bottling process. We can't expect Coca-Cola to push out everything for free. Hell, getting to their bottling plant is gonna be the linchpin to this whole deal, so we gotta have some capital flexibility. Don't ya think it'd be smart to be prepared?"

He seemed to ignore everyone else in the room as he zeroed in on Will, "I think I'm gonna get three a side from your sandbaggin' ass Kavanagh. Ten in the morning at Riviera, and don't get all hungover on me and start cryin' the blues. I'm seeing lobsters for lunch!"

"So how'd it go with Zig?" Johnny asked as they all dove into Oysters Rockefeller at Emilio's Steakhouse across the street from his Century Towers condo.

"Everything's nailed down except the deal with Coca-Cola. You wouldn't happen to know the CEO in Atlanta by chance?" Will posed with sarcasm.

"Elliott Richardson? No Will, I can't say that I'm armpit buddies with him; sorry man."

He looked over at Sam, who was looking very good in her little black Givenchy cocktail dress, and figured he'd pump her, "Our OB/GYN associate was quite taken with you today Mrs. Chessereaux. He thinks Johnny is a very lucky man."

"Is that so?" She replied with a wink. "He reminds me of Julio Iglesias, just younger and better looking. How in the world did you pair him up with Kelly?"

"Actually, he was Carmen's OB/GYN and she steered us to him. He is quite the intrepid fertility specialist, as he introduced us to an experimental procedure that worked the first time. After William here subjected him to his Cajun comradery, we became social acquaintances and Will brought Kelly in to save me from abandoning our marriage outright," Dom related with a furtive grin.

Will shrugged and then frowned as Sam scarfed up the last oyster. After he signaled the waiter for another dozen he responded, "He's definitely a hot commodity, but is somewhat intimidated by female veterans of the sexual revolution."

"So what'd she do, put him through boot camp?" Sam wondered.

"Believe it or not, she had to browbeat the poor guy to give him his first blow job! And he's 32 years old for Christ's sake!"

"Now that's a late bloomer if I've ever heard of one," Johnny grimaced. "So Zig just rolled over and copped a guilty plea on this charity? I find that hard to believe as much as he's fumed about getting revenge on your ass for that shellacking you put on him at Brentwood last year."

"He remembers, and wants three strokes a side—fat chance! Hey, we met the Ambassador down in Buenos Aires, pretty good guy; you remember he helped us with the taxes, tariffs and fees issues. His last name is Richardson too, Charlie Richardson. I wonder if he and the Coke guy are related?"

A light bulb must've gone off in Johnny's head because he was instantly looking for their waiter, "Any chance I can get a phone at the table? I need to make an important call."

"Hi Gordon, sorry to bother you at home, but I need to check out a prospective sponsor for this humanitarian project Zig's signed up for. I remember that you did some work for Coca-Cola a while back." He listened for a moment and said, "Right, Richardson's the CEO you lit up like the rain man. Do you know if he's by any chance related to the US Ambassador down in Argentina?" He looked at Will and asked, "What was his first name?" "Okay Gordon, his name is Charlie Richardson, which I guess is Charles." He got a huge smile on his face and said, "Thanks Gordon, that's what I needed to know. Have a good evening." Johnny looked at Will in triumph and reported, "The ambassador is his brother. How'd you figure that one out?"

"Think we can make an international call from that phone?" Will asked as he dug into his wallet for Richardson's card with his private line that was good at the office and home.

"Hell yeah, you can call anywhere Ma Bell operates from right here. Business talks and worries walk; what's the number?"

"Hi Charlie, this is Will Kavanagh, sorry to bother you at home but we're in LA coordinating our 'Help the Helpless' charity and really need a line into the Coca Cola organization. So do you think, no, would you be willing to call your brother and grease the skids for me to contact him tomorrow and enlist his aid in getting the formula bottled at their plant in Buenos Aires?"

"Where are you? I'm still at the embassy…oh, you said LA, right? Man, that charity campaign you guys started has really changed our relationship with the Archdiocese. Talk to me; what exactly is your plan?"

"We're in LA at sort of the launch for 'Help the Helpless,' and the devil's in the details, ya know? Now infant formula is like manna from heaven for the malnourished slum-dwelling new mothers, but it's widespread acceptance in the US is largely based on potable water availability…"

"Jesus, my cultural attaché says waterborne diseases are the biggest killers in the slums Will…"

"Right, but the soda and beer distributors have solved that problem by delivering the product ready-to-slake. We wanna do the same with infant formula, but we ain't got a bottling plant in our hip pocket," Will offered as Sam watched him closely, her eyes bedeviling him.

"So you want Chip to offer up his Buenos bottling plant to mix and bottle infant formula ready-to-drink?"

"Right again, we're tracking Charlie. Now tell him we ain't trying to glad hand him, and we've got cash to participate in a line share if Coke can possibly find a way to accommodate us within their production schedule."

"Explain the line share please."

"Jesus, I kinda leap-frogged a bit. We fly in the Enfamil formula mix and *Caritas Argentina* gets it to the plant…"

"So all you're asking for is potable water for the mix and bottling process?"

"My LA mole says Enfamil also sells it premixed for quick fixes with hungry young'uns. It's sold in dark bottles here—and I ain't done all the engineering due diligence—but it might require unique bottling. If this unfolds as fact, we'll have to pony up a line share to make it happen."

"That's too technical for me Will; Chip's the engineer, let his folks wrestle with the 'how to.' Chip is a bottom-line sorta guy though; what's in it for Coke?"

"Coke gets prime sponsor billing for the 'Help the Helpless' campaign if he can help us out. Think he'll bite?"

"What's in it for me?"

"Grilled lomos on the *parilla* with Grand Marnier for the final course," Will said, laughing.

"You do know they're one of if not the top net business in America, right?"

"Hmm, sounds like they need to balance profitability with spirituality *mi buen amigo Carlos*," Will offered, winking at Sam.

"I'll offer that as his primary reason for supporting 'Help the Helpless' Will; when you get the call from his R & D honcho you'll know it's a go."

"Thanks a million Charlie and have a good night."

Sam was looking at Will like he was a zombie, "I cannot believe you just called the US Ambassador in Argentina from our table at Emilio's! What did he say?"

"He said, and I quote, 'Listen Kavanagh, this is gonna cost you a grilled *lomo* and some Grand Marnier, think you can hold up your side of the bargain?' He'll make that call. He's just so relieved to find somebody treat him like a real person that he took to us." *Sam was literally radiating lust, so Will just closed his eyes and shook his head. How in the fuck can she be thinking about getting it on with Johnny around? Now I'll admit I'd probably sacrifice my first million to fuck her tonight, but be realistic!*

Dom just shook her head in disgust and offered, "I wouldn't be surprised to find that he has some Coonass Cajun blood somewhere in his family tree Sam. But I must admit, Charlie is a nice guy."

As Dom and Will were passing off into slumber land, four hours behind their body clocks and exhausted, they were stunned into an adrenaline rush as Sam climbed into their bed. Will jumped at Dom, holding her until she quieted, "The Walther's not there Dominique." She finally nodded that she was okay and looked around at Sam with concern. Will pulled her glorious blond hair aside and whispered in her ear, "Where's Johnny?"

"The poor darling; two seconals were too much for him with the Grand Marnier."

"Where's Willy?" Dom asked with mild concern.

"I just checked on him and brought the remote monitor with me. It's time for playback Mr. and Mrs. Kavanagh. I don't get such opportunities very often." Will barely heard her as he desperately searched through the bedroom closet, finally emerging triumphant with a heavy scarf. "What in the world are you doing Will; we need you here in the bed."

After he'd wrapped the scarf around her face reasonably tightly he smiled, "Say something." All he and Dom heard was a muffled, incoherent and most importantly very quiet mumble. "Okay, now you're ready to launch Mrs. Chessereaux."

Will was already moving down her body with glee as Dom attacked her breasts. He looked up just before launching into her vulva, "Right you are about opportunities with my living breathing kryptonite, and we're not gonna waste it! Good job with the seconals Samantha dear; you might make a commando yet!"

———

The scene at the first tee at Riviera Country Club the next morning was borderline comical, as Will wondered how many people followed the President around when he played golf. Besides the two carts for their foursome, Kelly and Rosita were in a third cart, with Dan Pierson and Jonathan following in another. "I can't give you three pops a side Zig; I've been stabbed, shredded with shrapnel and shot since we played Brentwood. How about we play it straight up?" Will offered, figuring he'd jack up Zig's blood pressure for good measure.

"Oh here comes the sob story. Tell ya what Kavanagh, since you're playing with my corporate counsel today, why don't we make it four shots a side. That should teach you not to take advantage of your elders," he said, breaking up into laughter so bad he started coughing.

"Alright dammit, we'll give you two a side, but that's the absolute vertical limit Mr. Hollywood CEO. We mere swine play bend over enough as it is," he played him, enjoying the banter.

He considered Will like a coiled snake for a moment, "Okay Mr. Walking Wounded, we'll make it two a side. By the way, what'd ya find out about the Coke thing? Bet they're just jumping with joy that we're gonna break into their production schedule down in Gaucho Land."

Will motioned for Kelly and Rosita to come closer. "Whoa, did I hear you say Gaucho Land? Dam Zig, you must be studying up on Cliff's Notes or something. Kelly just got off the phone with the Coca-Cola Research & Development VP. What'd you find out Kell?"

"They've made the commitment to accommodate our bottling within their Buenos Aires plant, but the nature of the infant formula requires a different type plastic container than they currently use with their own line of products. Dan is working with their engineering staff to locate suppliers of the resin and bottle specs so we can prepare an estimate of set-up costs. Coke has committed to partner up all other expenses associated with the bottling," she delivered in such rapid fire that she took in a huge gulp of air when she got the last word out.

Zig held up his finger and said, "Hold that thought." He stepped up to the tee and promptly sliced the ball so severely it hit a golf cart parked next to the adjacent ninth green. The golf ball caromed off the windshield, ricocheted off the roof of the cart in front of it and bounded back to the first fairway perhaps twenty yards shy of the Ladies Tee.

"Drop 'em Kowalski; you didn't make the Ladies for Christ's sakes," Will called out between fits of laughter.

Will was halfway through his downswing when Zig let out a tremendous 'Achoooo,' but to no avail as he ripped it 250 yards straight down the fairway. Will smiled at him as he looked at Rosita and asked, "So what'd you find out about the distribution down in Buenos Aires?"

Zig started to take a full swat at him with his traitorous driver, but halted when Rosita reported, "Minister Rojas has requested that we use El Palomar Airport at Campo de Mayo for transit associated with 'Help the Helpless,' as he can insure secure receipt and transfer to the *Cáritas Argentina* chapter of the Catholic Relief Services. He has provided them space at the air terminal to manage deliveries and is even making a warehouse available for temporary staging and storage. The Coca-Cola bottling plant is located near El Palomar and this arrangement will prove very advantageous."

Now Will was alarmed, "Rambo, we gotta find out what the runway requirements are for a loaded DC-10 bro."

"Already done Tonto; Palomar's just under seven thousand feet and if we limit cargo to seventy tons we can make it in and out, given the runway. Since we're carrying down powder instead of formula, I don't think that'll be a problem," Pierson reported with confidence. "Keep that number in mind for the return cargo, as it will not be powdered."

"So you gotta load all the cargo in FedEx shipping boxes, right?"

"Yep, so your guys can load the boxes up at Palomar; we'll do a test weight on the first one and figure it out."

"Damn, I gotta get ahold of Kellor and find out if he's ready to receive!"

Kelly pulled Will to the side and whispered, "You fucked her last night, didn't you, you asshole?"

"What are you talking about, fucked who?"

"You know who I'm talking about; the only woman that drives you into animalistic behavior."

"What the fuck Kelly? I slept with my wife; did things not work out between you and Jonathon last night or something?"

"You can't bullshit me Kavanagh; you drove it two-fifty down the middle on the first hole. I just want to know how you managed to pull that little sleight of hand off in the condo last night?"

Johnny glanced over at them with a sneer, the talking disrupting his address to the ball. Will put both hands over Kelly's ear, French-kissed it and told her, "Seconal, and she came like Mount Vesuvius erupting; all happy now?"

Zig's molars were grinding as Johnny followed with a bullet drive right down the middle, but reined it in enough to ask, "So what about this press conference? I saw the release that was supposed to go out."

"It's set up for tomorrow at two o'clock in front of the Cathedral of Saint Vibiana, and the Director of Catholic Relief Services is flying in for the event.

Dan's coordinating site setup with our publicity department and the Los Angeles Police," Kelly advised as Pierson gave two thumbs up from his golf cart.

"Okay," Zig finally said when Carlos had ripped his drive out by Johnny's, "sounds like everything's a go for the project. Good work you guys. Now if you'll excuse me, I've got to concentrate on my golf game before Kavanagh skins me alive!"

———

"So whatdya think about this shit?" Zig asked Will out of the side of his mouth as they stood on the top step of the courtyard entrance to Saint Vibiana Cathedral. Bartholomew Hynes, the director of Catholic Relief Services, stood next to James Cardinal Arrington who spoke about the 'Help the Helpless' project to about two dozen reporters and a few dozen interested bystanders. Rosita and Jonathan were standing on the other side of the podium from them, to the right of Arrington. Will couldn't help but notice that Saint Vibiana had been almost swallowed by encroaching progress, not unlike the Alamo in San Antonio or the Georgia State Capital in Atlanta. It made him wonder about the relative wealth of the Archdiocese of Buenos Aires, whose Metropolitan Cathedral was a huge monument to the Christian faith. The glass and steel skyscrapers visible in almost any direction paid testimony to the commercial dominance of Los Angeles.

"I'd say we're building a lot of good will for the *Norteamericanos* Sir Kowalski," he offered.

"Yeah, as long as you don't suck me dry buying plastic resin Kavanagh. And I would like to express my appreciation for the delicious lobsters yesterday at Riviera. Boy do you know how to throw a party," he whispered, but then broke into such laughter that the Cardinal paused and looked over at them.

"Right, that's the last strokes you're ever getting out of me Zigster. New rules for old mules," Will said as they smiled for the camera shots that were peppering the five of them. In spite of the four stroke handicap Zig had extorted from he and Johnny, Zig's partner Carlos made a twenty-footer for par on the last hole to decide the match. Although Will had started out straight and long, by the final six holes he was dragging serious tail feathers, telling Johnny the jet lag had him. In truth, his gorgeous wife Samantha didn't leave Dom and Will's bedroom until four-thirty, and two hours' sleep wasn't quite hacking it. How in the hell Johnny hadn't been woken from his drug-induced sleep considering his wife's even muffled pleadings to her maker was beyond him.

Zig glanced over Will's shoulder and asked, "Hey, I'm not going to lose my ace Producer over her Latin lover am I? I'd hate to see her head off into the sunset just after I get her trained."

"I don't see that happening Zig. I mean he may be the hottest thing since Julio Iglesias but she's set on building her career with Great West. Give her some credit for managing her life for Christ's sake."

———

That evening they were all out at Zig's Malibu beach house for the celebration party when Will smiled at Jonathan, "You don't mind if I borrow your girlfriend for a minute, do ya?"

He looked alarmed until Kelly told him, "It's okay Jonathan, Will and I need to talk business in private for a moment. We'll be right back."

When they had walked down to the beach behind a dune he grabbed her, pulled her into him and gave her a withering French-kiss. They were both getting happy when she pulled back and asked, "I don't know what that was for, but you sure surprised me!"

"That was for pulling off the miracle Kelly; damn did you play Houdini on this one."

"Really, for a moment there I thought you were missing your harem." She then rolled her eyes and began all but berating him, "It must be my ego tweaking the jealousy monster; I still don't know how you managed to pull off the *ménage* with Sam last night. Jesus, we've been there a lot and I know how loud things can get."

"Nah, I'm good; I couldn't be allowed a spoiled life like that forever. As for Sam, you gotta remember she's not the G spot Cossack Queen. She actually toned down the histrionics a bit considering the circumstances." He remembered and grimaced, "I almost forgot about the heavy scarf I wrapped tightly around her mouth. What I wanted to talk to you about is how things are going with Jonathan."

She smiled and told him, "Oh, I'd say they're going along swimmingly. Why do you ask?"

"Because Mr. Kowalski is growing alarmed that he may lose his prized Producer to the Southern Hemisphere. God I can't believe you just met him before Thanksgiving last year—you have applied yourself admirably. Now I told him you were intent on making a career of the movie business, so I covered your rear; but I'm curious as to how you see things going?"

"He actually called me his prized Producer?"

"Nah, that was my interpretation; he actually called you his ace Producer. You didn't answer my question."

"Well," she said, rolling her eyes dreamily, "he's the first man that's gotten my attention since a certain acquitted Air Force officer swooped me down to Diego a while back. Does that answer your question?

"I'd say that's fairly obvious to everyone who knows you, but isn't he a bit naïve compared to my worldly Cossack associate?"

"Oh yeah, he's already told me he loves me, but that kinda scares me. I'm not ready to leave Los Angeles and shuck it all to be a doctor's wife. Like you so aptly pointed out, I've only been with this Hollywood business for seven months."

"Okay," Will said as he pulled her back, grabbing both of her hind quarters in his hands, "that's what I needed to know. Now you know Dom—and especially me—will support you no matter what decision you make with your life. But I like to know what's going on in that pretty little head of yours. Now I think we'd better be getting back before Jonathan puts out an APB on us."

She smiled wickedly as she grabbed his burgeoning member, "It's good to know that all of you still cares about the Cossack Queen. After last night's workout I'm actually flattered."

He pecked her on the lips, "You think the Midnight Cowboy doesn't care about the minx from Kansas? Perish the thought!"

———

"Hey Bob, how are things in Washington?" Will asked from the study of the Century Towers condo. He just shook his head and pointed his index finger at Sam when she hit the speaker button.

"Hey Will, where the heck are you? I tried calling you in Argentina but the maid said you were in the US. What gives partner?" Bob Kellor replied from his office at Buzzards Point where the Air Force Judge Advocate General's offices had been relocated, mostly successfully.

"We're in LA kicking off a major charity drive for the peasants in the Buenos Aires slums; you might have heard about it, 'Help the Helpless'?"

"Have I heard about it? Jesus, General Melson is about to have a cow over the fact that you greased some skids via his buddy Charlie Richardson."

"All above water my friend, and just about to launch, which brings us to this urgent call. Please tell me you and Roberto Fabiano have been in touch about things. We might be having an empty FedEx DC-10 at El Palomar Air Field in less than two weeks *mi amigo*."

"Okay, so far as initial marketing approach is concerned, we decided an indirect absorption by retail establishments gives the best payback for the projected impact on demand. I've become friends with Ron Wood, owner of King Street Distributors in Alexandria, and he's agreed to serve as our agent of record with the ATF—that's the Bureau of Alcohol, Tobacco and Firearms…"

"What, the FDA isn't into alcohol yet?" Will asked, shocked.

"Not yet, but they're lobbying the hell out of Congress to have it added. In the meantime we've only got to keep ATF happy, and their General Counsel is a retired USAF JAG type. So Ron Wood's umbrella's gonna cost us a flat fee of five cents per gallon imported, or $365 per DC-10-10 load of 18,432 Magnum bottles of wine…"

"Why Magnum bottles? I take it you're hoping the restaurants will use it as their table wine and wait for diner's compliments to raise the bar?"

"You got it Will, and we're having to half load the FedEx SAA cargo containers so we don't exceed total cargo weight of seventy tons. This is due to the runway length at El Palomar, but with FedEx charging us only variable direct costs—they had to fly it back anyway—it works out to $3656 for the one-way shipment…"

"Which would have been charged to Great West if we hadn't stepped in?"

"Correct, so the transport cost works out to twenty cents per Magnum bottle for a net cost at destination of two twenty a bottle. Ron says customs is going to run less than eighty cents a bottle, so we're essentially delivering it to the Alexandria warehouse at three bucks a Magnum bottle."

"Damn, sounds pretty impressive so far; how you getting it out to the restaurants?"

"Again, Ron Wood is best buds with the Vice President of the Washington Restaurant Association, and they're all excited about this new vintner coming onto the scene. Ron's not carrying any Argentine wine now, so it only competes with his reds; that's my story and I'm sticking to it."

"Sounds too good to be true; I guess Roberto's got things ready on the other end?"

"Yep, and he told me about pushing that air commuter business to you; damn Will, how are you getting any sleep?"

"We also got the best pilot and E-9 maintenance superintendent from their equivalent of the 89th MAW bro; Capital Air Services is all but running itself, with no recurring overhead as we're leasing facilities and reservations services from the FBO. What about whiskey? Don't shoot me for asking because man, you have blown me away getting the wine piece operational Bob."

"Good news for modern man Mr. Kavanagh; there is a single distributor licensed by the Argentine Economic Ministry for all imported spirits—that's anything with an alcohol by volume exceeding twenty percent."

"Why is that good news? I thought we wanted to be that man," Will offered as Sam and Dom hovered around him like moths.

"Konrad Keller used his influence with Juan Perón to gain the license in 1973 as a favor for political campaign contributions. When the licensee became known by wealthy Jewish merchants in Buenos Aires, Konrad became scarce and all but disappeared into the countryside west of San Carlos de Bariloche…"

"Oh shit, don't tell me Roberto knows the guy?" Will shouted as he started cutting a jig with Sam and Dom.

"When the Israelis came looking for him—turns out he was a senior officer of the *Waffen-Schutzstaffel*—he died in a horrible motorcar accident in the Andean hills…"

"Say no more Sir Kellor; how much does he want for the license rights?"

"A *Señor* Aleandro Sosa has indicated that he is willing to convey the license rights to all but the premium liquors for fifty thousand US. Whatcha think?"

"I think we just hit paydirt brother; we happen to know this man fairly well as a matter of fact."

"That's what Roberto said, and he thought it best to keep the licensing rights away from his family name, with an eye towards the future."

"Okay, so we'll wire in a hundred thousand to Destination Partners for services rendered *mon ami*. By the way, you ain't doing this shit gratis bro; I'm thinking seventy-five hundred a month oughta keep you in beer until we get this thing generating a net profit. I know you've been making magic Robert; am I being a tightwad as my wife always accuses me?"

"Seventy-five hundred a month, are you shitting me?"

"Okay, sorry, what number should it be?"

"You idiot, that's more money than Howard Hughes has; damn, can you really afford that before we're operating in the black?"

"Robert, go buy your wife something very special and tell her you've been a good boy. I will be in touch my friend!"

When he hung up, totally satisfied with life, Sam and Dom sat in his lap in an odd triangle. "So the wine's set up and you've got your liquor license; what's not to celebrate?" Samantha said as she pulled his hand inside her blouse.

"Jesus Christ woman, didn't you extract all there was of me last night, excuse me, early this morning?"

She ignored him as she kissed Dom rapturously, then proceeded to unzip his trousers. "Listen here cowboy; I only get a shot at you once every blue moon. Here, swallow these little pills after I chew 'em up lover boy."

34

MAKING 'IT'S RAINING IN MARRAKECH' A REALITY

THE 'HELP THE HELPLESS' PROJECT was running very well, with almost daily publicity in the Buenos Aires *Herald* extolling the compassion and virtues of *Cáritas Argentina* in ministering to the poor and underprivileged of BA. Things were going so well back in the States that the manufacturers, FedEx and Coca-Cola were extending their efforts as the third plane of supplies arrived at El Palomar. Dom and Pierson were closely watching the costs associated with bringing the polymer resin into Argentina for Coca-Cola to manufacture the opaque bottles. Will had already told Zig by phone that it was ironic that the only real cash outlay for the project—the resin—was going to determine how long the effort would last. It was also noteworthy that the United Nations Children's Fund, or UNICEF, had taken special notice of 'Help the Helpless' and was encouraging a wider branching of the program's reach via the Catholic Relief Services. The entire effort had become a source of tremendous personal satisfaction for Circle Entertainment, although Hal and Carmen insisted on being out of sight background participants.

International Delights was surprisingly working well on both ends. The Washington Restaurant Association had embraced Argentine vintners hugely, as another full load went out on the second charity drive DC-10 return flight. Pierson was smiling as Roberto's fork truck operators set down the SAA boxes in the warehouse, other workers quickly unloading the airline containers with pallet jacks. A Fabiano SA step van was pulled up to one loading dock as the contents of one of the boxes was offloaded directly into the van. Dan saw an

Argentinian Customs agent sign off on the bill of lading and the step van full of bourbon, scotch, Canadian whiskey, vodka and rum drove off to the secure warehouse in Recoleta. If the DC oenophiles kept up their praise of the Cabernet and Malbec, they'd be shipping out in 750 milliliter bottles soon.

Dan Pierson was now supervising planeloads of set equipment, wardrobes and props into BA and Bariloche from LA as Hal served as the Argentine ground manager. Kelly had all but moved down to Argentina and was hopping between BA and Bariloche to oversee set developments. It was a great day for all when the Pan Am Airlines 747 arrived in Buenos Aires and they got to meet the cast for the first time.

Circle Entertainment hosted a kickoff party at *Casa Fabiano* their first night in town. Dom and Will were anxious to meet the primary cast members out of purely voyeuristic interests. Carmen had discreetly left the house before the visitors arrived to help obscure her identity from all except Zig and Carlos, who knew her from the initial debriefings and had executed non-disclosure forms concerning her real identity. "Dom, I'd like you to meet Tressica Martin, who is playing your alter ego in *It's Raining in Marrakech*. Tressica, this is Dominique Kavanagh, who really was exchanged for her mother during the actual operation in Algeria," Kelly explained by way of introduction.

With the two of them standing next to one another, Will got a glimpse into how casting for movies played out. Tressica was maybe ten years younger than Dom and was slightly prettier, but her hair was a dead on wringer and they were about the same height. "My goodness, they certainly reincarnated me into a beautiful woman, what do you think Will?" Dom gushed.

The hopelessness of answering her question became apparent when he replied, "I suppose Tressica's a good person to cast as Dominique; you're certainly both drop dead gorgeous. So who's playing Tony Marantz?"

"That would be me," a good looking guy about Will's height said. "I'm Justin Farraday Will, and it's great to finally meet you. I've been studying the script for a week wondering what you were like."

Will shook his hand as he gave him the once over, "I see they've cut a few years off and made me damn near irresistible in the transition. It's nice to meet you Justin. So who's playing Lucifer, you know, the antagonist Algerian warlord?"

"Ah Sandrigan; that would be Alphonse." He turned and motioned a tall, handsome man in his late thirties over and said, "Alphonse, I'd like you to meet Will and Dominique. This is Alphonse Sentiro, who will be Sandrigan in the movie."

As he shook their hands Dom looked at him in studied amazement, "The likeness is startling. Tell me Alphonse, are you Mediterranean?"

"No, I am from Cuba," he replied, pronouncing it 'ku-bah.'

Will got Kelly's attention via the mini-upjerk with his head, "So who's the smoking hot blonde over there?"

She smirked at him and waved the blonde over to where they were standing, "Patty, these people are Dominique and Will Kavanagh. Guys, this is Patty Smithson, and she will be playing the part of our assassin, or Angel Masterson in the movie."

Will was borderline overwhelmed by her smoking hot beauty, and was momentarily stunned when she asked, "So who is this Angel Masterson? I've been waiting to meet her since we signed the contract. The script certainly makes her seem dangerous."

"She's too dangerous to meet actually Patty. But I can assure you that you are cast perfectly for her. How do you keep the guys off of you?"

"Come on Will, I'm not that glamorous. I cannot believe that we came down here to shoot the movie and I'm not going to get to meet her," she pursued.

"Sorry Patty, that's the way the contract reads. She's a very private person. I would think that after you read the script you could understand that."

"So the script is accurate?"

"I wrote it, so I think you can make your own assessment. Want something to drink?"

"Sure," she said, cutting her incredible blue eyes at him, "make it something she would drink."

As he was making his way to the patio bar, Hal walked up with a man who looked like he was a refugee from the Haight-Ashbury days of the Flower Children. "Willy, I'd like you to meet John Forsman. John is the Director for Marrakech. John, this is my homeboy Willy Kavanagh. We go back a long ways."

Will was stunned when John shook his hand with a strong, manly grip, "It's nice to finally meet you Will; Zig Kowalski has told me some interesting things about you."

He gave him the once over, long hair going gray tied behind his head with an almost bushy beard, but there was something about the focus of his eyes that got Will's attention. "So are you a golfer?"

He smirked and said, "Pretty much a hacker; I carry a ten at Brentwood. How about you; do you chase the pill around fairways?"

"A ten! Jesus Christ, I bet Zig hates your ass! Hold on a minute, I gotta get blondie a drink."

"Pour up four of 'em partner, it's time to celebrate," Hal instructed.

Will grabbed one of the snifters of Marnier along with a glass of ice water and turned to go find Patty, but she appeared like a siren in front of him, "Is this Grand Marnier? I seem to remember it is your drink of happiness. Cheers!"

He was very impressed with both her recall and her zeal as she took a healthy swallow, looked at the glass of water and asked, "What's this for?"

"Oh I like a water back to cleanse the palate, to get ready for the next sip. You know, like smoking a cigarette before the next round of sex," he replied, watching her closely for a reaction.

She looked at him coyly and replied, "Is that so?" Then she took a slug of the water and smiled.

Hal was looking at them like they'd both just stripped naked, but collected himself enough to say, "John here admires our tastes in music Willy."

This snapped Will out of his lustful reverie enough to ask the Director, "Is that so?"

"Ken Banks, my music director looked over the notes you two made on scoring the script and couldn't believe you hadn't worked in the business before. I gotta tell you, you two guys are rock and roll freaks. Man it's a relief to find kindred spirits," he told them as they high-fived one another.

"So are you gonna actually consider them for the movie?" Will asked in disbelief.

"Consider them? Ken's securing the rights to use them in the movie at the precise moments you two indicated in your notes. This might be the first time I've ever had the actual participants in a scene tell me what songs were playing in the back of their minds when the shit was hitting the fan."

"Well, to be honest," Will told him, "Led Zeppelin might have been playing on the radio when the back window in the car exploded, but I think that's the only outside help we had scoring it. Glad we could enhance the realism."

Patty cozied up next to him and challenged, "If you're so good with music, why don't you put something on that takes you back to when the 'shit was hitting the fan?'"

Taking her gambit immediately, within a minute he was queuing up Led Zeppelin's *When the Levee Breaks* and told her, "I think I've got you cast in the perfect role for when this one was playing out in my life."

She was rocking her whole body and shaking her head to the song when she looked at him through smoky eyes and asked, "What role would that be?"

"My unattainable, invulnerable lust target; you fit her to a 'T.' Whatdya think Patty, couldn't you see yourself doing the most exotically erotic strip tease to this song?" Will asked, unable to help himself as he sang along with Robert Plant.

She smiled viciously before leaning in, "As long as it wasn't a tease I think I could get into it."

———

At La Cabrera's the next afternoon, the transformation of the restaurant into a Hollywood movie scene was amazing. Inside the barricades there were lighting props set up in key places, the shading effects incredible. Will snuck up behind Jonathan Calvatori, "So you're neglecting your patients once again Doctor Calvatori? It would seem a certain raven-haired minx is wreaking havoc on CIRVIDAR."

He grimaced and defended himself, "Actually, I was enlisted by the Tourism Ministry as on-scene medical support for the production."

"Right, like Patty Smithson's really gonna kill Sidi. You know Jonathan, I still can't figure out why Rosita has never made a pass at you. The two of you seem hot enough for one another." Will smiled inwardly, remembering how close Rosita had come to joining he and Dom in the ménage, her bra and panties the only remaining barriers when she decided she was too attached to Rambo for such hijinks. Will knew she'd come to regret that decision someday.

"So you would choose Rosita over Kelly?" he posed.

"That's a tough one, but you had Dom and me channeling Ms. Dupree right into your wheelhouse. So you aren't attracted to Ms. Cabrera?"

"Oh, she's a very interesting female, let there be no doubt. But I must ask, how many such women do you think one man can accommodate at one time?"

"Life's all a matter of timing Jonathan; don't miss out on the good deals because you can never go back. Hey, there's Patty Smithson. Jesus, they've got her made up almost as hot as Catwoman!"

He snickered, "Yes, she is incredibly attractive. She has already approached me as to the true identity of her movie character. She told me you were making it a secret."

"But you didn't tell her anything did you?"

"I absolutely did not. Kelly assured me that I would die a gruesome death if I did so."

"Good girl; she knows the important issues ma man. See you later."

He snuck in behind John Forsman's seat to observe a movie scene for the first time. Although he was energized and animated, calling out to assistants controlling everything, the actual process of shooting the scenes seemed so repetitive and boring that Will concluded watching grass grow would be more entertaining. When he finally said "Cut, wrap it up," Will was shaking his head when John noticed him, "That went incredibly well Will. I can't remember many scenes wrapping after only two takes. What did you think?"

"To tell you the truth John, the finished product bears no resemblance to the component parts. Man, that was about as boring as watching grass grow!"

He smiled knowingly and nodded, "Welcome to my world. The action begins on the cutting room floor after all of this is over."

The 'prick' scene in the garden behind the restaurant was shot after dark, and the effect was very alluring. Will could easily imagine himself in that park outside Farouk's in Algiers, the shadows and lighting effects were so perfectly balanced. He was projecting himself into that park imagining Carmen's seduction move when a female voice asked, "So what did you think?"

He turned to find Patty Smithson, hotter'n a sunspot in her outfit, "I wasn't actually in Algiers for that event, so I can't relate how it replicated the original. But the lighting effects were extraordinary, and you look like a million bucks. I guess you're off to Bariloche now?"

"No, they don't need me again until the factory scene in Ksar, which is going to be the last scene shot in Bariloche. A friend told me I should check out the beach here called Punta Del Este. Have you been there?"

"Yeah, but it's too cold down here even for getting a tan now, which I might add you don't seem to desperately need. If you want to go to the beach, I'd head up to Rio for the Copa Cabana thing," he told her.

"So are you going to be in Bariloche for the filming?"

"I don't know, after observing my first movie making scenes today I think I might just hold out for the big blast. You know, when the casbah goes boom at the end of the prisoner exchange."

"If you're not going to Bariloche, what are you going to do?" He had no clue where she was going with this line of inquiry, but he wasn't letting it drop off the cliff unattended.

"Live my life maybe? Just kidding; we've got a huge humanitarian project going on here in Buenos Aires. As a matter of fact, Zig and I are sort of the parents of it. Think you might want to see how we're helping some poor people?"

She looked at him in total disbelief, "You and Zig are involved in a humanitarian project helping poor people? Tell me about it."

"It's called 'Help the Helpless,' and we've set up a network to deliver baby food, diapers and infant formula to the impoverished *Porteños* who live in the slums. We sure could use a *Norteamericano* movie star's glamour in getting the attention of people. Whatdya think?"

"Sure, why not," she said as she slipped her hand under his arm, "it doesn't sound like it's good beach weather down her right now anyway."

He gave her a nod, patted her hand and told her, "That's my girl, good decision. We need your help."

———

Dom and Will went to see the cast off the next afternoon, with Pierson working with the set crew most of the night getting it packed up for shipping across Argentina to Bariloche. They were kicked back relaxing on the patio when Carmen asked, "So how did my stand-in do with the restaurant scene?"

"I wasn't at Farouk's with you, so I don't know how lifelike it was, but she seemed to pull it off believably. It took the dedicated efforts of all concerned to keep Patty Smithson from discovering the identity of Angel Masterson, I can tell you that." He smiled sardonically, "Of course if you'd wanted it to be spot on you'd have had your pregnant self out there coaching Catty Patty."

"Well, it would seem we have a respite from such worries now. I assume everyone has flown on to Bariloche?"

"Actually, Patty's not needed again until the end of the Bariloche shoot, so she and the actor playing Mustafa are hanging out in Buenos Aires to do what they can for 'Help the Helpless.'"

"Really; she actually cares about the poor? I assumed she was a spoiled, pampered diva from Hollywood. You certainly seem to be attracted to her Mr. Kavanagh," she said with a furtive smile.

"In my humble opinion, she looks so damn edibly good that it's easy to assume she's a diva. But she hasn't waited for me to open doors for her or anything. She was interested in the project's mission to try and help the newborn children in the slums."

Carmen was nodding her head in thought, "If I can arrange it, I would like to meet this woman. She sounds as though she is more than a glamour star for the posters. What do you have her scheduled to do?"

He grabbed the clipboard and checked, "Tomorrow she's shooting some commercials for the two main television networks here in Buenos Aires. Rosita will be with her, and Kelly and I looked over the recorded message and it looks fine. The only crap shoot is the adlib interview. That should show what she's made of. Then after that we're taking her down to *Ciudad Oculta* to hand out some formula to new mothers. It'll be my first glimpse into the *Villa Miseria* Rosita talked about some author making famous."

"Yes, that was the slum Bernardo Verbitsky described in his novel," she provided. She stopped to give Will the once over, staring at him menacingly.

"What, what is in that lizard brain of yours Belen?"

"You don't know this, but Rosita certainly does; the remnants of the Revolucionarias slithered off into the slums to hide after the Junta crushed them. It is not safe to travel without a shield in such places as Oculta. I shall coordinate with Rosita to make sure we have adequate coverage to insure your safety."

"So you're saying SIDE's gonna be pulling surveillance in Oculta?"

"Not surveillance Will, they will be on full counter-terrorism alert in Oculta. I will see if there is a discreet way in which I can meet her, this Patty Smithson; perhaps I can do this as the aunt of a young woman who has recently given birth."

"And just how in the hell is a smoking hot *Porteño* gonna pull that one off pray tell?"

"Do you not think I could get next to you Will, if I meant deadly harm?"

"Oh yeah, I didn't mean to doubt you Carmen, it's just that...."

"Just don't act like you know me when you see me; agreed?"

———

Oculta was a shanty town on the southern edge of Buenos Aires, and per prior arrangement the soldiers and police escorts left the 'Help the Helpless' convoy and remained at the entrance to the 'city', marked by high corrugated sheet metal walls erected as a barrier. The transition from Buenos Aires proper to Oculta was so dramatic as to be startling. The narrow streets were reddish clay and the houses—if you could call them that—opened directly onto the street. Yards and green spaces were apparently vestiges of the affluent. The tangles of wires streaming overhead added greatly to the feel of confusion, and 'junctions' streaming off in every direction from 'base' meters for power or telephone redefined the term jury-rigged. It became quickly apparent that sanitary sewers were nonexistent here, as the stench was so powerful that it took a good thirty minutes to get accustomed to.

Their only shell of protection—ostensibly from the gangs that preyed here—was the *Cáritas Argentina* trucks painted brightly with the organization's logo they were traveling in. The logo consisted of a red square with a blue cross inside with red arrowheads pointing to the center of the cross from the four quadrants. Will thought it fitting that the outline of the square itself looked like it had been brushed on vice stenciled, and the red color gave it the illusion of Christ's sacrifice on the Cross. The words *Cáritas* and *Argentina* were stenciled above and below the logo, and it made for a very distinctive symbol. They had no idea how expansive Oculta was, but they seemed to drive very slowly through the crowded streets for perhaps thirty minutes before pulling up in front of a church. The church was the first real building they had come across since entering Oculta, as even the stores on the street corners were constructed of plywood and sheet metal.

When they came to a halt, the trucks were immediately surrounded by hundreds of people, and Will looked at Dom to make sure she was okay. She smiled at him and patted his shoulder, "Welcome to my world Will. Do not be afraid of these people because they know we are not here to harm them."

Nour Fayed, the Egyptian actor who was playing Mustafa, nodded his head as he looked out the window and agreed, "This is the world I come from too Will. This place reminds me much of Cairo."

He nodded his head wistfully, "I've been in some bad parts of Manila—where I was the only white boy for miles—and I never smelt any place like this before." Dom suddenly cleared her throat as Will wondered if he'd said something wrong.

"I suspect you may modify that opinion once you've visited the Jemaa El

Fna in the old Medina of Marrakech. Our group was not in condition for tourist attractions when we passed through in February, but we will go there soon and experience a souk that has been in existence for millennia."

Patty Smithson was looking a bit shaky when she surmised, "So this is what the Third World is like, huh?"

Rosita looked at them and nodded, "This makes you appreciate running water and sewers, *n'est pas?*"

Will winked in appreciation of the French student, "Like nothing else could Rosita. Are we ready to begin unloading the boxes?"

"In a minute," she cautioned. Ramon Sanchez, the *Cáritas Argentina* site supervisor traveling with them had gone over the distribution process—what Will called the rules of engagement—before they left the warehouse at El Palomar airport. Once they arrived at the distribution points (there were seven groups of three truck convoys heading out to the various churches in Oculta) the site supervisor would set up a table next to the last truck and deliver individual paper bags to each woman who walked up. They would unload the trucks and pass down boxes of bags as Ramon handed out the goods to the recipients. Each paper bag had four liters of infant formula, two dozen jars of assorted baby food and a dozen disposable diapers. They had unloaded most of the last truck when it dawned on Will that they were innocently contributing to the rampant trash accumulation in the ghetto, but that was a distant consideration compared to malnutrition. As they handed out the last box and started to head to the middle truck to begin unloading it, some loud or excited Spanish could be heard at Ramon's distribution table.

"What's going on Rosita?" Will asked as he drew next to her, looking at Dom with concern.

She listened for a moment and told them, "One of the *barras* is demanding that Ramon give him his watch." They had been briefed about gang violence potential in the slums before departing the airport, with one of the 'ROE suggestions' being to remove all jewelry from their bodies and leave it in a safe place. Dom was wearing both their wedding rings and baht chains in her underwear for safe keeping.

"I thought SIDE had this operation under control *Señorita* Bond," Will whispered into her ear.

"Oculta is huge Will, and we cannot deploy helicopters due to the hidden sightlines. *Señorita* Bond, is that what you called me?"

"Jesus, Ramon didn't even listen to his own orders?" Will hissed as he climbed down out of the truck to see what all of the commotion was about.

When he jumped down to the dirt street, it became apparent that there was more than one 'barra' doing the intimidating, with four teenagers fanned out around Ramon. The leader was getting more excited by the minute, pointing a switchblade knife and demanding that Ramon give him the watch. Will stepped towards them and said "Hey!"

The sum total impact of his bravado was that the barras were now focused on all of the visitors as the leader snatched Ramon's watch and took two steps towards Will. He yelled something in Spanish, but Will was clueless so he looked back at Rosita for help. "He wants your wallet."

"Well tell him I don't have one," was all he got out of his mouth before the blade was at his throat."

Will very slowly rotated his head to look at the barra, and he was filthy, his eyes so dilated that he had to be high on something. By now the other barras were circling in, the baseball bats and sections of pipe in their hands. The barra leader yelled again, and looked like he was enraged with Will.

"He doesn't believe you Will. Give him something," Rosita pleaded with him.

Will shrugged and started to take off his shirt, but the point of the knife under his chin proved he hadn't guessed right. "Give him what he wants Will," Dom pleaded from behind.

Will looked back at him and said, "What the fuck do you want?"

He pointed down at his shoes and shouted again, "You want my shoes?"

He didn't see the baseball bat until it was too late, the back of his thigh suddenly blaring with pain. He looked back at the punk and started to swear at him, but was interrupted when a woman's voice in front of them could be heard speaking quietly in Spanish. Will was amazed to see the woman, filthy and wearing ragged clothes, dirt smeared on her face and her two front teeth missing, assuming control. She was however, holding a Walther PPK under the barra leader's chin and giving him instructions in Spanish. He slowly dropped the switchblade into her other hand and smiled at her right before she kicked him viciously in the groin. He fell over onto the ground, screaming in pain as everyone looked on in total bewilderment. Will quickly looked back at the woman and almost missed it. Her eyes were a deep green with golden flecks sprinkled around the irises, and he knew who their Gideon Angel was today. She reached down to the punk's pants, retrieved Ramon's watch and handed it back to him. She then gently kicked the leader and hissed something in Spanish to them, causing the others to drop their clubs and flee. She then said something to Ramon, and he nodded for them to resume unloading the boxes.

When they had finished unloading and handing out all of the goods, they climbed into the middle truck as their angel climbed into the truck in front, apparently to provide security until they left the slum. They were about two blocks from the entrance to Oculta when the lead truck stopped to let the angel out as everyone waved and saluted her as they mercifully re-entered Buenos Aires proper.

"My God Will, are you alright?" Patty Smithson asked breathlessly.

"Yeah," he said flexing his sore right leg, "that had to be an hour ago and I don't think anything's broken. Welcome to charity in the real world Patty. Are you beginning to see the need here?"

"The need for guns, that's for sure. Who were those guys?"

"I don't know, some punks high on something. That leader's eyes were as dilated as hell," he told her, exhausting his knowledge of the attackers.

"They were *barras*, the local gangs that began in support of their local football team. They commonly smoke *paco*, which is a paste from the manufacture of cocaine. I truly apologize for this, but I am afraid that is what the slums are like," Rosita advised them.

Not feeling the love of charity yet, Patty intoned, "We sure could have used Angel Masterson today in that ghetto. We're lucky that woman came to our rescue."

Will smiled at her, "Congratulations, you just met Angel Masterson. What'd ya think?"

She punched him playfully in the arm, "Oh come on Will, that woman didn't look a thing like me."

"Right you are Patty, I must have been mistaken. You did know Angel Masterson is an expert at disguises, right?"

Now the glamorous Hollywood vixen looked at him closely, "I just can't imagine that good a disguise, and I've been through some heavy duty makeup preps before. But I will give her props for disarming those thugs like they were playthings."

He put his arm around her shoulders, leaned in and said, "Now you're coming around baby; no wasted motion and she coulda killed all four of 'em in five seconds. Does that sound like a pregnant peasant in a slum to you? If so you didn't notice that Walther PPK she had was spotlessly clean. You just met her Patty; she told me last night she was impressed with you for your willingness to go to the slums. That was our little reward today; felling better about helping out now?"

To his amazement, Patty Smithson pecked him on the lips and smiled, "I am, are you?"

———

"Now those missing front teeth were pretty damn convincing," Will told Carmen as they toasted with margaritas back at *Casa Fabiano*.

The women were playing it straight with lemonade as Carmen replied, "My trainers in the 601 were quite skilled in the ways of disguise. What gave me away?"

"They'll have to invent colored contact lenses before I can't recognize those incredible green eyes of yours babe. Actually, a lot of people have green eyes, but you're the only one I've ever known with those golden flecks sprinkled around."

"I'm afraid this is the last time I will be able to bail you out for a while Will. The baby's due in six weeks and undercover operations are about over for me."

"About over for a lifetime I hope," Hal said, not too convincingly.

"So how did our friends from Hollywood like their introduction to Oculta today?"

"Patty Smithson was incredulous when I told her she had met Angel Masterson today. She said you didn't look a thing like her," he told her, smiling at Dom. "I think I convinced her when I suggested you coulda killed all four of the *barras* in five seconds. She was still giving me that grimace when I asked her if she noticed how clean the Walther PPK was."

Carmen laughed and replied, "Between the wig, the mud and the mouthpiece I suppose she didn't think so. Now why did you even tell her that?"

"Because I knew she wouldn't believe me. Well done Mrs. Rayfield, and thanks for the rescue."

"My pleasure," she said, then tossed him the switchblade she had taken off the *barra*, "give this to her as a souvenir of her visit to Oculta."

Dom chimed in right on time, "Will's already gotten his; I saw Patty kiss him on the lips as we passed back into Buenos proper."

"Hey, she was lost then found and didn't have Angel Masterson to thank, so I was next in line. Well played Mrs. Rayfield, well played."

———

"Jesus Christ, now that was something," Will all but shouted to John Forsman after the Catalano mansion imploded to the ground thanks to three well-placed shaped charges Pierson had planted around the foundation. "Not only did you make the building light up in those starbursts as each rocket landed, but the smoke trails overhead were incredible!"

"Don't congratulate me, tell Dan what a job he just did," John said as Pierson walked up to them, radio in hand confirming that fire suppression efforts were successfully underway.

"You only get one chance to do that right Rambo, and I gotta tell you, that was pretty damn close to how I remember Sandrigan's casbah going down. Man you even remembered to include that RPG round coming back towards the helicopter right over our heads."

The 'helicopter' for the reenactment was comprised of a stand twenty feet in the air with an M129 grenade launcher hard-mounted onto it, firing smoke rounds at the mansion instead of the high explosive rounds used in Algiers. The beauty of using actual 40mm rounds—even if they were benign smoke rounds—was that Dan got the realism of the smoke trails streaming overhead. They had discussed optimal camera angles for the final takedown, and John had played overkill with eight cameras filming the sequence from various angles, including one from the ground where Pierson, Hal and Will had watched the real show. John had compensated for the lack of an adjoining airstrip by having a Cessna 172 hug the tree line on the way in to simulate the low takeoff over the casbah.

"How'd you like that propane tank going up on the side? Pretty realistic compared to what we saw in Algiers, eh?" Dan said as Will high-fived him in congratulations.

"You didn't actually use propane did you?"

"Nah, propane's too unstable. That was some C4 and a tank of diesel fuel."

"Right, wouldn't want to take any multi-million dollar estates down unnecessarily now would we?"

It had been three days since the Oculta visit back in BA, and John had driven the cast pretty hard for the exteriors and interiors for the Algiers Casbah scene. "You actually shot interiors on location?" Will asked in disbelief.

"We'll look at them when we get back and see how the lighting looks," Forsman offered as Rambo listened closely.

"I don't know John, it was pitch black in that house we cleared room by room; you might have gotten the right effect here," Rambo offered.

Now Forsman laughed, "The right effect in your memory might not translate into the right effect on the big screen Daniel. We'll look at it before shooting it again inside." The Director looked at Will and smiled, "All Patty's been talking about since you guys came in is that switchblade knife you gave her as a souvenir from that slum. Is what she told me true, that Angel Masterson gave you that for Patty as a souvenir?"

"Yep, it's all true John, and before you leave Bariloche you'll meet her too and not know it," Will said as he laughed and slapped Rambo on the back.

35

WRAPPING A MOVIE, AND A RELATIONSHIP

THEY WERE GRABBING SOME LUNCH in the commissary tent when Dan walked in with the news, "Hey John, I just got the weather update. There's a storm coming in from the northeast and it might be ideal for the landing in the port of Algiers scene."

His report surprised Will, "From the northeast huh?" He looked around to find Rosita and asked her, "Is that normal, that weather systems come into Argentina from the northeast? In the eastern US, everything seems to come in from the southwest."

To his surprise she instructed them, "Actually, the two circulation patterns are similar. The Coriolis Effect moves air toward the poles in both hemispheres." She turned to John and inquired, "How much filming has to be done on board the boat? There might well be watercraft advisories issued for Haupi Lake with the weather alert."

"We only need the entrance into the harbor, which here will be clearing the quay wall that extends along the waterfront from the yacht club. All of the other shots, including the interior scenes will be filmed on the lot back in Burbank," he replied. Their glimpse into the film-making world had been somewhat like drinking through a fire hose, but it had been interesting to learn how much of what otherwise might seem a uniquely outside event could be shot inside a soundstage in California. Only the scenes that were more economical to shoot outside were considered for location shooting. Set design in Hollywood had been developed to an incredible level, but the backdrop of the Andes was so overwhelming that Bariloche was an easy sell to the Director.

330

"So everybody you don't need for the Ksar scene is heading back, eh?" Will wondered.

John nodded his head, "Yeah, all but one of them has another movie coming up, so they need to get back and gear up."

His comment about heading back reminded Will that Jonathan's clinic was closed waiting for his return. He then noticed Dr. Calvatori was nowhere around so he asked Dom, "Have you seen Jonathan today? I figured he'd want to see the casbah implode. That's gotta be the biggest boom in this movie!"

"No I haven't, and Kelly has been out of sight as well. Perhaps I will investigate their disappearance," she posed as she got up to begin the search.

"Hey, they might be holed up at the hotel you know?" Will offered but was immediately chastised with a scathing frown from his now obviously pregnant wife.

"Will, you know Kelly is taking her job seriously; how many times has she even taken a break to eat dinner with us in the last two weeks?"

As they walked out of the commissary tent Will spotted Kelly darting into the mobile trailer that served as her office on location. They walked over and just as he was about to open the door, Dom put her hand on his arm and knocked instead. Will grimaced at her and opened the door, only to find Kelly slumped at her desk with her head in her hands whimpering. Dom and he were immediately on either side of Kelly, cradling her as Dom asked, "What is it Kelly? What has happened?"

She looked up at them, tears streaking down her face, "I told him no and …" she halted, breaking down into sobs as Will pulled her into his arms.

Dom and Will knew it wasn't time for fifty questions, so they let her sob as Dom got her a glass of water and some tissues. After a couple of minutes she stopped crying, faded into stuttered coughs and finally told them, "Jonathan asked me to marry him and I told him no. It was just awful Dom, he was totally heartbroken and I felt so bad for him. What am I going to do?"

Dom looked at Will and half-nodded towards the door, so he kissed Kelly on the cheek, "Kell, I'm going to get something for you. Dom will stay here with you." He then gently grabbed her face in both hands so that she would look at his eyes, "We both love you very much. You will live through this. I'll be right back."

As he closed the door to her trailer, Dan Pierson was heading towards the door with a head of steam so Will held out a hand to stop him, "What's going down Rambo?"

"We're heading over to the marina to begin setting up for the port landing scene. Kelly needs to get going," he said as Will gave him the raised eyebrows. It took all of two seconds for him to know something was wrong, "Tell me."

"Jonathan asked Kelly to marry him and she turned him down. She's in the shits for the moment. Can you go ahead and get things rolling down by the quay wall?"

"Sure, no problem; Jesus I can sure sympathize with her; I got my own dose of humility not too long ago. Anything I can do to help?"

"You got any whisky on set? What I have is back in the hotel room."

He rolled his eyes and nodded, "Sure, I got a bottle of Stoli in my desk in the trailer. Sorry I don't have any scotch or brandy. Want me to grab it for you?"

"Nah, I'll get it. Why don't you start your wagon train convoy and we'll bring her there as soon as she's stable again."

"No *problemo* Tonto, I will head 'em out. See ya soon."

"Here you go babe, drink this shot of vodka, it'll help," Will told Kelly once he got back to her trailer with the Stoli and two coffee cups from Pierson's desk. Dom looked up at him with a wink, so he poured her a small shot and handed it to her as well.

The alcohol made Kelly flush slightly, but she seemed to come around a bit, "Thanks, I needed that. I should have known this was coming, especially after our little seaside chat in Malibu." The inevitability of the parting must have suddenly dawned on her, as she started to huff a bit, so he poured her another shot and helped her get it down.

"There was nothing you could do baby, except enjoy the time you had together before he made the fateful play. If I were you I'd take it as the ultimate compliment; Jonathan is quite the catch. That is if you're looking to become a doctor's wife in Buenos," he told her, earning a scowl from Dom.

The vodka was apparently having the desired effect, as she gave him a grimace, "Oh it was worse than that. You know that he is accredited in the US, so he countered my reluctance to become an Argentine housewife by offering to move to LA and find a new life there."

Will thought he had gotten the impression she just wasn't ready for marriage, but Dom wasn't buying it, "So why didn't you take him up on his offer Kelly? If he was willing to move and disrupt his life for you I would say that's a pretty big commitment."

This all but caused her to start sniffling again, "It's not that Dom; I'm just not ready to get pinned down. It was only nine months ago that Will introduced me to Zig, and now I'm already a Producer for a major motion picture. I have to be ready and able to pick up and move to places unknown for months at a time. I can't deal with the commitment that a marriage takes when I'm giving this job my every waking moment. I know I must sound like a self-absorbed bitch, but that's what's important to me at this moment in my life."

"Good," Dom said as she kissed her on the lips, "you know exactly where you want to be—and you're there! Not many people other than Will and I can say that right now. What you said makes perfect sense and I want you to forget about what anyone else but Jonathan may think about this decision. I do not believe that you have been deceitful with him, so I am sure that his self-esteem will rebound from this blow. Will and I will make the necessary effort to insure that he understands what considerations were behind your decision—just in case he forgets in his sorrow!"

Will was already wondering if Rosita might help Jonathan with his rebounding efforts but throttled that to tell Kelly, "Did you know there's a major motion picture scene about to be shot over at Haupi Lake? I just happen to be charged with getting your hot little body over there so that Zig's world will not implode. Ready?"

———

"So how long before *It's Raining in Marrakech* is ready for the big screen?" Will asked John Forsman as they waited at the gate for his flight home to LA.

"Oh we've just completed the easy parts here. We've still got to shoot the studio portions and begin weaving everything together. I wouldn't want to tempt fate with a projection at this point, but it will be several months before we're ready to screen a test for Zig and the Board," he surmised.

"Well, if there's anything we can do to help things along just let us know," Will said as he shook his hand following the last call to board.

He wrapped Dom in a hug and told them, "You've already done it Will. I can't thank the two of you enough for the way you've made us all feel welcome here in Argentina. It is never like this on location. And please pass along our best wishes to Hal with his new child. How is his wife doing? I'm sorry I never got to meet her."

Will smiled at him and let him in on the secret, "Actually you did John; she was the woman that Mustafa allowed to live to go tell the world that Sandrigan was no longer a threat in the final scene. I told you last week you'd meet her before you left. I'll give her your regards."

"You mean the extra that was very pregnant?"

"One and the same John. I'll see you back in LA; have a nice flight."

———

"Love's just a pisser sometimes," Kelly shrugged in bed later that night. She told the crew she needed to hang back a couple of days to wrap up details, but Will knew she wanted to vent some steam and get her head back together after the blur of the location shooting. She had surprised him by wanting to be with them naked, as if she had some burning interest in checking out the very pregnant Dom *sans* clothing. He couldn't be sure if she wanted to file it away for future orientation, but what the heck.

"Hey, it seemed to be a magical mystery tour ride 'til the end sweet cheeks, so it coulda been far worse, right?" Will offered, trying to help her see that the front end of the relationship was the pearl in the oyster.

She tossed this around in her head for a moment and concluded, "I guess you're right, but the end of it was so painful. My God, I should have listened to you on the beach that night in Malibu."

"And done what? Tell Jonathan that you were taking a hike because Kavanagh asked you about your future? Nobody takes the hard plunge over mere advice Kelly. What do you think you're gonna do when the shit really does hit the fan?"

She looked at him askance and posed the question, "Yeah, what am I gonna do when the shit really does hit the fan?"

He smiled at her, leaned down to lick right up her slit and announced, "Well, when there's no tomorrow, the shit really has hit the fan. If I ever call you and tell you that, you'll know it's time to fish or cut bait."

On the way back from dropping Kelly off at Ezeiza for the bittersweet ride back to her 'new' life, Dom looked over at Will obviously flummoxed. "I'm not sure about Kelly."

"In what way?"

"I'm not sure I trust her completely," she replied as Will jerked at her in surprise.

"Did I miss something, or did she tell you in private that she hated you because you're having a child and she isn't?" He knee-jerked, throwing out the most bizarre reply imaginable.

"It's never that simple Will; you should know that by now."

"Okay, I give. What makes you suddenly think you can't trust Kelly anymore?"

"She didn't want to have sex even though we slept together for two nights. Doesn't that strike you as unusual?"

"Jesus Dom, she just came off the adrenaline ride of the shoot and she had to tell the Latin Robert Redford she didn't want a life with him. Don't you think it might just be possible that she's shell-shocked and wanted to be near humans she could trust unconditionally? You know, without any expectations?"

She reached over to pat his hand, sighed and said, "I suppose you're right Will. Perhaps I'm being overly sensitive with all of these hormonal shifts that are occurring within me."

"Heaven perish the thought my dear," he told her but ducked to avoid the slam she was aiming for the back of his head.

36

NO GOOD DEED GOES
UNPUNISHED

"HELLO, THIS IS MARY RHINEGOLD calling from Washington, is Charge D'affairs Robales available for Secretary Vance?"

"Yes Mary, this is Mark Robales; we're still adjusting to the chaos down here. Joan Reynolds couldn't subject her family to it any longer and I haven't found a replacement yet. Please connect me with the Secretary, thanks," Mark Robales said as he looked at his Regional Security Officer Bob Matthews, who along with a handful of employees made up the Charge D'affairs key staff at the US Embassy in Managua, Nicaragua.

The regime of President Anastasio Somoza had finally become too repressive for Jimmy Carter to tolerate, even though he knew the rebel Sandinistas were Marxists with considerable support from the Soviets as well as Cuba. Carter had officially notified the Somoza regime on February 26, 1979 that due to intolerable human rights violations, normal diplomatic affairs between the two countries could not be maintained. With that Ambassador Maurice Pedrano was recalled to Washington, and Mark Robales had assumed the principal role as U.S. senior representative. Peter Mora, Vance's new candidate for Ambassador, was undergoing U.S. Senate approval as Carter had notified the Sandinista Regime that the US was reaffirming normal relations with Nicaragua.

Over the past twelve months of complete insanity surrounding the Nicaraguan federal government's implosion, capitulation and replacement, Bob Matthews had been Mark's 'go-to' guy on the staff. Matthews had seemingly bridged the gap to the Sandinistas well before Somoza's departure, and was

336 ·

their primary interface for intergovernmental unofficial communications. Robales knew he could not hope to survive the transition to Daniel Ortega's minions without Matthews running interference. Although Matthews technically worked for Colonel Paul Lawrence, the Military Attaché, Matthews was the one who could 'swim among the sharks' and survive. Robales had been told early on when Pedrano left not to even look for his CIA Station Chief Berny Mendoza because he was totally involved in highly classified activities.

"Hey Mark," Cyrus Vance's voice suddenly materialized, "I've got a meeting with POTUS in an hour and the word Sandinista is going to be on the front of his inquiring mind. Give me the highlights of the last twenty-four hours; I'll interrupt if I need more detail. It's your nickel Sheriff."

"Okay boss, I've got Bob Matthews with me as usual…"

"Oh, you mean your eyes and ears amongst Ortega's faithful?" Vance said with a chuckle.

"That would be more correct than you could ever know Cy. What to mention first? Okay, at least the Junta is solidifying so that we can see it. Daniel Ortega's calling the shots obviously, but his brother Humberto has taken over what will become their Defense Minister…"

"Christ, this five minute broad brush stroke is gonna end up delaying the Security Council, but I'm not going in there naked dangit. What's he the Defense Minister of? I remember you telling me the *Guardia National* was essentially decapitated when every officer above the grade of lieutenant fled the country two days after Somoza. Please fill in the missing intel Robert," Vance said, obviously shifting directly to Matthews for the straight skinny.

"The senior guys weren't the only ones that fled to Guatemala Mr. Secretary. The Sandinistas captured possibly seven thousand of the most senior GN officers and enlisted men they could find. Of course the GN's equivalent of the Nazi SS, the CSGN Security Company troops were long gone before they could be snatched and held to answer. So they've got the fortress San Bracinto max security prison jammed to the rafters with the most strident of Somoza's regime that didn't manage to escape. Humberto's not the cancer cell sir, Tomás Borge is. In case that name doesn't ring any bells, Tomas was with Danny Ortega when they went to Markus Wolf's little Shelepin National Liberation Movements course for beginners in Havana in 1972. He's the mouthpiece back to Raul Castro via Silvio Coralles of the DGI and

Shelepin's disciple Andropov. There are some other names floating around as Junta members, but the Ortega brothers, Tomás Borge and Henry Ruiz are the 'Fearsome Foursome.'

"So who the hell's in charge down there? This thing sounds like a soup sandwich—that's what I heard the DCI call it the other day. Is anybody stamping passports at the airport?" Vance asked in frustration.

"Fortunately, Ortega and the Sandinistas were really focused on the *Guardia National* as their primary target, so some of the other Somoza departments didn't get the ax as badly. As for the new keeper of the peace, the *Policia Sandinista*, or Sandinista Police, has taken over the offices and functions of the old National Police—whose sole jurisdiction was greater Managua. Like I mentioned earlier, Humberto is the head of the new *Ejército Popular Sandinista*, or the Sandinista Popular Army—EPS for short. A Colonel Armando Vargas is the head of the Sandinista Police—I think he was a Sandinista cell leader previously. His enforcer is his former aide, now Lieutenant José Rivas. Rivas can be a real pain in the ass, as he brought a healthy dose of ego with him…"

"Listen Bob, I can't copter over to the White House from Foggy Bottom, so we've gotta cut this off. Is there anything involving American citizens with these new Sandinista overseers? Also, it'd be great if I could take a list of your briefing notes with me to the Council meeting," Vance interrupted, beginning to show impatience.

"I just faxed them to Mary Rhinegold Mr. Secretary. There is one issue that might become a festering sore sir. Lieutenant Rivas arrested an American Lutheran missionary last night on trumped up suspicion of insurrection charges. Now it's all unofficial at this point, and I'll try and work some underhanded magic to spring him. But if something or somebody makes a stink of it, I'll lose my ability to nip it in the bud with, say, two thousand *Córdobas*—if you know what I mean. That's like two hundred fifty bucks, so let's hope nothing disturbs the nest before I can get to Rivas."

"Okay guys, that's a good intel dump. By the way, just in case somebody on the Council's Lutheran, what's the missionary's name?"

"Colton Kavanagh, and he's from some Podunk town in Louisiana called Gastineau," Robales said, reinserting himself back into the conversation.

"Kavanagh, why does that name seem vaguely familiar?" Vance asked as Robales held his hands up in surrender.

"Let's hope nobody asks Cy; his brother William led a band of my former

Phoenix commandos into Algeria six months ago and destroyed the empire of the biggest drug and weapons smuggler in Africa. Guy's name was Sandrigan el-Boukhari until Will put a bullet through his brain. I don't think there's any connection to his brother being arrested, as he was indirectly putting the heat on Bolt Sportswear—they've got a huge factory down here that visiting *Norteamericanos* refer to as a sweat shop…"

"What the hell did you just tell me RSO Matthews? You fill me with ho hum bullshit until you mention the one thing Carter would throw me in the hoosegow over? Why was he putting indirect heat on the sweat shop?" Vance asked, now angry instead of impatient.

"Believe this or not—as I got it from the barrio church priest where Kavanagh's been doing great work—but our missionary man got concerned when children attending Sunday School didn't show up for school during the week. He found out they were child laborers at Bolt's Sportswear factory and started rallying the parents to take a stand. Bolt musta complained and Bolt is a major source of income for a lot of families here—whether it comes from child labor or not. So this Lieutenant Rivas magically turns up at a rally Kavanagh was holding for parents of the kids who weren't getting schooled. To make this a complete clusterfuck—and you might want to adjust that term for POTUS— the primary goal of Ortega and his Sandinista junta is to implement Cuba's successful National Literacy Program to improve job opportunities for the peasants. Now I've got my guy working on this seeming disparity, but I don't like where it's leading at all Cy," Matthews reported as Robales cringed.

"And where might that be? I can see the Nicaraguans being upset about the possible publicity on the sweat shops."

"It ain't the Nicaraguans Cy, it's the fucking drug cartel out of Cali, Colombia, that sends a lot of their product through a nearby seaport called Masachapa. I know, I know, what's that got to do with school kids, right? Unfortunately, some of the same kids are employed as lookouts for the cartel transit teams. If Kavanagh gets in their crosshairs, I wouldn't give a plug nickel for his chances in prison, that's for damn sure."

"Well, as much as I don't need additional problems I'm glad you told me about missionary man Kavanagh's plight. I take it you're working it from the inside, right?"

"Yes sir, with all due diligence; we'll provide a report at the next status call sir," Matthews replied as Robales hid under his desk.

"Good, keep up the good work down there in the soup sandwich. Gotta go; talk to you guys later."

———

"Hello Comandante Daniel, how goes the revolution? I notice that you are answering Anastasio Somoza's telephone, so things must be progressing well, *sí?*" Silvio Corrales asked as the new power broker of Nicaragua sat down at his sworn enemy's desk and opened the humidor.

Corrales was a senior officer of the Cuban *Dirección General de Intelligencia,* or Intelligence Directorate, in charge of exporting former KGB Director Alexander Shelepin's vision of national liberation movements in Central America. The rebellious Sandinistas had been in the Communist camp since 1959, when the KGB recruited Carlos Fonseca Amador, the founder of the *Frente Sandinista de Liberación Nacional,* or FSLN. Of course, with the success of Fidel Castro's revolution and overthrow of the Cuban government in 1959, Havana became the hub of KGB efforts in Central and South America.

"Silvio, I should have suspected you would be the first to call me here. Things are going very well, but it is also very hectic trying to capture the rats before they leave the sinking ship. San Jacinto is full of Somoza's manipulators but we are filling up the prisons too fast; who would have thought that a problem two years ago, no?" Daniel Ortega replied, lighting the Cubano cigar and smiling at his brother Humberto sitting across the desk from him.

"No one, except possibly you and me Comandante. Our friends in Moscow are most pleased with your work; though they suspected Somoza's own greed would do him in. The Politburo is still taking bets on who assassinated Pedro Chamorro last year, setting off the powder keg as it were. Is there anything we can help you with Daniel?" Corrales offered, hoping Ortega would breach the arrest of the American.

"Nothing I can think of at the moment Silvio, although at some point we expect Somoza's Guardia officer's that fled to Guatemala will form a counter-revolutionary force to come after the Sandinista government. When that happens we will be most appreciative of any information concerning American help they may receive," Ortega said as Humberto winced. They were supposed to be basking in victory, not looking over their shoulders for the ghost of Somoza to reappear.

"I suppose congratulations are in order for two things Daniel; our KGB rezident Colonel Kravchenko just advised me that the United States has rees-

tablished full diplomatic ties with Nicaragua following your overthrow of Somoza. This is a very positive development, as staying off of the *Norteamericano's*
radar screen is a valuable survival attribute," Corrales told his golden-haired
revolutionary boy.

Humberto heard that last sentence and began to squirm, giving his brother a hand signal. "Hold on Silvio, I must speak with Humberto for just a moment; please hold the line."

After putting Corrales on hold Daniel looked at Humberto, "What is it?
What has happened that I do not know about? Silvio almost seems as if he's
setting me up for some bad news."

"Armando advised me that José Rivas detained an American missionary
last night and is holding him in the Municipal Lockup. He was apparently
fomenting insurrection among the poor by rallying children's parents because
they weren't attending the school he set up at the Lutheran Church in Barrio
Pomares..."

Daniel was suddenly impatient, "Humberto, is not our predominant
campaign issue the Universal Literacy Program that the Castro's mastered
following their takeover in Cuba? What in the world was Armando doing allowing his hired lackey Rivas to do such a thing?"

"It is more complicated than that brother; the children were not attending
school because they were working in the Bolt Sportswear factory. This missionary man Kavanagh told the parents that child labor was not allowed in
the U.S. and they should not have to tolerate it," Humberto added, but Daniel
was now livid.

"I do not care; this runs counter to our sworn goals and objectives Humberto. We must release him and call it a mistake," Daniel said as he reached
for the phone. He was not prepared for the swiftness with which his brother
clamped his hand over Daniel's.

Before he could utter a word, Humberto said with fear in his face, "Unfortunately this American Kavanagh's advice was overheard by one of the
neighborhood defense committees and word quickly filtered back to José who
in turn advised Enrique Constanza. José was acting on the orders of *Señor*
Enrique Daniel."

Daniel Ortega looked like he could scream, "What possible interest could
Enrique Constanza have with a Lutheran missionary?"

"Apparently some of the children that work at the sportswear factory also serve as lookouts for his transfer operation in Masachapa. The potential for international focus on the Bolt factory apparently caused our friend some serious concern." Daniel rolled his eyes and shook his head. He knew it was suicide to offend the Cali Cartel's Celeno, or cell leader, responsible for the entire transshipment route from Colombia to the Mexican border with the U.S.

He shook his head as he punched the button, "Silvio, so sorry to keep you waiting, but Humberto was advising me of the arrest of an American missionary who was fomenting insurrection with the poor of greater Managua. It would seem this missionary has posed a problem for our friends in Cali due to threats to expose the child labor issue internationally. I will have to give this situation some study before acting. Considering our goal is universal literacy—from the superior Cuban program—we must be very cautious about how we deal with this missionary schoolmaster."

"You just passed my first test for trust Daniel; odds were fifty-fifty between here and Moscow that you'd deny it and allow it to become your first international diplomatic crisis," Silvio Corrales told him as Ortega's blood pressure spiked.

"Forgive my ignorance Silvio, but why is an obscure missionary of interest to our friends in Moscow?"

"Because his brother wiped out their main African arms distributor six months ago right before shooting him between the eyes. I suggest you make this missionary Kavanagh hard to find and then allow him to have a regrettable accident. If he is allowed to live outside your prison again, you will likely have all manner of international press descending upon Managua like a plague. Please let me know how that is going, as I am now under orders to report via Kravchenko how this problem is being resolved. Until then Daniel; what a fine, fine start for a revolutionary hero."

37

TAKING THE GOOD WITH
THE VERY BAD

"*Cohiba Lanceros*, eh?" Proclaimed Hal as he lit up in the waiting room outside the maternity ward of the *Hospital Alemán*, causing the few others in the room to frown at he and Will.

"Nothing but the best for Wade Rayfield's debut into the world of oxygen breathers," Kavanagh said as he happily puffed the incredible Habana cigar. "Well I guess this is gonna trim your wings, eh Kemosabe?"

Hal tried but failed to slap the back of his Cajun buddy's head, "In your dreams Willy boy. Hal Rayfield ain't ready to hang up the spurs yet!"

Will was about to remind him of his gimp leg when the door from the ward opened and Dom came walking out with a bundle of baby blankets, "Would you like to say hello to your newest godson?"

Will was instantly on the little guy, immediately surprised by his head full of soft blonde hair. "Hey big guy, how you doing? Welcome aboard. The girls ain't got a chance!"

Baby Wade didn't seem to focus on his godfather but made a 'gah' sound as Hal reached out, took him and opined, "He's got his momma's eyes, that's for sure."

Will looked at Hal's very brown hair and surmised, "That ain't all he got from his momma. That boy is gonna be one oversexed cowboy!"

Now Hal was pleased with the assessment and agreed, "Damn right; the women don't stand a chance around my little stud!"

"Yeah well, your ass has about two thousand diaper changes before you have to worry about that!"

Hal grimaced and retorted, "Willy, why do you always have to try and play funsucker ma boy? I believe Henrietta will assist in such matters."

"Hey, that's why you keep me around Harold. And you'd better apprentice up buckwheat, 'cause your ass ain't always gonna be in the comforts of *Casa Fabiano!*"

"Here, hold your godson you little prick. I need to go check on Mrs. Rayfield," he said as he quickly threw on a surgical gown and headed towards the delivery room.

"How's Carmen doing Dom? I'm not well-versed in the nuances of childbirth."

She rubbed her now very noticeably pregnant belly and reminded him, "I would suggest you pay close attention William, as we will be revisiting this event in three months. She was in labor for about two hours, which Dr. Calvatori told us was an incredibly short time for a first pregnancy."

"So how's Carmen doing? What was it like?" He asked since Dom had been all but railroaded into standing in for Hal during delivery. Will had hounded him so doggedly about being a wimp during labor that he still sported a hard knot on his right triceps that withstood Hal's best right cross.

"She is doing fine, but is tired and happy. I am glad that I was able to assist her during labor as I now know what to expect when it's our time." She then looked at him closely and asked, "You're not going to become afraid like your friend Harold when our daughter arrives, are you?"

"Jesus I hope not Dom," Will said as he rocked Wade lightly, "but childbirth seems like a terror-filled experience compared to—say—taking down a well-defended, crazed warlord in a distant land."

She leaned in to kiss his cheek, "You'll do just fine Will."

They both turned as Jonathan Calvatori walked out of the ward, still in his scrubs, surgical booties and face mask dangling from strings over his neck. "Hello Will, I see you have met our newest arrival at *Alemán*. What do you think?"

"Well, Dom thinks I've got three months to complete my training. She just told me that Carmen's labor was a South American land speed record," he told him as he handed Wade back to Dom.

Jonathon looked confused until Will took him by the arm and led him off to a quiet alcove. Dom was having none of this as she followed. He glanced back at her as he asked, "How's my favorite fertility specialist doing in the post-Dupree era? Man I'm sorry it had to work out like that."

He got a pained expression on his face, looking at them both forlornly, "I was and still am heartbroken. Kelly was everything I thought I ever wanted in a wife. But I have to accept her decision that her career is most important to her at this time."

Will was shaking his head, relieved that Jonathon was taking it so well, but if he was as good looking as Calvatori, he'd roll with it too. "Here's my advice to you Doc: keep your friends close, your enemies closer and prospective par-amours like Rosita Cabrera in sight. You gotta seize the moment sometimes."

He smiled at Will, shook his hand and said, "Thank you Will, I will keep that in mind. I will see the two of you next week for the third trimester pre-natal checkup."

Almost as soon as he turned to head back into the ward, Carmen's par-ents walked back in carrying drinks from the downstairs cafeteria. "Look who we have for you Carlita," Dom said as she hugged Wade gently before hand-ing him over to the proud grandmother.

"Here you go George, Havana's finest," Will said as he handed him a cigar.

Carlita looked up from googling over her grandson to scold her husband, "George, you know you don't smoke those anymore."

He was inhaling the stogie deeply, savoring the rich tobacco aroma and finally looked at her, "I don't believe that having one to celebrate the birth of our only grandson will send me out early to the Pampas."

"So the Pampas is heaven huh? I learn something every day I'm here in lovely Buenos Aires," Will admitted, having heard numerous references to the fertile Argentine lowland plains.

"It is if you're from there!" George replied as he signaled for a light.

———

That evening they were kicked back after dinner, extolling the virtues of Chil-ean salmon steaks as Will snuck George another stogie and signaled to follow him out to the patio. Just as they had made it safely to the refuge of the smok-ing area Henrietta poked her head out of the sliding glass doors, "There is a call for you *Señor* Will. I believe it is your Mother."

He looked at George and said, "I gotta take this one George. Hopefully she's just checking up on Dom and the baby. Go ahead and torch off that *Cubano*."

"Hi Mom, how's everything in Gastineau? Guess what, Carmen had a baby boy today! Hal's a daddy!"

"Oh Will, that's wonderful news. Is Hal there? I'd like to congratulate him."

"Nah, he's still at the hospital. How in the world did you know they had the baby today? Word sure must travel fast!"

"I didn't, but I am so happy for them," she said, as he instantly detected trouble.

"What's up Mom, is everybody okay back there?" His mind was working on flash drive now, trying to remember any health crises his grandparents or aunts and uncles might have been suffering through.

"Yes son, we're all doing fine here in Gatineau. I'm not sure about Colton though. I tried to reach him at his church in Nicaragua and the priest there told me he hasn't been back since some rally he was at two days ago. I know I am probably overreacting, but it's not like him to stay out of touch if he knows we're trying to reach him."

Will instantly scanned the house until he found Dom and gave her a nod, "It's probably nothing Mom. He may be out away from the church on some mission activity. What's that number for the church? I'll call up there and see what I can find out. I'm with Hal's in-laws and they can help me with the Spanish if I need them."

Dom had a concerned look on her face as he covered the receiver and told her, "Colton's missing in Managua." His mother Jan on the other hand was obviously worried, as she quickly assumed the worst.

"If that were true, don't you think the people at his church would know about it? I can't help but worry about your brother Will. These missionaries go off into places they aren't familiar with. Your father just told me there was some news about a revolution in Nicaragua that ousted their President. I remember horror stories of those missionaries who ran into cannibals in Africa. I'm so worried Willy." Will tried desperately to control the panic rising in his brain, as Colton's disappearance in conjunction with a *coup d'état* had nothing but clusterfuck or worse, written all over it.

"Come on Mom, there aren't any cannibals in Central America. Tell me that number and I'll check it out and let you know what I find. Will that make you feel better? We'll hit 'em from both directions until we find the boy."

"Oh thank you Will. I so hope it's nothing but a mother worrying about her son in a foreign land. You will call and let me know what you find out, won't you?"

"I promise Mom, you'll be the first to know. Now try not and worry about it for now while I check it out, will ya? By the way, have you talked to anyone at the Lutheran church who knows about Colton's mission work?"

"I called the Seminary he attended in Houston, but they referred me to the headquarters in St. Louis. I spoke with a Reverend Spiker there, and he seemed to know about where the missionaries were in Central America. I've got his number too if you want to call him."

"Great Mom, you did good. Give me that number too. You say his name was Spiker, like a railroad spike?"

"Yes, that was his name. Please let me know what you find out, please Will?"

"I will Mom, trust me. Now I need to see what I can find out. I love you Mom. I'll be in touch soon."

He all but threw the phone down at the receiver as Dom followed him to the study where the satellite phone resided. He looked at her with controlled panic, "Somebody's nabbed Colton in Managua. I need to find out what the fuck's happening."

———

"Hey buddy, are congratulations in order?" Alex asked when he picked up the LST at ROUST in North Carolina.

"Yeah, he's got a bouncing baby boy named Wade Alex. Is Rico around by chance?"

"You sound a little stressed Will, is everything alright down there?" He asked as Will heard him whistle in the background, hopefully signaling Rico to come over to where he was.

"Maybe not, where's Rico?"

"He's right here, good luck buddy. You know where we are."

"Don't think I don't know that brother; let's hope this is nothing."

"Hey Will, what's going on?" Rico asked as he came on the line.

"My brother Colton's disappeared down in Managua from this church he's been a missionary at for the last two years or so. I just got the call from my mother in Louisiana, and she's in a huff and didn't get diddley shit when she called down there. What I need you to do for us is call the church and find out all you can through either charm or intimidation. If we've got to move out, the sooner we know there's trouble the better. Oh shit, I almost forgot, Hal and Carmen had a seven pound bouncing baby boy today named Wade Fabiano."

"Okay, what's the number you have for the church?"

"Here it is bro; the name of it is St Timothy's Church of Hope in Barrio Pomares in Managua. Mom said the Minister's name is Geovany Morales. Thanks a million bro; sure is nice to have somebody who speaks the language when you desperately need it!"

"Yeah, you should think about learning it Mr. Kavanagh; it might come in handy for the kind of things you get yourself involved with. I'll be in touch."

Will glanced at Dom and said, "Rico's on it." He grabbed a house phone in the study dialing the number from memory, which was nearly unprecedented, "Hey Charlie, Will Kavanagh here, and I'm in a pinch. I hope you're not up to your ass in alligators right now."

"Actually Charlene and I just saw President Videla off after a wonderful dinner and conversation. Now that woulda never happened before you and 'Help the Helpless' came into my life. Talk to me son, you have my undivided attention," Ambassador Charlie Richardson told him, which for some reason had a calming effect on the panic.

"Okay Charlie, my Mom called to tell me my brother Colton—who's a Lutheran missionary in Managua—disappeared from the church he's been working as a schoolmaster for two years. She said Dad saw some news program that a *coup d'état* had occurred in Nicaragua. Dom and I will be flying up as soon as we get a lay of the land, but I knew you'd probably know the situation on the ground there better than most; so whatcha got?"

"Holy Mother of Christ…"

"Do what?" Will screamed, interrupting him and causing Henrietta and Carmen's parents to run to the study. "Jesus Christ Charlie, what the fuck over? What's got you so keyed in?"

"Nicaragua, and Managua in particular, is in a state of emergency due to the abdication of longtime dictator President Anastasio Somoza. Holy Jesus Will, the new leader of the *Sandinistas*—Daniel Ortega—just assumed power today and POTUS has already granted Nicaragua full diplomatic recognition with Somoza's departure. Mother of God, I just read the diplomatic flash override message not two hours ago from Foggy Bottom. How in the world could your brother get arrested in the middle of a revolutionary takeover?"

"I ain't got a fucking clue Charlie, but I bet somebody in Managua does. I've already got my guy onto the priest of the Lutheran church Colton was the schoolmaster at, so he'll be giving me a real-time readout on pre-arrest details soon. Are you buds with the Ambassador in Managua by chance?"

"There isn't one Will…"

"Fuck!" Will screamed again, grabbing at his hair now.

"Hold on Will, it's not that bad; President Carter accused Somoza of serious human rights violations and recalled the Ambassador to Washington this past February. The Charge D'affairs, which is like the Deputy, a guy named Mark Robales, has been the senior U.S. rep there since then and in charge of the chancery. So at least we've got a foot on the ground there. Let me call Mark right now and see if they know about your brother's arrest. What's his full name?"

"Colton Johnson Kavanagh, and the church he was working at was St. Timothy's Church of Hope in Barrio Pomares in Managua. The priest at the church, and I guess Colton's boss, was Minister Geovany Morales. My mother gave me the name of the Missionary Coordinator at the Lutheran Church-Missouri Synod in St. Louis, so Reverend Spiker's my next call. Can you find out what Robales knows about this for me Charlie?"

"I'll call the Crisis Center at State if I need to Will, but we're three hours ahead of Managua, so everybody should still be on post at the Embassy. Remember, all hell's breaking loose there, but we've got maybe the best RSO in the Western Hemisphere there, so he'll know what's happening on the street. What's the best number to get back to you, this local number which I assume is at *Casa Fabiano?*"

"Roger that on the number Charlie—not many people drop everything to react when you need 'em ya know. What's an RSO by the way?"

"Oh, that's the Regional Security Officer assigned under the Military Attaché. Forget the attaché, the RSO there—a guy like your pals that went to Algeria with you—named Bob Matthews is the most connected guy we've got in the Americas. If anybody knows, Matthews will and I'll call you back. I promise Will Kavanagh, your brother is the top concern in my life right now."

"God bless ya Charlie; there ain't many people like you in my life," Will told him, glanced at Dom and knocked on the wooden desk for lying.

"We're wasting time; I'll be in touch soonest Will. Keep the faith son, bye for now."

Will looked at Dom as he grabbed the sat phone, "Charlie said it's a clusterfuck in Managua and can't imagine an arrest happening in the middle of a revolutionary *coup d'état*. He's pulling the string on that and will get back. I'm calling this Lutheran Missionary Coordinator guy." He took a breath while he keyed the sat phone for the St. Louis number, "Rico's onto the priest in Managua."

"Yes ma'am, I apologize for calling after hours, but I was wondering if I could possibly speak with Reverend Spiker? My name is Will Kavanagh."

"Actually Mr. Kavanagh, it's only 4:30 here in St. Louis, but may I ask if you are any relation to Colton Kavanagh?"

He remembered suddenly that they were two hours ahead of St. Louis, "Yes ma'am, he's my brother and my mother said she'd spoken with the Reverend earlier. Would it be possible to speak with him?"

"He's right here Mr. Kavanagh, please hold on."

"Mr. Kavanagh, it's good to hear from you. I spoke with your mother just a while ago."

"Yes sir, that's why I'm calling, and please call me Will. What can you tell me about what's happened to Colton?"

"First I would like to verify that you are related to Colton Kavanagh. Can you tell me your grandfather's full name?"

"Of course. I suspect the one you know about is Johnson William Colvay, and he's the minister at the First Lutheran Church of Lafayette, Louisiana. My other one is...."

"That's quite enough Will, I believe you. Your brother Colton has been affiliated with the St. Timothy Church of Hope in the *Barrio Pomares* in Managua for the past two years. Minister Morales called earlier today to convey his concern that Colton had not returned from a family counseling session two nights ago. That's when we notified your mother; I hope she's not taken to a panic attack."

"Okay, that check's out with the info Mom had on him. What's he been doing down there at the church? Mom said something about him being a schoolmaster but I ain't got a clue. But I know my brother, and it is highly unlikely that he has involved himself with any illegal activities. He's a straight arrow sir; as a matter of fact he married me and my wife last December."

"No, I agree that Colton is above reproach. He has focused his efforts on trying to reach out to the children of the barrio. I understand he has been quite effective in incentivizing participation by the children with assurances of minimal meals and basic necessities. After he got the children to start attending church he discovered they were illiterate, as they could not read the simplest written Spanish text. He sought and was granted an additional five thousand dollars to build and outfit a rudimentary primary school on the church grounds. He's quite an innovative young man. "

"Yeah, I get that sir. From my conversation with the Ambassador here, I learned there's been a *coup d'état* in Nicaragua and some outfit called the Sandinistas is now in charge. Now here's the deal, what kinda craziness could he have gotten himself into that could make him disappear? Ambassador Richardson was clueless on how he coulda gotten arrested in the middle of a *coup d'état.* Got any ideas on that?"

"I have no idea whatsoever, and I just learned of this overthrow of the Somoza government twenty minutes ago. I have not been to Nicaragua myself, so I am naïve regards the political issues. I am sorry but that's about all I know. What Ambassador are you speaking of? Where are you calling from Will?"

"Oh, I'm in Buenos Aires, so Charlie Richardson's the Ambassador to Argentina. Now he's turning hell upside down trying to find answers for me, and I've got a Spanish Spearchucker Jones interrogating Minister Morales via long distance. So when's the last time you spoke with him?"

"Actually it was late last December, perhaps when he was home for your wedding."

"And he didn't mention anything out of the ordinary?"

"Nothing I can recall, but he did ask me for information about some garment manufacturers on Madison Avenue in New York. He didn't tell me any reason why he wanted the information."

"Madison Avenue huh? Isn't that where the high-end clothing industry is located?"

"Yes, as well as the major sporting line of athletic clothes. Is there anything else I can possibly help you with Will?"

"Not at the moment Reverend, but thank you so much for speaking with me. I'm gonna find my brother and I may be back in touch for some help."

"Please do so at any time Will. And please let me know what you find out about Colton."

"Will do sir. Have a good evening."

"Well, you heard all that; any ideas?" He posed to Dom who had been listening in on the remote headset.

"Only that I wonder if there's a connection between the clothing industry and Nicaragua? But what that could possibly have to do with Colton escapes me."

Will was pondering this connection when the sat phone trilled, "Whatcha got Rico?"

"Okay, I spoke at length with the minister of St. Timothy Church of Hope, a guy named Geovany Morales, and I gotta tell you that your brother Colton is well liked. So anyway Colton was installed as an adjunct minister with the church focusing on outreach efforts towards kids. He ended up setting up a school at the church for kids because there apparently isn't a public school system in the barrios. Colton noticed that there were fewer kids at school than attended Sunday services with their families and began to investigate. What he found is that the missing kids were working at garment factories, more commonly referred to as sweat shops, which employed almost exclusively child labor. His efforts to entice them to attend school ended up making him a somewhat controversial figure with the parents, who were divided between needing the income from the kid's labor and wanting their children to go to school. Colton was attending a rally for the parent's two nights ago and hasn't been seen since. That's about all I got for now."

"All you got? You gotta be shitting me bro! Jesus Christ, you put together a hell of a lot for someone who wasn't on the ground there." Will came down off of the high to begin thinking tactically. "So what you got cooking Rico?"

"It's pretty quiet up here at the moment. We don't have another class starting for three weeks. Alex and I have been doing some mods to the dormitory to split out some female rooms and such."

"Are you in for some adventure? We'll pay you the going rates," Will proposed.

"Hell yeah, I'm in. Alex might have to step away from this part though.

Ask Hal about the last time they were in Managua. Where you wanna meet up?"

"I'm thinking Cozumel. Let me see about some private wheels and get back to you. How about pack up a lunch for three, and we need to eat light on this one. Tactical stuff only."

"You got it Will. You already suspecting trouble?"

"You never need a gun…" he began.

"…Until you need one really badly. I get it. What timeframe you looking for ETA?"

"He's been gone two days, so we better get in there before the trail goes completely cold; we'll launch from here in 24 hours for Cozumel. I'll be in touch about airlift. Thanks bro."

"Will, you still there?" Rico asked as Will snatched the handset back.

"Yeah, did you forget something?"

"No, but Alex just walked up and overheard us talking. He says one of our armpit buddies works at the Embassy down there and will ring him up to squeeze the blood from the turnip."

Will smiled at Dom, "The former commando's name is Bob Matthews; the Ambassador down here already told me about his rep—that he was the best in the Western Hemisphere. Anyway the Ambassador's calling the Embassy in Managua now for intel, but ask Alex to see if he can get to his buddy Matthews and get us the straight skinny. Big dogs don't always know the good shit; we good bro?"

"Alex is listening and is shaking his head; he can't believe you know about Matthews but will make the link, over and out."

Will looked around as Hal walked into the study and told him, "Trouble in paradise. Dom, how about fill him in while I call Johnny."

"Hey buddy, how you doing?" Will asked Johnny Chessereaux at his office in San Diego.

"Not bad Will; I heard you guys wrapped up in Argentina, and John Forsman is a happy camper. What's shaking?"

"There's trouble in paradise bro. My brother Colton's gone missing in Nicaragua. I'm in need of some private airlift between an obscure airport in eastern North Carolina and Cozumel. Any chance of tagging on Great West airlines for a hassle free lift?"

"Your brother this time huh? Man, I hope you're not getting in the shit again. You check with your buddy Pierson yet?"

"Not yet, but he'll need the nod from above before he can make any magic happen. Think you could sprinkle holy water on him for me?"

"You got it buddy, I'll call him right now and cut him free like the bird. After the hosting job you guys did for John's crew in Argentina and that charity job that made Zig look like the saint he ain't, your credit is somewhere close to infinity around here."

"Man I really appreciate the help. Once again Johnny Chessereaux comes through in the clutch."

"Who the hell you think you're talking to Kavanagh? Not the guy who took a flawless five carat diamond ring to his wife on our anniversary and made her the happiest woman in San Diego? You really know how to stack up credits buddy. I'll call you back with the info; no better yet, I'll have Dan Pierson call you and you guys can work it out, okay?"

"Thanks a million Johnny; I owe you one bro."

"Bullshit Kavanagh, I owe you one. Think electric blow jobs ma man."

Will laughed as he signed off, "*Sayonara Yoko-san* Chessereaux."

"I don't want to go back to Managua unless I really, really have to partner," Hal said without preamble after he hung up with Johnny.

"Yeah, I get it that you need to stay here with your wife and son. I've already got Rico cooking on it and he's free to come out and play. Man it sure is nice to have a Latino on staff when it's time to go to work in Central America. What exactly did you do to earn *persona non grata* status in Nicaragua? You may or may not know that they just switched governments today, so you may not have the devil to face anymore Kemosabe," Will told him with a half-hopeful smile. Dom was already moving to slap him considering Hal had assumed fatherhood mere hours ago.

"Willy, the only way me and Alex can show our faces there again is with a sex change operation…" When Will stopped laughing he continued, "So we go in for this nice clean little job to make a problem go away for Lindstrum and end up burning all bridges. This Guardia National General named Miguel Arguello was in charge of the Managua Region and was hitting the Agency up, charging Air America or Flying Tiger, I don't remember, a hefty surcharge when they landed to refuel for Christ's sakes. So we get a hop on a

Huey in from Tegucigalpa and fly into the first city in Nicaragua called Ocotal. That's where we meet our Sandinista intel mole, Colonel Sergio Prado. Instead of just giving us the surveillance intel on Arguello for his five hundred bucks, the bastard wants to go with us to León where we drop off for vehicles. So he gets all pumped on the flight to León and demands five hundred more bucks or he'll radio us in. So that earned him and his two bodyguards a freefall dive from a thousand feet and our Sandinista connections go to shit. But his intel was good and we invented 'The Managua' the next day when General Arguello comes driving down the entry road to the Nejapa Country Club to hook up with his mistress. So we burned the Sandinista bridge when Prado got smashed so Managua's a no go for me and Alex."

"Well, Dom would kill me if I tried to pull you in, but losing Alex too means Rambo's front and center. It sounds as though our idea to gift Mr. Chessereaux a perfect and very large diamond for his wife's anniversary ring was a wise investment." Will stopped to consider his statement, "At least it will be if we can get a Stanley case into Cozumel without a lot of fanfare. He's setting Rambo on the chase even as we speak."

"What you got cooking, a tactical package?"

"Right, lunch for three. Right now I'm thinking Dom and I will go in as tourists and Rico can come in separately in case we feel the need for speed. By the way, why did 'The Managua' sound familiar?"

Hal got a gleam in his eye, "Remember when we were fighting off seasickness in the Med that night and Alex asked if we wanted to pull off a 'Managua' in front of Sandrigan's casbah?"

"You mean the broken down car routine? So that's where it came from? You guys perfected it in Nicaragua? Let me guess; there was smoke pouring out from under the hood and a certain smoking ass hot blonde was waving for him to pull over and help her?"

"Good thing he was a heterosexual, right?"

"Hell, at least his last glimpse of life was a beautiful woman!"

38

MADNESS IN MANAGUA

"*QUE PASA AMIGO*, HOW WAS THE FLIGHT IN?" Will asked Rico Suarez as he climbed out of the Boeing 727 painted with the bright colors of Great West Studios.

He looked around and asked, "No customs?"

"It's amazing how the airport customs guy values an American C-note my friend. I take it the Stanley case is in with the luggage?"

"Man, that is the way to travel; General Aviation terminals unlimited."

"You got the plan ready for discrete travel?" Will asked, wanting to know the ingress and egress details they were getting ready to execute.

"After the bird gets fueled, it's dropping me off at an obscure place called San Carlos at the south end of Lake Nicaragua. My Cubano friend Chico will meet me there and has a boat chartered to take us up to Granada on the north end close to Managua. I'll reconnoiter the area and meet you guys at your hotel after you fly in."

"Sounds good; the things we do sometimes to get a little hardware in country. So how's Chico gonna make the big bird seem invisible? I doubt they get many flights into such a small place?"

"Chico's also the owner of a fishing charter business on the lake, and I'm a big adventure high roller coming in to challenge the only landlocked billfish in the world."

"So the Stanley case holds your fishing gear; cool. By the way, what'd Alex find out from Matthews? My ambassador buddy in Buenos actually talked with him and Robales, the guy in charge, and said things were still looking negotiable because nobody's made a stink about it yet. Of course, that was twelve hours ago; what's the latest?"

Rico closed his eyes and shook his head, "Not good Will; the Lutheran guys in Missouri made an official inquiry to the Sandinista Junta via their Senator so we lost the shroud of fog. According to Matthews, and he's only guessing because they snatched Colton during a fucking *coup d'état*, but they were primarily focused on rounding up all the former army guys from the *Guardia National* they'd been fighting for years. He suspects the cartel cowboys are somehow involved because otherwise it makes no sense. They've got way bigger fish to fry right now than a missionary man teaching school kids. Sorry Will, but that's the latest from Managua."

"Alright warrior, I guess we'll unfold this riddle over the next twenty-four hours," Will said, grabbing his hand in a warrior clasp. "I guess we should feel lucky they're allowing Americans in during a state of emergency. We'll see you at the Managua Hilton when you get there. Be safe bro."

———

"These airplane rides are becoming more uncomfortable the further along I get with the pregnancy Will," Dom said as they were waiting for their bags at Managua International. Will noticed the armed men around the Terminal, not a one in a uniform. He guessed it was still too early for the Sandinistas to have worked out the kinks—like official uniforms.

He looked at her with considerable empathy and offered, "I know, and I apologize baby. We've got first class booked out of here to Miami." The trip over from Cozumel had not been optimal for her, as the small planes did not have a first class section and was crowded and loud. During their last visit with Jonathan Calvatori he had noted a slight increase in Dom's blood pressure and counseled her to avoid stressful circumstances for the remaining months.

She stroked his face lovingly, "We should be fine here in Managua. I wonder if it is like Buenos Aires? I believe the Spanish were involved in the development of both places."

"We'll see babe, but besides the *coup d'état* Rico told me they had one hell of an earthquake here in the early 70's. I don't see us spending a lot of time on the ground. Thank God they at least have a Hilton."

The Hilton turned out to be one of the only modern buildings within the city center when they got there. Although it had been over seven years since the devastating earthquake of 1972, large portions of the old city were open where the rubble of buildings had no doubt been cleared. Interestingly, the National Palace appeared undamaged and intact, and Will had to wonder what architect had designed it and oversaw construction. As they checked into the hotel, he found the concierge and asked, "I guess taxis are safe to travel in here?"

"Oh yes sir, quite safe. The conflict between the Sandinistas and Somoza's National Guard is over and you are safe here. Have you been to Managua before?"

"No, so I guess they don't have the gangs like in Buenos Aires, eh? Is there anything to see around here, maybe outside the city? The place looked like a war zone on the way in from the airport."

"It has been a very difficult time since the earthquake *Señor*, and the capitol is slowly rebuilding with stronger construction codes to protect against the loss of life that happened in 1972. If you are interested, there is an interesting volcanic park only ten miles from here known as Masaya Volcano and Lake. There is a museum there that details volcanic events that have shaped the Managua district if you are interested."

"Yeah, sounds interesting, maybe tomorrow," he told him, discreetly slipping him a ten. "Do you think you could have a taxi for us, say at about two o'clock?"

"Of course sir," he said with renewed vigor, "and where would you be going *Señor*?"

"St. Timothy's Church of Hope in a *barrio* called Pomares. Is that far from here?"

"It is only two miles from the hotel *Señor*. I will have a cab waiting for you at two."

Will looked down at his nametag and nodded, "Thanks for the help Robert."

"I am so happy to make your acquaintance Mr. and Mrs. Kavanagh," Minister Geovany Morales welcomed them in his office in back of the church. On the short ride in Dom and Will noticed with relief that 'barrios' in Managua were fairly modern and orderly compared to the slums seen during their trips for 'Help the Helpless' in Argentina. Nicaraguan barrios were definitely more like neighborhoods than the Philippine rural villages called barrios.

"Please, I am Will and this is my wife Dominique, and thank you for seeing us. What can you tell us about the disappearance of my brother Colton? I believe you spoke with my friend Mr. Suarez on the phone?"

His face lit up at the mention of Rico's name, "Oh yes, Mr. Suarez is a very persuasive person and was most interested in Colton's outreach efforts here in Managua. Is he some relation to Colton?"

"No, he's a close personal friend. I find that his fluency in Spanish is often times helpful in getting to the bottom line about things. Have there been any developments? Have you heard anything else about Colton's whereabouts?"

"Actually, a member of the Sandinista Police, a Lieutenant José Rivas, left shortly before you arrived. He asked me a number of questions regarding Colton's work with the children. I wasn't aware that the Police were so interested in our mission here," he told them as Will glanced at Dom.

"So this Lieutenant Rivas—you said—what was his interest in Colton? Was he investigating a missing persons report or something?"

"No, he didn't mention anything about an investigation. He did ask me if members of Colton's family had been in touch."

Will was scribbling down the info on his notepad when Morales added, "I was almost concerned when he asked if Colton had been involved in organizing workers against their employers. Of course I told him such activities had nothing to do with our mission here in Pomares," he added almost as an afterthought.

"Jesus Christ man, didn't you think that was cogent?" Will all but screamed. Dom quickly reached out to calm him back down, but his mind was in overload.

Will reached into his wallet, pulled two one hundred dollar bills and asked, "Minister Morales, would it be possible for my wife and I to make a contribution to your mission here?" Before he could answer he continued, "I really need to use your phone to make an international call. Would that be possible?"

Thankfully Morales had left his office affording them some privacy, "Yes Mrs. Arrington, this is Will Kavanagh and I need to speak with Ambassador Richardson right away. Think you can get him on this line?"

"Do you have an appointment with the Ambassador Mr. Kavanagh?"

"Listen Mrs. Arrington, I'm in kind of a bind in Nicaragua. How about tell Charlie I'm on the phone would ya?"

"Please hold for a moment Mr. Kavanagh," she said as she put him on hold.

"Will, what the hell's going on in Nicaragua? Are you there?" Charlie Richardson's reassuring voice came over the phone.

"Yeah, I think so. I mean we are in Managua, and Dom and I are scoping out the details of Colton's disappearance so we won't be laying out hearsay as evidence when we meet this Sandinista Police department. We just learned that a police lieutenant was at the church asking a lot of interesting questions about possible involvement with organizing workers against their employers. Now before I go to the police, I need to know if the Nicaraguans have notified the Embassy about a detained American. We heard the Missouri Senator made the inquiry to the Sandinista Junta, so any chance of smoke and mirrors is gone. You got any late breaking news?"

"Yes, Mark Robales, the *Chargé D'affairs,* and I just spoke. I suspect Senator Danforth didn't do you any favors with the inquiry, based on my chat with the Embassy guys. The latest they've got is that the Sandinista Police have not filed any charges against Colton Kavanagh. I know that's not what you were hoping to hear, but it's the latest I've got. Mark and Bob Matthews will be waiting for you when you get to the embassy. Take care of yourself Will, and give Dominique my best. Bye."

———

"Hello Mr. and Mrs. Kavanagh, it's so nice to meet you. Ambassador Richardson asked me to speak with you," said Mark Robales as they walked into the U.S. Embassy, easily the most modern looking structure in the neighborhood still standing. He led them over to a seating area to the side of the entrance lobby.

"Good, Charlie's a squared away guy." Will looked at Bob Matthews and held out his hand, "Man I've already heard about you, and you my friend are probably the difference between success and failure here in Managua," Will said, blowing right past the pleasantries.

Robales just looked on with amazement as Will and Bob shook hands warmly, "Yes he is, but this is about your brother Colton. You have arrived in Nicaragua at a very volatile time."

Will looked at Matthews and smiled, "A very volatile time; how about the Fall of Saigon?"

Robales actually had the temerity to roll his eyes, "The previous regime was ousted after a concerted bloody insurrection, resulting in the new ruling Junta of National Reconciliation appearing yesterday. The new *Sandinista Po-*

lice just set up in their captured offices two days ago so things are in a state of flux, to say the least."

Will was shaking his head, thankful for the insight and trying to be patient, "So we just heard a Sandinista Police lieutenant was snooping around St Timothy's Church in Pomares asking about Colton's past history in inciting labor unrest. We assume he was arrested, so do you know where he is being held?"

"The new federal guys, the ECP or Sandinista People's Army don't, but my contact in what will become the Justice Ministry told me on background that your bother is being held by Sandinista Police, in charge of the Managua region. Now before you ask, I know it's confusing, but the local capital district operates its own system and their detainees are not treated as federal prisoners."

"Prisoners?" Will shrieked as Dom tried to restrain him. "Well, that sounds convenient; the Federales don't know what the local yokels are doing, is that about it?"

"I'm sorry Mr. Kavanagh, would you rather we discuss this in my office?" Robales asked, making him suddenly aware of his temper.

"No, I'm good, sorry about that. This whole thing just seems to be growing like a snowball down a hill. Okay, who's got him? The minister we talked to mentioned a Police Lieutenant named José Rivas. Is that the guy? Where's this precinct they're holding Colton at?"

"That would be the main Police Center on Brevatta Boulevard. I would caution you Mr. Kavanagh that given the emergence of the Sandinista regime within the past two days, the Police are very sensitive about intrusion into their oversight of criminal cases," Matthews advised them.

"Goddamn it Bob, my name's Will; didn't Alex explain that to ya? Now who said anything about criminal cases? What the fuck are they charging him with?"

"I believe 'charge' might be a slight misnomer given their tendency to confuse terms we accept as standard to the justice system. Colton is being 'held for investigation' of fomenting insurrection," he said to Will's total disbelief.

"Fomenting insurrection? The Lutheran guy told me he was meeting with the parents of some children who had been working in sweat shops. How the hell is that insurrection?"

Robales was being unusually patient, Will had to admit, "Mr. Kavanagh, please understand that the term 'sweat shops' is a vilified American term for what the poor people of Central America consider to be a valid employment arrangement. Efforts to disrupt such economic endeavors are considered intrusion into sovereign matters here."

"Oh yeah? Well just wait until the United Nations hears about this shit! These Sandinista mothers are going to get a whole lot more than mere intrusion into their affairs. Don't they have any decency down here?" He fumed as Dom once again tried to calm him down.

"I'm sorry Will, but besides being in the middle of a cauldron, this is a different culture than ours. We've got to at least understand how they think if we're going to be able to be effective," Matthews intoned.

Will looked at him with a newfound admiration, "At least understand, eh? I think I just saw why you're on the A team; I like the way you think. Do you have any suggestions on how to approach Lieutenant Rivas at the Police Center?"

At this *Chargé D'affairs* Robales looked down at his watch and announced, "I have an important meeting I must get on the phone for, Mr. and Mrs. Kavanagh, I will leave you with RSO Matthews if that would be acceptable?"

They stood up to shake his hand as Will said, "Good to meet you Mark, and thanks for agreeing to see us. I'm not sure where I'd turn to if you two hadn't come through."

"Oh don't thank me Will, it seems as though you have a good friend within the senior Foreign Service ranks. Best of luck to you, and please let Bob know if we can be of further assistance."

After Robales left Will looked at Matthews and said, "So what's the best way to work this Bob?"

He just smiled and shook his head, "You're buddy Alex Manatos called and said I should be expecting to hear from you. He also said that when I did it wouldn't be gentle. But guess what, that's about where we are in this circle jerk right now. I'll go ahead and admit I was stunned when the ambassador in Buenos Aires called, all but demanding Robales take your brother's case on as his first priority. Man, what'd you do for Richardson? You got pictures of him with a transvestite or something?"

"Nah, it was nothing like that. We made friends in Argentina and he wanted to make sure we weren't some counterculture revolutionaries or

WHEN THERE'S NO TOMORROW • 363

something. He's a squared away guy; we bailed him out with some steaks and libations at our place. So what's the lay of the land here?" Before he could answer Will interrupted and asked, "So how do you know Alex?"

"We knew each other in Vietnam," he said and waited for that to gestate.

"So you know Rico too?"

"And Hal Rayfield and unfortunately Marty Lindstrum as well; that was some band of vagabonds over in the jungle," he said with a hint of a grimace.

"Well Hal or should I say his wife Carmen just had a baby before we left Buenos, so it'd seem indecent of me to pull him in, right?"

"He didn't know I was here until Alex made the link. I assume he knows by now. We sort of lost contact with each other after Cambodia, but I ran into Alex at a gun show in Richmond a couple of months ago," he told them as Will pondered the possibilities.

"So you got an LST-5B?"

He was shaking his head and smiling, "Alex said you had become a convert. No, I don't have a sat phone but we've got encrypted phones. Wanna come up to the office?"

"So tell me, how am I gonna get Colton out of this jam he's in?" Will asked once they were comfortably ensconced in Bob's office with two very tasty coffees.

"I don't know, spring his ass? Just kidding, but this judicial system down here doesn't work—hell, who am I kidding, it doesn't even exist yet with these Sandinista pricks. They make American due process look like the Enterprise going to warp-drive on Star Trek."

"Alright, how about short-term objectives; what's the Police Center like? Doesn't sound like Dracula's castle," Will wondered.

"Don't let the name fool you. The lockup at the Police Center will remind you of that Turkish jail in *Midnight Express*. If it were my brother, I'd want him moved over to the Federal Detention Center; at least they have real guards there, and clean water."

"Hold the damn phone a minute Bob; somebody told me the Sandinistas had the big prisons cram full of Somoza's boys. So where the fuck are they gonna put Colton? I mean he ain't shot at 'em for the past twenty years like the GN, right?" Will shook it off and exhaled, "Okay, I buy your recommendation. How do we make that happen?"

"Listen, I know you've got the ability to piss people off, so…."

"Now where did you hear that bullshit?" He interrupted with a smile.

"Alex told me the story about you pissing Lindstrum off so bad he about had a heart attack."

"He's a very deserving person of such agitation Bob, so how do we get Will's brother moved to the other prison?" Dom asked, redirecting the conversation.

He looked at Dom considering something and said, "Okay, I want the two of you to go in together, otherwise they might throw Will in just for pissing them off, but what I would do is…"

———

"That's right Lieutenant, I want to see my brother Colton Kavanagh within the next ten minutes. And before you ask, here's the Letter of Request from the US Embassy, duly signed by the *Chargé D'affairs*," Will told a rather oily looking forty year old police detective dressed in a poorly fitting brown suit.

He looked at the letter and asked, "And your passport Mr. Kavanagh?"

As he handed it to him he said, "Don't get too comfortable with that, it's my ticket out of here."

"I will be right back Mr. Kavanagh," he said as Dom and Will stood in the main Reception Center. Unlike its name would imply, it was the main induction room for incoming detainees, at least a dozen of whom were hanging around the outside walls in handcuffs awaiting processing. Will glanced at the line of men, all in their late twenties or early thirties and concluded these weren't pickpockets or street urchins. They were probably the lucky ones who were in one of Somoza's government departments other than the hated *Guardia National*.

Rivas soon returned and told them, "I am sorry, but your brother is charged with a serious felony and is being held in our secure wing. A visit is not allowed by Police Center rules."

"Fine buckwheat, just countersign that there Letter from the Embassy saying your pompous ass is violating international treaties and I'll be happy to leave and watch your snarky ass get demoted to a traffic cop. Oh, and plan on moving to Ocotal, because it's bumper to bumper traffic trying to get out of Nicaragua. Jesus, what is it about these banana republics that makes it so hard to extend simple human courtesies?"

Will could see that he had achieved his goal as Rivas bowed up and his breathing became noticeably shorter, "Your brother has been charged with a serious crime under the Emergency Declaration of the Sandinista Junta of National Reconstruction of Nicaragua Mr. Kavanagh. As such, you may not have access to him until his arraignment before a judge of the Supreme Court."

"Fine, give me a copy of that charge sheet if your lying ass isn't making this up just to stick it up the *Norteamericanos*," he said, challenging him almost to the point of spitting. "And if you ain't charged him, I demand to see my brother right this minute!" Will was pissed now so he added, "Oh, and while you're at it, how about get me a copy of that Emergency Declaration if it says anything other than arrest any member of the former GN, like those poor schmucks lined against the wall over there." He was on a roll as he leaned over the counter, "Oh, and how about provide a list of those Supreme Court justices buckwheat; best I can tell justice other than a bullet to the head is the only jurisprudence I see being performed around this place."

"You will not be allowed to see the prisoner before arraignment Mr. Kavanagh," he said with so much angst that Kavanagh sounded like three words. Will watched with interest as he slammed a rubber stamp down on a piece of paper with such force that the countertop bounced.

"I believe this is the charge sheet you asked for Mr. Kavanagh, now if you would leave our Police Center, we have important business to conduct."

He looked down at the charge sheet to make sure he wasn't bluffing, and he was impressed that the rubber stamp had hit it so hard there were ink splatters radiating out around the word 'OFICIAL'. He smiled at him and said, "Thank you so much Lieutenant, have a nice day."

———

Once outside they walked over to Matthews' car and handed him the charge sheet, "How long is the transfer gonna take?"

He looked at the charge sheet to make sure it was duly executed, "What the hell did you say to him to make him cough this up?"

Dom stepped in and provided the intel, "I thought that Will's insistence that Colton's incarceration was against international treaties impressed the lieutenant, but I believe his use of the terms 'buckwheat' and 'banana republic' were effective in elevating Lieutenant Rivas' blood pressure."

Matthews was laughing his ass off as he started his car, "I'll take this straight over to the Ministry of Justice; Robales has already signed the Writ of

Correction. I'd expect your brother will be transferred sometime tomorrow. I bet that bastard's in there trying to find somebody to tell him what 'buckwheat' means! Man was Alex right about your ass Will."

"So you really think getting him transferred to San Bracinto is a good thing? Alex relayed some Matthews intel that it was stuffed to the rafters with GN officers and such."

"Right," Bob said as he put the ten year old Ford Fairlane in gear, "but at least they aren't a bunch of murderers—at least not the sick kind we have in our max security prisons. And it's not operated by the Sandinista Police; the EPS runs it because of all the GN inmates. Trust me, getting him away from Rivas and his 'local connections' is the best move. I'll let you know how things go with the Justice Ministry."

"Who've been in office two days, right? Thanks for the help Bob, we really appreciate it."

———

"I'm really too tired to eat in the restaurant Will. Do you think we can order something in the room?" Dom asked as they returned to the hotel.

"Sure babe, no problem. I guess it has been a long day. Sorry if I've been distracted," he apologized. "How about a grilled steak; would that fit the bill?" He asked her after comfortably tucking her into a chair in the sitting room of their suite with her feet on an ottoman.

"I really don't care Will, you pick out something from the menu," she replied in what seemed near capitulation.

As he was carefully considering the prospect of ordering fish or beef there was a knock on the door. "Do I surmise our associate Mr. Suarez has made it into Managua?"

"Hey buddy, how was the…" Will was saying as he looked up and saw Lieutenant José Rivas standing at the door. "Oh, good evening Lieutenant, did we forget something today?"

He smiled wickedly, "Yes, it would seem that you did Mr. Kavanagh."

"And what might that be pray tell?"

"I believe your passport has been improperly processed," he said, still smiling.

"Bullshit, what kind of crap are you trying to pull Rivas? What kind of fucking improper…." was all he got out before he remembered that he hadn't given his passport back after he asked for identification at the police station earlier.

"It would seem that your departure from your last port of debarkation was not properly noted."

Will's brain was wringing out the details of what Rivas could be talking about when he remembered that Carlos, their cooperative customs and immigration associate in Cozumel, hadn't stamped their passports when they left. He started to bluff him and tell him Buenos Aires was their port of debarkation, but there weren't any direct flights to Managua. Connecting flights might sound believable so he gave it a shot. "So you're now an immigration officer Rivas? For your information, we had a connecting flight out of Jorge Newbery Airport in Buenos Aires on our way in. Now how about that passport Lieutenant?"

"Fine, please show me your round trip tickets and we'll be able to resolve this matter," he said with a smirk. *Now the fucker's calling checkmate huh?*

"What'd you do, have your mole at the airport doing surveillance on every American entering? As you may not know, the American President Carter extended full diplomatic recognition to the Sandinista Junta yesterday. You want me to advise the Ambassador that he needn't come down here because the Sandinistas seem to have a target on the back of every *Norteamericano?*" The fucker didn't even react, so Will tried hard ball with him, "Tell ya what Rivas, get me my passport back and I'll tear up this letter I was writing to the United Nations Centre for Human Rights. Are you sure you want a bunch of liberal bastards swarming Managua looking for the sweat shops like Bolt Sportswear operates?"

When Will mentioned Bolt Sportswear he saw the jerk in Rivas' body. "We are merely doing our job for the revolution Mr. Kavanagh. You may appeal this egregious oversight with the Minister of Immigration at their earliest convenience. Until then, please do not make any attempt to leave Nicaragua. You will be stopped by any federal officer if you attempt to do so. Have a nice evening sir, or should I say Mr. Buckwheat?"

He fast-forwarded past anger at having not retrieved his passport earlier and was considering options when there was another knock on the door. Figuring he'd take a bite out of the smart-ass policeman's rear this time, he jerked the door open and blasted, "Now what do you want Rivas….." He did a double take to find Rico standing there, and in disbelief said, "Come on in buddy."

"What was that all about?" Rico asked as he walked in and closed the door.

"Just another fucking asshole in a banana republic trying to play dog dick, how was your day?"

"Rather interesting actually," he said as he took off his backpack, "any chance we could get some food? I'm starving brother."

In consideration of Dom's depleted condition, they settled on baked chicken, sautéed vegetables and fried plantains. As they were inhaling them Will asked, "So what have you discovered today Mr. Suarez? I had the opportunity to meet Bob Matthews face to face, and it turns out he's all but one of us. Can you imagine what a pleasant surprise that was?"

"Yeah, he actually is one of us," Rico said as he washed down the last plantain chip with a slug of Corona. "He just graduated to a semi-legitimate job."

"Semi-legitimate; don't tell me he's another of Marty Lindstrum's zombies?"

"No Will, he's semi-legitimate because he isn't beholden to the Foreign Service types. He works for the Defense Intelligence Agency, which supplies all of the military attachés. He's plugged in around here," Rico informed them.

"Well that's good; we obviously need a friend on the ground around Managua."

"You don't know how true those words are buddy," he said, causing Will to sit up and focus in on the conversation. "It turns out our associates from the underworld lurk just outside the periphery here."

"Which associates might that be? I heard there aren't any gangs here like they have in Buenos. Oh, hold on; Bob mentioned something about the cartels, but I don't know what interest they could have in Colton."

"The ones who make and distribute cocaine are the only peripheral group of immediate concern my friend. Masachapa on the coast not far from here is a major transshipment point leading up the coast to the land of unlimited demand."

"Jesus, once again your intelligence gathering abilities are to be admired Ricardo. How does that impact our situation?"

"The cocaine guys and your lieutenant friend are close business associates, and Rivas' number one job is making sure nothing draws attention to the activities of one Enrique Constanza, who is what the Cali Cartel refers to as a *celeno*. Enrique's job is to ensure the hassle-free passing of valuable powder from Cali to New York City without delay."

"Okay," Will said, glancing at Dom, "I still don't see what trying to spring my brother from prison has to do with the cocaine cartels. What am I missing?"

"What you are missing is that some of the children involved with the sweat shop exploitation are also involved with Constanza as lookouts. Colton Kavanagh's stirring up the pot and drawing attention to the sweat shops has the potential of drawing unwanted attention to all child labor issues. Now I know this is at best tangentially related, but you need to know the lay of the land you are treading upon."

"Yeah, trapped within would be a better phrase. Rivas kept my passport until he found something wrong, so now he's threatening to keep me hostage until we clear it all up," Will said in dismay.

Rico was looking at him with concern as he implored, "Having a passport in one's possession is not paramount to survival Will. Staying off the cartel's radar on the other hand, could very well be." He looked at Will closely and closed his eyes, "I've seen you lose your temper around people that piss you off Tonto. What exactly have you demeaned or threatened this Lieutenant Rivas with? Your brilliantly profane curses can sometimes be particularly bothersome to the target of your rage my friend."

"Tonto; when did I become Tonto instead of Will?"

"All Hal calls you is Willy or Tonto; I suspect you prefer Tonto since I haven't known you very long, and we are on an op, so to speak." Will nodded his agreement, "So how have you angered Rivas?"

Will glanced at Dom who nodded, "Unfortunately you are right, but Bob Matthews wanted Will to anger Rivas at the police station today so that he would give us the charge sheet just to be rid of us." Rico nodded and waited, flexing his eyebrows at her, knowing there was more. "Okay, I know William very well, and he uses his rants and profanity almost strategically at times. Unfortunately I believe he let his testosterone battle with Rivas free his tongue a bit. Just before you arrived he threatened Rojas with a letter to the UN complaining about Bolt Sportswear's sweat shops if he didn't get his passport back."

Rico shook his head at Will as if he were a misbehaving child, "That kind of rhetoric will almost surely be reported to Constanza; when he's not traveling along his route playing bad cop he lives in an affluent section of Managua called Los Robles…"

"Why Managua," Will wondered. "there's got to be classier digs along the twenty-five hundred miles between Cali and New York City?"

"Classier but not necessarily more secure; both Somoza and now Ortega fear the man, and he pays them off handsomely for their support. What are your plans for tomorrow?"

"Hopefully we can get in to see Colton once they transfer him to the federal prison tomorrow afternoon. As for tomorrow morning, we were thinking about heading out to Masaya Volcano Park. The concierge said it could be educational for us."

"Masaya eh? I passed it on the way in from Granada where Chico's boat is tied up at the marina. I will go check out Masaya Volcano Park in the morning," he said with a smile, "you know, to make sure there aren't poisonous snakes waiting to attack you, *comprendes?*"

Will wrapped him a bear hug, "*Comprendo mi amigo*, I don't know what I'd do without you brother."

"Hey, we've got to look out for each other, *si?*"

39

MEETING THE CALI CARTEL AT MASAYA VOLCANO PARK

THEY SAT THROUGH THEIR FIRST and hopefully last video presentation of the volcanic origins of Managua and its environs—in Spanish no less—when they decided to check out the flora and fauna described so vividly in the video. Thanks to an English language pamphlet the guide handed them, Will wondered why earthquakes weren't a more frequent event in the Nicaraguan Depression as the geologists called it. Managua itself sat upon the convergence of four separate tectonic faults or fractures. A volcano or earthquake seemed as likely for Managua as Old Faithful spewing its geyser of superheated water every sixty-three minutes.

They found the flora and fauna boring so Will suggested, "Let's go on up to the volcano and see what all the fuss is about. The shuttle's just over there."

Dom was still hedging on the side of caution when they got off the tram, only one other tourist couple joining them for the ride up the low mountain.

When they got to the turnabout at the end of the paved path, Dom was wiping off perspiration. "Why don't we walk over here Will," she said, pointing to a trail that led off to the side, as opposed to the climb up the wall of the crater.

"Sure babe, I guess you don't need all of that exercise after all."

They had walked along the trail perhaps fifty yards when Will heard footsteps behind them. He turned to find two bearded Latinos, fairly thin and scrawny looking with smiles on their faces, but both of them were holding pistols and pointing for them to continue further along the path.

Will glanced at Dom, and was surprised to see she was noticeably nervous, very unlike her normal fiercely calm self under fire. He leaned in, put his arm around her and said as calmly as he could, "Let's see what they want Dom. We've got the rings and necklaces, and I've got a wallet full of cash. Don't panic yet baby."

They walked perhaps another fifty yards and came to a clearing that included a scenic overlook of the surrounding mountains and valley. Across the clearing were two more men; one looked much like the scrawny sidekicks behind them but the other was larger, clean shaven but for a moustache and neatly dressed with an expensive leather jacket. The jacket seemed strange, as the weather in Managua reminded Will somewhat of the Philippines. The thugs behind prodded them until they were about twenty feet from the apparent leader. When Leather Jacket Man took a step towards them, one the thugs behind them said '*Para.*'

Will looked around as one of the thugs roughly frisked them, apparently looking for weapons. Will looked at Leather Jacket and told him, "We are tourists my friend, and mean no harm. You can take whatever we have on us if that is what you want."

The leader walked up, stopped two feet from his face and smiled sickly, "I believe you are lying Mr. Kavanagh. I believe you are here in Nicaragua to indeed do harm."

"How do you know us, we have not offended anyone," Dom replied, but the leader ignored her.

"That apparently is about to change, especially if you insist on publicizing your brother's plight to those outside Nicaragua," he said, this time pronouncing it *nee-ho-rah-wa*.

Will immediately understood that his big mouth had gotten them in the shits. *Why the fuck did I have to mouth off to Rivas last night about the letter writing dammit?* Rico's warning about the child labor issues echoed in his ears, "Mister, all I want to do is get my brother out of prison and leave the country. I don't see how that interferes with anything you are doing."

"I am sorry Mr. Kavanagh, but I do not see that happening. It seems as though your brother is determined to expose this tragedy of children earning precious money to stay alive. I am afraid he will stay in prison until he unfortunately perishes of an ill-timed accident."

"Well, I guess you have me at a disadvantage, because I don't even know your name. But I really can't stand idly by and let my brother die in prison, now can I?"

His smile turned to a deathly serious stare as he took another step to get in Will's face, "My name is Enrique Constanza, and I want you to remember that for the rest of your life." Will didn't even see the switchblade open or come up before he put the point against his cheek just below his left eye and slowly pulled it down his face. It stung like the devil being cut with the sharp knife, but Will refused to utter a sound, choosing to stare at his foe instead. Constanza locked onto his stare as he told him, "Do you understand me Mr. William Kavanagh?"

"Oh yeah, I get it loud and clear Constanza. You want me to run away and forget about my brother rotting in some God-forsaken prison in the middle of the jungle. But I can assure you, that ain't gonna happen."

He merely smiled at Will as he took a step to his right, stood in front of Dom and put the point of the knife right against her pregnant belly. "I beg to differ with you; do you not value your wife and child more than a brother?"

Okay Enrique, it's time to see if we're playing hard ball today or not. Come on Rico, I know you've got my ass covered brother. Will's eyebrows flexed as he half-smiled at Constanza, "Oh I value them all, but you don't have the brains to see that's none of the Cali Cartel's business buckwheat."

The words took a moment to register. When they did he looked at Will with anger bordering outrage right before the back of his head blew away, the gore splattering all over Will's face and arms as he grabbed Dom and pulled her down, shielding her with his body. They heard the muffled sounds of bullets whizzing past and then it was deathly quiet again. Will looked up to find Bob Matthews walking up from behind them on the trail, the suppressed muzzle on his H&K MP5 still trailing smoke. He quickly glanced back and saw the other three bandits lying on the ground very dead. Will pulled Dom away from what was left of Constanza, the blood and gore now moving slowly towards them, "Rico?"

Matthews nodded further ahead as Rico came down off the side of the hill and jumped onto the path, the automatic rifle in his hand looking unfamiliar. Will looked back down at Dom, her face flushed and she was huffing trying to regain her breath. "Baby, what is it? Did you get hit?"

He started feeling around her for blood but there wasn't any as she looked up at him like she was drunk, "I don't feel well Will, I don't…"

"Oh shit, you got any water on you Rico?" Will asked as he ripped open her blouse to pour some water in a mad attempt to cool her off.

Rico was beside him in an instant, made a quick battlefield triage assessment, "She's suffering some kind of panic attack Will. We gotta get out of here right now."

"Alright, Bob lead us out, Rico and I will do a fireman's carry with Dom." As Will leaned down to clutch her he caught a reflection of the switchblade in the sun. He picked it up, closed it and put it in his pocket. He got next to Dom's ear and whispered, "Honey, we're gonna lift you up and take you to the car. Try not and worry."

"God I'm glad this car's got air conditioning; whose is it?" Will asked Rico as he sat in the back seat giving Dom sips of water as she nodded for them. "You okay baby? We're heading out of here, don't worry. Hold on honey."

"Chico 'rented' it from the marina owner. How's she doing?"

"She's holding on; how far to the boat?"

"Not far, we'll be out of here in fifteen minutes," Rico assured him as he flew down Nicaragua Highway 4 slowing only to avoid any motor police going through the city of Masaya.

"Damn it's nice to have connections partner," Will said as the sport fishing boat pulled up into a cruising plane on Lake Nicaragua. "You did bring an LST I hope to God?" Rico had made hasty introductions once Will had Dom lying down on a comfortable berth in the boat's cabin.

"Yeah, already set up with the antenna; who you need to call?"

"We better start with this doctor down in Argentina," he said, his lizard brain in full tactical mode now. He bent down to Dom and asked, "Did you bring Jonathan's number with you baby?"

She half-smiled at him, "Don't you remember stuffing the cards from the Rolodex in my purse Will?"

"Hell yeah, for once I remembered the damn Rolodex, sort of."

"Hey Lita, it's Will Kavanagh; is Jonathan available?" He asked once he had the CIRDIVAR clinic receptionist on the phone.

"Hi Will, he's in with a patient at the moment, can I give him a message?"

"Lita, tell him it's an emergency. Dom's in distress and I need his help."

"I will get him, hold on."

"Will, what is it?" Jonathan asked in a panic not a minute later.

"Listen, we got in a tight pickle in Nicaragua and Dom had some kind of panic attack. She's been real woozy ever since. What should I do for her?"

"Is she conscious? Let me speak to her," he said as Will held the headset to her face.

"Dominique, this is Jon Calvatori; please tell me how are you feeling right this moment?"

"I feel very warm Jonathan."

"What about body temperature? Are you perspiring?"

"Yes, I am sweating."

"Are you experiencing any pain in your abdomen?"

"No, but I feel very confused; what has happened to me?"

"I see. Tell me, how does your head feel; is it aching?"

"How did you know about the headache?"

"I want you to remain calm, as I am going to give Will some instructions, okay?"

"He wants to speak with you Will."

"Whatcha think?" Tonto asked in combat readiness.

"It appears she is suffering from moderate hypertension, and the lack of discomfort in her abdomen would indicate that the child has not suffered any trauma. Do you have any medicine where you are? Where are you, by the way?"

He did a quick check with Chico before responding, "Nothing but booze and a small galley aboard the boat we're on Jonathan. Oh and we're out in the middle of Lake Nicaragua moving as fast as we can. We'll be leaving Nicaragua later this afternoon. What can I do?"

"It sounds as if we must administer some basic therapy to Dominique. Are there any of these items aboard the boat. You'll need to start with some hot water......."

"*Yish*, what is that you are feeding me Will?" Dom asked as she took the first swig of nature's own hypertension remedy.

"It's a tea Jonathan said would help with the elevated blood pressure; until we can get you to a hospital that's the best we can do. He said it may be critical to the baby's health to get your blood pressure down a bit. Think you can stand it?"

To his complete shock, she took the coffee mug and with a terrible expression on her face drank the entire mug down. He watched her closely to make sure it didn't come back up, but like the trooper she was asked, "What is in that vile tasting concoction?"

He smiled at her combativeness, "Let's see Dominique, there's tea, honey, garlic powder, ginger, basil and a dash of sesame oil thrown in for good measure. Whatdya think?"

"I think it tastes terrible, and I would never drink that voluntarily. Would it be too much trouble for you to fix me another glass of it?"

"That's my girl, coming right up!"

"Hello again Will, was Mark Robales able to help you find your brother in Managua?" Charlie Richardson asked once Will got him on the line.

'Yes sir, very much so but my brother's gonna be in prison for a while. I've got another problem now, and I hate to keep asking for these silver bullets sir. I'm kinda between a rock and a hard place."

"I see, how hard?"

"We got in a bit of a jam back outside of Managua and we're getting the hell outa dodge. Now I think we've got the egress under control, but this damn prickhead policeman confiscated my passport. We're gonna be flying back into New Orleans sometime tonight, and I've gotta take Dom straight to the hospital so I ain't gonna have time to dicker with the immigration folks. Do you think there's any way you could call off the dogs until I can get a replacement passport?"

"Slow down Will; how is Dominique, is she alright? How big of a jam did you and Bob Matthews get into? I'll need to know that for plausible deniability you understand."

"Yeah, her blood pressure went through the roof during the firefight, but we've got her drinking this herbal blood pressure remedy. We don't think the baby is in trouble, but I'm gonna get her butt straight into the hospital when we land. Come to think about it, I need to hook up an ambulance too. Think you can call off the passport police? Jesus, I didn't even think that maybe they weren't State Department people," he spit out in a continuous stream.

"I'll take care of the passport problem Will. What flight will you be coming in on?"

"Oh shit Charlie, we left our tickets in the hotel room back in Managua, along with our luggage. Damn it, why the hell didn't I…." he saw Rico giving him the timeout sign and nodded. "Hold on a minute Charlie, I gotta check on something." He looked at Rico, "What?"

"In all the excitement you must have forgotten Pierson's waiting for us to call him on the ground at Cozumel. We'll be flying back on the Great West studio bird."

Will high-fived him as he relayed the message, "Okay Charlie, I just found out we'll be coming into the General Aviation side of Louis Armstrong Airport in a Great West Studios private bird. I guess they've got the passport snoops over there too huh?"

Charlie half-laughed, "Don't worry about the passport snoops Will, I'll get your entry waived until you can obtain a valid passport. And I will have an ambulance waiting at the ramp for your plane when it gets in. Now I will be very unhappy if you don't call me back and let me know how Dominique is doing. Now before you exhale in relief, I wanna know what happened in Managua; I take it Bob Matthews was with you?"

Will looked at Rico and rolled his eyes, "Listen Charlie, FSOs aren't supposed to get into the shit, you know what I mean? If I tell ya what went down, Matthews could get his tit in a ringer with Robales, ya know?"

"Will Kavanagh, my loyalty is to you, nor Mark Robales. I know what Matthews does to keep life in Managua manageable. I just need to know what happened in case you killed somebody and this thing turns into some international crisis. We just normalized relations with the Sandinistas, remember?"

"Okay, this conversation never happened then, okay? By the way, is prickhead Cappeletti anywhere near ya? If so order his ass outa your office," Will told him as Rico looked on in disbelief.

"Ron's off trying to repair damage with my Deputy Chief of Mission at the BA Country Club; fire away."

"Oh shit, what'd he do, call the guy's Spanish wife a floozy?"

"Dammit Kavanagh, so we're trading secrets now, are we? You have him completely wrong, she's from Greece…" When Will came out of the near hysterics Charlie said, "Okay, you've seen mine, now tell me a story I'll never see in the newspapers."

Will rolled his eyes, shaking his head no at Rico as he exposed his flank, "Okay, Matthews and my guy did a little sniffing around and my brother Colton got across the breakers for essentially publicizing the sweat shops like Bolt Sportswear's factory. Then I pour gas on the fire with my big mouth and threaten this piece of shit police lieutenant with a letter to the UN Centre for Human Rights if he didn't give me back my passport. So here's the part that's sensitive and you can never claim knowing about. You are encrypted, right Charlie?"

"Hell yeah, and don't interrupt this story again; it never gets this exciting in Argentina."

"You can thank your lucky stars for that Charlie. So this traffic management director for the Cali Cartel—they call him a *Celeno*—lives in Managua as it's halfway between Quito where the coca leaves are collected and the Mexican border. So after I mouth off to the cop about flooding Managua with liberal Jane Fondas looking for sweat shops this *Celeno* by the name of Enrique Constanza jumps me and Dom at the Masaya Volcano Park about an hour or so ago with three of his thugs." Will brushed the back of his hand along the cut, but the blood had dried. "So Enrique tells me my brother ain't making it out of prison alive 'cause he'll blare the news far and wide. Before you ask, the Cali Cowboys have an interest in child labor because they use some of the same kids as lookouts for their big transshipment point at Masachapa, a port near Managua."

"So to them any news is bad news and he introduces himself staring me in the eyes as he pulled a switchblade knife down the side of my face. I obviously wasn't repentant enough so he stepped over to Dom and stuck the point of that blade on her pregnant belly. The bastard has the balls to tell ME—Will Kavanagh—that I gotta choose between my brother and my unborn child living. I stared that motherfucker in the eye and told him he didn't have the brains to see that was not the Cali Cartel's concern. When he realized what I told him, a seven-point-six-two NATO round went supersonic right through his right eye, blowing the back of his head off and making a huge mess of my face and clothes. That's when Dom went into the panic attack. Jon Calvatori—you met him—gave me a recipe for a voodoo blood pressure concoction and Dom's doing okay now."

"Holy Mother of Christ..."

"That's why I didn't want to tell you Charlie..."

"No, what about the three thugs with him?"

"Oh, Bob Matthews took out two of 'em with a MP5 and Rico finished the other one off; it was a fucking mess, especially with Dom's panic attack, let me tell ya."

"So the net sum of this little 'go check on my brother mission' is that he's now valued by the Sandinista Police slightly lower than Anastasio Somoza himself, and four Colombian Cartel members are dead lying on the ground near Masaya Volcano?"

"You're oversimplifying things Charlie. The fuckwad buckwheat police lackey kept my passport, but I pissed him off enough to get a copy of the charge sheet. So Matthews took that and is gonna pull the official strings with the Justice Ministry—what a fucking farce, what Justice Ministry?—and get Colton transferred to a bigger prison where the Cartel Cowboys don't have buckwheat on their payroll. So it's a net draw for a visit; we found out what's going on, but for the time being can't help my brother."

"I think you left out the part about earning the ire of the Cali Cartel by blowing the brains out of the Cartel leader's brother's head, right?"

"Did I have any fucking choice with the asshole pointing a knife at my unborn child?"

"No, of course not Will; it's amazing to me you had backup waiting for the Cartel guys to jump you."

"Charlie, we ain't still alive because we don't anticipate things."

"So you're saying that…"

"No, I'm saying that we had backup just in case the Cartel assholes tried to extort us with little things like summary executions. Are we all good now?"

Will could hear him exhale, "Just listening to that account of your recent life is like a rush, I can tell you that William. Better'n any book or movie I've ever seen!"

"Yeah, good thing you weren't there Charlie; but we got some time to figure out our next moves. Now don't be telling Keith Melson all about this shit because he gets nervous when I start thinking about what he calls 'extrajudicial' solutions. Now, as evidenced by one Order of May award, extrajudicial solutions are sometimes the only ones available. Are we good Charlie?"

"Only if you call me as soon as you get Dominique in a hospital; is that clear young man?"

"Yes sir, I will call you from the hospital as soon as the doctor gives me the high sign. Oh, and thank you a million Charlie; I don't know anyone else that would bail me out of this one. Later on Mr. Ambassador."

"So what was that assault rifle you had back at the volcano Rico? I don't think I've seen one of those before," Will asked now that the most emergent crises had settled. The three mugs of herbal voodoo concoction must have worked because Dom was sleeping soundly in spite of the constant lifting of the boat as they slashed through the mild seas on the huge lake. Even cruising at 27 knots it was going to take five hours to cross Lake Nicaragua along its axis.

"That was an FN FAL light automatic rifle. It's a Belgian design and is popular among all of the NATO armies."

"So why not the AK-47 throwaways; I noticed that Bob Matthews had an MP5?"

He smiled at his pilot buddy, "Because Chico didn't want any damn Russian trash, and he's going to take the Stanley case as payment for getting us out of dodge. Getting the picture?"

"Loud and clear brother. So I gotta ask, why'd you let that bastard give me this tattoo on my face if you had the shot? Did you think I needed to look more like you?" Will asked, touching the scar running down the left side of Rico's face.

He almost laughed but got deadly serious as he provided the after action report, "Dom's head was directly in my sightline when he was standing in front of you; sorry bro."

"So let me get this straight, if the bastard had wanted to rip open my belly, I was on my own?"

"I know it was a tough call buddy, but Dom had a little more riding on her belly than yours, sorry."

Will just shook his head, "The shit I get myself into sometimes, Jesus." He thought of something and said, "Let's get Hal on the LST, okay?"

"Hey buddy, how's it going in Sandinistaville?" Hal Rayfield asked, Will surprised to catch him at home.

"The shit hit the fan big time. What're you doing home, are Carmen and the baby already back?"

"Did you forget we're three hours ahead of you Willy? I was just getting ready to go pick her and Wade up and bring 'em home. So what kinda firefight did you get into up there?"

"What makes you equate the shit hittin' the fan to a firefight?"

"I just got off the LST with Alex, and he had a VERY interesting call from

Bob Matthews. Where the fuck are you?"

"Flying across Lake Nicaragua at flank speed bro. Dom had a panic attack so I gotta get her to a hospital."

"Slow down Willy. Matthews didn't hear what was going on between you and the brother of the Cali Cartel leader. Speak to me."

"Fucker said Colton wasn't gonna live through imprisonment and then the asshole pointed a switchblade knife at Dom's pregnant belly and asked me whether I valued a brother or a child more."

"Holy fuck, I guess that's when Rico pulled the trigger?"

"Right; I'd just told asshole Enrique Constanza he didn't have the brains to see it was none of the cartel's business. The look on his face was truly murderous when the seven-six-two round tore through his right eye. That pink mist cloud ain't real cool if you're downwind of it."

"So what's the play?"

"We wait until we can get 'em to transfer Colton to another prison, then we snatch his ass and scratch Nicaragua off the bucket list like you and Alex already did."

"So you're heading to Nawlins and plan on staying put for a while?"

"Yep, and you can bet I ain't staying at my parents' house bro. We'll be looking for a homestead, I can guarantee you."

"Smart move Tonto; just remember you're old buddy Rayfield is from the same place and suffers the same hometown disease you do. So bigger is better if you're looking for domiciles, got it?"

"Loud and clear Kemosabe; give that wife and boy a kiss for me. Later on bro."

40

NEW ORLEANS, LOUISIANA

THE FLIGHT BACK FROM SAN CARLOS at the south end of Lake Nicaragua had been a small reunion of sorts for Rico, Pierson, Dom and Will, together again for the first time since the casbah raid in Algiers. Rambo took one look at Will's face and quickly squeezed some antibiotic cream before applying a thin stream of translucent paste from an unlabeled tube. It was stinging slightly when Will asked, "What the fuck is that shit Rambo?"

"Super Glue, and with these butterflys you'll have a thin line instead of a Suarez Signature," he said as he pulled the tabs and applied three small Band-Aids shaped like outsized butterflies.

For once they had plenty of time to catch up on things, and since Rambo had missed the Masaya Mayhem he demanded a thorough debriefing. The ride had smoothed out after they skirted to the north of a tropical depression that was stirring up the Caribbean off the Nicaraguan coast, but it sure beat staying on the ground knowing an all-points-bulletin was forthcoming. The link between their disappearance and the dead Cali Cartel thugs would soon be too coincidental for the Sandinista Police to ignore.

"Having your own bird is too good. I gotta make another call," Will said as he reached for the satellite phone. The last call was to Johnny Chessereaux in San Diego, thanking him profusely for pulling their ashes out of the fire once again.

"I really apologize for waking you Mom, but I wanted to let you know we're back in the States. Think you and Dad could come to New Orleans tomorrow?" Will said, wondering why he hadn't waited until morning to call his parents.

382

"Nonsense son, when did you get to New Orleans? Why didn't you let us know you were coming home?"

"Actually, it's a long story, but the short version is that Dom and I went to Nicaragua to check up on Colton and Dom had a little blood pressure crisis so we flew back to New Orleans and we're at Tulane Medical Center."

"Is Dominique alright? What happened for her to get in this crisis?"

"She and the baby are fine Mom, but I suspect she's going to be taking it easy the last three months of the pregnancy. Now don't be trying to get here first thing in the morning, because we'll be here for a couple of days at least. There are two blue suitcases that we left in my bedroom Mom. Could you possibly bring those over with you?"

"Why, don't you have clothes with you?"

"We kind of left Nicaragua on the spur of the moment, so we could use those suitcases we left our winter clothes in. We'll figure out what we need to go buy once you're here."

"Okay Willy, I'm just so glad you're home. What did you find out about Colton while you were in Nicaragua?"

"He's safe but he's been detained for questioning in conjunction with some labor unrest down there. I'll tell you more about it when I see you tomorrow. I'm really looking forward to seeing my Momma again," he sucked up, hoping to end the interrogation for the night.

"Alright son, we'll see you both tomorrow."

"I'm not looking forward to that conversation Mr. Kavanagh," Dom said after he hung up.

"Me neither baby, but the three of us are alive and back in the States, so I'd say we're doing alright for the time being," Will told her as he kissed her and sat beside her in the bed until she fell off to sleep.

My God Kavanagh, what in the fuck are you going to do now? Lord knows when or if you'll ever get back to Argentina. Going back to Nicaragua, at least officially, is out of the question. I guess we could go back to Gastineau and stay with the folks; Jesus, why does that sound like Chinese water torture? And what the hell am I going to do to get my brother out of the hoosegow? What about Constanza's statement that Colton would experience an untimely accident in prison? Was that going to abate now that Constanza was swimming with the fishes, as they said in The Godfather? Lord knows it's a strange web we weave.

"Hey Sis, guess what; we're back in the States!" Will told his sister Alex, knowing he'd promised to call when they got back stateside.

"Really where?"

"We're in New Orleans, at the Tulane Medical Center. I promised I'd call when we got back, so I'm off the hook, right? How's it going?"

"What are you doing in New Orleans in a hospital? What have you gotten yourself into now Willy?"

"Let's see, we went to Nicaragua to find Colton and got into a little jam, then Dom's blood pressure spiked so we came to New Orleans where we knew we'd be close to family and friends," he replied, pleased with his ability to encapsulate.

"So what'd you find out about Colton? Did you talk to him?"

"Nah, he got himself across the breakers with the authorities down there by rallying some parents against child labor in the sweat shops. Who'd have thought Bolt Sportswear's havin' their tee shirts made by Nicaraguan children? Anyway, he's stuck in purgatory for now, but we got him moved to as safe a place as possible. How goes it in the Florida panhandle?"

"Funny you should ask. Do you remember our discussion a few months ago about Casey and me wanting to have a baby?"

"Uhmm, not really; things were going hot and heavy down in Argentina. As a matter of fact Carmen just gave birth to Wade Fabian. So how about refresh my memory Sis," he asked but had an unsettling feeling about the direction the conversation was taking.

"Well, I told you that Casey and I had discussed surrogate fathers for the baby and you were…"

"Okay, I remember. You wanted me to whack out a donation, right? So what's the deal, are you two finally getting around to making plans? You know I'll help you out babe, just say the word," he offered, knowing full well the chances of him being anywhere near them would be a crapshoot.

"Actually Willy, Casey's been tracking her temperature for the past few months and she's going to be ovulating tomorrow; can you believe it? This must be a sign from above that you magically reappeared right when she's fertile. Think you can make it over to Pensacola tomorrow afternoon?"

"I don't know Alex, Dom's touch and go right now, and I don't want to leave her when she and the baby are in jeopardy," he hedged, thinking he could slither out from under this circle jerk.

"Touch and go? I thought you said her blood pressure went up; don't they have that under control by now? Maybe we should head your way if things are that serious."

Wondering how he'd kicked the top off of that anthill he desperately fought for traction, "It's really not that much of an emergency Sis, at least for you guys to head this way. Listen, I'll ask Dom about it, and if she's good with it I'll head out to Pensacola in the morning. Mom and Dad are heading this way, so she won't be alone if I do have to go. Where's this place at?"

"Oh Willy, I knew you'd come through for us. Call me back after you talk to Dom and let me know if you're going to make it, will you?"

"Sure thing babe," he said with half-hearted enthusiasm.

He looked at Dom as he hung up, shaking his head in annoyance. "Oh Will, don't be such a pill; at least they're asking for a sperm sample instead of your unborn child," Dom offered in an attempt at sound reasoning.

"Right," he said, rolling his eyes.

"At least your sister's request is once and done; your brother's situation on the other hand could become increasingly problematic."

"Thanks for putting that in perspective for me love," he told her, his voice dripping with insincerity.

———

"Hey Mom, God it's good to see you," Will said as his parents walked into Dom's hospital room.

"Oh my God Willy, what's happened to your face?" Jan Kavanagh all but shrieked as she repulsed his attempt at a hug and kiss.

She was holding his face in her hands, and he had all but forgotten about the knife cut after Rambo put the butterfly strips on it in the Great West freedom bird. "I caught a sticker bush in Nicaragua walking on a trail at this volcano park Mom; how are you?"

Seemingly satisfied with his explanation she immediately diverted over to Dom, who was giving him flexed eyebrows for the cover story, no doubt. "How are you Dominique, how is the blood pressure now? Warren and I were worried sick the entire trip over here."

"I am fine now Mrs. Kavanagh," she replied, nodding at the IV line delivering fluid into her on a continuous basis.

"How did this happen to you dear? Did my son have you eating and drinking something he shouldn't have?"

"No ma'am, I just got overheated while we were walking in the volcano park. I am feeling much better now."

"I was worried to death when Willy called us last night. You know this will be my first grandchild."

"And your granddaughter wouldn't think of denying you the pleasure of her company," she replied, cutting a glance at Will. The gender of their offspring had been an inside joke even though they had steadfastly refused Jonathan's offer of an ultrasound to determine its sex.

"How you been Dad?" Will asked almost as an afterthought.

"Fine," he said as he looked his son over, "that must have been some sticker bush you ran into. It made a straight cut down your face. Good thing it wasn't anything bigger."

Will gave him a hug, "The good Lord works in mysterious ways."

"Nice work Mr. Kavanagh, I believe you sold that story," Dom said after his parents left to get lunch in the cafeteria.

"Yeah, let's hope I can do as good a job with lights and mirrors in Pensacola," he reported, less than thrilled about the prospect of driving 200 miles to jerk off into another petri dish.

"Oh Will, it's the least you can do for Alex and Casey. I realize I won't be there to assist you with the extraction this time, but I'm sure your efforts will be appreciated by your sister. I would think you should be flattered that they selected you as the surrogate father," her attempt at placating him failing miserably.

"Let's just hope this is 'once and done' like you said; I don't really aspire to being a professional masturbator," he groaned, the thought making him wonder who he'd fantasize about while doing the deed.

"Oh, I'm sure it will work out Will; now come and rub my feet if you would be so kind to a fat pregnant woman you are in love with."

41

SURROGATE CITY

WILL WAS DRIVING OVER TO PENSACOLA, listening to the radio about the tropical storm in the Gulf moving towards the Mississippi coastline. He found it interesting the tropical depression they had dodged leaving Nicaragua was now bearing down on the U.S. Gulf Coast as a borderline hurricane, radiating concern from Texas to Florida. The projected path was farther west than Pensacola, so he figured he was driving away from probable landfall, then remembered New Orleans wasn't out of danger. Suddenly reminded that his sum total of food intake was a stale donut and two cups of coffee some six hours hence, he exited I-10 at Biloxi and went hunting for a restaurant. He was trying to find a decent radio station, continuously dialing as he got in and out of FM range. Just as he pulled up to a light, he found one playing David Bowie's *Suffragette City*. He turned it up loud as the frenetic pace got the juices flowing in his rock and roll brain.

He was singing at the top of his lungs and playing drums on the steering wheel so intently he almost missed the car of girls in a Mustang convertible next to him waving desperately. He rolled down the window as the cutest brunette teenybopper in Mississippi yelled, "Hey man, what station are you listening to?"

He glanced at the radio, "FM 104.5."

Almost instantly, he heard the song booming from the other car, as they sat there in stereophonic twilight singing to beat the band. When the light changed, three of the girls all but leaned out of the car, smiling. "Hey man, thank you a lot! You know, hey man, we all think you're hot, you know, hey man…." to the tune of the song. Will laughed and gave 'em two thumbs up.

As he was pulling into Denny's he thought, 'Hey man,' that ought to be the anthem for this op I'm on, Surrogate City. The 'Hey man,' repeated throughout the song certainly seemed to fit his role in today's little endeavor.

As he was eating a turkey club he became concerned the storm might be upgraded to Category 1; if so, it might be turning to more of an easterly course. He called Dom to check on her, and she was growing more concerned by the minute, "I'm not comfortable with you being out there in this storm Will."

He glanced up at the TV behind the bar and replied, "Actually honey, it may be more of a problem for New Orleans than Florida. I'm driving away from it at least. Is everything alright there?"

"So far, they haven't issued imminent danger notices for New Orleans. You drive safely Will Kavanagh, we've got a baby on the way and she needs a father."

He flexed his eyebrows, "Yeah, so does everyone; it must run in the family. I'll call you after dinner and check on you baby; love you, bye."

He called Alex next to confirm both ends of the trip were still a go, "I've got to go to Orlando for a job interview early in the morning, but Casey will be waiting for you at the fertility clinic in Pensacola."

He looked at his watch, noticed he had plenty of time to get there and pondered his 'rest overnight' locale. "Hey, how far is Fort Walton Beach from Pensacola? I might just get a room in Pensacola rather than drive if it's a ways."

"It's about thirty miles, but it does take you farther from Louisiana. It's your choice, you're welcome to stay if you'd like."

"Alright, I'll see what this storm decides to do; good luck with that job interview."

"Yeah thanks, and thank you Will for being such a good sport about this. We really appreciate it; talk to you soon bro, bye."

He considered the thirty miles and knew he didn't want to put in the extra road time, as dinner options at Alex' would be slim to none. He got directory assistance to the Pensacola Marriott, and the receptionist sounded hot, "Hi, I'm Will Kavanagh and I'd like to make a reservation for this evening."

"Yes sir, that'll be no problem. The hotel's almost wide open with the storm coming."

"Hey, that reminds me, how are you guys fixed for emergency power?"

"It's no problem sir, the hotel has a high capacity diesel generator; we anticipate no problems for guests. Perhaps I can interest you in a free upgrade to a concierge level suite; we really appreciate your patronage Mr. Kavanagh."

Wondering what she looked like, and just how much she really 'appreciated' his patronage, he replied, "Okay Ms., what was your name?"

"It's Molly, Molly Randolph."

"Okay, Ms. Molly Randolph, your heavy-handed sales approach has made rain; sign me up for that free upgrade, smoking please."

As she took his credit card data he shivered, thinking he'd lost control of his damn libido. *Kavanagh you dog, you've got a pregnant wife and all you think about is pussy.* "Thank you so much for your business Mr. Kavanagh, and we hope to see you again soon."

He was swatting the devil back over his shoulder, "Thank you Molly, be careful out there this evening."

———

As he passed by Mobile, the city was battening down as a precaution. Will felt the heat around his ears as the first tremors of doubt regards the storm's path washed through his brain. Trying to ignore the damn storm, he finally found the fertility clinic in Pensacola where Casey was pacing back and forth beside her car. As he pulled in, she jerked his door open, "They just lost electricity on this block Will! Can you believe it? What the fuck are we going to do?"

He shook his head in dismay, "Jesus, I'm sorry Case. Why don't we go over to the hotel; I called and it's damn near deserted and they've got backup power."

She looked at him in disgust, "Oh alright, the electricity is probably out in Fort Walton anyway." She followed him over to the hotel; but as they walked up she stammered, "Jesus Will, what happened to your face? How'd you cut yourself?" Her query harkened recent memories, albeit in New Orleans.

Dom's doctor at Tulane Medical had noticed it too, and was on him like white on rice. 'Exactly how did you get this wound Mr. Kavanagh?'

He knew it be best not to bullshit the Doc, "A very nasty thug pulled a switchblade knife down my face earlier today."

The doctor examined the wound closely, "Whoever did this repair knew what they were doing; is this Super Glue?"

Will rolled his eyes, "That's what he told me Doc; it was sort of a battle-field kinda thing."

As he pulled off the Band-Aids and applied some ointment he was truly impressed, 'You're going to have a very distinguished mark instead of an ugly tattoo on your face.'

"So, distinguished at twenty-eight is where I'm at, eh?'

The doctor smiled sardonically, 'Based on what I see, you're fortunate to be around for twenty-nine Mr. Kavanagh.'

"I was half asleep trying to shave a couple of days ago, it's nothing." The coming storm had emptied out the hotel, as they were the only guests in the restaurant. Will snickered as Casey carefully evaluated the menu, finally deciding on the broiled wahoo that no doubt complied with her pre-natal dietary regimen. As they launched into their entrées, he asked, "So what do we do now Case, reschedule?"

"That's twice you've called me Case; what's that all about Xav?"

"I know dozens of people named Casey, but Case has a slick detective sound to it."

She scowled, "Right; today I'm ovulating and you're here and the fucking clinic is closed. How the hell does this shit keep happening to me?"

"What keeps happening to you?"

She grated her teeth as she grouched, "Oh, you know what I mean. I finally decide that I want to have a baby, Alex and I talk it over and you're the only donor we even came close to agreeing on. Now it's all gone to shit."

Wondering if the devil was peeking back over his shoulder, he smiled, "So you really want to make this happen Casey?"

She had more than a touch of angst in her voice now, "Of course I do, more than anything in the world; but now it's all gone to shit."

He put his hand over hers, "Well if it's that important Casey, we still have one option."

She stared in disbelief, but then ratcheted down the scowl, "You can't be suggesting what I think you are Will Kavanagh?"

"I didn't mean to insult you Casey, it's just that you seem like you're be-tween a rock and a hard place. I certainly wouldn't have any problem consid-ering a direct donation—you know, doing it the old fashioned way?"

"I could never do that with you Will; I mean, I'm in love with your sister."

"I completely understand Casey. It's just that we're in dire straits here, and if you really want this to happen it might be the only time the two of us are together when you're fertile." She arched her eyebrows considering his point when he added, "We sort of live in Argentina, but now I'm gonna be flitting around Central America until we get Colton home."

She stood up, walked across the room to look out at the roiling ocean. She suddenly turned and posed, "It'd be our little secret?"

Will broke into a broad grin, "Casey, don't you remember I told you I always wanted to make love with you? And you told me thirty minutes before Dom and I got married that you secretly always wanted to have sex with me? It's not like I'd have any problem getting it up for you. I heard somewhere that fertile women are superior hunters, you know, they pick out the best stud to procreate with. So what's the big issue?"

The impish grin gave her away, "You wouldn't have a problem getting it up for me?

He rolled his eyes, "Right Casey, as if I had to explain basic human sexuality; there is no chance in hell I would offer to make a 'direct donation' if I wasn't attracted to you big time. This attraction facilitates the excitement factor associated with the delivery of the donation, getting my drift?"

She turned and walked away, her face blushing then whipped around and got right in his face, "So you think we can do this? I thought you had some sperm problem that meant they had to inseminate me?"

"It was a serious issue when I was smoking a bunch of pot in college, but the fertility specialist in Argentina told me my motility factor was only moderately impaired, and that I could impregnate a female through normal intercourse. With Dom's issues, we still had to go the inseminated egg routine, but there's a chance we could pull this off if you want to give it a try."

She put her finger under his chin, "Show me the way Romeo."

They stopped and grabbed a bottle of Grand Marnier and a couple of snifters at the bar, then headed up to the room hand in hand. Once inside, he poured two shots and proposed a toast, "I always dreamed about doing this with you, so it's time to celebrate."

She was already hedging, "It's been ten years since I had sex with a man, so go easy on me will you?"

He couldn't wipe the smile off as he unbuttoned her blouse, "You bet."

She threw him on the bed as they fought each other getting clothes off. Will stopped, taking Casey Mooneyhan's nakedness into account for the first time. "You're fucking crazy beautiful." The naked Casey was almost as sensuous as Samantha Chessereaux, being a little shorter, but the breasts were perfect and she had that incredible little tuft of golden pubic hair that proclaimed her blondness. Owing to her competitive canoeing efforts, her muscle tone was incredible.

As he drank in his incredible fortune, she frowned, "Are you just going to look at me, or did you have other things in mind?"

Will was truly stunned at how quickly Casey Mooneyhan transitioned into heterosexual lovemaking. Within moments they were inhaling each other in a devastating French-kiss, and he was metering up to a blue-steel hard on. Casey looked down laughing, "I remember something like that once in a parking lot."

"Yeah, and I remember telling myself 'what a waste.' I can't believe the mountain has finally come to Mohammed." As she made a darting motion for his erection, he caught her, "Un-uh." He gently rotated her onto her back and began the wondrous procession downward, taking his time to all but ingest her beauty.

When he got to the golden tuft, she was already panting, "Please be gentle Will."

He paused to glance up at her face, "Don't you worry Case; you won't even know I'm here." With that he began the vulva sensitivity test ending up at the nerve-bundled sexual switch, and then turned on the low vacuum drive. As she arched her back he found the wondrous D spot and began changing Casey Mooneyhan's attitude about sex. When she blew through the first orgasm, he pretended not to notice and kept at it until she began screaming. The earth-tilting shiver that ended with her skin turning clammy cool had him feeling really good about life.

He was in her face when she came back to earth, "Won't even know you're here?"

He shrugged and offered, "Hey Case, I wouldn't want to build up your expectations unnecessarily."

"Yeah right cowboy; I overheard Dom and Kelly at your reception comparing notes about Freelancing, whatever that is." He didn't bite, but merely smiled, apparently intent on keeping her in the dark. "Goddamn it Kavanagh,

I know Dom's turned you into her Freelancing stud, is what Kelly said; time to fess up to your object of lust, *n'est pas?*"

He couldn't wipe the smile off his face, "Dom was my love mentor for Freelancing with Freud; you just experienced the welcome to Freelancing bell ringer. Why don't you climb on top and kiss me, and we'll explore it further?" As the words left his lips, the lights flickered and suddenly went out. He instinctively picked up the phone to check it, but there was no dial tone.

As she rolled over on him, a smile was pasted across her face, "I guess we're all alone in the world now, aren't we?"

"Yep, there'll be no interruptions and we have the perfect alibi for disappearing all night."

As she slid onto him, they both shuddered with a groan. He shook his head, "We can't be doing that quite yet Casey. We must have some fun in conjunction with this insemination project. I want you to ride me a bit, nice and easy like you just took a ten year sabbatical."

With that, she broke into a wicked grin and became the piston demon, gaining speed and momentum with every stroke. Sensing the limit approaching, he grabbed her hips and pulled her forward before slamming her backward into the fulcrum. She made a garbled grunt, but with the third fulcrum impact he gave her a hard vertical thrust as she whimpered. It took two more thrusts, but then she completely lost it and began crying out, slamming down on him as hard as she could. Further resistance was futile as he gave her one final upward thrust. When the passion abated enough for him to make sense of his surroundings, seemingly every muscle in her body had stiffened into a brick. Will didn't know how long it took the two of them to get through the aftershocks, but when she came to, collapsed on his chest, she was a changed human being. "My God Will, what in the hell was that? I've never felt anything like that in my life!"

He was smiling like a Cheshire cat, "You know Case, we might just have gotten you pregnant on that little elevated fulcrum maneuver, but we shouldn't take a chance on once and done, now should we?"

She was smiling wickedly as she reached for the Grand Marnier, "Right cowboy, wouldn't want to take a chance on missing out on any sperms, now would we?"

As the lights flickered back on, he headed to the bathroom, but didn't make it far. Casey suddenly announced with alarm, "My God Will, what happened to your back?"

It suddenly dawned on him the Algeria-Sandrigan battle to the death had been fought and won since they'd last seen each other in Charleston. "Don't you remember that Hal, Carmen, Dom and I had to go rescue Dom's mother who had been kidnapped in Morocco?"

She had a confused look on her face, "Yeah, I remember, but what does that have to do with those scars on your back?"

Hoping he could quickly appease her he smiled, "I took a few hits during the rescue operation. Hal and Bob Kellor took rounds in the leg too. It was a very dangerous operation that we all lived through thankfully."

Clearly not satisfied, she pursued, "What kind of hits?"

Hoping against hope that he could nip this in the bud, he surrendered. "I took a piece of shrapnel across the back, see that long horizontal tattoo across my shoulder blades? I took a curved Arab dagger through my left shoulder when a hidden guerilla sprung on me in the dark; that one required major surgery to correct. And I took a nine millimeter bullet through a bound ledger that broke two of my ribs on the right side—see the brown burn mark? Oh, and I got this beauty mark on my face in Nicaragua a couple of days ago when a cartel thug wanted to convince me he was the boss."

She was now thunderstruck, "You have got to be shitting me Will Kavanagh. What happened to the cartel thug?"

Sensing he was about to be delivered from interrogation, he told her the truth, "After cutting my face, he put the point of that switchblade on Dom's pregnant belly. The asshole had the temerity to ask if I valued my brother's life over my unborn child's. A buddy of mine was waiting with a high-powered sniper rifle for him to step clear of Dom. I watched his goddamn Colombian Cartel head explode in a cloud of pink mist. I hope Enrique Constanza rots in hell, and that's all I've got to say about that cocksucking bastard." She stared at him in stunned disbelief as he finally got to the sweet relief of the bathroom.

While catching his second wind, he lit a cigarette hoping to marshal the forces of stamina for the next round. Trying her best to reconnect with the romance of the evening, she asked him whimsically, "Jesus Will, that story completely freaked me out, but this is our only night together. What would you think about indulging me in the one fantasy that gets me wet just thinking about?"

Her reference to fantasy was rewarded by a naughty smile, "And what might that be, any special way?"

She laughed as she climbed on top of him, playfully slapping at his thigh, "I've always wanted to feel like I was suffocating during sex. Your sister would never even discuss it with me; she thought it was so repulsive. Are you repulsed?"

Will was smiling for a living, "So how do you want to play it? It seems like something to pull out of the hat at the very end, you know, like just as you're coming. Help me out here Case, my project planning partner."

She was beaming now, "Damn, I should have known you'd be a player, you wild man. So do you and Dom get into any kinky stuff?"

Her voyeuristic compunction amused him, "Casey, neither of us are having sex with our mates tonight; this one is a freebie. So how do you want to play this Ms. Mooneyhan?"

She scrunched her face into a perplexing grimace, "Well, I've only seen it in a porn movie, but the thought of it gets me wet. They actually used a soft rope to strangle her just enough to trip her panic button, but I don't think we can chance something like that; I wouldn't want any bruises on my neck to have to explain away."

Will was getting focused now, "No restraints for the neck then; Jesus, I got tied down once for a massage fuck, and it was brutally sensuous. And I must admit that Kelly Dupree is the Cossack Queen of restraints."

Casey was suddenly alive with excitement as she began the interrogatory, "You got tied down? Maybe we should try that, you know, you tie me at the wrists and ankles and then take me. Maybe you can muzzle me when I can't take it anymore; what do you think?"

He didn't even answer her as he was off the bed, searching his overnight bag for some article of clothing he could sacrifice to the event. Spotting none, he darted into the bathroom and returned with two huge bath towels, no doubt adequate for the pool or the bath. He thanked his lucky stars that he'd packed the switchblade taken from Constanza, and was soon cutting narrow strips of the soft terrycloth towel. "Is that the same knife the cartel thug cut your face with?"

"I already told you Casey; fuck that cocksucking cocaine cowboy," he was saying when he heard himself. "Sorry babe; yeah, this is the same knife. I kept it as sort of a souvenir."

He was gauging the suitability of the strips for the job when Casey crawled onto his back, "God Will, I'm already hot as hell for this; let's do it."

As if fortune were smiling on them, the head and foot boards comprised vertical spindles, not unlike small balusters. He turned to tell Casey to lie down, but she was already happily spread-eagled. He tied her wrists and ankles off carefully but snugly, not knowing how violent her resistance might get during the upcoming horizontal hijinks. He tickled her body with the point of the switchblade, causing her to gasp as he examined his bound paramour, shivering as he ventured downward towards her crotch. He thought she was going to overheat during the D spot, and barely balancing on the brink when he entered her. She began screaming so loudly he was worried about the hotel security staff. He put his hand over her mouth to stifle the outburst. When he did, her eyes became as big as saucers and the screaming did not abate, albeit in garbled decibels. She was trying to lunge up at him, but was completely stymied by the restraints.

Sensing victory—and becoming more and more excited himself—he gently pinched her nostrils closed with his other fingers. It was then that the entire room seemed to be shaking. Casey was screaming, lunging and shaking almost uncontrollably as the orgasm completely overwhelmed her. The passion level was clearly off any scale, and Will came violently as the sexual bliss grasped her unabated. As he lifted his hand from her mouth, her screaming was at the alarm level, so he quickly began kissing her to quiet things down. When she found his mouth, she began kissing and biting him with fury. When he tasted blood for the first time since his Philippine days, it so angered and aroused him that he began pounding away again without any recovery. She was at the edge of hyperventilating when he figured it was time to stop and take stock of their little experiment.

Casey was huffing from the exertion and looking at him like a wild animal as he untied her hands and feet. He sat down next to her and inquired, "So how'd it work out?" Instead of answering him, she launched into him and climbed on top as she began a devastating French-kiss that transitioned immediately into fellatio. It was all he could do to pry her off of him. When he finally did he tried the interrogatory once more, "Do I take it that means we gained positive traction?"

She was making a guttural sound, not unlike Malina Garcia's catlike purr, when she finally threw him down on the bed and climbed on top of him. "That was the most incredible thing that has ever happened in my life! I knew I was going to have a heart attack when you pinched my nose shut. Jesus, I came so hard I know I busted something loose."

He smiled at her with knowing insight, "It's lucky you're in such good shape Case. I have never seen anyone get that excited in my life! I'd say you made a good call on wanting to explore that little fantasy of yours."

She was calming down enough to smile as she summed up Round Two, "It was my life's fantasy and you played it like a maestro. God Will, I can't believe that happened."

He smiled smugly, "Well it did sweet cheeks, and you might just have gotten pregnant seeing as how you were so brutally receptive. Jesus Casey, sex doesn't get any hotter than that. My God woman, that was history book stuff."

As she got up for the bathroom, the sultry glance over her shoulder spoke volumes, "Right cowboy; now it's really time for some of that Grand Marnier."

As he tilted the snifter for a well-deserved swig of Marnier, he glanced at the clock and thought it strange they'd only eaten a couple of hours ago, "You hungry?"

"I'm starving; didn't we just eat?"

"What do you feel like? I'll call room service and have them bring us a feast; just name it."

She was smiling wickedly now, "We had seafood for supper, but now I'm in the mood for some rare beef. How about you?" He smiled inwardly at her abandonment of the light side, but had to admit that a steak sounded damn good.

"Sounds good to me," he said as he picked up the phone, "Hi, this is Mr. Kavanagh in Room 715, is it too late to make a dinner order?"

"No sir, what did you have in mind?"

"Can we get two filet mignons, medium rare, and some steak fries? And how about send up a bottle of your best cabernet with that please?"

"We'll have it up in twenty minutes sir; you'll be our last service of the evening."

While inhaling the last of the delicious rare steak, Will felt his energy levels rebounding and looked at his previously unattainable blonde co-conspirator. "Clock's tickin' baby; any last requests?" Before she could respond he admitted to her, "God almighty Casey Mooneyhan, if you only knew how badly I wanted to do this with you the day I met you. Making love with you is like a planetary mind fuck."

She just sat there, rocking her head, biting her bottom lip so very seductively, "Yep, it's been like the most incredible mind fuck for me too; who knew you could unlock my fantasies like a map reader?" She was smiling as she conjured up the final flickers of unexplored fantasy, "I wouldn't mind doing that asphyxiation thing again, but the restraints were almost too frustrating— I was borderline psychotic by the time you took them off. Think we could do it without them?"

He forced himself into project mode, trying to work his way through the geometry. "Without the restraints, you're going to be harder to control, so I'll need at least one free hand to manage horizontal shift. Maybe if I attacked you from behind we could pull it off, you know with only one hand on your face."

"Jesus Will, ever the engineer, but I guess I knew that a long time ago. Want me to lie down on the bed?"

"Yeah, but sideways, we gotta get ourselves ready first."

As she was shifting into place, he looked at the TV, "Hey Case, you were pretty loud that last time and I was worried hotel security might break down the door to see who was being assaulted. Maybe a little background noise?"

"Yeah, but I ain't listening to those constant storm updates; is there a radio?"

"Hey, this is a suite, I'm sure there's a radio. Here we go, maybe they have a decent station around here."

"Hey, what's that?"

"David Bowie's *Space Oddity*; feel like blasting off again?"

She was moving against him, rolling her head from side to side, the blond tresses flowing across those perfect breasts, "Fuck me Major Tom."

———

To say he was surprised at how fast an erection grew from the well-played sixty-nine warm up must have been evident, as Casey purred, her chest heaving with excitement. "Are we compatible or what?"

Her question gave him pause; it did feel as though they'd been lovers for years considering how quickly they'd adapted to nakedness and relaxation. "Incredibly compatible Case; I'm fucking in heaven."

"I could fuck you forever Will Kavanagh; God if I'd only known what I was missing," she said, waxing melancholy.

"Well, to be completely honest, when we first met I didn't have a clue how to please a woman in bed. Dom has been my apprentice instructor; she actually taught me how to turn her into the Princess of Orgasm. So, it was probably serendipitous that we waited this long."

She was licking his neck now, "I am so ready for you."

"Let's find out. Get on your knees and lean over the bed," he told her, beginning to see the path to that stairway Robert Plant had sung about so long ago. As she assumed the position he cozied in behind her and began lightly spanking her lovely derriere. She was reaching back between her legs to direct him in when he found her nipples and began a slow but deliberate pull. She gasped and none too delicately thrust him into her steaming hot wetness. He reached up to her neck and began a slow, delicate grasp, resulting in another gasp as she began pounding against him as the moans transitioned into low shrieks. When he moved his hand around and lightly grasped her throat, she began bucking savagely against him and her breathing became shallow. Sensing it was time for the *coup de grâs*, he covered her mouth with his other hand and pinched her nostrils closed. He quickly shifted his free hand to her exposed clitoris as the dimensions of their universe began to stress at the seams. Not five seconds later she started pounding the bed with her open palms screaming, followed quickly by what seemed like a desperate flail to tear his hand off her face. He let go of her nose and mouth, only to find her gasping desperately for air. She pulled in a huge breath and then all hell broke loose. She let out a scream and slammed down so hard he thought his knees would give. Will was wondering if she could possibly achieve any deeper penetration when she shook into a rigid brick and he heard the stream of liquid splatting on the floor.

As he tried to shift around to see what was happening, she screamed "No!" and this time she slammed down so hard he did go down on his butt. Casey was in the midst of the most violent orgasm he had ever witnessed. Will was right on the brink of losing control when she slammed down one final time. He exploded in her like an erupting geyser, the two of them on fire together. Will tried to establish what was happening within his realm of experience, but there was none—they were exploring new cosmic territory. They were together, the flames flying off of their joined souls. He heard himself yelling something as the aftershocks rolled across his consciousness, so intense he couldn't even think. When he came to Casey was lying across his chest bleating almost uncontrollably. He was close to panic trying desperately to regain his breath when he looked down and saw a sizable pool of clear viscous fluid between them. He had shared orgasms with more than a few lovers, some quite violently, but female ejaculation was rare indeed. He quickly dialed back and remembered Carmen ejaculating all over his stomach by the hot tub in that realistic Buenos dreamscape. But this seemed different; it being the first time both of them had been consumed in the slick viscous fluid. *My God, what the hell just happened here?*

As she regained consciousness, Casey clutched him and began crying. Will struggled mightily to keep from breaking down emotionally as he held Cayce close. *What in the name of God have we unleashed here?* Finally he managed to ask, "Are you alright baby?"

With tears flushing her face, she looked sideways at him, "God I love you Will; that was the most soul-rendering event of my life. I cannot ever imagine anything more intense than that. I am totally and forever in love with you Will Kavanagh."

He had to look away to hide the tear that was escaping down his face, but it would have been unfair to deny the pure emotion they had not only shared, but created. With tears running down each cheek he told her, "I can't believe it either baby. I'm shaking from it. This is as close as I've ever come to compromising myself spiritually. God I love you woman."

She leaned her head back just slightly, "You mean with Dom?"

Now he was sobbing as he nodded his head, the truth so evident it could not be denied, "Yes."

"Say it to me one more time while you really mean it Will," she asked, seeking confirmation they had shared the same transformational experience.

He took her face in his hands, "I'll go to hell for saying it, but right this moment I love you more than anything on this earth Cayce."

———

Will had never seen Casey Mooneyhan smoke, but she grabbed his cigarette and inhaled deeply before she asked with a nervous edge to her voice, "What are we going to do Will?"

Thanking his lucky stars he was becoming more lucid by the moment, he got right in her face, "We're never going to do that again."

She was nodding her head as she took another long pull on the Marlboro. When she'd exhaled a long column of blue smoke, she spoke with crystal clarity, "Not unless we want to fuck up a lot of people's lives."

"Right, we came here to get you pregnant, not change the universe. God Almighty that was very nearly transcendent. I, I, I feel as though we went somewhere and came back Cayce."

"I sort of feel the same way but can't put it to words Will; what happened to us?"

He rolled his eyes and shook his head, "I'll be declared criminally insane if anybody else ever heard me utter these words, but it almost felt like we crossed into another dimension." He shook his head, "Am I making any sense?"

"No, you're putting to words what I feel. My God, I was sitting in front of the sun with you, and our universe was composed of pure love."

"So we somehow crossed over the mythological membrane separating regular life from pure love, is that what you're saying?"

"No, you said it, but it's absolutely the truth."

He slapped her playfully on her world class ass and laughed, "I'd say we did a pretty fair job of improvisation, *n'est pas?*"

They were both sitting up in bed smoking cigarettes and sipping Marnier when he looked at Casey and told her, "It's time for me to be completely frank with you Casey, and this is the only time I really ever want to talk about it ever, got it?"

She nodded her head in assent as she put her arm around him, "Go ahead Will."

He glanced up at the ceiling to compose his thoughts, "What I said to you about compromising my soul tonight is absolutely true. I have only felt that type of connection with one other human being, and that is Dominique. We have committed ourselves to the betterment and welfare of each other, and that is my absolute guiding light in life. I have killed people to protect that bond. I have felt a connection, albeit subliminal, with you since the day I first laid eyes on you. I have wanted to make love with you, not necessarily fuck you, since that first day. I was not aware of nor prepared for the emotional onslaught that would accompany what we just did. I was naïve, but I should have known it was going to be something other than predictable and controllable from the start. I probably made a mistake by leading both of us into this situation, but I saw this as an opportunity to achieve two very different goals; help you and Alex with a baby and fulfill my pent up desire to be intimate with you. I want you to know one thing, and I want you to believe it with all your soul," he said, turning so that their noses were touching, "I do not regret what just happened between us. It might have been inevitable. Would it have made any difference if it had happened when we first met, who knows? I will love you until the day I die, and I will do anything I possibly can to help you and Alex. And I will deny this took place for the rest of my life. It's very, very personal between you and me."

Assuming it was her turn, she grabbed both of his hands in hers and began, "First of all, I need to be completely honest with both of us and say that, in spite of my certainty that I am attracted first and foremost to your sister, I have known from day one that I had an almost overwhelming desire to make love with you, and it has been a burr in my saddle, so to speak, in being completely comfortable with the term gay. I'm sure you understand that it has also been a source of misgiving in my relationship with Alex, whom I love completely. And I'm sure you saw me completely compromise my soul with you tonight, and I'd feel better if I were ashamed of it, but I'm not. It was singularly the most incredible moment of my life, and I must always suppress the desire to repeat it by remembering the perfection of that moment. I'd like to be selfish and think about a life with you, but we are who we are and it's going to have to suffice to remember that I experienced that one sublime moment, that event, in my life. I know I'm lucky to have seen that pure light. I will love you like no other man for the rest of my life, and you will always be more than a friend, and you can always count on me for anything, anytime, anywhere. I can't make a more personal commitment to you than that Will; it's just not possible in humans. I don't want you to feel uncomfortable when I tell you this, but I adore you."

Recognizing this was the last of the good deals, he looked at her and winked, "Come on woman, the night ain't over yet." They luxuriated in the warmth and intimacy of the shower, washing and testing each other until Will had to plead with her to wait for the bedroom.

Fortunately the suite had a pair of queen-sized beds, so they opted for the 'unsoiled' one and quickly got comfortable with one another. The lead in—it couldn't properly be classified as foreplay—was excruciatingly sensual, as all pretense of ego had vanished between them. Casey had very nearly ruined their chance at making love when she dedicated herself to *quid pro quo* after Will once again turned her into a screaming D spot aficionado. And then the slow, intensely reactive love making began in earnest.

Will couldn't tell how long it lasted, but they were covered in sweat when they finally surrendered to the passion, looking into each other's eyes as they spoke the forbidden words, "I love you." Will grimaced inwardly at the sacrilege of it, but was confident that Casey had as much to lose as he did by ever revealing the truth.

As they were passing off into wasted happiness, Casey nuzzled his ear, "You know I'll always love you. But I love Alex more, and in a different way. I can't imagine doing this with any other man. Thank you for being so thoughtful and caring."

He shrugged in warm nothingness as she spooned him from behind, "You're everything I thought you would be Case. You better be glad I took it easy on you, being a rookie at this heterosexual sex and all."

She rallied enough to slap his butt, "Yeah, right cowboy."

———

He awoke with a start, knowing he hadn't checked in with Dom since the stop in Biloxi the day before, but didn't know how much of today was going to be out of control once they left the hotel. He opted to take a shower, leaving the new Princess of Orgasm sleeping soundly in the now moderately soiled second bed. As he was beginning to moan with relief from the pulsing hot water, the shower door opened and Casey stepped in, "Trying to sneak away, are you Mr. Kavanagh?"

He turned around to engage her, wiping water from his eyes, smiling like a Cheshire cat, "Naw, I just needed to wash the Casey Mooneyhan off of me before I head back west."

She reached for the soap and began lathering his back, resulting in instant karma. "Maybe you shouldn't wash it off just yet; I'm wondering if you might have manufactured any more of those impaired sperm overnight?"

Quickly taking stock of his very unhappy Johnson, he grabbed the soap from her and began foaming up her lovely breasts, "Casey, you have rendered me an empty, sore shell casing. I'm not sure there's any lead left in the pencil."

She smiled coyly as she dropped to her knees and took him in her mouth, and his concern with soreness quickly dissipated, "You know, for someone who loves a woman, you demonstrate incredible fellatio skills."

With that she stood back up and replied with a smirk, "Well, for someone madly in love with his wife, you donate sperm incredibly well."

He was frowning at her clever rejoinder, and then gave the devil her due, "Touché!"

Thinking of a trick probably not part of lesbian love, he asked, "Casey, have you ever been introduced to the slow screw up against the wall?"

She was smiling wickedly now, "No I haven't; is that something I might enjoy?"

He was already lifting her up to clutch her legs around his waist, "Hard to tell Case, but never up never in, right?"

They were both heating up rapidly when Casey shuddered, no doubt the muscle memory of last evening kicking in. Acting on impulse, he took his right arm from around her butt and placed his hand over her mouth, leaving the thumb and index finger to squeeze her nostrils shut. Her eyes immediately got the size of saucers, but with nothing restricting her movements she grabbed at him violently. He could feel her fingernails digging into his back not far from where his broken ribs had not quite mended. He screamed in pain and immediately flung his arms out at her hands, resulting in her falling straight down into the bathtub. She immediately looked up at him in horror, "Are you alright Will?"

Trying to catch his breath, he looked down at her, staring past his amazingly resilient manhood, "Just an old war wound. Sorry about that, now where were we?"

They both knew this was going to be the last time they ever made love, so they took it slow and luxuriated in the hot shower pulsing on them as they moved through the wonderful machinations pulling them towards the inevitable cataclysmic implosion. They were lounging in each other's arms in a warm cocoon when he told her, "That wasn't exactly the slow screw up against the wall, but my God, what a last dance! We are the royalty of improvisation my dear."

He watched as Casey dressed, in total disbelief that seeing her slip into a bra and panties brought a stir to his loins. "Get thee behind me Satan," he said to himself as he turned his head and shivered.

"What's the matter, that damn lust thing won't go away and hide where you want it to?"

"No dammit, it won't; Jesus, fate sure did step in when we met. The golf gods decided I couldn't put up with a steady dose of something as hot as you blondie."

"Sure you could, but you'd be dead by now the way you look at gorgeous women."

He nodded, "I am indeed fortunate to have a bride who shares my tastes in life Casey Casey."

42

RECOVERING FROM A HURRICANE

AFTER DRYING OFF, HE CALLED the front desk for a travel advisory. The receptionist was the sexy one who had taken his reservation the day before, "I believe you came in from Louisiana, didn't you Mr. Kavanagh?"

"That's right, how in the world did you remember that Molly?"

"There were only three reservations made for last evening, but I'd remember your voice anywhere. I take it you're returning to Louisiana?"

"Right you are Ms. Randolph, what about road closures and any communication outages?"

"Well sir, the storm did not strengthen before it came ashore at Pass Christian, Mississippi, but we experienced wind gusts of 50 miles per hour here in Pensacola. As you noted last night, the entire area lost power when a major distribution line went down in Jackson County in Mississippi. We were able to regain power in the hotel when maintenance discovered contaminated diesel fuel and switched to another tank. Electricity is out through coastal Alabama and Mississippi, so I would suggest you stay on the Interstate going back west."

He quickly digested this and asked, "So what about telephone communications. I had difficulty dialing out during the night."

"I apologize for the inconvenience sir, but the storm surge resulted in AT&T shutting down their main exchange in Mobile, with all telephone traffic in the region rerouted through Birmingham, Alabama. It was several hours until AT&T rerouted the lines to bypass the flood-threatened exchange in Mobile."

He nodded as he filed away the intel, "So the lines are back operable now?"

"Oh yes sir, please let me know if you experience any further difficulties calling out."

Casey was pacing the carpet when he hung up, "So what are the power and comm issues?"

"Okay, they lost power throughout Pensacola, plus all of coastal Alabama and Mississippi. Winds here peaked at 50 mph, making local travel very hazardous, especially between Pensacola and your house in Fort Walton Beach."

"Right, got it; too dangerous to drive back home after the 'successful' insemination procedure. The hotel was empty and rooms were easy to come by. What about communications?"

"AT&T lost regional comms for several hours, shut down the Mobile switch and rerouted everything to the Birmingham hub. No telephone connections at the hotel for most of the night."

She reached for the phone when he stopped her, "Shouldn't you coordinate with the fertility clinic about our 'direct donation'? Is the clinic doctor the one who is going to be your obstetrician?"

"Jesus, you're right Will. How many lies is it going to take to keep the lid on this?"

"Maybe just one; you'd better check if that clinic is open, then go by and explain to the doctor what happened. You'll have to enlist him in our conspiracy, but if you're pregnant it doesn't make any difference how the sperm got to the egg, right?"

"Now I understand prostitutes and call girls; it was worth $1200 to have the ride of my life, that's for damn sure."

"It was going to be $1200 anyway, so why not a transcendental ride to the fallopian tubes, *n'est pas*? Just make sure you get a money back guarantee in case the first insemination doesn't take!"

"Before we make these calls, I'd like to hear how taking me to the sun ranked up there for you. I'll be honest; it was the greatest experience of my life."

Will took a good look at Casey, figuring he could play it straight, "Okay Casey, I'll lay it out but not a word ever leaves this room, agreed?" She nodded so he began thinking out loud, "After the tie down round last night it felt like we'd been lovers for years. Did you sense any of that?"

She laughed, "I felt like I was your fiancée, strutting around naked without a care in the world. How'd that happen by the way?"

"It was always right below the surface Case; when we finally removed the moralistic restraints we discovered we'd been spiritual lovers for years. That has never happened to me before."

"So, what I'm hearing is that I'm really a bisexual person, is that what you're telling me?"

"Did last night happen, and happen with wonderment?"

She nodded, finally accepting it. "Okay, put last night into your life's sexual hierarchy."

Though Will considered ranking emotional relationships a spiritually devoid exercise, Casey wanted to gauge intensity like it was a separate metric. "The night Dom and I first hooked up was the most electrifying fuck of my life, and I quickly figured out why." Now Casey was excited and prompted him to continue.

"I shared a night of abject debauchery with a gorgeous call girl in DC, and that was the most uninhibited I have ever been with anyone. She taught me about anal sex by the way." Casey was now in his lap, eyes wide open nodding for more.

"I met this jet-set international stewardess in the Philippines who was the wickedest lover I have ever had, and she orgasmed for minutes at the time."

"Kelly Dupree was possibly the most depraved lover I have ever known, but she and Dom were so into one another I couldn't tell what the impetus was."

"So she was your first *ménage a trois* partner?"

"The first one that counted anyway," he couldn't believe he was telling anyone such things. "I really believe I was most turned on the night Dom and I had the ménage with Samantha Chessereaux, and I was literally gagging with passion as we imploded into one another."

"I'd otherwise say you're lying, but I've seen her literally slobber over you; God, I can't imagine how hot that was," Casey shivered.

"Now I come to Pensacola and experience the biggest mind fuck of my life; I've always wanted you so badly but who could predict what happened? My God, I'm glad I lived long enough to experience pure three dimensional love and passion. That was without parallel Casey!"

Seeing inside his mind really keyed her up, "It'll be hard not thinking about how you, oh, Jesus, you've spoiled me forever. It's blasphemous, but

I'm cool with the moral implications; I will never forget what perfect sex is. Nobody can take that away from us."

He nodded his head, "I believe we understand each other now Casey; ready to make those calls?"

With a pregnant wife in crisis, Will made the first call to Dom's room, surprised when he was transferred to a nurse's station at Tulane Medical Center. A nurse supervisor said, "Hello Mr. Kavanagh, I'm glad you got through. Your wife Dominique, along with most of the ambulatory patients, checked out of most New Orleans hospitals yesterday as the storm approached. She has been transferred to, let me see, yes, she has been transferred to Lane Regional Medical Center in Baton Rouge."

Stunned, he stammered, "Holy shit, is she alright?" The look on his face must have been unsettling, because Casey was immediately by his side giving him the prompt as to what was happening.

"Yes Mr. Kavanagh, she was fine and your parents transported her to Baton Rouge. Here is the number for Lane Medical Center in case you want to call there."

He was wildly dumping the contents of his wallet on the coffee table as he told Casey, "Queen Nurse said they evacuated all ambulatory patients from New Orleans as the storm approached yesterday. Dom's at a hospital in Baton Rouge."

He found the Sacramento number for Penny Martindale and quickly dialed it, the voice message saying she was on vacation. Guessing she might be in Baton Rouge, staying at her brother's place, he got directory assistance to patch him through and Bobby answered on the third ring, "Hello?"

"Hey Bobby, this is Will Kavanagh, how you doing?"

"I'm fine Will; Jesus what time is it?"

"It's seven o'clock Bobby, and I'm sorry for waking you but I'm in a little pinch. Is Penny by chance in town?"

"How'd you know, she's sound asleep upstairs; man we had a barn burner here last night."

"Listen Bobby, I'm kind of between a rock and a hard spot here, can you wake her and tell her I need to speak with her?"

A very sleepy Penny Martindale answered, "Hey Will, how did things go after the wedding?"

Fast-forwarding past pleasantries, he launched, "Hey babe, I'm in a bit of a tight spot and could use some help."

By now fully alert, she replied, "What kind of tight spot? What can I do to help?"

"Listen, I'm in Pensacola right now getting ready to head to Baton Rouge. Dom is six months pregnant and had to be hospitalized in New Orleans a few days ago, but they evacuated the patients they could in front of the storm and she's at Lane Medical Center. Do you think you could possibly go by and check on her? My parents have been shouldering the load and could probably use some moral support." He heard what he'd said and grimaced, "By the way, is Lane close by? I ain't got a clue."

"You're in luck Will; Lane Medical is in Zachary, which is north of Baton Rouge. But my parents live in Zachary so it's no big deal. I'll head over to Lane as soon as I shower; that was some blowout Bobby put on last night. What are you doing in Pensacola?"

"I'll tell you when I see you later today. Thanks a million Penny Lane, you're a life saver."

Casey looked at him as she reached for the phone, "Who's Penny Lane?"

"Penny Martindale is a reporter I met after my court martial; didn't you meet her and my attorney friend at the wedding?"

"Oh yeah, that other gorgeous blonde, how could I forget. How well do you know this one?"

"Actually, there were three gorgeous blondes at the wedding," he replied making an exaggerated bow to Casey, "but I had only seen two of them naked by that point in time. Now don't you have to find Alex and let her know you're safe and hopefully pregnant?"

"Yikes, you're right," she shrieked as she dialed up the hotel in Orlando.

Since it was early, she caught Alex just as she was leaving for her job interview, "Hey babe, how's it going in Orlando?" She listened for a minute and then replied, "Yes, the insemination went well and I may just be pregnant. I'm still in Pensacola though; the highways were too dangerous to chance driving back to Ft. Walton last night." After another minute of no doubt frenzied monologue she said, "He's right here; we're making these calls from his room. Hold on, I'll let him explain," she said as she handed Will the phone.

"Hey Sis, how you doing down there in the land of sun?" He asked, hoping to invoke some levity.

"How is Dom doing? I saw the weather reports on television last night, and it looked like New Orleans was the target for landfall."

"They evacuated the ambulatory patients out of New Orleans as the storm approached, and Mom and Dad took her to Lane Medical in Baton Rouge. We lost power here along with telephone, but thankfully the hotel had its own generator. Everyone is shaking off the storm this morning, and I'm getting ready to drive up to Baton Rouge."

"Will, thank you so much for doing this for us. You will never know how much I appreciate your willingness to help, especially with what Dom's going through."

Rolling his eyes at Casey, he replied, "Think nothing of it Sis, I hope the insemination takes the first time. Listen, I've gotta scoot; I'll call you when I get a lay of the land in Louisiana. How long are you going to be in Orlando?"

"I'm flying back tonight, take care of yourself."

Casey looked at him perplexed, "How much of the insemination routine do we keep under wraps? It might make a huge difference to Alex if she knew the truth. What about Dom, are you going to tell her the truth?"

Will nodded, "Maybe not today, but as soon as we have some privacy and can discuss it alone. She and I have no secrets until now, and she did tell me to 'go and do this favor for Alex and Casey.' We just improvised when confronted with formidable impediments."

Casey was shaking her head in amazement, "How can you be so trusting with anyone Will? Is there no limit to what you two can endure?"

"Case, Dom and I have been to hell and back together. She watched and participated while I absolutely devoured Samantha Chessereaux, even when she screamed out that she loved me when we climaxed together. She did that for me to help me cure myself of the lust I harbored for that woman. She is absolutely sure of my love for her, and I would never betray that. If I didn't think you and Alex shared a similar love, I would not have come here to be a sperm donor, I don't think."

She was smiling wickedly, "So did it work, the curing of the lust for Samantha? I've seen the two of you together."

"Casey, I don't know if fucking Samantha cured me any more than finally doing it with you. But at least neither of you are unknown, forbidden sexual fantasies any longer."

"Okay, keep a lid on it from your end. I'll see if there's any way I can come clean with Alex without ruining our relationship. Jesus, just when I get pregnant!"

He stopped the feverish packing and stared at her, "Casey, if it even has the slightest risk of splitting you two up with you pregnant, don't even go there. Dom and I will cover you for eternity, so all you have to lock down is the obstetrician. Maybe he can write you a fake billing for the insemination procedure."

She snickered, "My God Will, you survive a military court martial and you think like a criminal."

He suddenly remembered a dangling piece of intel, "By the way, what was Alex doing in Orlando? Job interview you said?"

She was all smiles now, "Damn Will, I completely forgot to tell you. I'm being reassigned as the Facility Manager for the Test Range Support operation at Patrick Air Force Base!"

He stared at her in amazement, "Casey Mooneyhan is going to be the facilities weenie for the NASA Eastern Test Range off Canaveral? Well congratulations girl! I'll have to come down there and check on the three of you!"

Pinching his ass, she dared him, "You'd better get down there to meet your daughter Will Kavanagh."

He smiled then winked, "And just what makes you think it's going to be a girl?"

Wondering if he'd gone insane, Will held his hand up as he dialed the Lane Medical Center in Baton Rouge, "Yes, I'm looking for a patient who was admitted yesterday from the Tulane Medical Center. Her name is Dominique Kavanagh, and I am her husband,"

"Just a moment Mr. Kavanagh, I'll connect you to her room."

"Hello?" Dom answered in her lilting French accent.

"Hey baby, it's been a hell of a twenty four hours, *n'est pas?*" He replied, surprisingly relieved to hear her voice.

She was crying now, stuttering through sobs, "I was terrified I would never see you again Will Kavanagh; you didn't call me and I could only imagine the worst."

He rolled his eyes at Casey, "Everything is fine baby. We lost power and telephone when the storm came ashore, and they're just restoring everything now."

"Oh Will, I miss you and they made us leave and your parents have been so wonderful. When are you going to be here?"

Casey saw him exhale with relief, "I'll be leaving here in a few minutes and will drive straight to Baton Rouge. Are you alright, I mean, you're not, the baby's not, in crisis are you?"

"No Will, we are fine. I can barely wait to see you. How did everything go with the fertility procedure?"

His eyebrows were dancing now, "You know me babe, I was asked to do a favor and I did it. We'll see if nature cooperates from here on."

"Good, I can't wait to see you. Drive safely love."

Remembering another dangling participle he quickly added, "Hey that reminds me, Penny Martindale is back home and will be stopping by to see you."

He could hear loud noise in the background as Dom all but yelled in glee, "She just walked in the door! See you this afternoon love."

They eschewed the concierge level offerings for more privacy in the restaurant. As they were eating breakfast, Casey had that impish grin, "I was asked to do a favor and I did it?"

"That's right Case; sometimes you just have to go above and beyond the call of duty. If you think about it, that bondage episode was one of the most extemporaneous and improvised sexual acts ever conceived and executed."

"Executed to perfection I might add. I'll never be able to look at you again without thinking about last night."

"My experience in life is that once I share intimacy with a woman, we communicate almost transparently from that moment on. You and I will never misunderstand the other's intent. That's pretty special, don't you think?"

As he was climbing into the rental car to head back, Casey pulled him in for a sweet kiss goodbye, "You are something special Will Kavanagh. I will always be indebted to you for coming here and preventing this from being a fiasco."

He noticed she was holding a plastic trash bag with the towel strips used in the 'securing' portion of the bondage episode. "And you are everything I ever thought you'd be in bed Casey. Little did I know all those years ago in Denver that I would one day experience that pure ecstasy with you; you didn't disappoint me. What's that, trash you need positive disposal of?"

She was snickering as she kissed him one last time, "I kind of want to hang them up for a wall mounting, but then I'd have to explain them to you-know-who. Take care love, and call me when you get to Louisiana."

———

The return trip was really quite simple; he jumped on Interstate 10 and it was four hours direct to Baton Rouge. He set the cruise control and settled in for the journey.

My God Kavanagh, what have you done now? Not nine months after marrying the love of your life, and six months after you share the miracle of conception with two lost causes of fertility, you fuck the only woman you really ever wanted badly but hadn't slept with, and you did it again and again, and you enjoyed it immensely. Is your moral foundation a bottomless pit? I don't think so, why couldn't there be a warning sign flashing in my mind, 'Caution: You are about to enter the Twilight Zone?'

Now what about your brother in prison down in Nicaragua; what are you going to do about that? Neither Dom nor you can travel openly there again, and you won't ask Carmen to put herself at risk with her newborn son. Jesus Kavanagh, who are you fooling? Didn't she go to Algeria and save your life—and Dom's—while she was pregnant with the child she just bore?

And where in the hell are you and your family gonna live? It's all going to depend on what Dom wants to do, so you can punt that one for the time being. Jesus, we gotta get Colton out of jail. But first, you idiot, you've got to reunite with your wife!

43

ESCAPE IS A RELATIVE TERM

"WHAT ARE YOU TELLING ME JOSÉ? Please speak more slowly this time. I obviously misunderstood you to say Enrique had suffered an accident," Hector Constanza said into the phone, trying to make his brain accept what the Sandinista lackey policeman was telling him. He quickly looked up at Aleandro Muñoz, his bodyguard and signaled him for another round of cocktails.

Hector was hosting a meeting of the *Triumvirato*, or Big Three, of the Cali Cartel at his mansion outside of Cali. The *Triumvirato* had emerged in 1976 when they joined forces to dethrone Victor Rodriguez, one of the founding members of the Cali Cartel. Victor and his brothers were unfortunately focused on the manufacture and distribution of marijuana exclusively, even though it was bulky and cocaine was infinitely more profitable considering the threat/reward. Hector Constanza had emerged with his close compatriots Pablo Restrepo and Juan Diego Loaiza as the rulers of the 'cone' of leaders that remained following the unpleasant purge. They were meeting today to discuss the rising threat of the M-19, or 19th of April Movement. The urban guerilla group was becoming more threatening as they expanded their base of operations. The urgent telephone call from Managua had disrupted the *Triumvirato's* emerging plans to subdue M-19 and slowly absorb them into the Cartel's security and transportation cells.

"*Lo seinto mucho Señor* Constanza, but your blessed brother Enrique has died, here in Nicaragua right outside Managua. It was a terrible calamity *Señor* Constanza," Lieutenant José Rivas told the man as he tried mightily to control his bladder. Among other duties, Rivas was expected to provide Enrique Constanza with advance warning of danger. Of course, Enrique had taken it upon himself to terrorize the *Norteamericano* Kavanagh into leaving and forgetting about his brother, but something had gone terribly wrong at Masaya Volcano Park. A careful search of the crime scene had produced exactly nothing; although Enrique's head was nearly blown off, each of his three lieutenants had suffered at least five bullet wounds each. No shell casings or any other evidence was discovered.

Hector was now standing, his fists clenched as he put the call on speaker phone, "Lieutenant Rivas, were we not paying you to protect and provide warning to my brother?"

"Yes *Señor* Constanza, and I did that, just as I was ordered. I reported to *Señor* Enrique two nights ago that this *Norteamericano* Kavanagh was in Managua trying to obtain bail for his brother. I also told him that Kavanagh foolishly claimed he would signal the United Nations Human Rights Centre over child labor in Nicaragua. *Señor* Enrique saw this as a very big problem, but insisted that he would take care of it when I told him Kavanagh's itinerary for the next day. I really have no idea what happened *Señor*; Kavanagh was traveling with his very pregnant wife."

"Who the hell is this Kavanagh? He and his pregnant wife somehow blew my brother's brains out and riddled his guards with bullets?" Hector was now having difficulty processing words, much less tactical issues.

"All I can tell you sir is that I have his passport, and he is from Louisiana, in the southern part of the U.S. He was in Argentina for several months before he came to Nicaragua, apparently because of his brother's disappearance."

Hector was reeling from the loss, as Enrique had been his Celeno of the Trafficking Cell. The compartmented nature of the Cali Cartel made it less prone to cataclysmic violent response to individuals being arrested. "Lieutenant, would you please make sure the bodies are preserved and prepared for shipment? I will send a plane to Managua arriving at eight o'clock tomorrow morning—and send that passport with the bodies. Is that clear Rivas?"

"*Si Señor*, I will assure that your wishes are complied with," Rivas said, hoping against hope that he could survive this clusterfuck. The line went dead before Rivas got confirmation that Hector had even heard him.

44

REENTERING THE ATMOSPHERE

WHEN HE WALKED INTO the hospital room, Dom was sitting up in bed and Will ignored everyone greeting him as he went to her and engulfed his bride in a passionate hug. She was crying when she finished kissing him, "My God am I glad to see you Will Kavanagh. I missed you so badly."

Risking certain death, he glanced down at his watch, "I've been gone for about twenty-three hours honey; you didn't think I'd abandoned my family, did you?"

She was wiping away tears as she slapped his arm, "I didn't know whether that storm had taken you from me, and you can joke about it?"

Fighting back the devil he smiled, "I was fine baby. All I had to do was hunker down and wait it out. Did you get up here okay?"

With that, Mom, Dad, Penny and Dom chimed in for the chorus, "No!"

He looked back at Penny and gave her a hug, "Thanks for coming over Penny Lane." He glanced back at his parents, "So how was the trip up from New Orleans?"

Warren took over, wrapping an arm around his son's shoulder, "There was a mad exodus from New Orleans after the Weather Service issued the storm warning and voluntary evacuation call. It took us four hours to get here even on the Interstate."

He gave his Mother a kiss, "Thank you so much for covering for me; you'll never know how much I appreciate your being here to help us."

She looked at him strangely, "How'd things go at the fertility clinic? It seemed like it was a near emergency for Alex to get you down there."

He tried mightily not to roll his eyes heavenward, "That's because Casey was on a tight window and I had to be in the same time zone to make it happen. I was asked to do a favor, and I accomplished it as promised. Mother Nature has to take it from here." He looked at Dom and inquired, "How long do you have to stay in the hospital? When do they plan to release you?"

Dom was nodding, obviously ready to leave, "They want to keep me for observation overnight to insure my vitals are stable, and if everything checks out, they'll release me tomorrow. Where are we going by the way?"

Her question hit Will strangely, so he smiled like it was a foregone conclusion, "To Gastineau of course, that's home!"

She was patting his hand as she beamed, "Good."

He put his arm around his parents' shoulders, "Mom, Dad, why don't you head on back to Gastineau. There's no reason for you to stay now; I've got the watch. We'll come on down tomorrow when they release Dom."

After they bid their goodbyes and departed, the dietician brought Dom her lunch. Thinking this might be a good segue, Will looked at Penny, "You hungry?"

With a resurgent smile she almost gushed, "I'm starving."

He just smiled and rolled his eyes, "Hey hon, Penny and I are going to step out for some lunch. Is there anything I can bring back, you know, something you can't get here in the hospital?"

She looked up from her first bite of uninspiring braised carrots, "I'd kill for some pistachio-banana ice cream."

He was about to make an unflattering comment about pregnant women's appetites when Penny bailed him out, "Come on Will, there's a Baskin-Robbins right next to the Silver Nickel." Then looking at Dom she intoned, "We'll find you some ice cream Dom, you can count on it!"

The Silver Nickel turned out to be a very classy steak house, and as they sat down to order Will narrowed a stare at Ms. Martindale, "Rough night last night Penny Lane? You look a little blue around the gills."

She rolled her slightly bloodshot eyes and explained, "The Martindale boys decided we had to have a Hurricane Party, and made Hurricanes for hours. I've still got a headache to balance out the low grade hangover."

Remembering the Typhoon Party they had hosted at the Palace one time, Will smiled, "Hair of the dog; perhaps a Bloody Mary?"

Her eyes suddenly came to life, "Only if you'll have one with me."

He winked at her as the waiter magically appeared, "Abso-fucking-lu-tely!" Without glancing up Will held up two fingers in the victory sign, "*Dos Bloody Mary's por favor?*"

She closed her eyes, since shaking her head made it hurt, "You've been in Juan Valdez country too long cowboy."

As they were inhaling the first bites of absolutely delicious medium-pink grilled burgers, Penny looked up and asked, "How in the world did you get roped into being a surrogate father?"

"Alex and Casey talked it over and I was the only person they could agree on as their Johnny Appleseed."

Her eyes bulged as she tried but failed to keep from blowing a piece of hamburger bun across the table. She managed to choke out the words, "I really can't see you masturbating into a petri dish Will; I'm sorry, it just doesn't compute."

With the devil peeking over his shoulder he smiled, "Oh, I had some help."

With her eyebrows almost touching her hairline, she blurted, "What'd they do, tie you up?"

He was just able to turn his head to keep from spewing Bloody Mary on her. Wiping off his sleeve he bowed slightly, "Touché."

She looked startled, "What kind of fertility clinic provides restraints? You didn't get tied up…did you?"

"Sort of; I got to provide the sample into a nice warm receptacle."

Shaking her head, she postulated, "They must have some good health insurance; sounds like the golden goose laid an egg for you."

"You know how it is; with FarmState you get the blow job while second best only pays for used Hustler magazines."

Now she was letting out little shrieks of laughter, grabbing her Bloody Mary and sucking the straw until the ice cubes gurgled. Will gave the waiter the high sign for another round as she finally stopped laughing. "Come on now, they don't do blow jobs in fertility clinics…do they?"

"Can't fool you; fellatio wasn't on the menu but let's say it was a very arresting experience. How's Captain Jones doing these days?"

She stopped eating, folded her hands into a tent under her chin and smiled, "Now isn't that an interesting subject to bring up?"

He looked at her like she'd farted, "What's so interesting about it? Did he ask you to marry him?"

She rolled her eyes, "Oh no, nothing like that, but we had a very frank discussion about past paramours, and your name came up."

Will considered Penny Martindale, what her qualities were and what she might want to make of her life. He decided to take a chance on the real deal. "Penny, you're playing with me about sexual issues, and I want to resolve them all for you; Dom and I have had sex together with other gorgeous women and you'll be there someday depending on timing." He paused to wait for the quasi-shock to pass and continued, "Life has gotten deadly serious for me since the wedding..." She shook her head and blinked her eyes, "You didn't know about the raid in Algeria?"

"Yes," she said, eyes wide open, "Trip told me what Bob Kellor told him about it. What else has happened?"

"The Sandinistas have kidnapped my missionary brother Colton in Nicaragua, and we got across the breakers with the Cali Cartel when we went in to investigate. That's how Dom's blood pressure went wacko—when this thug cut my face and threatened to cut her stomach open. He died suddenly and things are gonna get deadly serious before they get quiet again. That's not what I want to talk about, okay?"

"Sure, what's on your mind?"

"Do you want to be something more than a pretty talking head on the nightly news in Sacramento for the rest of your life?"

Now she was stunned bordering on an attitude, "What, that's not good enough for you?"

"No, and it's not good enough for you either." He stared into her soul until she got the message and nodded. "Trip's not right for you either; if I'd met you the day I did and fell in love, we'd be making serious marriage plans by now—trust me."

"Jesus Christ Will, what has happened to you?"

"Life, and it's coming whether you like it or not. Do you have any interest in becoming a journalist of note, as opposed to a hot blond that leaves all the beer bellies thinking what if?"

"I'll have you know I majored in journalism William Kavanagh. I'm not sure I follow your thinking though."

"What if I needed or wanted or offered you the break of a lifetime on a very interesting news angle? Ever had an interest in Pulitzer Prizes?"

"Ah, I see where you're coming from now. How would I work that out, assuming such a very interesting news angle presented itself?"

He leaned across the table, deadly serious, "You'd have to drop everything you're doing and take off for places unknown. Take vacation, a sabbatical or threaten to leave—shit, you're the hottest reporter on the left coast."

"How can I do that; I'm contractually obligated…"

"For how long? Next time you renegotiate that contract you limit your nightly news to weekdays, require the station or network to develop weekend, spelled back-up, newscasters and you stipulate that a minimum notice will be provided when you must leave suddenly. If you do not have a passport, apply for one tomorrow."

"And just how the hell do I do that, can you tell me that?"

He fished a business card out of his wallet, "Call Patty Smithson and tell her you're a close friend of mine. She owes me a favor, and she's got an ace agent that's looking out for her career. Talk to Patty and she'll know you by then because I'll have spoken with her. You need an agent at least part-time who can whisper sweet nothings to the LA stations and have you an open-ended job offer. With that in hand, your negotiations with your present employer will be greatly facilitated. Are we good now?"

She reached across the table and grabbed his hand, "Why are you doing this to me?"

"Somebody had to; you're heads above your competition, but reading news ain't your manifest destiny Penny. I knew that the day I met you and I knew that in your condo that night. Put that pretty little mind of yours to work and map out your life."

"Will we ever…"

He smiled as he glanced at the waiter for the check, "You bet, and it'll be the crowning achievement of your sex life up to that moment. After that you'll be too aware of the possibilities to put up with selfish males anymore."

She just draped her arms around his neck at the car outside, "Wow, who sent you to kick me in the ass?"

"You did Penny, and we finally got there." She kissed him somewhat inappropriately before he told her, "Now go make us all proud girl."

———

When he walked back into the hospital room with a pint of pistachio-almond ice cream, Dom was sitting anxiously with a spoon and a napkin in her hand

and said, "Well that took long enough. What'd you two do out there?"

He rolled his eyes and fessed up, "We had a nice relaxing lunch at her favorite steak house and had an interesting chat about Penny getting her ass in gear and pursuing a fulfilling career. Sorry, they didn't have the pistachio-banana flavor babe."

Disregarding the flavor substitution, she tore off the lid and began desperately eating the ice cream, finally looking up to ask, "You told Penny she needed to get her ass in gear? How did that go?"

He smiled as he supplied the intel, "Oh, she was hungover and wanted to talk sexy shit, but I put the cabash on that by telling her that yes we had experienced ménages and that yes she would one day experience it with us. Once the sex issues were set aside she was more conducive to listening to real life stuff."

She stared at him with a surprised look on her face, "Exactly how intense did you get with Ms. Penelope?"

Will was nodding his head, "I told her she and Trip wouldn't work because if I'd have met and fallen in love with her when he did, the two of us would be making serious marriage plans. I think it almost relieved her to hear the words out loud."

She looked at him suspiciously between bites and continued the interrogation, "My God, how did she take it? Did you endanger our friendship with Penny?"

Thinking he'd pump the ego of his enlarging pregnant wife he offered, "She actually thanked me at the end for kicking her in the ass; I helped her with her job structure. I told her to call Patty Smithson to discuss agents; I have got to make that advance call." He paused to see Dom canting her head sideways for the rest, "She also said she'd never, ever miss out on another chance to have a *ménage a trois* with us."

"Flattering, but highly unlikely. Now tell me about this sperm donation you made. By the way, your mother's reticence about your sister's lifestyle was somewhat attenuated when I advised her that she'd now have two grandchildren by you."

"Hey, that was good! The chances of my other two siblings contributing are somewhat diminished."

Dom put down the spoon long enough to give him the finger twirl, "What in the world did you think about while you were masturbating into that petri dish? I'll not be pleased if it was Samantha Chessereaux, although your mind would likely go there by default."

The furtive grin told her he wasn't going to lie, "Actually, I didn't have to use a petri dish."

She frowned at him before swallowing a large dollop of ice cream, "Okay, how did you deliver the sample?"

Will was grinning from ear to ear now, "We took a more direct path to the insemination procedure."

With this, she put the container of ice cream down on the lap tray in front of her, "I should have known you couldn't do anything straight Will Kavanagh. Tell me what happened, and where was Alex?"

"Do you remember how Johnny Chessereaux was conveniently busy that night we got to know Sam better? Well, Alex had to be in Orlando for a job interview today, so she flew out yesterday and left Casey to get inseminated at the fertility clinic."

She was getting exasperated at his pace of parsing, "So Alex was gone, and Casey was having the procedure. What went awry?"

"They lost power throughout Pensacola and the fertility clinic had to close. Getting the picture?"

With this, Dom leaned back on her pillow and looked at the ceiling, "Okay, the clinic was closed down. What did you do?"

"Well, since Alex and Casey live thirty miles on the other side of Pensacola, I made a hotel reservation in town, making sure they had backup power. So Casey comes over to the hotel, we had supper and she was all down and out about this being her one day ovulating and that I was available and that everything had turned to shit."

A snicker of a smile was leaking from Dom's face when she asked, "So what solution did you craft, my enterprising industrial engineer?"

"Well," he smiled furtively, "I sorta reminded her we kinda lived in Argentina and would be hovering around Central America until we got Colton home…"

"Right, right, right," she interrupted, "the chances of you two being in the same time zone again while she was fertile no doubt triggering an anxiety attack. Do not make me redirect my inquiry again William."

"I looked at Casey and told her if it had to happen right then, the only option left was *au natural*."

"God Will Kavanagh, you cannot do anything by the books! So what did she say? I mean she's in love with your sister."

He grimaced at her and glanced to the side, "Right, and I'm desperately in love with my beacon Dominique. So she marches off to look out this big window at the roiling ocean—the hotel was nearly empty because of the storm—turns around and says, 'So this can be our own little secret?'"

By now Dom was rocking gently, enjoying the story, "I take it Casey was exposed to some of the Freelancing nuances?"

"You bet, and the second heterosexual sex of her life," he said, incredibly relieved that Dom was taking this so well.

She shattered his aura of innocence with her next volley, "I know you Will Kavanagh, and if you had to compromise your moral boundary, you'd make sure to not take it half-heartedly. Was there anything unusual that occurred during the apparent multiple times you two had sex?"

Shifting uneasily, he tried lobbing a curve ball, "Well, we did discuss that we should go ahead and fire all of the ammo that was reasonably available, that being the one and only time you know."

With this she rolled her eyes up, looked back at him and repeated, "Did anything unusual occur while you and Casey were transferring all of your available supply of ammunition?"

It had been a dialogue replete with all manner of tripwires and land mines, but Dom took the whole asphyxiation during orgasm remarkably well. Will was thanking Sweet Jesus he'd met a level-headed mate.

Dom was looking at the ceiling, contemplating something when she said, "We may have to try that at some time in the future Will; it sounds as though the helplessness precipitates extraordinary emotional response. Now how will your sister Alex react when she learns of this alternate insemination procedure you used?"

"Casey thinks Alex would leave her if she ever found out. I told her you and I could keep her secret between us forever, but that she couldn't take the chance on a breakup with her just now getting pregnant."

She looked at him, smiled and said, "Possibly pregnant. Okay, you two did the only reasonable thing you could, given the circumstances. You are also correct about your availability for any transfer, direct or otherwise. Your brother Colton's situation isn't going to get better from long distance, that's for sure. Can we stay at your parent's house, or should we find our own place?"

He almost collapsed with relief at how well she had absorbed the facts, and was beside her on the bed, arms wrapped around her, "Only you could be so assured of our love Dominique. You have proven to me time and again that ours is an incredibly strong bond. We'll stay at my parent's place until we figure out where we'd rather be, and we can always get our own place in Gastineau if we want. I love you so much baby."

She leaned up to kiss him and smiled, "You know I love it when you call me baby."

Just then the room telephone rang, and Will was curious when Dom answered it, "Why that would be very kind of you Penny. Are you sure it won't be an imposition?" He was more than a little curious as the conversation continued and Dom asked, "Does he know how to get there? Okay, give me that address." When she hung up he looked at her in total confusion when she said, "You're going over to stay over at Penny's parents' house tonight Will. They live only ten minutes from the hospital. Here's the address in case you have to stop and ask for directions."

He snickered and threw out a stink bomb, "Aren't you concerned that Penny might sneak around during the night, you know to get an advance on the *ménage*?"

Without hesitation his wife-therapist imparted her typical wisdom, "Not a chance; I suspect you're so depleted from last night that sex isn't high on your priorities right at the moment."

He was shaking his head in wonder as he kissed her goodnight, "What would I do without you Dominique?"

45

PREPARING THE NEST
IN GASTINEAU

As THEY TRAVELED ALONG State Road 1 the next morning Dom asked him, "Do you think it will be a bit crowded at your parent's house Will? I mean, the bedrooms are probably small from what little I remember."

Nodding his head in agreement, he pondered, "Yeah, you're probably right. Want to get a hotel room when we get into Houma?"

"What do you think about maybe buying a house in Gastineau; you know we'll be back there a lot, and we don't have any home to take this baby to when she's born."

He frowned at her insistence that it was a girl, "That's a good point. I seem to recall that young nymph Johnny was misbehaving with is a realtor; why don't we call her when we get in and see what's available?"

"You mean the one he was fucking during our wedding reception? Okay, let's give her a call, but no sneaking off to the game room William."

He gave her his best shit-eating grin, "Perish the thought my dear."

———

"So what do you think? Is this too big for what you had in mind?" asked Alana Morgan after they had walked through the fifth house of the afternoon. The fact that she was dressed to kill, with her legs in that miniskirt so inviting, made Will extra vigilant with regards to 'attraction avoidance' techniques previously etched into his consciousness.

Dom was looking around the great room, checking its access to the adjacent kitchen and dining area and finally responded, "It is a bit bigger than what we had in mind, but I really like the layout. The twin master bedrooms

426

are a very unique feature, although at this point I have no idea what I'd do with the space. But with my family in Morocco, a bit of extra space might be an excellent idea…"

"Uh, Dom, sorry to interrupt, but Hal mentioned that we should go bigger vice smaller since this is his hometown too and he suffers the same Protestant moralistic strictures," Will added as Dom nodded. Alana on the other hand had to turn her head to smother the laughter.

"How much did you say this listed for Alana?"

As she examined the realty listing she engaged her brain, "It's listed at $115,000, but it's been on the market for several months. It's a fairly large ranch at 2500 square feet; do you want to look at something smaller perhaps?"

Without a moment's hesitation Dom instructed her, "Make the seller a cash offer of $100,000 and let's see how serious they are about wanting to sell it."

Alana and Will both stood there with mouths gaped open in surprise, but Alana quickly recovered, "Cash offer? I'll call him as soon as I get back to the office. Where can I get in touch with you?"

As they were driving to the Will's ancestral residence, Dom was obviously making plans, "Where is that furniture we bought in the Philippines stored? Is it around here?"

Her transition to 'delivery king' startled him, as he came alive for the new project, "I'm not sure babe; Dad had mentioned maybe putting it in the lake cabin, but I don't know if he's done that yet. Hey, all of our wedding presents are in my old bedroom; we'd better take stock of them and see what we need. I think Chambie's got a truck we can use to move stuff around. Jesus, I wonder who I can get to keep the place up when we're not here?"

Dom began laughing, "My God Will, when you get the scent of a project, you turn into a demon. You didn't say a word when I made that offer on the house, why not?"

He reached over and patted her enlarging stomach, "It's your nest Momma, and I actually kind of like it too. It'll be interesting to see how the seller responds."

She was beaming as she leaned over with a hint of effort and kissed him, "That's the correct answer Mr. Kavanagh. If Momma is happy, everyone is happy!"

Jan and Warren Kavanagh were caught between being thrilled and concerned when Will told them about the offer on the house. The ringing telephone finally provided some relief, "Hello? Yes Alana, you are kidding me! That's great news. Just a minute, let me put my negotiator on the line." Dom was already moving for the phone when he told her, "They bit."

Dom was now smirking, "Hello again Alana. It would appear that the buyer and seller have similar objectives. How soon can you get the property surveyed and the requisite title insurance issued? Tomorrow, my God you work quickly here. Can you suggest a good closing attorney? Okay, I'll trust you with that one. Tell your broker that I expect you to get the full listing and selling commission on this, and if he or she has any problem I will come in personally and discuss it. Please set the closing up for this Friday and call me back with the details. Thank you for your very capable help with this Alana; I insist on your being fairly rewarded. We will talk to you soon."

Will and his parents were in open-mouthed wonderment when Dom hung up the phone. She deftly deflected it however, "I used to be a real estate broker in Colorado. I could tell the seller was ready to unload the property and guessed correctly at the current market here. Now where is that furniture?"

Still bewildered at the suddenness of the sale, Will got his head back in the game, "How are we going to pay for it; Kelley Field or AMEX?"

Just as she was about to reply the phone rang again. Figuring it was Alana calling back Will answered, "Good news already Alana?"

"Jesus Willy, who the hell's Alana?" Hal Rayfield asked.

"Hey buddy, where in the hell are you?" Will asked excitedly before glancing at Dom, who had a hateful scowl on her face, his parents recoiling from the profanity.

"I'm here in Gastineau at my parent's house; who's Alana?"

"Oh, she's our realtor; Dom and I put an offer down on a house here in Gastineau. When did you guys get into town? How are Wade and Carmen doing? Things got dicey on the egress brother," he said, immediately wanting to kick himself for letting out any hints about Nicaragua within earshot of his parents.

"Yeah, that's the big reason we flew up. Things aren't going to get easier until we figure out how to spring Colton out of banana land. We need to chat buddy, you know, more casually," he said, clearly in the same boat with his overly curious mother hovering about.

"What are you guys doing tonight?" Will asked, feeling the need for speed—away from his mother! His survival instincts kicked in just in time, cringing as he looked sheepishly at his mother who expected to cook supper for the son she hadn't seen since his wedding.

"Don't have any plans at the moment. Mom and Dad are out at Bingo Night, so we're free like the bird."

Will quickly hatched a mutually workable stealth plan, "Good, how about we meet over at Beudreau's at seven? I'll ask Mom if we can have you guys over for supper tomorrow night."

On the drive over to the restaurant, Dom smirked at her husband, "That was some maneuvering you did back there Will, I am impressed!"

"Did you notice I angled her for the pork loin roast? I knew we could get the country fried shrimp at Beudreau's."

"Right, one clever bait and switch accomplished my enterprising husband. Now if you can just get your sister to swallow that smoke and mirrors show you and Ms. Mooneyhan concocted for the insemination!"

"Dominique my dear, Sister Alex has not been subjected to my major domo, my master love therapist as of yet. There is always hope."

When Hal walked into Beudreau's with Wade in his arms and Carmen lugging the baby bag along, Will thought Tamara Beudreau, a former *objet du désir*, was going to pass out. "My God, you go away for a year and you return a domiciled married father. Carmen must be some kind of woman to pull you through the eye of the needle Hal Rayfield!"

Hal leaned over to peck her on the cheek, which Tamara tried to turn into an open-mouthed kiss. Will glanced at Carmen to see her thankfully checking on the baby's diaper, "Hey, is Ricky still fixing that shrimp dish Willy turned us on to last time we were here?" Hal asked innocently enough, but there was lust boiling below the surface. Tamara had longingly enlisted Will in her flight from virginity; when he thought about it he still kicked himself for turning her down because he was still in love with Danielle. *What a fucking mistake that was; damn, that toxic pairing was doomed to failure, and I fended Tamara off like some valiant prince. What a fucking bozo I was.* Hal of course had followed up on Will's declination and provided Tamara with all of the insight she desired into lust-driven sex.

"You bet; it's now our best-selling entrée!"

"You gals up for country fried shrimp?" Hal asked with a wide smile.

Carmen just scowled at him, "Of course, Dom and I are going to change your matador-in-training."

As The Who's *Behind Blue Eyes* began softly playing on the sound system, Hal started nodding his head, "Let's go to the bar for a minute." He gave Tamara the high sign to follow, and when they were somewhat obscured within the empty bar he leaned into her ear, "Jesus you still look good woman; any chance we can find some place with a little privacy around here?"

Will was wondering if Hal had suffered a jolt to the head, as Tamara had the same confused look. "Sure, there's an office in the back." Then she blushed and continued, "What'd you have in mind?"

"I believe you know what I have in mind babe, but Willy and I need to make a call to a friend. Would that be a problem for maybe ten minutes?"

"Sure, no problem; feel free to use the phone on the desk," she offered, ready to accommodate.

"Nah, thanks though; we brought our own. How about show the wives back when they finish in the powder room. Oh, and how about a couple of Johnnie Walker Blacks on the rocks for Willy and me. Better make it chardonnay for the women."

"Jesus whatcha got there bro?" Will asked as Hal put a hard plastic case about the size of a large shoe box on the desk, the PANASONIC label prominent.

"Can't travel without music now can we?" He asked as he opened the case to reveal what looked like a miniature stereo receiver and two speakers that took up most of the box. He pulled out one speaker and flipped a latch, revealing their old familiar friend, the LST-5B. As he opened the other speaker, he took out the antenna, a headset and a small box Will hadn't seen before; all of the hidden items were snugly bound in cut Styrofoam for a secure fit.

"Damn bro, where'd you get that? I am impressed!" Will said as the girls walked in with a freshly changed Wade the Matador.

"How about open that window Willy and let's get Bob Matthews on the phone. Let's see what's happening in Managua."

Once he got the antenna unfolded Hal wasted little time getting their Managua connection on the phone. "Hey buddy, how goes it in Managua? I've got Willy, his wife and Carmen with me. What's happening?"

"Well, I've got some fair news and some bad news. The good part is that Colton was moved to the Federal Penitentiary and I have almost unfettered access to him; so that situation is far improved over him being in the Municipal Lockup," he reported, causing Will to exhale with relief.

"And what's the bad news?"

"Minister Morales was seriously burned in a fire that completely gutted the St. Timothy Church of Hope in a very suspicious blaze. Morales hasn't regained consciousness for questioning as to the source. He had second degree burns over half his body, so his prospects are guarded. Does that seem too much of a coincidence?"

"Why was it suspicious, other than the fact that it occurred right after I was there grilling him about Colton's missionary efforts?" Will asked, the angst building as they talked.

"Exactly; my guy tells me the Managua Sandinista Police have questioned every person that even had minor contact with you while you were here, including the hotel concierge and the taxi drivers you used. It definitely looks like they're investigating Constanza's death, but there have been no news reports in the paper here about it. Given *Señor* Constanza's pedigree, I am not surprised that his demise has been squashed in the local press."

"Yeah, well fuck him, putting a knife to my wife's belly. So you think Colton's safe for the time being? What'd he say when you saw him?"

"He said he was at another church's social hall meeting with parents whose kids worked at the Bolt Sportswear factory when a dozen people came in and began shouting at him. He's pretty sure they were sent by the factory manager, but he has no proof. By the way, he was pretty pumped to learn that you and Dominique had been down here looking into it."

Will was instantly alert and posed, "So did he have any knowledge of Lieutenant Rivas, our fan club leader?"

"Oh yeah, it was Rivas who arrested him. He also said Rivas spit on him when the Federales were leading him out of the city lockup."

"So did you tell him how we got the charge sheet out of that aggravating prick?"

"As a matter of fact he asked me to tell you that purposely infuriating the Lieutenant wasn't going to help him. He is a man of the cloth you know."

"So he's safe for the time being, eh? How slow can the wheels of justice turn down there? If Rivas is any example of Sandinista efficiency I'd say he might make arraignment by the next ice age."

'Hey, he's with the Federales Will, so we've done the most we can for now short of breaking him out. And don't even go there, the San Bracinto facility is like a castle. The only chance we'd ever have is if they moved him someplace. But let that thought gestate for a while; he's okay for the time being."

"Alright Bob, call us, oh shit, call Alex if there are any developments okay? Thanks a million brother. We'll be in touch," Hal said by way of signing off.

As he was packing the LST back into the 'music box' Will was curious, "Does that thing play music?"

He looked at him like he was a rookie, "Of course it does Willy. Jesus Christ son!"

As soon as they sat down, Tamara had a second round of drinks for them as she grabbed her order pad. "Do I suspect four country fried shrimp plates for the table?"

Will looked at the others as he nodded, "You bet. You'd better send over a couple dozen Oysters Rockefeller for warm-ups."

As they were appreciating the Scottish elixir, Hal looked disparagingly, "Willy, I'm not sure about those oysters buddy; things are a little tight over at my folk's place."

Will nodded knowingly, thinking he might just have to endure the electric blow job tonight, "Hey, this house we made the offer on, I mean that we're buying, has two master bedroom suites in it. Want to make it a ROUST home away from home? We don't know when we'll be back here or whatever, but it'd sure beat the hell out of staying with the folks."

"Willy, I never cease to be amazed at your insightful ways. We need a nest around here, so hell yeah. Let's see, you have a kid on the way and Wade's already here, how much room does it have?"

"We can go by tomorrow and take a closer look, but there are two small bedrooms in addition to the master suites, we'll see how it fits."

Hal nodded in assent, "Sounds like it would work perfectly for our brood."

"Our two kids and Alex and Casey have one cooking too. So a Gastineau nest probably looks good for all of the wayward offspring," Will added, his interest growing in the Gastineau roost.

"What the fuck are you talking about? How the hell can two lesbians have a kid?" Hal asked in complete disbelief.

Will was already breaking into a smile, "With a little help from their friends, of course."

"Help from whose friends?" Carmen asked after giving Wade a pacifier.

"I was just telling Hal that Alex and Casey were going to have a baby."

"So just how the hell did they pull that off Willy? Did some fox sneak into the hen house?" Hal asked as the women started giggling.

Dom took over, "Willy served as the sperm donor just two nights ago."

Still not catching on, Hal blurted out, "I cannot believe my ears Willy; you impregnated your own sister?"

Will shook his head in disgust as Dom offered, "No Hal, Casey's having the baby, and yes, Willy did supply the seed for the deed."

Seemingly mollified, Hal retreated enough to pronounce, "Well, she is smoking hot, so that makes a lot more sense even if you did have to have it inseminated."

Dom couldn't help herself, much to his horror, as she spilt the beans, "Hal, your pal Willy had to divert to a direct donor program at the last minute when that storm took the power out in Pensacola."

He and Carmen were staring at Dom bewildered, "Hey, we were between a rock and a hard spot, so I did what I agreed to do."

Will wondered if Dom was drinking in the ladies room when she blurted, "Right, while she was tied up and being asphyxiated!"

Hal looked at Will, shaking his head, "Willy, you and I have got to have a serious discussion son!"

———

"So this is it huh?" Hal said as he and Carmen toured the house the next day, clearly impressed with Dom's Momma's Nest.

"I really like the twin master suites; I don't think I've seen many homes laid out as such," Carmen added, taking advantage of Hal's mother looking after her grandson.

Dom was already projecting into the future, "Will, it might get crowded in here when all of us have our families down at the same time. Do you think you might be able to build an annex onto the back for a children's playroom expansion?"

"Hey buddy, she brings up a good point. You are after all, the master problem-solving engineer," Hal sniped.

"I don't know, we're buying this with cash, so an addition could get expensive," Will noted, ever the pragmatist.

Hal looked at the women with dismay, "Willy, do you remember that

Destination Partners took a windfall of one million dollars as a result of a recent obscure rescue mission in Algeria? I'd say they may be quite interested in investing in a promising real estate property in Louisiana, even if it carried, say, a $50,000 expansion addendum."

Will shook his head in ecstatic disbelief, "I'll get started on the drawings for the addition. Maybe we should add another master suite for Alex and Casey."

Dom suddenly joined the discussion by insisting, "That sounds like a prudent investment Hal. Why don't you let Will and I furnish it as our contribution? The Partners are saving us $100,000 in the process."

They all four joined hands in a circle and shouted, "Done!"

When they got to the closing attorney's office Friday morning, Will was surprised when Catherine Chessereaux greeted them with muted politeness. He had completely forgotten that she worked for an attorney until he remembered the divorce writ she had prepared for Danielle on grounds of adultery. Thinking it was karmic justice playing out since Dom had been the object of the adultery grounds, he smiled at her in greeting, "Hello Catherine. You do remember my wife Dominique, don't you?"

She looked at Dom, barely concealing her surprise at Dom's pregnant belly, and merely replied with a nod. He turned to Hal and Carmen, "Hal, you remember Danielle's mother Catherine don't you? Catherine, this is Carmen, Hal's wife and mother of his bouncing baby boy."

With a pasted on smile she offered, "Hello Hal, good to see you again after all these years. Why are you here?"

Before he could reply, Will jumped back in, "Hal and I are buying a house here in Gastineau as directors of Destination Partners."

By this time Dom and Carmen were seeking comic relief as Dom welcomed a very happy face, "Hello Alana, glad you could make it."

She gave Dom a hug, "This will be the biggest payday I've ever had in my life. I wouldn't miss it for anything!"

As soon as the closing attorney passed the keys, they stood to head out and begin the move in. As he was walking out the door, Alana caught him by the arm, "Will, thank you so much for remembering me. Dom's insistence that I get the full commission on this sale means I can breathe easier for a couple of months."

He smiled as he bent over to kiss her cheek, "Your earned it babe. Take care of those incredible legs."

By late Friday afternoon, the Lafayette Interiors van had offloaded enough furniture to nicely outfit the house, added to their Philippine rattan which Papa Warren had kept in a local storage warehouse. The Sears Delivery Truck came in as they were leaving to set up all new appliances, including a 36 inch color television. Will was fussing with the TV antenna controls when the delivery guy asked, "That's everything Mr. Kavanagh; do you want me to schedule a technician to install those two garage door openers?"

"Naw, leave the boxes in the garage and I'll install them later. We're going to do some renovations in the garage, so it's best to leave them for now. Thanks much ma man."

Mom, Dom and Carmen were busying themselves with the curtains, kitchen and bathrooms when the phone rang, their first incoming call. With nominal anticipation Will answered, "Hello, Gastineau Roost."

"Hey Willy, we got your message about the house, where is it?" Alex asked by way of introduction.

"It's three miles from where we grew up, in Carrington Subdivision. Do you remember where that is?"

"Sure, but I don't know that street address. What did you mean when you said it was our place too?"

"Alex, this is Dom's Momma's Nest, plus the primary home away from home for us expatriate Gastineau exiles. That includes you, Casey and your baby whenever she or he shows up."

"I can't believe it Willy. I've always felt a little strange at Mom's; you know how she is about Casey and me. That is wonderful, when are you moving in?"

"The furniture was just delivered and Mom, Dom and Carmen are putting up curtains, stocking the kitchen and getting the bathroom ready. We're staying here tonight, although it may be a little like camping."

She was all excited now, "Can Casey and I come over tomorrow? I've just got to see this nest of ours."

"I love it Sis, you're already taking ownership. Hell yeah, get your asses over here and let's toast the new nest!"

"Great, see you guys sometime tomorrow afternoon."

As they were stretching out the kinks from having slept their first night in the roost, Hal looked at Will through bleary eyes, "Damn Willy, I know what was missing in the house last night. We didn't have any whiskey or weapons. I think Mrs. Rayfield and I are going to go out on an acquisition mission today and correct that deficiency."

Before he could protest the implications of having loaded firearms around children, Dom said, "As much as I hate to say it, you're probably right on both counts Hal. I always sleep better with a Walther close by."

He smiled and tilted his head, "Right, and we didn't even have any Marnier to celebrate the housewarming either. Jesus Willy, we must be getting old if we forgot the whiskey!"

Carmen swooped in to sit on his lap, wagging her finger at him, "If your performance last night was any indication Mr. Rayfield, I'd say you're not too old just yet."

As they headed off to the shower, Dom put in her two cents, "Don't forget to get some Stolichnaya while you're out you two."

Alex and Casey were pulling into the driveway as Hal and Carmen drove away, so Will went out to greet them. When he got close, they were slamming their doors as he sensed a rarified emotional state. Casey blew past him with a red, tear-stained face muttering, "Hi Will."

He looked over at Alex, a hateful scowl on her face as she managed to grouch, "Inside."

He followed them inside, catching Dom with a raised eyebrow and turned to find Alex and Casey standing across from each other, hands on their hips like they were facing off at the OK Corral. He ventured a greeting by saying, "Welcome to the Gastineau roost ladies."

Alex glared at him hatefully, "Well that's some welcome you had in store for me brother. I hear you had a fucking good time with my supposed love partner here."

He looked at Casey, and the expression on her face told him everything he needed to know. Thankfully, Dom stepped in and said, "Alex, Casey sit down. I will go get us some water and we, the four of us, are going to have a heart-to-heart discussion." Alex took a stuffed leather chair to separate herself from her alleged cheating partner, while Will took a seat on the couch opposite Casey and Dom assumed the judge's role in the middle chair, everyone separated by the coffee table. Dom looked at Alex, "Alex, what do you think has happened that has damaged your relationship with Casey?"

Alex glanced at Will, then glared at Casey before turning to Dom, "Maybe you don't know it yet, but my brother—your allegedly loyal husband—and Casey had sex together in Pensacola; and I wouldn't be surprised if you want to divorce the cheating bastard!"

Without any expression whatsoever, Dom asked her, "Why do you think they had sex?"

With that, Alex jumped up out of her chair and began pointing at Casey, but Dom calmly but firmly told her, "Sit down Alex. We're going to discuss this like adult human beings. Now tell my why you think Will and Casey had sex?"

"Because she told me she did," she said, pointing at Casey, "and I don't see Mr. Righteous over there denying it."

Dom nodded just perceptibly and continued, "Alright Alex, if Will and Casey had sex together, why do you think they did it?"

It was all Will could do to keep from shaking his head in open-ended admiration at how Dom could cut through to the core issues so quickly. The question gave Alex pause, but she threw herself right back into it, "Because they've always secretly wanted to fuck each other's brains out."

"So why haven't they already done that, fucked each other's brains out? It seems that there have been many opportunities before now; what changed the stakes?"

Knowing she had Dom on the ropes, she blurted out, "Because they were all alone in Pensacola and that storm gave them the perfect cover; sneaky little bastards."

Again without any emotional reaction, Dom inquired, "Why were they all alone in Pensacola?"

At that, Alex glanced back at her brother, then at Casey, and finally replied, "I thought it was so Casey could get artificially inseminated with Will's sperm, but no, they had to act like a couple of sex-starved teenagers and fuck each other into oblivion. Look at this!" Will had to fight hard to keep from flinching when she pulled out one of the terrycloth towels strips and held it out as Defense Exhibit One.

To her credit, Dom didn't even glance at the restraint, but instead continued the interrogatory, "So if they went there for Casey to be artificially inseminated, why did they not execute that plan?"

"Well, according to my slut lover, the fertility clinic was closed because the storm had knocked out the electricity, but I know better than…." she said with a load of steam when suddenly she stopped and looked at Will but didn't say another word.

Dom picked right back up on the discussion, "So the fertility clinic was closed and then what?"

"Well, they obviously saw the opportunity and dove right into it," she said, but she was losing some of her angst along the way.

"What was the overriding priority in your lives before Casey went to Pensacola Alex?' Dom asked, the truth flaring like a heat-seeking missile.

For the first time, Alex paused, looked over at Casey and said, "We wanted to have a baby more than anything in the world."

"Do you think she shared your common goal?"

Will noticed the first tear forming on Alex' eyelid as she replied, "Yes absolutely."

"So did Casey do everything she could, given the circumstances and the fact that Will may not be available, to execute your overarching mutual goal?"

A tear was trickling down her cheek as the truth dawned on her, "My God, what have I done?" Dom glanced at Will and he was nodding his head in absolute astonishment.

"What they did Alex, was adjust to the circumstances they faced and had to make a decision whether they would cross the moral boundary that has always existed in front of them in order to accomplish the objective. In the process, there is some likelihood that Casey is pregnant and Will delivered his part as promised. Does this moral boundary issue overcome all of the potential good that could come of it?"

"When you put it like that," she said, and then continued, "it sounds like a cold-hearted decision based on logic. But don't you see, they always wanted to have sex and now they have!" Alex blasted as Will fought to keep from rolling his eyes at her crushing insecurity.

"So what's more important in your life Alex; having this baby or the two of them having sex to facilitate it?" Dom implored.

Obviously getting frustrated with her lack of traction, Alex picked up the towel strip from the table and announced, "Well don't you think it was just a little beyond the call of duty to play fantasy games? They used this to tie her to the bed so she could experience her dream come true."

Will was growing curious as to how Dom was going to parry this thrust when she answered, "Why, was that Will's fantasy or Casey's?"

He could see the veins in her neck bulging when she responded with venom, "Oh no, that is Miss Slut Casey's little dream. She tried to get me to do it to her but I was too disgusted to even think about it."

"So why is that disgusting? Isn't that something that would possibly have pleased her?" Dom asked, relentless in her cross examination.

"Oh yeah, she claims she had the greatest orgasm of her life doing that sick little pretend game. Don't you find that disgusting Dom?" Alex posed, desperate for some understanding.

Instead of answering her, Dom looked pointedly at her husband and said, "Will?"

"Alex, I'm going to tell you something that is very sacred to my relationship with Dominique. Dom was brutally sodomized under restraints in an hours-long torture session she endured at the hands of a deranged madman in North Africa. The only reason I'm telling you that is to demonstrate her revulsion with the prospects of restraints of any kind. After I described the event Casey and I extemporaneously concluded, she has amended her hard stance regarding restraints and possible breathing restriction during sex," he said, risking a glance at Dom.

With a look of total confusion, Alex looked at Dom and asked incredulously, "And why would you even consider that Dom?"

"Because the sense of helplessness apparently stimulates a strong emotional response. Performed in a secure environment with a trusted mate, I can see that the sense of sexual release could be dramatic," she said, and he was never prouder of his medical examiner shrink. She surprised all of them by adding, "And I think that you should try it with Casey. What have you got to lose?"

She was about to respond when Casey spoke up for the first time, "So did that madman get away with it. What happened to him?"

Dom looked at Casey until her eyes bored into her soul, "Will blew the son of a bitch's head off just as he was about to slit my throat." He had to turn his head to shield the incredible emotion her description cast over him, but Alex and Casey were staring at him, shocked. A tear was trickling down his cheek when Dom continued, "So you see the devotion and love that man embodies? If he makes a commitment to assist you in any endeavor, he will do his very best to live up to his commitment. He has never let me down, and I know he didn't let either of you down either. Lord only knows what it will take to bring your brother Colton home safely, but I can assure you he will do whatever is humanly possible to make that happen as well. Would anyone like some wine, I know I certainly would?"

Before anyone could move, Alex blew out of her chair and flew into her brother's arms, wailing, "I'm so sorry Will, I didn't mean to call you those hateful names."

He grimaced and shrugged at her, "Hey, you're my sister baby, I'm good with it. Don't you think you should apologize to Casey? She loves you more than anything."

With that she moved just barely as Casey was in her arms, buried in what he had to admit was a very sensuous open-mouth kiss. When they came up for air, they pulled him into the hug and Dom soon joined them to commemorate yet another Dominique Lefebvre lesson in love.

Just then the front door blew open and Hal was moving through with a box full of whiskey bottles. He took one look at them huddled together and said, "Jesus, this crowd looks like it could use a drink!"

Everyone was busy putting away bottles and glasses, talking color schemes and possible configurations for the addition. Will went to the kitchen to grab a snack as the first thoughts of a scale drawing took form, then supper crossed his mind. He was looking out the window thinking of what they could do with the alcove above the garage when he detected movement behind him. He turned and Casey buried herself in his arms, clutching so tightly that he wondered if there was a problem, "What is it baby?"

She wouldn't look at him but talked into his chest, "My God Will, I had no idea what your life has been like. I'm humiliated that we brought this idiotic love spat here to air out in front of you and Dom."

He tried to push her away to see her face, but she held on tightly, "It wasn't idiotic Casey. If Dom wasn't the world's most unrenowned love therapist, we'd still all be in the shits."

"But you've killed people to protect your friends; Hal just told me you killed a bad guy just before he was about the shoot him in the back. Don't you think our little surrogate father dispute seems ridiculous?"

"They're really no different on the surface Case. You go on a mission, and even though you plan it best you can, we still get shot and people's lives irreparably harmed. I didn't properly prepare for the Pensacola trip; I let my ego get in the way, and that was almost fatal."

"Well, I think we've turned the corner on that," she said as she finally looked up at him. "God, what if it is twins?"

He pecked her on the lips, "It'll be so much easier if it's a boy and a girl."

Just as he was kissing her, Dom walked in from the great room, saw them and asked, "Boy or a girl?"

Casey made a self-conscious turn away from Will, "Dom, I was just telling Will that I am humiliated that we brought this lover's quarrel here for you to referee. It is so obvious now that what we asked you to do was so insignificant compared to the things you two have been through."

"Well, it obviously is not insignificant to Alex, and neither is it to Will or me. You are our family, and we treasure every one of you. What was that about a girl or a boy?"

Will smiled at Casey, "It seems to me that this gender debate that precedes childbirth could be nullified if she had a boy and a girl."

Dom shivered just slightly, "Heaven forbid. What do you want for dinner?"

46

YOU CAN RUN, BUT
YOU CANNOT HIDE

DOM AND WILL WERE BASKING in the afterglow of having christened the new king-size bed, during which he had become concerned for the baby's health when Dom over-heated in the grand finale of an orgasm. They were cuddled up in a warm embrace when she said, "That was some session we had with the lovers today. I hope everything settles down between the two of them."

"Yeah, me too; Alex was sure packing an attitude when she showed up," he offered. "I haven't seen Dominique Lefebvre in such top form since you broke my stud warrior down at ROUST that night when you cleverly described Carmen as that gorgeous woman who loved him."

She pinched him mischievously, "It's very admirable how you have throttled your desire for Carmen all this time; I'll give you a pass for the morphine-induced overture you made on the ride out of Ksar that night. I'm not as sure about Casey however; you two seem to share magnetism, not unlike the way you are around Samantha Chessereaux."

He shivered inwardly, "Casey and I know the line we cannot cross; the moral boundaries are rigidly back in place."

"That's good to know. I wasn't so sure when I saw the way she was clutching you in the kitchen today."

Ignoring the panic spike he replied, "You've got to admit Dom, those were some cuttingly nasty things Alex was saying about both of us. Casey just felt totally humiliated to hear herself referred to like that when she has never been anything but a devoted lover of Alex'."

She looked at him wearily, "But she never had reason to until she discovered that restraint in the car. Now that was a foolish mistake on Casey's part."

"Keeping the restraints was stupid. Now it might have leaked out around the edges eventually, but I have never known Alex to be such an insecure, immature person before."

"She's got a lot at stake now. Goodnight my love."

He laid staring at the darkened ceiling, unable to sleep, thinking how he had crossed the line badly with Casey, and was now protecting the lie by not being truthful about it with Dom. He knew that in his soul the very fact that he wasn't being truthful was more dangerous than having executed the perfect act of love with Casey. The thoughts were haunting him that he could destroy what he had with Dominique.

"What is it Will?" Dom asked as she held him in her arms, alarmed that she had awoken to find him sobbing disconsolately beside her.

He could barely see her through the haze of tears as he offered the mea culpa, "I'm so sorry Dom."

Now fully alert and sitting up, she tenderly kissed his ear, "What are you sorry for Will?"

He took one look at her and began crying openly. Finally he told her, "I lied to you Dom."

"About Casey?"

"Yes," was all managed before breaking down again. She was holding him, gently rocking them, too wise to say another word. "I'm so ashamed of what happened with Casey in Pensacola that I have made a weak and futile attempt to keep it from you. I finally couldn't take it anymore, and I knew it would grow like a cancer between us and destroy the purest love any human has every felt for another. I am so sorry Dominique, and I want you to know that."

"So you crossed a line?"

"Yes we did."

"And did you step back across that line?"

"Yes we did, but I'm not going to leave it at that; perhaps if you know what happened you can help free me from the nightmare of guilt."

She nodded knowingly, "Okay, tell me."

He shuddered at what must come next, "I told you about the lovemaking session when I restrained Casey and closed off her breathing, resulting in an almost unbelievable emotional reaction on her part. She was all but worshiping me for granting her the realization of her fantasy."

"So there was another session you have carefully protected in your mind?"

He merely nodded his head, "So we ordered room service and the food rebounded our energy. I asked if she had any other fantasies to explore. She told me the restraints had nearly rendered her psychotic, and was there a way to execute the asphyxiation part without the restraints."

Dom held up her hand to pause, looked briefly up at the ceiling and said, "So she wanted to experience the pleasure—the rush—without the fright dragging her down emotionally?"

"In retrospect that seems almost obvious, but at the time I was too fixated on how to execute the challenge."

"Of course you were; you solve problems Will, please continue."

"So it dawned on me that if I didn't have to use two hands to close off her airways, it would be easier to execute at the moment of rapture."

Dom looked at her hands, "So what solution did you arrive at?"

"I decided it was an easier task if I was attacking from behind, so I had her lean over the bed with her knees on the floor."

Dom was nodding again, "That was a better attack attitude than if she had laid on her stomach on the bed. It sounds as if you arrived at the optimal positioning. How did it play out, and what led to the lie? You haven't told me anything that sounds out of the ordinary."

He shivered again, "The lie came from the reaction to the orgasm."

Dom's eyebrows actually danced, "I'm terribly interested, please continue."

He grimaced slightly, "Okay, I began spanking her ass, and she got about as excited as Kelly Dupree did that night. Next I pulled on her nipples, and her reaction to that was to grab me and thrust me inside her. I then gently grasped her throat and she got more excited and began pounding down with incredible vigor. When I covered her mouth and nostrils with my hand and fingers, she lost total control and began screaming and slamming down on me so hard I fell back on my butt on the floor. She made two more extremely violent downward thrusts, screamed 'NO,' went rigid into a brick and began ejaculating on the floor. This almost incomprehensible combination of events caused me to orgasm so hard that I felt I was sort of on fire, and I had this sudden recognition of Casey's soul, and we were on fire together. She was crying uncontrollably afterwards on my chest and we both recognized the pure love we had just experienced. We were proclaiming pure love for one another and she said it was the soul-rending event of her lifetime, and I couldn't disagree."

Dom was looking at him with a slightly open-mouthed stare, so he asked her, "So what do you think?"

She shook her head lightly to refocus, "I think we must do that as soon as we are able Will. My God, your souls were on fire together?"

He almost collapsed with relief, "That's what it felt like to me, and Casey agreed. You can see where that would create confusion in the minds of two people who were intent on transferring sperm instead of altering the universe. I felt as though I had spiritually compromised my soul by allowing myself to feel that intense a love for Casey."

Snapping out of her prurient fascination with the act, she replied, "I absolutely do understand your panic. You entered the arrangement intent on fertilizing her, probably satisfying the subliminal lust you two shared. But what you encountered was pure love without even seeking it or knowing it was a possible outcome. That would confuse anyone. How did the two of you resolve it between yourselves? I can just imagine the inclinations such an intense sharing of emotion must trigger."

He was limp with relief, "Well, we both knew we couldn't let it interfere with our lives, although that could easily be a choice given the intensity of the event. We both acknowledged the love we had shared, and refused to feel guilty about it because neither of us had any idea that could happen. Finally, I told her we would never, ever do that again, and she agreed totally. I later jokingly told her that it was a shame my mind couldn't have flashed a warning sign, 'Caution: You are about to enter the Twilight Zone.'"

Dom smiled, "Yes, wouldn't that be nice. So if I'm reading you correctly Will, you didn't want to tell me about this because you were ashamed that you had experienced this completely unexpected and unsolicited feeling of love for and with Casey?"

He now felt like a complete fool, "That's about it Dom. But I did hide it from you, and I lied by not telling you about it. Casey and I even agreed we could never tell anyone that this had happened. It was so foreign to our love relationships, but now that you dissect it down to its component parts I feel like an idiot."

"So what is really bothering you about this Will? I don't see that you did anything disloyal to our love, our relationship, our marriage. You just somehow stumbled upon the magical method of making love."

"I let my ego get in the way of good common sense. You would probably say my id overrode my ego and inspired me to do something imprudent. When I made that indecent proposal at the hotel, I was leading her towards the conclusion that she was almost compelled to make. Once I succeeded in winning her over, I was morally compromised and was susceptible to unexpected surprises like those I encountered."

Dom was shaking her head, "You are discounting the fact that Casey invoked free will in choosing to accept your indecent proposal, as you call it. Don't you think she's at least as responsible as you for going down the path you chose? I'll put this in your terms Will: don't you think she wanted to fuck you as much as you wanted to fuck her? By the way, how long have you known Casey? There seems to be an unnatural familiarity between the two of you; the clutch in the kitchen made this quite apparent."

He rolled his eyes slightly, "Nothing gets past you Dominique. I actually met Casey two weeks before I met you back at Lowery AFB. She was a student at the school the same time I was. I asked her out the day I met her, and over drinks that evening she decided she trusted me and confessed that she was a lesbian. As fate would have it, she was assigned to the same unit I was in DC, and she made a significant contribution to the success of that legal project I was heading up. About a month after you were deported, I took her to Champagne Brunch at Bolling AFB; she couldn't realistically be seen with her girlfriend at the time. When we drove up, Danielle and her boyfriend were walking towards the O' Club, so she got pissed and decided she'd play the part of a hooker to give Danielle a dose of her own medicine. When I went home on vacation from the Philippines after I'd been there a year, my sister Alex confessed to me in my parent's back yard that she was a lesbian, and that Casey was her lover. And she made me strip naked in front of her for inspection on our wedding day to insure I was properly dressed for the occasion. So you see, there's a rather long history of intersections along our lifelines for the past four or five years, and yes, we have always felt comfortable around one another. The unstated issue of mutual lust remained suppressed until the indecent proposal."

Dom was ready to render judgment, "Okay William Kavanagh, I forgive you for not telling me all of the truth. I do not forgive you, however, for falling into this intense love encounter with Casey Mooneyhan; there's nothing to forgive, and you didn't know it could happen." She paused, smiled that furtive grin and asked, "Did you test out this line you drew in the sand?"

He was flushing slightly when he told her, "Yes, twice. She followed me into the shower the next morning to see if I had manufactured any more ammo while sleeping. And the last two encounters were in the prohibited missionary position; no airways obstruction allowed!"

As she rolled over to return to dreamland, she said, "We can't take a chance on exciting me that much while I'm pregnant. I will be waiting for you the moment the doctor gives me the go ahead following childbirth. You have made a significant contribution to the nuances of Freelancing William. Good night."

———

Everyone was in a festive mood the next morning, Hal and Will checking out the garage for converting the attic space into a loft apartment. "What'd you have in mind for this place if we do convert it to a loft Willy? I know your enterprising mind is working overtime."

Will pointed out that the overhead was open, and that the builder had opted for buttressed rafters instead of pre-fabricated trusses, so the attic had decent headroom potential as a loft. "I don't know buddy, but with our travel schedules subject to severe and sudden changes, I thought it might be good to have someone living here, you know, like a live-in keeper. Somebody like Chambie who already lives in a nest and shows no signs of hooking up with a woman any time soon would be ideal."

Hal acted like a light bulb had gone off in his head, "Now that idea has real potential Willy. We could probably lure him over here just with paid utilities, but we should offer him a monthly stipend for being our overseer. That'd leave plenty of time for him to do whatever else he does besides hunt."

"Right, all we'd have to do is put him on restricted hours for smoking pot. Let's go by and see if he's interested?"

"Maybe later," Hal responded, "Carmen and I are going out in search of some baby furniture this afternoon. We can't be lugging those carry-on cribs and all if we've got a permanent base of operations."

"Righto partner, want Dom and I to watch Master Wade while you guys are shopping?"

"You know, I never thought I'd see you embrace domesticity this eagerly Willy, but we'll take you up on that offer, thanks!"

When they walked back in the house, Alex was on the phone, and her body language along with the wrinkled forehead and grimace foretold it must be their Mother. "Okay Mom, I'd love to have lunch with you and chat about things, whatever they are. I'll pick you up at noon and we'll go grab lunch at Beudreau's." As she put the phone down with a *humph*, she turned to her brother, "I don't know what your Mother is up to Willy, but I can just imagine what this little girl talk can be all about."

Casey looked at her and headed for the bathroom, "We're leaving at noon? Yikes, I've gotta go take a shower!"

Alex rolled her eyes, "Oh, you can cancel that. Mom wants it just to be her and me. I can't imagine what news she's got in store for her only daughter!"

Dom peeked around the corner and offered her two bits, "Alex, she was much more accommodating about you and Casey when we were at the hospital in Baton Rouge. I think she's happy that you're taking on parenthood."

Alex looked at Dom with a smirk, "Yeah, especially since she thinks Willy's the father."

As she was leaving, she looked at Casey and said, "Hey babe, how about peel some carrots and celery sticks for a snack on the drive home. I'll be back whenever my mother is finished with me."

Will could barely restrain himself, "Jesus Alex, you'd think you were going to have a root canal instead of lunch with your mother; ease up for Christ's sake!"

She was snarling when she yelled at him from the front door, "Right, get your sorry ass over there and have a nice chatty lunch big boy. Later!"

As Alex burned rubber out of the driveway, no doubt excited to share some quality time with Mom, Casey closed her eyes and shook her head. "I might as well get started on those veggies; Lord knows we wouldn't want to snack on anything that tasted good!"

As she began peeling carrots in the sink, Dom gave Will her mysterious Mona Lisa smile and nodded, "Why don't you go see if you can put Casey at ease Will; I think it's time for us to have a nice little chat, what do you say?"

He kissed her sweetly, "I don't know what you have in mind Dom, but I know it will be interesting!"

Casey was cheerfully peeling carrots, rocking out to the Floyd's *Comfortably Numb* on the radio when he snuck up, stepped right in behind her and whispered in her ear, "Hey baby, how you doing today?"

He noticed her exhale just perceptibly and move her ass back into his crotch as she cooed, "Better now." He was almost pissed when he started getting an erection just from the proximity, but ignored it and nuzzled her ear as he eased his hand around her neck, just touching her throat with his fingers in a little flutter. He was surprised and pleased when she suddenly gasped, dropped the peeler and the carrot in the sink and started to turn around. When she did, Dom was standing there watching them with that wicked smile of hers. Casey quickly recovered and took a step away from him, blurting out, "Hey Dom, I didn't hear you come in."

It was somewhat awkward to pretend the obvious reactivity wasn't radiating, but Dom merely smiled, "Casey, do you trust Will explicitly?"

To her credit Casey didn't hesitate, "Yes."

She nodded just perceptibly, "Good. Will, why don't you thank Casey for the gift she gave us." He winked at Dom, turned to Casey, took her in his arms and began kissing her until she opened her mouth and entered into a devastating French-kiss. When he had tested her resolve suitably, they slowly disengaged, both flushed and on the edge of panting. His previously nominal erection was now a full-fledged blue-steel hard on, and Dom did glance down at his crotch, "Let's sit down and have a chat you two, and Casey, you have nothing to be anxious about. I want to pick your brain, so to speak."

They sat at the kitchen table, Dom on one side of Casey and Will on the other as Dom just perceptibly winked an eye towards Casey's hand on the table. He covered her hand with his, closed the fingers around hers and looked at her with a smile. Dom nodded and smiled, "Casey, what do you think we are having this discussion about?"

To his surprise, her faced flushed red as she blurted, "If I didn't know better I'd think you two want to have a *ménage a trois* with me."

Dom laughed just lightly, "No Casey, that would cross the line you and Will established, wouldn't it?"

He watched her face turn almost purple, but she got it back under control enough to say, "Cross what line?"

Instead of replying, Dom looked at him and said, "Will?"

He touched her chin very softly, pulled her face around to look him in the eyes and said, "That would cross the line you and I agreed never to visit again babe. It was necessary for us to establish that boundary because we experienced complete and total love for one another, and we knew we could never go there again if we wanted to have any semblance of normal lives."

She visibly gulped, then looked at Dom, "He told you about that?"

Ignoring her question, Dom pursued, "Didn't you hear him crying last night in the bedroom?"

With a look of horror on her face, she looked between Will and Dom. "I didn't know if that was the baby crying or what." She turned to look at him and asked, "Why were you crying Will?"

He couldn't trust his voice to work, so he punted, "Dom, could you…"

"I'd be happy to. Casey, Will was so distraught by the fact that he had lied to me—actually lied by omission—about what happened between the two of you when you joined souls in orgasm that he broke down and told me all about it last night in bed. Does that surprise you?"

Casey managed an awkward grimace, "I guess it actually does. We had agreed that we would never mention anything about that to anyone, ever. But since it's out in the open here, I'll be a resolute bitch and tell you neither one of us regretted it. It was too pure and spontaneous to deny."

Will held up his hand to Dom and leaned in close to Casey's face, "Why do you think you're being a resolute bitch? You don't have to admit anything here babe, this isn't about hate; this is about love."

He could see a tear breaching her lower eyelid when she said, "Does she know that at that moment of ecstasy that I loved you more than life itself? Did you tell Dom that, were you completely honest about what we experienced?"

He looked at her with a cold emotionless expression and gave her the answer she wanted to hear, "Yes, and I told her I loved you more than anything at that moment Casey. Dom can deal with truth, but not with lies."

A tear was leaking down her face now, "How can you withstand that kind of truth Dom? Doesn't that make you hate me, and hate Will?"

Dom could have been playing poker, "Not in the least Casey. What you two experienced was nothing short of remarkable."

By now the tears were flowing, and she all but pleaded, "Please tell me why you don't hate me, or hate Will? Didn't we undermine every precept of loving commitment when we did that?"

With that Dom moved out of her seat and pulled Casey into a warm hug. Then she surprised the hell out of them when she held her face and kissed her passionately on the lips. Will had to chasten the devil to get behind him, as the sight of it turned him on big time. When she sat back down, Dom resumed the discussion, "Tell me Casey, when you proposed this asphyxiation fantasy exercise, what were your expectations?"

This seemed to sober her up slightly as she glanced at Will, "I just wanted to feel what it would be like, you know, whether maybe the orgasm would be more intense than routine lovemaking. I had seen it done in a porn movie, but Alex would never agree to try it; but Will seemed more than willing to take me there."

Dom nodded her head again, "That sounds reasonable; a new and different position and unfamiliar stimulus would reasonably be expected to be more exciting. So you entered into this exercise with the expectation of a superior orgasm, is that right?"

Will was smiling on the inside as he saw where Dom was leading this, and Casey predictably replied, "Exactly."

"So when you modified the routine so that it was less confining to you, the second time you experienced the asphyxiation, what were your expectations?"

Now getting more comfortable with the exchange, Casey laid it out simply, "That I could enjoy the orgasm without being on the edge of a psychotic episode."

"Don't you see Casey, I think and Will thinks, those are reasonable expectations. And if that had happened, we wouldn't be having this discussion. What happened, much to your shock and terror, was that you experienced a life-altering union with another human. That is the most extraordinary thing that can ever happen to a soul. You were caught totally by surprise, and that is what Will finally came to the understanding of at one o'clock this morning. You might believe you subordinated your moral boundaries to have sex in the first place, but you had damn worthy reasons for doing so. You have no reason, and neither does Will, to be ashamed of what happened between you because you had no idea that the very extemporaneous steps you two put into play would result in the spiritual equivalent of a nuclear explosion. What to me is most incredible is that the two of you, not knowing the first thing about how to execute this method, somehow perfected it the second time you attempted it. I told Will he had stumbled upon the most magical method of making love, and that the moment I'm physically able to participate, the two of us are going to try and achieve the almost unbelievable results that you and he did."

Casey and Will were both momentarily stunned at the prosaic countenance of Dom's recitation, but he shook it off to ask, "Aren't you feeling better about yourself Casey?"

She slumped into his chest as he put his arm around her, sagging with obvious relief. Finally she looked up and said, "Yes, for the first time since that spiritual equivalent of a nuclear explosion occurred—as you so aptly described it Dom—I don't feel like a low life slut about it. And you made me almost feel like I should file a patent, because it was incredibly unlikely that Will and I could figure it out to that level of perfection."

"Are you willing to answer some questions about your personal reaction to that event Casey?" Dom asked, more confident now that the corner had been turned on Casey's reticence.

She smiled and said, "Sure, what would you like to know?"

Dom glanced at Will and then ventured forth, "Will described the feeling he had when the explosion occurred as if he were on fire, and that was closely followed by the sensation—no the reality—that at the two of you were joined together on fire. How do you describe it?"

She gazed up at the ceiling to orient her recollection, then refocused on Dom, "When he held my nose shut for what seemed like eternity, I became hysterical to take a breath and when I beat his hand off of my face and took that breath, I suddenly felt like I was looking directly into the sun, but it wasn't blinding me. Instead it was sort of welcoming me. I got scared and yelled 'NO' and then Will was there with me and the sun turned into bright pastel colors. I had the sensation—maybe the reality—that the world was a total cascade of love and I was breathing in the love and it was the most incredible happy feeling I could ever imagine. And then I was laying on Will's chest sobbing uncontrollably until he asked me if I was alright. Then came the treacherous aftereffects, like the worst hangover you can imagine. I didn't understand what had happened, and Will couldn't explain it either. I believe that we were both terrified that we had somehow ruptured the dynamics of our own universes, and that if we didn't enter into immediate denial that our relationships with you and Alex would be all but damned. It was singularly the most extraordinary and the most excruciating experience of my life, and I got the distinct impression that Will felt the same way." She focused suddenly on Dom and asked, "Does that sound like anything you have ever heard before?"

Dom was staring wide-eyed at Casey and didn't seem to hear the question, so Will asked, "Dom, are you okay?"

She shook her head slowly and looked at them strangely, "Did you ask me something?"

Casey looked at Will with a weird expression on her face, "Where were you Dom? Did that take you to some other place?"

Dom shook her head again and finally replied, "Yes, as strange as it may seem, your recollection was so vivid that I was nearly able to be there with you. That was incredible, and I can see that you must know you're going there in order to be receptive and comfortable with it."

"So does that sound, or seem, like anything you've heard about before?" Casey inquired.

Will was clearly mesmerized at the tack this adulterous conversation had taken, so he was all but pleading for Dom's response. Finally she said, "Yes. In the most advanced forms of Kama Sutra meditation, practitioners are supposedly able to experience the presence of love as a sort of three dimensional force. I believe you might have penetrated some time-space continuum, otherwise described as another dimensional aspect. The other two situations that come to mind are near-death experiences and trips taken on LSD. All I can tell you for sure is that must have been one hell of an orgasm, my God!"

Now Casey smiled as she glanced at Will, "That is almost incredible, because when we were sitting in bed afterwards trying to make sense of it, Will said something quite similar. Did he tell you?"

"No," Dom replied, glancing at Will quizzically, "what did he describe it as?"

"He said we may have penetrated some membrane between the third and fourth dimensions. It's amazing you thought something so similar."

Ever the pragmatist, Will tossed in the stink bomb by asking, "So how can Casey ever resolve this experience with Alex?"

Casey scowled at him because of the intrusion into the existential realm, "Alex is too grounded to even smoke pot. She is not comfortable with altered states, and cherishes a predictable orientation. This discussion would totally freak her out. She would wonder if we had simultaneously experienced brain damage due to that cabernet we were drinking."

Dom considered this and said, "You're just going to have to take it one step at a time. It is apparent to me how you two get along—you are almost opposites except for your sexual orientation. If you were too much alike, you would irritate each other constantly and easily find fault with every nuance of the other's lifestyle. Perhaps the best you can hope for is to convince her that this sexual fantasy convention is a viable alternative to predictable sameness. It certainly seems to have worked for you and Will. I still cannot believe I haven't been tempted to try this previously."

Will suddenly had a hysterically funny thought, Dom and Casey prompting him with their finger rolls, "Well?"

"There sure was a lot of subliminal attraction lurking between the exterior visages wasn't there? Once we resolved the moral tripwire, there was instant relaxation between the two of us. We even admitted to one another that it felt like we'd been together for years. I'm not sure I would have felt comfortable attempting some of the process steps—which I might add, I had no reason to have confidence in—with almost anyone else but you Dom. Makes you wonder about pre-ordination doesn't it?"

Dom seemed contemplative for a moment, and then ventured, "Yes it does. I have only seen you this comfortable around one other woman, Samantha Chessereaux, and there were very similar magnetic resonance aspects. I suppose it would be interesting to discover just how you've known each other previously."

Casey was suddenly alert, saying, "You mean past lives? I've sort of wondered about that myself, but I was trying to beat down the devil by denying I really had the hots for Will. So I never pursued it further. Now that I'm freed from my denial, I might just look into that. I know a lady at ARE who gives readings. Who knows?"

"So, in summation, what have we learned here today? Will, you go first," Dom the moderator instructed.

"I believe I recognize that I shouldn't select me being a dumb ass as the first choice when something doesn't register within my realm of understanding. There may be other factors in play, like spiritual nuclear explosions."

When they both stopped laughing, Dom looked at Casey and said, "Any lessons for you?"

She was nodding her head as she began, "I've always wanted to hate myself for this lust, this thing I have for Will, but now I recognize that I love him because he's a wonderful human being. I felt as though my feelings for him were a deadly poison to my other relationships. But now I see that if you talk about them—acknowledge the realities—that you can reasonably coexist if you merely establish behavioral boundaries. I'm not saying I would never entertain the prospect of making love with him again, especially the three of us, but I know the rules and I know the dangers."

Feeling like a third wheel, he grouched, "Hey, I'm sitting right here next to you for Christ's sake; you can pretend I can hear you!"

She gave him a hateful stare and proved her point by asking Dom, "Do you foresee a *ménage a trois* possible for the three of us?"

The surprise on Dom's face was unmistakable, "I saw the way you two reacted to one another when he kissed you in the kitchen. There is no doubt in my mind that we could have a successful and mutually rewarding *ménage a trois*. But given the dynamics of your relationship with Alex—and the fact that she's Will's sister and a very unlikely candidate for participation—I consider the likelihood of that happening to be very slim. But as Will's Gideon Angel is wont to say, 'hope springs eternal.'"

With that Dom stood and announced, "We've got an appointment with that local obstetrician who was so kind to see us on his day off William. I am going to clean up and get ready. I expect you two have a few things you want to discuss with each other after that little séance. We are leaving at three o'clock Mr. Kavanagh, and I expect you to accompany me to this appointment."

He looked at her like she had wounded him, "Of course I'll be there with you Dom, go do what you must."

Once Dom took her leave, Casey and he chatted about innocuous things until she heard the shower running and turned to ask, "How have you been love?"

"It's been busy Case; a lot has been going on since I got back, or didn't you notice?"

"I mean, how have YOU been about US?" She snickered furtively as she began rubbing the inside of his thigh.

A hint of a tremulous shiver went up his spine, "Fine."

"Oh come on Will, when you touched my throat I was ready to bunk over that kitchen counter and do it all over again right there. And don't try and play coy, I saw that baseball bat in your pants."

In spite of himself, he visibly exhaled trying to suppress a burning desire to bunk her over the table and take her right there. Instead he took a deep breath, "You seem to have the same effect on me as Samantha Chessereaux, and the last time she was seducing me with those galactic blue eyes I told her very clearly, 'Goddamn you woman.'"

She brandished that Mona Lisa smile, no doubt pleased, "Good, so we share the same damnable desire. You unleashed some wanton animal in me, and I have trouble not thinking about it."

He was trying mightily to rein in his rampant libido. Failing miserably he looked at her, "Goddamn you Casey Mooneyhan." He took her head in his hands and tried to French-kiss the life out of her, but she was up to the task and attacked his mouth with fury, biting his lip and tongue as he tasted the blood. He suddenly stood up and was just able to control his rage, "This is not going to work Casey. We cannot be doing this; you will drive us both crazy if you cannot figure out how to rein it back in! Remember, your life is with Alex!"

She suddenly relaxed and smiled, "Yeah, I get that Will, but do you remember saying we didn't initiate that nuclear explosion to change the universe? Well guess what, I think we triggered a revolution, and I cannot let it go. I will make love with you any time, any place, anywhere, anyhow, just so you know where I stand on the matter."

Will didn't know how he was going to bring this incendiary conversation to an acceptable conclusion. Shaking his head like a wet dog drying himself, he looked back to find her smiling self-contentedly. "What the fuck do you want me to do? Divorce my wife, turn my back on my family and ruin this entire world I live in? That's not going to happen Casey; but damn you, you're probably pregnant with my child so I'll never abandon you or the baby. We have got to reach an amenable position baby, or we're both doomed."

"Well, you know what position I want you in, directly behind me. But I know we can't trigger a real nuclear explosion. Did I accurately convey to you what my feelings are about this matter?"

Hoping against hope that she had finally turned the corner from channeling Princess Shiva, he smiled sickly, "Perfectly. And I believe you understand what almost supernatural magnetic force you exert upon me. So I beg you please exercise restraint so we can all have a chance of living peaceably."

"No problem William, now that we understand one another. Oh, did I mention that I adore you?"

He was beginning to wonder if Casey was the latter day incarnation of Evelyn Draper of 'Play Misty for Me' fame. "I believe you did mention that.

Didn't you have to get some healthy snacks ready for the trip back?"

Proving that karma was smiling on them, Alex drove up just as a happy and smiling Casey Mooneyhan returned to the sink to peel the veggies. As she walked in Will greeted her warmly, "And how was your quality time with our Mother?"

To his surprise, Alex had lost the angst and irritation she had left with, "We actually had a very nice time together. Your mother seems to have lost her hard edge regarding my 'alternate life style' and is anxiously looking forward to being a grandmother."

The look on his face must have mirrored his difficulty believing her, so she added, "Due no doubt to the fact that she hopes with all of her Lutheran sanctity that her precious son is the father of said grandchild."

"Well, that's the way you and Casey wanted it to happen, *n'est pas*? So it's a win-win, right?"

She swooped in to kiss him, no doubt signaling that the war was over, "We'll see when it's time for Casey's next period."

He managed to block the lingering doubt regarding *Evelyn Draper* Mooneyhan, "Let's hope for the best Sis. Need a hand loading up?"

As the two lovers were heading out to leave, Dom was looking especially radiant with her glowing perfect pregnant persona. As Casey stopped by for a hug, Will was curious to see Dom kiss her on the lips without reservation. Alex got the more traditional cheek buss, and at the car Alex stopped to say, "I love the roost Will, Dom chose well. I'll be interested to see what you come up with for the addition. Let me know the first you hear about Colton."

Casey saved Will for last, and surprised him when she leaned up to kiss his cheek. Instead she hesitated for just a moment by his ear, "Any time, anyplace, anyhow or anywhere cowboy. See ya."

Trying to remain emotionless, he smiled at her, "Yeah, good luck with those snacks; you won't be risking happiness with those!" Alex was shooting him the bird as they pulled out, burning rubber for good measure.

———

On the drive to the obstetrician, Dom looked over with a baleful expression and asked, "Well?"

He shook his head lightly, "Not good baby."

"How bad?"

He laughed at the way the conversation was playing out, the fewest words ever spoken to relate a complex subject. "Real bad."

She twisted in her seat to face him, "Please explain."

He scratched his head, shook it lightly and told her, "Casey thinks the spiritual nuclear explosion sparked a revolution."

She was nodding her head knowingly, "That's always one of the dangers of raw emotional exchange. I suspect her relationship is less grounded than ours; this could be problematic."

He shook his head in resignation, "I suppose every relationship can't be grounded in past life frustration and redemption. As much as I don't want to sound like an asshole, they did choose each other."

Without missing a beat, Dom added, "And you chose Casey."

It was no time to bluff, so he bit the bullet, "I know. Just like I chose Samantha, but at least she exists in a more normal lifestyle."

"That's not going to help you, or me. What was Casey's bottom line?"

He slowed down to look Dom in the eyes, "I'll paraphrase for you; she'll fuck me anytime, anyplace, anywhere and/or anyhow. Oh, and she adores me."

Thankfully his confessor tolerated vitriol well, "We can only hope she does not become obsessive. There is potential here for tragedy."

"Why couldn't I have seen this coming baby? I feel like a rank amateur."

"Nonsense, the animal was caged and under control until that sublime union released it to the outside world. You couldn't have seen it coming; I know I certainly didn't."

"I apparently didn't do the situation any favors when I went up behind her to 'relax' her earlier. I merely touched her neck and she gasped, and she convinced me she would have recreated the entire nuclear explosion right there on the kitchen table. If I had to characterize it, I'd say she's like heart pine tinder; ready to combust with nominal excitation. Perhaps once and done would have been safer for seed transfer."

"That's ridiculous Will; you had no idea you were going to do anything but procreate and have some fun. Besides, there's no guarantee that even once would have been a safe margin; she seems to have taken quite naturally to heterosexual musings."

Her supposition actually made him laugh. "That my dear, is an understatement. I told her in Pensacola that she was bisexual."

"Really? It could well be that what is really at play here is a deep psychological conflict over her sexual identity awareness."

He once again nodded his assent, "I would say once again my dear, that is an understatement!"

Jan Kavanagh had referred them to her OB/GYN in Gastineau, and he was happy to see Dom on a Saturday, so they gave him an upcheck on attitude right up front. Dom refused to allow Will to sit in the waiting room, reading incredibly boring magazines, so he ventured in with her for the initial exam and assessment. He was admittedly bored trying to keep up with the blizzard of potential blood chemistry issues the doctor was relating. Will lost interest and found himself replaying the wickedness of Jessica Walter's character in Clint Eastwood's movie *Play Misty For Me*.

"Nothing other than a longing for pistachio-banana ice cream," she reported humorously.

"Well that's very impressive, normally......" he was saying when Will interjected himself rather rudely.

"Excuse me Doc, back up there for a second. Those symptoms you were describing for psychological problems almost sound like what we've traditionally chalked up to the nesting instinct. Are there any typical or common triggers for such symptoms in the first trimester of pregnancy?"

He looked at Dom's obviously protruding stomach when Dom chided him, "What on earth does that have to do with our situation Will?"

His poker face gave nothing, "Who said anything about our situation?"

Dom appeared frustrated, "I don't know what you're talking about Will, what could that possibly..." The potential hit home dramatically, as she said, "Oh my God."

She turned back to the Doctor, "Yes, what could trigger off psychological problems in the first trimester of pregnancy Dr. Paul?"

He looked at both of them with a frown, "Well, such symptoms at the outset of pregnancy are almost always a result of the endocrine system releasing hormones for the support of fetal development. Morning sickness is a common..."

"I'm actually more interested in the delusion and persistent longings symptoms Doctor. Is there any specific endocrine or hormonal aspect that manifests itself in those types of problems?" Dom was all but interrogating

Dr. Paul now.

He looked confused but shrugged, "Sure, if the patient does not have Graves's disease, mild hyperthyroidism could result in elevated hCG levels and…"

"Elevated what?" Will asked, feeling dazed and confused.

Dr. Paul narrowed his focus, "Human chorionic gonadotropin is a hormone secreted by the embryonic placenta villi. It's presence in a mother's blood is used as a predictor of pregnancy." Will shook his head, "That's why we refer to it as hCG; it's a lot easier to record and so forth."

"So the first screen of the mother is for Graves' disease and the second is for the presence of hCG?" As he asked, Dom was actually leaning forward in her seat to hear the doctor's response.

"Actually, they're the same blood test. The thyroid screen will pick up all of that, but your charts show no abnormalities…"

"Right, so if a mother hadn't gone through the tox screen, I'm sorry the thyroid screen, you wouldn't or couldn't diagnose the problem, am I correct?" Will asked, but Dr. Paul shook his head in confusion.

"Actually Mr. Kavanagh, that is part of the initial consult, and any obstetrician would be looking for such issues, I can assure you."

Dom gazed at Will with a look of true admiration, "Well played Mr. Kavanagh; your investigative instincts are as sharp as a razor."

———

They flipped a coin to see who would make the call that night; it came up heads, so Will dialed up Fort Walton Beach. "Hey Sis, how are you doing, Have an otherwise uneventful journey?"

"Sure, except you-know-who was as moody as I've ever seen her. I think you were right about the snacks; I was ready to kill for some French fries by the time we came off the Interstate at Pensacola."

He laughed, suppressing the urge to tell her 'I told you so', "Hey is Casey handy? I'd like to say hi."

"Sure, she's right here, hold on."

Dom had picked up the extension phone when Casey came on, "Hey Will, how's it going? Is everything alright back there? We just this moment got in off the road."

Fast-forwarding past pleasantries, he launched, "Hey Case, remember you couldn't make that appointment with the obstetrician at the fertility clinic that day?"

He could hear the tremor in her voice when she replied, "Yeah."

"Listen babe, did you ever go back and have that appointment with the doctor?"

He could tell she was uncomfortable, but hung in there to reply, "Actually they were still closed the day after the storm. I was supposed to have my initial consult. Why are you asking?"

"Because you're pregnant!" Dom's voice boomed over the extension.

"Congratulations Casey, we did it. One of those rascals made it through to the finish line!" Will added for good measure.

"What?" She almost shouted over the phone. "How in the world could you know that from two hundred miles away?"

It was Dom who provided the key data, "We believe you are displaying symptoms of mild hyperthyroidism.

By now Alex was on the phone, "What in the world are you two talking about? Casey's about to pee her pants!"

"You could do us all a huge favor if you two would schedule that initial consult as soon as possible. Will and I believe Casey is pregnant."

"But how in the world could you know that? Did you two go to a palm reader?" Alex asked in obvious disbelief.

"I had my first appointment with Dr. Paul, the OB/GYN here in Gastineau this afternoon, and Will picked up on some symptoms that would be discovered during the initial consult and the associated blood work they do for screenings. I don't want to presuppose my sorceress abilities, so it is my heart-felt suggestion that you two make that appointment," Dom intoned, trying not to scare them.

"Okay, we'll make that appointment first thing in the morning. I am more than a little curious if you can possibly be right about this, making the call from Louisiana."

Will's stealth comment closed the call, "Hey, never up never in. Make that appointment and we'll be waiting to hear from you two."

They were lying in bed, pleased with the day's efforts when Dom smirked, "Never up never in? My God Will, you couldn't have been more blatant."

"It's a golf expression Dom, it means you've got to get the ball to the hole if you…"

"Yes, Mr. Kavanagh, I know what it means in that context. I couldn't believe that your sister didn't kneejerk over that little gem."

"Hey, we heterosexual types just seem to prefer the natural form of insemination, that's all," he said, but couldn't hide the shit-eating grin.

"Well let's see Mr. International Stud, you impregnated your wife via artificial insemination, *n'est pas?*"

"Hey, it wasn't because I was partial to that delivery medium, if we…"

"Yeah, right cowboy. We all better hope two of those little rascals didn't find friendly eggs at the finish line."

47

INTO THE CALI CARTEL'S CROSSHAIRS

WILL WAS DRAFTING THE FIRST ROUGH sketches of the addition, having taken measurements to confirm the blueprints they'd received at closing. Hal walked up to the kitchen table and looked at the first assumption at room configuration. "You know Willy, since we're building the addition from scratch, we ought to figure out where to fit in a panic room."

He looked at him like he'd spoken Russian, "A panic room? What the fuck is that?"

"A panic room is a hidden place, no windows or doors, that we can escape to if everything should turn to shit. That little exit Sandrigan had off of his bedroom would be a decent example."

"You mean the door that led off to the tunnel to the airstrip?"

"That's it Willy, but this will be a secret little room that we can escape from the house in; it'll need separate air, power and comm leads from the rest of the house, and it will be our own little armory. Beginning to see the light?"

Will was rubbing his chin, trying to get his head around it, "So no windows, no doors, how the hell do we get into it?"

"Hidden trap door ma man, and you get to design that into the plan. My guess is that it would be next to impossible to detect from the outside if we put it behind a walk-in closet at the very corner of the addition. It doesn't have to be real big, just enough room to get into and access whatever trapdoor you design leading under and out of the house crawl space. I'd also block that crawl space around the panic room walls so that it's not accessible by anyone getting into the crawl space. I'd build a tunnel over to a companion panic room for

463

egress; probably in the garage considering the layout here. Plan on racks on the walls for the weapons and you'd better harden the walls around the panic room; I'd design it to stop a 7.62 mm round; if somebody hits us with .50 cal, we're toast anyway."

The challenge of the design intrigued him, but Will had to question the intent, "Jesus Hal, do you really think it could get that dicey here in Gastineau?"

"Hey, you never know, and if we can get a decent panic room for, say five grand, it'll seem like chump change if everything turns to shit. In case you haven't noticed, we've been dealing with some bad hombres, and is it beyond comprehension to think that Sandrigan's associates might not like the way you blew his brains out?"

Will was jolted out of his contemplative state when Dom walked up behind him, "Hal's absolutely right Will. It's better to be prepared, and we can pull this off without anyone but the construction workers knowing that it's even there. I also like the idea of having an AR-15 handy if I need one to protect my family."

Recalling the hot LZ at Sandrigan's casbah, Will nodded, "Yeah, and I'd like to have a Mossberg 500 Tactical handy; Pierson sure convinced me on that point in Algiers."

"Now you're talking Willy; you remember how that Mossberg took the fight right out of those assholes. Once we get the room ready, I'll have one of the guys drive down here with what we need to outfit the armory."

"Okay, sounds good, I'll put together a preliminary design and take it from there."

———

"So Robales says let him rot in jail, eh?" Hal exclaimed after Will had debriefed he and Carmen on the latest news on Colton at lunch the next day. He had called Bob Matthews earlier to check in and Bob described the situation as diplomatic purgatory.

"I know, the State Department's impotence prevails once again," Will replied, confident in their inability to do anything 'actionable.'

"So what can we do to help the situation Will?" Carmen implored.

"I really don't know; Matthews said his boss was especially emphatic that we do nothing 'extra-judicial,'" he said in disgust, smirking.

"Well, breaking him out of prison in Nicaragua might not be the worst situation we've ever found ourselves in," Hal pointed out.

"You're probably right, but the *Chargé d'Affairs* assured us that Colton was being humanely treated, with food and water delivered regularly by the Red Cross," Will added benignly. "That pretty much mirrors the reports we got last time."

"Yeah right," Hal grouched, "those fucking wimps at State don't know how to do anything other than roll over and cop a guilty plea. If it wasn't for Matthews we wouldn't know jack shit about what's happening on the ground down there."

"So what do we do?" Will asked, open to any suggestions.

"Matthews will have somebody down there watching the prison for anything out of the ordinary. Jesus, I'm beginning to feel like a State weenie myself," Hal protested.

"Perish the thought; you're no weenie, believe me," Will offered in protest.

"I know Willy, you capped that guard that had me dead to right too. Maybe if they move Colton to another location we can snatch him when they make their move."

"Yeah his goose is cooked for Central America; burn that fucking bridge for good!" Will said as everyone agreed. "We need to position some assets closer to Central America so we'll have a reaction force when we do catch a break."

"Yeah, you're right but where? I suppose we could launch from Cozumel if we absolutely had to," Hal grimaced. "You think your buddy Johnny Chessereaux could come through for us again?"

"I'm sure he would, but we gotta tell him where to send it."

"I'll make the call," Hal offered, "Cozumel's 1400 miles closer than ROUST. And they don't ask a lot of questions about what you've got in your bags when you get there."

"So how are we set up for a little deployment partner?" Hal asked when he got Alex on the horn.

"Oh school's out, if that's what you wanted to know. Do I hazard a guess that you're pointing south?"

"As a matter of fact, we need to set up house as close as we can to Managua without letting the cat out of the bag. Willy and I were thinking Cozumel; got any better ideas?"

"What'd you have in mind by keeping a close eye on things? Matthews said San Bracinto was damn near impregnable. You're not thinking of going in there are you?" Alex asked, clearly incredulous.

"Hey, we both know San Bracinto's the Alcatraz of Central America but whatever happens we're going to need to be in the vicinity. You got any buds in the neighborhood? Cozumel's kinda our fallback right now just because it's 1500 miles closer for you guys. Logistics in and out of there still aren't ideal," Hal pondered.

"Yeah, Will's favorite word 'suboptimal' comes to mind. Hold on, I'll get Rico on the horn," he said as they heard a shrill whistle in the background. "Okay Ricardo, Hal and Will are on the line and we're trying to figure out a base of operations somewhere near Nicaragua that we can come and go in relative obscurity. Cozumel's on the table, but do you know of any better options?"

"Sure, Jimbo Meaux owns damn near all of Butila Island. That'd be our best bet if we gotta be close to Nicaragua," Rico announced as Hal and Will gave each other the Italian Army salute.

"So where's Butila Island, I ain't never heard of it? Jimbo Meaux you say; sounds like a coonass to me?" Will asked.

"It's right off the northeastern coast of Honduras, and more importantly Jimbo's lord and master of it. I don't know if he's Cajun, but he's got some sweet disability deal with the government. He was a Medal winner in 'Nam," Rico reported as they nodded their heads impressed.

"So we can come and go without upsetting immigration types, is that what you're telling us Rico?" Hal asked with considerable interest.

"Absolutely Kemosabe, Jimbo's our kind of guy."

"Make that call Rico. Butila sounds like our new home away from home. Go ahead and plan on packing heavy for the trip; we don't know what kinda shit we're gonna find ourselves in before this is over. Willy will see if he can arrange airlift. I like your contacts Mr. Suarez."

"It's for you Will, it's your Mother," Carmen called out as he was poring over the floor plan of the addition.

"Yeah Mom, how's it going?"

"Oh Will, I just got off the phone with Reverend Spiker, the missionary coordinator in St. Louis," she said excitedly.

"So what news did the Reverend have?"

"He wanted to tell me that his Lutheran Missionary Office had appealed for mercy for Colton with the government in Nicaragua, and that they had dismissed the appeal. I cannot believe those people could be so heartless."

"Did they give a reason why Mom?"

"They said my Colton had been charged with a serious crime and that he had to stand trial in the Nicaraguan courts before anything could be considered," she said, now beginning to sniffle.

"Okay Mom, let me look into it. Those people in the government down there didn't impress me a lot, to tell you the truth. I'll make a call and let you know what I find out. I want you to try and relax, and you know I love you. Hang in there Mom."

"What was that about Will?" Dom asked as he hung up the phone.

"Ah the Sandinistas have stiff-armed the Lutherans in their appeal for clemency for Colton. I wonder if our Catholic friends might have better luck. Remember they're the ones who first set out to convert the New World heathens; the Catholic influence is still pretty predominant."

"Well how are you going to approach the Catholic Church? It seems like it's a competitive thing for saving souls," she posed.

"We'll try an end-around," he said, reaching for the contact cards from the Rolodex.

"Why hello there *Mademoiselle* Tourism Minister," Will offered by way of greeting Rosita Cabrera.

"Actually I believe it's *Señorita* Tourism Minister Mr. Kavanagh, and how are you? I heard from our friend Daniel that life has once again become interesting for you."

"I'm fine Rosita, and I take it Rambo told you we had been in Nicaragua together?"

"Yes, he said he played steward for you and Dominique on your flight out."

"Right, I don't know if he offered background intel, but my brother Colton's been arrested there on a trumped up charge of sedition. The court system there's more screwed up than Hogan's goat, so we're trying to improve his situation as best we can. I was thinking that our friends in the Catholic Relief Services might be willing to help out, seeing as how a couple of *Norteamericanos* saw fit to help the innocent in need in Buenos."

"I'm sure they would be interested if they could help. What exactly do you want them to do?"

"Well, they've got him in this maximum security prison with Lord knows what kind of criminals, and if we could have him moved to another place my Mother would be greatly relieved. You know some minimum security place where at least he could get outside and get some exercise," he told her as Dom, Hal and Carmen all nodded.

"So tell me Will, what he did that got him in prison? Our friends in *Caritas Argentinas* would want to know that they're not asking to help a dangerous criminal."

"Okay, here's the short version. He was setting up a school for barrio kids and found that children weren't attending school because they were working in sweat shops instead. When he met with their parents he was arrested by the police for fomenting insurrection. Now he's hopelessly mired in their judicial system rotting away in a prison where the hard core criminals are kept. My family and the Lutherans are pretty much helpless at this point. Think you could approach someone for us?"

"If what you say is true, I'm sure someone from within the Church would be willing to petition the government there for leniency. What is his name again, and where is he being held?"

"His name is Colton Johnson Kavanagh and they have him in San Bracinto prison outside Managua. Do you really think *Caritas Argentina* could make a difference?"

"Actually, we might get intervention from a higher power. How can I reach you? By the way, where are you?"

"We're in Gastineau, Louisiana, and here's the number. Thanks a lot for your help Rosita."

"It's the least I can do for a former dance partner, *n'est pas?*"

"Damn, I am impressed babe; you picked that French up on the first try. Let me know when you know something. Thanks a million!"

He looked around for a high-five, but Hal was shaking his head, "Not yet partner, don't you have to make airline reservations?"

"Alright Rico, we've got Great West Airlines scheduled to arrive ROUST at 1000 hours tomorrow. Willy's just called in a marker with the fish-eaters— oh shit, sorry bro—to request clemency from the Sandinistas to have Colton moved to a minimum security prison. We need to be ready with a plan to snatch him if and when that transfer takes place. Whatdya think?" Hal asked.

"I think I'll need to go in for a reconnaissance run and scope out the locations of the prisons and the route between them. Why don't I take Rose in with me? We can be a vacationing couple for all the world knows."

"Who's Rose?" Will wondered, clueless.

"Jesus Willy, do you not remember our receptionist at ROUST, Rose Cordes?" he snarled. "Perfect Rico, I guess Alex can set up at Butila Island, eh?"

"Righto, and Rose and I can fly out of Managua later to La Ceiba. That's the closest big city up along the Honduran coast. It's not easy getting to Butila Island without a private plane, I can tell you that."

"Alright, I'll call Bob Matthews and let him know to expect you two. Try and stay out of the Sandinista's crosshairs while you're down there."

After the call Will shook his head, "Jesus Hal, you're gonna send a receptionist into an undercover op?"

Hal smirked as he looked at Carmen, who told him, "She's no mere receptionist Will; Rosario Cordes was a secret member of the ELN in Colombia. She was quietly soliciting support from the Cubans, Venezuelans and Panamanians before the Colombian government got interested in her travels. Don't worry, there are no 'civilian's' working at ROUST."

He shook his head in amazement, "I shoulda known. So she can shed her skin on demand, eh? Working for the ELN? What exactly is the ELN? I remember Charlie Richardson telling us the big revolutionary groups in Colombia were the FARC and the ELN."

"The ELN, or *Ejército de Liberación Nacional*, is the National Liberation Army of Colombia. It was founded as a Marxist-Leninist revolutionary council with Castro Cuban subversives in the early 1960s. Upon the death of the ELN founder, it was headed by Roman Catholic priests who abhorred the inequity of income distribution and political corruption that maintained the ruling class in Colombia," she explained.

"Now that is interesting," Will admitted, "so the Catholics have a stake in the ELN? I wonder if our proactive Archbishop Villaponteau is aligned with them?" He glanced at Hal, shaking his head at some disconnect. Finally he remembered, "Didn't Charlie Richardson say something about the Archbishop rubbing elbows with the FARC?"

"Yes he did, but I did not comment on his rumor because he was relying on either poor information or disinformation. I do not know if the Archbishop is aligned with the ELN, but there is much competition for the peasant's allegiance between the ELN and another communist-inspired revolutionary group. They call themselves the *Fuerzas Armadas Revolucionarias de Colombia--Ejército Del Pueblo,* or Revolutionary Armed Force of Colombia--People's Army (FARC-EP). From what Rose told me, the FARC is involved with the Cali Cartel in providing protection for coca farmers and distribution routes to processing facilities. The ELN has for the most part kept their hands clean of the drug trade and instead resorts to kidnapping and ransom as their primary funding source."

"Jesus, one side's into kidnapping, the other into protection rackets; fine citizenship building characteristics. So the Catholics are aligned with the ELN to some degree, and the Cartel is joined at the hip with the FARC. Politics does indeed make strange bedfellows," he observed.

Carmen was nodding her head in agreement when she added, "And Rosario Cordes retains vital contacts within the ELN."

"And just how did you meet her?"

Carmen was shaking her head coyly when Hal interjected, "Hey Willy, those guys you encountered at the volcano were Cali cartel types, right, not the Medellin cartel?"

He shrugged as he replied, "I really had no idea to tell you the truth. Rico told us the night before that shady Sandinista Police Lieutenant Rivas was the cartel's stool pigeon within the Managua government. Now since then Matthews has been bringing up the Cali Cartel a good bit, but I thought it was about the sweat shop bad press. All's I know for sure is he said his name was Enrique Constanza and he was wearing a nice leather jacket in 80 percent humidity." He reached into the desk drawer and pulled out the switchblade, "Oh, and he used this to give me this beauty mark on my face. His biggest mistake in life was placing the point of that blade on Dom's stomach. I told him he was making a mistake, but he just looked at me with a sick smile as that 7.62 round went supersonic right through his grey matter."

"So tell me again Willy, what did this Constanza guy want with you and Dom?" Hal wondered.

"Well first of all he knew who we were, which wasn't common knowledge. He said it was unfortunate that we wanted to publicize Colton's plight outside of Nicaragua, as our insistence on exposing the child labor issues would result in his meeting a fatal accident in prison." He shivered suddenly, "I almost forgot; he had every intention of killing us if we didn't go away timidly and never mention Colton again. When I told him I didn't even know his name, that's when he cut my face and told me I'd never forget it. I haven't so far."

"So he basically knew everything about Colton's activities and your intentions. He had to be pretty well connected just to know that much." Hal glanced at Carmen before adding, "I'm not so sure you and Dom were supposed to leave that volcano park alive Willy."

"Yeah he did seem to know everything come to think about it. I wonder if he might have big dog connections with the Sandinistas? Maybe we need to check in with Bob Matthews; I bet he'd know," Will said as Hal reached for the sat phone.

"So you gotta be shitting me; Enrique Constanza was tight inside the Cali cartel?" Hal asked in disbelief. "Some Agency nerd said the Medellin Cartel was headed up by the real antichrist."

"No Hal, he's not just tightly connected, he was their *Celeno* for Transshipment, responsible for the safe passage of product from Colombia all the way to the New York City," Matthews told them as the new dimension of the hit at Masaya Volcano Park registered. "He just had a mansion in Managua as his *pied-à-terre*; sorta halfway between the labs and wholesale customers."

"Holy shit; then why would he be concerned about a priest looking into kids not attending school? How much blow do they flow through that port close by?" Will wondered.

"From what my guy tells me, some of the kids were lookouts for the cartel shipments. The local port Masachapa is a big hub—think five hundred keys a week big—and Constanza saw the danger to his operation if the international press came looking into Bolt Sportswear's tee shirt factory. But the bad news doesn't stop there. Enrique Constanza is the brother of Hector Constanza, the head of the Cali Cartel. Those are some mean hombres brother," he told them, and they could hear the '*phew*' in emphasis.

"Well that would explain how he prophesied that my brother would die in prison of an accident," Will said, putting two and two together. "Is there any way we can put a shield around Colton? Or do you think Enrique Constanza's demise will put a damper on their efforts?"

"It'll be temporary at best. When his brother Hector figures out what happened, all hell will break loose. The cartel's money can buy anything around here Will, sorry."

"So how long do you think we've got; days, weeks, hours?"

"Who knows? The sooner we can do something to help your brother the better," Bob warned. "But we ain't gonna be out on the windy corner by ourselves bro."

Hal was instantly on top of Matthews, "What the hell does that mean? You didn't call anybody in the Agency did you? Tell me you didn't give that fucking Lindstrum another chance to fuck with us, please?"

"No Hal, we know he's the plague and avoid Marty whenever possible. I spoke with a mutual friend at the Stockade; as a matter of fact, he said to say hello…"

"Tony Franklin?" Hal asked, amazed and a little concerned. "What interest do the snake eaters have in our little issue south of the border?"

"It would seem that our Hector Constanza has approached Umberto Rodriguez seeking an alliance. Rodriguez is Commander of the FARC-EP, in case you didn't know," Matthews provided as Will shook his head at the multiple tentacles this simple snatch appeared to be growing.

Hal was trying to weave together the common threads, "So the fact that the Cartel has allied itself with the FARC has the Cali guys on the Delta's radar screen?"

"You got it, and they are in-theater Mr. Rayfield. The snakes have eyes and ears on Constanza now, who rarely travels but is in Costa Rica at the moment…"

"So you're saying he's getting closer to Managua because of this snatch? What the fuck are we walking into Bob?"

"No, he's relaxing at a very private beachside mansion with his mistress. What gave Tony pause is that Hector's shadow bodyguard Aleandro Muñoz wasn't with the boss in Costa Rica."

"Well, somebody's got to guard the fort while the boss is away playing, right?" Hal posed as Carmen rolled her eyes. "So Tony's got eyes on Constanza in Costa Rica?"

"Yep, but I wouldn't draw any hard conclusions that's connected to Colton Kavanagh; Tony thinks the Cartel will become direct players in their little war with FARC at some point."

"Okay, Rico and his 'girlfriend' are heading your way to reconnoiter things. How about look out for him when they get down. We gotta start planning for a bust-out if we can," Hal advised.

"As much as I hate to admit it, I think you're right to push the envelope on this. Those cocaine cowboys are the worst I've seen. And you know what kind of crazies we dealt with in 'Nam. Those Korean mothers might have been brutal when they skinned Cong alive, but these cartel dudes have their Colombian necktie for stoolies. Look it up bro, it ain't pretty. I'll be on the lookout for Rico. This one ain't looking like a walk in the park partner," Bob said in parting.

"Hi Rosita, have you been able to interest *Caritas Argentina* in a Lutheran priest being held incommunicado in Central America?" Will asked once he'd gotten their contact in Buenos Aires on the line.

"I'm sorry to tell you this Will, but *Caritas Argentina* has limited reach within their organization's charter," she reported.

"Well, that's not exactly what I was hoping to hear," he replied, fighting back snippets of hopelessness.

"However, a certain Roman Catholic Archbishop has enlisted his counterpart in Colombia to intercede on behalf of the family of Colton Kavanagh with the Sandinista Junta," she added, all but stunning him.

"I see, and how did this intercession take place, and when?"

"I believe the request for clemency was delivered to the Junta for National Reconstruction this afternoon. Is that responsive enough for you?"

"Man, I'll say; remind me to get *Sara Smile* put on the next time I see you. I owe you a dance *Senorita* Tourism Minister!"

"What a flattering thought Mr. Kavanagh, but I suggest you coordinate that with our friend Daniel. By the way, *Tio Guillermo* passes along his best wishes regards your brother's plight."

"Please tell the Archbishop that I am deeply in his debt. Once again, he has proven himself as a caring person who will go the extra mile for humans in need."

48

AN EYE FOR AN EYE

"YES JOSÉ, ALEANDRO INDICATED that you had some important information for me," Hector Constanza said from his patio overlooking the white sand of Cocles Beach in Puerto Viejo, Costa Rica. He was stroking the hair of a beautiful Venezuelan woman who was focused on her efforts to facilitate another erection.

Consuela Diaz, his dark-haired mistress, was also the wife of Colombian Foreign Minister Gianfranco Diaz, as well as the mother of their two children. With her husband away at the Organization of American States' week-long workshop at the newly created Inter-American Court of Human Rights, she was free to take the children home to Caracas, or so everyone else thought. After pursuing Consuela doggedly for two years, she was finally tempted to 'test the waters' when she discovered Hector was in a torrid affair with the gorgeous Colombian television star Marta Cruz. He had been the beneficiary of unknown jealousy, but now he and Consuela were deeply in love. It was more than a little ironical that Gianfranco was attending the OAS workshop in San Jose, Costa Rica, while Consuela and Hector were ensconced on the beach at Limon, a mere seventy-five miles east on the Caribbean coast.

"Indeed *Señor* Constanza, I have some good news indeed. The Justice Ministry has decreed that Colton Kavanagh be moved from the San Bracinto maximum security prison to a minimum security facility some twenty-five kilometers north in Tipitapa as a humanitarian gesture. It would seem the Junta reacted to a Clemency Appeal from the Archbishop of Colombia, for some reason."

This was indeed good news, but Hector didn't understand the link to the activist priest Villaponteau. He had already dispatched Aleandro Muñoz, his most trusted bodyguard and security advisor, to Managua in anticipation of an opportunity to snatch Colton Kavanagh. Rivas had promised to work a means of getting access, but the Holy Roman Church had intervened instead. "I take it you have already communicated this to Aleandro; he is my eyes and ears in Nicaragua now José."

"I did so as you ordered *Señor*, but he insisted that I call you with the news. The move is scheduled two days from now, and I have alerted *Señor* Munoz as to the details of the prisoner transfer," Rivas related, feeling a little more comfortable communicating with the Colombians now.

Hector was already aware of far more details of the transfer and its interception than Rivas would ever know of, especially dead. He did not know who had gotten to the Catholic Archdiocese, and this might become critical intel as the scheme Hector had planned for William Kavanagh played out. "So José, are there any rumors on the ground there in Managua about who asked the Archbishop to intercede?"

"We assume it came from the missionary's family, but the Appeal for Clemency was jointly requested by both the Archbishops of Colombia and Buenos Aires. From reviewing William Kavanagh's passport, it was noted that he had been in Argentina for at least nine months before coming to Managua," Rivas reported.

Hector thought out loud in front of an underling for once, "But Kavanagh is Protestant and he is married to an African Muslim woman. I must look further into this matter."

"Comandante Ortega was in touch with the Cuban," Rivas reported as Hector's attention shifted so swiftly he pushed Consuela off of his lap.

"Yes, and what did Silvio Corrales have to say?"

"It would seem that William Kavanagh and his associates were in North Africa before heading to Argentina, where he and his close friend had major surgeries for battle wounds. Apparently the Argentines greatly rewarded *Señor* Kavanagh's courage for having killed the Barbary warlord Sandrigan el-Boukhari. They made him a hero of Argentina, so the Cuban presumes Kavanagh made close friends with their bishop during his stay there."

"Excellent field work José," Hector told him, almost regretting that Rivas had only forty-eight hours to live. "Aleandro advised me that you will be in the lead vehicle for the prisoner transfer to insure no problems, am I correct?"

"*Si Señor*, I will be on my post to insure no problems," Rivas told him, almost saluting at his desk in the Managua police station.

"*Muy buena* José, now we can proceed with teaching this would be hero a lesson he will not live to regret. Goodbye José," Hector said and hung up. There was something about the way he had said 'Goodbye José' that froze Rivas' blood. He shivered and wondered if Buckwheat Kavanagh would return to Nicaragua to rescue his missionary brother.

———

"You get it?" U.S. Army Special Forces Master Sergeant Ferdinand 'Fergie' Marko asked his man on the camera.

"Yep, got shots of the woman giving him a blow job with the mil-dot right over his heart," U.S. Army Special Forces photographer Staff Sergeant Henry Lopez replied with a nod. "Got the same shot without the reticle too Sarge."

"Good, take a few wider angle to show they're sitting on the patio of the beach house. There won't be any debating this shot Hank, I can assure you," the Master Sergeant said, patting his understudy on the back. They were stationed under a spiny palm mangrove in tropical camouflage ghillie suits a hundred yards south of the mansion. Constanza's guards patrolled along the perimeter of the estate grounds only, preferring not to chance an encounter with the feared Eyelash Palm Pit Viper.

"I'll get a couple of close ups of the faces too in case the boss needs ID placards," Lopez said as he clicked away on the specially modified Nikonos IVA. Nominally a 35 millimeter single lens reflex camera body, it had been transformed into the surveillance gold standard with the 300 millimeter Nikkor Rangefinder lens and lightweight aluminum rail-mounted pistol grip. Attached to the mounting rail was a collapsible stock for the user to brace against the shoulder to stabilize the camera. The trigger on the pistol grip served as the shutter release and advanced the film, but the most dastardly feature was the reticle option on the camera's program nob. There were three options for different types of reticles—the crosshairs in a gunsight—to overlay the exposure, giving the exposed photograph the appearance of a photo taken through a high power sniper rifle scope. The shock value of the option was obvious should its owner choose to utilize it in conjunction with high stakes extortion or blackmail. Lopez looked up at Marko to indicate he had all the shots, "Man, DARPA did one hell of a job on this baby; they took the Soviet Zenit spy kit we got in Medellin and gave it some teeth." The Defense Advanced Research Projects Agency had carefully examined the

KGB Zenit spy camera kit Delta's Cobra Team retrieved from a safe house in Medellin, Colombia, and enhanced it considerably. Not only did the DARPA Long Range Surveillance System have the reticle overlay option, but they had wisely selected the Nikonos IVA, Nikon's latest underwater model, taking environmental considerations out of surveillance in high humidity environments subject to unpredictable rainfall.

"Yeah, let's go make sure that's true. Bravo Squad is approaching from the south to relieve us, so we'll have that film on a plane to Bragg within the hour. Pack it for transit Lopez," Marko said as he glanced to his left to see a tree branch move, signaling their relief was on site.

49

LAST SHOT AT FREEDOM
IN NICARAGUA

"YOU GOTTA BE KIDDING ME? The Sandinistas reacted that quickly? The Holy Roman Church certainly must hold considerable sway with the Nicaraguans," Will all but shrieked when Bob Matthews told him Colton was being remanded to the penal reformatory in Tipitapa, some twenty miles northeast of Managua around the shoreline of Lake Managua. Bob was in his office at the Managua Embassy calling in on a secure line.

"Right, our guy in the Justice Ministry said it's going to take place two days from now. Looks like the perfect opportunity for an interception," he related the obvious.

"Great, what we got in the way of assets Rico," Hal asked, assuming the leader role. He covered the handset and motioned for Will to get on the Gastineau roost house phone and make reservations to Cozumel.

"We've got me, Rose and Bob, along with his two guys. We ought to be able to pull it off with the broken down car routine, supplemented by a school bus blocking the road," Rico reported.

"So how are we gonna get him out of Nicaragua? Are you taking a cruise down the lake again?" Will surmised, shooting Hal the bird. The flight reservations could wait until he knew the latest 'straight skinny.'

"Right, Chico's on standby in Granada like last time. I wish we had someone to trail the prison bus, but I think we can pull it off with what we've got."

"Dammit, Willy and I'd fly down if they didn't have an alert out to shoot us on sight. You sure you got what you need to pull it off? We'll alert Pierson to be on the standby for San Carlos," Hal said, once again assuming the role of George Patton.

"Already done Kemosabe; we'll be practicing for the snatch and keeping an eye on San Bracinto between now and then. Where you gonna meet us?" Rico wondered.

"Cozumel; I'll make the reservations right now after I get off the horn. Good going guys. We'll check back in tomorrow. I can't believe it; we've got a line on springing my brother!" Will said joyfully as Hal shook his head and reached for the scotch.

"You want me to call Alex and Casey and have them come up?" Will asked Dom as he threw a few clothes into a travel bag for the trip to Cozumel.

"No love, Carmen and I will be just fine here looking after Wade. I so hope this rescue comes off without anyone getting harmed," she said as she wrapped her arms around his neck.

He looked at her and grimaced, "Jeez babe, the plan is to ambush a prison van on an open highway. You know that's not exactly a civilized negotiation, but the threat Constanza made has to be taken seriously. I'd rather some prison guard spend a week in the hospital than have to explain to my mother how her son died in a high security prison when he went to Nicaragua as a missionary."

"I know Will; at least we won't have to worry about you being there in the danger. I've almost lost you twice now, and I really don't want to face up to that terror again."

He was about to tell her no sweat when the phone rang, "Just the person I wanted to talk to. Would you care to explain why Dan Pierson streaked out of Zig's office with his hair on fire?" Kelly Dupree demanded with a head of steam.

"Probably in a hurry to get to Cozumel would be my guess. By the way, hello Kelly, how have you been?" He asked, slightly flummoxed by her phone manners. He really didn't want to get into a long explanation about Butila Island, so Cozumel was a destination she was familiar with and was close enough to the truth that he wouldn't need to seek recompense for it.

"I'm busier'n a one-armed paper hanger. Zig didn't even need to use the intercom to summon me when Dan left. He wants to know, and I quote, 'What the hell is Kavanagh up to now?' Care to fill me in, or is this some hush-hush caper?"

"Yeah, I think I'd like to fill you in sweet cheeks, but since that ain't gonna happen suffice it to say that my brother Colton's been arrested for sedition in Nicaragua and the Holy Roman Church has interceded on his behalf. Rambo and I are going down to bring him back home," he told her, hoping against hope she'd buy it.

"Well what do you need Rambo and the Great West chariot for? Doesn't American Airlines fly to Nicaragua? Zig's more than a little curious about this. He still doesn't know about that last 'emergency' airlift flight you had on Great West's nickel. You guys were lucky we were filming that college reunion flick in South Carolina when that happened. So what gives? Come clean with me Mr. Kavanagh; I am your partner in crime you know."

"Dammit woman, I've gotta catch a flight outa Nawlins in three hours and it's a ninety mile drive from here. Okay, here's the deal, and not a word of this to anyone but Zig; Jesus, tell Johnny too if he pins you down. So Colton's gotten himself in the shits down there—totally innocently—and we gotta spring his ass while the window of opportunity is open to us. We really can't get him out on a commercial flight because the 'springing' is gonna piss the Federales off big time. But I've been assured he's gonna die an accidental death in prison if we don't snatch him. So Rambo's the key to whisking him out of Nicaragua from an obscure airfield away from the capitol. Got all that?"

"Can I expect that William Kavanagh is once again going to be playing commando on a dangerous rescue mission? You really shouldn't subject your pregnant wife to such shenanigans at a time like this," she replied, half pissing him off.

"For your information Mother Teresa, Hal, Alex, Dom and I are on the Nicaraguan arrest-on-sight list, so we can't go in as *touristas*. Our associate Rico will be looking after our interests in our stead."

"Rico, you mean Che? Now there's one of your mystery friends I'd like to meet. Alright, I think I've got enough intel to satisfy the boss. He'll probably want to know why I'm not there taking notes."

"No fucking way Jose; your ass stays in Tinsel Town for this one. This is way too shaky to have you on sight distracting the bejesus out of us with that smoking hot bod of yours. I'll make sure Rambo clues you in about the outcome. I gotta go Dupree; keep the sharks off our ass will ya?"

———

"So this is Butila Island huh?" Will said as he looked out the window at the beautiful little Caribbean gem as they turned onto final approach at sunset. It had been a round-robin flight, heading off to North Carolina after picking Hal and Will up in Lafayette, Louisiana. Once at ROUST, Alex, Rico and Rose quickly loaded the Stanley cases and they were back in the air in thirty minutes after taking on fuel. It had been the first time the four commandos had been together since the takedown of Sandrigan's casbah in Algiers, so it was an opportunity to catch up on life as well as show off battle scars. In a rapid and unanimous vote, they had added Dan Pierson as a Director on the board of Destination Partners. This greatly simplified the inevitable discussion that would follow any clandestine operation about how to equitably compensate Dan for his nearly invaluable contributions.

"Yeah, and it gets us within three hundred miles of Managua. It's a shame we can't fly in from here," Rico noted with a sigh as he looked down at the Stanley cases holding the Dragunov sniper rifle, three AK-47s, four Makarov PM pistols and interestingly, an RPG-7 rocket propelled grenade launcher with two high explosive warheads.

It had been an interesting ride in, as Will had never spent a lot of time around Rose Cordes before. "So you actually know Juan Villaponteau? This FedEx pilot had us thinking he was from the dark side when his name first came up down in Buenos Aires."

She gave her characteristic half smile and explained, "That is not an altogether incorrect description of the Archbishop. He was an active proponent of the ELN after the loss of Jorge Torregos in a battle with the Colombian Army. He is very much revered by the poor people because he wages political war against exploitation and indecent wealth among the plantation owners. It is obvious that his influence extends beyond his Archdiocese based on the reaction of the Sandinistas to his overture concerning your brother."

"I gotta tell you Rose; these Holy Roman men of the cloth have been very accommodating of this Lutheran boy from Louisiana. I have been very impressed with their willingness to help."

"That is because you sought their assistance Will. Other *Norteamericanos* do not display the same sense of inter-cultural sensitivity as you," she said, giving him pause.

"Hey, remember Rose, I'm married to a Moroccan Bedouin; she keeps me grounded on such matters. And I believe you would be impressed at how our friend Harold there launched into the Buenos Aires CIA Station Chief with both feet when he accused us of getting in bed with the locals. He won't make that mistake twice! I thought Hal was gonna grab his Colt after that breach of etiquette."

"Ah, you can't equate those spooks with normal humans," Hal interjected. "Let's go meet your buddy Meaux before you ride off into the sunset Ricardo."

James 'Jimbo' Meaux was perhaps the most gregarious and engaging coonass Cajun Will had ever met; easily outdoing Penny Martindale's brothers in Baton Rouge. He was late-thirties with a strong build and his full beard was already showing signs of grey, even though his long brown hair curled without a wisp of aging. He couldn't help but notice that Jimbo was missing the first two fingers of his right hand as he shook theirs aggressively. There really wasn't much you couldn't like about Jimbo Meaux, so Will asked, "Where'd you get that limp Jimbo?"

He pulled up his right pants leg to show them his prosthesis, attached just below the knee, "Lost feeling down there when I tackle-blocked a buddy who was standing on a mine outside Can Tho in '68."

Will shook his head in amazement and asked, "Did he make it, your buddy?"

"He's one lucky *hombre* that he only lost a foot in the deal. You guys thirsty by chance?"

"Damn right, but we gotta get Rico and Rose back in the air before we wear the pilots plum out."

"Give us a call when you get the lay of the land tomorrow partner," Hal said as he gave Rico a bear hug. He looked at Rose, kissed her cheek and told her, "Thanks for helping out down here Rosario. I'll check in on your sister to see if everybody's behaving back at the ranch." Rose's sister Lorena was normally employed as the scheduler and receptionist for the Rayfield Driving School, but covered for Rose at the main ROUST Reception Office when Rose was away for any length of time.

"Hey, you guys enjoy Butila. Rose and I have a boat to catch in San Carlos," Rico told them once Jimbo Meaux' airfield mechanic/jack of all trades got the Great West 727 refueled.

Will looked at Pierson, "You coming back here or heading back to North America Rambo?"

"Nah, after the day this crew's put in, we gotta RON so we'll be laying low in San Carlos overnight."

After they left and the Great West bird was spooling up towards the end of the airstrip Will asked, "I never met the sister, Lorena you said? What's she like?"

"Lorena? Oh she's too hot for you to go out on a decoy trip with, that's for sure," Hal related.

"She's too hot huh? So why isn't she down here with Rico? Seems like she might make a more believable married couple with Rico, don't you think?"

"Don't even go there partner. Rico's wife was brutally tortured and murdered by Castro's thugs when she wouldn't give him up, and he's been very careful to avoid getting serious with any woman since. He thinks that if he allows himself to fall in love with a woman that she gets a big bull's eye painted on her back. Besides, Lorena's not battle-tested; she does a hell of a job for us back at the School though."

Will considered this for a moment. "Sex without love huh? It could be worse ma man; I flourished in that mode for a full year in the Philippines, but it's gotta be a drag over the long haul though."

"Rico gets his share of the women buddy, don't go crying for him."

"Yeah, I bet. Our friend Kelly seems to be intrigued by him."

"Well maybe we'll just have to see how the two of them hit it off sometime," Hal agreed.

"Right, with their schedules it'd be like the planets aligning or something. Hope springs eternal though."

———

"So what do we have, ladies and gentlemen?" Hal asked to open the call between he, Alex, Jimbo Meaux and Will at Butila and Bob Matthews, Rico, Dan Pierson and Rose in Bob's office in Managua. The thought wasn't lost on any of them that they had more firepower cooling their jets on Butila than on the ground in Managua, where they were desperately needed. Pierson had made a last minute decision at the airport in San Carlos to join the ambush team, and once again Will could only admire his gallantry. The Great West 727 had then returned to Butila to await the extraction alert.

"Okay San Bracinto is located about two miles southeast of Managua off of the Masaya Highway. The only route that makes sense is Nicaraguan Road 11, the direct route to Tipitapa and the minimum security facility. About a mile up from the Masaya Highway intersection there's this crook in the road as it passes through some low hills. That's the place to hit 'em," Rico reported.

"Yeah, sounds about right. What's the tactical plan? I presume Rose is gonna be along the road in the broken down car spewing smoke from under the hood?" Hal opined.

"Correct, and Bob found us a 'borrowed' dump truck that can stop the prison van even if they try to ram us. Rose scatters fleshettes under the prison van if they sense a trap and go for it. Pierson's the hotshot with the M79 grenade launcher with tear gas that'll incapacitate the riders in the van. As long as we don't have traffic showing up at the wrong time, I'd say we've got a good chance to pull this off."

"You may want to use one of your guys as a road blocker from whichever direction the predominant traffic flows that time of day. Speaking of which, when's the move taking place?" Will asked.

"Firm ETA is 0930 based on the Justice Ministry's memo, so we'll set up no later than 0800 in case they get unpredictable."

"So all's well in the world eh?" Will wondered, trying to imagine what could fuck up. "Are there any flies in the ointment?"

"Only that your fan club president Lieutenant Rivas has been instructed to accompany the van to make sure your brother gets to Tipitapa safely," Rico advised.

"Alright guys, it goes without saying that Willy, Alex and myself would rather be there with you than here, but it sounds like a good plan. How close hold is the plan to move him? Have the Sandinistas told the Archbishop it's a go?" Hal wondered.

"No, it's tightened up within the Justice Ministry. The last thing they want is to have to tell the Archbishop that they lost Colton enroute to the country club," Bob explained.

"Alright then, it sounds like Bob's got one hell of a mole in the Justice Ministry. Call us on the LST once you're underway across the lake. Good luck and Godspeed ladies and gentlemen. I owe you one big time," Will said as they closed off the satellite link.

50

SLIDING SIDEWAYS IN NICARAGUA

"SLOW DOWN RICO, what the fuck happened?" Hal asked as they sat in stunned silence around the LST on Butila the next day around noon.

"There was another ambush squad, and it was bigger and badder than us, I can tell you that," he said, obviously upset.

"Jesus Rico, is everyone alright? Any casualties? Where's Colton?" Hal asked in rapid fire as Will's stomach turned sour.

"Yeah, we're fine, but that's only because the prison van got jumped a couple of hundred yards before it even made it to Rose's broken down Datsun. Jesus, there were two Suburbans flying down the highway from Tipitapa and they formed a wedge to block the prison van on the highway. Marco, Bob's guy, was following the prison van as a traffic shutoff, but another Suburban blew past him and hemmed in the prison van. Altogether there were a dozen armed shooters and they didn't come in light. The trailing Suburban had a sun roof they popped a .50 caliber machine gun out of to ward off evil spirits. It was something to behold Kemosabe, sorry," Rico explained.

"So what happened to Colton? They didn't kill him, did they?" Will asked with foreboding.

"No, he was the prize the ambushers were after. We were looking at the whole thing through binoculars, and the prison van seemed to stop almost voluntarily. Strangest fucking thing I've seen in a long time, but that Lieutenant Rivas seemed to know the kidnappers because he was walking towards them smiling. The attackers in the trailing van got out with AK-47s and promptly shot the driver and the guard in the back of the van, then grabbed Colton and put him in their Suburban. Then the real ugliness began. Those guys are real animals boss," Rico said as they looked at each other bewildered.

Knowing that Pierson, Rico and probably Matthews had seen some grisly stuff in and around Vietnam, Hal asked him, "What kinda real ugliness? Did you see this too Dan?"

"Well, it was at least as bad as the ROK guys in the Central Highlands boss. Two guys held that Lieutenant Rivas while another cut his clothes away. The lead ambusher then came up and did something we couldn't see, but the next thing we heard was a gunshot and Rivas was on the ground," Pierson told them.

"Sounds like they shot him, but what was taking the clothes off about?" Hal said, shivering slightly remembering the 'Colombian necktie' Matthews had told them about previously.

"Jesus boss, when we got up there after they left, Rivas was lying on the pavement naked, his genitals in his mouth, shot through the forehead and Will's passport on his chest. They cut him up pretty bad, which we assume means they were displeased with the job he did protecting Constanza's brother," Pierson reported, but everyone could tell it hadn't been pleasant to witness.

"Damn, how could you know that? Did they look like Colombians or something," Hal asked, although Will wondered what Colombians looked like, as opposed to other Central American natives.

"No, Kavanagh's passport had a note clipped to it, that's how we figured it was the Colombians."

"So what'd the note say?" Will all but shouted in pure panic.

"I'm reading it right now, and it says, 'An eye for an eye. The Jesuit is your recompense. From your friends in the South.'"

"Sounds like the shit's gonna hit the fan down there brother, let us know when you're in the air. We'll launch the freedom bird straightaway," Hal told him.

"Okay, see you guys this evening," Rico said as he signed off.

"So what do you got Bob? We just got off the horn with Rico and Dan Pierson," Hal asked once they had Matthews on his office phone.

"Damndest thing I've seen lately. Talk about a double cross! The snatch was obviously set up in advance through Rivas, but man did that bastard get the surprise of his life! The Sandinistas apparently don't know what's happened, as there are no advisories or BOLOs out on the wire yet. Based on that note they left, it would appear Hector Constanza expects Will to come take his brother's place. What a fucking mess!" Bob exclaimed.

"You are the master of understatement Mr. Matthews. We'll be in touch; I'll be curious about the chatter this causes amongst the Sandinistas. It sounds like our area of operations has just broadened into Colombia. Thanks for the help today. Things could have worked out even worse if we'd been the first to stop the prison van. You tell the *Chargé d'affairs* about this?" Will asked.

"No way Jose; he'd freak fucking out. This ain't no game for the timid. Let me know if I can help you out with anything in Nicaragua compadre. And good luck with finding your brother."

51

WHEN THERE REALLY IS
NO TOMORROW

"Okay," Will said, the four of them leaning over the huge detail map laid out across Jimbo's ping pong table, "it looks like it's at least a thousand miles between Butila Island and Cali, Colombia. We can use Butila as our base, but we're gonna have to have a tactical jump-off point somewhere closer in; any ideas?"

"Jesus Willy, what do you think we're gonna do, invade 'em?" Hal snarled.

"Of course not, at least not on a large scale basis. We're gonna have to figure out how to exploit existing political differences if we're gonna have a snowball's chance in hell of surviving these nasty bastards. Watching 'em cut your dick off and stuffing it in your mouth ain't my idea of a vacation brother. So the question remains, do you guys know of any friendly oasis between Butila and Cali?" Will reiterated.

"Well, I spent a couple of months at Fort Davis in Gatun before I went back to 'Nam. That was the Special Forces jungle training base. It's at the Atlantic end of the Panama Canal near Colón. I'm not sure if we're still there with this Canal turnover and all, but it'd sure be a decent staging base if we had to be nearby for whatever. That is, other than being on an aircraft carrier off the Pacific coast of Colombia," Alex advised.

"Fort Davis huh? Sounds like an Army base," Will pondered. "You got any residual contacts inside the fraternity brother?" he asked Hal. "I thought Bob Matthews mentioned some buddy of yours when he told us we were not out on the windy corner alone."

"Hell yeah, Tony Franklin's my main man at Camp Mackall. If this Ft

Davis is being used, he'll know about it. If not, I'm sure our Delta brothers have a tactical base somewhere south. But what are we gonna do when we get there Willy, twiddle our thumbs?"

"Dammit you're right; here we go with air support again," Will moaned, remembering the struggle to get Mustafa's men into Algeria.

"That's one thing I admire about the Deltas, they get the best rides known to man," Hal replied with a shrug.

"I guess we need to check on the availability of helicopters while we're at it. Now I see why force projection's such a bitch, that is if you ain't got a handy aircraft carrier you can send in," Will grumbled.

"And what exactly do you need a helicopter for Willy? If we ain't invading the place, what's the plan? Help me out here brother. Oh, and we'd better tell the women something about this too," Hal said, adding to the complexity needlessly.

"What we're gonna need the chopper for is hotfooting our asses out of there once we grab Colton, but I ain't worked out all of those details just yet General Eisenhower. Why don't you call your Zen master at Camp Mackall and see what the possibilities are down south, and I'll get the women on the horn and hustle them on down here to Butila. You know they ain't gonna wanna hang around Gastineau when the action's down here."

"Alright, I'll make the call, but we ain't engaging the gals in the shit this time around. Jesus, when does all this crap calm down enough to have a family, that's what I wanna know?"

Will glanced at Jimbo and Alex—both confirmed bachelors—and replied, "Look around and tell me if you see anybody to answer that question oh wise one. And don't forget to ask the Delta Prince about helicopters while you got him on the phone!"

"I know babe, but there doesn't seem any way out," Will told a distraught Dominique after reporting the straight skinny on developments.

"How can these things keep happening Will Kavanagh? Wasn't Africa enough drama for one lifetime?" She caught herself ranting and then rebounded, "I'm sorry honey, I just hoped we could have this baby in some semblance of peace." He heard some chattering in the background before Dom said, "Hold on, Carmen wants to be in this conversation also."

"Will, I only caught part of that discussion. So these narco-terrorists have your brother and are holding him hostage until you appear?" Carmen asked.

"I have no idea if they're terrorists, but from what I've heard so far, the drug cartel based in Cali has kidnapped Colton. Why, do you know some players in the mix?"

"No I don't, but Rose Cordes is linked into that confusing framework called Colombia, and I would utilize her as a key contact. Have you been in touch with the kidnappers yet?"

"Nah, and I ain't got a clue how to do that. You got any ideas?"

"If it were me Will, I'd stake my life on Rose getting to the kidnappers. If she doesn't know how to get you there, she'll know someone who can. Now where are you and Hal staging your strike from?" She asked, all but shocking him with her insight, knowing they were in Butila.

"Damn, who said anything about a strike?"

"Come on Will, even if you were trying to find a way around it, your partner in crime Harold would have none of it. Since your brother was kidnapped by the Narcos, I take it you'll be focusing on Colombia?" She asked, boring down into his psyche.

"Right, and we're set up on Butila Island off the coast of Honduras at the moment," he replied, helpless against her insightful onslaught.

"Butila Island; that doesn't sound like an airline hub, now does it? In that case, Dominique, Wade and I will be flying to Panama City tomorrow and will reserve a suite at the Intercon. Do you think you can meet us there?"

"Jesus babe, we got some hardware we gotta get in-country, so we gotta work through the logistics before we can make the leap. Hal knows about this army camp on the other end of the canal, and he's talking to his old buddy about it now. So you guys will be at the Intercontinental?"

"Yes, we will be there by sundown tomorrow. I suggest that you and Harold find a way to join us. Dominique and I get concerned when you two spend too much time apart from us together," she intoned.

"Okay, we'll do our dead level best. We'll be in touch after we get a fix on things."

Will looked over at Hal, still hunkered down with his Delta contact on the sat phone, so he made the call he knew he'd regret later if he didn't. "Hey baby, how's your day going?"

"Well it just got better, I'll tell you that. And what are you up to Mr.

Kavanagh?" Kelly Dupree answered from her office in Burbank.

"Get your ass on a plane to Panama," he told her without fanfare.

"And just why would I do that? In case you didn't know, I'm up to my eyeballs trying to keep Mr. Kowalski happy these days."

"Well, when there's no tomorrow, you gotta go where the action is," he told her.

"Oh shit, not that again. Where do I meet you?"

"I might not be there; but Dom and Carmen will be at the Intercontinental. See you soon."

Hal all but slammed the LST headset into the table as he looked at Will hatefully, reached out for the bottle of scotch and relayed, "Ft Davis is there and is still being used, but Tony Franklin says we can't do shit there because the Air Force runs the show in the Canal Zone."

"Well, if the Air Force was to smile on us, could we use the base or not?" Will asked as he looked around for the number for Keith Melson.

"Right, and just who do you know that could sprinkle holy water on that?" Hal groused as he slammed a shot of Johnny Walker Black down.

"Well, it's worth a call to my former Gideon's Angel, that's for sure," he said as he grabbed the LST-5B and dialed up Keith's number in Hawaii.

"Yes sir, that's about the crux of it, but I don't know how things are gonna play out once we make contact with the kidnappers," Will told Melson, who was cleaning his desk out as he prepared for his trip back to DC the next day.

"Okay Will, your lucky star seems to be shining," Melson told him, raising his expectations suddenly.

"How's that?"

"Goodie Stilton just went down to assume command of the Southern Air Division at Howard Air Base in Panama City. I suspect that is his last assignment before retirement."

"Great; he's got a chance to make up for not giving me the Meritorious Service Medal. Let's hope I still have a silver bullet left over from that one. What's his number down there?"

"Here's the number, and I wish you the best of luck. As you know, Goodie's a squared away guy. If he can help you I know he will."

"Thanks much Keith. Lord knows how this'll play out, but it seems that Panama is our land link since we can't call in an aircraft carrier for support.

How's Bob Kellor doing by the way?"

"I just saw him last week, and he's walking without a cane now. He hardly has time to give a turnover to his relief, he's so busy meeting with wealthy restaurant owners in Washington. Man, that wine import business has taken off like a rocket."

"That's good news Keith, but I need to find Goodie Stilton."

"Jesus Will, it doesn't sound like things are calming down for you."

"You got that right, especially with Dom six months pregnant. But hey, when it's your brother's life in play what choice do you have?"

"I can only say best of luck and God bless you Will. Do let me know how things work out."

"Will do General, what would I do without my Gideon's Angel?"

"Let's hope you don't have to find out. Take care and say hello to Dom for me, would you?"

"Will Kavanagh, what in the world are you up to? The last I heard your name you had dodged a bullet big time at a general court martial," Major General Thurgood Stilton asked after Will had satisfactorily played fifty questions with his aide-de-camp. It wasn't until he called the aide a dog robber that he was finally convinced that Will had known the general.

"Jesus General, that seems like ancient headlines sir; but I suppose it was all of a year ago. Since then I got out, reunited with the woman of my dreams, got married and now we're expecting a child in three months. How about yourself General, glad to be rid of DC?" Will asked, remembering that he had arrived at the Pentagon just in time to save him from the wrath of Stilton's predecessor.

"Once again glad to see the Pentagon in my rear-view mirror, and this time it was for good! They offered me this assignment as a peace offering, but enough about me. What can I do for you Will? Forgive me for suspecting you didn't call to check up on my health," he said, effectively ending the small talk and reminding Will he was still a busy commander with a large area of responsibility.

"Actually General, I'm kinda between a rock and a hard spot. My brother Colton was a missionary in Nicaragua until he got across the breakers with the Sandinistas and found himself in the hoosegow. His grievous offense was becoming concerned that some kids couldn't attend school because they were child laborers in Bolt Sportswear's sweat shop. The Sandinistas looked the other way when the Cali Cartel snatched Colton and took him to Colombia. Now we gotta go into Colombia and try and extricate him from the Narcos, and I need a launching spot close to the action."

"Back up, why in the world were the Colombians interested in a missionary? What am I missing here?"

"Oh that, the brother of the head of the Cali Cartel, one Enrique Constanza, lost his mind and put a switchblade to my wife's very pregnant stomach at Masaya Volcano Park outside Managua," he explained.

"Sorry if I seem a little slow here Will, but why did this Constanza character threaten you and your wife? Lost his mind you say?"

"Constanza wanted the two of us to forget about my brother—whom he assured us would meet his death in prison—and leave Nicaragua and never look back. The knife was the final straw though; he made the fatal mistake of asking me if my brother's life was more important than Dominique's and our child's."

"So what'd you tell him? That'd be a tough one on anybody."

"I told him he didn't have the brains to make me to decide just before a 7.62 NATO round caught him in the right eye and took the fight out of him. Fortunately I had backup sir," Will told him, hoping he'd covered the bare facts.

"Jesus Will, life didn't ease up on you when you left the service, I can see that. So what's your plan now?"

"Well, the dead guy's brother, Hector Constanza, is insisting that I come and take my brother's place so that he can exact some revenge for Enrique's demise in Nicaragua. Now I haven't perfected the plan, but at a minimum we're gonna need a staging spot close enough to get a chopper into the exchange site to extract us once the play goes down," Will offered, knowing the details were painfully scarce still.

"So where were you hoping to stage this rescue from? I suppose Panama is the closest land link."

"Right; one of my commando buddies spent some time at Ft Davis when he was a Green Beret and said it'd be as close as we could hope for. Now all of us are former military, either Air Force or Army, so it's not like we're strangers to the bureaucracy. I realize I'm asking for the impossible General, but I thought it'd be worth a try," Will said, hoping he was stating his case with the proper level of angst.

"The cartel's holding your brother eh? I gotta tell you, that don't sound encouraging. Those are some ruthless characters in the cocaine trade, and they seem to have friends in the strangest places. What exactly are you planning to do anyway? You know these cartel types have a lot of muscle around them," he replied, reminding Will that the President of Panama was also rumored to have ties to the cartels.

"We've gotta figure that one out pretty quickly General, but we're also aware of the competitive nature of the two revolutionary groups down there too, the ELN and the FARC. We've got a trusted partner who's still keyed into the framework down there, so we'll use that conduit as best we can. Whatever we do we're gonna need to get out of Colombia quickly once the exchange takes place. I don't see this happening with a handshake sir," he offered. "So is Ft Davis still active? Since Jimmy Carter gave the Canal away I don't have a feel for how the military is deployed down there."

"Actually Will, the Army runs Ft Davis. Tell you what, I know this Colonel Daryl Funstrom, he's the CO of the 101st Aviation Group at Ft Campbell. His guys are in and out of Ft Davis all the time and he'd have a better handle on that. Tell you what, if he questions your credentials, tell him I put you in touch with him and for him to call me if he needs me to vouch for you. As you can imagine, I've gotta maintain a little distance from whatever you do down here, but I want you to know I'm pulling for you to get your brother back. And ideally be alive to celebrate with him. Let me know if you run up against a stone wall with anyone in the military down here, okay?" He offered, and Will was impressed that he'd go that far out on a limb. Perhaps Melson's comment about this being his 'sunset' assignment made him more amenable to things that actually made sense, as opposed to things spelled out in regulations.

"Thank you so much for being willing to listen to my sad tale of woe General. I'm kinda in dire straits at the moment. You should try and find a silver bullet when you really need one; they're not for sale! And I'm sure the mere mention of your name will do wonders at Ft Davis sir. Take care and good luck with the Southern Air Division."

"No, good luck to you Will. Let me know how things turn out; I'll be very interested. And be sure to check your six; this sounds dicey from the word go!"

"Will do sir, but I kinda suspect you'll figure it out from the prop wash when it all goes down. Take care General, and thanks for your help with

Colonel Funstrom."

"That sounded encouraging Willy; who was that anyway?" Hal asked, circling like a buzzard as he finished the call to Stilton.

"That was Major General Goodie Stilton—who pinned the Commendation Medal on me—and he just took over command of the USAF Southern Air Division at Howard Air Base. He'll run interference for us, but it's gonna be indirect from the sidelines. He can't have the shit get on his shoes over what we do, but he put me in touch with this bird colonel that runs an Aviation Group at Ft Campbell. What's with an aviation group stationed at a tank base? I obviously don't understand the Army's organization."

Hal's wrinkled forehead told him he must have said something important, "Damn Willy, I cannot believe it. I know you ain't got a clue, but this Air Force guy just hooked you up with the Army's super specialized helicopter group, and their claim to fame is getting Green Berets and Delta types in and out of hairy places. They're just taking delivery of the new chopper that replaces the Huey of Vietnam fame; they call it the Black Hawk. Let's call the guy; man I cannot believe it!"

"Jesus Hal, try to remain calm. What the fuck are we gonna ask him to do? We ain't got a clue what we're gonna do yet. When are Rose and the guys getting back? We need to hatch a plan and get her plugged into whoever can put us in touch with Constanza. We gotta figure out how we're gonna play this," he said, sobering the brief flash of optimism.

"Dammit you're right Willy. So I guess the first thing we've gotta do is make contact with Constanza…" he was conjecturing before Will rudely interrupted.

"Right, and what are we gonna tell him? That we know he's got Colton and here's our phone number? We gotta think this thing out, and Rose, Rico and Rambo need to be part of the discussion. Hell, they're gonna be crucial to the resolution right? What's their ETA?"

"Not soon enough apparently," he said as they all moved to fix a drink.

Will turned to Rose, "What do you think the next move is Rose? Carmen says you're the key to this whole operation."

"I'd say we need to give them a means for communicating with us. No direct contact; I wouldn't put it past them with their cash to find a way to make a hit if they knew where you were," she replied, immediately impressing him with her ability to boil the confusing situation down to its essence.

"So how do we do that? Even a pay phone can be traced out and watched; any ideas?"

"Sure, we impose upon Archbishop Villaponteau to be our pass-through—at least initially—and communicate with him via an untraceable telephone number."

"Dammit she's right Willy," Hal declared, "we need a commercial satellite phone. One we can have two-way contact without the DC switch and code words being involved."

"I just happen to have one of those," Jimbo Meaux interjected, "do I take it my phone has now become more valuable? You know at five grand a pop they're not cheap."

Will didn't smile as he told him, "Order another one—shit, make it two, no three—as soon as possible. Okay Rose, if we set up this communication path via the Archbishop, what do you see as the next logical move?"

"The ultimatum from Hector Constanza is the only move that counts right now. The thing we need to consider is that after we establish the bridge to Constanza, he is essentially in charge of the timeframe. If there are any actions we can take before we make the link, I suggest we make them," she added.

"I really think we should at least visualize how this scenario will play out," he postulated. "What can we do to improve our position at this point?"

Hal stepped up to the plate, "So let's visualize it. Constanza's gonna set a time frame for us to react to, and it may or may not be negotiable—a la Sandrigan. So what we need to do is anticipate what advantages we need to have when the clock starts ticking."

"Let's think it through; he'll set a time frame for the exchange of Colton for me. Is that gonna take place in Cali? I mean, that's where he's operating out of, right?" Will wondered, obviously clueless.

"No way," Rico interjected, "he'd never set that up in Cali or Bogotá—too crowed and too many Federales looking in. He'll set the prisoner exchange for somewhere he feels safe and away from prying eyes."

"So how many soldiers can he bring to the table? I mean, I understand the power of cash, but how powerful is he outside the manufacturing and distribution systems? Does he lean on any one or organization for support?"

he pondered.

"Of course," Rose suddenly blurted out, "he'll lean on the FARC; they're the ones with the true muscle, outside of the Colombian government. So my guess is the exchange will take place at one of their strongholds."

"That makes a lot of sense. So considering the commercial airline hubs serving Colombia, it'd have to be somewhere near Bogotá the capital, right?"

"Probably within driving distance," Alex added.

"Okay," Will said, leaning across the map once again, "so we strongly suspect it'd be within driving distance of Bogotá since that's where I would have to fly in. Any other thoughts Rose?"

She was smiling when she replied, "Yes, if the exchange is to take place within one hundred miles of Bogotá, our friends in the ELN are within range to help us. I will make contact with them now if it's possible. Can you dial up an international number for me?"

"Sure," Jimbo Meaux said, "why don't we use my satellite phone for this first important call?"

"By the way, since we just ordered three of 'em, what the fuck's a satellite telephone?" Will wondered. "I know what a lightweight land satellite terminal is," he said, pointing at the LST.

"It's a phone that works off of satellites in geosynchrous earth orbit picking up the signal and transmitting it to another phone number," Jimbo explained, showing them a device that looked like a hand-held portable radio with a foot long retractable antenna. "They just came out last year and they're prohibitively expensive, but the signals are encrypted and they're safe to use if you're trying to hide."

After listening to a withering one-sided exchange in Spanish, Rose hung up and said, "My cousin believes the prisoner exchange will occur in Pereira. There is a plantation there belonging to Umberto Rodriguez, the head of FARC."

"Okay, let's say we've guessed right on the interface and allegiances thus far, how do we open the line up to Villaponteau? And how much time do we need to be ready for the deadline? Are you proposing that we make overtures to Villaponteau and the ELN Rose?"

"Oh, we can do it at the same time; Archbishop Villaponteau is well-connected with the ELN. What do you want to propose?"

"I'm really not sure I trust Villaponteau, even though his appeal for clemency got Colton out of the torture chamber at San Bracinto. I think I would prefer the initial contact to him come through Archbishop Acosta in Buenos Aires. I know I can trust him, hell he granted me absolution. Lord knows he may have to do it again before this is all over. Under the circumstances I think he would be willing to make the call to Villaponteau for me," he said and winced remembering his inquiry of Acosta as to Villaponteau's intentions.

"What is it bro?" Hal asked, lighting on his body language.

"Well, in spite of Carmen's warning that I not get diarrhea of the mouth around the Archbishop, I asked him about Villaponteau's militant intentions—based on some rumors Rambo had heard."

"Hey, that might actually play out to your advantage now that your worst fears for you brother have been realized," Rose postulated. "In hindsight, you certainly seem less paranoid than you might have appeared at that time."

"Right," he replied then turned to Hal. "What message do we ask Acosta to pass? I guess we need the time and place for the exchange."

"Jesus Willy, the first thing we demand is a proof of life. Now I'd be shocked if they'd go to all the trouble of snatching your brother and hauling him out of Nicaragua just to kill him. But we gotta start with the understanding that he's still alive. I'd be surprised if Constanza gave up the exchange location with his first play, but that can maybe be a negotiating point based on safety," he provided.

"Safety? Shit, it sounds like he intends on killing me as revenge for his brother's demise, don't you think? I mean, there's the note; I'd say his intent is fairly obvious," Will said, looking at the note and his passport, which now would become a keepsake memento of their Nicaraguan escapade.

Hal rolled his eyes before refocusing on him like a zombie, "I think we got that Willy; I mean we gotta at least make Constanza think it's Colton's safety we're most concerned with. We might can force his hand by insisting that we know where the exchange site is to motor Colton out of there. That should seem like a reasonable request. So why don't you make the call to Acosta and tell him we must have a proof of life and the time and place for the prisoner exchange. As soon as you finish that call, we need to make contact with the Army colonel in charge of helicopters. We need to move our operations base to Ft Davis as soon as possible."

———

"She's doing very well with the pregnancy Archbishop Acosta, and I'm sure she'll be thrilled you asked about her," Will told his mystical link to the Holy Roman Church. He had enlisted Rosita's help in getting to her godfather, extorting her with a promise that she'd get a call from Pierson if she could get him through quickly.

"So my goddaughter tells me that you're brother has been kidnapped and is being held in Colombia. How can I help you in this hour of need Will?" He asked, the sincere piety displayed bringing a lump to his throat.

"Meaning no disrespect whatsoever Archbishop, I don't know Archbishop Villaponteau and I kind of need him to be the interface—at least initially—between myself and the kidnappers, which is the head of the Cali Cartel by the way. But I do know you sir, and I trust you completely; I believe in my heart that you would help me in this very deadly standoff I find myself in. So what I'm asking you for sir is to contact Archbishop Villaponteau directly for me and convince him I'm not some heathen who ripped off the cartel or something."

"Before I make this call for you, tell me what are the kidnapper's demands? Have they already made some overture?" He asked, and Will cursed himself for not providing the critical background.

"I suppose I should give you a quick rundown on the situation Your Grace. My brother was a Lutheran missionary in Managua as an outreach coordinator for children, specifically trying to encourage them to attend church. When he discovered children weren't attending school because they were laborers in sweat shop factories he started meeting with some parents, and was subsequently arrested for fomenting insurrection. When Dom and I went to Nicaragua to see him we were denied access and treated abruptly by the authorities. When we went on a sightseeing trip we were accosted by cocaine cartel thugs who threatened Dom by sticking a knife at her pregnant stomach. A friend who was covering my back shot and killed the cartel leader, and he turned out to be the brother of the head of the Cali Cartel. Now the cartel has snatched my brother from Nicaragua and they are demanding that I be exchanged for him. I assume it is their intention to kill me as an eye for eye retribution. So now we're trying to prepare for this nightmare and I decided the Archbishop would be the safest person to act as my emissary in Colombia. After the initial contacts are made, I assume communications will be made directly between us and them."

"I am very concerned for your safety Will. The cartels are brutally vicious businessmen who show little respect for human life. You mentioned us. I take it you have friends supporting you in this matter?"

"Yes sir, my friend Carmen that you helped retire permanently from SIDE is married to my best friend from high school, and he is highly skilled in the art of combat. He and his friends assisted Dom and me during our problems in North Africa. We really didn't ask for this fight Archbishop, but I can't abandon my brother in his hour of need."

"Of course you can't Will. I will speak with Archbishop Villaponteau about your dilemma, and I feel confident that he will agree to assist you in any way he can. What number can he reach you at?"

"Here's the number sir, and we really appreciate your willingness to help us out. The church is the only organization that I have any faith in when it comes to Colombia. This narcotics trade has infected everything with their guns and money."

"May God look over you and yours in this quest you find yourself involved with Will. I feel confident that Archbishop Villaponteau will be in touch in short order. Take care and please let me know how things turn out?"

"I'll do it sir, and thanks a million."

As soon as he got off the phone with Acosta he turned to Rose and asked, "So when are you going in? I take it you want Rico to go with you as a vacationing couple?"

"I'm afraid your unfamiliarity with Spanish handicaps you Will," she replied, "I would assume you would want Rico with you wherever you must go to help with communication."

"Willy, forget personnel assignments for the moment and let's call this Army colonel at Fort Campbell. If he can't hook us up with a launch pad we're toast so far as any kind of forays into Colombia are concerned," Hal cautioned.

"Alright Kemosabe, Fort Campbell it is," he said as we dialed up the LST, saving the high-priced satellite phone for necessities.

"Yes sir, I completely understand that Ft Davis is an active duty military installation, but I was hoping given the extenuating circumstances you might could allow a visit by some philanthropic activities, you know sir, to maybe help out the poor children of the surrounding barrios," Will pleaded, sweating bullets that the overture to Colonel Funstrom was sliding sideways, much as the failed snatch had.

"Philanthropic activities? I thought you wanted to stage some kind of hair-brained rescue operation out of an active DoD installation?"

"Well, it's a bit of both sir, could you hold on for a second?" Will said as he turned to Hal. "What's that guy's name you know at Mackall?"

Hal raised his hand to slap him, but instead grabbed the handset and launched, "Colonel Funstrom, this is Hal Rayfield and I'm a friend of Will's. We're in this together sir, but I was in touch with Tony Franklin and he…"

"You know Tony Franklin?"

"Sure, Tony and I go way back. All the way back to Cambodia as a matter of fact. Now Tony told me that…"

"Hold on, you're Army aren't you? I've heard your name before. Do you have a friend named Pierson?"

"He's right here Colonel, want to talk to him?" Hal asked, a smile piercing his stone visage.

"My God, your buddy Kavanagh sure has some strange friends. So what exactly do you want to do out of Ft Davis?"

"Fly a chopper in support of a prisoner rescue mission sir. Know of any choppers we might be able to grab a ride on?"

"I'd be court-martialed if I let you involve one of mine, but I just happen to know of a possible link for you. Where are you planning on going Rayfield; how far from Davis?"

"Maximum sortie range is four hundred fifty miles one way in sir. I know that means external fuel tanks for a chopper. What's available from that link you mentioned?"

"Well, this is on the QT, but Sikorsky's doing some testing on the UH-60, you heard of that?"

"Sure, the Black Hawk. Are you guys happy with the new bird? I guess the Huey has its limitations," Hal offered, getting into the exchange.

"The Black Hawk's the rotary wing aircraft of the future; I can assure you of that. Now the Sikorsky guys wanted a humid jungle environment to test their new bird out in, so the Army agreed to provide them access to Davis, which they've been taking ample advantage of. Now if you could come to some understanding with the Sikorsky people, I believe we could authorize visitors to the manufacturer's test site."

"So there'd be no problem bringing in some hardware for them to test out on their airframes?"

"I don't think that's a serious problem, as they're testing armament configurations at our test range down there nearly every day."

"So what's the name of the Project Officer for Sikorsky Colonel? We'll make direct contact since you have no problem with our doing so."

"The PMO guy at Sikorsky Corporate is who you'll need to talk to. His name's Curt Webster, and he's one of us. Here's his number in Connecticut. Just tell him you've talked to me. And good luck with whatever you've got going; General Stilton called and said you guys are on the up and up."

"Thank you Colonel; I'll call Curt Webster. You have a nice day sir!" Hal said in closing, jumping for joy as he hung up the handset.

With renewed vigor Hal looked at Rose and said, "Okay, it's time for you to return to your homeland for a visit Rosario. Why don't you take your new husband Alex with you, eh? Show him around the wonders of Colombia; never know when a sharp pair of eyes might come in handy, right?"

"How am I going to do that? There aren't any scheduled airline flights out of Butila Island," she replied.

"Dammit you're right. I need to grease things with this Sikorsky character. Any of you guys ever heard of a former operative named Curt Webster?"

"Curt Webster? Hell yeah, he's one of us," Pierson responded.

"You know him good enough to enlist his help in our little foray into Ft Davis?"

"Shit yeah, give me the phone."

"Okay, the spook community prevails. Let's pack up and head down to Colon. We're gonna need to take that sat phone with us Jimbo," Hal directed before flinching. Pierson had been the perfect candidate to talk to Curt Webster, as the two of them were reliving Vietnam War stories within a minute of greeting one another.

"And just what are you gonna offer up as collateral?"

Hal looked at Will and gave him the high sign, as he pulled the small cloth bag of diamonds out of his pocket, selected a five-carat beauty and handed it to Jimbo Meaux, "Think this'll cover it?"

Jimbo stared at the rock, walked over to his desk and grabbed a jeweler's loupe, "Damn right, this'll do. Did you guys want me to order some more phones for you?"

Hal flexed his eyebrows, so Will shook out ten more large diamonds and handed them to Jimbo, "Actually, we appreciate your hospitality Jimbo and we owe you for some jet fuel. Think these will get you past cash flow considerations?"

As he examined each of the carbon sparklers he shook his head in amazement, "You guys really know how to strike a bargain. I'll order three more phones, two for you guys. Where you want 'em delivered?"

"How quick can you get 'em shipped?"

"Probably the same time I call 'em; at those prices the manufacturer delivers in a hurry. We're actually tagging on to a DARPA delivery order. You want them delivered to where?"

"Make it our room at the Intercontinental Panama City. We'll have someone to accept delivery even if we're not around. Thanks a bunch Jimbo, you have been a Godsend," Will reported.

"I'd say hold that thought," he rebounded, "you guys haven't taken on the Colombians yet. Lord knows what kind of intercession of the Gods you're gonna need before this is over!" Little did any of them except possibly Rose know how much truth Jimbo had just spoken.

52

FORMING STRATEGIC
RELATIONSHIPS

"IF YOU WERE IN ONE PIECE Jimbo, I'd recruit you to come with us; Lord knows we need another commando for this op," Will told their Butila Island host as they turned at the steps to the Great West 727.

"I'd love to come with you, but my warrior days are just about behind me. I gotta stay here and protect my little piece of heaven. I sure wish you all the best of luck, 'cause you're gonna need every bit of it going up against the Colombians. Let me know if there's anything I can do for you back here. You'll always have a coonass Cajun brother covering your back."

He gave him a bear hug, as did Hal, Pierson, Alex and Rico and then they climbed the steps leading to the great unknown.

As they assumed cruising altitude Will looked at Hal, "What are we gonna do to get ready partner?"

"Priority number one is sex; it's time for overdosing Willy," Hal spewed the first thing that came to his mind. Rose swatted him in the back of the head to emphasize how self-centered his chauvinistic comments were. "You mean aside from what we've already done? Well we've gotta make contact with Bob Matthew's counterpart in Panama and see what he knows about the lay of the land. I've been to Bogotá a number of times, and it's actually a pretty nice modern metropolis compared to the Third World that awaits outside the city limits." He looked around the plane at the crew and began his predictable take-charge bravado, "Okay, I want Rico and Alex to stay at Ft Davis and get synched up with Curt Webster with as many check rides as you can get on the

Black Hawks. Evaluate how we can mount any offensive weapons on 'em, but Curt'll know all about that. Will, Rose and me will fly on to Panama City and get the straight skinny from the Embassy Regional Security Officer—Jesus I hope he's half as good as Bob Matthews. We'll also figure out how to infiltrate and who's gotta go which way once we get the straight skinny. Alex, I want you guys to keep the LST-5B and I hope to God Jimbo's relationship with Motorola is good enough for them to have the sat phones there in time for us to use them on this mission." He reached into his pocket and handed Alex a slip of paper, "Here's the main incoming number to the Intercon, so ring us up about an hour after we're wheels up from Colon."

As he handed off the phone number, their new satellite phone trilled, "Will Kavanagh speaking."

"Hello Mr. Kavanagh, I am Juan Villaponteau and my dear friend Guillermo Acosta tells me that you are in need of some assistance," a pleasant but forthright voice with a noticeable Spanish lilt announced.

"Yes sir Archbishop Villaponteau," Will said loud enough to get everyone's attention, "thank you so much for calling. I am indeed badly in need of your assistance. I trust Archbishop Acosta relayed to you the general nature of our dilemma?"

"He indicated that your brother who is a missionary is being held as a hostage by the Cali Cartel, and that you badly needed a way to get in touch with them about hostage negotiations. Would it be imprudent of me to ask how this occurred?"

"Forgive me for asking Your Grace, but are you speaking on a secure telephone?"

"Actually, I am speaking on an encrypted line reserved for the College of Cardinals Mr. Kavanagh, so please feel free to communicate openly. May I ask where you are at the present time?"

"Yes sir, we're on a plane flying across Honduras towards Colon, Panama. Please forgive me if I retrace things you might already know…" Will was saying when his brain tripped off. "Thank you so much for dispatching the plea for mercy for my brother to the Sandinistas Your Grace. The plea worked, but the cartel snatched my brother while being transported to the minimum security prison. Our team was on the ground watching, and they butchered their Nicaraguan snitch and left the note pinned to my passport saying 'The

Jesuit is your recompense.'"

"I see," Villaponteau offered before redirecting, "please tell me more of this mission your brother Colton was on Mr. Kavanagh."

"Colton was a Lutheran missionary focusing on outreach efforts to bring young children into the church in Managua. When he noticed most that showed for Sunday services didn't attend the school he started, he investigated until he found the ugly truth. He met with some of the kid's parents when it became clear they were working in garment factories as child laborers, and was subsequently arrested for fomenting insurrection by the Sandinista government, actually the day they took over. After your successful appeal to have him moved from San Bracinto, their maximum security prison, he was abducted by heavily armed Cali Cartel soldiers. Constanza's interest in Colton was no doubt triggered by the death of his brother Enrique, who accosted my pregnant wife and me while making a tourist visit to the Masaya Volcano. Before his death, Enrique told us that Colton represented the potential for unwanted international interest in the employment of children in Nicaragua, some of who were no doubt participating as lookouts and such for the cartel. He further explained that this would not happen and that Colton would die in prison from an unfortunate accident. To reiterate the point that he meant business, he sliced my face with a switchblade knife and then held it to my pregnant wife's stomach before an associate of mine took him out with a rifle shot. Now Hector Constanza wants me to travel to Bogotá and take the place of Colton so that he can kill me in revenge for his brother's death."

"I see. First of all, the cartels represent the most vicious and brutal organizations known to man. Is it your intention to go directly to this exchange and face certain death at the hands of Constanza?"

"Actually Archbishop, we were hoping to set in place some plans to improve my odds of surviving this suicide mission and to get my brother safely out of Colombia and back to the United States."

"And how were you planning on preparing yourselves against such overwhelming odds?"

"Well, we were hoping that you'd serve as our initial contact with Constanza, and then hopefully gain some key intelligence from some associates in Panama," Will told him, feeling totally unprepared and inadequate to relay how they could possibly succeed.

"If you will forgive me my impertinence, I'm not sure that merely hoping will improve your odds of succeeding in your quest. I am a native of Colombia and know this country and its culture quite well. Before I make any overture to Mr. Constanza, I would suggest that you and I meet here in Colombia, as it might appear odd if I were to travel abroad on short notice. The port of Barranquilla is a relatively safe place to travel to, away from the cartel activities of Medellin or Cali, and I can guarantee your safety here."

"But what about the ELN Archbishop, I've heard they make most of their cash from kidnapping and ransom," Will blurted, hoping he didn't insult the Cardinal with what were only suppositions.

He actually half-laughed, "I can assure you of safe passage here in Barranquilla Mr. Kavanagh. Let's just say that I know the Ejército de Liberación Nacional hierarchy from past association. We can meet in the Maria Reina Cathedral, which is but a few miles from the airport, and I would like to introduce you to some friends who might be very interested in helping you out with your mission."

Will high-five Hal, "What about tomorrow Archbishop, would that be too soon?"

"Actually, I was hoping you might be willing to come at once. We should not delay making contact with the Cali Cartel for long, but we must formulate our plans before that call is made. Things could move very quickly once their demands become known."

"So you say it's safe, eh? I was gonna leave my wife in Panama City because she got so traumatized when Constanza put that knife to her belly she ended up in the hospital. I'm sure she'd like to meet you sir, the Holy Roman Church has been quite good to us over the past few months."

"Please do bring Dominique," he said, shocking Will, "Guillermo Acosta told me of the blessing he gave the two of you for the child in her womb. I would very much like to see her and report on her progress to Guillermo. There is a ten o'clock COPA flight in the morning that is but an hour in duration. Do you believe you can possibly come to Barranquilla tomorrow?"

"We'll be there Archbishop, as close to ten o'clock as possible, but we'll be flying our own bird for the time being. I am quite fortunate to have a friend in the film industry that provides opportune airlift from time to time."

"Ah yes, Guillermo told me of the splendid things you did in Argentina in conjunction with Great West Studios. *Caritas Argentinas* is forever in your debt for the incredible kindness you showed for the destitute in the slums of

Buenos Aires Mr. Kavanagh. I very much look forward to meeting you and your friends."

"Archbishop, we might as well get this out of the way right now; when you refer to me as Mr. Kavanagh I think about my father. Could I impose upon you to call me Will? That's my name and I'd sure feel more at ease."

"As you wish Will, and please call me Juan. I will meet you at the airport in the morning."

"That'd be most kind of you Archbishop Villaponteau, we'll see you then!"

"So he's on our side?" Hal all but shouted.

"I'd say Acosta worked his magic, and that little 'Help the Helpless' charity project has come back to us in spades partner," Will all but yelled as he went around and hugged everyone, even kissing Rose in his exuberance.

"Will, this is far beyond what you could ever imagine. The Archbishop is a man of extraordinary influence. You said he wants to see Dominique as well? What about safe passage, Barranquilla wasn't the safest port I've ever visited," Rose offered.

"Juan says he's got it wired with the ELN, and they'd never do anything without his say so. Makes you wonder just how closely he's aligned with the Marxists, doesn't it?"

"They are both trying to help the disenfranchised, so I can see where there could possibly be mutual interests in spite of the theological disconnect," Rose said as the LST trilled once again.

"Kavanagh, how may I help you?" Will asked, his game face on.

"You mean like invading another sovereign country?"

Will looked at Hal, "Didn't we say goodbye to Marty the Loser Lindstrum a while back?" Hal let out a 'Fuck Lindstrum' as Will held out the phone before re-engaging. "I'm sorry, but this sounds vaguely like a CIA section chief who didn't want his name muddied with evidence of narcotics trafficking," Will replied as he signaled Hal to get on the remote headset.

"Last week's news Kavanagh; don't be making any travel plans to Colombia in the near future," Lindstrum said unequivocally.

"I'm not sure what you're talking about Marty. What interest does the CIA have in a missionary hostage held by the Cali Cartel?"

"So which devil have you taken a blood oath with this time Lindstrum?"

Hal all but snorted.

"Actually the DEA approached me to warn you the fuck off of any involvement with the Cali Cartel, and specifically Mr. Hector Constanza."

"Let's see, the New York Times was concerned with U.S. Embassy hostages six weeks ago, but they need something new and exciting. How about a front page banner that reads 'CIA and DEA Lock Arms with the Cali Cartel.' Have you started using that poppy powder we gave you or something?" Hal asked in complete disbelief.

"I don't know what powder you're talking about Rayfield, and this time you're pissing up a rope against a National Security Finding. Now put that in your pipe and smoke it," Lindstrum replied as they heard him lighting a cigar.

"I'm dialing the Times number right now Marty unless you can concoct some bizarre scheme that doesn't sound as if it were hatched at Timothy Leary's acid factory," Will added.

"It just so happens, even though neither of you are cleared to know this, that the U.S. government has hatched a deal with the Colombian National Police to begin eradication efforts of the endemic coca overgrowth in the southwest Andean provinces of Colombia. Now if you've got the number of Jimmy Carter, go right ahead and call him; but this is his pet project. Sorry, you lose. And you've been formally advised by the US government not to interfere, so you can call off whatever little escapade you've got planned down in Juan Valdez country."

"I hope you're in your office motherfucker, because your ass is gonna get a call in ten minutes. Fuck you!" Hal shouted with extreme animosity as Will ended the call.

Hal looked at Alex and said, "You got Bernie Jepson's number handy partner? We're gonna stick a hot poker up Lindstrum's ass he'll never forget!"

———

"Yes sir General, sorry, General Selectee, Hal Rayfield here, how are you this fine day?" Hal asked once he'd sweet-talked Jepson's first shirt into passing him through.

"Hal Rayfield, I'm not sure I know that name. Oh yeah, it's coming back to me now; I've got a steel plate in my shoulder from my last encounter with you, you sorry scoundrel. How in the hell are you?" The departing Commander of the Army's Airborne School at Ft. Benning, Georgia, replied. Rambo had provided the intel that Colonel Jepson was on his way to Ft.

Bragg to take over the 7th Special Forces Group and the 1st Special Forces Operational Detachment-Delta. Between the 7th SFG and Delta Force, Jepson commanded the only reputable counterintelligence force in Central and South America.

"Are you presently at Ft. Benning or Bragg sir?" Hal pursued.

"Neither; let's just say I'm in transit. How can your country serve you today Mr. Rayfield?"

"As usual General, I wouldn't interrupt your busy day unless I had my knickers in a knot. You remember prickhead Lindstrum, don't you?"

"That motherfucking excuse for a human? Is that the Lindstrum you're referring to? What the fuck did he try and do to you this time?" Jepson asked, and Will was blown away at the rapport Hal had with him.

"This buddy of mine named Kavanagh is trying to put together a rescue op to get his missionary brother away from Hector Constanza of all people. Hector wants to trade the brother for Kavanagh so he can give him a Colombian necktie. Pierson and I are going in to try and convince 'em that's a bad idea, and save the Kavanagh boys at the same time. So Lindstrum calls and tells me there's a National Security Finding to eradicate coca plants that cover the mountain sides down there and we are forbidden from doing a goddamn thing regards the Cali Cartel. Now have you ever heard such shit in your life General? Hell, we'll all have a good shot at getting killed during the op, but we can't leave a missionary down there with the cartel heathens. Whatdya think?"

Jepson suddenly became serious, "I actually know about that; those DEA assholes are leaning on the Ft Campbell copter spooks to pull it off and reducing my available assets. So where are you having to go get the brother from? As I recall, the eradication effort is in the far southern parts next to Ecuador and Peru."

"Exactly General, but do you think Lindstrum wanted to know that? Hell, we paid him twenty million in heroin for a shitty ride on a C-47 outa Algeria into Morocco as a New Year's present. Our op is gonna be centered 120 miles northeast of Bogotá for Christ's sake, 250 miles from the nearest paraquat spraying. You know those bastards, if they don't come up with the op they're obstinate obstructionists. Think you can get him off our backs?"

"Hmm, sounds like you're gonna be using mobile air assets. How the hell'd you get around Daryl Funstrom? I know he'd have a hard time with unsanctioned ops."

"Kavanagh knew this guy Stilton down here at the Air Division, so Funstrom didn't tell us just to go to hell when we called. He put us in touch with Curt Webster, do you know him?"

"Hell yeah, he's the project guru on converting the Black Hawks into offensive gunships. Don't tell me you got him on board?"

"Jesus General, he's one of us for Christ's sakes! Of course he's on board. As a matter of fact we're on our way down to Ft Davis right now. I talked to Tony Franklin about Davis a couple of days ago. Webster's gonna put our guys through training on some Sikorsky birds he's got down there. He's even got external fuel tanks to make the jump over into Colombia. Think you can pull the rug out from under Lindstrum for us? He's the fly in the ointment at the moment."

"More like the turd in the bathtub. Don't you worry about a thing Sergeant Rayfield; I'll take care of Marty Asshole Lindstrum so far as your little operation around Bogotá is concerned. By the way, Tony Franklin's been keeping watch over *Señor* Constanza for me until I get seated at Bragg. Were you by chance aware of that?" Jepson asked with a hint of the devil in his voice.

Now Hal was tap-dancing, "Bob Matthews—another graduate of the Laotian insanity—kind of let that out the bag by telling us we weren't standing out on the windy corner all alone regards Constanza. Does that mean you're willing to help a couple of your famous graduates extend their life expectancy with some shared intel?"

"Goddamn it Rayfield, let me get into my new office before I commit to selling the barn with the cows in it. Now do me a favor and tell Dan Pierson that I expect the two of you to come by Bragg and have a drink with me; got all that!"

"I got you loud and clear sir, we will be there for the drink—if we're still alive. Thanks a million General!"

———

"Hey baby, how's the hotel?" Will asked an effervescent Dom as she answered the phone in the penthouse suite of the Intercontinental Panama City.

"It is wonderful Will, when are you going to join us?"

"Who's us by the way? I was expecting a couple of visitors," he inquired.

"Us is Wade, Carmen, me, and Kelly. All we're missing are the husbands;

where are you?"

"We're on final approach into Colon; that's on the other end of the Panama Canal from you. After we drop off Alex and Rico we'll be zooming your way. Man am I ready to see my baby?"

"Is that so? Did you forget that I am now twenty pounds heavier than when I was your formerly seductive bride?"

"Well, you did say that Kelly was there, right?"

"I am going to make sure you never have sex again after that remark Mr. Kavanagh! How dare you insult a fat pregnant woman in such a manner," she said with some venom.

"Hey, I was just testing your mood; I've got a head of steam built up for my Bedouin chickadee. We should be landing in about 30 minutes, how about put Kelly on."

"Hold on, she's about to beat the phone out of my hand."

"Well, it's about time you came up for air Mr. Kavanagh. What's so important that I had to leave LA for? Mr. Kowalski's about to bust a gut waiting to hear back from me."

"Keep panty hose on Dupree, all will become clear very soon. And I'm putting your ass on the fastest chopper known to man for the extraction. Bring any film with you?"

"Fifteen rolls. By the way, do you know an Adam Chennault? He's called twice looking for you."

"You have got to be shitting me! Call his ass back up and tell him he's gotta be at our suite in forty-five minutes. And I don't care if you've got to go seduce him to get his ass over there; he's got critical information on Constanza and it could be the difference between me living or dying on this suicide mission we're about to jump square in the middle of."

"So take one for the team, is that what you're telling me?"

"Kelly, I don't care if you have to give him the electric blow job, just do it inside forty-five minutes. I, no we, need to hear what that guy's got to say. Think you can do this for your Midnight Cowboy?"

"He'll be here, trust me. See you in forty-five cowboy."

"Hey, how about put Carmen on the phone," he asked, remembering a critical point.

"Hello Will, what can I do for you?"

"I can't answer that question in present company Belen, but let your imagination ramble. Jimbo Meaux ordered up a couple of newfangled satellite phones for us and they were supposed to be delivered to the hotel suite. Have you by any chance seen them?"

"Those things are the most interesting toys I've seen in years. And for your information they are presently plugged up with their AC adaptors charging up the batteries. Where in the world did you get them? I've never seen anything like them."

"They cost us some very hard carbon sparklers, but we'll need them soon enough; see you guys in a few."

53

INCUBATING A BLACK OP
IN PANAMA

"Wow, you missed me that much?" Will said as Dom smothered him in the master bedroom of the penthouse suite.

"When you leave me these days William, I never know when you're going to return, if at all. Now do you think you can entice a fat, pregnant woman with the emancipated fulcrum?"

"I take it that's the pregnancy variant of the elevated fulcrum?"

"I'm sure my problem solving engineer can see the angles, *n'est pas?*"

He was flexing his eyebrows, "Never up, never in my dear."

He was beginning to wonder if their child was experiencing trauma as Dom orgasmed so hard, but relaxed once he heard the heart beating in her stomach once they'd concluded. "That's one tough cookie we've got there Dom; no mere orgasm's gonna scare him away!"

"It's a her, and I should think she enjoyed it as much as her parents did. Now who is this Adam Chennault that you're so interested in that you sent Kelly out on a call girl assignment to abduct?"

"He's the key to the future; that is if he's got his shit together. Bob Matthews said he's the man in the know down here, so I'm expecting a lot out of him to prepare us for our Colombian adversaries."

When Kelly walked in she had a hateful scowl on her face, totally ignoring the man walking behind her, presumably Adam Chennault. Adam was late forties, somewhat overweight with a bald head and a reddish beard. With the eyeglasses he looked like a government computer nerd, but Will offered his hand, "Adam Chennault I presume?"

514

His attitude changed abruptly as he grabbed Will's hand, "Glad to finally meet you Will. Bob Matthews all but threatened my life if I didn't brief you the minute you stepped foot in Panama."

"Bob's a good man; he saved my bacon more than once in Managua. How do you know him, State Department?"

"Oh no, I was his comm guy back in Laos. He insisted that I inform you 'I ain't one of those Foreign Service Officer flunkies.' So I understand you're going to have to go up against Hector Constanza; man I do pity your ass!"

"Yeah, that's what I've got to milk your brain about. Tell me about Constanza; where from, how he worked up the line, what he's worth now, family, friends, mistresses, we need the whole ball of wax."

As Hal, Carmen, Dom, Pierson, Kelly and Rose circled around the table Will signaled for Pierson to fix the drinks as Adam began his tutorial. "Okay, Hector Constanza was born in Armenia, in the middle of the Colombian coffee triangle, one of seven kids in a coffee harvester's family. He grew up in the coffee fields and attained some notoriety for his energy and loyalty—apparently he didn't skim like the other pickers did. He became a trustee to the supervisor at age twelve and grew into a trusted subordinate until one day he witnessed his supervisor get shot by a FARC scout who became incensed when the supervisor refused to pay a tax for a shipment of coca leaves traversing his plantation roads. You all know what FARC is, right?"

Kelly immediately jumped in, "No, what's a FARC?"

He smiled at her, making Will wonder what she had to do to induce him to the meet, "The *Fuerzas Armadas Revolucionarias de Colombia—Ejército del Pueblo*, also known as the Revolutionary Armed Forces of Colombia—People's Army, was inspired by the Latino liberator hero Simon Bolivar and had as their roots the Marx-Lenin socialist philosophy of the proletariat rising against the bourgeoisie. Anyway, after the supervisor got killed, the plantation owner made Hector his supervisor and, learning from past mistakes, he made an accommodation with the FARC regarding unimpeded transit through the coffee plantation with their coca leaves bound for the cocaine laboratories further into the mountains. When the plantation owner died of mysterious circumstances attributed to food poisoning, Hector became the de facto operator of the plantation and was made an offer he couldn't refuse to become an adjunct member of FARC."

"This synergistic relationship lasted only until Hector became the owner of several coca processing labs, which were insanely more profitable than coffee growing. Hector was wise enough to maintain the coffee plantations as a front while he developed more coca processing labs, and after narrowly avoiding being assassinated by one of his competitors, he began to grow an armed force for his protection. This armed force defied the FARC from collecting taxes for their transit through his territory, but since they had done business in the past they resolved to allow each other's business to go on without interference since they were dependent upon one another. When the U.S. DEA nabbed Jorge Herrara, the then head of the Cali Cartel, a nominal power struggle ensued and Hector Constanza ended up being the least disliked member among the cell leaders who formed the cartel."

"Hector showed business acumen by convincing the other cell leaders to move their first-stage cocaine processing labs further away from the Colombian National Police—and by association the U.S. DEA—into Peru and Bolivia. Hence the transit pattern became much more simplified by transporting kilos of semi-refined coca paste instead of bulk coca leaves. With this development, the Cali Cartel became focused on downstream distribution and even sent a trusted associate to establish a distribution point in New York City. Hector further streamlined his distribution routes by hiring the FARC as his pipeline policemen, hence the close association between the Cali Cartel and FARC."

"Okay, I have a much better understanding of the rise of Hector Constanza and his relationship with the FARC now regards the cocaine business," Rose intoned. "How is this going to help us with the kidnapping and retrieval of Will's brother?"

Adam smiled and continued, "In the course of his business ventures, Hector met and fell in love with Mariana Manrique, the daughter of the mayor of Armenia. They made the coffee plantation located between Armenia and Pereira their home and had five children as Hector's stature grew both financially and politically. Seeing the benefit of making important allies, Hector donated $500,000 to the Bogotá Archdiocese with the caveat that the money be used to build a university in Armenia with associated junior schools for the younger children. The hypocrisy of this was amply demonstrated when one of his underlings turned on him during a National Police investigation and was found lying against a police precinct building sporting a Colombian necktie. Are you familiar with this?"

Alex and Pierson rolled their eyes to the heavens but the women were rapt with curiosity, "No, what is a Colombian necktie?

Adam looked to Will for guidance, but he figured they were due the shock therapy and nodded for Adam to continue. "Actually, Hector was one of the first to employ the Colombian necktie as a warning to would-be informants as to their probable reward. The person's throat was slit so severely that the tongue was pulled through the opening in the throat to look like a very bloody and obscene necktie. The point was well taken, as numerous suicides were subsequently unexplained but it was suspected the informants preferred a gunshot to the head as opposed to the agony of the necktie."

"Okay Adam, we're all convinced this guy's a brutal maniac," Will redirected. "So how do we get to him? And hopefully prevent me getting a necktie as my reward?"

He smiled as his eyebrows danced, "Okay, Hector has two known weaknesses; women and the ELN."

"I think Villaponteau is gonna brief us on the ELN aspects tomorrow, but what are the weaknesses so far as Constanza is concerned? We know he was with his mistress in Costa Rica recently," Will offered up without thinking, as Chennault merely stared at him aghast. "Sorry, that's a rumor we heard on the flight in; please provide details Adam."

"The weakness is that he has cast his stake with the FARC with regards to revolutionary causes in Colombia. For one, he grew up around them, and another is that they are predominant in the western part of Colombia. With Cali being along the southwestern section of Colombia, and the FARC pipelining the semi-processed paste from Peru and Bolivia in the southwest, the FARC and the Cali Cartel are almost brothers-in-law. But they still mistrust one another due to the FARC's political agenda and the cartel's purely profit-driven interests. Now the ELN, which you will apparently learn more about soon, have relied to this point on kidnapping and ransom as their revenue-generating activity. As such they are not in direct competition with the Medellin Cartel, and do not attempt to extort taxes from them. The potential for cooperation between the two is, or should be, an item of interest to you in your current impasse with Constanza."

"Okay, we'll take that up with Villaponteau. What about the women thing; who are they and how can we get to them?"

He smiled. ready to launch the *coup de grâs*, "Mr. Constanza, in spite of his pronounced love for his wife and family has always had an eye for beautiful women. Thus far he has been able to contain all aspects of his extramarital affairs."

"Oh really; and who was he hiding the salami with in Limon?" Hal asked in anxious anticipation."

"Gianfranco Dias, the Colombian Minister of Foreign Affairs is married to a gorgeous Venezuelan woman named Consuela. Although the Dias' have two children, Hector has made it his life's ambition to seduce Consuela into bed, and her husband's hectic international travel schedule has apparently served as the perfect window of opportunity. Hector succeeded in bedding the lovely Consuela three months ago during Gianfranco's visit to Cuba to discuss cutting ties to the communist revolutionary groups in Colombia. From the reports I've received from Brad Covington, the RSO in Bogotá, the affair has taken a very serious turn and both Consuela and Hector are very much in love."

Will looked at Hal like they'd been given a Mercedes for Christmas, "So whatdya think about them apples?"

Hal turned to Adam and asked, "Do you have a picture of her?"

Adam was flexing his eyebrows as he pulled a surveillance shot of Consuela getting out of a car, but the enlargement of her face was clear. "Damn, she's a dead ringer for Carmen," Will said before the words registered in his brain.

Hal snared at him, "How tall is she Adam?"

"Oh, she's not very tall by American standards; I'd say five-three or five-four."

He looked at Rose, who was five-three and asked her, "How'd you like to grow another couple of inches and become a blonde?"

"I don't see that as a huge challenge. Do I detect that I am to become Constanza bait?"

"With glasses and a raincoat hood, I don't see it as being that difficult since we're gonna be there during the rainy season. As long as we've got lines of fire covered." Will turned to Adam and asked, "So I guess this Brad Covington knows Mrs. Dias' comings and goings? Does she travel with bodyguards?"

Adam handed him another photograph and nervously glanced back at Kelly. Will looked at the photo, shaking his head in disbelief, "Where in the fuck did you get this pix?" He handed it to Hal and told Adam, "Man, I thought Matthews was on top of his game, but you fuckers actually pulled surveillance on Constanza?"

"Obviously she doesn't have her bodyguards with her at all times. That was taken by the snake eaters hiding under some spiny palm mangroves along the beach at Puerto Viejo, near Limon, Costa Rica eleven days ago." He narrowed his stare at Will, "How'd you know about that already?"

"We're desperate men Adam," Will offered with a grunt. The women were now coming alive as they let out mild gasps. Will smiled at them, "Come on, Hector's not hung that well ladies." He looked at Hal and Pierson, "Think that photo might save my life at some point during the limo ride with Hector?"

"Pull it at the wrong time Tonto, and it might get you and Rico killed on the spot," Hal warned. He looked at the ceiling and nodded, "But if the fucker tells ya he'll kill ya both if you don't provide proof he's other than a righteous married man, you've got your silver bullet."

"Okay, so it gets sewed into the jacket lining." He looked at Adam, "So Bogotá's considered as lethal as a snake pit?"

"Oh yeah, everyone of prominence travels with bodyguards and Kevlar down there."

"What the fuck are you talking about Kevlar? Isn't that what they're making the new military bullet-proof vests out of?" Pierson asked, suddenly alert.

"Hell yeah, there's this tailor in Bogotá that has almost a patent on making coats out of Kevlar fabric and it can stop a nine millimeter parabellum. Not so sure about a 7.62 rifle round, but it'll sure slow one down. I think his specialty is having the ability to cut the fabric precisely and then sew it so that it looks almost like a normal outerwear garment."

Hal was jumping up, "Jesus, what's his name? We gotta go see that guy!"

Thinking through the last hour's discussion, Will asked Adam, "So you said he was a womanizer. Is this Consuela his only squeeze, or does he have an alternate when she's busy with state functions?"

Adam nodded his head, "He actually was banging this Colombian TV star named Marta Cruz, but he seems to have cooled off on her since Consuela's come around to his charms. Man, I'll tell ya, I'd sure like to get close to Marta Cruz—she's smoking hot!"

Will nodded towards Kelly, "Sorta like her?"

Adam frowned before replying, "Maybe, but Marta Cruz might actually be approachable; I think your friend here hates men."

Will knew the devil had him by the balls, but he walked to Kelly, took her face in his hands and gave her a passionate kiss. He leaned back, smiled at her and told Adam, "Are you sure?"

He shook his head in total disgust, "It's late, I gotta go."

"Hey Adam, aren't you forgetting about Brad Covington's phone number? We gotta get ahold of that Kevlar tailor too. And I'd really appreciate it if you'd call him first thing in the morning and tell him we'll be in touch with him soonest. Could you do that for us?"

"You bet, goodnight."

Will reached out to grab his hand, "Thanks a million for the briefing buddy, you have been invaluable. I will remember you for helping us. You might not be Bob Matthews, but you sure know your shit around this neck of the woods, and I appreciate it!" Before he let go of Adam's hand he reminded him once more, "And we need the name and address of that Kevlar tailor."

He actually smiled, glanced whimsically at Kelly and offered, "You're welcome Will."

54

CLOSING THE DEAL IN

BARRANQUILLA

"So THIS IS COLOMBIA, EH? My first glimpse of the land of Juan Valdez?" Will offered as they peered out on final approach into Cortissoz International Airport.

"Actually Will, the coffee triangle is in the middle part in the mountains. This is the original port city of Colombia, and was the capital for decades," Rose advised.

"Looks green and hot from where I sit. It seems like I have a penchant for equatorial lands; the Philippines, Africa and now South America. But what the heck, it beats the hell out of freezing your ass off, right?"

"We'll see Willy," Hal advised, "freezing your ass off might just include not being shot at."

Will couldn't remember the plane being as full as it was today. On board were Dom, Carmen, Wade, Hal, Dan Pierson, Kelly, Rose and Will, and it seemed as if they were almost testing fate by having so many of the Posse together in one place. He dismissed the paranoia as he saw a tall, thin man dressed in the black attire of a priest with a white collar waiting for them on the tarmac where a ground crewman was motioning to park. Will grabbed Dom and was the first down the stairs to greet their host, "Hello, may I presume you are Archbishop Villaponteau?"

"I am, and may I presume you are Will Kavanagh and this is your lovely wife Dominique?"

Before he could grab his hand and bow, Dom did so and kissed his ring, "It is my distinct pleasure to meet you Your Excellency."

He smiled at her as Will did the same, "And it is an unaccustomed pleasure to make your acquaintance Your Grace."

He smiled and told them, "I see that Archbishop Acosta was quite right about the two of you. You seem to hold the Holy Roman Church in high esteem for two who are not of the faith. Welcome to Colombia. And who are you traveling with?"

Hal and Carmen were right behind them, as she bowed just perceptibly, kissed his ring and said, "Thank you so much for coming to meet us Your Grace; it is a totally unexpected pleasure."

Hal shook his hand and said, "It's a distinct pleasure to meet you Archbishop Villaponteau, and this is our son Wade. We are much in need of your counsel and wisdom in this dangerous plight in which we find ourselves. May I introduce you to our friends Dan Pierson, Rose Cordes and Kelly Dupree? They have come with us to meet the person who can help us in our quest to survive the dangerous mission we must now embark upon."

He smiled as he shook everyone's hand and offered, "Please, accompany me to our Cathedral so that we can have a heart-to-heart discussion about this most serious situation you find yourselves in."

As they approached the Maria Reina Cathedral they were all astounded at its unique architectural visage, with triangular edifices that looked like geometric counterpoints to the flying buttresses of European cathedrals. The city of Barranquilla seemed to have a clean European feel to it, although Will strongly suspected impoverished slums stood nearby housing the peasants who had flocked to the city seeking better lives. As he ushered them into a comfortable conference room in the rear of the cathedral, they all eagerly accepted the mugs of rich smelling Colombian coffee presented for their refreshment. "I realize that you did not travel here for a tourist visit, so I will forego the pleasantries and discuss matters that concern you in the immediate circumstance. You are all under intense danger here in Colombia because you challenge the most powerful man in Colombia, Mr. Hector Constanza, the leader of the Cali Cartel. Let me say that he is the most brutal and heartless man in this country—if not the world--and many men have lost their lives for doing nothing more offensive than asking him a question. I believe we can markedly improve your chances of survival, but you must be circumspect in following our suggestions. Are there any among you who is unwilling to listen to the harsh lessons I must impart unto you? Are you all prepared to face immense danger in this noble effort to free Colton Kavanagh, an innocent man?"

None of them moved so much as a twitch so he continued, "Mr. Constanza has many enemies among the Colombians, the most significant being the poor peasants who do not share in his vast wealth and lifestyle. He has proven time and again to be a covetous man given to greed, power and corruption. These will prove his undoing, and I will assist you in understanding the parts that make him weak and vulnerable."

"Sorry Archbishop, but we understand he has made large contributions to the church. How do you reconcile his largesse with the church and his obvious penchant for evil?" Will asked.

"That is a fair and reasonable question. His donations to create institutions have no doubt helped many Colombians further their education and improve their lots in life. What we cannot tolerate is the brutal violence he employs pursuing his business objectives. As you all know, killing another human being is one of the prohibitions contained in the Ten Commandments handed down to Moses on Mount Sinai, and these are to be complied with without exception. Do not mistake me for a naive man, as I understand that such actions are regrettable but necessary in the pursuit of God's instructions. These should not be the norm for behavior however, and I see that you have been forced into a scenario where killing may well be justified if not necessitated. I would like to introduce my trusted colleague Daniel Gomez, who has been with me since my early days supporting the Ejército de Liberación Nacional, or the National Liberation Army. Before you ask, I will say that the ELN is founded in Marxist-Leninist principles that run counter to the precept of the Holy Roman Church. I know you must think these are strange bedfellows or allies, but the disparity of wealth among the poor peasants and the wealthy landowners is indeed obscene and the life expectancy of the poor is forty years less than the wealthy. This is due primarily to a lack of clean drinking water and basic sanitation practices. Cholera and malaria take so many newborns that it is all but genocide here in Colombia."

"Now you may wonder why I tell you these things when you are trying to rescue a man of God, not necessarily overcome a powerful warlord in Cali? I would offer that you cannot achieve one without achieving the other. But I can tell you that I will help you in any way I can because of my desire for the poor and disenfranchised to share the economic comforts and realities of the most basic forms of human needs. What we are willing to help you with is overcoming the wealth and arrogance of the wealthy as characterized by Mr. Constanza. We will assist as necessary to confront this powerful snake that professes to be his own God and cut off its head."

"And just how do you propose to do that Juan? I don't see but two people here who are willing to mount your admittedly socially admirable ambitions. Are there more that are willing to take up your beliefs and willingness to fight?" Hal asked.

Juan smiled and asked, "Are you willing to travel a short distance to find out the answer to your question Mr. Rayfield?"

"Sure, let's go, I'm game," Will answered for them, looking back at the enthusiastic group.

When they arrived at the Howard Johnson's Versailles Barranquilla, Will wondered if it was the home to the merchant marine officers who docked at the industrial wharves and rail yards surrounding it. Juan and Daniel walked straight around the hotel to a medium-sized warehouse with the wide doors rolled completely open, giving it the look of a large work shop used for repairing boats. There were perhaps one hundred blue collar workers, apparently dockworkers who managed the warehouses surrounding the ships tied up along the long wharf. They collectively had the air of men who made their living through toil, hard work and sweat. Will glanced at the women, but only Kelly moved just noticeably closer to Pierson as they walked up to the assembled throng. Juan stepped up to them and to their amazement greeted each of them individually and bowed his head in blessing as he did so.

He then took the lead by addressing them in Spanish as Rose translated for the Posse, "Good day my brothers, I have brought some *Norteamericano* friends to meet you. Before you begin to judge them on their appearance, let me say that Mr. Kavanagh here"—he touched Will's arm and motioned for him to step out in front of the workers—"has been threatened with death by the Cali Cartel because they want him to replace his missionary brother so that he can be brutally murdered by Hector Constanza. Let me say that Mr. Kavanagh's heinous crime was trying to extract his imprisoned missionary brother from Nicaragua when the Cali Cartel's celeno confronted him outside Managua, threatening him, his wife and his missionary brother. He protected his wife Dominique here when the Cali celeno put a switchblade to her pregnant stomach and asked him if he valued his brother more than his unborn child. Now they want to kill him in revenge. How many of you would protect your pregnant wife if she was to be cut in the stomach? I dare say every one of you would protect your wife, and that is the crime that Will Kavanagh is accused of. Now they want him dead and he has come to us for help."

"Do any of you know the land around Pereira? That is where the execution of Will Kavanagh is to take place. I will be there with a rifle in my hand, trying to prevent a son of God from being shot down like a beast for protecting the sanctity of his child in the womb. If any of you are willing to help us out, we would be proud and eternally thankful. Now I recognize that Mr. Kavanagh is not one of us, but he deserves the chance to raise his son in spite of some madman thinking misguided revenge is the only way of life. He who is without sin let him cast the first stone! Will Kavanagh needs our help, and more importantly, his wife Dominique needs our help if their child is going to have a father. This unholy event will take place within the next few days, and I ask that you pray in your hearts whether you can assist this pious man who kisses the ring of the Church in humble appreciation of our mutual ideals."

Before anyone could move or say anything, Will took one step forward holding Dom's hand and asked Rose to come and translate for him. When she was standing beside Dom, he began, "I come before you a stranger who has been blessed to have met and married this woman whose hand I hold. We are not members of the Holy Roman Church, but the church has been overwhelmingly kind to Dominique and me by blessing the child she carries in her womb. I do not know if I will survive this task before me, but before you and God I declare my undying love for this woman and the child she bears." As Rose completed the translation, he reached for Juan's hand, knelt slightly and kissed the ring on his finger.

Dom quickly followed by taking Juan's hand and kissed the ring. She then stood to embrace him in a hug and told him, "Thank you Your Grace."

And then a most unexpected thing happened; every one of the dock workers walked up to them and either shook their hands or touched their shoulders saying, "*Que Dios los bendiga*," or "*Estamos con ustedes*." Dom and Will acknowledged the greetings and told each of them "Thank you so much," or "God bless you." When they had greeted the last worker they turned to find

Juan Villaponteau smiling and bleary-eyed. Their friends of the Posse who made the trip were all wiping their eyes with their sleeves. Will looked at Juan smiling, "I guess we made some new friends today, wouldn't you? Man, that speech you gave them really turned the tide in our favor. Thanks a million Archbishop."

He shook his head no, "The piety you and Dominique displayed by kissing the ring resonated all the way to their souls Will. They will go to the gates of hell for you and your unborn child now. Let's go back to the cathedral and plan this telephone call to Mr. Constanza."

When they returned to the Maria Reina Cathedral they were all ready for a glass of wine. Juan noticed this and ordered lunch to be sent to the conference room. As they settled into the delicious swordfish quesadillas he asked, "So what plan do you have to prevent Hector Constanza from murdering you as soon as he gets you into his limousine? He's not known for inaction, as you may be aware."

Will nodded to Hal, so he took over, "It turns out that Hector has fallen in love with the wife of the Minister of Foreign Affairs, one beautiful Consuela Diaz. Once we grab her, Willy can let Hector know it's a tit-for-a-tat in yet another exchange, this one Constanza didn't know about."

Juan stroked his chin approvingly, "So how do you plan to 'grab' the Minister's wife? I'm sure she moves under armed guard and there are paparazzi snapping pictures of her on a regular basis."

"Hmm, I hadn't thought it that far through," Hal acknowledged, then looked at Will. "Any thoughts on how we can make the grab?"

"Jesus partner, we don't even know where she hangs out for Christ's sake!" he said, but Dom was already flinching. "Sorry Juan, my American slang and vulgarity is a weakness. So I guess she moves in pretty fashionable circles if she caught the eye of Hector the Molester. We can't make it a shootout when we take her, that's for sure." He looked around the table and asked, "Any thoughts on how we can sequester Mrs. Hotness off to the side for an interview?"

Kelly jumped in and offered, "Dammit Willy, you got it all in one fell swoop! We'll get Penny Martindale to come in and do an interview on prominent South American political wives; it'll be the best thing since Evita!"

"Who is Penny Martindale?" Juan asked innocently, but was roundly ignored.

"We'd have to make it one in a series of interviews for it to appear legitimate," Dan Pierson added. "What about the President's wife, what's she like; not uglier'n a bulldog I hope?"

Then they had the unique opportunity to see what an Archbishop looked like when he lost his shit and broke into uncontrollable laughter. When he came around he looked at Pierson and told him, "I wouldn't call her uglier than a bulldog, but she is not as charmingly enchanting as Mrs. Diaz. But she is socially prominent with charitable work, so she would also make a good interview candidate. Who is this Penny Martindale?"

"Can I use that phone Juan?" Will asked, motioning for Dom to give him the mini-Rolodex she kept in her purse.

"Hey babe, how's my coonass Cajun sister?" Will asked, all but shocked to find Penny at her desk.

"Will Kavanagh, is that you? Where in the world are you?"

"It is indeed, and I am calling from the wilds of Colombia, and that's not the one in Missouri or South Carolina. Now listen up sweet cheeks, I've got my ass in a crack and need a big favor," he said, but grimaced an apology to Juan for the language.

"How big a crack, and what kind of favor?"

"Remember our little chat at the Silver Nickel? Have you perchance renegotiated that contract yet?" Seemingly the prominent reporter's life mentor, the Posse stared at him in disbelief.

"The answer is yes; how did you know about Lib Garrison?"

Will quickly assumed a meditative state before opening his eyes, "I take it you called Patty and she got you in touch with her agent?"

"Yes, how could you have known to hook me up with her?"

"Good, it sounds like you're ready for the Pulitzer. I need you to convince your station director, nah hell, make it the regional network czar that you've got the inside track on prominent South American political wives—think Evita Peron. So anyway, you get that smoking hot little body of yours and a camera man down to Bogotá, Colombia, and our man on the ground here, oh shit, hold on…" he said as he looked at Hal. 'What's the name of that RSO in Bogotá?' When he told him Will resumed the conversation, "So your guy here's a man named Brad Covington over at the Embassy, but in reality your guy on the ground's gonna be Rambo. Getting the picture?"

"Will Kavanagh, I'm a news reporter but…damn you, okay I'm on the same page. By the way, who made you my life mentor?"

"You did, in so many words. Okay, if you can't do this, I'll probably be eviscerated by the head of the Cali Cartel, but we'll probably get to meet in our next reincarnation—whenever that happens! Now listen Miss Hotness, I ain't trying to overplay this, but we need you to interview this admittedly smoking hot momma and we'll take care of the rest. Here's the deal; Cowboy Kavanagh pays all expenses, including first class airfare, and if your director tells you to piss up a rope, tell him you're taking the evening news anchor for the CBS affiliate in LA. This ain't costing them a dime—which I'm providing by the way. Oh, and your cameraman needs to be fluent in Spanish. Doesn't your new contract call for Spearchucker Jones substitutes that come in for you on the weekends anyway? What's a few days in beautiful downtown Bogotá? As long as you've got American press credentials nobody'll fuck with you. Whatdya think?"

"Will Kavanagh, if I didn't know you I'd tell you to go to hell. By the way, how's Dom doing with the pregnancy?" She suddenly stopped to ponder, and he knew it was fortuitous.

"Hold on, she's right here," he said. He looked at Dom and pleaded, "Sell it please."

While the girls were talking, he looked at Hal, "If we can make this interview happen, you and Rambo can snatch her afterwards and get all of the info/data we'll need to masquerade Rose well enough to fool Constanza. To protect Penny, we'll schedule another interview right before Consuela's to give her total deniability. The last thing we need is for these cocaine cowboys to come after Penny back in the States. But I'd like Penny on the plane out of Colombia before I advise *Señor* Constanza that his mistress has been snatched."

Juan Villaponteau's face was frozen in wide-eyed amazement. "I can hardly believe what I am witnessing. Were you just demanding that a prominent news reporter in California abandon her job and fly to Bogotá to participate in this operation? I am totally unfamiliar with such planning tactics."

Kelly was smirking as Will had to throttle back, "Yeah Juan, we're setting this up on the fly *mi buen amigo; estamos todos bien?*"

"*Eso creo,*" he nodded, still dumbstruck by the seemingly lightning pace the Posse was hatching their frantic plan.

Carmen was there for the rescue, "Your Grace, perhaps you are not used to such operational planning. As you know, this situation developed rapidly following Colton Kavanagh's kidnapping…"

"So what am I witnessing before my very eyes?"

"These commandos have the ability to think outside the boundaries of social structure. Right now Will, Hal and Dan have engaged their lizard brains to the total exclusion of other considerations." He stared at her dumbfounded so she tried it in Spanish, "*Que se su cerebro de lagarto conspirar a la velocidad de la luz.*"

He shook his head, "*Cerebro de lagarto?*" She smiled and shrugged her shoulders, the Posse not even breaking for air.

"So where we gonna hide her out?" Rambo asked.

"Brad Covington's safe house of course, we can explain it away as protective custody after the fact. It's gonna be up to Mrs. Diaz to figure out if she can save her marriage to the Foreign Minister. Listen, how about I tell Penny we can hook her up with an interview with Alicia Videla down in Buenos Aires; I bet Rosita can hook that up for her main squeeze. By the way, that's still an active association I hope?"

"You bet, but do you actually expect Penny to go down there for the interview?"

"Probably not; we'll need to get Penny the hell outa dodge after the Diaz séance. Let's see what magic Dom the Mental Master has wrought?"

As they walked over Dom, was closing out her chat with Penny, "That's right Penny, Kelly Dupree will be greeting you and the cameraman at the Bogotá airport and Great West Studios will arrange the interviews for you. We'll have first class round trip tickets waiting for you at the American Airlines counter at San Francisco Airport. I would suggest you begin doing research on Eliana Jiménez, the wife of the President, and Consuela Diaz, the wife of the Minister of Foreign Affairs. Hold on," she said as she looked up at Pierson.

"Tell her to add Alicia Videla to the list; she's the wife of the Argentine President."

"Also Penny, add Alicia Videla to the list of prospective interviews, as she's the wife of President Jorge Videla in Argentina. Kelly and Will met her at the Presidential Palace."

Dom shook her head, "Right, you probably can do that one by telephone. I would suggest you put together a short synopsis of what you hope to learn from these very determined and strong-willed women who survive inside of a decidedly male-dominated world. Your producers back in Sacramento might actually get interested in this vacation pursuit of yours. Plan on getting to Bogotá as quickly as you can; this unpleasantness with Will is gaining momentum. I can't wait to see you back in Panama City. Bye."

They were all fairly happy with the results of the Penny Pursuit when they turned to find Juan standing with a thin bearded man who appeared to be in his late thirties and was dressed in the clothes of a horse stable or ranch hand, his thin leather chaps prominent. "Ladies and gentlemen, it is my pleasure to introduce you to my dear friend Marco Pintoles. Marco is the manager of a cattle ranch not far from Barranquilla. Marco, I would like you to meet Will and Dominique Kavanagh, Hal, Carmen and Wade Rayfield, Kelly Dupree, Rose Cordes and Dan Pierson."

They were somewhat flummoxed as to who he was, but any friend of Juan's was a friend of theirs so Will shook his leathery hand, "It's a pleasure meeting you Marco. Is it leather, dairy or meat that your ranch specializes in?"

He smiled at him and nodded, "A bit of all of them, but dairy and meat are our primary markets. Leather tends to be a byproduct of aging."

With that Hal let out a hoot, "I'll say, at least there's not a lot of waste associated with your industry Mr. Pintoles."

He shook his head just slightly and told them, "My men were very impressed with your sincerity today *Señor* and *Señorita* Kavanagh. We are not often in contact with *Norteamericanos* who act with such respect and consideration for our ways. Archbishop Villaponteau tells me that you are in dire trouble with the narco-terrorists in Cali, and that this trouble is not of your making. I will do everything that I reasonably can to help you, if you would be so kind as to tell me where you expect your troubles to occur."

Will glanced at Juan totally confused, so the Archbishop put things in perspective, "Marco is the head of the Ejército de Liberación Nacional, what is routinely referred to as the National Liberation Army or ELN. As you can imagine, many people would pay much money to learn of his identity, but after he spoke with his men today, he feels as though you are worthy of his trust and will not betray him."

"Oh my God, you are the guy, the leader of the ELN?" Will asked, thunderstruck.

Pintoles smiled and responded, "What did you expect Will, John Wayne or Che Guevara to ride down out of the hills with a thousand horsemen? We are but simple people trying to survive this difficult world we live in."

"So how far does the ELN's area of influence range Marco? I am a novice in the geopolitical matters of Colombia."

"Our base of operations is nominally in Maracaibo, across the border in Venezuela, and we maintain influence within roughly the northeast portion of Colombia. The Cordillera Mountain ranges essentially form the western boundary of our influence and we have a presence down to just south of Medellin. Juan tells me it is the Cali Cartel that is causing you problems with the kidnapping of your brother. If he is being held in Cali, our chances of infiltrating are greatly lessened. Cali is too far south compared to our area of operations."

Will looked at Juan, "We haven't made the first call yet, so we are still trying to map out how things can work to our advantage. So far as my friends are concerned," he said as he pointed to Hal and Pierson who were listening as they closely searched a detailed map on the wall, "we're trying to keep things as close to the central part of Colombia as possible. We have airlift opportunities the closer we can keep the action to Panama. Given the international airline schedules, it would seem probable that we can insist on my initial arrival into Bogotá, since that's the airline hub. We know Constanza is from Armenia and that his friend Umberto Rodriquez has both a hacienda and coffee plantation in and around Pereira. We are hoping that we can set up the final showdown at Rodriguez' hacienda in Pereira, but our friend Rose here is a native Colombian and can perform surveillance for us as necessary." He shifted to look Pintoles in the eyes, "Is the ELN familiar with Pereira?"

He smiled and replied, "Oh very much so. That is the home of Umberto Rodriguez, who is the leader of our bitter rival the FARC. Because of this, Pereira is well defended by FARC paramilitary troops."

Juan nodded at him, "I do not doubt the capabilities of *Señorita* Cordes, but I believe her surveillance capabilities would be enhanced if she were to travel as a married couple with Father Daniel Gomez."

As they looked at him strangely, the good looking young man with a full head of wavy black hair and a slender physique they had met earlier walked in from behind a hidden door. He smiled at Rose as he said, "This will be my first assignment as a married man, but I promise to behave."

Will was looking at Hal suspiciously when Juan told them, "Do not let Father Gomez' appearance deceive you; he is highly skilled in survival techniques, both defensive and offensive. Do you believe Daniel is prepared for a surveillance mission Marco?"

The ELN leader sneered his reply, "Are you kidding? I'd take him on as one of my officers if he weren't a committed man of the cloth. I have known very few men as brave as Father Gomez."

"Okay, we need Rose in Bogotá for the swap with Consuela in a couple of days, but perhaps she and Daniel can begin their honeymoon through the Coffee Triangle of Colombia and surveil defensive preparations in Pereira. I would be especially interested in elevation points around the Pereira Hacienda that would make good sniper posts. If we bring a helicopter onto the hacienda tennis court, a sniper could wreak havoc, so sniper nests are key. Marco, we'll probably be depending on you to neutralize the FARC and National Police troops on the ground if it comes to that. So are we ready to make that call into the hornet's nest?" Will asked Juan, his mind reeling at 3000 rpm.

"At a minimum we will need; proof of life, number to call, voice confirmation with the brother, and date and time for the exchange. Your preference is a public place in Bogotá, but let them make the first proposal to see what their defensive plans are. Are we ready?" Juan asked as he placed his hand on Will's head.

"I believe so Archbishop."

"May God bless and protect you my son," he pronounced and then picked up the telephone.

To their amazement, the Archbishop was able to connect with Constanza on his second call, and they were guessing that the first one was to his Cathedral in Bogotá. As the conversation was taking place in fast but polite Spanish, they were all surrounding Rose as she translated bits and pieces she picked up from the one side of the conversation she could hear. Finally she looked up at Will and said, "They're talking over when you can be at the exchange point. Archbishop Villaponteau is arguing that you are at your parent's house in the United States and that it will take a few days for you to get to Colombia. I believe he is doing his best to convince Constanza that you will arrive as they agree, but Constanza wants you to come to the meeting alone. Juan cannot reasonably argue that point, but that will be a point of negotiation once you and Constanza converse directly."

Will suddenly wasn't listening to her as he turned to Kelly, "Why don't we make Penny an award-winning journalist with this trip she's about to take? Between Archbishops Acosta and Villaponteau she can surely get a fix on the plight of the masses in South America who have surged to the big cities in order to scratch out a living. Getting the perspectives of the three wives and the two Cardinals will surely give her article some serious credibility, and with the Latino population around Southern California it will surely get some attention. Whatdya think?"

Carmen suddenly piped in and added, "I'm not sure how you can think of such things at the moment, but if the two Archbishops can enlist the Archbishop of Rio de Janeiro, she can cover three of the most populous cities on the continent and make it seem an almost universal blight for South America."

"I want somebody with her if she's traveling like that though," Will protested.

Kelly looked at him with a scowl, "What's the matter, you don't think she's a big girl?"

"Oh yeah, she's a coonass Cajun girl and smoking hot. But these are some dangerous places we're talking about. Maybe Rico would take her on as a bodyguard," he said with a smirk.

"Actually, with his Spanish skills he might be the best person to accompany her," Carmen agreed.

"So when am I going to meet this mysterious Che? You seem to have hidden him from me thus far?" Kelly pouted.

"Just as soon as we get back to Panama...." he was saying when Juan interrupted.

He crossed himself as he began, "It pains me to deal with such blasphemous men, but *Señor* Constanza is very anxious to make the exchange for your brother Colton, and all but insisted that you fly to Bogotá tomorrow. I told him that you were in the United States caring for your depressed mother, so he agreed to delay the meeting until Saturday, which works in our favor."

"Why Saturday Juan, how'd you get it pushed back that far?"

He smiled and told them, "Fortune is at least smiling on us for that part; Saturday is the 89th anniversary of the founding of the Colombian National Police, and there are parades and fiestas scheduled in all of the major cities. *Señor* Constanza is well aware of the reduced police presence on Saturday, as well as the unlikelihood of vehicular checkpoints along highways except for the secondary roads leading into Bogotá. He agreed to send a proof of life to the Embassy in Panama to confirm your brother's condition, but was adamant that you come to the meeting alone. I am not comfortable with this last demand."

"That ain't gonna happen, as I need Rico there with me for a couple of reasons—my ignorance of the Spanish language being front and center. So, did you get a number for communications purposes? I think I'll give him an hour, as that's about what it'd take you to find me in Louisiana, and call and tell him I ain't coming alone and that I insist on speaking with my brother as a secondary proof of life."

"I would suggest you delay that call until you receive the package at the Embassy. I would presume he'll have a picture taken of your brother holding that day's edition of *El Tiempo*, Bogotá's leading newspaper. Once you have that proof, it would seem prudent to want to hear his voice as reassurance, and then you can make your demand to be accompanied to the meeting. By the way, why do you want to subject another person to the murderous plans *Señor* Constanza has in mind for you?"

Will glanced at Hal who took over, "Archbishop, we have a trusted friend named Ricardo Suarez, who was a Cuban freedom fighter and lost his wife tragically to Castro's thugs. If I were Hector Constanza, I'd be much more worried about Rico—even unarmed—than I would be a rattlesnake coiled next to me. He has already saved both Will's and my lives during our mission to take down Sandrigan. I personally recommended he accompany Will due only partly to his fluency in Spanish."

Villaponteau was rubbing his chin as he said, "I only hope you are not sending him to his death. Now what other plans must we initiate before you head back to Panama? I also must return to Bogotá before my absence is noticed."

Will looked at Rose and Daniel, "Okay, are you two ready to begin your travels into the interior of Colombia? What do you need to take with you?"

Daniel smiled as he replied, "I believe we have everything we need to insure a safe journey Will. We have friends at every town along our path."

Will looked at Juan and asked, "How about some working capital Archbishop, are you going to need any lubrication incentives?"

He smiled and offered, "Actually Will, the ELN does not extract taxation from the drug cartels, so funds are always a consideration. Are you in a position to help us?"

Before he could answer, Dom jumped in front of him, "Do you have a bank account in the Cayman Islands Your Grace?"

He smiled as he glanced at Gomez and replied, "As a matter of fact we do. Bank accounts in Colombia are subject to expropriation at the most inconvenient times due to political instability."

Without giving Will the slightest consideration, she asked, "Would fifty thousand US dollars assist in facilitating the effective conclusion of this dangerous mission we are about to undertake? If you need more, just name the amount."

Juan's eyes got wide as saucers as Daniel Gomez actually knelt to the floor before the Archbishop responded, "I cannot believe your charitable graciousness Dominique. What you offer is far too much considering the nature of the assistance you require. We would all offer our efforts freely to allow this child you carry to have its father."

Will looked at him with a wicked smile, "Fine, if you're gonna play hardball we'll make it an even hundred thousand dollars, and you can use it to drill some wells in the barrios around Barranquilla and do something to really help these people who are willing to lay down their lives for us."

Dom then reached for Archbishop Villaponteau's hand, "Archbishop, would it be appropriate for us all to say a special prayer at this time. Will and I recited the Lord's Prayer during our marriage vows, and I feel that is appropriate given the present circumstances."

He nodded to her, put his arm around her shoulder and his other around Will's as the rest including Daniel did the same. Then they prayed those eternally comforting words:

"Our Father, who art in heaven,
hallowed be they name,
thy kingdom come
thy will be done
on earth as it is in heaven.
Give us this day our daily bread;
and forgive us our trespasses,
as we forgive those who trespass against us;

and lead us not into temptation,
but deliver us from evil.
For thine is the kingdom,
and the power, and the glory
forever and ever, Amen."

When they finished Will looked at Juan and told him, "I've been delivered from evil twice in my life Archbishop, so I hope I've got one more coming my way. May God bless you for the assistance you have rendered unto my family and friends; I will never forget you Your Grace."

He smiled at him and opened his arms as Dom and Will embraced him and hoped they could be spared one more time.

At the plane at Barranquilla's Cortissoz Airport, Will gave Rose and Daniel a hug and told them, "Take care of yourselves; I guess I won't see you two until Pereira on Saturday. You've got the sat phone and charger, right?"

Rose patted her cargo pants pocket and replied, "Oh yes, right here. And take care of yourself Will. I cannot imagine a more dangerous situation than you are getting ready to step into."

"Hey, with friends like you, I've got a chance. By the way, where's Hal?" He asked, looking around to find him bounding down the stairs from the airplane.

When Hal got to where they were standing, he discreetly pulled a white envelope and gave it to Rose, "Here's a little grease money in case you find yourself in a sticky situation. Be good, and never forget that I love you." With that he stunned them all and kissed her sweetly on the lips, making Will wonder whether there had been some more intimate contact in their previous association.

55

HAIL, HAIL THE BLACK HAWK

As soon as the Great West 727 was in the air Will called Adam Chennault at the Embassy in Panama City, "Okay Adam, we've made contact with Constanza. He's express shipping a packet for me to the Embassy with the proof of life we demanded. How about call me on this number the minute it comes in; can you do that for me?"

"Hell yeah, I'll do anything to help you Will. What in the hell has happened since I saw you last night? The Ambassador called me into his office first thing this morning wanting a full report on what was going on with you and your brother. For all I know, he didn't know anything about your situation when I left work yesterday."

Will smiled at Dom and guessed, "We had to make some contacts back to our South American friends; it sounds like my buddy Charlie Richardson caught wind of what's happening. So what'd the Ambassador have to say?"

"He said for me to get my ass in touch with you and provide any—and I mean any—support we could possibly render in helping to get your brother back from Constanza."

"Really, he was that helpful was he? That's really rather surprising for a career Foreign Service Officer, but Charlie Richardson's sure the exception to that rule. Here's the deal, we're gonna need some ambivalence out of the Colombian military when we overfly their territory for making the snatch by helicopter. How about figure out who we've gotta sleep with to make that happen, okay?"

"Damn, you don't ask for much do you Kavanagh? Does the term Bilateral Mutual Cooperation and Security Treaty mean anything to you? Jesus, this shit takes place at the Presidential levels normally," he said with a *phew*.

537

"Yeah, yeah, I get all that, but maybe we can get a one-time only good deal exception. How about check with the Military Attaché and see if the Colombians owe him any favors. We've gotta find an angle in there somewhere. My ass sure doesn't want to entertain the prospect of getting shot down after we've somehow managed to thwart Constanza's blood oath against me. Do you know that guy, the Military Attaché?"

"Jesus Kavanagh, he's my boss for Christ's sake. I'll go fall on my sword in front of him and see what he says. You got any silver bullets that might make him sit up and take notice?"

Will looked at Hal, asked him the name of his buddy at Benning and then continued, "Why don't you tell your Colonel that Major General Goodie Stilton knows what I'm doing here, even though he can't directly participate. And while you're at it, tell him Colonel, that would be General Selectee, Bernie Jepson is forming a big shield around us to ward off evil spirits. Think that'll help your cause?"

"Damn right, I'll be back in touch as soon as I talk to the man."

Next he called Brad Covington, the RSO at the Embassy in Bogotá, and was relieved to catch him at his desk, "Hey Brad, it's Will Kavanagh. Did Adam Chennault get ahold of you?"

"Oh yeah, he told me all about your suicide mission into the heart of the Cali Cartel. What can I help you with Will?"

"Listen, we've made initial contact with Constanza and he wants the kidnap exchange to take place at some museum building at the Bogotá Botanical Gardens. Are you familiar with that place?"

"Oh hell yeah, that's actually a beautiful place and well hidden from the surrounding urban blight by a veritable jungle of huge trees. Are you planning on hitting him there, right in the middle of Bogotá?"

"Nah, I'm sure he'll grab me and Rico and drive us away from the city to wherever he plans to do his dirty work. Listen, I need to make sure I get my brother out of dodge as soon as possible, as I wouldn't put it past Constanza to double-cross us and snatch Colton again as insurance against a trap. Is there any place close to the Botanical Gardens that's semi-secure and has a helicopter landing pad?"

Will sensed him thinking out the geography as he came back, "Yeah, the Botanical Garden is right next door to the Simon Bolivar Military Academy.

I can't remember whether they've got a helo pad there, but there's a huge ass practice soccer field just to the south side of the Academy buildings. What's the plan, drive him to the soccer field and fly him out from there?"

"Yeah, but I'm not sure we'll have enough av gas to make it back to Panama. Any friendly airfields we could make an interim landing at for refueling?"

"I guess the refueling stop would ideally be along an imaginary line between Bogotá and Panama City, right?"

"Right, how are things between the Colombian military and your boss the Attaché these days?" He asked, grimacing as he remembered Marty Lindstrum's warning of a National Security Finding for the coca crop eradication program.

"You really don't want to go there, as there's a highly classified joint operation between the Americans and the Colombians on the books even as we speak."

"Listen, I've already reamed the CIA's ass over trying to pull my simple little rescue op into their massive coca crop eradication project down south. Now you and I both know nothing I'm planning to do will interfere one iota with that crop dusting. So what about a friendly gas station along the way; whatdya think?"

"Jesus Christ Kavanagh, who the fuck are you? How the hell did you know about that?"

"Fuck 'em, I really don't care about a billion gallons of paraquat raining down on some jungle. I'm trying to get my brother and me away from the most evil presence since Adolph Hitler. Where can I refuel the birds?"

"Did you say birds, as in more than one? What the fuck Kavanagh? Anything else I can do for you?"

"Yeah, as a matter of fact, I need the name of that tailor who sews coats made out of Kevlar. And, I'm gonna need some surveillance on one Consuela Diaz, the torrid mistress of one Hector Constanza."

"What the fuck? I can get you to the tailor, but what are you gonna do with Ms. Diaz?"

"Stash her in your safe house until I can use that info to keep Constanza from cutting my nuts off for starters. Were you aware that she's banging Constanza big time?"

"Damn where do you get your intel? Now just when do you plan on snatching the Foreign Minister's wife? You know she's got a bodyguard right?"

"Right after she gets finished interviewing with an American reporter for a special story on South America's unfortunate and impoverished children who reside in filthy barrios. Now how about research out that airfield we can refuel in and find me that tailor's address and phone number, can you?"

"You bet Will, I'll be back in touch."

———

When they landed at Colon's Jiménez Airport, Alex and Rico were standing beside a black Suburban that they presumed was a Sikorsky vehicle. "How'd things go in Barranquilla?" Alex inquired.

"Great; Alex, Rico, I'd like you to meet our friend Kelly Dupree. Kelly's down to hopefully document the rescue op we've got to make over in Colombia."

Will and Dom watched with barely disguised curiosity as she first shook Alex' hand and then paused when she shook Rico's. She smiled and said, "So I finally get to me Che? How are you? Will and Hal certainly kept you hidden away for a long time."

He looked at her curiously and asked, "Who's Che?"

"Oh that's your name in the Algerian op that you guys were involved in last year, or was it earlier this year? Anyway, Will and Hal had this huge board up with all of the player's pictures and nicknames. You were Che!"

"Oh, I see," he said politely. He then turned to Hal and told him, "The Black Hawks are supreme birds Kemosabe. Curt's got 7.62 Gatling guns pod-mounted."

"How about the external fuel tanks? Willy's still working on a refueling stop enroute for us coming out of Bogotá."

"Good, we can make it there with the extra av gas, but we'll need replenishment for the ride back. When's all of this going down?"

"We've made initial contact with Constanza, or at least our Archbishop friend did, and we're awaiting receipt of a package with the proof-of-life in it. I'd say we'll be moving by early Saturday morning based on our latest intel," Will told them.

"So I'm going in with the choppers?" Rico wondered.

"You could only be so lucky; your ass is going in with me to Bogotá for the suicide mission. Feeling special?" Will asked, giving him his best shit-eating grin. He then looked at Alex and told him, "I'm gonna need you and Hal on the choppers; by the way, can Curt cough up two Black Hawks for the op?"

Alex smiled as he nodded, "He's got four down here flying jungle acceptance tests. He's flying lead by the way." He then looked over at Dan Pierson and asked, "What's Rambo gonna be up to? Sure could use him on one of the guns."

"Sorry Alex, Dan the Man's flying out to Bogotá in the morning to set up surveillance on a certain key asset. Listen, I want you and Rico to take Kelly under your wing and show her the ropes around here—evasive chopper rides and all. And get her at least minimally checked out on small arms while you've got her."

"Hey," Kelly started to object, "what are you talking about? You're not leaving me out here in the jungle all alone are you? I didn't sign up for all of this shit Kavanagh."

With a very insincere smile, Will looked around at everyone, "Could you excuse the two of us for a moment?"

After they were hidden by the right-side landing gear, Will swirled Kelly around by an arm and got right in her face like he was gonna kiss her. "Which part of a suicide mission were you hoping to watch? When they bring the bodies back? It's time for you to see how one of these things is set up, and I want you on that backup bird when we ruin Constanza's day in Pereira. Now are you a pussy or what?"

She got a hateful scowl on her face and was just able to control her temper, "Who the hell put you in charge?"

"I did, since I'm the one likely to die," he told her, but at least she was listening. 'And Zig thinks it's a good idea for your hot ass to be at the scene of the action this time. Now I want your sexy little world class ass to become a quasi-commando groupie over the next 24 hours, and you're gonna do it three miles from here at Ft Davis. Rico will not let anything bad happen to you, and if you just so happen to become better friends with Che so be it. Now I've gotta beat feet to Panama City and set this mission up on its hind legs. Now, are you in with us studs or are you the pussy?"

She got a furtive smile on her face then moved in to kiss him passionately as she squeezed his manhood, "I'm part pussy mister, but I've also got an ass that'll kick butt as well. When are you gonna come back here?"

"Maybe tomorrow; I need a check ride on the Black Hawk, and I've gotta get some detailed maps for the guys to use inside Bogotá and Pereira. If you get time, why don't you call Penny Martindale and talk about the synopsis for her research piece on South American poverty? I'll try and get ahold of the Archbishop in Rio so she can tie the story together. You bring your boots?"

"Yes Mr. Kavanagh, I brought my boots, jeans, camera and fifteen rolls of film. Satisfied?"

"What a question from the Cossack Queen. Let's go find the others."

When they got back to the 727 Will looked at Alex, "We've gotta head back to PC and set up some details—not the least of which is the flyover clearance. How about have Curt fly over to Howard Air Base tomorrow around noon, and I'll take a check ride on the Black Hawk. I should have the city detail maps of Bogotá and Pereira for you by then. Am I forgetting anything?"

Alex looked like he had lost his best friend, "Any ideas on how we're gonna keep from getting shot to shit when we fly into Pereira?"

"I'm working on that. Rose and a rogue priest set out on the trail to Pereira an hour ago, and there will be significant ground support irregulars keeping Constanza's thugs at bay. I just hope we can find the sniper's nests before we go in." He suddenly remembered something and looked at Alex, "Curt need any contributions for the good and welfare? He's saving our asses out here."

"Are you shitting me? He's eating this up; the active duty guys won't let him do shit, so this is his time to shine. Sikorsky's footing the bill; they plan on selling thousands of these birds to the DoD."

"Alright, we're outa here. Make sure you keep the LST plugged up; I promise I will be in touch. And good luck showing Ms. Dupree the ropes; she's been known to get a little cranky. *Adios!*"

———

"So how we doing on the smoke and mirrors show *compadre?*" Will asked Adam Chennault after they got airborne.

"You'd better call Brad Covington on that one, but I cannot believe how Colonel Mixon came around for you."

"Who's Colonel Mixon?"

"He's my boss, also known as the Military Attaché to the US Ambassador to Panama. Care to plug me in as to how he became your best friend overnight?"

"I haven't a clue, unless he's drinking buddies with Goodie Stilton. Listen up Adam; I need detailed maps of Bogotá and Pereira in the worst way. Any clue how I can get my hands on them?"

"Once again, I haven't a clue how this happened, but a special pouch came in from Ft Bragg's Command Section with your name on it. What the hell is that?"

"Maps maybe, can you patch me through to Brad Covington over your secure embassy net?"

"Yeah, hold on, when are you gonna be in town? Colonel Mixon wants to meet you in the worst way."

"He got any Special Ops experience?"

"Hell yeah, he worked Phoenix for two years in 'Nam, why?"

"Tell him to be at Howard's flight line tomorrow at noon. He and I are gonna take a joy ride in a Black Hawk."

"You interested in this Federal Express package that came in posted from Bogotá this afternoon?" Chennault asked, risking certain death over his non-chalance.

"Okay, I'm fifteen minutes out from PC now; patch me through to Brad in Bogotá, and then get those pouches to me ASAP Adam. See you soon bro, and thanks!"

"Hey Brad, Will Kavanagh here; have any luck with the Colombian's on the flyover issue?" Will asked, jumping past formalities.

"You can forget that Will; it ain't gonna happen. My boss says the Colombians are all jammed up over this coca eradication project they're 'participating' with the Yanks on. He won't even approach them about your little excursion."

"So what's his punch button? Everybody's got one. The Colombian's can't be that hyped up about a couple of copters flying across."

"He says, and I quote, 'If Kavanagh thinks he's coming across scott free he'd better be Bernie Jepson's son-in-law.'"

"Now why would he say that? Are the Colombians friends with our Special Forces brethren?"

"As far as the Colombians are concerned, Jepson's boys are the only Americans that deliver what they say they will; so good luck with that. Anything else you need, it's getting late?"

"As a matter of fact, how's surveillance on Mrs. Venezuela coming?"

"Business as usual with her now. She and her lover hooked up this afternoon during some kid's international soccer match at the national stadium. Her bodyguard's pretty sharp though."

"Good, you are worth you weight in salt my man, way to go. See you soon, or should I say be on the lookout for my man Pierson when he shows tomorrow."

"How will I know him, what does he look like?"

Figuring Rambo would show up in disguise, he smiled, "Don't worry about it, he'll find you. And if you feel a gun barrel in your back don't do anything stupid. Thanks a million bro!"

———

Will carefully opened the FedEx pouch from Constanza as Hal opened up the package from Jepson, but Will was the first to report, "So anybody got a copy of El Tiempo from yesterday?"

Everyone was immediately at his side looking at the snapshot of Colton holding a newspaper in his hands, looking very uncomfortable.

"Yeah, Adam Chennault sent one over just in case we needed to use it for comparison purposes," Carmen said as she held it up next to the snapshot, confirming that it was yesterday's edition.

"So we know he was alive as of yesterday. It says in the note that I am to come alone to the museum of the Bogotá Botanical Garden Saturday at noon. No surprises there, when should I call him back and tell him I ain't coming in alone?"

Pierson spoke up and offered, "Alright, I'm out of here on the first bird to Bogotá tomorrow morning. We'll want to wait as long as possible for the follow-up proof of life, but we don't have but one more day to get set up. Flight time's an hour, so I'll get there by mid-morning. Make the call to insist on being accompanied by Rico and the live conversation with Colton at 1400 hours. That should piss Constanza off to no end, but what choice does he have?"

"Alright, sounds good." Will turned to Hal and asked, "Any good news from our friends at Mackall?"

Hal was smiling nodding his head in the affirmative, "I'll say! They've cleared the flyover with the Minister of Defense and have included their best maps of the two cities. Better yet is that they're setting up their man in Bogotá to help Pierson out in his snatch job. Believe it or not, they've even got a safe house there that the CIA doesn't know about. Talk about hitting the jackpot!"

"So all we need is a gas station, is that what I'm hearing?" Will pondered.

"Tony Franklin says there's a Colombian Special Ops unit stationed at Moreno Air Base in Puerto Salgar, which is about 90 miles northeast of Pereira. He says he'll make the call for us, but we've got to pay them off for the fuel. He suggests gold coins."

"Anybody got any gold coins on them?" Will asked rhetorically.

"Um, Willy, don't you have a little sack with some hard carbon sparklers?" Hal inquired.

"Damn right, but we'll take along some dollars just in case," he considered.

"Right, we'll take along about 10,000 rounds of linked 7.62mm just in case," Pierson added, "we can't be taking any chances once we've got everyone on board."

Hal was holding up a white envelope smiling, "Now we know who took the shots of Constanza and Consuela in Costa Rica." As he passed the shots around he held up one and looked at the note. "Damn, if Constanza claims Consuela was his only venture out into the land of adultery, check out this shot of his former main squeeze." Will was instantly beside him, looking at the photograph of Constanza standing beside a golf cart, an incredibly hot blonde snaked all over him in a passionate embrace. "That my friend is Hector with Marta Cruz at the Tierra del Sol Golf Club on Aruba."

"Damn, she's as hot as Casey Mooneyhan easy," Will said in obvious admiration. He glanced at a scowling Dom and added, "Only to be used in emergencies my dear."

Hal was considering his buddy carefully, "If you have to use these pix, the reticle is gonna freak Constanza. You'd better have a cover story for that Tonto."

Will looked to Pierson, "Whatdya think Rambo; why would we be shadowing Constanza and not take the shot?"

Pierson was going through the six photos carefully now and suddenly smiled, "Damn, Tony Franklin sent the same shots with and without the reticle overlay; now that was good planning." He looked at Carmen and nodded, "Will takes the shot of Hector and Marta on Aruba without the reticle, since that was before the encounter with Enrique in Masaya. This other one, with Consuela in Costa Rica was taken almost a month after Enrique Constanza died in Masaya, two days before Colton was snatched…"

"Right," Carmen nodded, now on his wavelength, "now we have the opportunity for disinformation, and there is no price to pay." She had everyone's undivided attention as Will gave her the finger roll prompt, "So we shook Rivas down at gunpoint, assuring him of death if he told the Cartel about the conversation…" Will was now pumping his fist as she smiled, "So Rivas tells of his conversation with Hector, and that Hector is beside himself with rage. We anticipated blowback from Constanza and put the tail on him. We didn't shoot him in Costa Rica because that was before Colton was snatched by Aleandro Muñoz." She touched Will's chin to focus his eyes, "This is deadly bluffing Will; only go there if your life is at stake. Since there are no other shots of Hector after Costa Rica, we can presume he did not leave Colombia again. He was too well protected in Colombia for a positive firing line, as we refused to harm anyone other than Hector, including his family and lovers. That should give him pause."

"What if he demands to know who took the pix?" Will asked, staring at Carmen so intently they were alone in the universe.

She smiled, "The demise of Sandrigan should have come up by that point in the conversation, so attribute the shadowing to your Posse."

"Who are nameless," Will nodded, then kissed her on the forehead. Will looked around the room, "Okay everyone, we've just about planned this one out as best we can for now. The best we can do for ourselves is try and get some sleep and charge up the batteries. By my count, we've got 32 hours until Dan flies out on Saturday morning. Let's hit it again tomorrow and iron out the details we've missed. It goes without saying that I cannot possibly thank you all enough for being here. May the force be with us."

"Here we are again wondering if we're going to live to see another week Will. How can this keep happening to us?" Dom asked after she'd gotten comfortable around six pillows bolstering up her admittedly large belly.

"Hey, don't seem so down in the mouth honey; this time we're assured of the continuity of the dynasty. At least you and our son aren't going into harm's way," he replied with a smirk.

"It's our daughter, and I cannot even ponder the future without her father there to love and spoil her. I am so worried I'm not sure I can sleep," she moaned.

"Well why don't you roll over onto your side and I'll see if I can't reduce some of that tension for you Mrs. Kavanagh."

As she rolled over with considerable effort, she asked, "Do you think Kelly and Rico are mating tonight?"

"I have no idea my love, but we certainly put them in position to give it a shot. I had to have a tough love chat with Kelly when she thought we were abandoning her in the jungle."

"Well, you were! What else was she supposed to think?"

"She was supposed to think that she was finally getting her shot at Che without any aggravating people around asking too many questions. Besides, she needs to toughen up if she's gonna follow us around the world."

"I suppose you're right," she exhaled, "now what was that relaxation exercise you were talking about? I believe I'm ready to try that."

56

THE CALM BEFORE THE STORM

WILL ACTUALLY HAD TO CALL General Stilton's office from the Howard Air Base front gate guard shack to get them in the next morning. By the time Hal, Pierson and he got a ride to the flight line they saw the beautiful black bird glinting in the sunlight with a civilian and an Army Colonel standing beside it. When they pulled up Will jumped off the jeep and greeted the civilian, "You must be Curt Webster?" Curt was a little shorter than Will, maybe five-nine, in his early forties with a chiseled body that announced he took life seriously. He wore his dark hair in a Marine cut, shaved up each side above his ears. His grip was strong and his grey-blue eyes seemed to focus instantly on his target.

He smiled as they shook, "Right, you've gotta be Kavanagh. This is Colonel Dale Mixon, the Military Attaché here in Panama."

"Good to meet you Colonel; your man Chennault's been a big help to us. These are my good friends Hal Rayfield and Dan Pierson; they're coming along for the ride."

Hal and Dan immediately narrowed their gaze on the Colonel until Hal finally had it, "I'll be damned if it ain't Slickshot Mixon; how the fuck are you buddy?"

"No one's called me that in many moons Sunshine," he said, then turned to Pierson, "and what the hell is Rambo doing out of retirement?"

"Duty calls Colonel; 'bout ready to check out this starship?"

"Not before we finish topping off the tanks we're not," came a familiar voice that had them guessing until Bob Matthews bounded down out of the cabin.

"What in the fuck are you doing here?" Hal and Will echoed out a shout.

"Heard you boys needed a hand down here; these odds don't look especially inviting."

"So you're going with us to Colombia?" Will asked in disbelief.

"Can't send a rookie in without some backup, now could we?"

Will looked at Curt Webster, "We need to check on our guys over at Ft Davis; think you can show us how this bird flies between here and there? Man, I ain't never seen a helicopter with wings before; what the fuck, over?"

Curt acted like it was his newest Christmas toy, "This is a little experimental design the spooks are interested in." He pointed to the short wings that were attached to the top of the fuselage and said, "We actually designed the stub wings ourselves at Sikorsky so the bird could have flexibility. Each stub wing has two hard points that we can attach guns or external fuel tanks to." He walked over to a scary looking six-barreled machine gun attached to the hard point closest to the fuselage on the port side, "Now this little sucker can just about ruin anybody's day."

"Damn, that's a M134 mini-gun," Pierson said with admiration. He studied the 7.62 mm linked ammo belt streaming back into the fuselage, "Jesus, I didn't think the Black Hawk was supposed to be a gun ship!"

"It ain't, but they haven't gotten the Apache past prototype testing yet, so we made a little modification to cover our brothers until the attack copters are ready."

"So we're gonna fly out with the mini-gun and external fuel tanks on this mission?" Pierson wondered.

"We'll have to if we're gonna make it to Pereira without a stop. We'll jettison them before we get into tactical ops," Curt told them. "You guys about ready to see how she flies?" When everyone nodded excitedly he added, "I just hope nobody had a hearty breakfast this morning; you're not gonna believe what this bird can do!"

Webster's cautionary warning proved prophetic, as Bob Matthews and Dale Mixon threw off their headsets within minutes to lean out the door and blow chow. Neither Hal, Rambo nor Will would even look at them because they weren't feeling rock solid themselves. The Black Hawk had almost unbelievable maneuverability and could easily fly inverted as they hung from their shoulder belts. About fifteen minutes outside Howard Air Base, Webster took a southerly turn and flew towards a seemingly uninterrupted expanse of jungle until a clearing appeared with an old farmhouse on it. Webster half turned and pointed, "Watch that farmhouse and see what this pea-shooter has in it." He came in from the north at a fast pace and just as they were abreast of the farmhouse Webster jinked the copter ninety degrees and opened up with the 7.62mm mini-gun. They watched the upper half of the farmhouse quickly dissolve into splinters. Will was giving Hal and Rambo the thumbs up when Webster called over the headsets, "There's another one of my birds coming in at eleven o'clock." They watched with interest as the other bird closely parroted their approach to the farmhouse and further demolished it down to about knee height. They looked over at the Black Hawk as it flew by and noticed the crew chief standing in the door waving, but with the helmet and safety visor it was impossible to tell if Rico was giving them the high sign or not.

As they feathered down at Ft Davis, the other Black Hawk settled in alongside as everyone unhooked shoulder harnesses, doffed helmets and jumped out of the bird to go greet the other crew. As they walked up to the second helicopter Will was amazed to see Kelly Dupree unsnap her safety strap, doff her helmet and jump down to greet them. "So whatdya think about the Black Hawk?"

"Damn woman, that was you in the doorway? Jesus, you've taken right to this combat business eh?" Will said as he gave her a twirling hug.

"She's taken to this flying better than most recruits I've been around," Rico said proudly as he came up to shake hands.

"Kelly and Rico, I'd like you to meet Colonel Dale Mixon and this other gentleman is Bob Matthews, who's AWOL from his post in Managua." It was a reunion of sorts for Bob and Rico, so after exchanging greetings Will asked, "So who's piloting the other bird?"

Rico was smiling like he'd just gotten laid—which he might just have—as the other pilot walked over and only then took off his flight helmet. Pierson almost had a heart attack as he grabbed Vinny Sanders in a bear hug and screamed, "I can't fucking believe it! How the hell did you get here Vinny?"

"Hell, I heard you were going on another Kavanagh suicide mission, so somebody had to come bail your ass out! How the hell you been brother?"

Will was trying to understand the reference to 'another Kavanagh suicide mission' when it dawned on him that Vinny had been piloting the chopper that blew Sandrigan's casbah all to hell with the M129 grenade launcher. He jumped at him and gave him a bear hug, "Man am I glad to finally meet you Vinny; that was some job you did back in Algiers brother!"

It was smiles all around as they walked into the crew briefing room where a waitress was eagerly awaiting their drink orders. As they sat down around the table Will couldn't help but notice that Rico and Kelly were sitting beside one another chatting quietly. He smiled until they looked up as he gave Kelly two thumbs up. When the others saw him doing so he covered, "Man am I proud of Annie Oakley hanging out of that chopper like Slim Pickens riding the nuke in Dr. Strangelove. You guys don't know this, but Kelly Dupree is a Hollywood producer for Great West Studios when she's not out playing jungle survival games. Think we should put her through ROUST for some more formalized orientation?"

Hal, Pierson and Rico were all shaking their heads in the affirmative when Kelly asked, "What's ROUST?"

Hal took over and answered, "It's a combat survival training school that I run, and Rico and Alex are my department heads. And if you're going to pal around with this crowd when we go out for excitement, I'd say you probably could use a couple of weeks of training. I can assure you that when you graduate from ROUST there ain't a man alive that'll ever lay a hand on you again—unless you want him to!"

They were all laughing up a storm when Kelly replied, "I believe you may have a point after the education I got putting together that screenplay for the North African Invasion. I'll have to see what my boss says when I get back to LA. It lasts two weeks you say?"

Will was smiling for a living, "Right; and Rico's the department head in charge of close combat, survival training and assassination. Now don't those sound like pretty valuable skills to have around all those sharks hitting on you every day in Tinsel Town?"

"We'll see what Mr. Kowalski's got to say about that when I get back."

"So what's the plan of attack Kemosabe?" Rico asked Hal.

Hal and Will tacked up the large scale maps of Bogotá and Pereira on the walls as the others moved in to eyeball the targets. Will spotted a large map of Colombia that someone had already tacked to a chalkboard and moved it over as well.

Hal looked around the room and said, "I guess we've got all of our players here except Rose, and she's gonna be picked up for the primary descent into Pereira, where she's gonna impersonate Constanza's mistress. Now for everybody else, Copter One, which we'll dub Castle One, will fly directly to Bogotá from Colon; that's 540 miles. Is that within extended range Curt?"

"Yeah, we can make it no sweat with the reserve fuel tanks. You got a refueling site picked out?"

"Yeah, Tony Franklin and the boys at Mackall came through with a Colombian air base where their Special Operations unit is based. It's called Moreno Air Base in Puerto Salgar. That's 90 miles northwest of Bogotá and 90 miles northeast of Pereira. We can decide between now and then whether you want to stop there on the way in or the way out. By the way, Franklin says they like gold, but all we got is dollars and diamonds, so Rambo says we'll have 10,000 negotiation points if they don't like it."

"I heard they've got some gold coins in the Fort Quartermaster's vault. Think they'll consider a swap?" Curt Webster asked with a dastardly smirk.

Hal looked at Slickshot Mixon, "Why don't you take that one on Slickshot, I mean Colonel. They might listen to you and how many dollars do we have on us Willy?"

"Fifty thou," Will said as he heaved up the gym bag, "but I wouldn't think we'd need that much av gas. You know we need some for insurance money." He pulled a banded ten thousand stack and handed it to Mixon, "Why don't you see if the Quartermaster is willing to help us out?"

After Mixon left, Hal turned back to the crowd, "Alright Curt, as much as we all want you to high tail it out of Colombian airspace as soon as you have Colton on board, we're gonna need you to fly west over to here," he said pointing to a spot between Pereira and Armenia, "and fly into this coffee plantation that may be the alternate holding spot for Will and Rico. Pierson will hopefully have the Consuela snatch under control and can jump on Castle One at the Military Academy when we transfer Colton to the chopper from the Embassy limo. I want Alex and Pierson on Castle One for the plantation approach, as things might get a bit dicey on the ground there. Rose says the ELN's got two dozen soldiers surrounding the place, so at least we won't be going in naked. I'll take Bob Matthews with me on Castle Two to drop off Rose in Pereira, and I'm sure Vinny can save us if things start sliding sideways. Of course, we're going to have Will, Rico and Rose on board for the trip out after Constanza hopefully loses his life. Any questions or thoughts?"

Will was looking at the fax Brad Covington had sent, "Okay, we got some names here Kemosabe. The plantation is *Hacienda Cardona* in a small place called Tres Puertas; that's in Risaralda Province. The mansion is *Casa*

Manrique, Pinares, Pereira. Do you see them on the map?"

Vinny and Curt were eyeballing the two maps like heathens, "Okay, here's Pinares subdivision I guess, and here's the only mansion with tennis courts anywhere near. You see the hacienda on there Vincent?"

Vinny snatched the fax and smiled, "Hot damn, coordinates." He actually tracked longitude and latitude manually off the map axes and pointed to a spot, "Here we go, looks awful lonely around the hacienda, which should work in our favor." Pierson was now next to him tapping the shaded area, "Yep, looks like some tree cover around the coffee fields Rambo."

Hal was nodding now, getting into pre-launch mode, "Any other items of interest?"

"As a matter of fact yes," said Kelly with a dose of attitude, "what about me? Which copter am I going to be in? I didn't bring all this film to take pictures of helicopters taking off and landing."

"No fucking way you're going in Dupree, and that's final. Now if you've got to go pout in the corner, go right ahead. You ain't dying on my fucking mission," Will said with conviction.

"Oh yeah, what if something happens and Rose can't make the trip to Pereira for the swap; how are you going to cover your ass if that happens? I don't see any other women in this mission brief."

He wanted to slap the living shit out of her, but caught himself walking over and touching her raven black hair, "It might not take too much of an impersonation for you to be Consuela Diaz; I've seen a picture of her. What do you think Rambo?"

He shook his head, "They're both hot, there's no doubt about that. And Kelly's probably only a couple of years younger than Consuela. I think it's a good risk; I mean if Rose gets hung up we're fucked from the get-go unless we come in with blazing guns, and then you and Rico become shark bait as well. Now don't get me wrong, I ain't for sending non-coms into battle, but Kelly might just be the silver bullet for this mission."

Will grabbed Kelly's shoulders and got two inches from her nose, "Goddamn it, I'll rot in hell if anything happens to you Kelly. Jesus Christ, I love you like my sister. Dom will skin me alive when she finds out about this. Motherfucker, the shit I get into!"

"So we won't tell her until after the fact, deal?" Kelly said with a self-satisfied smirk.

"Hey, you love the rest of us like brothers, so what's the difference? It's almost come down to either she plays ball with us or we fail, potentially. I say we take her along." Hal then went to Kelly, kissed her on the forehead and said, "And my ass will rot in hell with Willy if anything happens to you dammit."

She smiled at them, "Well then, we won't let anything happen to me will we?" She looked at Curt and asked, "Think they have any wig shops in Colon? I'm supposed to be a hot blonde, right?"

"So what's zero hour?" Curt asked.

"What's the flight time to Bogotá?" Will replied.

"With our light loads, we can make it in three hours," he said after some quick mental math. "In fact, with the external tanks we might just be able to make the entire trip without refueling."

"Okay, weather's supposed to be overcast after clearing the coast a hundred miles, and the forecast for Bogotá and Pereira is for light rain most of the day. That's gonna help us from sniper considerations, unless the pricks have thermal sights. With the rain, Rose or Kelly can wear raincoats with the hoods on, and that'll help with the swap. Okay, Rambo's flying out when we get back to PC and set up his surveillance." He looked at him and asked, "You got the name of Tony's mole in Bogotá?" When Dan nodded he added, "I think I'd trust Delta's mole more than the embassy's RSO—no offense Bob."

"So where's the snatch gonna take place? Have you talked to Penny lately?" Pierson asked as Will went into a panic.

"Oh shit," he said as he pulled out the sat phone and couldn't raise Penny. "Shit, she's in the air now flying in to Colombia. Shit, shit, shit."

Kelly looked at him like an imbecile, "Didn't you ask that Embassy guy in Bogotá to serve as her chaperone? Don't you think he'd know?"

This time he kissed her on the lips as he dialed Brad Covington and was greatly relieved when he answered on the second ring, "Hey Brad, Will Kavanagh here."

"Yeah, I wondered when you were going to call, what's up?"

"Hey, I've sorta lost track of when Penny Martindale was going to arrive there, and I was hoping you'd know."

"She's right here in the airport. I just met her, want to speak with her?"

"Please."

"Hey babe, how's everything going?" Penny asked, sounding completely refreshed after her $6000 first class luxury ride.

"We're kinda busy at the moment. Did you already schedule your interviews with Eliana Jiménez and Consuela Diaz?"

"Of course I did Will; I wouldn't have flown here without having those two meetings locked down. Why, don't tell me you want me to reschedule!"

"Of course not, you're gonna be my Pulitzer Prize-winning reporter. When and where are the interviews? I don't want to try and call you while you're with these important women."

"Let's see, both of them are in my suite at the Tequendama Intercontinental near the Presidential Palace. I'm having Mrs. Diaz over for a working lunch at noon and Mrs. Jiménez at one o'clock."

"Nice digs for the interviews Penny Lane; I take it you're staying in the penthouse suite?"

"Of course, since you made it so convenient for me. By the way, what am I going to owe you for all of this?"

"Not what I want, I can guarantee you that. Listen, I'm gonna try and hook you up with the Archbishop of Rio de Janeiro as part of your investigation. That's the largest city in South America; what do you think?"

"I cannot believe you are being so kind William. We'll talk more when I've finished with these two important ladies; any last requests?"

"Yeah, fly back to the US as soon as you can after the interview with Señora Jiménez. Call me if anything interferes with your interviews, okay? And do us all proud, will ya?"

"You got it cowboy, take care."

———

"It's two o'clock Mr. Kavanagh, don't you think it's time to make contact with Hector Constanza?" Hal prodded.

Will tried to free his mind of everything before he dialed the number, but Hal handed him a piece of hotel letterhead that included the three things he wanted to get across during the call. First, to speak directly to Colton to prove he was still alive; second, to confirm the exact time and place of the exchange; and third, insisting to bring along an associate. He could hear the call being routed through several relays, which told him it wasn't a satellite phone.

On the third ring a voice answered, "Señor Kavanagh I presume?"

"This is Will Kavanagh, to whom am I speaking?" Will asked as Hal became a second set of skin listening in on the call.

"I am Hector Constanza Señor Kavanagh, and I salute your punctuality.

Are you prepared to complete the exchange for your brother?"

"Well that all depends on whether you can prove he's still alive, now doesn't it? Please put my brother on the phone so that I can ascertain his condition."

"I am sorry *Señor* Kavanagh, but that was not part of the arrangement I spoke with Archbishop Villaponteau about. And besides, your brother Colton is being held in a secure location to insure his safety until the exchange."

"Well, I guess we don't have a deal then do we? Do you think I am foolish enough to surrender myself to you if you cannot prove my brother is alive? Now put him on the phone or this deal is off, and I mean off for good."

"And just what are you prepared to do if I do not *Señor* Kavanagh? I seem to be holding all of the trump cards, as I believe you *Norteamericanos* are so prone to expound.

"If he's already dead, so are you Constanza. So spare me the melodramatics and put the phone in his hand."

"So you are threatening me *Señor*? Do you know how many men I have protecting me?"

"I would never be so presumptuous as to threaten you Constanza; I'm telling you what's going to happen to you if you have already killed my brother."

"I see, so you are assuring me of my death if I do not comply, is that my understanding?"

"Yep, put him on." Hal was looking at Will with dread but he kept a stiff upper lip and waited. As he did Will pantomimed rolling the dice on a craps table. Hal just closed his eyes and shook his head.

"Will, is that you?" Colton's voice finally asked, a bit flustered but sounding fairly normal.

"Hey buddy, what's your mother's father's middle name?"

"The same as yours Will, where are you?"

"Never mind that, have they hurt you in any way?"

"No, but they're keeping me in some dark room; I'm alright if that's what you're asking."

"Do you have your assurance now *Señor* Kavanagh?" Constanza asked suddenly.

"That's the first one, so the deal's potentially on."

"And what else could you possibly want to know?"

"The exchange is to take place tomorrow at the Bogotá Botanical Gardens Museum at high noon, is that correct?"

"That is correct *Señor*, and I would warn you against trying to station armed men; they will be shot on sight. What is high noon?"

"High noon is when your clock starts tickin' Hector. And yeah I get the fact that you'll have the place surrounded, but I ain't coming alone. I'm bringing an associate with me who will also be unarmed."

"That is not what I insisted upon *Señor* Kavanagh. Do you wish to sentence your brother to death?"

"Not at all Hector, but I am an ignorant American, and I insist on bringing an associate with me who is fluent in Spanish. That way I at least have a chance of knowing what is being communicated."

"I believe you are not so ignorant *Señor*, please hold the line for one moment." Will could hear some quiet chattering in the background before Constanza came back. "The request for an associate is granted, but I must warn you that he will be dealt with in the same manner as you. Are you familiar with the biblical concept of an eye for an eye?"

"Very much so Hector, but I also believe in the inevitability of good over evil. I assure you that neither of us will be armed with anything but God's trust. I very much look forward to meeting you in person tomorrow *Señor* Hector Constanza. I believe it will prove a momentous day for both of us; until then."

"Yes, Mr. Kavanagh, I suggest you enjoy your last night on this earth."

"And you as well Mr. Constanza; be sure and kiss your wife goodbye."

"Now that was an Oscar worthy performance Mr. Kavanagh," Kelly said as she swooped on him. She turned with annoyance as Pierson was holding a tape measure up the length of her body and making notes. "And just what in the hell are you doing Rambo?"

"Taking your measurements of course. I'm going to purchase a nice Nehru vest for you to keep you safe during this escapade. What color do you prefer?" He asked, swooping the tape over her shoulders and hips.

She seemed put out with the measurement taking, "Some earth tone will do fine. Is it gonna be that dangerous where we're going?"

"Yeah from what I hear it is, but we've got to give you an extra layer of protection," he said as he smiled at Hal.

"Good thinking partner, we might all need some of those come to think about it. Who'd you find to make the vest?" Hal asked.

"There's this guy named Miguel Caballero in Bogotá who specializes in bullet-proof clothing. Brad Covington knows him and says they've got a couple of Nehru vests that a customer didn't need."

Will thought about 'didn't need' and offered, "I see why he'd insist on paying in advance. Let's hope one of the vests fits my Cossack Queen."

Kelly was frowning as she said, "Jesus, you think I'll get shot? Now I see what you mean about going into combat. It didn't sound as though you and Constanza will be swapping Christmas cards."

"We got what we wanted, now let's hope he allows us to stay alive long enough for me to tell him his mistress is missing. That ought to get his attention," Will said with a glance to heaven.

Hal was the sobering influence now, "Let's get in touch with Rose and see how things are developing with our on-the-move ELN associates."

On the third ring Rose's voice was muffled as Hal asked, "You alright Rose, I can barely hear you?"

"It's raining so hard here in Pereira that I can hardly hear you either Hal. Is all in place for tomorrow?"

"That kind of depends on you and Daniel's friends, now doesn't it? Have you been able to conduct any surveillance?"

"Oh yes, our friend The Horseman is also in Pereira, and has brought many of his compatriots."

"That sounds very good; has he been able to surveil the *Hacienda Cardona* that is near Tres Puertas as well?"

"Yes, he has placed two dozen of his fighters there, but the level of activity in the plantation house appears abnormal. The Horseman described it as a human bee hive."

"So that's where he's holding Colton until the exchange in Bogotá tomorrow. Is there a possibility that one or more of The Horseman's men can infiltrate to gain a better feel for the interior configuration?"

"Our friend the priest is taking the lead on that infiltration even as we speak. I have a very bad piece of information to pass along to you however."

"Okay, what is it? You cannot make it to Bogotá to facilitate the exchange for Mrs. Diaz?"

"How did you know this Hal? The roads over the mountains are impassable in this rain. I am truly sorry to let you down like this. Is there anything I can do to make this up to you?"

"You bet, tell The Horseman that we must—absolutely must—find the sniper nests before we enter the *Casa Manrique* grounds in Pinares with the helicopter. If the sniper is in place I am afraid the mission will fail. Can you communicate that request to The Horseman?"

"Of course I can, is there any other information you need to know to make the mission a success?"

"Yes, I need to know if you and Daniel are getting along all right."

She snickered before replying, "If he wasn't a priest I would marry him. He is the most captivating man I have been around in my life."

"Good, that's what I wanted to hear. Do not worry about missing the swap with the mistress; we have found a suitable replacement. Please focus your efforts on neutralizing Constanza's forces around the Hacienda and especially the Casa in Pereira. If you do that we will all have an excellent chance of surviving this dangerous mission. Please call me if anything changes for the worse, will you?"

"I promise I will, and I wish Will God speed in his encounter with the Satan's angel tomorrow."

Hal felt the tug on his sleeve and nodded, "Hold on Rose, Will wants to speak to you."

"Thank you for everything Rosario; I will never forget what you have done for my family. I love you Rose, goodbye."

Will looked at Kelly through a fog of tears, "Okay Kelly, your role in this just went from backup to primary. Are you ready in your mind to do this?" He looked around the room and nodded at each of his veteran compadres, "If you have the least bit of doubt in your heart about doing this, we'll find another way. God knows I love you woman, and it nearly tears my heart out to put you right in the middle of ground zero here. But I can assure you that Rose, Marco Pintoles and the rest of us will do everything in our power to keep you safe."

She stepped up to him and put her arms around his neck, "I'd do it a million times to keep Dom from raising that child of yours by herself. I won't pretend I'm not terrified, but dammit, there are some things you just have to take a chance on. How soon can we get that Nehru vest?"

Will glanced at Rambo who reported, "I'll have it on Castle One when we rendezvous at the safe haven." He looked at Will and said, "We'd better get back to PC, I've got a bird out in an hour."

"What safe haven?" Will suddenly wondered.

Hal and Rambo had an arm around each shoulder as they led him out the door to the Black Hawk. Hal leaned in and whispered, "If you don't know certain things Willy, then Hector can't torture 'em out of ya, right?"

Will merely nodded as he gave Pierson the warrior grip, "See you in Colombia on the way home tomorrow Rambo; you're the man."

Curt Webster had the Black Hawk at full military power blasting back across the Isthmus at over 180 mph, setting the big black bird down softly outside the cargo terminal at Tocumen International. Curt reached across to the copilot's seat and shook his hand, "Only a lifer would have his go bag with him eternally. Don't take no wooden nickels Rambo, and we'll see ya tomorrow for some fun and games in good old Colombia."

Pierson smiled at his buddy, "Yeah right cowboy; let's hope those ELN dudes come with their game faces on. Thanks for the lift hombre."

Outside the other copter back at Ft Davis, Will had Vinny hemmed in as he unwound his brain. "Okay, we'll need Castle One at the Military Academy by 1215 hours, and don't forget to pick up Pierson and Blondie at 1415 wherever Hal told you to keep me in the dark. That'll put Alex and Pierson on Castle One, and I sure wouldn't want to tangle with either one of those boys. I want full combat packs on each bird, including a Remington 700. Gauge fuel consumption as you cross to determine if and when we need to refuel. Here's nine Canadian Maple Leafs for each bird—that's seventy-two hundred in av gas credits. Vinny, I want Hal and Bob Matthews with Castle Two, and that'll be our combat information center. Kelly goes on Castle Two. Hal calls all the shots once Rico and I are wheels up out of Tocumen tomorrow morning at 0930. Anything I forgot about?"

"Yeah Willy, I believe it's time for you to wear your own shield," Vinny said as he handed him something in his closed hand.

He accepted the oval silver medal suspended from a long chain and asked, "What is it Vinny?"

"It's the Saint Michael Medal, and I want you to wear it for the rest of your life."

"Who was Saint Michael?"

"He was the Archangel who fought Satan in the battle of Armageddon, from the book of Revelations. You are now a warrior whose heart is pure and you do violence only to promote good. Please accept it as a token of our esteem for you in the coming trials you will face in Colombia. God Speed Will."

He put it around his neck and told him, "Thanks Vinny, you've saved my ass before. Let's hope God's on our side tomorrow. God Bless you brother."

Will didn't make it a step before Kelly was clinging to him like a vine, whimpering before she unleashed a shameful kiss on him. "Goddamn you Will Kavanagh, don't you die on me tomorrow or I will never forgive you."

He pulled back to see her eyes as he pinched her ass, "Oh come on Dupree, I've still got a couple of thousand orgasms left in me. It would be a sin before all womanhood to waste such a gift, *n'est pas?*" She was still standing at the helo pad with Alex and Rico as Hal, Mixon, and he watched the slick black bird slowly rise up and quickly disappear over the jungle and wondered if this would be the last sunset they'd ever witness.

———

"Please don't cry Dom, we've got a good chance of pulling this off tomorrow. It's time for optimism, not dread. We've done everything we possibly could have to get ready for this other than bring in the Special Forces to spring Colton for us. We've got to trust the friends that got us this far, and I'm not sure there are four people more effective at war than Hal, Dan Pierson, Alex and Rico. I know this scares you, but I must go return Colton to his home alive, so I really don't have any choice in this matter. By the way, Vinny the copter pilot gave me this today, whatdya think?" He asked as he handed her the St Michael's medal.

She looked at it curiously and asked, "What patron saint is Michael to our Catholic friends?"

"According to Vinny, he was the Archangel who fought Satan during Armageddon as portrayed in the Biblical book of Revelations. He told me that my heart is pure like Saint Michael, so I will prevail over the evil that stands in front of me now."

She held the medal against her pregnant belly and intoned, "May God spare my husband in this struggle between love and hate."

He smiled as he laid his head on her stomach and told her, "It's up to God, friends and Sikorsky helicopters now baby. I love you more than anything."

57

INTO THE HEART OF DARKNESS

THE FINAL APPROACH INTO Bogotá was interesting, because he'd only seen maps of it before, and they hadn't broken cloud cover until they were 1000 feet above ground level. Will was impressed with the city and its surroundings, as it seemed to be situated between mountain peaks and ravines. The vegetation was a deep dark emerald green, and the city center of high rises with adjacent mountains looked a bit like Los Angeles from the air, with residential neighborhoods extending out in all directions bounded only by the mountains.

"So whatdya think?" Rico asked.

"Looks like a nice place, but I could have done without that turbulence coming down through the clouds. Is it always this way?"

"Nah, there's a storm working its way in, and that might work out well for us. You sure that RSO is gonna meet us?"

"Yeah, he'll be here; we're his big excitement for the month. Oh shit, I just remembered, he's chaperoning Penny Martindale around. As hot as she is, I wouldn't be surprised if he completely forgot about us!"

"Well fuck him if he does; we can find the Botanical Gardens on our own."

Since they'd checked no baggage, they were heading straight out to the taxi stand when someone said, "Will Kavanagh!"

He looked around to find Penny Martindale dressed to the nines trying not to stumble in her four inch heels as she made her way over to them. "Hey baby, welcome to Bogotá. When'd you get in?"

"Last night," she said as she kissed him sweetly on the lips. "Brad showed me around the night life here; this is a happening place!"

He shook Brad's hand and introduced him to Rico, "So what's on the agenda now? Heading straight over for your interviews?"

"Yeah, but we're dropping you two off at the Cathedral; it seems a certain Archbishop would like an audience with you," Brad said as he led them to his Embassy Suburban.

Once underway, Brad pulled out a bag and said, "Dan Pierson ordered this vest and asked that I pass it to you. Who's it for? Looks a little tight for you ma man."

Will took out the Nehru vest and examined it, impressed with the toughness of the fabric, even though it seemed to weigh twice as much as a sleeveless vest should. "A friend of ours needs it for a business meeting in the near future. Tell me, do you have a lead into this Miguel Caballero's clothing business?"

"Sure, we have an Embassy account with him; nobody goes out on the street without one of his blue blazers on."

"So what's the deal with this guy's blazers? Are they some fashion statement here in Bogotá?" Penny asked.

Will got next to her sexy nose and replied, "They're all bullet-proof baby; this is a dangerous place to be. Hal and I are most interested in setting up a business relationship with *Señor* Caballero."

As the Embassy driver pulled up to the Archiepiscopal Palace, Penny pulled him in close, "Please be careful Will, don't let this be the last time I ever see you."

He smiled, gave her a passionate kiss that ruined her makeup and replied, "What, and miss out on my coonass Cajun sister's wedding? Perish the thought. And good luck with those interviews. I want to see your article in Newsweek; think Pulitzer Prize baby doll, later!"

A smartly dressed bellman opened the door to the Archbishop's residence as Rico asked, "What's this all about? I don't remember this being on our agenda."

"Who knows brother, but I can assure you Juan Villaponteau is our ally."

They were startled when Villaponteau appeared behind them, "Welcome to our house of worship gentlemen. How was your trip in?"

"Fine," Will said as they shook his hand, "did you want to give us some last minute advice Your Grace?"

"No, actually I wanted to accompany you to the Botanical Gardens. I feel a special empathy with the quest you are about to undertake." He looked down at his watch and said, "It would appear that we should leave now to make your appointment with *Señor* Constanza. Please follow me."

Neither expected papal transportation to the exchange, but were impressed when they got to the back of the Palace to find a black Mercedes limousine waiting with the back door open. As they climbed in, Juan motioned Rico and Will to sit on the rear-facing seat and were soon underway the short distance to the Botanical Garden. He looked at Will and asked, "How do you plan on avoiding Constanza's revenge, knowing what his intentions are? And I see you have brought an associate to also endure this agony?"

He half-smiled, "Actually, if Hector can restrain himself from killing me quickly, he will discover with certain horror that his mistress has been abducted and is being held as ransom for our safe return."

Juan was shaking his head in admiration, "I must salute your excellent investigative skills Will; you are aware that this abduction will result in the dissolution of two marriages don't you?"

"Forgive my impertinence Your Grace, but the intensity of the affair between the lovers would indicate that the two marriages were on tenuous grounds at best, wouldn't you say?"

"Yes, and I realize this might be the only thing that could enrage Hector enough to consider letting you live. Now, if the two of you would indulge me as I bestow a blessing upon you in preparation for your dangerous venture," he said as they both kneeled in front of the limo bench. Villaponteau put a hand on each of our heads as he said:

"Holy Michael, the Archangel, defend us in battle. Be our safeguard against the wickedness and snares of the devil. May <u>God</u> rebuke him, we humbly pray; and do you, O Prince of the heavenly host, by the power of <u>God</u> cast into <u>hell</u> <u>Satan</u> and all the <u>evil</u> spirits who wander through the world seeking the ruin of souls. Amen."

When Will looked up at the Archbishop through tears, he pulled the St Michael's Medal out of his shirt and showed it to him. "Thank you Your Grace, as you see others have also invoked the spirit of Michael to assist us in our journey today."

———

As they pulled into the gate of the Botanical Gardens they could see three armed gunmen watching the Archdiocese limo approach. When they got to the portico of the museum, they saw a man assumed to be Constanza stand-ing next to Colton. Will looked at Juan, "I almost forgot, please drive directly to the Simon Bolivar Military Academy next door and deliver my brother to the men who will be flying a large black helicopter." He handed him the bag with the Kevlar vest and asked, "Please have Colton take this with him on the helicopter. It will hopefully save a friend's life."

He smiled and nodded, "Your friend Mr. Covington advised us earlier of the plans for your brother. Do not worry about him, worry about your own self Will. Hector is an unpredictable murderer."

Will hugged him tightly, "At least we don't have to worry about my soul Your Grace!"

They could see the surprise on Constanza's face as Archbishop Villapon-teau exited the limo with Rico and Will and walked towards them. Constanza was about what one would have expected for a field worker who had moved up in an organization via a long series of treacherous acts; he was about five-six, early forties and bald but for a bowl of graying hair surrounding his head. His life of wealth was beginning to show as well, as his growing midriff bore witness. They stopped about ten feet in front of him as he said by way of wel-come, "I did not expect you to be accompanied by the Archbishop of Bogotá *Señor* Kavanagh. To what do we owe this pleasure Your Excellency?"

Without expression Villaponteau replied, "I am here to provide for the safety of this innocent Christian missionary *Señor* Constanza. I trust he is in good health?"

Constanza took one arm and pushed Colton forward saying, "He is fine, take a look for yourself."

As Colton walked away from Hector, Will grabbed him and hugged him tightly, "Go with God brother, I will see you soon. You can trust Archbishop Villaponteau. I love you Colton."

Colton was crying as he broke the embrace and walked to Villaponteau, who motioned him to get into the limousine and then turned to Constanza, "This man Will Kavanagh has done nothing to harm you *Señor* Constanza. I beg that you show some empathy for his plight."

"The sins of the father must be atoned for priest, isn't that what is says in the Holy Scripture? This man was the catalyst for the cold-blooded murder of my brother Enrique, and he must reap what he has sowed. Do not concern yourself with such matters priest, for there are many in your flock in need of your compassion and attention."

"But he only reacted when your brother threatened to cut open the womb of his pregnant wife. How is that cold-blooded murder? He was only trying to protect a child who had already been blessed by the Holy Roman Church. Can you hold yourself in such sacrilege?"

Will was wondering if Villaponteau might be enraging Constanza bad enough for him to shoot the Cardinal himself, "You have no proof of what you say priest. I, however, have the body of my only brother, or what was left of it after *Señor* Kavanagh had his head blown off. Now I would suggest that you depart with this Christian missionary and be grateful for the compassion that is being demonstrated by a grieving brother."

Juan considered him for a moment and then started to get into the limo before looking back, "Be careful what you wish for *Señor* Constanza, for the wages of sin is death."

———

As Villaponteau's limo pulled away, two of Constanza's guards came up and roughly frisked Rico and Will, even making them take off their shoes to examine them for hidden weapons. Will was quietly pleased when the shoes passed muster, as Jimbo Meaux had outfitted him with a special pair of ordinary looking ankle high boots that contained a secret compartment where the steel shank of the shoe would normally reside. Unlike other stealth boots, the hidden compartment could only be activated by pressing down on the top two shoe lace eyelets at the same time. Will hoped he would have an opportunity to utilize the hidden knife, which in fact was the switchblade Enrique had used to cut his face and press against Dom's stomach. They looked on with curiosity as a white limousine pulled around to the museum portico and a guard tied their hands behind their backs just before pushing them roughly into the rear-facing seat. Constanza climbed in, sat in the rear seat with a bodyguard on each side and smiled at them.

As they pulled out into traffic, Will noticed the sounds of a helicopter taking off from somewhere nearby and smiled inwardly that Phase One of the operation was now complete. Constanza heard the same sound but ignored it, "If you had a choice *Señor* Kavanagh, how would you like to die?"

"Well," he considered, "if I had my choice I'd like to go out in a nitrous oxide cloud, but I don't plan on going that route until the doctor tells me I have dementia."

Constanza laughed at his response, "I can assure you that it will be no such comfortable circumstance. But since I have your undivided attention, could you please tell me why you killed my brother Enrique?"

"Listen Mr. Constanza, I didn't even know your brother's name until he was slicing my face open with a switchblade knife. That's how he made his point that I'd never forget his name. He'd probably be alive today if he hadn't pushed the point of that knife against my pregnant wife's stomach."

"I have only your word to confirm your claim, but I was not aware that Enrique threatened your defenseless wife. But there must be revenge for this act, so you will still die at my hands. In consideration of your explanation, I will make it a quick and relatively painless death, unlike that experienced by Police Lieutenant Rivas who failed to warn Enrique of impending danger. Are you aware of how Lieutenant Rivas died?"

"Yeah, I heard his genitals were redirected to his mouth. I am interested Mr. Constanza, why was my brother—a mere missionary trying to improve the plight of the poor—such a threat to you and your brother?"

He got a harsh look on his face, "Because he was stirring up labor unrest and activism among the poor. Such activities unfortunately attract the attention of international news organizations, and we could not afford the notoriety given the importance of the area around Managua for our distribution network."

"You mean for the cocaine pipeline that utilizes children as lookouts?"

"Do not attempt to lecture me on the moralistic aspects of the cocaine trade *Señor* Kavanagh, for it is the undisciplined, spoiled Americans who create the limitless demand for our product."

"Well, I'm not sure the Americans have anything on the Europeans," he offered as counterpoint.

Constanza looked out the window as they made a turn onto some highway, "This is where we must blindfold you and your accomplice. You have proven cunning in your past escapades."

Will was wondering if he knew about the Sandrigan operation when black hoods were placed over their heads. He filed it away in his mind to practice being hooded as a torture method if he lived through this one. Interestingly, one of the guards removed the rope restraints, at least making the ride more pleasant without their hands tied behind them.

As they seemed to drive on endlessly, Constanza decided it was time to enlighten their understanding of the cocaine business, "Are you familiar with the cocaine trade *Señor* Kavanagh?"

Figuring he'd humor him he said, "Not really, I've tried it a couple of times, and I know it comes from Colombia but that's about it."

"Would it surprise you to know that two hundred-fifty kilos of coca leaves must be harvested to produce one kilo of cocaine hydrochloride?"

"Wow, now that is interesting; not a very efficient transfer then?" He asked, figuring it'd be beneficial to keep him engaged on his specialty.

"Actually, the coca leaves go through a transformation from paste to base to finally purified cocaine hydrochloride. It is quite a cumbersome process."

"Really, so where does the process begin? I mean where are the coca leaves grown?"

"The coca with the highest alkaline content grows on the eastern side of the Andes Mountains above 1500 meters elevation. Most coca harvesting takes place in Bolivia, Peru and Ecuador."

"So why is Colombia the cocaine capital of the world if the raw product comes from other places?"

"Because the laboratories that transform the paste and base are located here in Colombia. The final transformation process is quite involved and requires a tightly controlled environment to be performed on an efficiently high volume basis."

"So the raw materials are grown away from Colombia and the cocaine that is shipped out is refined in Colombia? That sounds like a lot of transportation across a large area? How do you manage to maintain an efficient flow of materials?"

"By use of our friends in the Fuerzas Armadas Revolucionarias de Colombia, what you might know as the FARC. While the FARC does not actually process coca, they are instrumental in assuring the safe transport of the paste and base to our labs here in Colombia. Do you find this interesting?"

"Very much so as a matter of fact. How do you manage to maintain a non-combative stance with the National Police?"

He ignored the question and asked in response, "And what is your relationship with Archbishop Villaponteau? I am very curious as to how you enlisted his services in this endeavor."

"I called an old friend in Argentina, Archbishop Acosta, to help me make contact. It's not like your phone number's in the book you know."

They heard a grunt and some unintelligible chattering right before the hoods came off. After Will had a moment to adjust his eyesight he looked at Constanza and said, "Thanks."

"So *Señor* Kavanagh, I would like to hear about the demise of my emerging business associate *Señor* el-Boukhari."

"Really? I thought he was only into peddling heroin, hashish and marijuana. I don't see the thread, other than you both deal in dangerous drugs."

Hector glanced towards the ceiling and continued, "Please my naïve, judgmental *Norteamericano* friend, we only deal in substances that are eagerly sought after for the purpose of decadent entertainment of the spoiled masses of rich people."

"So you don't believe that farmers chew coca leaves for stimulation or that the mules that move your paste smoke the paco?"

"This may be true, but members of my organization are forbidden from indulging in cocaine under threat of death. I need professionals with their heads clear doing the serious business of our enterprise."

Something clicked in his head about the southern European network distribution that Marty Lindstrum wanted from Sandrigan's codebook, "So Sandrigan's southern European distribution network looked like promising marketing territory for cocaine, eh?"

Constanza smiled, "The finest, with Nice, the French Riviera and Monaco with all the wealthy tourists. But you had to come along and ruin that for me *Señor* Kavanagh. Before I kill you, would you be so kind as to tell me what *Señor* el-Boukhari did to enrage you so? And how in the world did you get close enough to kill him?"

"You mean like as close as I am to you right now?" He asked just before a gun barrel slammed against his right eyebrow. When he came to and opened his eyes again, his right eye was blurry and blood was running down over it. A terrible headache suddenly overtook the right side of his head. He flinched when Constanza wiped his face with a handkerchief, causing darts of pain to spring from his eyebrow.

When he saw Will had refocused he told him, "My associates don't take such veiled threats lightly *Señor* Kavanagh. I would suggest that you refrain from inciting them further. Now would you care to tell me how you managed to kill a North African warlord in his own territory?"

He looked at Constanza imagining how he would kill him but instead answered, "He made a critical error in judgment Mr. Constanza—he openly declared that he wanted to brutally murder my wife. Now if he hadn't been so psychotically deranged, he might still be alive and entertaining your business proposition."

Hector nodded his head as he lit a cigar, "So it would seem that you react violently to threats against your women *Señor* Kavanagh. At least we won't have that to worry about here in Colombia. So how did you kill *Señor* el-Boukhari? I am waiting for your answer."

Will looked at him with a cold hard stare, "A nine millimeter parabellum right between the eyes took the fight right out of him. And he underestimated my ability to enlist friends, obviously."

"Such as the CIA? You won't be enjoying any such association here *Señor* Kavanagh; the CIA is watched by the National Police, the FARC and the cartels. We also keep close tabs on your Drug Enforcement Administration. You have no friends here in Colombia."

"Well, I suppose I'll have to look to God Almighty to help me out of this, eh?"

He smiled, "You mean your alleged friends in the Church? I'm afraid they will not come to your aid here in Colombia; we all try to peacefully coexist. Since you have been so forthcoming with information I am interested in, I will arrange that you also see a nine millimeter parabellum as your last view in life."

"I could think of worse ways to go, but I ain't quite ready to check out just yet Hector. I'm gonna have a baby girl in two months. Wouldn't want to miss out on seeing her come into the world, now would I?"

"Worthy and lofty goals, but alas you won't be there for the blessed event. You are in my home turf now."

"And where might that be? We've been driving for a while."

"Actually my home is in Cali, but a dear friend and business associate has agreed to let me use his plantation outside Pereira where we can have some privacy."

"And what's in Pereira, I've never heard of it? Does it contain some classic torture chamber? And please tell me why you insisted on this meeting on Saturday; are you by chance Jewish?"

He smiled and nodded to his henchman who this time delivered a punch to the solar plexus that he was only partially able to brace in anticipation of. As Will tried to catch his breath he told them, "The National Police is celebrating their founding today, the 89th anniversary as it was. Highway checkpoints and such are limited to main roads leading into Bogotá today. Do not worry *Señor* Kavanagh, I will entertain you at a fine hacienda this evening and will sacrifice your soul to the patron saint at noon tomorrow."

Will half-smiled, "And Aleandro Muñoz, your able-bodied understudy taking time off from his Celeno duties will perform it?"

This resulted in some harsh chatter between Hector and the bodyguards as Rico squirmed slightly. Finally Constanza said, "Who is this Aleandro man you speak of?"

"Come on Hector, that's him that hit me in the stomach. Are we such high priority targets that you forsake the transshipment cell?"

Aleandro produced the gun again, pointing it at Will and pulling back the hammer as Constanza smiled. "I'll give you one opportunity to explain how you know that *Señor* Kavanagh."

"Actually, you can call me Will; it's a lot easier. As for how I know about Aleandro, your mole on the Sandinista Police force, José Rivas, didn't stand up well to interrogation. We assured him he would die sooner than he did if he told you we'd talked. Obviously he didn't."

"Is that all he told you Will?" Constanza asked with a smile.

"Nah, he told us that Enrique was gonna kill me, my wife and our unborn child regardless of what we said or did. We were collateral clutter the *Celeno* didn't need managing the pipeline from Cali to New York City. Nice place you've got in Los Robles; Rivas told us about that too. You know, it's a shame your brother had to go to all the trouble; hell, we've already sent the article about Bolt Sportswear to the New York Times, sorry Aleandro."

Hector's breathing hastened as Aleandro grunted to him in Spanish. "Aleandro wants to shoot you now Will, but I told him we had to entertain you this evening. You see, we are not such uncivilized beings, no?"

Knowing it was time for the *coup de grâs*, Will told him, "I see, and will there be entertainment at this hacienda? I understand you are quite the ladies' man."

His expression turned deadly serious as he slapped Will, "I am a family man *Señor* Kavanagh, and a righteous father and husband. Do not insult me with such nonsense you heard from your CIA associates."

"Hmm, I guess my intel was all wet then Hector. I heard you were banging the hottest women in Bogotá; damn, I gotta tell Lindstrum he's got it wrong, *n'est pas?*"

"Martin Lindstrum?" Hector asked and laughed with his bodyguards. "Lindstrum knows only what I tell him *Señor* Will, so these rumors are quite slanderous, no?"

"So, you deny fucking the eyes out of Marta Cruz on Aruba this past August?" Will asked bracing himself for the assault.

The Colombian's once again chattered before Hector smiled, "Aleandro thinks your source of rumors is suspect, but your targets are certainly worthy. Whom else have you heard such rumors about?"

"Okay, let's try this one on for size Hector. Two days before Aleandro snatched my brother outside Masaya, you were entertaining a beautiful woman at Cocles Beach in Puerto Viejo. Oh, that's just south of Limon, Costa Rica."

Constanza grabbed the Sig Sauer from Aleandro and pointed it at him, "I'll give you thirty seconds to prove such lies before I kill you and your friend, Kavanagh."

"No problem," Will said, still smiling, "have Aleandro get the two photographs inside my jacket lining. I think you'll have all the proof you need Hector Constanza." Aleandro quickly pulled a knife and tore Will's jacket lining open, exposing the two pictures. Hector looked at them as his eyes got big as saucers. Will watched as his complexion turned from tan to darker, like the Inca in him was suddenly overriding the Spanish blood. "A picture's worth a thousand words, as they say."

Constanza was now near manic, "How did you get these pictures? I will once again delay ending your life while you explain."

"Fair enough Hector; you've been on our radar screen ever since you and Umberto formed the alliance. Now that wasn't really worthy of concern until Enrique turned up with three hitters to kill me and my wife. After that you became a serious target, but you were clever enough not to leave Colombia again after Colton was snatched. Otherwise, we wouldn't be having this conversation," Will told him, pointing to the reticle with crosshairs over Constanza's heart. He didn't mention that Consuela was sucking his dick a foot away.

Now the chattering between the three Colombians became very serious. Will glanced at Rico who just noticeably nodded. "So, why am I now pointing a gun at you if you could have killed me in Costa Rica so easily? Can you explain that Mr. Kavanagh?"

Will pointed to the woman giving him a blow job in the picture. "Sure, why don't you call your mistress and see if she's having a good day? I believe her name is Consuela Diaz, and her husband is the Minister of Foreign Affairs, Gianfranco Diaz. You apparently cover the domestic affairs with her."

To their shock, he snatched the silenced Sig Sauer P226 from Aleandro and shot Rico through the thigh, taking care to miss bone and arteries. The impact bent Rico over double as Will begged Constanza to let him take off his shirt to stanch the bleeding. As soon as he had Rico's wound under control he looked at Constanza and told him, "One more shot and Consuela dies a nasty death, with a suicide note written in her hand saying she couldn't go on without fucking you any more Hector. Sad to have to ruin two marriages and their families over some misunderstanding Enrique had back in Managua, wouldn't you say?

The look on his face was beyond murderous as he grabbed his cell phone from Aleandro and quickly dialed a number. When it was answered he got a demonic scowl on his face and demanded, "And who might I be speaking with?"

"Hello Hector, I suspect you are looking for Mrs. Diaz, your mistress that you are head over heels in love with? Oh, I'm Mr. Rayfield, a friend of Will Kavanagh's, so it's time to deal Chico. Isn't that what she calls you in bed, Chico?"

Rico actually managed a grin as Hector covered the phone and told Aleandro to have the call traced. Once Aleandro was busy he turned his attention back to his own call, "I see Mr. Rayfield, and what have you done with Consuela? If you have harmed a hair on her body I will kill you in the most gruesome manner imaginable."

"Come on Chico, you can't even find us, much less kill us. I'll tell ya what's gonna happen Constanza, you're gonna bring Mr. Kavanagh and Mr. Suarez in good health to the back yard of Umberto Rodriquez' *Casa Manrique* in Pereira tomorrow at noon. Then we'll give you Consuela in exchange for my two friends. Whatcha think?"

Constanza was clearly experiencing hypertension when he replied, "So you wish to exchange your friends for *Señora* Diaz, is that what I understand your proposal to be? And if I were to allow one of these murderers to go free, how would you propose exchanging them?" He held his hand over the phone and spoke in Spanish to Aleandro, who nodded his head before whispering something.

As the two were busy, Will glanced at Rico who whispered to him, "They're setting up a welcome party at *Casa Manrique.*"

"Hector, tell Aleandro the trace ain't gonna work so he can call his boys off," Hal told him, winking at the Delta communications specialist at the console at Camp Valdez. The Deltas had made friends with a local Indian tribe who provided a small valley with the surrounding slopes for their super-secret operational base.

"Prove to me you have Consuela in your custody Mr. Rayfield, or I will kill both of your friends within one minute."

"No sweat Hector, hold on," Hal said as he motioned Consuela over to the console. "Hey Connie, Hector wants to hear your sexy voice so he knows we haven't harmed you. Tell him hello," Hal said as Rambo smiled at her survival instincts.

"Hello Chico, it is me, Uela, and I am being treated well by my captors."

"Where are you? Where did they take you?" Hector asked as Will smiled at Rico.

"Chico, I have no idea where I am, but the *Norteamericanos* have been most kind to me; they are even learning poker tricks from the Venezuelans, *si?* Here is Mr. Rayfield again, *adios mi amor.*"

Hector suddenly became incensed, "I will expect you at *Casa Manrique,* east of Pereira, tomorrow at noon. It will be a pleasure to see you die with your friends *Señor* Rayfield."

"Right Hector, high noon; I understand there is a tennis court behind Umberto's casa?"

"What? Yes of course there is a tennis court, why do you ask?"

"Because we're bringing a helicopter in to deliver Connie and pick up our friends; please have the net removed from the tennis court, as it will make walking so much easier."

Now very pissed, he shouted, "I will have the net removed Mr. Rayfield, and await your arrival with considerable anticipation."

Hector said something to the limo driver as he turned off of the highway onto a gravel secondary road. Hector smiled and said, "It would seem your compatriot Mr. Rayfield is going to make a fateful attempt at kidnap and ransom."

Will shrugged and replied, "So where are we going, to that Casa place?"

"Nothing so charming for you two I am afraid; I believe it is time you learned more about coffee growing here in the area made famous by Juan Valdez on your American television."

"So coffee growing is a mountain country pursuit, eh? I often wondered where it came from. Most young Americans think only cocaine comes from Colombia. So is this your plantation Hector? How large is it?"

"It actually belongs to my friend Umberto, and it covers 5000 hectares. Unfortunately, you two will not be taking a tour of the plantation, just the basement of the Plantation House."

"And what form of entertainment do you have planned for us at *Hacienda Cardona*, Hector?"

This latest revelation lit the three Colombians off once again. "Oh, I believe you two know more about this abduction of the Foreign Minister's wife than you're letting on. He will be most thankful when I provide him information relative to her safe recovery."

Seeing the scale tipping against them, Will pulled one out of his ass and told him, "Right, actually there's a diplomatic pouch ready to be dispatched from Panama City with numerous pictures of you and Consuela, as well as Marta Cruz, in—shall we say—compromising positions much like those in your hand. This will be done if my compatriot and I were to meet some unpleasant denouement. I bet you thought nobody knew about that little hideaway trip you two took to Limón last month or the one to Aruba, did you?"

His rage was nearing the boiling point as his hands clasped into fists, telling them Adam Chennault's gossip and Jepson's pictures had indeed struck right on the mark. Will tried to redirect the conversation by telling him, "Listen, all's I can offer in my own defense is that I didn't go to the Masaya Volcano with any ill will towards you or your family. I had never met your brother Enrique until his thugs jumped us and he put this tattoo down my face. All I wanted was to rescue my brother and take him home, which I assume has now happened."

He snickered at him and pretended to be admiring his manicure, "Actually, we had a surprise waiting for the Archbishop's limousine after it left the Botanical Gardens, just in case you had some treachery planned *Señor*

Kavanagh. By enlisting His Grace's aid in this matter you have endangered his life."

Will glanced down at his watch, "It better have happened fast Hector, because the limo took him straight over to the Simon Bolivar Military College which was approximately one kilometer away from the Botanical Gardens. Don't you recall that helicopter we heard as we were pulling out? You may want to make a call and check up on that little ambush you had planned."

His agility completely surprised them as he sprung across the seat and slapped Will hard in the face, causing pain to radiate anew down from his right eye, now almost swollen shut. He didn't understand the Spanish curse Hector swore at him as he reached for his cell phone, "It doesn't matter; we had our man covering the departure terminal at El Dorado Airport."

Will half-laughed at him, the pain once again causing him to flinch as he managed to say, "You mean the one in Bogotá? The copter didn't stop there Hector, it went straight out to a U.S. Navy frigate waiting 100 miles offshore from Buenaventura. So it's all about you and us now, except that Connie Diaz is probably wondering why she's being held in some low rent hotel."

This latest revelation, even though completely bullshit, made him consider Will for a moment, "Perhaps we can learn some more secrets from you this evening *Señor* Kavanagh. I certainly hope you weren't planning on sleeping."

He looked at him seriously with his one good eye, "Not a problem Hector, we got a good night's rest before we came. Just remember that FedEx pouch is waiting to be sent to the New York Times and the London Mail so you not only have the other cartel, but the Colombian government raining down on you if you get trigger happy with me and my friend here."

He smiled sardonically and said, "Gunplay isn't what we have in mind for you tonight *Señor* Kavanagh."

They slowed on the gravel road, having traveled for miles inside the plantation when Hector pointed out the window and said, "Welcome to *Hacienda Cardona*. I'm not sure where you heard the name before Mr. Kavanagh, but I intend to find out tonight."

"Same place we took those pictures Hector; there's not an easy way out, but I'm sure you'll look for one. We've been on your trail now for six weeks; Lindstrum was beginning to think you'd become paranoid. Oh, and just so you know, Mr. Rayfield didn't tell me where he took Connie for the evening.

He thought that'd be dangerous information for me to have considering your penchant for torture and all."

Hector smiled and nodded, "We shall see what pain does for your memory *Señor* Kavanagh."

Compared to the main house at Carmen's *Estancia Fabiano* in Bariloche, *Hacienda Cardona's* main house was surprisingly small. It was neither surrounded by manicured landscape nor built of expensive stone, lacking in architectural appointments one would expect from the main residence of a huge agricultural operation. Instead of tractors and other farm machinery, the primary means of conveyance appeared to be horses, mules and oxen. The dusty outer walls of the house bore testimony to the frequent arrival and departures of horses and perhaps horse-drawn wagons.

The limo continued around to the back of the house, and Will was more than a little surprised by the number and size of warehouses supporting the operation. He was staring at one large warehouse which was completely different; all windows and doors were closed and there were commercial vent stacks protruding from the roof line at measured intervals. Hector noticed his interest and said, "That is our high-value warehouse operation *Señor* Kavanagh. Would you care to take a look inside at one of the finest cocaine laboratories in the world?"

He was stunned that Constanza would be so forthcoming about an asset many would love to know about—and either destroy or take over—but recovered enough to answer, "You bet; I'd be very interested to see how cocaine is made."

Rico was already grimacing, no doubt wondering why Constanza was being so cooperative when Hector laughed, "You two are probably wondering why I would show you such a valuable asset? You have no doubt underestimated the ways of the Colombians. When the helicopter arrives tomorrow with Consuela and your friends for the exchange, it will be obliterated from the sky, and you two will unfortunately be burned up beyond recognition in the explosion. You can never trust the National Police, who are my friends; in Colombia, everyone has their price."

"So you would violently murder the woman you are in love with?" Will asked, incredulous.

Hector shrugged resignedly and told him, "She is a special woman, but she is only a woman. And now she has become a liability for me. And do not concern yourself about this package of allegedly damaging materials you plan to send to New York and London; both regularly deride the Republic of Colombia and are of no local interest. So you are what we refer to as expendable."

Figuring it was time for another world class bluff Will told him, "The helicopter doesn't come within range of *Casa Manrique* unless they receive a cell phone call from me Hector. And if that doesn't happen, some unfortunate accident might rein on your little factory here. Ever heard of the American military weapon M129?"

The glint of fear that reflected off of his face indicated that he was, indeed, familiar with the M129, so Will added, "Sandrigan's palatial Casbah didn't stand up to a two hundred round belt of those 40mm darts from hell too well Hector. But I am curious, how do you foresee that we will meet our doom; rocket-propelled grenade or Soviet SA-7?"

He nodded his head at him, "I am impressed with your knowledge of such weapons. Actually, we will deploy both and end this little charade you have perpetrated." He then smiled and added, "But you knew nothing of this laboratory until just now, so I believe you are bluffing *Señor* Kavanagh."

"Actually Hector, my associates were very concerned about the shrapnel storm that would accompany the disintegration of *Castillo Blanco*, your state-of-the-art factory here. Stand-off weapons were considered the safest option. The M129s are for cleanup in case you have some *Federales* helping out."

Hector stopped in his tracks, "So you even know the name of my factory and its disintegration features?"

Inwardly sweating, and knowing he needed to somehow communicate this information back to Hal, Will looked at Hector and said, "Nah, it was just a lucky guess Hector; let's see what a real high-tech cocaine laboratory looks like."

As they walked through the secondary door, which sealed off any temperature or humidity from the outside, Aleandro handed them face masks, no doubt concerned that they not get a coke high to lessen the dread. To their amazement, the walls were painted glossy white, the floor had been covered with a reddish-brown rubber-like compound and the overhead lighting was bright and pervasive. The only place he'd seen anything even similar to it was a precision-measurement equipment lab back in the Air Force that was hermetically sealed to prevent damage to sensitive calibration equipment. There were perhaps forty workers busily going about their tasks, with large cylinders of hydrochloric acid and acetone along the outer walls connecting back to stainless steel vats via suspended tubing. Large stainless tables were laid out with high-powered sun lamps baking powder that they assumed was the finished product emitting humidity until it was at some packaging standard. Hector led them down the production line to what seemed like the back— or delivery—area of the building. Will was interested to see several workers removing what looked like plumber's putty from clear plastic bags. Before he could ask, Hector advised, "We receive the coca paste, which has been produced at the harvesting site. The complexity of the conversion process to cocaine hydrochloride is beyond the capabilities of the growers."

Remembering the wonderful high he had gotten from snorting cocaine, Will looked at the chemical tanks and asked, "So this cocaine hydrochloride— what we call cocaine on the street—has been processed with hydrochloric acid and acetone?"

Hector smiled and informed them, "Only in the final phase of the manufacturing process. Earlier phases utilize gasoline, sulfuric acid and diesel fuel to precipitate the coca alkaloid from the coca leaves. Step two further precipitates the solids via use of ammonia and potassium permanganate. As you see, the final refinement uses hydrochloric acid and acetone to scrub the remaining sediments from the alkaloid."

"Jesus," was all Will could manage, thinking about the trace chemicals ingested while using cocaine.

Hector was smiling at him now, "And to think you Americans so desperately desire to inhale such things. The exact process for manufacturing cocaine hydrochloride would seem troubling to Americans?"

"Well, the high sure is instant, so the rush is what they remember most. So you said it takes two hundred fifty kilos of coca leaves to produce one kilo of powder? Man, the *Federales* ain't gotta chance eradicating coca if it's that abundant along those Andean slopes."

Hector grimaced, "Aleandro has already said you have a formidable poker face." Will shrugged as he continued, "He says you were bluffing desperately trying to stay alive. Prove to me you know what you are speaking about, these Federales eradicating coca?"

"Don't take my word for it Hector; have Umberto call Brigadier General Tonzel, his Southern Bloc Commander, and see if airplanes are not raining down paraquat on the coca slopes. His 48th Front is at this moment trying to decide whether to fire on the aircraft," Will challenged, eternally grateful he had read all of the affiliated intel Fort Bragg had sent them.

Will could tell he was stressing Hector badly, as he grabbed his satellite phone from Aleandro and made a call. Constanza turned to walk away as he spoke with Rodriguez. Rico translated the parts he could hear, "Jesus Will, you just kicked to top off the anthill; the FARC soldiers are apparently afraid to fire on the herbicide sprayers as there's an AC-130 shadowing them."

Hector was becoming more animated and loud, "What the fuck, from the tone of it, Hector's cursing as badly as I ever have; what's happening?"

Rico managed to laugh, "I've heard you light off when somebody tries to brace you Willy, but Hector might be more craven than you..." He stopped talking to listen and smiled, "Rodriguez had to scramble reinforcements to the Southern Bloc, so Hector ain't getting the company of FARC soldiers he was counting on." Rico then exhaled loudly, "Man, that's gonna make him that much more desperate Willy."

Hector ended the call and snapped around at Will, "You seem to know about very sensitive operations Kavanagh; perhaps we will encourage you to tell us more."

"Anything you wanna know, except for the stuff Rayfield didn't want me to have access to—just in case you tortured us," Will told him with a shrug before glancing off to the south. "So you've got an airstrip here at the plantation?"

"It's a large plantation *Señor* Kavanagh; now please follow Aleandro to your quarters for the evening."

As they walked from the cocaine lab to the back of the house, Will counted ten guards armed with a variety of weapons. The ones closest to the house, no doubt tasked with protecting the leaders, were holding H&K MP5 machine guns supported by straps over their shoulders. They entered the house through a heavy wooden door and immediately noticed a set of well-worn stone stairs leading down to what they assumed was the basement. When they got to the bottom of the stairs, the basement opened up into a long hallway with doors leading off either side. As they passed one door, Will saw two men sitting at a table feeding a currency-counting machine, and the walls were lined with banded stacks of bills. Aleandro noticed his interest and roughly pushed them further down the hallway until they got to an open door. Hector held out his hand, "After you gentlemen."

The room stank of vomit and urine, and they looked on with dread at the far wall where two sets of shackles hung by heavy chains. The concrete floor beside the wall was brown-colored, and they didn't have to imagine what had happened there previously. Instead of taking them to the wall, Aleandro lead them to two steel chairs that were bolted securely to the floor. Hector then announced, "I would allow you the honor of the wall of pain, but I need you both to be able to stand tomorrow when our final show begins at the Casa."

With that Aleandro threw Rico down onto one of the chairs, resulting in a howl of pain from the gunshot wound in his leg, and took a roll of duct tape and began wrapping his legs and arms around each of the bars on the solid metal chairs. After he'd done the same with Will, Hector paused at the door, "I am hungry, so I will leave you for a while. When I come back, we will talk more about where I can find my dearest Consuela."

After they closed the door and heard their footfalls down the hall, Will looked at Rico, "How's the leg buddy?"

He shook his head slightly, "Man am I glad we did the vaccination boosters at Butila. Hector is either good or I'm lucky that he missed an artery."

"Don't forget about those two huge Doxy's we took on the plane ride in this morning. Jesus, why is it that every time we take those things we get the shit kicked out of us?"

He leaned as close as he could and whispered, "Lots of flammables in that lab bro."

Will smiled as he whispered back, "You didn't miss that propane tank outside did ya?"

"Nah, and they keep a lot of cash around here."

Will flexed his eyebrows, "Bet they'd hate to lose this place."

The door suddenly swung open as a bearded flunky wearing a coat three sizes too big for him walked into the room carrying a metal tray with some kind of unidentifiable mass that might have been food in it and placed it at their feet. Will rolled his eyes and said, "And just how in the fuck are we supposed to eat that shit with our hands tied down?"

The peasant got down on the floor, took the spoon from the tray and held it up to his lips and said, "*Por favor.*"

Will was so pissed at the crap in the spoon he was just about to spit in his face when he saw it was Daniel Gomez, the priest-warrior Villaponteau had sent along with Rose to do surveillance.

"I have only perhaps two minutes. What have you learned?" Daniel urged.

"Tell Hal they're gonna take out the copter with a SA-7 at the casa tomorrow. Tell him to level this place and the coke factory if they can plant it on the *Federales*. And tell him to get the cash out of here if he can before the place goes boom. Did they snatch Consuela?"

"Yes, but how do we defend the SA-7?"

"Hal's gotta come up with a diversion, something brighter than the exhaust on that copter. Now get the hell out of here. Hold it, did Kelly get that vest?"

"I do not know, but I will return if I can. Good luck," he said as he picked up the tray and left.

After Daniel left Will told Rico, "He's in for hell if they catch him. I spotted ten guards just walking back to the house from the lab."

"We're all in for hell if they catch him. If Constanza finds Consuela before the show, we're all toast."

"Yeah, how the hell did I get you into this brother?"

"Hey, nobody held a gun to my head forcing me to come Will; keep the faith man."

They heard the door opening as Hector and Aleandro came in smiling and looking slightly flushed in the face, no doubt having consumed an indeterminate amount of wine with their dinner. Hector stopped by a table, picked up a length of what looked like garden hose and said, "I believe it's time you gentlemen tell us where Consuela Diaz is being held."

Will glanced at Rico before responding, "I really don't know Hector; that wasn't part of my responsibility. I was merely supposed to come and replace my brother."

"So how did you know that Consuela was to be brought in for the exchange tomorrow? I believe you are not telling all you know," he said just before he slammed the hose down on Rico's wounded thigh. The only reason Rico didn't fall onto the floor was because he was taped so heavily to the chair.'

"I'll ask again, where is *Senora* Diaz being held?"

Will just shrugged before Hector swung the hose as hard as he could at his right side. He screamed with pain, wondering if his arm was broken but thanked God that his arm had been pinned to the chair arm giving his mending ribs a slight layer of protection.

Will figured he'd better give them something, so he offered, "They snatched her after an interview at the Hilton and took her off someplace safe. That's all I know except that she's gonna be on the chopper tomorrow for the exchange."

The matching slam on his left arm was even more painful, and after getting the tears under control he looked at Constanza, "I will kill you if it's the last thing I ever do Constanza. I just told you what I know dammit."

The next flail caught him across the right thigh, and he was actually getting used to the searing pain. Noticing this, Constanza wrapped the hose around Rico's neck and began twisting the loose ends together like a tourniquet. Will knew he'd kill him from the suffocation if he didn't offer up something so he blurted out, "Okay dammit, the plan called for her to be taken to the safehouse, somewhere near Bogotá. They said nobody could get into there, even if they could find the place."

Hector looked at him with a smirk of satisfaction, turned to walk out but suddenly stopped to get right back in his face. "I will go check out your story *Señor* Kavanagh. But tell me, who is your contact within the CIA? I know most of the underhanded ones who would sell their soul to impress their superiors."

Smiling inwardly he replied, "CIA?" Will let that trail of doubt set in before adding, "I think we've already established Marty Lindstrum as the man who'd sell out his own mother. Oh, that's right, he's a buddy of yours isn't he?"

Constanza smiled broadly and exclaimed "Yes, *Señor* Lindstrum is a dear friend of mine. And I just happen to know where his safe house is. I will go check this out, and either way things aren't looking too good for your future now that you've told me what I need to know."

After they had left, Will told Rico, "Things aren't looking too good for the home team bro. Still feeling right about coming along on this suicide mission?"

"Hey, the fat lady hasn't sung yet my friend. I suspect Hector's guys are gonna get a surprise when they try to break into the safe house. Jesus, those guys have that place wired big time!"

"My thoughts exactly; it's a shame Constanza won't make the breach himself. I sure hope Daniel gets the word to Hal about the SA-7. Man, that could ruin our day."

Rico nodded his head slightly, "Don't forget, Curt Webster's going to be flying that bird, and he's been through the shit before."

"Yeah, but they're gonna need a hell of a sunspot to distract that surface-to-air missile. Oh well, nothing we can do about that now, eh?"

They were dozing off later when the door burst open and Constanza and Aleandro walked in so mad Will wondered what could have possibly gone wrong. He did notice that Aleandro was holding his stainless steel Sig Sauer P226 pistol, which didn't seem too promising.

"I should shoot you right now you piece of horse manure," Constanza said for his opening blast.'

"Let me guess, Consuela wasn't at the safehouse? I told you that was what they told me they were going to do with her," Will said, wondering if he was going to take a nine millimeter parabellum in the knee for his insolence. He figured he'd fry Lindstrum again, "Hey Hector, now I remember; my guys got a call from this spook who works for the CIA sometimes and said Lindstrum had rolled over to Silvio Corrales. You know Silvio right, the DGI big dick in Habana?"

Hector grabbed the Sig from Aleandro, cocked the hammer back and held it to Will's head, "I'll give you one more chance to tell me the truth. Are you ready to die?"

"Been ready since I was born Hector, but I already told you what I knew about the snatch. What happened?"

"The only thing that didn't happen was that *Señor* Lindstrum was not present to die like all of the others in the house."

"Maybe that means it wasn't the CIA safehouse they were planning to use," Will offered, trying to buy some time. "I take it that means not all of your men died and are now being held by the National Police?"

Hector half pulled the trigger in front of his face when there was a commotion in the hallway outside the room. Rico and Will almost fainted with sorrow as two of Hector's guards slung Rose and Daniel into the room and made a report in Spanish to Constanza.

Rose made eye contact with Will and shook her head no, no doubt defying him to tell Constanza anything as Hector instructed the guards to shackle the two of them up to the wall of pain he had previously excused Rico and Will from. Once they were suitably shackled, Hector looked at them and asked, "I want to know where a woman named Consuela Diaz is being held prisoner. One of your team took her, and it is my intention to find out before the night is over."

To their amazement, Rose looked him in the eye and replied, "I do not know. My job was to surveil this plantation in case *Señor* Kavanagh was brought here."

Hector considered this and redirected, "And who gave you this order to surveil the plantation?"

Like the warrior she was, Rose merely shook her head no. She saw Hector's intentions as she shouted, "Hal Rayfield gave me the order."

Now Hector seemed humored, "And exactly who does Hal Rayfield work for *Señorita?*"

She wouldn't answer as Constanza grew increasingly angry. Suddenly Will told him, "He works for me Hector."

"Really, so this is all you operation Kavanagh?"

"Yep; I thought we established that earlier. Now we learned from you Hector that it's best to compartmentalize the operation so that no one person knows it all. Except of course Hal Rayfield; he's our *Jefe.*"

"Is that so *Señorita?*"

Rose was terrified, but replied, "*Si Señor, Señor Rayfield es el Jefe.*"

Without a second's hesitation, Hector aimed the Sig at Daniel's left knee and pulled the trigger, as the explosion inside the room and Daniel's terrified scream overtook their consciousness.

Daniel was now slumped to his left, the leg no longer providing any assistance as Hector once again implored them, "Who gave the order to have the plantation surveilled?"

Will couldn't watch this agonizing torture a moment longer and shouted out, "Marco Pintoles."

Hector now began nodding his head, no doubt trying to figure out how the ELN was involved, "So you are a communist pig?" Before Daniel could answer him Constanza shot him through the right knee as Will began to openly weep.

With tears raining down his cheeks, his body slumping now supported only by his shackled wrists Daniel calmly prayed his last words, "Father forgive them, for they know not what they…" Almost mercifully, the Sig fired one more time, right between Daniel's eyes, shattering the back of his head and splattering the wall behind him grotesquely.

Constanza looked at the three of them still alive, "We will see how many of your friends die before you speak the truth Kavanagh." He lined up on Rose's knee as Will was about to shout, to tell him anything to keep him from killing Rose. As if providence were intervening, one of Hector's guards opened the door to the hallway. Hector cursed at him in Spanish as Rico glanced at Will and almost smiled. The guard made a very tense report to the boss as Hector motioned for Aleandro to follow him. He stopped at the door to wipe the blood and gore from his face and neck. "I hope you have a wonderful evening. I suggest you prepare yourselves for the end of your lives tomorrow."

58

DARKNESS BEFORE THE LIGHT

"DID HE MAKE THE CALL TO HAL?" Will asked Rose after she had finally stopped whimpering. The sight and smell of Daniel's ruined body next to her served as a constant reminder to the three of them that Hector Constanza's life could now be counted in hours.

"I believe so; he was speaking on the satellite phone when I walked up behind him. He stomped on the phone with his boot just as the guards came upon us."

"So how many allies do we have around the plantation?"

"There are thirty spread out in a large perimeter. We have already spotted three National Police teams staked out, no doubt ready to destroy anyone threatening the hacienda."

"Did Daniel convey that info back to Hal when he spoke with him?"

She was shaking her head no but smiling when she told them, "He did not tell Hal that, but Marco Pintoles is here and is prepared to badly embarrass the National Police during tomorrow's activities."

Will glanced at Rico, "There is a God in heaven." He suddenly sobered as he turned to Rose, "That was by far the worst thing I have ever had to witness Rose. I promise that I will...."

She interrupted him, "You won't have a chance Will. Constanza is mine."

He smiled at her and nodded, "As you wish, but let me have a little heart to heart with him first, okay?"

The night passed in a nightmarish manner, with recurrent dreams of Dom and their baby girl standing on a precipice not a hundred feet away from Will, separated by a bottomless chasm. Rose's moans from her shoulders giving out had finally stopped when she went into semi-shock and they were awakened by the sudden silence. "You awake Rico?"

He blinked several times and nodded, "Yeah, what's up?"

"Both of Rose's shoulders are dislocated by now; if she cannot walk when the guards return they might shoot her."

Rico pondered that for a while and replied, "So what's the play?"

"When the guard unlocks her from the shackles she's gonna collapse on the floor. We gotta be quick and work the guards at the same time."

"Okay, what's the plan?"

"I kinda picked this up at ROUST, but here's what I think might work…"

———

The three were rousted from their terror-filled slumbers when two guards walked in and began barking orders in Spanish. Will looked at Rico in confusion at the absence of Hector or Aleandro, but Ricco merely shrugged, "Probably making last minute preparations at the kill zone."

Will half-smiled, "The question is whose kill zone?"

They watched as the guards unshackled Rose from the wall of pain, only to see her stumble to the ground, her knees unable to support her weight. Will noticed her discreetly pick up something from the floor. "*De pie o se muere perra,*" one of them said as Rico nearly pulled his chair from the bolts.

"*No, hay que fijar las hombros, por favor Jefe,*" Rico pleaded from his chair. "*Por favor Señor, vamos a ayudarle a su.*"

As the other guard cut their duct tape bindings loose from the chair, the lead guard—who had threatened to shoot Rose if she didn't stand—nodded his head towards her. "*Llevarla hasta entonces o te pego un tiro.*"

"*Muchas gracias,*" Will said as he bowed slightly towards the guard, and then looked at Rico as he held up her semiconscious body. "You ready?"

Rico got a firm hold around Rose's ribs and neck and nodded. Will put his foot against her ribs under the left armpit, grabbed her left wrist firmly and pulled hard and suddenly. Rose came shrieking out of her shock-induced blackout screaming obscenities in Spanish. She quickly quieted down and looked at Will. "You'll thank me later Rosario," he said just as he planted his boot into the ribs under her right arm and pulled it hard and fast from the wrist. The echo of profanity must have been impressive because the two guards were suddenly pointing and laughing. Will got in her face and said, "Slap me as hard as you can Rosario."

He just did catch her hand as she attempted payback with a vengeance.

Will glanced at Rico who turned to the guards, *"Estamos listos ahora, muchas por favor."*

The guards unceremoniously slapped handcuffs on them before marching them out and up the stone stairs. They had to turn their heads to keep from being blinded by the morning light. One of the guards muttered something in Spanish, as Rico smiled, "Welcome to your final day on earth asshole."

Will let out a hoot, "How'd you know he didn't speak English?"

"All the trained guards have left for the Casa Tonto; I'm beginning to feel better about the day."

As they were marched outside, Rose could barely stand, so Will put his shackled arms around her and duck-walked them to the van, "Hang in there baby, the best part of the day is yet to come."

She managed to look at him as she put a piece of metal in his hand, which he closed and put in his pocket for later examination. The guards change-out got Rico's mind working, "Hector called in reinforcements; what are you thinking *Jefe?*"

Will turned on him, *"Jefe?"* Rico merely shrugged as Will smiled, "Good, I bet between Rambo and Marco Pintoles they've got a surprise or two waiting for 'em back here."

59

RECOMPENSE FOR THE RIGHTEOUS

WHEN THEY GOT TO *CASA MANRIQUE*, which was on the southeastern outskirts of Pereira, Will was impressed with the place, a total aberration from the plain functionality of the country hacienda. The Casa was three stories, made of stone and glass on what appeared to be four or five acres of rolling terrain, and there was a pool and a regulation-sized tennis court behind the house. As he looked to see that the net was taken down from the tennis court, Will noticed that there was a church perhaps a half-mile away with a very tall spire, not unlike the minarets he had seen on the mosque in Algiers. There was a huge clock face in the middle of the spire, no doubt serving as the community wrist watch.

They were marched to a spot on the patio so that Will, Rico and Rose were side by side, with Aleandro behind them holding his trademark stainless Sig Sauer P226. Standing on the ledge of the deck leading out of the house was Hector Constanza, dressed in his finest cream-colored *Guayabera*, the Colombian alternative to formal men's wear. To their surprise, he was holding a silver Sig Sauer P226 down to his side as he smiled at the surrounding terrain. Will could only imagine what his expectations were, having moved his entire security detail over for the coming showdown.

As they were standing there, they heard the unmistakable whooping of a helicopter's blades. Strangely, there was nothing in sight from the northwest where the sound seemed to be coming from.

Will saw Hector glance up to his left, and followed his gaze to see a man crouched down on the roof of the guest house holding a shoulder-fired surface-to-air missile. He was praying word had gotten out and precautions had been taken when the whooping sounds seemed to all but disappear.

Will glanced back at Hector, who was surveying the sky in a semi-circle,

590

the sudden silence making the bizarre scene seem like a modern day standoff at the OK Corral.

———

And then it happened, just like that day in Menara Park in Marrakech; time seemed to slow down for Will. The vision in front of him seemed completely surreal until a loud explosion to their left shattered the silence, leaving only a cloud of smoke trailing off in its place. They heard a strange sound behind them as Hector's face took on a mystified look. Without any warning at all, a huge black monstrosity came streaking over their heads at tree-top level, faster than any helicopter could fly. The chopper seemed to pull up and change speeds about a half mile away, seeming to nose down slightly.

Will's dread factor was at an all-time high when he noticed Hector nod his head and a small blast preceded a streak of steam blowing across the sky at the Black Hawk. As the copter quickly dipped into an adjacent ravine, everyone was stunned beyond belief when the spire of the church suddenly exploded into a blazing fireball as bright as the sun. They watched in wonder as the SA-7 flew straight into the clock face and exploded, sending the bricks and other material in the spire in a wide circle of shrapnel. Hector suddenly looked up at the shooter, but he only shrugged and nodded in the direction of the Black Hawk. A self-satisfied smirk crept across Hector's face, and Will could only imagine that there was another trap set up for his friends aboard Castle One.

They watched with amazement as the Black Hawk suddenly appeared above the wall of the ravine, its nose pointed in towards the Casa. Curt Webster was yawing it rapidly from right to left, the tail seemingly out in front of the nose. After a very slight change in direction, the 7.62mm mini Gatling gun suddenly came alive, red tracers chewing the top of a building to the right of the church as a streak of steam flew out above the copter. The RPG trailed its exhaust until its propellant was spent and disappeared, a distant explosion barely heard.

The Black Hawk remained stationary for a moment, no doubt checking to make sure the RPG shooter was dead, but the entire top floor of the building looked like a giant wrecking ball had hit it. The helicopter then slowly proceeded to the Casa, making a perfect landing in the middle of the tennis court. Will was surprised that Curt did not begin to shut down its engines, but merely remained in place twirling its blades in readiness. They could not believe their eyes when a woman stepped off the copter first, the hood of her raincoat pulled over her head as she made her way towards the deck in back of the house. Will caught the sudden protrusion of a gun barrel from the top of the chopper's side door. He glanced over his shoulder, knowing the SA-7's shooter was not otherwise in a sightline.

The sound of a huge explosion off in the distance distracted them momentarily, and when they turned back around Kelly Dupree was standing thirty feet away from Hector Constanza smiling. Hector was momentarily distracted when he looked behind Kelly and saw Archbishop Juan Villaponteau step off of the Black Hawk, his face totally expressionless.

Kelly took two steps closer to Constanza and said, "Hello Hector, I'm sorry but Consuela couldn't make it but she sends her best."

Without any hesitation Hector raised his Sig and shot Kelly as she fell down on the ground apparently dead. As soon as the shot rang out from Constanza's gun, an incredible staccato of gunfire sounded that felled the three guards standing post in the yard as well as Aleandro and all of the Cartel soldiers posted around the perimeter of the Casa. As Constanza knelt down to put his gun on the deck, Will reached in his pocket to find the cuff key Rose had given him earlier. He unlocked his handcuffs, then passed the key to Rico to follow.

They were all surprised when Constanza looked towards Villaponteau and pleaded, "Your Grace, have you no mercy on your fellow man? Please implore these sinners to do as the Good Lord instructed us all."

Ignoring the drama, Rico raced over to where Kelly lay on the concrete, bum leg and all and began doing everything he could to resuscitate her. Once she regained consciousness and it became obvious that the Kevlar vest had done its job, Will turned to Villaponteau to await his decision.

To their amazement, Villaponteau didn't move a muscle, his face a rock. Finally he looked at Will and slightly nodded his head, "The angels of Satan must be struck down where they stand."

Will reached down to punch in the two eyelets of his boot as the sole twisted sideways to expose the switchblade knife he had kept since the day he met Enrique Constanza. He walked calmly over to where Hector was standing, and noticed that he was trembling like a leaf in a late autumn wind. He put his boot on the Sig Sauer lying on the concrete and said, "I told you no one threatens my wife and gets away with it." He then opened the switchblade and stuck the point in deeply right below Hector's left eye. As Will pulled it down his face Constanza began crying, begging him to spare his life. "Enrique Constanza can burn in hell for involving my family in your unholy aberration before the Lord."

"Knife!" Rico shouted as Will caught a glimpse of Constanza's right hand coming up. He took a step to the left, slashing the switchblade, severing the tendons inside Hector's right elbow with all his strength. "Belt!" came the next warning as Will looked at Hector with a terrible grimace on his face.

"Go to hell," he told Constanza as he sliced across the tendons on the inside of his left elbow rendering his arm a limp stump. Hector was now standing helplessly, moaning and crying like a baby. "You're a fucking disgrace Constanza."

He stared into his soul as he told Hector Constanza one last thing, "Threatening my wife was one thing Hector, but threatening a child that had been blessed by the love of Christ is unforgivable." The look of hatred on Will's face was unmistakable as he slowly pulled the knife across Constanza's stomach; not deeply but far enough in to make him cry out in agony as the *Guayabera* reddened across his belly. He snapped the blade shut as he turned away, Constanza doubled over in pain. Will reached down and grabbed the Sig, walked over to Rose and handed it to her. "He's all yours Rose; send him to hell where he belongs."

As he walked away from Constanza, Hal was running past him to check on Rose. Will noticed a glimmer on the deck and bent over to pick up the spent shell casing Hector had fired at Kelly and put it in his pocket. He didn't look back as he grabbed Juan Villaponteau by the arm and led him towards the helicopter.

Hal was very concerned about Rose's condition, as she was having difficulty standing up. She brushed him away and said, "Just stand that coward up while I have my last words with him." Hal nodded and turned to find Constanza holding his arms over his stomach, bent over at the waist cursing in Spanish. He also was pleading for mercy now that his own plans for death had turned so dramatically.

Hal grabbed Constanza by the shoulders and stood him up straight. "Time to face up to your sins like a man Hector; Rose here's got a message for you."

Rico was helping Kelly to the helicopter but she told him to stop when she heard Hal's entreaty to Constanza. "Hold on Rico, I want to witness Rose Cordes' interpretation of 'an eye for an eye.'" Will and Juan also stopped and turned.

Will looked at Juan, "You would not believe what that man inflicted upon Daniel Gomez last night chained to the wall. Hector pointedly asked me if I was aware of the Biblical phrase. I actually want to see him reap what he sowed." Juan merely nodded as Will shook his head in the affirmative, "How about translate what Rose says please; you cannot imagine the horror of Daniel Gomez' death."

Rose shakily got the pistol up, holding it with both hands. *"Es to para asesinas brutalmente Padre Daniel Gomez,"* she said before the Sig Sauer exploded, shattering Constanza's right knee. He screamed in agony as he fell towards the obliterated joint. Hal caught him and moved to his right side as Rose waved the pistol directing him. Rico and Juan immediately crossed themselves, a tear running down the Archbishop's face. "This is for brutally murdering Father Daniel Gomez."

"Padre Daniel Gomez, el único hombre que he amado de verdad," she swore in vengeance as she shot his left knee, all but hacking his leg in half. She nodded over her head to Hal, who quickly cleared out of the way after pushing Constanza backwards so his head was facing Rose to witness the final moments of his sordid life. Again, Juan crossed himself and began praying in Latin as Rico teared up as well. "The only man I ever truly loved."

"What is it Rico; what happened at that hacienda last night?" Kelly implored him, not understanding Rose's declarations.

Rico could barely talk as he pointed, "Rosario is the Angel of Death; she is allowing *Señor* Constanza to die as he allowed Father Daniel..."

Now Juan looked to the heavens, his hand on Kelly's head. She bowed slightly as he looked down at her, "For whatever one sows, that he will also reap."

"Padre Daniel está en el cielo. Espero que usted se quema para la eternidad en el infierno," she said right before she blew the back of Hector Constanza's head off,

now splattered like a grotesque warning to the Cali Cartel. Hal took the gun from her, put it in his jacket pocket and signaled Will to help him. Juan was trying mightily to contain his emotions as he told Will, "Father Daniel is in heaven now; I hope you burn for eternity in hell." Will nodded before moving off to help Hal. Together they carried Rose to the helicopter and climbed in after her.

They were immediately into triage as Will shouted to Curt over the noise inside the Black Hawk, "Rico took a flesh wound in the leg, but it's been twenty-four hours now. Got any injectable antibiotics?"

Curt looked at him like he was crazy, "Antibiotics? That boy needs morphine now." Hal was already peeling the plastic off the murphy stick. Curt looked at Will warily, "Jesus Kavanagh, you look like shit; sure you're gonna be alright?"

He reached out to pull Kelly into the helicopter, "Hell yeah I'm alright! By the Grace of God I lived through this. Let's get the hell out of here Commander Webster!"

———

As they were accelerating out of Pereira, Hal put flight helmets on each of them and secured the chin straps. Finally able to hear and converse normally Kelly leaned into Will and asked, "How you doing cowboy?"

"Oh, I've been better; you a believer in Kevlar now?"

"Damn straight! But I am going to take you up on that survival school offer. Hanging around you guys can be hazardous to a woman's health."

He leaned in to kiss her, but even that hurt his face, and the helmets were problematic. "Now that was one hell of a first op Dupree! I knew you were a fighter!" As he winked at her with his good eye, she rubbed her chest where the bullet had failed to penetrate the Nehru vest.

"Yeah, well that eye of yours looks like you went through a title fight with Joe Frazier. Your wife is not going to be pleased."

"Hell, she'll have me there for the birth of our child, what more could she want! I guess you're gonna keep that Nehru vest as a little trophy from your Colombian escapade?"

"Hell yeah, this goes in the closet with my boots and camo fatigues; I am now a convert to protective clothing!"

"Well good," he said as he pulled the shell casing from his pocket and handed it to her. "Why don't you hold on to this as your little memento of the bullet that could not kill you?"

Once they got settled into the flight north to Puerto Salgar for refueling, Rico was holding Rose, speaking quietly to her as he tried to bring her back to the land of the living. Will moved over to look her in the eye, "You owe me a hard slap in the face Rosario; think we could call it even for a murphy stick? You must be hurting like holy hell woman."

She managed what could be a smile, "*Por favor Jefe.*" As he injected the morphine she sighed and quickly fell asleep in Rico's arms.

Will looked at Juan Villaponteau, "I'm not very good with Spanish Archbishop, thanks for translating Rose's interpretation of an eye for an eye." Hal was shaking his head no as Will pursued, "For what it's worth, she executed Constanza in the precise manner he murdered Daniel."

"Actually, I believe that was between Rosario and the Lord Will. Suffice it to say that she very much appreciated the wonder of Daniel Gomez' soul. May God bless the departure of his Earthly countenance," Juan offered the spiritual chastisement.

"So what made you come along on the takedown Archbishop? Do you have a particular preference for helicopter rides into unknown combat operations?" Will wondered with a snicker.

The Archbishop looked at him askance, "Don't you think you've earned the right to refer to me by my given name Will? Actually, I thought it might be to our advantage if Hector Constanza saw me present at the meeting."

"Okay Juan, I gotta ask this question since I had no clue what was going on until I saw Hector glance back at the guy firing the surface-to-air missile. Was that your idea to decoy the SAM with the exploding clock tower?"

He frowned slightly as he related the background story. "Marco Pintoles' people had spotted the nest from which the shooter was going to fire the missile, but he could not get a shooting angle on it from any surrounding vantage point. The sacrifice of the bell tower was my decision based on the very limited options and time constraints."

"So I guess we owe you for rebuilding that tower Archbishop," Will said as he frowned, "uh, sorry, Juan. But I gotta wonder what in the world Pierson came up with to create that blast; it looked like the sun exploded there for a moment."

"Actually, that was my idea Willy," Hal chimed in as he handed him a silver flask. "Nothing goes wow like a white phosphorous 40mm grenade. We were fortunate that Curt Webster had a couple with him on the chopper."

Will hung his head as he glanced at Rose, "I can assure you Daniel Gomez wasn't so fortunate. I had to watch while Constanza shot him through both knees trying to extract the location of Consuela—which he was totally ignorant of." Will began crying as he told them, "His knees were gone and he was hanging from his manacled wrists like Christ on the Cross..." He stopped to compose himself then continued, "But all he said was 'Father forgive them for they know not what they...' and then that bastard blew his brains out all over the wall. I have never felt so helpless and so enraged in my entire life!"

Juan put his arms around Will and held him until he stopped sobbing. "His sacrifice was not made in vain Will; we achieved our objective and cut the head off the snake of the Cali Cartel in the process. Your friend Dan Pierson and Marco Pintoles recovered Daniel's body and we have it with us for proper entombment in Barranquilla."

Will nodded in understanding and then looked at Hal, "What kind of entrance was that? I was totally shocked when the black bird came shrieking in over our heads."

Hal smiled as he nodded towards the pilot's seat, "It was really pretty scary to actually watch from inside the copter too Willy. Curt knew he had to give the SAM shooter an exhaust signature, so that's why we came in like a bat out of hell. But Curt had me watching for the second shooter as we blazed across, and I spotted a guy with an RPG on the roof of that apartment building. It really was a game of quick draw coming back out of that ravine brother; who could shoot who first. What'd that Gatling gun look like from where you were?"

"Jesus man, it looked like there was a red ribbon connecting the chopper and that building, the tracers were blowing out so fast. I guess the shooter was too stunned by the church spire exploding to pick up on you guys fast enough?"

"That's what we were counting on; if the shooter had been set up for us......well, it was dicey there for a few seconds. If you don't believe me, ask Juan or Kelly," he said as Kelly was nodding her head in the affirmative.

"I guess that explosion right before you guys came in was a distraction?"

"We had radio contact with Pintoles' guy at the Casa and he lit off a fragmentation grenade to mask our approach."

"So what happened to that hacienda where we were being held? Constanza actually had the gall to take us on a tour of his impressive cocaine laboratory."

Hal smiled at his buddy, "Poof! We'll know more when we get to the refueling stop and can talk with Rambo."

Will shook his head and tried to smile, then thought of something, "So where is Consuela Diaz? Hector Constanza tried to move heaven and hell to find her." He pulled up his sleeve to look at the black bruises, "I'll never look at a water hose the same again, I can assure you."

"She was at Jepson's Delta boy's safe house the entire time playing nickel ante poker with the guys. She took them for twenty bucks and was quite pleased with herself. The Deltas said she could come back any time; I think they liked her. By the way, what the hell happened with the CIA safehouse? Somebody attacked that place and made one hell of a mess; it was all over the television news," Hal wondered.

Now Will did manage to grimace as Hal flexed his eyebrows and redirected, "Don't tell me you had anything to do with that Willy! Jesus, if Lindstrum finds out we'll be in the shits for years."

Will felt like the little boy who'd been caught with his hand in the cookie jar, "Constanza had a stiff piece of garden hose wrapped around Rico's neck twisting it like a tourniquet to kill him. In desperation I told him the plan was to stash her at a safe house near Bogotá, but I didn't tell him CIA safe house—he just assumed that. By the way, he claimed to be best buddies with Marty Lindstrum. What happened at the safe house? When Constanza got the report back an hour later he came in ready to kill Rico and me, but then his guards brought in Rose and Daniel and distracted him."

"Well that explains it then," Hal began, shaking his head in disgust, "the CIA had that place wired at every door and window, and Jepson's guy told me they were holding some Medellin cartel informant there when Constanza's crew came in heavy. From the pictures on the TV news, every window and door looked like it had exploded off, and there were bodies all over the ground and street around the house."

"Jesus, so the CIA's gonna trace the hit back to Constanza, and then they're gonna put two and two together and come after us. Sorry bro, but it was the only desperate thing I could come up with to gain an extra hour's time on this earth," Will offered sheepishly.

"Not to worry ma man, the two survivors from Constanza's attack team died mysteriously in the hospital within an hour after being admitted. Dead men tell no tales," he smirked as he took a shot from the silver flask. Hal then stared at Will with a hint of disgust, "And your sorry ass is coming with me and Pierson when it's time to have a drink with Bernie Jepson cowboy. His boys saved our ass back there!" Suddenly noticing his lack of manners, Hal held the flask out to Juan, "Care to share a taste of celebration?"

To their amazement he took the flask, drank a respectable shot and said, "Thank you so very much for sharing; that is quite respectable Scotch whisky."

"Johnnie Walker Black Archbishop, and it's my pleasure to share it with you."

"So how'd Consuela get back to her other life?" Will wondered.

"Our Delta brothers really did take a liking to her. They delivered her to her favorite supermarket, where she took a taxi home. I think they hooked her up with a cover story of being temporarily kidnapped by M-19, but the kidnapper's lost their resolve when news of the CIA safe house broke," Hal provided. He saw the look on Will's face, "Jesus Tonto, she's gotta blend back in; big girls that have affairs have to think on their feet."

Just then they heard the pitch of the engines change just noticeably as Curt Webster's voice came over the headphones, "Okay folks, let's see what kind of welcome we get at Moreno Air Base."

———

As the two Black Hawks feathered down to the tarmac in front of the Moreno Base Operations building, Curt took off his helmet and informed them, "Looks like a less than friendly reception; someone didn't get the invitation that we were making a friendly stopover."

Everyone craned their necks to look out the cockpit window to see four jeeps full of guards armed with M-16s pull up within twenty feet of the helicopters and deploy in a perimeter around them. Will looked at Hal and asked, "What now Kemosabe?"

To their surprise, Juan Villaponteau opened the side door to Castle One and stepped out, walking towards the Colombian Air Force officer who was no doubt in charge. When the Commander saw that it was the Archbishop he said something to his troops, resulting in lowering their weapons but still holding them across their chests. The conversation between the Commander and the Archbishop lasted a couple of minutes as Juan pointed back at the helicopters and finally motioned for the rest to join him and the officer. When they got to where Villaponteau was standing he turned and smiled, "I would like you to meet Brigadier General Pasco Hernández, the Commander of Moreno Air Base. General Hernández, these are friends of mine who just rescued an American missionary being held by the drug cartels."

Hernandez projected somewhat of an imperious persona, "So who is this missionary who has been rescued; I would like to meet him."

Colton, who had been riding in the Castle Two with Pierson, made his way to the front of the group and offered his hand. "I am Colton Kavanagh General, and I am very happy to make your acquaintance. It has been a difficult two weeks for me until my friends came for me yesterday." In all the excitement of the mission Will hadn't noticed that Colton's clothes were dirty and ragged, and his two week growth of hair and beard only served to emphasize his frail condition.

General Hernandez nodded just perceptibly at him and opened his arm to point towards the Base Operations building. "Please come inside and clean up while my men refuel your aircraft. I believe we can find some clean clothes that will fit you." He then turned back to look at the choppers, "I have not seen this type of helicopter before; what is it?"

Hal stepped towards him and replied, "This is the new general purpose helicopter the U.S. Army will use to phase out the Hueys."

Hernandez walked towards Castle One as Hal motioned for Curt to get out. The General stopped next to the helicopter and touched one of the barrels on the Minigun. "General purpose you say? This looks like very much like the miniature Gatling guns your Special Forces utilize, no?"

Curt stepped forward, "Hi General, I'm Curt Webster and I'm the Senior Project Manager for delivery of the UH-60, called the Black Hawk, for Sikorsky Aircraft. We've been testing offensive capabilities on the Black Hawk as the Army's new helicopter gunship is several years from operational testing."

He walked to the other side of the Black Hawk and examined the M129 grenade launcher and the linked band of grenades on the feed tray. He shook his head and smiled, "It would seem you have a quite viable aircraft to bridge this delivery gap Mr. Webster." He then turned to motion everyone inside the terminal building.

Curt and Vinny refused to leave the helicopters as the base fuel truck came out to refill their tanks. The rest of them followed Colton and the General inside and were directed to a dining room while the General took Colton by the arm to his quarters. None of the raid crew had given the slightest thought to food during the adrenaline rush of the rescue mission. Now that they were sitting at a table with food being delivered, their appetites became apparent. "So what is this, some kind of soup?" Will asked a waiter who was delivering a large serving bowl of what appeared to be a soup of some sort.

He answered in rapid-fire Spanish, also pointing to a platter of what looked like fried chips, but Rose rescued him with a smile. "It is indeed soup Will, and it is called *Ajiaco*. It is made with chicken, corn and potatoes, and you eat it over the steamed rice. Fresh cream and capers are in those smaller bowls to add as garnish to top off the *Ajiaco*. Those chips are friend plantains, and are delicious."

They were all relishing the food when Colton came walking back in with the General, now cleanly shaven and wearing clean military fatigue pants and a pilot's leather jacket with a fur collar. Will smiled at him and asked, "Hungry brother?"

"No thank you, General Hernández was kind enough to have some food brought to his room while I showered. Are we about ready to head out? It seems like a long time since I've been home."

When they got out to the helicopters, Will handed a platter of fried plantains to Curt and Vinny, who accepted them with noticeable delight. Curt handed Will the gold Maple Leafs Colonel Mixon had scrounged for them back at Ft Davis and nodded towards the General. Will walked up to General Fernandez and bowed slightly, "We really appreciate your hospitality General, and we would like to offer you a token as payment for the aviation fuel you have been so kind to provide us."

He looked down at the Canadian Maple Leafs Will held out for him, but he shook his head no. "I cannot accept these as payment, as the aviation fuel is a government appropriation and there is nothing to repay. I am happy to offer you and your brother a moment of respite from the rigors of your last few days."

To their surprise Juan Villaponteau reached into Will's hand and grabbed the 18 gold coins, placed them in the General's and closed his hands around them. He smiled as he told Hernández, "In that case General, please see that this small contribution is used to build a canteen for the men who must work in the weather and keep this airfield open to needful visitors. I am sure that an informal break area would be much appreciated, and it would serve as a humble contribution on our part."

On the flight over to Barranquilla, Hal swapped birds with Dan Pierson so he could debrief what had happened with the 'backup' copter, Castle Two. "So I kinda lost sight of you after Colton took off with the Archbishop; by the way, everyone in Constanza's limo heard the Black Hawk taking off from the academy grounds," Will said to begin the debrief.

Rambo was smiling when he said, "Actually, you're brother had never been in a helicopter before, so we went on a little joy ride. Then Hal wanted to get Consuela out of sight after that snatch, so she joined us on a little joy ride as well; she's actually a lot of fun."

"So where'd you hide her? Constanza was going bugshit trying to find her; I guess you know about Daniel Gomez?"

"Yeah, Marco Pintoles and I put him into a body bag to carry back to Barranquilla. We kind of kept the lid on the exact location of Jepson's safe house, just in case Constanza put the screws to you. The Deltas actually have this remote ranch near a town called Girardot, about 50 miles outside of Bogotá. That's where we hid Consuela as well as the Black Hawks overnight. Man, you talk about going native, the Deltas who run that place look like Colombians, talk like them and even smell like them."

"Okay, so how'd she manage to make her disappearance seamless? Hal told us the Deltas dropped her off at a grocery market in Bogotá. I guess you know Kelly took her place at the exchange?"

"Jesus I'm glad Constanza shot low, that was super risky for Kelly to take on. So anyway, as if fate was smiling on her, Consuela's husband Gianfranco was in Havana of all places, and didn't even know about the snatch or the put back. Believe me, that woman knows she was given a second chance on life and her marriage."

"So did she and Penny hit it off in the interview? Did she mention anything about that?"

"She loved Penny, and the interview went over their schedule by an hour. I got the impression they'll hook back up again at some time in the future."

"That's good, I think Penny's gotta make a trip down to Rio; Lord knows we can't let her go there without a shield around her."

Pierson smiled and said, "Oh, I think I'll be more than happy to provide her security for that trip. We might even be able to drop down to Buenos

Aires where I know a certain Tourism Minister." He nodded over to where Kelly was hovering over Rico and asked, "You see the two of them hooking up seriously?"

"I sure hope so; she surprised the shit out of me playing Annie Oakley hanging out of that Black Hawk back at Ft Davis. By the way, what happened back at *Hacienda Cardona*? Hector had just killed Daniel and was aiming the pistol at Rose; I was about ready to tell him the Deltas had the place surrounded just to buy us another hour. Some guard came in and completely distracted him. Do you know what that was about?"

Pierson actually put his hands together and looked upwards, "Man, talk about timing; Marco Pintoles called in to tell us they had captured Rose and Daniel. Which reminds me; we gave Pintoles one of the satellite phones for indefinite contact. Anyway, when we got the word that Rose and Daniel were captured things started getting more than a little paranoid back at the Delta House…"

Will actually laughed, even though it shot lasers of pain through his right eyebrow. "Sorry, Delta House was debauchery headquarters in the movie Animal House. Please continue."

"Right, and the Delta leader tells Hal to cool it, that they had his six covered. So the Delta guy gets on his radio and talks to some guy in Bogotá. When he hangs up I give him Tonto's Italian Army salute so he tells me, 'No sweat Rambo, Constanza's home in Cali just got an anonymous call from a pay phone outside the Cuban Embassy. Silvio's street thug told them M-19, this revolutionary group, was enroute to kidnap Constanza's wife and kids.'"

"You gotta be shitting me!" Will said and high-fived Rambo.

"Nope, so I suspect that Constanza found out about that little threat right before he was gonna get really ugly."

Will bowed over with his hands held out, casting the Indian Shaman blessing to the Deltas. He looked at Rambo and told him, "Constanza actually gave us a tour of his high-tech cocaine laboratory. Man, were there a lot of flammables stored in that place! I tried to get word back to you guys via Daniel; did he get through?"

"Like a champ bro. So we knew about the lab, the cash vault and the National Police spotter teams before we went in. Man do those guys of Pintoles know stealth."

"Whatdya mean stealthy? They must've been able to sneak up on the guards protecting the place," Will figured.

"Not only that, but they had visuals on the police spotter teams, who were armed with RPGs I might add," he said with a smirk.

"Okay, we've nibbled around the edges now; take me through the whole thing. I guess Constanza had Rico, Rose and I moved around ten o'clock."

"Right, we had Pintoles giving us live status as things went down. As soon as you guys pulled out of the plantation, Pintoles guys took out everybody but the police spotter teams. As soon as the guards were neutralized, we flew in at treetop level and landed on the front side of the hacienda so the police spotter teams couldn't see the chopper."

"Why'd you do that?"

"Because we needed to load up a few things on the chopper before we induced our National Police friends to fire off their RPGs into the Cali Cartel's most important refinery. Getting the picture?"

Will was rubbing his hands together, imagining the brilliance of the plan, "So how were you gonna prove the *Federales* torched the place?"

"All in good time my man. So we grabbed all of the dollars in the vault, man, I ain't got a clue how much was there. It wasn't banded up real nicely for easy loading. But of all things, Constanza, or maybe it was Rodriquez the FARC guy, had this impressive collection of jade stones—you know that's the gem Colombia's famous for. So the ELN guys snatch all of the packaged coke from the lab—maybe 200 kilos—and load it up in the chopper as we're hauling out the satchels of cash. During the last sweep, we spotted the bag of jade stones and a brief case, so we took that out with us and Vinny lit off the engines on the chopper. Once he had it revved up to eighty percent, he jumped the bird up above the house for maybe five seconds. I saw the flash from the RPG just as Vinny put her back down hard on the ground. Remember, we had the house and the warehouse between us and the shooters."

Will was getting excited by the story, "So then what happened?"

"The dumb fuckers shot too low and hit that huge propane tank on that side of the hacienda!"

"You have gotta be shitting me! That must be what we heard over at the Casa. I guess the shrapnel was blasting everything on the back side of the house?"

"Yeah, especially the acetone and generator fuel tanks supporting the lab; man, that concussion almost tipped the Black Hawk over, but Vinny felt it coming and got her up and facing into the blast at the last possible second. That was actually a pretty close call, but I've seen worse."

"So back up here Rambo, how are the *Federales* implicated in the destruction of the Cali Cartel lab? Did you have Penny Martindale out there with her video camera?"

He was smiling smugly now, "Kelly gave Pintoles her backup Nikon and three rolls of film, and our ELN associates took full color pictures of the National Police teams firing RPGs into the plantation and coke lab. Unfortunately, the members of the police teams were killed in the ensuing shrapnel storm but their bodies were photographed with the launchers still in their arms."

Will high-fived him, "Man, it don't get any better than that!"

Dan was grinning like the cat that ate the canary when he reached down to open the brief case, "How about a stake in British Petroleum?"

"What kind of stake?"

"How about twenty-five million in bearer bonds ma man; think that'll buy us some gasoline?"

Will reached over to close the case securely and said, "OPSEC as of this moment Daniel. We've got to get to the Caymans."

He stared at Will's one good eye and replied, "Roger that."

———

When they got to Cortissoz Airport in Barranquilla, Villaponteau insisted they come into the Dignitary Visiting Lounge while the helicopters were being refueled. Will pulled him to the side and said, "Juan, we collected approximately three million dollars from the hacienda cash room before the place was incinerated. We'd like you to take this ill-gotten wealth and make something good come out of it."

He was nodding his head, "Do you have any preferences on how this money might be dispensed?"

"First of all, we need to repair that church clock tower that saved us back in Pereira. Next, I'd like to see Daniel Gomez appropriately memorialized by the construction of a church in his name. And finally, I'd like the rest of it to be used to provide for clean water and sanitation for the poor people of Barranquilla."

He smiled and nodded, "So it will be done Will. Do you have any plans for the future? Would you like to come and oversee this water and sanitation improvement effort?"

"Actually Archbishop, I've gotta go be there for my wife when she brings our daughter into this world, and that's the most important thing in my life. But I do know a capable engineer—a Sicilian Catholic no less—who has performed just such a task in the central Philippines for the past three years, and he would like to come back closer to his home. Perhaps I can contact him on your behalf?"

Juan smiled at him as he asked, "What is his name, and what is your relationship to him?"

Will smiled and shook his head, "I should know you can see through me Juan. His name is Tony DeLuca, and he is from Fort Monmouth, New Jersey. And I was in love with his daughter Christine at one time, but she is now married and expecting a child of her own. I know Tony to be a man of severe principals."

His smile became a grin now, "Did these severe principals impede your relationship with his daughter?"

He rolled his eyes and came clean, "Let's just say I learned that a Sicilian Catholic didn't think a divorced suitor was appropriate to marry his daughter, that's for sure!"

He touched Will's face gently, "I have met your miracle of the flesh Dominique, so everything has worked out for the best?"

"Right you are Juan, now thanks for everything you've done; I don't know how we coulda pulled this off without you. You are a true friend, and you can always count on me to come through for you when you need me."

He smiled as he pulled a box from his pocket and said, "Good, come with me so that I may appropriately commemorate the actions of these heroic friends of yours."

Everyone was thunderstruck as Juan placed the Saint Michael's Medal around their necks, but when he started to put one on Will, he grabbed his hands and leaned over to kiss his ring. "Please Your Grace; place this St Michael's Medal on Daniel Gomez when he enters final rest. He was not only a man of God, but a hero in the truest sense. I am honored to have known him and fought with him."

Will thought he saw a trace of a tear on Juan's lower eyelid when he responded, "It will so be William Kavanagh, go with God my son."

60

PUTTING COLOMBIA IN
THE REAR VIEW MIRROR

WILL CALLED DOM while watching the Caribbean through his good eye, as Curt had invited him to sit in the copilot's seat on the flight back to Ft Davis. "How you doing baby?"

"Eihh! *Mon Dieu*, Carmen, come, it is them!"

"My God Will, where are you? Archbishop Villaponteau called us to tell us that Colton had been rescued, but we have been sitting in total fright for two days. Tell me everything is alright!"

"We're all fine baby, at least for the most part. It got a little dicey there for a while, but we made it out by the grace of God, and Juan Villaponteau."

Carmen grabbed the phone and shouted, "Tell me my Harold is alright Will, we have been going crazy waiting in this hotel room for news."

"Well, that's actually good that there's no international news of strange things happening in and around Bogotá. Hal is fine, and he didn't even get wounded this time."

"What do you mean HE didn't get wounded this time?" Dom screamed, obviously on an extension phone now. "What has happened to you Will?"

"Oh, it's nothing a little plastic surgery and a few Percodans can't manage. I'll tell you what, I'll never look at a water hose the same way again; man can those things hurt like shit."

"Plastic surgery for what? What has happened to you Will?" Dom blurted, sobbing now.

"I'm fine baby. I took the barrel of a Sig Sauer hard up against my eyebrow, but thank God a little pistol-whipping didn't crack my hard head."

Having fed the women the most important details he added, "Alright, listen up because I can't go into a lot of detail. I need you two to call Chris Campion and schedule a roundtrip flight between Panama City and George Town, Grand Caymans, with a stopover in Colon to pick up a passenger. If possible, I want Carmen and Hal making the trip to George Town, and we'll watch Wade until you get back. I might even have Pierson ride with the two of you if Hal thinks that's necessary. I'll get a helo ride over to Howard after you get here on the 727 Carmen, and we'll probably be bringing everyone back to the Intercon. This mission is just about over. Got all that?"

"Hey, we'll see you when you touch down, how far is Ft Davis from Colon?" Carmen asked.

"Don't worry; we'll be in two beautiful black helicopters on the General Aviation side of the field at Colon, just tell Chris to pull up next to us. We've got about 300 miles to go and we'll be in Colon in less than two hours. See you there!"

After the call, Curt looked at Will and asked, "I take it this trip was profitable as well as successful?"

Will regarded him warily, but figured if he couldn't trust him by now he'd already be dead. "Actually Curt, I believe you have proven the Black Hawk is the chopper of the future. I might just be in a position to make a little investment in Sikorsky. What are your thoughts?"

"Hey, if I were a man with money to invest, I'd call my broker and say buy Sikorsky Aviation. DoD has made their selection and Sikorsky's gonna be delivering them as fast as they can produce them. Before this is over, all of our allies are gonna be getting 'em too. Sikorsky's as close a thing to a sure bet as I've ever seen."

Hal slithered through the cockpit opening and asked, "You call the girls yet?"

"Yeah, Carmen's gonna be waiting for you on the Great West 727 at Colon. You and she are gonna take a little delayed honeymoon ride over to George Town. You want Rambo to go along?"

He looked at him weirdly, then the light bulb came on, "Nah, Carmen and I can handle it. It's time for the rest of you guys to see a doctor and get patched up. Rico's gonna need surgery."

Will nodded towards Curt and told Hal, "Curt here says Sikorsky's gonna be selling thousands of these Black Hawks over the next decade or so. Sounds like a pretty wise investment for Destination Partners, wouldn't you say partner?"

Hal was shaking his head as he replied, "Damn right. I sure would like to have access to one of these birds when I need one. I don't think we can justify keeping one around ROUST just for joy rides."

Curt smiled as he made the pitch, "You and a few hundred other people; at $15M a copy, these birds aren't cheap. But we've already formed up an Elite Partners Program where the S-70, which is the commercial version of the Black Hawk, can be leased on a part-time basis. Besides the New York City area, plans now are to have Partner hubs in Washington, Miami, Houston and Los Angeles. There's some stockholder threshold where program fees are waived. I'll get my guy in touch with you about it if you're interested."

"Hell yeah, we need to know the program specifics before we make our investment too. I bet my cunning attorney in San Diego would be all over this. Who's your guy Curt?" Will asked, now very interested in the entire Sikorsky relationship.

"I'll have him call you on that satellite phone of yours. Do you know where you're gonna be in a month?"

"Hell yeah, my ass is gonna be in Gastineau, Louisiana trying to keep from freaking out during the birth of my daughter! But I'll keep the sat phone around for obscure contacts. Man have you ever been a life saver Curt! I really don't see how we coulda pulled this off without you," Will said with genuine admiration.

"Hey, when the going gets rough, who you gonna call? The guys you've been through the shit with before. And I might add Mr. William Kavanagh, welcome to the club!"

Hal patted him on the shoulder and corrected, "Oh, he's been a member for a while Curt. He's collecting scars now like a tattoo master!"

———

The welcome awaiting them when they feathered down fifty feet from the Great West 727 in Colon was like a small reenactment of the troops coming home from World War II. Will was holding Wade as Hal twirled Carmen around in sheer joy. Pierson was doing his typical sleight of hand with the immigration official, telling him they had nothing to declare but some test weapons used on a training mission into the interior of Panama. Dom couldn't stop crying as she continued to touch Will's face, which was swollen from the beating Hector had given him. His swollen shut right eye was now a collage of yellow, purple and red where a spot of infection had somehow overcome the large doses of antibiotics they'd taken before and since the encounter with Hector Constanza. His arms were striped with black bruises where the garden hose had flailed him, but he was so glad to see his extremely pregnant mate that he momentarily didn't really care. Kelly was staying next to Rico, reapplying a dressing to his thigh that'd taken Hector's nine millimeter shot thankfully through the flesh and muscle. When Dom went to check on them, she all but fell back in horror as she noticed the very black and blue bruise in the middle of Kelly's chest showing around the tank top tee shirt she was wearing with her camo fatigue pants. Will looked around to find Bob Matthews collecting his things and grabbed him around the shoulder, "Man it sure is good having some experienced warriors around when the shit hits the fan. You gonna come on back to Panama City to get out?"

"Nah, I'll take a COPA bird out of here to Managua. My boss is chomping at the bit to have my butt back on the ground there. He says the Sandinistas want to question me about some roadside killing that took place a couple of weeks ago. Go figure."

Colton walked up and instead of shaking his hand, engulfed Bob Matthews with a bear hug. "I can never thank you enough for all you've done to give me my freedom back Bob. I guess all of the people in the Embassy aren't completely without means."

He smiled as he replied, "I wouldn't bother coming back to Nicaragua any time soon Colton; as a matter of fact, why don't you put Nicaragua on your list of 'been there, done that?'"

"I think I already have; Nicaragua and now Colombia have just about cured me of foreign travel for possibly the rest of my life."

They moved everything to one helicopter for the ride back to Howard, so Will got Vinny and Curt together and pulled out the envelope that still had $40,000 in clean 100 dollar bills and pushed it inside of Curt's flight suit. "That's just a little something Colton, Dom and I want to pass along for the two of you for saving our lives. I will never forget that white phosphorous sunspot distracting that SA-7; man, that had to tighten your sphincter up Curt!"

Curt glanced inside the envelope and said, "Scary ain't exactly how I'd have described it, more like split-second timing. Hal picked up the flash as soon as the SAM left the launcher, and waited one second before detonating that grenade. Sometimes it's better to be lucky than good!"

"We were both today brother, I can guarantee you that. Listen, I'll have my guys talking to your Partners program guy. Also, the next time I talk to you, we'll all be owners of that company!"

Will looked at Vinny and told him, "That's twice now you've pulled my ass out of the fire brother; let's not make it a habit, okay?"

Vinny gave him a bear hug, "Not until the next time brother. Take care and good luck with fatherhood—your ass is gonna need it!"

When they got to Howard Air Base, Will called Major General Goodie Stilton and explained Rico's gunshot wound and wondered if there was any way they could get him patched up in the base hospital. Goodie was ever the deal maker as he told him, "Let's see, Staff Sergeant Suarez is a veteran of the United States Army, honorably discharged. I believe we can have an ambulance over to the flight line in, say, sixty seconds."

"I can't thank you enough General, it's been one hell of a two day foray into Colombia, but we got everybody back almost in one piece.

"So when are you gonna head back to Zigville Dupree? I'm sure he's about to have a coronary to hear back from you."

"Not before tomorrow, that's for sure! My ass is getting drunk in your penthouse tonight big boy!"

"Good," he said as he kissed her lips, "see you when Ricardo's all sewn up again. Nice work babe; you sure surprised the shit out of me!"

She narrowed her stare at him, "And that's the last time you're setting my ass up to be shot! What if he'd aimed a little higher?"

He slapped her on the ass, "He was focused on those beautiful tits of yours Dupree; that perfect body of yours once again saved the day!"

"Yeah right cowboy, you'd better have some Grand Marnier!"

"That's right Johnny, we want to become stockholders in British Petroleum and Sikorsky, which is part of United Technologies Corporation," Will told their West Coast attorney as Dom, Carmen, Wade and Hal sat around the master bedroom with the speakerphone on the middle of the super king-sized bed.

"I see," he replied slightly lubricated, interrupting the Board's happy hour. "And just what kind of investment do you want to make?"

"Well, I've got the principals of Circle Entertainment right here, and we figure ten million apiece in each company," Will said as he clicked rocks glasses full of scotch with Hal.

"You have got to be shitting me; don't you think that's kind of a large investment? And just where am I to obtain this capital for that you wish to invest?" he asked, starting to sober up a bit.

"From the Cayman's operating account you set up for Circle Entertainment of course. I'll give you a one-time access code for the purchase transaction," he replied, knowing he was driving Johnny crazy with the limited background information.

"Would it be too imprudent of me to inquire as to where you obtained this investment capital?"

"Actually, Hal and Carmen took care of that, so I'll let them explain," he said, opening his hand to Hal for the *coup de grás*.

"Let's see John, the twenty-five bearer bonds had maturity dates of 1984 and the coupons were all still attached, so we were able redeem them for just under $27.9 million."

"Jesus Christ, where the fuck did you get bearer bonds?"

"Where have Kelly Dupree and Dan Pierson been for the past week Johnny?" Will posed.

"Oh, they blew out of here for some crazy ass thing down in Panama…. hey, did you have anything to do with that?"

"We did Johnny ma man, and the prize for participating in that crazy ass thing was some misplaced bearer bonds. Now it would be a violation of our attorney-client relationship for you to ever utter one word about this, but it might behoove your major domo Zigster to perform due diligence on United Technologies which is about to deliver a godzillion UH-60 Black Hawk helicopters to the US military over the next two decades. I for one can attest to the amazing aeronautical capabilities of the Black Hawk, as it pulled my ashes out of the fire constantly over the past three days."

"Okay, I'll get my investment guy on the stock purchases first thing in the morning. Which way you wanna go, common or preferred?"

"Jesus Johnny, he's your investment guy; let him tell us which way is the smartest to go with this. You know us; all we want is ten percent a year forever.

Nothing greedy," Will said as Hal burst out laughing.

"Alright, I'll get on it; any little bonus for your armpit attorney friend?"

"As a matter of fact Mr. Chessereaux, my fellow Directors did manage to bring back a bag of extraordinary jade jewelry quality gem stones. So if you were hoping to gain favor with that gorgeous wife of yours, we may have something of interest for you," Dom added.

"Now we're talking; I'll call you when we've got an investment plan ready to present to you tomorrow."

When he hung up the phone, Will looked at Hal, 'You know, Dan's been more than a friend in what we've been through for the past year."

Hal smirked at him, "Make that the past seven years bro, sort of BK: Before Kavanagh."

"So we gotta reward him in the proper way. What do you think, a million for the Colombian Op or a full share in Circle Entertainment?" Will asked as he looked around at Carmen and Dom who were the other partners in Circle Entertainment.

Carmen was the one to propose first, "Why not both? We can make him the offer, so he can decide if he wants to invest half of the million as a share-holder."

"Yeah, it seems as though we're gonna be earning some decent interest income in the coming years from the stock purchases, so it is an interesting investment," Will added. "Go ask him to join us for a few minutes."

As Dan somewhat uncomfortably leaned against the dresser, Will looked to Dom who was technically the President of the organization. "Daniel, we think you are one of us, and have been for some time. Every time the call for risking lives goes out, you are the first to come forward."

Dan shrugged self-consciously and replied, "It's just an old habit I have, but not everyone's got that emergency number to call."

"Right, just Hal, Carmen, Will or I come immediately to mind. We are also the Directors of Circle Entertainment, and have decided to assign you a one million dollar stipend for your contributions during the Colombian Operation. Do you consider that adequate, or should we reconsider this?"

Poor Dan was shaking his head with embarrassment, "No, no way can you pay me like that. I was only one member of the team. I am a mere warrior who hasn't met that misdirected bullet just yet."

Will saw Hal jerk, but he put out his hand to steady him as he told Dan, "Well if a million is too much money for your contributions to the suicide mission I just survived, how about you use half of it to become a full partner with Circle Entertainment? That'd leave you a payday of a mere half-million in tax-free money. Does that sound more reasonable?"

"More than reasonable, but I've got to ask you; what does Circle Entertainment do besides go out on the most dangerous missions this side of the Delta Force?"

"Well, we seem to be under contract right now with Great West Studios to deliver the screenplay for an incredible North African action movie. Oh, and before I forget, we just made a commitment to invest heavily in British Petroleum and United Technologies not ten minutes ago," Will added, wondering if he'd make the connection.

Dan was rubbing his chin, "And United Technologies would be?"

"Parent firm of Sikorsky Aircraft, which is under contract to deliver thousands of Black Hawks to the DoD over the next two decades.

"Okay, I'm in for the partnership and I'll take the money. How is it tax-free?"

"Via an American Express Card drawn on your account in the Cayman Islands ma man. Just use it outside the United States to be safe," Hal advised.

Dan was thinking about something when he finally asked, "So how much stock are we buying? I guess the plan is to harvest the interest off the stock?"

Will smiled as he slapped his back, "Ten million in each company ma man. That was some find you made in that brief case back at the hacienda! Now how about go find Kelly and send her in."

Kelly was popping a Percodan with a sip of her Grand Marnier when she walked in, "What's up? Not another suicide mission?"

Will shook his head from side to side as Dom walked over to her and was barely able to bend in far enough to kiss her. "Close your eyes and hold out your hand."

When Kelly opened up her eyes again she looked curiously at the black credit card in her hand with her name on it, "What's this?"

"It was actually everyone's idea, but Will insists on telling you what it's good for," Dom advised her.

When Kelly turned to him with a blank expression, he told her, "It's good for buying, say, seven top line Lamborghinis."

They could see her doing some mental math before she replied, "Those cars are over $150,000 apiece. What are you talking about?"

"Well, there's nothing wrong with your brain," Will said pointedly looking down at her bruised chest. "That my dear is Circle Entertainment's way of thanking you for taking a bullet for us today. Without you, this would not have turned out well. Oh, and you should only use it for overseas purchases; it's kind of our little present from an obscure Caymans Island account. You my dear are a million dollar baby!"

———

Hal, Pierson and Will were reasonably hungover when they reported to Major General Stilton's office the next morning, the final curtain call in Panama before heading home. To their amazement, Colonel Mixon, Adam Chennault and Curt Webster were already sitting around the General's conference table when his aide ushered them in. Stilton saw them and asked, "And how are you gentlemen feeling this morning? If it's no better than these three, I'd say it's about time for the hair of the dog!"

Hal and Will shivered at the prospect of drinking any more alcohol, but to their surprise the General's aide magically appeared with a tray crowded with Bloody Marys in grotesquely huge crystal glasses. Picking his up and taking a satisfying sip, Stilton led off the debriefing by asking, "How'd the Black Hawk hold up in combat operations?"

With reluctance, Hal and Will reached for their drinks as Curt Webster reported, "We didn't take any small arms fire sir, but aerodynamically she is awesome. With the external tanks we extended combat range out to 600 miles, but you'd better have a tanker or a gas station when you get there. We even evaded an SA-7 through clever use of a 40mm WP round serving as a flare."

Stilton looked around the room and surmised, "I suppose I'm looking at the invasion force. How in the world did you guys hold the Cali Cartel at bay?"

"If you thought politics made strange bedfellows General," Will said, spilling Bloody Mary on his clean golf shirt, "how about the Catholic Church and the ELN joining forces?"

"Now you have got to be shitting me? What do the Holy See and Karl Marx have in common?"

"A desire to help the peasants overcome the wealthy, or at least obtain minimal measures of supportable life such as clean water and sanitation. Actually, a priest was the head of the front-end surveillance team the ELN sent out in advance of our arrival in Bogotá."

"So the ELN countered the Cartel soldiers? What about the priest, did he actually kill people?"

Will looked at Stilton with a narrowed gaze, "I watched Hector Constanza shoot both his knees out as he was shackled to a wall, and then blow his brains out when the priest tried to forgive him as Christ had done."

Stilton shook his head, then took a gulp of his Bloody Mary, "Why'd Constanza shoot this guy? What was he trying to find out?"

"He was trying to find out where we had hidden his mistress, who happened to be married to the Minister of Foreign Affairs. If he could have found her, we were all gonna get the Colombian necktie, or worse. The hell of it was that Daniel—the priest—didn't know where the mistress was being held!"

"So the return of this mistress Constanza couldn't find was crucial to your being here today for this debriefing?"

"Yes sir, except we had a stand-in for the mistress at the final takedown. It got a bit scary when Constanza shot her in the chest with a Sig Sauer P226," Will offered, slurping the last of the Bloody Mary and suddenly feeling much better.

"Shot her in the fucking chest? You got a stand-in killed during the shakedown? Jesus Christ Kavanagh, that doesn't sound like a smooth operation."

He reached down into the grocery bag he'd brought in, took out the Nehru vest and passed it around the table to Stilton. When he examined it, he saw an indentation and asked, "So this is where the bullet hit? And you say it was a 9mm round? What's this vest made of?"

Hal took over and reported, "It turns out there's this tailor down in Bogotá named Caballero who specializes in making clothes out of Kevlar. He had this one from some unfortunate client who didn't make it to his store in time. Our friend Kelly Dupree wore it and took the shot, even though we think he'd have shot his mistress if she'd have shown as well."

"So where is she? I'd like to shake her hand."

"Actually she went to the base hospital to hopefully get our friend Rico discharged so we can take them both home," Will replied.

Stilton punched a button on the phone in front of him, "Chief, how about roust up two of Kavanagh's interlopers on the installation. Names are Kelly and Rico, and they were at the base hospital. Bring them in as soon as you find them."

Will smiled at Hal because Stilton hadn't handed off the task to his aide, instead relying on his Chief Master Sergeant. "So I guess you took Mr. Constanza to meet his maker after witnessing this torture of the priest?"

Will stood up and walked to Stilton, bent down so he could see the scar down his face, and told him, "I gave him a slice just like this one, then pulled the knife right across his fat belly before I threw the coward's Sig Sauer to Rose and told her to send him to hell."

Just then a knock on the door caught Stilton's attention as a burly Chief ushered in Kelly Dupree and Rico, who was leaning on a crutch but seemed happy to be under his own power again. Will got up and introduced them, "General Stilton, this is Rico Suarez, former Special Forces, who took a round in the leg when I advised Constanza that his mistress had been abducted. In retrospect, I could possibly have conceived of a better way to break him the news."

Rico looked at him dispassionately, "At least he missed the bone and arteries."

Will took a step to put his hand on Kelly's shoulder, "And this is Kelly Dupree General, who is a movie Producer from Hollywood and served as our stand-in for the real mistress."

Stilton stood up and shook each of their hands, thanking them for their bravery and stopped in front of Kelly, who was again wearing one of her tank tops with fashionable camo capris. He looked closely at her badly bruised chest and said, "How badly did that shot hurt with the vest on. Will showed us the vest earlier."

"Once I regained consciousness, it hurt like hell General. And I can assure you that I will never volunteer for such a mission again; one is enough for me."

"I can certainly understand your point young lady. Now before you all leave, I want you to know that I met Will Kavanagh several years ago, and I can truly say that difficult situations don't seem to avoid him as he goes about life. But I can assure you that his ability to surround himself with incredibly capable friends and to somehow get access to the most advanced military equipment known to man is absolutely difficult to believe. I am so pleased that this operation worked out for the best and I wish you all the best of luck."

As they turned to leave, assuming they had been dismissed, General Stilton said, "I have one more order of business to conduct here today before you leave." He turned to his Chief Master Sergeant and nodded, prompting the chief to hold out a navy blue case. "Captain Xavier William Kavanagh, who has served this nation with valor and distinction, would you please come stand before me." Will looked around at Hal who shrugged and walked to stand before the General. He had a smile on his face now, "Captain Kavanagh, I believe the United States Air Force did you an injustice many years ago in conjunction with a 'career buster' assignment, which has since proven to be a shining example of urban renewal and efficiency. It is with great pleasure that I correct an injustice perpetrated by a well-meaning but ill-informed system of standards and measures by presenting you with the Air Force Meritorious Service Medal. Congratulations Mr. Kavanagh."

Will opened the box to find the Meritorious Service Medal and the associated ribbon shining brightly and did the only thing that seemed appropriate. He came to attention, resplendent in his jeans and golf shirt and saluted him smartly, holding the pose until he saluted him in return. They then shook hands as the room burst into applause and congratulations. Will looked at the box and then told Goodie Stilton, "Keith Melson always said you were a squared away guy, but this medal is nothing compared to the assistance you provided my family in safely returning my brother from the gates of hell. Thank you very much sir."

He put his arm around Will's shoulder as he led them out of the room, "And that little bit of assistance you just mentioned shall remain our little secret; I still have to retire from this man's war."

61

THE LONG ROAD HOME

THE GREETING PARTY AWAITING their arrival at Louis Armstrong International Airport was overwhelming to say the least. Will's entire family was waiting anxiously for a glimpse of the 'miracle man' as Reverend Spiker had tagged him, along with a number of complete strangers. As Will stepped to the tarmac, his father was the first to grab him, "My God son, what in the world happened to your face? You look like you've been in a street fight!"

"Actually, I was pistol-whipped Dad, but they tell me the swelling will go down eventually. How's Mom been holding up?"

"I thought the doctor was going to put her on tranquilizers she was so distraught, but that was yesterday. How in the world did you pull this off? The newspaper said you rescued Colton from Colombia," he asked, almost immediately interrupted by a rude TV reporter shoving a microphone in their faces.

Will was momentarily stunned when CBS 60 Minutes host Morley Safer used his 'aw shucks' persona to move past the other media types and introduce himself. Will politely told him 'Pardon me Morley' as he glanced at Kelly and announced to the throng, "Sorry folks, but NBC Reporter Penny Martindale has exclusive access to this story, and you may contact her at her offices in Sacramento, California. Now if you don't mind, I've got a family celebration to attend to."

As he turned away from the reporters to find his Mom, he was mobbed by Alex and Casey who immediately began touching his face and giving him the devil about not taking care of himself. He rolled his eyes at the relative idiocy of their chiding, "Jesus, I'm walking aren't I? Those Colombian bastards aren't the friendliest people in the world, but we made it back." He then nuzzled his face in Casey's hair and asked, "Everything going along okay with the other pregnancy in my life?"

She squealed with excitement, "YES! I haven't even had morning sickness. My doctor's been giving me vitamin B-12 injections and things are going along perfectly. How's Dom doing?"

"I don't know, let's go find out," he said, taking them by the hand in search of his pregnant bride. When they found her she was in a wheel chair being attended to by an Emergency Medical Technician. "What's wrong baby?"

Her face was flushed as he took the iced-downed washrag from the EMT and began dabbing her face, "What is it baby? What happened? You seemed fine on the plane?"

Her weak smile had him on the edge of panic, "I don't know Will, I guess all of the excitement from this huge throng got me over-heated. Did you know a miracle man celebration was awaiting us?" She lost the vitriol as her complexion paled, "I'm feeling a bit nauseous at the moment."

Will looked at the EMT, "Can we take her to the hospital? It's been one hell of a last two months on her pregnancy."

The med tech took one look at Dom's face and began wheeling her to the ambulance, directing people to clear the path. Jan Kavanagh came running in another tizzy, "What's wrong with Dominique Will?"

"I don't know Mom, but I'm going with them on the ambulance to the hospital. We gotta make sure the baby is alright."

Enroute to the hospital, one EMT started an IV drip as the other took Dom's temperature and blood pressure. They were working so fast and communicating in such shorthand that Will finally had to ask, "How is she?"

"She's moderately hypertensive and her heartbeat is elevated, but we've started her on IV fluids and she will be stable until we can get her to the ER."

"ER?" He blasted back. "What the fuck for? What's happening? Come on man, come clean with me, I'm her husband."

"Remaining calm is the best thing you can do to help your wife Mr. Kavanagh. She is not in critical danger, but a doctor should make an assessment of her condition. How far along is her pregnancy?"

"Jesus Christ," he swore, stopping to think. "I'd say seven and a half months; is that a problem?"

"No sir, we just need to collect the facts to present to the ER physician when we get to the hospital."

"We're going to Tulane Medical Center, right?" Will asked, trying to remember the cogent issues.

"Actually, that's not the closest medical center to the airport sir. We're mandated by state law to take the patient to the closest...."

Will interrupted him with some ferocity, "If the patient is in dire straits, right? Now I want my wife in the Tulane Medical Center. You want some cash or something?"

"No sir, that'll be adjusted on the bill." He leaned against his shoulder microphone and made some unintelligible remark to the driver, as the ambulance turned at the next intersection.

With the lizard brain fully engaged, he pulled out the business card for Jonathan Calvatori in Buenos Aires and called. Lita the receptionist answered, "Oh hello Mr. Kavanagh; how is your wife doing?"

"Listen, is Jonathan anywhere close by? I'm in an ambulance with Dom enroute to a hospital in New Orleans—once again—and I need to talk to the MAN!"

"One moment please, Mr. Kavanagh, I'll go find him."

"Will, what's wrong? Lita said you're in an ambulance in New Orleans; tell me exactly what's happened," an alert and concerned Dr. Jonathan Calvatori said.

"Well, I ended up going on this rescue mission to retrieve my brother in Bogotá and everything seemed okay until we landed in New Orleans. Completely shocking us, a huge throng had gathered to welcome us home. I think the shock of the crowd was too much excitement for Dom and her blood pressure spiked and she's got an elevated heart rate. We're on our way to Tulane Medical Center; whatdya think?"

"My God Will, she wasn't with you in Bogotá was she?"

"Nah, she and Carmen were kicked back at the Panama City Intercon waiting for word on the rescue op. I guess she was somewhat stressed by the suicide mission I was on, but it all worked out; whatdya think?"

"I think I would like to speak with the attending physician in the Emergency Room when you get to the hospital. Can you arrange that?"

"Sure, but I ain't part of their brotherhood; you know these ER guys get kinda stiff if they think you're trying to give 'em too much advice," he opined, having learned from their first visit to Tulane after the Managua debacle. "So is there some secret handshake, or maybe a classified code that normal humans ignore but physicians panic over?

He could hear Jonathon suppress a snicker, "Tell the attending physician these two words: CODE OMEGA. As he's catching his breath, please call me back at this number and I will make sure that I am immediately available to converse with him."

"Code Omega, got it doc. Thanks a million, and I'll be back in touch shortly."

Dom was watching him closely, ignoring the cannula feeding oxygen through her nose, "What does Dr. Calvatori suggest?"

"He wants to talk to the attending physician when we get to the ER; don't worry about a thing baby, we'll figure out what's best for you and junior in there."

"Actually Mr. Kavanagh, I believe it's a little sweetheart in there," she said with a smirk.

"So where's this doctor located that you want the ER trauma physician to consult with?" The EMT asked. "They've got all kinda restrictions in there with whatever kind of phone that is you have sir," he cautioned, pointing at the satellite phone.

"Fuck 'em, unless they want to direct-dial Buenos Aires. But I could really give a shit, that's my wife and child whose lives are on the line," Will said, the smugness unavoidable.

"Buenos Aires, as in Argentina; what kind of phone is that?"

"A very fucking expensive one, but it really doesn't matter. My wife's safety and the health of our child is what are important, right?"

He was shaking his head, "Right you are sir. We'll make sure we get you all there in good shape."

To their amazement, Dom blurted out "Y'all."

Predictably, the Emergency Room at Tulane Medical Center was a zoo when they arrived. The nurse who was pulling Dom's gurney through the swinging doors grabbed a curtain that opened to an ER examination station and told Will quite curtly, "You'll have to leave sir."

He merely shook his head, "I ain't going anyplace until the ER doctor shows his face, and then we'll discuss my location relative to my wife. Her name is Dominique Kavanagh by the way."

The nurse looked frayed, and in her defense he didn't know how long she'd been on duty, as she pressed a black button on the wall behind her. About twenty seconds later a black guy in scrubs who looked like he could have been the starting linebacker for the Tulane Green Wave looked at the nurse who glanced towards Will and nodded. The linebacker said in a very pleasant voice, "Sir, please come with me, the doctor will be out to give you a report after he has examined the patient."

It caught Will as hilarious, as he had a swollen face, one eye completely swollen shut circled by yellow and purple bruises, so he asked him, "Which patient?"

This rejoinder caused the orderly/bouncer to inhale deeply as he put his meaty hand under Will's right armpit, "Please come with me sir."

Will looked up at the giant, knowing his options were limited as a doctor in a white smock stepped into the examination room, "Is there a problem?"

Just as the ER enforcer was about to jerk him away, Will blurted out Jonathan's secret code words, "We've got a Code Omega here doctor."

Without another word, the doctor grabbed a phone from the wall and announced, "OB/GYN to the ER STAT!"

He looked back at Will, "What is the nature of the emergency? Are you a physician?"

He smiled at him and said, "Standby one doc; I'll have her OB/GYN on the phone in just a minute."

"We really don't allow phones in the Emergency Room sir. What number can the doctor be reached at?"

"Forget that shit doc, Jonathan Calvatori's waiting to speak with you from his clinic in Buenos Aires. I'll have him right on the line."

Jonathan answered on the first ring, "Damn Jonathan, your magic code words worked. I'm patching you through to the attending physician in the ER now; they've already called in an OB/GYN guy. Talk to you soonest bro!"

He watched with barely suppressed amusement as first the attending physician and then the obstetrician took turns discussing areas so technical he knew the rocket scientists at NASA had nothing on them. After about fifteen minutes of frenetic discussion, the obstetrician handed Will the sat phone,

"Dr. Calvatori wishes to speak with you Mr. Kavanagh. Now would you be so kind as to excuse us while we perform a detailed examination of your wife and child?"

As he walked out through the ER waiting room, he noticed it was jammed with anxious family members. He walked outside the ER and sat down on a curb, "So what's happening in there Jonathan? Those fuckers won't tell me shit."

"First of all, you are quite fortunate to have access to Doctor Sanderson, the OB/GYN who I spoke with just now. He has agreed to be Dominique's primary obstetrician throughout the remainder of the pregnancy. I certainly wouldn't consider moving her again, such as that plane ride you just had from Panama City. She must remain in guarded condition for the remaining four or five weeks of the pregnancy, but it is time for me to tell you the delivery implications of Dominique's pathology."

"Okay, if you can explain that in coonass Cajun I think I can follow you Jonathan. What part of Dom's pathology impacts the delivery issues?"

"As you recall, Dominique experienced a traumatic injury when she was a small child, which resulted in her development of polycystic ovary syndrome. This condition manifested itself in unpredictable menstrual cycles for Dominique, and that was the most notable symptom of the injury that impacted your daily lives. Unfortunately, the trauma of the childhood injury also partially ruptured her uterine wall, and the subsequent development of scar tissue makes it impossible for her to deliver the fetus via normal childbirth."

His head was absorbing the information as quickly as possible so he blurted out, "So if she can't give birth normally, she's gotta have a ...""?

"Right Will, Dominique must have a Caesarean section in order to give birth. Are you familiar with this procedure?"

"Jesus, not in the least. How in the hell do you give birth if you can't give birth?"

"Doctor Sanderson, assisted by myself, will make an incision along the lower abdominal wall, and then carefully open the uterus to retrieve the child."

"My God Jonathan, is she gonna die giving birth this way?" Will asked in horror.

"No Will, a Caesarean section performed in a reputable hospital is not a high-risk surgical procedure. Most fatalities associated with C-sections are related to other, pre-existing health problems with the mother. Dominique has none of those, so it should be quite safe."

"So I gotta ask, what ARE the risks associated with the surgery?"

"I really do not like to get into potential issues for which I have no evidence of, but based on the uterine wall rupture, the complications of repairing the incision made to deliver the baby may prove problematic. If this were to occur, there is a chance that we might have to perform a hysterectomy on Dominique, which would quickly shift her into menopause. But all of this is highly speculative, based on unknown issues that will not become apparent until after the procedure is begun."

Will was trying mightily to process the information when Kelly sat down beside him with a vacant look on her face. He grabbed her, needing someone to hold onto badly and asked Jonathan, "So from what we know now, Dom will have a Caesarean section and we won't know about retention of the remaining ovary until it's time to close her back up. So, I guess this is once and done....." he was saying but suddenly became overcome with emotion. The irony of him avoiding fatherhood in any fashion through most of his life had been an immutable barrier in his mind. Now he was becoming all but despondent over the probability that this was the one and only chance Dom and he would procreate. The reality overwhelmed him, and he fell to the sidewalk and began sobbing uncontrollably. He regained his senses when he noticed that his head was resting between Kelly's legs, her hand stroking his hair as she spoke to Jonathan with the other. He looked at her and held his hand out for the phone, which she did and then held him tenderly. "So that's the reality of it Jonathan? This is our one chance to have a baby?"

"We do not know that for a fact Will; what is more important to me as a gynecologist is that if we can spare Dominique's remaining ovary, her quality of life will be much better. Delaying the onset of menopause—while not of paramount importance—can be important to quality of life issues. Considering the dramatic hormonal changes that take place during menopause, I would consider that to be our most compelling challenge. I believe Dominique will be fine, but I will be in contact with Dr. Sanderson on a regular basis until it is time for me to come there for the procedure. By the way, it is my opinion that Dominique should remain physically close to Dr. Sanderson and the hospital for her remaining weeks of pregnancy. Do you think you can make this arrangement?"

"Fuck it doc, I'll rent a penthouse if I need to. So you're actually planning on flying up to New Orleans for the birth? Is that standard practice for your patients?"

He laughed and replied, "Actually, it's a service I only provide to patients who ply me with *lomos* and excellent wine. And please tell Kelly that it was the highlight of my day to hear her voice. How has she been?"

In all the confusion, he'd completely forgotten about Kelly giving the Latin heartthrob the 'Dear John' treatment, but he told Jonathan, "Kelly? Actually she's been up to her ass in alligators down in Colombia with us. She's a tough little cookie, let me tell you. She took a nine millimeter in the chest to save my ass and walked away from it. By the way, how will they know when it's time for the operation, does Dom look at me and tell me 'I can't take this anymore?'"

"Unfortunately, there is no 'ready switch' that mothers have available. If Dominique shows no further complications, Dr. Sanderson and I will schedule the birth during the 40th week following the ZIFT, or in about one month. Please keep Dominique from doing any strenuous labor between now and then, although walking some every day will help her blood pressure. Other than that, follow Dr. Sanderson's advice on pre-natal activities. By the way, did you say Kelly got shot in the chest with a gun? How is this possible?"

"I'll explain it all to you when you get here Jonathan; it's a long, painful story. Suffice it to say that I blew the bugle and she came running, like the saint she is. Thank you so much for attending to the patient's husband; I'm not sure if I coulda put up with these yahoos inside the ER. I will be in touch, and thanks again!"

Will looked up at Kelly from between her legs, the tears not quite dried on his face, "Thanks, I needed that."

"Jesus Willy, nobody could have dealt with what you just did and not collapse."

He climbed up her torso to kiss her sweetly, "Jonathan said you made his week just hearing your voice. I don't think that flame has been extinguished my dear."

She smiled furtively at him, "Yeah, we'll see. I seem to get along well with your friend Rico, or couldn't you tell?"

"Who the fuck gave you permission to call me Willy?"

"You did about thirty orgasms ago, or did you forget in all the excitement?"

He shook his head at the sky, "Thank God for small miracles. I guess I gotta find a comfortable pad somewhere around here 'cause Jonathan says Dom's gotta stay close to the hospital and Sanderson until the baby gets here. Any ideas?"

"Well, let's go ask the crowd that's waiting for you in the hospital lobby Mr. Hero. You never can tell, somebody might be willing to put you up."

He pinched her lovely ass as they stood up and told her, "What in the fuck am I gonna do in New Orleans for four weeks?"

"Well," she said, discreetly brushing the front of his jeans, "I'd say you're number one objective is to stay out of trouble! Oh shit, I overheard Morley Safer say that Penny Martindale's on her way here since she's been designated the exclusive news source for the Columbian rescue mission." When he didn't react she added, "Christ Almighty Kavanagh, you've got an Archbishop as your personal spiritual mentor, have Dom and Mando as your life guides and every gorgeous woman you meet falls madly in lust with your wife. If 60 Minutes doesn't impress you, what the hell is it gonna take?"

"The Gipper," he replied so quickly that she couldn't respond. "When Ronald Reagan—yes, the Governor of California—becomes President I will find a way to offer my services."

She was clearly incredulous, "Willy, the Republican National Convention's over a year away; what makes you say such crazy things?"

"When an incumbent President—albeit one who pardoned Nixon—can't beat the peanut farmer, the GOP is DOA. The only answer is a politico that wasn't tainted by the Viet War, and that's Reagan; trust me on this one my jaded lover."

Before they turned the corner of the hospital, he pulled Kelly in for a more passionate embrace—that immediately sent a shimmer of pain up his head—and told her, "We're gonna make Penny famous baby; and you get to produce the movie. It's all good!"

She leaned back just enough to look him in his one good eye, "And what do you get to do?"

"I get to manage my money!"

When they rounded the corner to the front of the hospital, they were stunned at the assemblage of reporters and celebrants eager to learn more about the rescue. Kelly pulled him over to where Hal and Pierson were standing, looking very uneasy. Will asked the rhetorical, "Carmen disappear with Wade?"

Hal nodded as Will's attention was displaced by a commotion, only to find Penny Martindale jump from a taxi and make a bee line for the microphone bank. Reverend Arthur Benson was giving thanks to the people who had returned his Lutheran son Colton Kavanagh to him. Penny took one look at Will and tersely ordered, "Inside!"

Once they were uncomfortably ensconced in the hospital administrator's office her eyes were daggers flying straight at Will. "And just what in the fuck did you think you were doing designating me as the spokesperson for this little undercover operation of yours?"

Will glanced at Colton before replying, "I just selected the most worthy newsperson in the US and told the rest of the buzzards that all statements would come through you."

"Did you also forget that I have a job with WCAZ in Sacramento? Do you think I might have some trouble with my managing director saying to hell with my job and following your wayfaring ass around the world?"

"I believe Ms. Martindale, that you will notice that you have an exclusive drop on the most sought after story since JFK's assassination."

"Alright, let's assume I do. What the fuck am I gonna tell those news hounds outside when I get back out there?"

He glanced at Arthur Benson through the window, "You're gonna tell them that a very much respected missionary of the Lutheran church was miraculously returned to them after facing extraordinary conditions of captivity."

She seemed to soften just perceptibly, "So how am I gonna tell them he was miraculously rescued? I doubt you and your band of pirates want the notoriety of the world press."

"Quite right Ms. Martindale, you are gonna tell them that the Church came up with a charitable benefactor and was able to meet the kidnapper's rescue demands."

"And how did that take place?"

"The ransom exchange took place at the Museum of the Bogotá Botanical Gardens two days ago, and that Mr. Colton Kavanagh had to follow a circuitous journey out of Colombia."

"And why was Mr. Kavanagh being held against his will by the, who was he being held by?"

"He was being held by a counter-revolutionary group that was unhappy with his Christian efforts in Central America. They propose a Marx-Leninist option for making the peasants more like rich people."

"So why an obscure missionary; why not go after some higher member of the Christian leadership?"

As if scripted, Rose opened the door to the office just as the words left Penny's lips, "Turn on the television to CNN, now!"

Once they had it tuned to CNN, Will was horrified to see a the video of Juan Villaponteau lying on a stretcher next to an ambulance with a bloody shoulder, paramedics working over him feverishly. A very attractive Colombian reporter was breathlessly breaking the incredible news, "Not twenty minutes ago, the Archbishop of Colombia, His Excellency Juan Cardinal Villaponteau was the target of an assassination attempt as he departed the Maria Reina Cathedral here in Barranquilla. We can only thank God that the attempt was unsuccessful. Cardinal Villaponteau was shot in the shoulder but is expected to recover from his wounds…"

Will turned to Penny, "It would seem that Colton Kavanagh was not the only target of the FARC in trying to absolve Colombia and Central America of Christian influence. I believe you have the basis for your story Ms. Martindale; and I assure you it is timely."

62

UNFINISHED BUSINESS

WILL PULLED OUT HIS SATELLITE PHONE as it trilled and was surprised to hear Marty Lindstrum's voice, "And just what kind of hell are you trying to bring down on yourself Kavanagh?"

He motioned for Hal to follow him over to the far corner of the room, "I'm afraid you've got the wrong number Marty. I just got back from rescuing my brother in Colombia; what could you possibly be talking about?"

"Why don't you walk out behind the hospital and let's have a private chat; got time for that?"

Hal looked to Alex, Rico and Pierson and quickly huddled them up before they disappeared, Hal's only clue as he left was to pantomime 'SHADOW.' Will turned back to the phone, "I've always got time for a CIA rat who took twenty million in heroin for a shitty plane ride. What in the fuck are you doing in New Orleans Lindstrum? I had this vague notion the Agency was OCONUS."

"I was instructed to come pay you a visit and give you a message. You gonna come on back here or are you gonna hide behind the skirts up there making you out to be some kind of hero?"

"Well you know me Marty, given the choice I'd always hang with the pussy, but since you made a special trip and all, I'll come on out and chat. Now I'm warning you, I ain't armed."

"It won't make any difference Kavanagh; we just need to settle up some business from Bogotá."

"I'll be right out," he said as he motioned for Kelly.

"Where's that Nehru vest you wore in Pereira?"

"It's in my roller bag right outside, why?"

"Go get it and bring it to me; don't say a word to anyone, okay?"

They went to the women's room, to the stares of at least a dozen hospital staff, and he was just barely able to button it over his chest. He then pulled his golf shirt and jacket back over it. Kelly looked at him and asked, "Jesus Will, who is it this time?"

"You don't wanna know babe, otherwise you'd lose faith in the Constitution. See you in a little while, and thanks so much," he said as he kissed her lightly on the lips. "Just tell me you'll always love me."

Instead of answering she enveloped him in the most salacious embrace short of full fornication. She broke it off as a blue-haired elderly woman entered the bathroom. Will flexed his eyebrows, "Thank you my dear, and I hope you enjoyed the audition!"

———

When he made his way to the back of the hospital where the trash dumpster enclosures were he didn't see anybody. Not knowing what to do, he turned around to head back inside only to find Marty Lindstrum standing in front of him holding a Walther 380. "What's this, a greeting party Marty?"

"No, they're the greeting party," he said, nodding to three other men who suddenly appeared from around the backs of the dumpster enclosures.

"So what's with the gun Marty? What the fuck is all the drama about?" Though playing along, he had a sneaking suspicion that it was directly connected to the CIA safe house in Bogotá getting obliterated by Constanza's boys who were desperately in search of Consuela Diaz.

"The gun represents the paranoid part of me that never knows the location of Dan Pierson. Now would you like to tell me what you know about a certain safe house and all its occupants being annihilated three nights ago in Bogotá?"

"Now how the fuck would I know about that Marty? I was being tortured in the plantation basement of one each Umberto Rodriquez outside a little country town near Armenia. I can assure you I would much rather have been on the streets of Bogotá than watching that bastard Hector Constanza blowing holes in friends of mine."

"Now that's all of a sudden starting to match up with the word our Station Chief in Bogotá sent out. He says it was Constanza's men who attacked the safe house for some unknown reason. Now why would Hector Constanza, who is a business associate of mine, attack our safe house? Can you possibly answer me that?"

"Beats shit out of me Marty, maybe he wasn't that good of friends with you," Will said as one of the Lindstrum's muscle boys whipped something at his leg, sending a shooting pain straight up his body like he'd been hit by shrapnel.

'You like that stun snake, eh? Tell you what, we'll take it easy on you if you'll tell us how it happened. Those might have been Colombian employees, but they were still ours, and damn good ones. They took out a dozen of Constanza's men before they gave up the ghost."

"Well who the fuck were they holding in the safe house? Did you ever think it might have been a hit on whoever was being protected?"

He saw Marty glance at one of his guys, "It was the informant from the Medellin Cartel. No way Constanza woulda wanted to get to him."

"And just why wouldn't Constanza want to get his hands on an informant from his rival cartel Marty? Jesus, why the hell did you look at me for this?"

"Because Constanza called me wanting to know where you were hiding Minister Diaz' wife, that's why Kavanagh. When I told him we didn't have her, he said he already knew that because you had already given our safe house up. Any last words before I shoot your ass as a traitor?"

"Let's see Marty, the head of the Cali Cartel calls you for operational information on a rescue mission sanctioned by a US Special Forces Group. Weren't you supposed to be concerned with spraying paraquat on coca slopes? Besides, Hector told me you'd become best friends with Silvio Corrales, so I figured you were playing both sides against the middle. Do these guys know they're working for a double agent? I'm not sure how you can call me the traitor. *Et tu, Brute?*"

"Doesn't matter, you fingered our guys and now it's time to pay the piper. Goodbye Kavanagh," he said as he raised the Walther and shot Will right in the chest.

When he came to, Hal was holding him in his arms and it seemed like daylight, even though he knew it couldn't have been much past sundown when he left the hospital for the meeting. Will was confused by the blaring of police sirens echoing everywhere.

He looked up at Hal drunkenly and asked, "What happened?"

"The New Orleans Police department just arrested Marty Lindstrum for attempted murder and assault with a deadly weapon on a decorated US Air Force veteran. We wrapped up his sidekicks until the cops arrived as well. I'd say we've solved our little Marty Lindstrum problem forever bro."

Will touched his aching chest, wondering if he'd broken more ribs and asked, "How'd you know I had on the vest?"

"I saw you and Kelly sneaking into the bathroom with it. I figured if you could put up with the pain of getting shot through that vest we could put Marty away for good."

Will shook his head and asked, "How is he put away for good? Won't he just come back for us again?"

Hal smiled at him smugly, "Bro, the CIA does not operate domestically, at least not to the point of getting arrested for attempted murder. He'll never make it out of lockup bro; my guess is with his long and faithful service they'll hit him with about 10cc of succinylcholine. Couldn't happen to a nicer guy."

"So what about the hired help?"

"We just offered them a job; they'll have to change their appearances, but the CIA wouldn't let them live very long once this came to light. We always need guys to go to places you wouldn't send a dog to."

Hal was helping Will walk when they got back inside after midnight, the police reports seeming to go on interminably until Hal's call to Bernie Jepson finally sprung them. Kelly took one look at Will and said, "What did you do, test out the vest again?"

He smiled at her sheepishly, "Yep, wanna compare bruises?"

She swatted him on the ass, "Actually, your wife is waiting desperately to speak with you."

"And I was so hoping she'd want you to stand in for her tonight," Will said as Kelly winked at him. Two steps later his sat phone trilled again.

"Kavanagh."

A strange voice with a Spanish accent announced, "Hello Mr. Kavanagh, my name is Umberto Rodriquez, and I am so sorry that we didn't have an opportunity to meet while you were here in Colombia."

He gave Hal the pantomime for RODRIQUEZ as Kemosabe jumped off to make a call on his sat phone. "And what can I do for you *Señor* Rodriquez?

I understand you recently lost a dear friend Hector Constanza."

"Actually, I am calling you on his phone, since he obviously doesn't need it anymore."

Will relayed that information to Hal, which sent him off to make another sat phone call. "Yep, he just didn't know when to leave well enough alone Umberto. So why did you call me, to tell me how much you miss him? I understand the two of you were partners of sorts."

"I am calling to inform you that you are a dead man William Kavanagh. No one destroys my coffee plantation property and escapes justice. I will follow you to the ends of the earth until I kill you."

Hal came back and gave him two thumbs up, so Will continued the banter, "Now Umberto, you know it was the National Police who blasted rocket-propelled grenades into your property and destroyed it. Have you even seen the remains of the property? Hector's cocaine lab went up in the blast as well."

"I do not know how those pictures appeared in *El Tiempo*, but I know they are doctored. And yes, I am standing beside my airplane this very moment looking at the smoldering remnants of a once thriving business."

"Listen Umberto, I'm a little pressed for time here, but did you know that a brave man named Daniel Gomez died in your basement, shot to shit at point blank range by Hector Constanza?" Will asked as Hal rubbed his hands together in anticipation.

"No, I did not know Daniel Gomez, but I assume he was an enemy if Hector killed him."

"Listen Umberto, I know you're a communist, but Daniel was a man of God, does that mean anything to you?"

"No, I do not care for the Christians. An associate attempted to take out the Archbishop this afternoon and I was sorry he failed. Why do you care so much about this priest named Daniel?" Umberto said as Hal whispered into Will's ear and gave him two hands open—a solid ten count.

"Tell me something Umberto; do you see that red light off to your left in the woods?"

"I see something like a smoldering piece of charcoal, why?"

"Because Daniel Gomez was Marco Pintoles' favorite nephew; see you in hell Umberto," he told him and heard a loud crash, then silence.

Will was trying to dance in sheer joy as Hal gave him a bear hug that hurt like holy hell, "Two satanic angels in one night partner, that was some going?"

He held up his hand, hit redial on his sat phone and listened, "Just consider that Remington 700 with the night scope a present along with the satellite phone Marco. You have done well my friend, and you'll want to know this. Umberto Rodriguez just admitted it was a FARC hit on Juan Villaponteau today a few seconds before his head exploded. So we both know who the enemy is *mi buen amigo*. Please keep an eye on our friend the Archbishop; he is indeed a special man. If you ever need a favor, you just let us know; Juan will always be able to find us. Be careful my friend."

"So I gotta ask, partner, how'd you set that one up?" Will asked Hal with unbridled admiration.

"Pintoles was so pissed when Pierson and he cut Daniel Gomez' body down off that wall that he swore eternal revenge to both Constanza and Rodriquez for not having the basic decency to at least execute a man in a humane manner. His ass sat out in those woods for two days waiting for Rodriquez to fly into the hacienda with his Lear jet and inspect his destroyed property. I told him to get a shot of Rodriquez through the cell phone if he could so that the SIM chip would be destroyed and no one could trace any numbers that had been dialed or received on it."

"So it would seem the Cali Cartel and the FARC are now looking for new leadership?"

"And the CIA's looking for a new asshole to torment the world as we know it; don't you think it's about time for a cigar?"

"Just as soon as we go check on Mrs. Kavanagh. She is not going to be a happy camper!"

Kelly suddenly appeared at his side, lacing her arm around his shoulder, "See if you can get a little dispensation for tonight cowboy; I'm feeling a little randy."

63

THE MIRACLE IN THE FLESH

IT HAD BEEN FOUR LONG WEEKS living in the Hilton Riverside Hotel. When they initially checked in, Will inquired about getting the penthouse suite for a long term stay and was asked if he was an Elite Partner with the Hilton chain. He gave the clerk the Italian Army salute as she beckoned the front desk manager who advised him that only Elite Hilton Partners could reserve the penthouse suite for longer than a week at a time. Will just shrugged his shoulders, "So how do you become an Elite Partner?"

He nodded apologetically and advised, "Elite Partners are those who have either been frequent guests over many years or are stockholders in the corporation. I apologize sir, but can we interest you perhaps in a suite on our concierge floor? It includes a panoramic view of the river and Lake Pontchartrain."

"Actually, I travel a lot, so the Elite Partner thing sounds like a good idea. Hang in there for a minute," he said as he punched up Johnny Chessereaux' number at his office in San Diego. "Hey buddy, how you been?" After listening to an exaggerated version of Tinsel Town dalliances he asked him, "Hey, are you an Elite Partner with Hilton? It seems like it'd be a good idea."

"Yeah, our firm is and Great West is, but why do you want to become one? Is some counter jockey giving you shit about a penthouse? Where the fuck are you?"

"Listen Johnny, I think Hilton fits into my preferred stock portfolio plans; Lord knows they're building one in every place on earth you'd want to visit. What say you buy me a million worth of their preferred stock, based on the closing price as of today? Think you can do that for me?"

"Actually, that's a pretty good investment idea; shit you seem to be coming up with good ones lately with BP and United Technologies. Man, Zig followed your lead on UT and is one happy camper. Okay, I'll make the buy in the morning. Now please hand the phone to whatever desk jockey has told you that you can't have the penthouse. By the way, where are you?"

"New Orleans Riverside, ever been here?"

"Oh yeah, and they get all the high rollers off the gambling boats trying to blow smoke up their ass. Put the hotel manager on the phone; just tell him Great West Studios is on the line. And hey, stay in touch tiger, I heard about that little one man war you had down in Colombia, Jesus Christ Kavanagh!"

Will looked at the desk manager and smiled sweetly, "Would it be possible to get the hotel manager on the line? Mr. Chessereaux, the Vice Chairman of Great West Studios would like to speak with him for a moment."

———

"Jesus," Will shuddered as Jonathan Calvatori made the first incision across Dom's lower abdomen. Jonathan, Dr. Sanderson, Dom and Will had participated in a lengthy and lively discussion about the relative merits of general or regional anesthesia, but Dom had made the final determination that she wanted the regional, or neuraxial blockade, which he had heard of before as epidural anesthesia. This method offered effective pain relief and allowed for the mother to be awake and interact immediately with the baby. Jonathan was so focused on his work that he didn't seem to notice Will as he continued across Dom's belly perhaps making a ten inch long cut. He had to remind himself that he had recently watched a man being brutally tortured hanging from a rack on a wall to seek rapprochement with his mind over the blood issues. For some reason, the butchering job he did on Hector Constanza didn't count; that was pure recompense. He held Dom's hand and tried not to look shocked, but she merely smiled at him, "How's it going?"

He put on his Academy Award winning act and smiled, "Looks pretty smooth so far baby."

To be in the operating room, he had to wash up and dress just as any of the doctors or nurses, including a cloth mask to contain airborne contaminants. Will humorously asked the anesthesiologist if he had a valium for him, but the bitch merely laughed and pointed to Dom as the important patient in the room.

After Jonathan made the incision across what Will assumed were the skin and abdominal muscles, he obtained a different scalpel from the nurse's tray and began carefully cutting through the uterine wall, which looked so messy and bloody he had to look away a few times until the nurses blotted the excess blood. Sanderson saw him blanching and reassured him, "This is going extremely well Will; Dominique is experiencing a very slight level of bleeding. Dr. Calvatori is extraordinarily skilled in penetrating the uterine wall. I have never seen it done with more precision."

Once the uterine wall was cut through, it seemed to Will that the two doctors and the nurse were doing their best to stretch the uterine wall opening as widely as possible. When he eked out another 'Jesus,' Sanderson looked at him and explained, "We must make the uterine opening as flexible as possible to allow for the baby to exit with minimal distress. Do not worry; Dr. Calvatori will take extraordinary care in suturing up the uterine wall when we have removed the placenta."

The reference to the placenta gave him a nauseous feeling, even though he had steadfastly refused to eat since dinner the night before lest he become THE problem patient in the operating room. He watched with concern as Jonathan began to very carefully make snips in the placenta wall, no doubt being extremely careful not to cut or injure the baby as he gained precious access. If Will thought the stretching of the uterine wall was dicey, he almost had to turn his head a couple of times as Calvatori and Sanderson stretched the placenta as they continued to carefully snip and open it further. When he finally glimpsed the baby's form, he was aghast at how it was seemingly covered with splotches of blood and slimy fluid. This continued until Jonathan said simply, "Coming up." With Jonathan holding the placenta open, the obstetrics nurse and Sanderson lifted the baby out of the cavity as a second nurse expertly cut the umbilical cord and quickly clamped it off.

The next word he heard was "Suction," as another nurse began pushing a plastic bulb into the baby's mouth, sucking out fluid. After she had done this three times, another nurse put a bag-valve mask over the baby's mouth, quickly ventilating her lungs. "I take it this is part of transitioning the baby from fluid breathing?" Will asked and chuckled, "I guess birthing transforms them from fish to air breathers?"

Doctor Sanderson noticed Will's interest and explained, "During natural births, the onset of labor induces the fluid producing cells in the lungs to cease production. Residual lung fluid is expelled during the confined movement through the birth canal. Most full term babies usually take their first breath within a minute of clamping the umbilical cord."

"So Caesarean Sections deliver the baby with lungs which the fluid producing cells have not ceased production?" Will asked, thinking he was catching on.

"Exactly Mr. Kavanagh; that's why you see the suctioning of fluid and
manual resuscitation used to ready the baby for breathing…" he was saying
when they were interrupted.

As they looked on, yet another nurse spanked the baby on the butt. The
sharp cry caught him so off guard he jumped back, but Dom was holding
onto his hand tightly and smiling expectantly. "Jesus Christ Dom, we've got
a baby!"

The two nurses now took the baby and began thoroughly cleaning her,
wrapping her in a small warm blanket as they continued to use some fluid to
clean the baby's hair. Finally content with their handiwork, the chief nurse
glanced at Sanderson who nodded, as the nurse handed the swaddling bundle
to Dom. The look on her face was precious, so Will took at least a dozen
pictures of her holding their brand new miracle of life. Dom looked for Jonathan, "Dr. Calvatori, I'd like you to meet Sofia Alexandra Kavanagh, our
miracle of life!"

Jonathan merely nodded as he said something to a nurse who put a hood
on his head with a light and two scopes that looked like giant jeweler's loupes.
The wires leading from the back of the hood gave him an alien-like appearance, but he was concentrating so hard on instructing the obstetrics nurse and
weaving the suturing material that Will was nearly mesmerized. He snapped
out of it when Dom asked, "What do you think of our little bundle of love
Will? Is she not the most precious thing you have ever seen?"

He took little Sofia in his arms for the first time and kissed her forehead,
for which he was rewarded with a sharp cry. He placed her back in Dom's
arms as she quieted down and seemed to be at peace with the world. Will
looked around at one of the nurses and asked, "Did you get a chance to weigh
her?"

"Sofia arrived into the world at seven pounds, eight ounces and she is a
beautiful healthy baby girl. Congratulations Mr. and Mrs. Kavanagh."

Will leaned down to kiss his happy but tired wife and told her, "I never
ever thought I'd see this day come, but I met the miracle of my life and now
we've done the miracle ourselves. I couldn't love you any more than I do right

this minute Dominique. You are indeed an incredible woman."

She smiled at him as he expected some Dominique Lefebvre life-altering wisdom, only to be surprised to hear her ask, "I'm very thirsty Will, can you get me something to drink?"

He looked around at the nurse, who smiled as she handed him a cup of ice chips which he fed to Dom one at a time as she luxuriated over the cold wet treat. After she had sated her thirst, she asked, "Well, what was it like?"

He glanced at the nurse—who was giving him the flexed eyebrow stare—and replied, "I have gained a true admiration for the skill and professionalism of our operating room crew. Jonathan Calvatori is a master weaver."

At this, Calvatori looked up for just a moment, "We were very careful with the uterine wall incision and now the closing. There is no apparent damage to your functioning ovary Dominique. It would appear that we have accomplished what we set out for. You have been a model patient."

"Hey, it's time to show off Sofia to our closest friends, may I?"

Dom looked at him suspiciously, "I'm not sure if I trust you with our daughter just yet William, why don't you go ask Carmen to come in?"

"Oh come on Dom, I'm Sofia's father for Christ's sakes, I won't let anything happen to her," he said as he picked up their daughter. "We'll be right back."

When he walked out into the waiting room, Carmen jumped up and flew straight to him, grabbing Sofia and telling her all kinds of unintelligible things in Spanish. Will turned to find Hal slapping him on the back as he asked, "Now I can truly say that you have proven me a wimp Willy boy. What was it like in there?"

Will opened his mouth to describe the scene he had just witnessed and was confused when he opened his eyes to find his mother holding his head in her lap, "Are you alright Willy? You passed out like a light!"

He shook his head slightly until he focused on Hal, who was shaking his head in disgust, "Now who's the wimp? Jesus Willy, I thought you were the ice man."

At that moment Jonathan Calvatori walked out, still wiping his hands on a towel, took one look at Will and said, "Will, you are the first husband who has ever watched a complete Caesarean section performed. I've seen medical students pass out during that procedure more than once. Are you certain you don't have an interest in the medical profession?"

"Only so far as painkillers, tranquilizers and sedatives are concerned at the moment," he said, getting to his feet. He opened his arms as he embraced Jonathon with a bear hug and told him, "Damn, you did it buddy. We listened to you and you did it. I plan on telling the world about you brother!"

To their surprise Kelly came up and took over for Will hugging him tightly, but he managed a glance at Will, "Your wife would like a word with you, and she would like you to bring her daughter back when you do!"

———

Later that night, or probably early the next morning, Hal, Carmen, Rambo, Kelly, Penny, Casey, Alex and Will were all parked around a picnic table on the roof of the Tulane Medical Center smoking cigars and passing around a bottle of Grand Marnier. He opened another bottle of Marnier, tossed the cork signifying its past usefulness and proposed a toast; "To the happiest day of my life, I'd like to salute the best friends a man could ever hope for. And I never ever want to watch another live birth. One is more than enough. Here's looking at the people who keep me from doing myself in. Except Dom of course, but she sent along her best regards, 'cause she's with her new best friend! Here, here!"

As they all saluted Sofia the miracle, Will detected the unmistakable beginning of a song he'd heard Leon Russell play in concert so many years ago while in college at WestTech. "Hey, turn that radio up Case." When she did everyone turned to listen as Will smiled at Hal and told him, "*Stranger in a Strange Land*." He could remember some but not all of the words and picked it up in the second verse, "How many days till I'm done? It's only my confusion waiting in the night…" When the chorus started the second time around, everybody was standing and singing the incredibly appropriate refrain. By the time Leon got to the last chorus, they were all singing as loud as they could, right into each other's faces. When it was over there was a lot of kissing and hugging going on, and they all knew that, indeed, they had once again survived being strangers in a strange land.

GLOSSARY OF FOREIGN WORDS AND PHRASES

Chapter	Foreign Lanuage Term or Phrase	Language	English Translation (as used in this book)
1	*janbiya*	Arabic	an Arabian curved dagger
1	*dîtes-moi*	French	tell me
1	*n'est pas*	French	ubiquitous French parenthetical term; isn't it, doesn't it, you agree, aren't we
1	*Mon Dieu*	French	My God!
2	*Señor*	Spanish	Mister
2	*Porteños*	Spanish	Citizens of Buenos Aires, Argentina
2	*casa grande*	Spanish	literally, large house; (as used here), a mansion
2	*Avenida Junin*	Spanish	Junin Street or Junin Avenue
2	*desaparecidos*	Spanish	missing persons in the Dirty War
2	*Revolución Libertadora*	Spanish	literally, liberating revolution
2	*Montoneros*	Spanish	literally, guerilla fighter; 17th century civilian militia
2	*Alianza Anticomunista Argentina*	Spanish	Argentine Anticommunist Alliance; AAA, a brutal death squad
2	*Ejército Revolucionario del Puebla*	Spanish	People's Revolutionary Army of Argentina
2	*raison d'être*	French	literally, reason for being; in this case, the Army's actual charter
2	*Batallón de Inteligencia 601*	Spanish	601 Intelligence Battalion; Carmen was assassin for them
2	*Secretaria de Inteligencia de Estado*	Spanish	Argentine Secretariat of State Intelligence (SIDE)
2	*Dirección de Inteligencia Nacional*	Spanish	Chilean National Intelligence Directorate (DINE)
2	*Movimiento de Izquierda Revolucionaria*	Spanish	Chilean Revolutionary Left Movement (MIR)
2	*cause célèbre*	French	am issue or incident arousing widespread conrtroversy
2	*Islas Malvinas*	Spanish	The Falkand Islands
2	*Muchas gracias, compadre*	Spanish	Thank you very much, partner
4	*autopista*	Spanish	literally, motorway; a restricted access highway
4	*Casa Fabiano*	Spanish	Fabiano Mansion
4	*mi Chico favorito*	Spanish	my favorite boy
4	*Señorita*	Spanish	Miss, Ms
4	*Indefinido*	Spanish	Indefinite
5	*Conquistador*	Spanish	spanish conquerer of Mexico and Peru
5	*bife de lomo*	Spanish	beef tenderloin
5	*chef de maison*	French	executive chef of the restaurant
5	*¿En qué puedo ayudarle, señor*	Spanish	How can I help you sir?
6	*el bufet*	Spanish	Porteno smorgasbord buffet
7	*pomme frittes*	French	french fried potatoes
6	*parilla*	Spanish	large elevated metal grill for cooking
7	*Mio Dios*	Spanish	My God!
7	*usted semental*	Spanish	you bull stud
7	*vous taureau stud*	French	you bull stud
8	*mi querida Hermana*	Spanish	my dear Sister
8	*mi hermano*	Spanish	my brother
8	*desaparecidos mi querido Guillermo*	Spanish	disappeareds my dear William
8	*muchas gracias mi querida Belen*	Spanish	thank you very much my dear Belen
8	*titiritero*	Spanish	puppet master, behind the scenes enabler
8	*cómo se llama eso Belen*	Spanish	how do you say it Belen?
8	*Precisamente*	Spanish	Precisely
8	*Una vez, más, precisamente*	Spanish	Once again, precisely;
9	*Su Excelencia El Presidente*	Spanish	Your Excellency The President
9	*De hecho mi valiente amigo, Salud, Salud!*	Spanish	Indeed my brave man, Cheers, Cheers!
9	*La Casa Rosada*	Spanish	The Pink House; Presidential Palace; Government House
9	*buenas noches*	Spanish	good evening
10	*Norteamericanos*	Spanish	North Americans, esp US Americans
10	*Estancia Fabiano*	Spanish	Fabiano Ranch
11	*Circuito Chico*	Spanish	literally, small circuit; Route 77 north of Bariloche
11	*hors d'oeuvres*	French	literally, apart from the main work; appetizers or starters

Chapter	Foreign Lanuage Term or Phrase	Language	English Translation (as used in this book)
11	*tapas*	Spanish	literally, to cover; a small plate of appetizers
11	*cojones*	Spanish	a man's testicles
12	*Español Abuela Diaz*	Spanish	Spanish Grandmother Diaz?
12	*Adios Abuela Diaz*	Spanish	(as used here) Bye Bye Granny Diaz!
12	*Madre*	Spanish	Mother
13	*por favor*	Spanish	please
15	*Punta del Este*	Spanish	literally, Eastern Point; beach resort in coastal Uruguay
17	*Gracias a Dios*	Spanish	Thanks be to God
17	*su querida hermana*	Spanish	your dear sister
17	*Auf wiedersehen*	German	Until we meet again
18	*Circulo de la Vida Realce*	Spanish	Circel of Life Enhancement, Calvatori's fertility clinic
20	*Lagar*	Spanish	winery
21	*coup de grâs*	French	(as used here) the disabling blow
21	*Edificio Libertador*	Spanish	Libertador Building, Argentina's Pentagon
23	*Si, esto es verdad*	Spanish	Yes, this is true
23	*meister*	German	someone who is expert at something
24	*Muy buena*	Spanish	Very good
24	*faux pas*	French	an embarrassing or tactless act in a social situation
26	*Aerolíneas Argentinas*	Spanish	Argentine Airlines
26	*mi querida Ministria*	Spanish	my dear Minister
26	*culto*	Spanish	fraternity of acolytes, following a charismatic leader
26	*Escuela de Mecánica de la Armada*	Spanish	(Argentina's) Navy Mechanics' School; torture facility sueinf Argentina's Dirty War
26	*excusez-moi*	French	pardon me
26	*Circulo Militar*	Spanish	Military Circle; Argentine Defense Ministry's Grand Officers Club
26	*Mais oui*	French	litterally, But yes; (as used here) Of course
26	*no diabólica; que es su cerebro de lagarto*	Spanish	(No Rosita), not diabolical, it is his lizard brain
26	*muy buenos amigos*	Spanish	very good friends
27	*mi heroina Belen*	Spanish	my heroine Belen
27	*no mas*	Spanish	no more; I surrender
29	*Cuba Libre*	Spanish	literally, Free Cuba; a cocktail of rum and coke
29	*coup d'état*	French	suddden, illegal seizure of a government
29	*Fuerza Aérea Argentina*	Spanish	Argentine Air Force
29	*aeroparques*	Spanish	airports
29	*Casa Militar*	Spanish	literally, Military House; Argentina's central command & control center
29	*Agrupación Aérea Presidencial*	Spanish	Argentine Presidential Air Group
29	*Destacamento Aeronautica Militar Aeroparque*	Spanish	Arentine Military Aviation Detachment Buenos Aires Airport
29	*la mula*	Spanish	(in aviation parlance) a towing tractor for ground movement of aircraft
30	*Orden de la Sociedad de Mayo*	Spanish	(The Argentine) Order of May Society
30	*Sociedad Anónima*	Spanish	(In Argentina) literally anonymous society; a public joint stock company
30	*mi mejor amigo*	Spanish	my closest friend
30	*Sociedad de Responsibilidad Limitada*	Spanish	(In Argentina) a limited liability corporation
30	*Escribano Publico*	Spanish	(In Argentina) a notary public
30	*Suboficial Mayor*	Spanish	Argentine enlisted rank of Chief Master Sergeant (E-9)
30	*Contador Público Certificado*	Spanish	a Certified Public Accountant
30	*Ejército de Liberación Nacional*	Spanish	National Liberation Army of Colombia (ELN)
30	*Fuerzas Armadas Revolucionarias de Colombia–Ejército Del Pueblo*	Spanish	Revolutionary Armed Force of Colombia--People's Army (FARC-EP)
32	*Tio Guillermo, esta soy yo Rosita*	Spanish	Uncle William, it is me Rosita
32	*Caritas Argentina*	Spanish	Charity of Argentina (Catholic enterprise)

Chapter	Foreign Lanuage Term or Phrase	Language	English Translation (as used in this book)
33	Waffen-Schutzstaffel	German	Hitler's armed wing of the hated SS secret police
34	Ciudad Oculta	Spanish	Town of Oculta (shantytown)
34	Villa Miseria	Spanish	(as translated by the author) Povertyville; literally a shanty town set in famous novel about Buenos Aires' slums
34	barras	Spanish	slum gang member, orig football zealot
34	paco	Spanish	Cocaine paste, an intermed form in process
36	Chargé d'affairs	French	diplomat serving in absence of ambassador
36	Guardia National	Spanish	National Guard under Nicaraguan President Somoza
36	Policia Sandinista	Spanish	Sandinista Police, who took over for the National Police
36	Ejército Popular Sandinista	Spanish	Sandinista Popular Army—EPS for short
36	Córdobas	Spanish	Nicaraguan currency; 1980 exchange rate; $1 = CS 7
36	Frente Sandinista de Liberación Nacional	Spanish	Sandinista National Liberation Front (FSLN)
36	Dirección General de Intelligencia	Spanish	Cuban Intelligence Directorate (DGI)
36	celeno	Spanish	litterally, cell leader; in charge of total distribution path
36	Cohiba Lanceros	Spanish	Elite Cuban cigar made in Havana
36	Barrio Pomares in Managua	Spanish	Pomares neighborhood in Managua
37	Sayonara Yoko-san	Japanese	Goodbye Mister
37	persona non grata	Latin	literally, person not appreciated; diplomatic equivalent of excommunication
38	Que pasa amigo	Spanish	What's happening buddy?
39	Para	Spanish	(as used here) Stop!
43	Triumvirato	Spanish	Triumvirate, or Council of Three in the Cali Cartel
43	Lo seinto mucho Señor	Spanish	I am so sorry Mister
46	objet du désir	French	object of desire (as in a former romantic interest)
54	Que Dios los bendiga	Spanish	May God Bless You
54	Estamos con ustedes	Spanish	We are with you
54	Adios	Spanish	Goodbye
54	estamos todos bien	Spanish	are we good (you and I?)
54	Eso creo	Spanish	I believe so
54	Que se su cerebro de lagarto conspirar a la velocidad de la luz	Spanish	It is his lizard brain conspiring at the speed of light
57	Si Señor, Señor Rayfield es el Jefe	Spanish	Yes sir, Mr. Rayfield is the Chief
58	De pie o se muere perra	Spanish	Stand up or you die bitch
58	No, hay que fijar las hombros, por favor Jefe	Spanish	No, we must fix her shoulders, please bossman
58	Por favor Señor, vamos a ayudarle a su	Spanish	Please mister, let us help her
58	Llevarla hasta entonces o te pego un tiro	Spanish	Get her up then, or I will shoot
58	Estamos listos ahora, muchas por favor	Spanish	We are ready now, thank you very much
59	Guayabera	Spanish	Colombian formal outerwear shirt
59	Es to para asesinas brutalmente Padre Daniel Gomez	Spanish	This is for brutally murdering Father Daniel Gomez
59	el único hombre que he amado de verdad	Spanish	the only man I ever truly loved
59	Padre Daniel está en el cielo	Spanish	Father Daniel is in heaven
59	Espero que usted se quema para la eternidad en el infierno	Spanish	I hope you burn for eternity in hell
59	Ajiaco	Spanish	a Colombian soup made with chicken, potatoes & herbs

ABOUT THE AUTHOR

X. W. KAVANAGH IS THE PSEUDONYM FOR ME, the author of the seductive action adventure escapades of Will Kavanagh. The third helping is *When There's No Tomorrow*, featuring the dynamic pairing of Will and Dominique as they navigate life's ups and downs before things get scary, hairy and downright homicidal.

Will's alter ego also escaped humble Southern roots, traveled the world, discovered love and tragedy and then lived to write about it. Having lived inside the US defense establishment as an officer, a civilian employee and finally a consultant, he takes you places with the hardened shell of a government mule. He also gets to have fun and be a real person, which makes him so different from typical characters in action novels. Why write only about the brutal conflict when that's just part of your life, right? While this is a work of fiction, many of the places and events described in this novel are in fact familiar to us and such familiarity helps sustain the fantasy.

So what's Will's alter ego like for real? Let's just say he thinks and talks exactly like Will Kavanagh. Stunned? If you write a book the way people think and talk it's got to be more relevant, *n'est pas*?

Since Will Kavanagh gravitates towards that incontestable axiom of the enemy of my enemy is my friend, you could make the presumption that when he lives long enough to meet Ronald Reagan the two of 'em get along just fine. But that's for a whole other series out on the horizon. First we've got to see how Hollywood and Circle Entertainment really mix with one another. I really, really think you're gonna enjoy *A Rainbow On the Sun*, Will's next step along the yellow brick road. If that title seems vaguely familiar, you're a leg up on the new sensation.

Feel free to contact me about your reactions, impressions or even ideas about where you'd like to see Will go to next. From where I sit, it's always late at night anyway! Email me at xwkavanagh@gmail.com or visit my website for a glimpse of the next incredible adventure at www.xwkavanagh.com.

Made in the USA
Middletown, DE
13 June 2017